'In!' Phelan commanded.

Vashti stumbled forward, almost tripping over her own coffee-table as he slammed the door behind them.

'Now,' he said. 'No telephones, no lying little switchboard operators, no screaming hysterics.'

Vashti could have laughed at the last, because she thought her legs would collapse beneath her any instant. 'Get out. Leave me alone,' she gasped. 'Get out . . . get out . . . get out . . .'

'Not,' Phelan said grimly, 'until we've talked this thing through!'

Dear Reader,

This month finds us once again well and truly into winter—season of snow, celebration and new beginnings. And whatever the weather, you can rely on Mills & Boon to bring you sixteen magical new romances to help keep out the cold! We've found you a great selection of stories from all over the world—so let us take you in your midwinter reading to a Winter Wonderland of love, excitement, and above all, romance!

The Editor

Victoria Gordon is a former radio, television and print journalist who began writing romances in 1979. Canadian-born, she moved to Australia in the early '70s and now lives in northern Tasmania. The founding president of the Tasmanian Gundog Trial Association, she judges retrieving trials for gundogs and is active in a variety of other outdoor activities when not chained to her magic word-processing machine.

Recent titles by the same author:

GIFT-WRAPPED

A TAXING AFFAIR

BY
VICTORIA GORDON

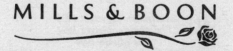

MILLS & BOON

MILLS & BOON LIMITED
ETON HOUSE, 18-24 PARADISE ROAD
RICHMOND, SURREY TW9 1SR

This for ROB BURR...

Who could never qualify as a heroine, even
under the most taxing circumstances.
But helped immensely.

*First published in Great Britain 1993
by Mills & Boon Limited*

© Victoria Gordon 1993

*Australian copyright 1993
Philippine copyright 1994
This edition 1994*

ISBN 0 263 78309 X

*Set in Times Roman 10½ on 12 pt.
91-9402-53120 C*

Made and printed in Great Britain

CHAPTER ONE

VASHTI stretched her throat as if for the sacrificial knife as she tipped her head back and stared upwards to an unseen heaven.

'But why *me*?' she asked, directing the question not at her immediate superior, who had provoked it, but past him, above him, to the nameless, invisible deity she half expected to reply in a barrage of thunderbolts.

'Because it was *you* that he asked for,' was the reply, but it came, of course, from Ross Chandler, whose rotund figure was all too visible, its Buddha-like attitude of benignity offset by eyes that never smiled, perhaps never had.

'And,' he continued with an attitude to match, 'since he apparently has friends in high places, it would be best to...'

His gesture upwards had vastly different overtones than had Vashti's. To Chandler, the only deity that existed was the Australian Taxation Office for which they both worked; the Commissioner for Taxation was the ultimate authority.

'But it doesn't make any sense,' Vashti argued. 'I don't know the first thing about writing, and certainly I'm no authority on the ways in which this office works. I'm just a field auditor. Surely there are people far better qualified for... for whatever this person wants.'

'He wants *you*. He is apparently writing a book in which the workings of the taxation office—and particularly the field audit side—play some significant role, and he wants someone he can consult regularly to ensure accuracy.' Her boss was unmoved by her concern. The request had been ratified from above, therefore she would follow through to the best of her ability. Or *he* would know the reason why.

'But that's just the point,' Vashti insisted. 'Why *me*? Surely there are much better people in this office to help Mr...?'

'Keene,' her boss supplied the name, through hardly moving lips. Vashti added his first name, but her own lips trembled noticeably, at least to herself.

'Phelan. Phelan Keene,' she whispered, shaking her mane of ash-blonde hair and clenching her teeth around the name as if to somehow subdue the memory it carried. 'Of course...of course it would be.'

And just knowing the name answered, at least in part, the manifold question of why. Vashti had spent the months just prior to his father's death working on a terribly convoluted—and still not complete—field audit on the family's wide-ranging Tasmanian business dealings. Phelan Keene hadn't been involved, except as a remote and distant partner in the overall scheme of things; he was a writer who spent virtually none of his time involved with the family's rural affairs. He'd only come home, she thought, for the funeral.

She narrowed her usually wide pale grey eyes and pushed time back a fortnight, back to a grave site...

The funeral for old Bede Keene had been held on a bleak Tuesday morning, the setting a tiny church that crouched on a high and windy ridge back in the hills behind Ouse. Once there'd been a settlement there, now there were a few isolated homesteads and a sign at the gravel-road junction. The aged church, refurbished in a dress of cream-coloured galvanised iron with a fresh-painted green roof, hunched in one corner of a small cemetery, as lonely as its setting. Many of the graves dated back to before 1900; some delineated entire family histories, and several were no more than humps in the ground, unmarked, with nothing to speak for those beneath.

Vashti had attended purely for personal reasons. Purely because during her months of dealing with the old man she had come to like and respect him greatly, and she'd been genuinely saddened by his death.

Emerging from her car after a horrendous drive through drizzle and fog all the way from Hobart, she had almost got right back in again and left, thinking how out of place she felt, and probably looked, to all those gathered round the tiny church, which was literally propped up by timbers on each side and seemed almost to cower beneath the huge old pine trees surrounding the cemetery.

She was only twenty kilometres from Ouse, barely a hundred from Hobart, but it seemed as if she'd gone back just as far in time.

These were country people. Work-roughened hands tugged at unfamiliar and strangling ties and collars beneath out-of-fashion pin-striped suits. Those who were hatless had pale foreheads above tanned and weathered faces. Most of the women, too, seemed from a different time, their clothing somehow dated, their very attitudes different. Given the unique setting of the place, Vashti wouldn't have been surprised to see Model-T Fords parked around the yard, but what she did see still held a country flavour of battered utilities and four-wheel-drives parked along the narrow dirt track to the churchyard with luxury vehicles that had seen better days.

Around her as she hesitantly sought out a glimpse of the family were the voices of rural Tasmania; the talk was of cattle and rain and sheep and drought and crops. And the very cadence of those voices was audibly different, so reminiscent of old Bede Keene's way of speaking that it brought a lump to her throat.

And as more people gathered—surely the little church couldn't hold them all?—she noticed that she wasn't totally alone in not fitting in. There were a few people in city gear, a few men who stood out from the crowd because of their noticeable veneer of sophistication.

Two, she noticed, were politicians, one of them a cabinet minister for the state of Tasmania. And of course Janice Gentry, the family's accountant, was there, classically clothed, classically beautiful, but, to Vashti's eye, with an expression that said this was a duty appearance, even if the accountant seemed comfortable enough in the rural setting.

Her expression had changed as the two women met, nodded, and then Ms Gentry was past and Vashti found herself face to face with Bevan Keene, the elder of the sons, and Alana, the surprisingly young twenty-two-year-old daughter of the patriarch, who'd died in his seventy-ninth year.

Their welcome was evident; Bevan smiled at her, murmuring her name as he nodded. Alana went so far as to reach out and take Vashti's hands in a warm greeting.

Vashti had to blink back tears and force a smile of her own that froze as Alana moved aside to introduce 'my brother Phelan' and Vashti looked up to meet grey-green eyes that fairly blazed with hostility.

No words. She, transfixed by his attitude, simply couldn't speak; he clearly wasn't about to.

Instead, he stared down at her, eyes fierce, mouth fixed in a bitter, angry slash. His pale eyes seemed to burn from a darkly suntanned face the colour of his crisply curled hair. It was a wolf's face; merciless and bleak.

Vashti was stunned. Never in her life had she seen such blatant bitterness. And for what? She'd never met him before—and certainly wouldn't have forgotten if she had.

Far from handsome, at least in any conventional way, he was the most intensely *alive* man she'd ever seen. Although he was standing still, it seemed as if he was poised, totally ready for action. His immobility shouted its own lie. And, she noticed quite irrelevantly, he too was in the country yet not quite *of* it. His dark suit was of European styling, his gleaming shoes a world apart from the dress boots worn by most other men present.

His haircut was of the city, his hands work-muscled, but more the hands of an artist than a farmer. Which, of course, he wasn't. Phelan Keene was a writer and a famous one, a man who'd kept his rural background in his fitness and carriage, but whose life now was centred round the international scene, travelling in Europe and especially in south-east Asia.

And he did not like her, to say the very least. But why?

She tried to match his stare, but found it almost impossible. Had it been a frank sexual appraisal she could have managed; she'd faced enough of them in her adult years to recognise such. But this was a predator's appraisal, so savage that she half expected to see him snarl, to see gleaming teeth slashing down at her trembling throat.

For what seemed like hours she felt as if there were only the two of them there, as if they were trapped in stillness within the quiet, sober bustle of the funeral crowd. Then he shouldered past her and it was as if she'd been suddenly returned to a strangely menacing present.

Moments later, the crowd began to take on a semblance of order as everyone moved to first fill, then overfill, the tiny church. Vashti, still shaken by Phelan Keene's silent assault, hung back, and stayed with the overflow outside.

The funeral, quietly dignified and somehow fitted to the setting, finally over, she found herself in the muddle of departing vehicles without seeing Phelan Keene again, and wasn't sorry. Finally, she managed to trail other vehicles southwards to Ouse, but didn't pause for the 'wake' at the Lachlan Hotel, despite overhearing compliments about the food and drink that would be on offer.

Instead, she had continued on to Hobart, wondering as she drove why Phelan Keene had seemed so angry, so hostile. It was, she had thought with no sense of understanding, as if he somehow blamed Vashti herself for his father's death.

All of which, she now thought, made his request all the more surprising, not to mention suspicious. Fair enough for him to write a book which might involve taxation office procedures, but why specifically seek *her* involvement?

'I'll do what I can, then,' Vashti assured her boss, but she kept her fingers crossed behind her back as she did so; there was something going on here that she somehow knew she wasn't going to like.

On her way home from work, Vashti bought a paperback copy of Phelan Keene's latest suspense thriller.

The reading of it occupied the next three evenings, but did nothing to reveal the logic of the remembered antipathy towards her. Even Keene's picture on the back cover held more mystery than information; it was unsatisfyingly flat and lifeless compared to her memory of the man himself.

The picture simply couldn't do justice to those eyes, she found herself thinking. Those icy grey-green eyes, so bleak in their hostility towards her, now seemed to mock her with their blandness in the picture.

Worse, the image of Phelan Keene revealed a surprising resemblance to the man's father; Vashti might have been looking at Bede Keene in his mid-thirties, she thought.

There was the same high-bridged nose, the same generous mouth and solid, determined jawline. It was easy to picture the old man's shock of still curly grey hair as auburn and even curlier. The photograph held none of the anger she remembered from her brief meeting with the man; indeed he looked almost friendly, with one quirked eyebrow and a hint of a wry smile for his readers.

A face with character, she found herself thinking. A lived-in face. A face too much like his father's for Vashti's taste. She had liked and greatly admired the father, a man of black and white principles, a man with little compromise, and no deviousness, no great subtleties except in the droll, dry sense of humour she'd come to relish.

Throughout their involvement, he'd established a joking pattern of trying to marry her off to one or the other of his sons, insisting she was getting 'long in the tooth' and overdue for marriage. The subject had first arisen when he'd spoken of the original family home north of Ouse. Now it was of only marginal significance to the family's vast empire, but it had been the beginning, and held great emotional significance to the old man.

He'd grown up there, married there, buried his wife there, and was far from joking when he told Vashti he'd 'get a measure of satisfaction out of dying in the same house I was born in. Not that it's really the same house—probably more new than old about it now—but still . . .'

'I can't imagine much satisfaction in dying anywhere,' she'd replied, adding, 'but then I've only got my poky little flat, and it's rented in any case.'

'And you're far too young to be thinking of dying anyway,' he'd said. 'You should be thinking of children and a home of your own. *I* should be thinking about grandchildren, by rights, but the way my mob's going I suspect I'll not see grandchildren in the house where I was born.'

He'd chuckled, eyes bright with inner laughter. 'Unless I could interest you in a fine, strapping lad like Bevan, of course. Might be handy having a tax expert in the family. Phelan,' he grunted, 'wouldn't be much use to you; he's never here at the best of times.'

Vashti had missed most of a muttered remark about the second son, but the look in the old man's eyes fairly shouted that although Phelan Keene might be wild and unruly, with little of the old man's steadiness, he was none the less a favourite.

'You'll outlive all of us,' she'd retorted, and now recalled the comment with sadness as she thought of him on that lonely ridge with generations of Bannisters and various members of the Harrex and Barry families, the many children from so long ago that were buried there with him, yet no grandchild of his own left to mourn.

A grand old man, a man worth the knowing.

But this son? She didn't know—couldn't know—could only speculate at the man behind the confusing dichotomy of picture and meeting. Phelan Keene clearly hadn't liked her, but his father *had*; of that she was certain.

When she'd finished the first novel, she searched out two others in a second-hand bookshop, and had read one of them as well by the time she finally heard from the man himself. Neither book did anything to ease her apprehensions; even less did they prepare her for the sheer seductiveness of his voice over the telephone.

'Phelan Keene,' he announced in tones that were pure chocolate fudge. 'I understand you've been designated to assist with this book I'm trying to work up.'

'I've agreed to help where I can,' Vashti replied, not exactly being evasive, but hoping at the same time to avoid sounding too eager.

It was difficult; Phelan Keene's voice fairly rippled with sex appeal, touching her as surely as if he had been there in the room, stroking, caressing, exploring.

'We'll have to get together in person, soon,' he was
suggesting, and that voice did more than simply
suggest. 'I was hoping to at least have lunch together
before we got into the details of my research, but I
seem to have got ahead of my own schedule for once,
and already I have questions that are slowing me up.'

'We couldn't have that, could we?' Vashti replied
without thinking, then could have bitten her tongue.
What a thing to say!

Phelan Keene seemed not to notice. He began, instead, to work through what was obviously a list of
questions he had already prepared. Most of them,
Vashti was comforted to find, seemed direct enough
and easy to answer.

But then she began to detect a pattern, or at least
the beginnings of a pattern. And it was a pattern that
did nothing at all for her peace of mind, harking back,
as it now clearly did, to her work with Phelan Keene's
father and family, to the field audit and the philosophy behind it.

Vashti shook her head, both alarmed and worried
by the direction the conversation was taking. There
was, she now knew, absolutely nothing drastic hidden
among the myriad accounts administered—in theory—
by Janice Gentry; indeed, the family business was
almost certain to emerge from the field audit with
flying colours. But something about the way Phelan
Keene now approached the subject was a red danger
signal to Vashti.

'Really, Mr Keene,' she finally had to say, 'I think
this is getting far off the track of being just research.
It seems you're getting on to fairly specific ground
here, and I'm not sure we ought to be discussing
such details.'

'Why not? Have you got something to hide?'

'Certainly not, but policy prohibits me from discussing specific cases, which it seems to me you're leading up to.'

'It's a case in which I'm personally involved. It isn't as if I were asking you to discuss somebody else's business.' His voice was still so smooth, so persuasive.

'I realise that,' Vashti replied, 'but again, Mr Keene, I have to say that I'm not comfortable about discussing this specific case outside a formal situation with your family's accountant in attendance. I don't . . . don't think we should go on with this at this time.'

'Too right you don't . . . *Ms* Sinclair.' Despite the rich, mellow sound of his voice, he managed to make the honorific 'Ms' sound somehow tawdry, or at the very least pretentious.

Vashti's temper flared, then was as quickly brought under control before she could snap a reply into the telephone. She suddenly guessed—and just in time— what he was on about and why the entire conversation had suddenly taken on a tinge of *déjà vu.*

Gotcha! she thought, and almost laughed aloud. The very nerve of the illustrious Mr Keene! He was playing games with her, had been all along.

'Could you hold for just a tick?' she asked, and, without waiting for an answer, she put down the telephone and turned to quickly rush across the room and grab her handbag.

Returning to her desk, it was the work of a moment to grab up the copy of the book she'd only just started reading and find the passage she wanted.

Forcing the book down hard in front of her, Vashti skimmed through the pages and fought to steady her breathing and still summon the courage for what she was about to try.

'You seem to have something against the use of the word "Ms", *Mr* Keene.' Vashti deliberately kept her voice rigidly calm, undramatic. It wouldn't do to give the game away by her tone of voice alone. 'I wouldn't have expected a man in your position to be such a blatant chauvinist.'

'Chauvinism has nothing to do with it. I just don't like having to refer to any woman by a word that's at best wishy-washy and at worst nothing more than an abbreviation for manuscript,' he snapped in reply, and Vashti could have cried out with delight.

He was following the script! Just as if he, also, had the book there in front of him; as if he, too, could read the hero's lines that *he* had written.

Vashti grinned to herself, silently wondering how far she could carry the performance. She forgot, for the moment, that she was working, and plunged into the game with a vengeance.

'A manuscript? Is that really the way you see me?' she purred, lost in a mental picture of the book's scenario as Phelan Keene had created it.

'Be an interesting concept—if I were blind—for both of us,' he replied, and now that rich chocolate-brown voice was softer, sliding into a resonance that was dangerously seductive.

Vashti, reading as he spoke, found herself mentally picturing Phelan Keene himself as the hero of the piece. And, strangely—almost dreamily—herself as the heroine. It wasn't all that difficult; the girl in the book was also short, with long ash-blonde hair, and wore glasses. Her figure...well, Vashti had never considered herself quite so voluptuous, but by the same token she was quite happy with her body. She did, she knew, have very good legs—at least as good as Keene's heroine.

'Braille? I'd...hate to think my skin was all *that* rough,' she replied, reading and yet not reading; acting.

'So would I.'

His voice was husky now, as he reached out to take her wrist in his fingers, fingers that brushed the thin skin of her inner wrist with the delicacy of a kiss...

She pulled away, suddenly fearful, her heart hammering. This man could too easily take control of this situation, she realised, could too easily take control of *her*!...

'The masculine honorific, after all, doesn't concern itself with whether a man's married or not,' Vashti said.

But even free, she could feel his touch like a burn on her wrist, could feel the tingle all the way through her body. She thought she was trembling, tried not to...

'Perhaps because it doesn't matter?'

His voice was still soft, his eyes now close—too close. She could see the tiny dark rays that ran through the startling blue, could actually see the desire in...

'Fair is fair,' she replied. 'If *Mr* doesn't tell me whether *you're* married or not, then I can't see why a woman should be forced to——'

'Forced?'

Now it was his eyes that touched her, and if anything that was worse. Because his eyes didn't stop at her wrist; his eyes touched all of her, brushed firmness into her nipples, crept enticingly along the flat plane of her stomach . . .

'Who said anything about force, *Ms* Sinclair?'

The pages of the book blurred before Vashti's eyes; she momentarily lost her place and found herself gasping for a quick breath, a shake of her head that left her wide-eyed at the strangeness she felt.

'You . . . you . . .' she faltered.

'. . . wrote the book!' he snapped, now departed from the script, no longer the heroic, fictional character in a book, now a too real voice on the telephone that threatened to drop from Vashti's suddenly nerveless fingers.

No chocolate fudge in the voice now. It snapped across the phone wires like a lash, flaying both her ear and her conscience.

'Credit for trying, *Ms* Sinclair. Inventive, to say the very least. But you should have *finished* the book before you started playing silly little games. You might have found out that she *didn't* win in the end, didn't get the hero in the end.'

The sound of him hanging up was like a physical blow; there was a dreadful sense of finality to it that was curiously mingled with foreboding.

Vashti sat there, staring sightlessly at Phelan Keene's book on the desk before her, the telephone receiver now humming. The book had flapped shut and his picture stared up at her accusingly, the half-smile caught by the photographer suddenly not a smile at all, but the beginnings of a predatory grin.

CHAPTER TWO

THE second time Vashti spoke with Phelan Keene started as another unmitigated disaster, improved not at all by the fact that Vashti knew it was all her own fault.

She was sitting in Janice Gentry's office when he arrived, along with his brother and sister, and had they come without Phelan she actually might have been quite glad to see them.

Being ten minutes early—Vashti had often considered her habits of punctuality to be a curse—had forced her into a lengthy session of supposedly polite chatter with the accountant. Polite on the surface, at least. Vashti hadn't liked Janice Gentry when they'd been at university together, and had since found little to change her mind about the woman.

Not that she would ever—during her time at university—have expected Janice Gentry even to know she existed. They had moved in vastly different social circles, to put it mildly.

Janice Gentry was 'old' money in Tasmanian terms. Her family had been among the island state's so-called 'squattocracy', descendants of early land-grant settlers at a time when, historically, most of the island's population was drawn from convicts or former convicts. Her family had left the land and formed a dynasty in Hobart business circles before Janice came on the scene, Vashti knew, but the dark-haired accountant's claim to social acceptance was solid enough.

While Vashti had worked her way through university with the help of a scholarship, Janice Gentry had used her father's money and social position to the utmost. No academic slouch by any standard, she had gained her degree by working only *just* hard enough; studies came a poor second place to the social opportunities.

She had moved into her father's firm, as expected, and then, also as expected, had gravitated to head the firm at his poor-health-forced retirement only a year before. But, even before Janice took over, the firm had been less than popular with the taxation office; her ascendancy to the top had improved nothing.

And if she hadn't noticed Vashti during their days at university, it was clear she wasn't about to start now. They had spent the ten minutes on reminiscences so startlingly different, they mightn't have been at the same university.

The enforced falseness of this polite time-wasting had done little for Vashti's already fragile mood. This would be, she hoped, the final official meeting required to tidy up all the loose ends in the field audit, but she had been dreading the meeting just on the presumption that Phelan Keene might attend; when he walked into the office she could only rise to her feet politely and hope her nerveless legs would support her.

Suddenly she knew, without even knowing why she knew, that it *wouldn't* be the final meeting, that somehow Phelan Keene was going to complicate things. And that the complications would have nothing at all to do with the book he was supposedly researching.

Bevan and Alana greeted her with their usual friendliness, Alana especially effusive in her greeting. Vashti had liked the 'baby' of the family from their very first meeting, and although both girls claimed compatibility because of their size—Alana was an inch shorter even than Vashti—it really went beyond that.

'You don't look all that well, if you don't mind me saying so,' Alana said with concern as she reached out to take both of Vashti's hands in her own. 'Have you got the dreaded lurg that's been going round?'

Vashti didn't dare look at Phelan Keene, who stood behind his brother and sister. How would he, she wondered, react to hearing himself described as a contagious disease?

'I'm fine,' she assured the diminutive Alana. 'I've just had a few . . . late nights lately.' She dared to look up then, only to realise she'd put her foot in it again!

Phelan's pale eyes fairly danced with satisfaction as he murmured, 'With a good book?' then gave a fierce bark of laughter as Vashti flushed with embarrassment.

The soft query brought questioning glances from his brother and sister, but Phelan ignored them, striding over to sit at the side of the room, where he fixed Vashti with his pale eyes and proceeded to thoroughly demoralise her.

He'd chosen his position, she realised immediately, just so that he could deliberately stir. The angle of his position let him watch Vashti's every move and, worse, force her attention to be diverted at his choosing, without the others catching him at it.

They were concentrating mostly on what Janice
Gentry was saying, and on Vashti's responses. Vashti
found herself attacked on both flanks, and unable to
defend either one adequately as a result.

This is a farce, she told herself, having had to ask
the same question for the third time as Phelan's
scrutiny and faint sneer destroyed her concentration.
Most of the discussion involved going over old
ground, but even that familiarity couldn't help her
forever.

'There just isn't the documentation,' she found
herself saying, again repeating herself. Oh, damn...
damn... damn, she thought, increasingly annoyed at
how easily Phelan Keene could get her goat, and
knowing it was all because she'd let herself be drawn
into playing silly games on the telephone.

The worst of it was that Phelan hardly said a word.
He let Janice Gentry and his brother Bevan carry the
arguments, with no more than the occasional slightly
cocked eyebrow, usually at Vashti's responses.

But he didn't really have to speak to be effective.
He managed that only too well, just with his eyes and
his overall body language.

If Vashti dared glance his way, it was to find those
knowing, icy grey-green eyes undressing her, peeling
away her clothing as distinctly as if he could physically touch her, could actually undo the buttons of
her sensible office blouse, could feel for himself the
whimsical lace of her bra, the soft swelling of her
breasts.

Certainly *she* could feel the physical manifestation
of his mental assault. Beneath the bra her nipples
throbbed, as sensitive to her thoughts as to his touch.

She had to consciously restrain herself from shifting in her chair, her thighs warm beneath her tights.

Damn him anyway, she thought, mentally squirming, because she couldn't do so physically. Bad enough he was able to manipulate her so—but the rotter was so obviously enjoying it!

By the meeting's end, she had conceded several points, mostly because she had intended to in any event. Even with sketchy documentation, old Bede Keene's intentions were clear enough, and there was no evidence even to *suggest* tax evasion on his part.

One major issue still remained, however, the ultimate interpretation of which could have significant effects throughout the wool-growing sector. It was this which had sparked the field audit in the first place, only to be submerged in the welter of partially related affairs linked to old Bede Keene's personal dealings. One more meeting, at least, Vashti realised, would be required to finally sort that one out, since Bevan Keene said he thought there might be a bit more documentation available.

'I'm sure I saw it when we were sorting things out at the farm,' he said, for the first time drawing Phelan into the discussion.

'More than possible; I'm still finding things I didn't know existed,' was the reply. 'The old man got to be even more of a pack-rat as he got older. I'm surprised we're having any trouble at all finding written evidence of his dealings; he kept everything else.'

'Phelan's staying on at the farm for now,' his brother explained to Vashti, who already knew Bevan and Alana lived on separate family properties—he in the northern Midlands and she on a smaller, intensively cropped property served by the new irrigation scheme centred below the Colebrook reservoir.

'We're off to lunch, Vashti. Why don't you join us?' asked Alana with her usual spontaneity. The invitation, to Vashti's great surprise, caused a noticeable flicker of annoyance to cross Janice Gentry's face.

Vashti's immediate reaction was an overwhelming no. Not just that it was rather against policy, not even that she'd had more than enough already of Janice Gentry... It was the look she caught from Phelan Keene.

But before she had a chance to say anything, *he* did.

'It isn't that I want to be antisocial,' he said. 'And I'm sure Ms Sinclair doesn't either. But we have further business to discuss, she and I, so if it's all right with you lot we'll be having lunch... together but without you.'

'I——' She got no further.

'You don't believe in lunching with *clients*, I suppose,' he interjected. 'But it is lunchtime and you do have to eat, same as the rest of us, and we *do* have a few things to discuss, do we not?'

'Yes... but...'

'Yes... but what? If you're worried about being compromised I suggest you think again. I don't compromise pretty girls in public, and I'm off back to the bush right after, so stop being all public service and *thing*, and come along. We'll go over the road, I think.'

He had taken her arm and was leading her from the office before Vashti could properly object, waving a farewell to the others and saying at the same time, 'I *did* mention on the phone that I'd hoped to have lunch with you; there's no need to seem quite so surprised.'

Vashti said nothing. She found herself struck mute, as if his fingers above her elbow had cut off some vital nerve to her tongue. They walked to the lift together, descended to street level, and emerged into Hobart's city centre without her saying a single word.

Phelan Keene didn't even appear to notice. He chatted on about something—she might have been deaf as well because it just didn't get into her ears— holding her arm in the meanwhile as if they were the best of friends or... or more.

And suddenly it was too much—too much and far too fast. Twisting free, Vashti gabbled out the first excuse that came to mind—anything to keep herself free of his touch.

'I...I've just remembered I have to get to the bank,' she stammered. 'In case I don't have time after work.' The light had changed, but Vashti was no longer paying attention. Half her mind was on walking back towards the Trust Bank of Tasmania building; all of her instincts were crying out to her to just run... run anywhere that would get her away from Phelan Keene.

Phelan Keene—who didn't appear to notice her confusion—was oblivious to her panic. 'OK,' he said. 'But don't be too long about it; I'm more than just a bit peckish.'

Vashti nodded her assurance, meanwhile reaching into her handbag for her wallet and the card that would activate the automatic cash machine.

Phelan stood back courteously as she fed the card into the machine, punched in the complicated series of identification numbers, and collected the notes that eventually emerged.

She stuffed the money into her wallet and turned to find him standing there, shaking his head and frowning slightly. 'You really ought to be ashamed of yourself,' he said.

'Why, for goodness' sake?' Vashti genuinely had no idea what he was on about, and wasn't, it appeared, to be told just yet, either.

'Later, maybe,' he muttered, shaking his head. 'It might just be me; I tend to get cranky on an empty stomach.'

They crossed the street and turned up Murray Street to an historic hotel, where Vashti was somehow unsurprised to find Phelan greeted by name when they entered, and they were courteously shown to a quiet corner table in the restaurant. She so seldom dined out that she'd be lucky to recognise a restaurant's name, much less have staff remember hers, Vashti thought, then shrugged the thought away as unworthy.

Phelan, she thought, looked perfectly at home here. He was dressed in the type of semi-casual clothes preferred by country folk in Tasmania—a Harris Tweed sports jacket, moleskin trousers and elastic-sided boots. And now that he wasn't glaring furiously at her, as he had during the funeral, he looked more the man on the cover of his books.

The crisp, curly dark brown hair was well cut and tidy enough, except when he thrust his fingers through it in absent thought. His grin was almost infectious, if rare. Only the eyes hadn't changed. Against the depth of his tan they were astonishingly pale, difficult to read.

They ordered, Vashti refusing a drink on the legitimate grounds that 'I wouldn't get any work at all done this afternoon; a big lunch will be quite enough of a shock to the system, thank you.'

'I can't imagine your system being that easily shocked,' was the response. 'But then again...' He let the comment drag out, stretching it much as he had persisted in stretching out the 'Mssss' whenever he addressed her.

'It's a very simple system, I assure you,' she replied, almost calm now, almost composed, despite knowing he could upset her composure almost at will.

Vashti sipped at her tomato juice when it arrived, too aware of his eyes upon her, of how he seemed to be ever watchful, attuned to her every movement and thought.

His telephone accusation, not once mentioned during the meeting or—yet—now that they were alone together, still grated. How dared he accuse her like that? she thought. And immediately felt her anger begin to push away her spate of nerves.

She took a deep breath, as subtly as she could manage it, then put down the glass and reached up to adjust her glasses as she looked at him squarely.

'Now, Mr Keene,' she said firmly, 'perhaps we can begin?'

'Do that again,' he replied, and she saw his eyes gleam with what seemed to be laughter.

'Do what again?' she countered, immediately cautious. What on earth was he on about this time?'

Now he grinned, and reached out to shove imaginary glasses into place on his nose. 'Makes you look all fierce and authoritarian, like an...a... schoolteacher.'

'What kind of schoolteacher?' She hadn't missed the hesitation, could have inserted 'old maid' easily enough herself, but suddenly wanted to see if she could push him into admitting it.

'A rather pretty one, actually,' he replied, his grin broadening but his eyes somehow making the comment far more intimate than it sounded.

Vashti shook her head, but said nothing. It was too dangerous to play word games with this man, she told herself, but couldn't help it.

Neither could she help the habitual gesture of adjusting her glasses, and, without realising it until too late, she did it again! And Phelan Keene, of course, nodded his approval with a quirky grin. She could have kicked herself.

'I suppose you're bound and determined this is to be all business,' he said then with an exaggerated sigh. 'Can't we at least wait until we've had the starter? I'm absolutely famished and, as I told you, I get fair-dinkum cranky when I'm hungry.'

And *I* get fair-dinkum cranky when I'm being stuffed around, she wanted to say, but didn't. She didn't say a word, in fact, just nodded agreement at the first part of his statement.

He frowned at her determination, but the frown changed to a wide grin of satisfaction as their starter arrived. 'Saved by the bell,' he chuckled, thanking the waitress, who—Vashti couldn't help noticing—was wondrously appreciative of every morsel of attention Phelan Keene deigned to proffer.

Style, she found herself admitting. And what's worse, he does it without even having to think about it. The man's a born womaniser; he flirts and flatters and *manipulates* just for the hell of it. So watch yourself!

Which she did, concentrating on her scallops, while being only too aware that *he* was concentrating more on her than on the scrumptious-looking Barilla Bay oysters he appeared to so enjoy.

But it was all too brief a respite. Vashti nibbled at the last tasty morsel and wished she'd claimed to be on a diet or something, so that this would be the end of the meal and she could then plead some excuse to return to work. And then asked herself why, because sooner or later she would have to deal with Phelan Keene and his damned book! Maybe the sooner the better, she thought; at least it'll be over and done with.

But it wasn't. While they waited for their main courses, Phelan showed no sign of wanting to get down to business. He commented on the quality of the food, solicitously enquired whether Vashti wouldn't reconsider and have wine with her duckling, but gave her no opportunity to force the conversation back on to purely business footings.

Nor was she as ready as before to force the issue. Now her instincts told her to be totally cautious, to volunteer nothing, expect only the unexpected. I'm being set up, she thought, but I don't know for what, much less why.

Thankfully, she was able to devote her full attention to the delicious roast duckling when it arrived, impatiently putting aside a mild feeling of envy when she looked over at the thick rib of beef he was consuming with obvious pleasure.

I'd feel the same way if *he* were having the duckling and I the steak, she realised; the issue wasn't the dish on offer but the fact that Phelan Keene had taken the privilege of ordering for her.

'You needn't look so envious,' he said with a wry grin. 'All that talk about having to work this afternoon, I reckoned a steak this size would have you dozing in your chair by smoko.'

Vashti nearly choked. What was it with this man? Surely he couldn't be reading her mind? Then she sobered and glared at him across the table. Observant, that was all. Logical for a writer, she supposed, but unnerving for all that.

She thought for an instant of asking him if he made a habit of verbalising his observations, then thought better of it; he'd probably only say what she'd been thinking, and she didn't feel up to any cryptic references to writing or—worse—books just for now.

'I'm a bit surprised at you,' he said after a moment. 'Either you hide your feminine curiosity rather well, or...'

'Or what?'

'Or I'm losing my touch,' he admitted bluntly. 'I would have expected some sort of question by now about my comment at the bank, although I realise you've been trying hard to keep our relationship totally businesslike.'

'Should it be anything else?' she replied calmly. Phelan Keene might need food to keep from being cranky, but Vashti had just discovered how much a good meal improved her whole mental outlook. For the first time that day, she actually felt totally capable of dealing with his attempts to stir her up.

'But OK, I'll play your litle game.' She shrugged. 'What did I do at the bank that so got on your wick? Wasn't I secretive enough while I was punching numbers into that stupid automatic cash machine or something? If I was, it's hardly anything surprising.

I hate the damned things with a veritable passion, but, the hours I keep, there aren't many alternatives.'

Phelan grinned. 'The issue wasn't secrecy—just plain old inconsideration,' he reflected. 'Although I suppose you didn't notice that there were six healthy, hale and hearty *human* bank clerks standing round that bank twiddling their little thumbs while you were standing out on the street in a line of people talking to a damned machine! It's worse than just inconsiderate—it's downright insulting!'

His voice rose gradually throughout the diatribe, to the point where one or two people at adjacent tables actually looked up. Vashti sat there with her mouth open, absolutely stunned.

All she could do was look at him, wide-eyed, a fork full of food halfway to her mouth, and—in her mind—gasp like a stranded fish. Phelan Keene, meanwhile, sat glaring at her as if she'd kicked his dog. They sat there for what seemed hours, silently looking at each other.

'Sorry about that,' he finally said, voice thankfully lower now, although without a sign of real remorse. 'One of my hobby-horses, obviously, and I *did* warn you that hunger makes me cranky.'

'It's a bit late for that excuse,' Vashti replied with a meaningful glance at his nearly empty plate. 'And don't you dare blame it on the wine, either; that's Piper's Brook, and I'm sure you know how good it is, considering you're paying for it.'

'And will end up taking most of it home with me,' he snapped crossly. 'You can see I've only had two glasses, and I'm damned if I'll lay myself open to a drink-driving charge.'

'I should certainly hope not. And don't change the subject,' she replied just as snappily, delighted at actually having *him* on the back foot for a change. 'Don't you think it's just a bit much to invite me to lunch—to coerce me into having lunch with you, not to put too fine a point on it—and then start criticising my banking habits, of all things?'

'I brought it up before lunch, actually,' he replied without the slightest sign of contrition. 'And, I might add, without so much as mentioning the fact that if you were going to use a machine that's available twenty-four hours a day there was hardly the panic involved you tried to portray. You could have got your money any time.'

'I don't care *when* you brought it up,' Vashti hissed. 'I think you've got a nerve bringing it up at all! It is none of your business. None!'

Vashti was working herself up into a frothing good rage, however artificial, when the waitress arrived to clear away their dinner plates. It was quite obvious that the woman was only too aware of the hostile atmosphere between them, but to Vashti's astonishment the waitress looked at *her* as if she were the sole cause of the argument. Phelan Keene got just what Vashti would have expected—a look which clearly took his side entirely in the matter.

And from the look on Phelan's face, he and waitress agreed!

That was enough to make her truly wild. Vashti found herself clenching and unclenching her fists beneath the table, her fingernails biting into her palms. Her breath came in short, sharp huffs, and it seemed as if the entire room were closing in around her, the very air electric with her anger.

She was conscious, as the waitress turned away, of actually holding her breath, waiting for the woman to get just far enough before she let fly.

'This, I think, is the moment where you're supposed to throw something at me, grab up your handbag, and stomp out in high dudgeon, whatever that is.' His voice was low, but with those rich chocolate-brown tones it carried across the table like a shout. Or a challenge.

'In some pulp fiction epics, written by people who shall remain nameless, and present company definitely *not* excepted.' Vashti spat out the words, her voice even more controlled than his. 'But this isn't fiction, *Mr* Keene; this is the real world. This is Hobart, Tasmania, and I'm a real person. I'm not so sure about you.'

Vashti pushed up her glasses, instantly regretted the gesture, but *only* for an instant, then returned to the attack.

'So how about *you* throw something and stomp off in high dudgeon? Presuming you can spell it. Try throwing money to pay for this ... this ...' She sputtered, but not to a stop. 'Because *I'm* going to have the biggest, richest dessert on the menu, and I'd like to be able to enjoy it without being hassled about my ... my banking habits!'

She was half out of her chair now, one lacquered fingernail aimed like a gun between those fathomless grey-green eyes, her own eyes blazing and her words hanging almost visibly above the table.

Phelan sat immobile, his long, craftsman's fingers splayed on the table before him. His jaw was clenched, and she could see the muscles flexing, as if he was gnashing his teeth in a fury that matched her own.

But when he finally spoke, it was in a voice of such soft, reasoned calm that she surprisedly became aware of her posture, and quite suddenly sat back down.

'You're right, of course. And I do apologise—honestly.' He threw open his hands in a gesture that would have been provocatively flamboyant except that his eyes told her the truth. Under her glare, he paused, then continued, and this time his words confirmed it.

'You said earlier you don't go much on those damnable automatic cash machines,' he said, steepling his fingers before him on the table. 'Well, I positively *hate* the things, although I have to admit my feelings aren't wholly altruistic. True, it really gets my dander up when I go into a bank and find half a dozen clerks standing around doing nothing while people line up outside to use machines. I think it's a tragic sign of the times that so many people would rather deal with a machine instead of a *person*.'

'When you work the hours I do, there often isn't all that much notice,' Vashti interrupted, only to have him shush her with one upraised finger, then at least have the grace to look slightly embarrassed when she obeyed.

'After hours isn't the issue,' he said, eyes now blazing with what Vashti thought a writer would call impassioned fervour. 'It's during the day that I'm talking about—during normal business hours, when bank clerks are being paid to be there, to be of service, to do their jobs, for goodness' sake. And nobody will let them. They have to stand there with fixed little smiles on their faces and watch—*watch*, mind you!—while people ignore them in favour of *machines*! How the hell can anybody get job satisfaction out of that?'

Vashti shook her head, uncertain what, if anything, to say, not certain, indeed, if she was to be given a chance, until the waitress arrived with the sweets menu and she was able to echo Phelan's earlier remark.

'Saved by the bell . . . again?'

His grin was infectious.

'Too right. And please, without any arguments, may I be permitted to order this wondrous dessert you're going to have? It's a small price for my sins.'

'I'd reckon! *Your* sins, I suspect, would have a far, far higher price than that,' Vashti retorted. But her grin matched his; she simply couldn't help herself.

'A deal, then? No names, no pack drill?'

'Deal,' she replied, but hesitated momentarily before reaching out to meet the hand he extended across the table. Their eyes met with, she thought, some unknown-as-yet message as his fingers closed around her own, and he held her hand just sufficiently too long, or was it not long enough?

She was saved the problem of deciding with the return of the waitress, and Phelan's grandiose announcement that he wanted the biggest, richest, most awe-inspiring dessert on the sweets menu.

'And my mother'll have the same,' he said, flashing Vashti the most mischievous, devilish little-boy grin she'd ever seen.

The waitress smiled; Vashti thought the woman would have smiled no matter what Phelan said. Chauvinistic bastard! Vashti bit her tongue but didn't smile. Instead she shot Phelan a look of warning, in the certain knowledge that it was wasted.

'You really do like living dangerously, don't you?' she muttered when the woman was truly out of earshot. 'What is it—a death-wish? Or do you just like to stir?'

'I sometimes wonder myself,' he replied, leaning calmly back in his chair, as if the knives she was glaring at him couldn't possibly get across the table. 'You do stir awfully easily, I must say. I'd have thought a decent sense of humour would be vital in your job.'

'And I'd have thought just *some* sense would be vital in yours,' Vashti retorted. 'Do you live your whole life in some fictional wonderland where you can just write your way out of trouble? I am the dreaded taxman, in case you've forgotten.'

She put on her sternest face as she said it, the face she used when the powers of her office were needed in full to bring some really difficult client into line. It was needed seldom, but when it was...

Stern look or no, it was supposed to be funny, supposed to match the mood Phelan Keene had created. But it wasn't, suddenly. Something...something she couldn't quite identify...came to life in his eyes, and Vashti instantly cursed herself for such an unprofessional gambit.

You fool, she cried inwardly. Fool...fool...fool! She recognised the predator, the wolf that had so fleetingly stalked out to glare at her. She'd seen that look before, in a lonely cemetery where she'd been the subject of a longer, more thorough inspection.

And just as quickly, the predator was gone. Phelan's eyes now were bland, placid. She'd seen that colour— exactly—in the water over shallow reefs, and once in the wild eyes of a blue merle collie just before it tried to lunch on her left leg.

Vashti shivered inwardly, still cursing herself for her transgression. She wanted to take it back, to say something—anything—but the chance had disappeared as quickly as that fleeting predator's glance.

'Yes, I suppose I should remember that, shouldn't I?'

Phelan's expression was as bland as his eyes now, too bland. 'Especially as we never did get to the real purpose of this luncheon, which was supposed to be business,' he continued, voice calm, strangely flat.

'Still,' he said with a grin that never reached his eyes, 'there's dessert to come.'

And come it did! The sheer size of the offerings was such that Vashti and Phelan could only stare first at their plates and then at each other, animosity forgotten—or so Vashti hoped—in the face of such gastronomic opulence.

Each of them managed half their dessert, eating in silence at first, then with timid forays into the kind of small talk that the meal had begun with. There was no business, and now Vashti was glad of that. She felt embarrassed at having come the heavy; however frivolous the move had been it had been a bad one, seriously misinterpreted.

Far easier to let Phelan relate the other reason he hated the automatic cash machines . . .

'So there I was, Friday night of a long weekend, with not a single soul whom I knew within a thousand miles and no money worth mentioning, the damned car with a flat tyre and a flatter spare—just the scenario they advertise as being the time your cash card will save you,' he said. 'And what did the automatic cash machine do?'

'It ate the card, of course,' Vashti answered. 'There's nothing surprising about that; it's hardly an uncommon occurrence. You probably didn't get the PIN number right or something.'

'I did too!'

'Well, you must have got *something* wrong,' she insisted. 'These machines don't just go around eating people's cards at random.'

'Want to bet?'

'No, I don't want to bet. What I want to know is what you did *after* the machine ate your card. It must have been a bit traumatic, to say the least.'

'Traumatic? I was fairly ropable, as you can imagine, and on the Tuesday morning I had meaningful dialogue with the bank, let me tell you.'

'And in the meantime?'

'Oh, I just checked into the best hotel in town and lived it up for the weekend.' He shrugged. 'They didn't ask for any money until I checked out, and of course, by then I had plenty.'

'Lucky for you.' Vashti didn't even attempt to sound sympathetic. She hardly knew anybody who hadn't faced similar problems with the technology. 'And I suppose you've never used a cash card after hours *since*, either?'

'Now you're being sarcastic,' was the reply. 'Of course I have; that's what they're for. But I also——' with a hint of smugness '—make sure I'm never caught quite that short of real, usable money. It meant I had to eat every meal in the hotel's restaurant, and while it wasn't bad or anything, it got a bit boring by the end.'

'Not as boring as going hungry would have been. Or having to sleep in the streets.'

'But the card, or lack of it, had nothing to do with that,' he protested. 'I could have stayed in the hotel and charged everything whether I'd had the damned card or not! And having the card stuck in the machine all weekend meant I *had* to stay. Even if I'd somehow managed to get the car fixed, I *had* to stay because of the machine. That's the point!'

Then he grinned, again with that light of mischief in his eyes. 'Still, I got a scenario for a book out of it, so the weekend wasn't a total waste. But that doesn't change the fact that I don't like those machines, never have and never will!'

'And you never, ever use an automatic cash machine during working hours, I know,' she concluded for him. 'And while I wouldn't want you to get bigheaded about this, you've actually converted me to that philosophy as well. I'm forced to admit it never occurred to me to consider how the bank clerks must feel about it.'

'Well, there you go! A taxman... person who's human after all,' he sad. 'Will wonders never cease?'

Vashti sighed. 'I do wish you'd let up on that,' she said. 'It's old hat to me, and I'm long past being offended by comments like that. Really.'

He raised one dark eyebrow. 'Well, let's just hope the chef's not easily offended either,' he said, with a meaningful glance at their half-full dessert plates. 'Because with the best will in the world I couldn't finish this, and I don't really think a doggy-bag is appropriate, somehow.'

After the lunch, they walked together back to the corner of Collins and Murray Streets, where Vashti would turn north to return to her office.

'It doesn't appear we're going to get much business done today, either,' he said as they prepared to part. 'Not that it matters much; I'm in no screaming hurry. It might be better, all things considered, if we waited on the book stuff until the family audit is finished. What do you think?'

Vashti wasn't about to create any new misunderstandings. 'If it has to be, it has to be,' she replied. 'This business seems to have more delays than real progress sometimes.'

Phelan Keene merely laughed. 'With the amount of provisional tax I'm usually up for, any delay is a blessing in disguise,' he retorted. 'I suppose I'd be in terrible strife if I somehow managed one year to have all my records just disappear in a puff of smoke?'

'You could try,' Vashti replied with a grin. 'Remembering of course that tax law is perhaps the only area of law where you're automatically presumed guilty until proven innocent—and the proof usually has to come from you!

'Records *have* been lost, of course. But I really would have to advise you to try and avoid it, and to have a very, very good accountant or tax advisor if it did happen.'

'Ah, but of course I have,' he replied. 'The very best, and extremely attractive in the bargain. I'll be right. And thanks for joining me for lunch, by the way. Even if we didn't get any business done, it was very enjoyable.'

As Vashti headed north towards her office she found herself reflecting not on the lunch—which had indeed been enjoyable—but on Phelan's coment about his accountant.

The ravishing Janice Gentry, of course, she thought, and shrugged off a vague sense of disquiet. Of course he'd have Janice Gentry as an accountant. It was only logical, since she handled the family's affairs. And certainly she was extremely attractive, no sense in denying that.

Too attractive, she found herself thinking on several occasions during what turned out to be a cow of an afternoon. Vashti put her bad temper down to too much dessert, knowing she was fooling nobody, including herself.

CHAPTER THREE

VASHTI didn't see or hear from Phelan Keene for more than a week—at least not in the flesh. He turned up on the ABC's book programme one night in what she thought must have been an old interview, but there was nothing old about the picture of him in the Hobart *Mercury* social pages.

He was resplendently dressed in evening wear, as was his predictable companion. Janice Gentry, if the grainy black and white picture was any guide, might have been wearing an evening gown—what there was of it—in leech-green, so tightly was she attached to Phelan's arm.

Vashi told herself it was irrelevant and none of her business anyway, and used that section of the paper to wrap up her rubbish.

The radio programme was quite a different story, sneaking up on her without warning as she was wishing herself to sleep after what had been a fair bitch of a day.

Having Keene's rich voice right there, next to her ear on her very own pillow, somehow sounded different from how she remembered it. It was gentler, more mellow. And, she quickly realised, it was a highly revealing voice—too revealing!

She'd turned on the radio part-way into the programme, at a point where he was reading bits of his own work and explaining some of the background.

Only after a few minutes did the interview itself begin, and Vashti was immediately wide awake with interest.

'Any man who says he understands women is either a damned fool or a liar—or both!' he was saying. 'In fact there are times I don't think *women* understand women; certainly *I* don't make any claims in that direction.'

'And yet your heroines seem...well...so well rounded—as people, I mean,' cooed the interviewer, and Vashti could literally *see* Phelan pouring on the charm. The interviewer's first few questions had clearly been designed to set Phelan up for something, but without even appearing to notice, he'd turned the entire thing round to his favour.

And he continued to do it. He's playing her like a piano, Vashti said to herself, fully awake now and fascinated by the whole performance. If she hadn't personally seen and heard Phelan Keene in action, his performance on the radio mightn't have been so obvious, she thought. And then she recalled how he'd done much the same to her both in person and over the telephone.

'Well, you won't do it again, and that's for sure,' she said aloud, then wondered if the opportunity would even arise.

As the interview continued, Vashti found herself swinging between anger, laughter and downright astonishment as Phelan manipulated the poor woman asking the questions.

'You should be in politics, my lad,' she found herself muttering after one exchange in which he deftly managed to appear to answer a particularly awkward question without really answering it at all.

And when the question came, as she had already come to expect, about money and how much a *famous* writer could make, it was no surprise to find him evading that one too. The real surprise came afterwards.

'The taxation system is enough to drive any sane person quite mad,' he said. 'One of these days I think I'll write a book about it, I think. Like every other businessman in the country, I spend half my time working for them anyway; it might be useful to get something back. Of course I'd have to find the right sort for a heroine, which might be tricky.'

It drew a chuckle from the woman interviewer. 'The tax—er—*person* as a heroine?' she asked. 'I'll look forward to reading that one, Mr Keene. I wouldn't have thought it possible.'

'Anything's possible in fiction,' he replied. 'That's what makes it so wonderful—the ability to create impossibilities like honest politicians and tax systems that make sense, and actually make people believe them.'

From that point, the brief remainder of the interview returned to discussions of his books, but Vashti didn't, couldn't, listen any more. She'd read the books, even enjoyed them. Now she found herself wondering—dreading the thought—if she was going to somehow be *in* one!

The concept, she realised with actual surprise, was worse than terrifying. A very, very private person, she found the whole idea so unnerving that she hardly slept all night. Because it was just what she might expect from Phelan Keene, she realised, especially considering his apparent opinion that she might in some way be responsible for having driven his father to his death. It was all too, too complicated. And scary!

You cunning, devious, rotten sod, she thought, staring past her morning coffee after a troubled night. Through the window of her small flat she could see cloud perched like a gay pink bonnet round the crown of Mount Wellington, heralding a day in which it should be safe to walk to work.

The radio confirmed it, only to become a liar when Vashti was half a block from the office. By the time she'd actually reached her desk and could begin work she had run her tights trying to open an umbrella that exploded into useless tatters, dropped an armful of papers into a muddled heap that clogged the corridor, and broken the back off an earring.

The entire week seemed to get worse from that point on, as Vashti found herself haunted by the entire concept of Phelan Keene's double-damned book.

She found herself hearing the interview over and over in her mind, then wishing she'd had the facilities to tape it, because she quickly became unsure of the accuracy in her memory.

How old had the interview *really* been? Had he decided to write this book before her field audit on the family business dealings? Or after? And was she to be purely an accuracy consultant, or did he have far more sinister plans for her involvement in the book?

The worries did nothing for Vashti's week and even less for her weekend, especially when she found herself face to face with Alana Keene in one of the city's second-hand book shops just before Saturday noon.

'What have you been doing to my big brother?' Alana asked, eyes wide with what Vashti thought might be astonishment that anyone, female at least, could be guilty of doing anything disagreeable to Phelan Keene.

'I can't imagine,' she replied evasively, tucking a copy of his very first book under her arm in the vain hope that Alana might miss seeing it. 'Why? Is he upset with me or something?'

'More *something*, I expect,' was the reply. 'He's been going round for the past few days like somebody kicked his dog. He's living alone out there in Dad's old house, you know, and he really shouldn't be. I think isolation is quite wrong for him, being a writer and all. You've got to observe if you're going to write about people, and out there the only thing to observe is himself in the mirror. I finally had to leave in the end, or else I'd have been saying something that would have got *me* kicked.'

'Oh, surely not,' Vashti answered, not one bit sure the remark was even half logical. Phelan Keene, she suspected, might be capable of almost anything when crossed.

'Figuratively speaking. He's a marshmallow, really,' was the bright reply. And then, in a whisper that carried like a cannon-shot through the shop, 'Surely you're not going to *buy* that? I've got all his books at home and I'd be more than happy to lend you one.

'Although,' she sniffed, 'that's the *last* of his books you'd ever want to read. It's nothing but sex and violence and sex and violence and *more* sex and violence. His later stuff is much, much better.'

Vashti was caught floundering. Indeed this was the 'last' of his books she'd want to read; she'd already read all the others, hoping against hope that he'd already done the tax book he'd mentioned on the radio. But she didn't dare tell Alana that!

'Well, if even his sister doesn't recommend it, perhaps I won't buy it after all,' she replied finally, only to contradict herself by then saying, 'Actually, I've got all his others, so yes, I will buy it.'

'Oh, not you too,' was the surprising reply, followed by a wide-eyed gasp. 'Open mouth; insert feet. I do a lot of that,' Alana said, shaking her head as if to deny any form of insult. 'I'm sorry, Vashti. It's just that every damned woman Phelan meets seems to fall for him like . . . well . . . you know! And he just laps it up like . . . like it was his *due*.'

Alana stamped one small foot, her eyes bright with feeling. 'What my brother wants is a woman who'll give him a bash around the ear occasionally; he's had things all his own way for far too long.'

Vashti didn't know what to say, which was obvious to both girls. Alana suddenly grinned, saying, 'I do love him and he's really a wonderful person, deep down inside. But I'm afraid he's going to get spoiled even more rotten than he already is, if everybody in a skirt treats him like . . . well, like that prize bitch Janice Gentry. Surely you saw that photo in the paper—she was all over him like a rash!'

Vashti had to laugh at the comparison between her own mental picture of leech-green and Alana's description. Then she had to explain her laughter—easy enough, because she truly did like Alana—then share it.

'He's leading a more dangerous life than I thought,' Alana said with a final giggle. 'Leeches and rashes and . . . speak of the devil . . .' She raised one eyebrow in a quick caution, but it was too late.

'Child sisters ought to have more respect,' said a familiar voice from behind Vashti.

She turned to look up into Phelan Keene's face, trying frantically to hide his book under her arm as she did so, but it was a futile gesture.

Long, tanned fingers reached out to pluck the book from her suddenly nerveless fingers.

'Shocking literary taste,' he growled, shaking his head in mock-dismay. 'And I suppose, having bought the thing second-hand—thus denying me my paltry royalties—you're going to expect me to autograph it.'

'I...was not.' Vashti managed to get out the denial, but she was wasting her breath. Phelan had already turned his attention to his sister.

'Give us a pen, little one,' he demanded, and was reaching out to accept the meekly provided object when Vashti managed to squeak,

'But I haven't even paid for it yet!'

'Oh! Well, you'd best do that first. Good thing you mentioned it, because of course an autographed copy would have cost you more,' he said sternly.

The book was thrust into her hands, then she was gripped by the shoulders, turned around, and quite forcibly shoved towards the cash register where a clerk—young, female and attractive—was staring wide-eyed at both the performance and at Phelan Keene.

Hardly surprising, Vashti thought as she hunched forward in an obvious attitude of self-consciousness. The man looked like an advertisement for a catalogue. His blue checked shirt was crisp and snug-fitting, as were the faded jeans he wore so well. His boots gleamed as brightly as the eyes that followed her. In the rather crowded confines of the small shop he loomed above the other browsers, fairly exuding a sort of roguish male vitality.

'Is that really...?' The sales clerk's whisper boomed through the quiet bookshop, her eyes never leaving the author as she took Vashti's money, rang up the sale, and counted the change.

Vashti didn't bother to answer. The photo on the dust-cover did that for her. All *she* wanted to do was somehow escape this ludicrous situation. But Phelan was watching too closely for that, unless she dared to just turn and flee, which would be adding insanity to ludicrousness, she thought.

To hell with it, she thought, and straightened her shoulders as she returned to where he and Alana stood waiting.

Suddenly aware of just how ratty she looked, in faded, paint-stained jeans and an over-sized sweat-shirt, her hair gathered loosely at the back in a rubber band, Vashti went overboard in her reaction now to Phelan Keene's stirring.

'Please, sir,' she wheedled as she reached him, and slouched into a totally subservient posture. 'Please, sir, if I pay the royalty may I humbly beg that you autograph this book for me poor old granny? Please, sir! It'd mean so much to her, sir; she's one of your greatest fans.'

Fumbling into her handbag as Phelan took the book with a scowl, obviously taken aback by her per-formance, Vashti found a two cent copper, virtually obsolete because of the country's most recent cur-rency changes, and had it ready when he returned the book to her after furiously scribbling inside it.

He handed her the book, accepted the coin without a glance, then *did* look at it, whereupon he fell into his own role with a vengeance, snarling, 'Foul little urchin ... Get away with you. Your granny probably can't even read.'

Vashti took him at his word, and scuttled from the shop, only to find him right behind her, a hand outstretched to catch her by the shoulder before she could continue her escape. Alana, convulsed with laughter, was right behind him.

Phelan, however, wasn't laughing. He stood, hand still on Vashti's shoulder, his touch burning, she thought, right through the bulky fleece of the sweatshirt. His pale eyes, edged with the tiny wrinkles of a man much out of doors, gleamed with a message she couldn't read.

'You two should go on the stage; you make a great act,' bubbled Alana, apparently oblivious to the tension between them. Vashti, having to meet his eyes and squint because of the sun high in the sky behind him, was hardly conscious of his sister's presence.

'You look about twelve years old.' His voice rumbled down like distant thunder, barely audible and yet impossible not to hear. The message in his eyes was something far more complicated, too much so. Vashti couldn't think of an answer. She was caught by his gaze, held by it.

The sunlight in his dark, coarse, curly hair threw up rainbows, she thought, rainbows tinged with dark auburn. She found herself thinking that it was almost criminal for a man to have such long, thick eyelashes.

'If you two are going to stare into each others's eyes, how about doing it over coffee or something?' Alana's voice, liquid with suppressed laughter, flowed in to break the spell, if spell it had been. 'Or better yet, lunch! I vote we trot down to the botanical gardens; they do a scrumptious luncheon there.'

'Oh . . . no. I . . . well, look at me,' Vashti replied.

'You look fine. I'm only talking about lunch, not a reception at Government House.'

Vashti looked at the younger girl, casually dressed, to be sure, but neatly so, in jeans and riding boots and a plaid shirt beneath a jumper that matched her violet eyes.

'I look like a grot,' she replied. Firmly. Uselessly.

'Don't be silly. It's Saturday, after all. Not as if anybody's working or anything.'

'If I'm awake, I'm working!' Phelan joined the conversation for the first time.

'Oh, stop being so dogmatic, brother, dear,' Alana sniffed. 'You're doing no such thing, and anyway, it's Saturday.' She then ignored him, turning again to Vashti and casting an appraising eye.

'Well, I suppose I have to take your point, but it's no problem. We'll just whip you home for a quick change on the way.'

Vashti had no chance to reply.

'Not so fast, baby sister,' Phelan interrupted, reaching out to take Alana by the shoulder and turn her to face him. 'I have no objection to having Ms Sinclair join us for lunch; indeed I'd welcome it.' This was said with a wicked grin tossed in Vashti's direction. 'But not if you're going to start putting words in my mouth, or, even worse, ignoring what I say altogether. You do enough of that. So let me repeat— if I am awake, I am working! Doesn't matter if it's Saturday or Shrove Tuesday.'

'But why should it matter anyway? Honestly, Phelan, you do go on about the strangest things.'

'There's nothing strange about it,' he replied grimly. 'You forget, dear sister, that, while Ms Sinclair may be a darling girl, she is still *the enemy*.'

And he said it with such fierceness that both girls reared back in surprise.

'All the more reason to give it a miss,' Vashti snapped, the words pouring out in a torrent as she rushed to get her two bobs' worth in first.

'Oh, don't be silly,' Alana replied hotly, her words muddled with Phelan's, saying virtually the same thing.

'Maybe we can manage not to disagree so often if we have a neutral buffer, provided, of course, we can keep her quiet—which is seldom easy,' Phelan said then, taking each girl by the hand and turning to start off down the footpath. 'But we *are* going to eat, because arguing on an empty stomach is bad for the complexion. You lot mightn't have to worry, but I'm too old to take risks.'

He smiled at each girl in turn, then cast a sideways glance at Vashti, mischief lurking in his eyes. 'And I think we will stop and let you change, Ms Sinclair. I don't want you to feel at a disadvantage if the arguments get really interesting.'

Vashti allowed herself to be led along like, she thought, a lamb to the slaughter. And although she was on one side of the trio, she quickly felt as if she were square in the middle.

Phelan and his sister seemed to have agreed to disagree about anything and everything. Even as they walked to where Alana's car was parked—'No room for all three of us in that excut a paddock ute I'm reduced to driving,' Phelan said, adding, 'My temperament will improve out of sight when my own car arrives from the mainland next week'—the siblings argued and scrapped like a couple of ten-year-olds.

Vashti, an only child, found it a quite astonishing performance, not least so because, despite the fervent passions displayed, there was a clear thread of familial love and affection that never wavered.

She already knew that Alana shared a similar rapport with the elder brother, Bevan, but, he being a less volatile personality than Phelan, the relationship was less flamboyant.

How wonderful, though, she thought. Three children so vividly different in temperament and yet so united as a family despite their differences. Old Bede Keene must have been proud; each of his children in their own way had obviously lived up to his influence.

Memory of the old man sobered Vashti, and by the time they reached her flat she was half tempted to try once again to beg out of the luncheon.

But no chance.

'You've got five minutes to make yourself presentable,' Phelan remarked with a stern glance at his wristwatch. 'We won't come in; doesn't look like there'd be room for all three of us——' this with a grin that supposedly showed he was only joking '—but if you dilly-dally, I warn you, I'll come in and get you, ready or not!'

Vashti got out of the back seat and ran for the door of her flat. There was nothing else for it! Politeness should have required her to invite them in for a drink, or at least coffee, but Phelan hadn't been far off in saying there wasn't room. And she didn't have a drop of milk in the place, much less any sort of drink to offer.

She was back in seven minutes, the last two of which had been spent applying minimal make-up while keeping one eye on the door, as if Phelan Keene might be expected to kick it in like some marauding vandal.

Her grotty jeans were replaced by tidy trousers, the sweatshirt by a jersey blouse in shades of greys and pinks. Her hair, normally gathered in a tidy knot or braid for work, cried out for similar treatment today, but instead was quickly brushed and allowed to hang free.

There was hardly time to intellectualise the reasons; Vashti just knew she felt better and looked better with her hair free, though it was an extravagance she seldom allowed herself. It certainly wasn't, she determined, anything to do with Phelan Keene.

He was the most contrary individual, one day treating her as if she were, indeed, the *enemy*, only to switch attitudes without logic or warning and treat her as...well...*not* as the enemy, despite his remark. Not today—or at least not yet.

'Yet', she discovered upon her return to the car, was a relative term.

'If you were going to take *that* long, you could at least have worn legs,' Phelan muttered over his shoulder as she got into the rear of the car. He cast a disparaging look at her trousers, then glanced pointedly out of the front window as if to forestall any reply.

'You look lovely,' said his sister with a smile in the rear-view mirror. 'And you, brother, dear, should be grateful for such attractive company and keep your chauvinistic remarks to yourself.

'He doesn't mean them anyway,' she cried over her shoulder to Vashti. 'It's just part of his "Aren't I wonderful?—I'm a famous writer'' role. He doesn't think it's proper to be a real, human man and write all that sex-and-chauvinism macho rubbish at the same time.'

'Girls with good legs shouldn't be allowed to wear trousers,' Phelan retorted firmly. 'It's all right for you; you've got fat ankles, and you're my sister anyway. I have to put up with you.'

'You have to put up with both of us,' Alana replied without taking her eyes off the road as she squealed into a minuscule hole in the traffic. 'So put a lid on it, or I'll throw my ladylike manners to the wind and we'll treat Vashti to a real Keene domestic over lunch.'

Phelan shrugged, obviously bored, and having made his point anyway. 'Just don't throw away your rudimentary driving skills,' he muttered. 'I'd like to get there in one piece, if it's all the same to you.'

'*He* taught me to drive,' Alana replied, turning to grin over the seat-back at Vashti.

'Only enough for you to sneak a pass out of an examiner who was blind-drunk at the time,' Phelan said, bracing himself as she flew into the railway roundabout like a rally driver.

'The examiner,' Alana confided over her shoulder with seemingly total inattention to the road ahead, 'quite liked my ankles.'

They swept round the back of the Domain and into the botanical gardens car park, where Phelan emerged from the vehicle, giving thanks to St Christopher, and only—or so it seemed—helping Vashti out of the car as a sort of second thought.

But there was nothing secondary about the way he swept his gaze over her figure as she emerged, nor about the look in his eye as he held her fingers in a firm, over-long grasp.

And when he gallantly took a girl on each arm and declared, 'I'll be the envy of every bloke in the place,' as he marched them towards the restaurant, Vashti didn't know what to make of him. Especially as she thought she heard a muttered 'Even in trousers' under his breath.

She was treated to what, for her, was a rare example of sibling bantering, throughout a splendid lunch, and Vashti kept finding herself thinking how lucky both Phelan and Alana were.

An only child herself, she found their constant point-scoring confusing at first, then realised it was simply their way of expressing very deep emotions while sharpening their wits at the same time.

She'd have been content just to sit back and enjoy the performance, except that both kept trying to draw her into their games, which would have been fine if she'd known how, known the rules. But the whole thing was quite beyond her experience, and Vashti finally had to say so.

'An only child? Your poor thing,' was Alana's immediate response. 'Not that there haven't been moments in my young life when I'd have envied you.' Then, with sudden seriousness, 'But not very many.'

'You're talking rubbish,' Phelan declared, throwing a very strange look across the table at Vashti. 'At least she'll be able to grow up and marry without making some poor fool's life a living hell.'

'You're a fine one to talk,' retorted his sister. 'You're *never* going to grow up, and any woman who'd have you wants her head read! Thirty-six years old and he still spends half his life in fantasy-land,' she continued with a quirky grin to Vashti. 'He writes about all these macho heroes and busty, steamy heroines and then gets round with a...an accountant!'

'Now hang about!' Phelan snapped. 'There's no call to get personal.' Then his scowl vanished, replaced by a broad knowing grin. 'And don't forget that our Ms Sinclair is an accountant, so watch your mouth, little sister.'

'Vashti is a person, not a walking calculator,' Alana replied, totally undismayed by her *faux pas*.

Vashti squirmed in her chair, wishing frantically for the waitress to return on any excuse, just to stop this line of discussion before it went any further.

Phelan, on the other hand, was clearly enjoying seeing her squirm.

'*All* women have calculating minds, so you'll have to be more specific than that. What have you got against accountants, anyway?' he demanded of his sister.

'You're a filthy chauvinist pig,' was the fiery response, drawing only a laugh, which even Vashti had to share.

'That round clearly goes to...Mr Keene,' she said haltingly, flustered at having nearly used his first name while so aware that he was insisting on not using hers.

'See what I mean?' he immediately asked, adding to her confusion. And his eyes twinkled with satisfaction as he declared, 'Vashti—obviously a woman of splendid breeding and exemplary manners— couldn't bring herself to call me Phelan on such short acquaintance, and is far too refined to call me a chauvinist pig, so her calculating mind took over and came up with a proper compromise.'

'She was just being polite.'

'Was she?'

'No!' declared Vashti, suddenly embarrassed and just a bit exasperated by being talked about as if she weren't even there. '*She* is going to the loo. And when *she* gets back, *she* will expect to have coffee and a change of subject, or *she* is going home.'

Whereupon *she* left the table and practically ran from the room, not sure whether to be truly hurt or insulted by it all, but dead sure she needed a break from Phelan Keene's persistent scrutiny.

Even when he'd been in full-bore verbal war with his sister, the man had used his eyes more as weapons against Vashti.

Without lifting a finger, he'd stroked her hair, caressed the long line of her throat, undone each and every button on her blouse and skilfully touched her nipples to an exquisite tenderness.

And by lifting only one finger, he'd quietly hitched up her glasses to ensure that she was unable to miss seeing exactly what he was up to.

Removing the hateful glasses, she splashed cold water into her eyes and stared at her reflection in the mirror. Her nipples still tingled from Phelan's gaze, and despite the excellent meal she felt empty, hollow, hungry. Stupid, she thought. Stupid to feel this way; stupid to be here in the first place.

'And stupid to let him *get* to you like that!' she snarled with a scowl at the myopic image before her.

She returned to the table determined to drink her coffee, pay her share of the bill, and then leave. It wasn't a long walk home across the Domain, and walking would do her good.

But when Phelan stood up at her approach and walked round to hold her chair for her, she found herself too readily noticing the easy, cat-like grace of the man, and when he smiled and said quietly after returning to sit down, 'My sister apologises,'—making not the slightest gesture of apology himself—she didn't know whether to laugh or cry.

Alana ignored him. 'I have to behave,' she said with a ten-year-old's scowl. 'Or he says he'll put me in a book. That's his *direst* threat, you know? And what's worse—he means it. You'll see, when you get round to reading that heap of sadistic garbage you bought this morning.'

She leaned across the table, ignoring Phelan as if he didn't exist, weren't there, weren't listening. 'I'm in *all* his books, but I never get anything exciting to do, never get any of the really dishy men, or the hot-shot lovers. I *did* get killed once, but that's about it. Such a boring existence.'

Vashti couldn't help it. She erupted with laughter so intense that it brought tears to her eyes and an ache to her over-stuffed empty-feeling stomach.

Because of course it was true! She hadn't picked it up, but probably would have; there had been something vaguely familiar about Alana ever since Vashti had read the first of Phelan's epics. Now she realised what it was.

She laughed, then laughed some more, deliberately not looking at Phelan, not daring to include him in what had suddenly become a girls-only joke.

'But surely you *enjoy* it?' she asked in a serious deadpan, leaning across to meet Alana's secretive gaze. 'I realise being killed isn't much fun, but surely the fame, the recognition ...'

'It's all right, I suppose. But you know what really gets on my wick?' Alana hissed in a conspiratorial whisper. Vashti, wide-eyed now and quite revelling in her part, sat with lips parted in anticipation.

Alana's voice dropped even further. 'The man's colour-blind! Or else he's just got no taste; I'm not sure which. So I ended up being dead in clothes you wouldn't be caught dead in!'

'Next time, you'll go in fat ankles and all; I've spared you that so far at least,' Phelan threatened now, too obviously trying to control his own chuckles.

His sister was totally nonplussed. Vashti could only sit with bated breath for the explosion she thought *must* come if this continued much further.

'Well, what about Vashti, then?' Alana demanded. 'You can't give *her* fat ankles; she'd have you jailed for tax evasion.'

Vashti felt her heart leap, her every cautionary instinct alert, poising her to flee, given half a chance.

But she couldn't, could only sit like a mesmerised prey animal, awaiting her fate. Every fear, every trepidation about Phelan's plans for the book with her involvement soared into flight inside her skull, making a roaring sound so loud that she could barely hear him reply.

'She might anyway,' Phelan mused, now turning his gaze once again to caress Vashti's throat. 'No, for Vashti I'd have to leave everything just exactly as it is. Even——' with one finger at the bridge of his nose '—the glasses.'

His eyes, oblivious to his sister's interest, moved lower, caressing Vashti's breasts with obvious pleasure. 'Except I don't think I could kill her off as easily as I did you. It would have to be *seduction*, with perhaps a touch of revenge involved, I think. Heavy on the seduction.'

'Thank goodness for that,' Vashti heard herself saying, wondering that she could speak at all for the turmoil inside her. And, astonished, continued. 'I mean, with the price of nail polish today, torture would be just *so* expensive.'

No mention of the torture already endured, the promise she read in his eyes of more—*far* more—to come. There was no longer any question in her mind; Phelan's alleged book was no more than an excuse. He was out to get her, and didn't mind what methods he used in the process.

'I'll remember that,' Phelan said, signalling for the account. And his eyes told her he definitely would.

So she was instantly on guard when they got outside and Phelan suggested Alana leave he and Vashti to walk off their lunch.

'We can have a good look at the gardens and then it's not that far through the Domain to where the ute's parked,' he suggested. 'Or I might even *walk* you home, if you're game.'

The offer was too sudden, too unexpected. Her instincts told her to refuse, but weren't quick enough to stop her tongue.

'I think that might be very nice,' Vashti found herself saying, feeling yet again that impossible feeling of emptiness in her tummy.

'You watch him,' was Alana's parting remark, made without, Vashti couldn't help noticing, the slightest hint of any argument. 'He'll be all shirty because we ganged up on him, and he's likely as not to get frisky on a full stomach. Just remember you won't be able to run very fast with tidy little ankles like that.'

'Racehorses do,' Vashti replied with a grin, and added, with a bravery she certainly didn't feel, 'Besides, could it possibly be *worse* than being put in a *book*?'

Which got her a speculative glance from Alana and a waved farewell; she didn't dare look to see Phelan's reaction.

Her own reactions concerned Vashti quite enough by themselves, starting the instant he took her hand in his and said, one eyebrow cocked in sardonic amusement, 'I've always wanted to be a jockey.'

CHAPTER FOUR

PHELAN continued to hold her hand, rather to Vashti's surprise, as he led her off into the Royal Botanical Gardens.

And he kept holding her hand—not that she was terribly disposed to have it back—as they wandered amid the vast array of trees and shrubs.

'I haven't seen these new Japanese gardens,' he said, thus breaking a rather long silence as they walked. Vashti hadn't either, but didn't say so. For some reason, the need to talk had been lessened with Alana's departure; she was content just to stroll and enjoy the experience in silence.

It wasn't until they paused on the bright scarlet bridge in the Japanese gardens, both of them staring down into the tranquil runs of water between the rock waterfalls, that words seemed necessary.

'I really envy you your family,' Vashti said without looking up at Phelan. 'It comes of my being an only child, I suppose, but you're all so...so vibrant, and so strongly supportive, even if you do pretend to bicker all the time.'

'What do you mean—"pretend"?' he scoffed. 'We do bicker all the time. Or at least Alana and I do. And she's even worse with Bevan, because he's more the strong, silent type, and my dear child sister simply can't *abide* silence, I sometimes think.'

'I quite like her,' Vashti replied.

'Which means what? That you don't like me? Or that you're not saying?'

She looked up to see one dark eyebrow cocked in amusement, and was suddenly only too aware of the hand that was captive in his lean, strong fingers.

'You really like a good stir,' she replied evasively, making the reply more question than comment.

'Of course.'

'It's not something I'm very good at.'

'Except over the phone, I've noticed.' And once again that eyebrow went up.

'It must help to have a good memory,' she quickly blurted.

'And you don't?'

'Only for figures,' Vashti replied, and then flinched at the innuendo as Phelan ensured she couldn't free her hand.

'Now you're even stealing my lines,' he chuckled. 'You don't need a great memory if you can read minds. And you don't have to be embarrassed about it, either.'

'I'm not,' she lied, then found herself stuck for words as she contemplated what he'd really said. It was too easy to remember when she'd thought he was the one able to read minds—or her own, at least, which was the problem.

But now she was faced with a quite different problem as Phelan turned to stand close to her, taking full advantage of the bridge rail at her back.

'You reckon you can read my mind now?' he asked, and his voice, though soft, echoed like surf in her head. His pale eyes seemed to expand until they were all she could see, as he lowered his mouth to capture her lips.

Vashti's first reaction had been to twist away, to somehow escape this intimacy she both wanted and feared. But his hands were on the rail, holding her body immobile without ever quite touching her. Only their lips touched, and his kiss was gentle, undemanding.

Vashti's lips parted, accepting his kiss without really replying to it. Her instinctive need to lift her arms, to touch him, was forestalled by an equally instinctive caution that thrust through her mind with his own words tumbling over and over and over. 'The enemy... enemy... enemy...'

But in her mouth was the taste of him, sharp and clean, in her nostrils the faint scent of his aftershave. No enemy taste, no enemy scent.

And then his hands were on her waist, pulling her closer to him, and her own hands were lifted, pressed between them in a barrier that did nothing against the warmth and firmness of his body.

She could feel his arousal as his hand slid down to hold her hips tight against him, and now his kiss was firmer, demanding a response she couldn't hide or deny.

'Vashti...' His voice was soft, a whisper lifting from his tongue as her mouth parted to accept his deeper kiss. Under her fingers she could feel the muscles flex as he breathed, could feel his nipples firm to her involuntary exploration.

Madness, this! As his lips left her mouth to trace a path of shuddering torment along her cheek, then down along the arched hollow of her throat, she couldn't stop herself twisting to ease his way. Her hands, thrusting against the muscles of his chest, were no barrier to the lips that wandered unerringly down the front of her blouse, much less to the fingers that now had slid beneath it and were lightly rippling upwards along the nubbles of her spine.

The gasping of her own breath thundered inside her head, the sound mingling with the warmth of his breath as it sighed and sang beside her ear. And with all, another sound—that of children's voices raised in play.

Vashti was struggling to free herself even as that noise became evident, struggling so fiercely that she almost tipped over the bridge railing as Phelan also heard, and stopped his plunder of her senses.

Her eyes blazing with embarrassment and anger, she had her blouse tucked in again and was running desperate fingers through her hair, not daring to look at Phelan, hardly daring to open her eyes, when the children gambolled into view from behind the French Memorial Fountain.

And when she did look up, it was to meet laughing, ice-green eyes that danced with what she could only construe as satisfaction.

It took her several deep breaths to recover any semblance of composure, to calm the waves of sensuous passion and fiery rage that surged side by side through her body. Her legs felt like limp ropes; without the railing to hang on to, she would surely have collapsed at the feet of this horrid, laughing man.

'I'm sure you think it's hilarious,' she finally managed to snarl. 'Saved by the laughter of the little children? How frightfully convenient! What chapter is that supposed to be, I wonder?'

Phelan met her glare squarely, his eyes darker now, somehow, totally unreadable except for the vestiges of passion that flared like sunspots against his irises.

'What are——?' He got no further before Vashti flung herself past his relaxed arm and stalked away, unwilling to hear his answer, wanting only to get away from the turbulence of his presence.

Her heels clattered on the bridge deck, then thudded along the pathway as she surged forward, head down, intent only on escape. But he was beside her in mere strides, and there he stayed as she plunged along the track, oblivious to her direction.

And he stayed beside her, not touching her, not speaking, but moving with cat-like grace, easily keeping up, and hovering like an extra shadow. Vashti tried to ignore his presence, couldn't, tried to freeze him by sheer force of will, failed.

And in the end she halted, breathing as quickly and frantically as she had in his arms. But not now with the unchecked warmth of his body against her; now she was icy-cold and shivering, despite the relative warmth of the day.

'You . . . you . . .' She couldn't even find the words, though they scurried inside her head like so many bumper-cars, bouncing off each other without pattern.

'I'm a rotter, I know,' he said with a half-grin. 'Or should we try something really literary, like "depraved lecher" or "scoundrel"? I've always quite liked "scoundrel", although I can't remember ever using it. Good lord, woman, what's so horribly awful about a stolen kiss in a park?'

The question stunned her into silence, thwarting the savage reply that had been forming on her lips.

Stolen kiss? Compared to her own feelings of having been literally *controlled*, it sounded so...so little. But in reality, she thought, what else had it been? She had indeed been kissed, but he hadn't actually touched her in any way that could be described as intimate. Except that he *had*! He'd touched her with great intimacy, but the touch had been in her mind, in her very being.

And she couldn't possibly describe, or indeed *admit*, just how intimate that touch had been, couldn't let him realise how easily he'd breached her defences, how he'd stirred feelings she hadn't *wanted* stirred.

'Stolen kiss? Is that what it was?' she demanded scathingly. 'That's a pretty simple description for some quite juvenile groping, I'd have thought. And I am not particularly impressed by such antics, *Mr* Keene, unlike your fictional heroines.'

'Ah.' He breathed the word softly, almost thoughtfully, as he stood at a respectful distance, meeting her fiery gaze with eyes as calm and still as glacial tarns.

His stare seemed to go on forever, as if he felt the calmness in his own eyes could somehow bridge the almost tangible link with her own.

'Especially,' he said then, still speaking so softly that she could barely hear, 'in public.'

'At all!' Vashti replied, trying to force into her voice a firmness she didn't quite feel. Damn the man anyway! All he had to do was look at her, and she could feel her resolve weakening.

'OK.' The reply was too quick, too simple. 'No more juvenile groping. And I apologise; I should have known better.'

The admission and the totally unexpected apology left her weaponless, not to mention speechless. She could only stand there and force herself to meet his eyes—eyes that now glimmered with hidden laughter, eyes that denied both admission and apology while forcing her to accept both.

'Let's continue on our way, then, shall we?' he finally said, and turned along the path towards the tropical glasshouse and the cactus house. Vashti, her anger with Phelan defused and her anger with herself boiling furiously but undisclosable, paused only a moment before joining his casual stroll.

They walked for half an hour in a sort of rigid silence, a situation that grew increasingly uncomfortable for Vashti. She kept seeing things she wanted to share, but stubbornly held to the seemingly agreed silence. Her anger had faded against the spectacular beauty in the tropical displays and the manifold shapes and colours of the cacti.

Only when Phelan paused on the bridge at the tranquil lily pond did a flicker of her former anger emerge, but it couldn't be sustained, not even when she stumbled in the cool depths of the fern house and his fingers leapt to steady her, only to release her with an unexpected suddenness before she could even think to object.

And even as she murmured her thanks, it was to his moving flank, drawing only a sort of grunted acceptance.

'This is stupid.' Vashti stepped up her pace, thrusting herself around to halt him, making him face her.

'What is?' The question belied the glimmer of amusement in pale eyes, an amusement made all the more obvious by one dark eyebrow cocked to reveal it.

'This ... this attitude! That's what.'

'Attitude? My attitude—or yours?' Now his eyes actually laughed; even his voice chuckled behind a wry half-grin.

'Ours, if that makes it any easier,' Vashti replied sternly. She was giving in, and knew it, but the alternative was a day totally ruined, and she didn't fancy that.

'If we keep going on like this it's going to ruin the whole day for both of us,' she insisted. 'And I . . . I don't want that. I really enjoyed lunch and, well, I don't want the day to end on a sour note, that's all.'

'Ah,' Phelan said, again drawing out the sound as he held her eyes with his own. 'But the day isn't over yet, is it? Who knows what's yet to come?'

'Well, I just wanted to say that I'm sorry I over-reacted back there; that's all.' Vashti had to drop her eyes to make the admission, but make it she must. She was not and never had been a vengeful person, and found it impossible to remain angry for any length of time.

'OK. And I'm sorry I gave you cause,' he replied soberly. 'Although I'm not one damned bit sorry I kissed you, even if I did apologise. You're far too pretty not to be kissed. I may even——' with a roguish grin '—do it again some time, and you can decide for yourself whether that's a threat or a promise.'

'Definitely a threat,' Vashti replied lightly, trying to maintain the conversation in a light-hearted vein.

And she felt a curious little lurch in her tummy when he grinned and replied, 'Only in public. And if we walk much further without a break, even that threat would be hollow, because I'd be too tired to be threatening. Come sit down in this wondrously named Wombat One picnic shelter and tell me the story of your life.'

'I'd much rather listen to the story of yours,' Vashti replied, thankfully moving into the shade. 'My life story's far too boring to bother with.'

Which, in her own mind, it was. Only somehow it didn't seem so under Phelan Keene's gentle but skilled probing. She found herself revealing more than she realised, especially when he adroitly turned the subject to her work.

They had left the botanical gardens and climbed up the steep slope to the children's playground and then downslope again towards Cleary's Gates before Vashti realised just how *much* Phelan had been pumping her about her job and the way things really worked in the taxation office, and the realisation made her stop dead in her tracks.

'I suppose you've been told before that you're cunning and devious and very, very clever at questioning people,' she charged. 'But I can tell you now that there's nothing to be gained by it.'

Which was as far as she dared go without coming out with a direct accusation that he was quizzing her merely to gather material for the book, that he really didn't care that much about Vashti herself, about how she felt, about how she feared his interest, feared for her privacy.

'That's what you think,' replied Phelan as they reached the edge of the busy Brooker Highway. Then he reached out to take her hand as he briskly gauged the traffic in both directions. 'But now isn't the time to yammer on about it; come on, before one of us gets run over.'

They dashed to the centre barricade, then on to the top of Stoke Street. By the time they'd wended their way through north Hobart to where Phelan had parked his utility, Vashti had mostly forgotten her concerns, deciding she'd told him nothing compromising anyway.

But a different caution took hold with his offer then to drive her home. If he did that, she'd have to invite him in for coffee—but she had no milk in the flat—or a drink—she didn't have a drop except for some aged cooking sherry—or...

'I'll only have time to just drop you off and maybe share a very quick coffee if you'd be so kind. I've got somewhere I have to stop before I head back to the farm,' he said, as if reading her mind. And if so, could he read the turmoil there? The incident in the park notwithstanding, she felt at least reasonably comfortable with Phelan here on the street.

But to be quite honest with herself, the thought of having him in her tiny flat, where his dominant personality would be overwhelming...

'All right, then, but I'll have to impose on you to stop so I can get some milk,' she replied, safe now in the implications of his remark.

She was leaving the milk bar, having decided on the spur of the moment to pig out on some rich chocolate biscuits as well, and was crossing the street to where Phelan was parked when the blast of sports-car exhaust warned her to leap back on the footpath.

'Fool!' she muttered, only half conscious that the passenger in the low-slung machine appeared strikingly familiar.

Phelan, having noticed the incident, was scowling into his rear-view mirror when Vashti slid into the passenger seat, but if he too had recognised Janice Gentry it went unmentioned.

It wasn't until they'd arrived in front of Vashti's flat that his scowl totally disappeared, but he was positively beaming when he walked round to open the utility's door for her.

'Now that you've got milk and bikkies, I reckon that cup of coffee would go down extremely well,' he said, his pale eyes a vision of innocence, backed up by the broad grin.

'I thought you had somewhere you had to be?' she replied hastily, forcing a smile of her own to cover the sinking feeling in the pit of her stomach. Of course he'd had somewhere else to go—until he'd seen that Janice Gentry wasn't about to be there!

'I did, but I've decided it wasn't that important after all,' he replied. And his bland expression covered what she assumed must be bitter disappointment.

She tried not to show her own disappointment as she met his smile and said brightly, 'All right, then, but you'll have to promise to behave.'

And could have kicked herself! What stupidity, to be instigating word games with this man after the day's earlier incident. But Phelan, as if perceiving her uncertainty, only nodded. Then he held up one hand, fingers crossed, and shot her one of those devastating little-boy grins.

It wasn't until they were inside the flat that he reached out, impishly, to push her glasses up into place, saying, 'You worry far too much, Vashti,' then turned away before she could reply and began to prowl the small lounge room while Vashti put the kettle on and began to spoon out the instant coffee.

She watched silently as he moved blatantly through the room, peering at her small collection of paintings, her records, and her eclectic range of books. These filled almost every available space in the small flat, and Phelan was still inspecting them when the water had boiled.

He glanced up to meet her enquiring eyes, then grinned hugely and remarked, 'I suppose it's rude of me, but nosing through other people's bookshelves is one habit I've never been able to break.'

'I don't mind,' she replied. 'It would hardly be fair, considering that's one bad habit we share.'

'Aha! Something in common. Now, at least, we've got a place to start.'

'What *are* you talking about?' She set the tray down on the coffee-table, then moved to sit in a single chair, leaving the couch to Phelan.

'Our relationship, of course. Or didn't you think we were going to have one?' There was mischief in his pale eyes now, and the start of a grin, as he sprawled on to the couch and reached for his coffee, waving a rejection of the milk and sugar.

'I'll have a bikkie, though. If you have to get through them all by yourself you're liable to get fat, and we wouldn't want that. Would we?'

'What relationship?' Vashti ladled more sugar than usual into her own coffee, suspiciously holding Phelan's mocking gaze as she did so.

'Ah,' he replied. 'Well, now, we'll just have to wait and see about that, I reckon.' But the look in his eyes said something quite different. There was again that slightly predatory gleam as his eyes moved to touch her lips, to prowl the long expanse of her throat.

'I do wish you'd stop that,' she protested, hoping the protest would distract him from noticing the effect he was having on her. Even before his eyes had reached her breasts, Vashti was aware of how her nipples were

firming, were tingling, almost as if he were touching
them with his lips, his fingers.

'Stop looking at you? Whatever for?' And his grin
was almost smug now. 'I enjoy looking at you, dear
Vashti, and I intend to do it every chance I get.'

Then the smugness was replaced by an obviously
overdone expression of pensiveness as he complained, 'Although I would prefer it if you'd give up
wearing trousers; that's almost a crime with legs like
yours.'

'You are incorrigible,' Vashti retorted, unable to
repress a chuckle at his deliberate put-on. 'How would
you feel if I started laying down the law to you about
what you wear?'

'Is that in the nature of a complaint?' And his grin
became decidedly devilish as she shook her head
without thinking. She had never seen him, either
casually, as now, or when dressed up, as he'd been
for the funeral and for business meetings, when his
clothes hadn't fitted to perfection and suited him
equally well. And he knew it, the rotter!

'And you've never even seen *my* legs,' he chuckled.
'Yet.' Those self-same legs, snugly encased in his
trousers, seemed to stretch halfway across her lounge,
and Vashti didn't need to see them to know their
strength, to recall the feel of them against her as he'd
held her close to him.

'I do wish you'd stop trying to work up these fictional scenarios,' she said, the crossness in her voice
more put on than real. 'You insist on mistaking facts
for fiction, which is a truly ridiculous way to go about
things.'

'Oh, I know the difference. Don't let my baby sister
steer you wrong on that score,' he replied. Then,

before Vashti could think to reply, 'And we're *not* going to talk business now and ruin a perfectly enjoyable afternoon, not when we're already scheduled to meet on Monday and finish off this damned family tax audit thing. For now, there are far more pleasant subjects, had we only the time to explore them.'

Draining his coffee, he was on his feet in a single, lithe movement. 'Thank you for that. Now I'd best go or you'll be having me for dinner as well as lunch, which might be altogether too much of a good thing.'

He turned in the doorway and reached out with a long forefinger to push Vashti's glasses back into place, grinning as she frowned at him for doing so. Then his finger traced a slow path down along her cheek and the side of her mouth before lifting her chin just enough so that he could bend down and kiss her. It was a brief kiss, light and gentle, as one might give a child, yet it somehow held a promise untold, a promise added to by his quirky grin.

'Been a lovely day,' he said quietly. 'But on Monday, wear legs; on Monday it's back to battle stations.'

Vashti had no chance to reply, could only watch as he moved down the footpath in his long, countryman's strides to get into his utility and drive off without so much as a wave.

She spent that evening quietly, reading his first novel and realising why Alana had advised her against buying it. By comparison with his later work it was rough indeed, yet already showing the complicated, tortuous mind of the author.

Throughout Sunday, that contrariness of Phelan Keene's haunted Vashti's own mind. One minute so friendly, the next too friendly by half, and yet just as quick to turn angry and savage, to withdraw into himself at some real or fancied slight she couldn't understand at all.

None of which, she thought, should be bothering her at all. She was, after all, in a relative position of power; whatever devious approach Phelan Keene or, more likely, Janice Gentry might dream up, it was *she* who had the vast powers of the taxation act to back her up.

But she slept poorly on Sunday night, her restlessness only added to by flickering nightmares that melted to nothing each time they woke her, leaving no memory of their content. When the alarm finally forced her awake, she felt haggard and looked worse.

'Power dressing; that's what's called for here,' she told the hollow-eyed image in her mirror, judiciously applying more make-up than usual to make that image appear bright-eyed and alert. Her hair went into its usual neat French roll.

'Power dressing...and legs!' She muttered the words like some sort of incantation as she sorted through her meagre wardrobe. It didn't take long; her best black shoes were in being mended, which left only the best grey ones. Her 'best' black suit was at the cleaner's anyway, and for the image she wanted today the soft dove-grey with the flaring lapels was probably better anyway, especially over the high-necked white silk blouse she had bought specifically to go with it. The skirt was perhaps a bit short, but all the experts had been predicting a return for the mini, she thought with a wan smile. And as for legs, she had one pair of tights that were perfect, with an almost invisible pattern that only enhanced their sheen.

She ignored breakfast—except for her mandatory three cups of coffee—and was ready early enough for a leisurely walk to work, carrying both raincoat and new umbrella just in case.

En route, she collected her morning papers and an egg and bacon roll, which she consumed carefully at her desk, ever aware of how the soft grey suit would stain. The papers told her nothing the radio at home had not; the egg and bacon roll sat like lead in her stomach.

And there just wasn't any reason for it! The work had been done; there wasn't a case to be answered, only a few final details to be tidied up and approved. But Vashti was tense, leery of what was to come. Janice Gentry—and if anyone was to blame for the confusion in the Keene family tax matters it was that woman—would be unable to put the matter to rest without some final blow, Vashti thought.

She was certain of it by the appointed deadline, but rather less sure why Phelan Keene and his accountant were late. And when they did arrive, complete with apology, she found herself wishing they'd been later still—like at least a full day later!

Janice Gentry's version of power dressing was almost identical to Vashti's own, but there was no compliment in that—not when it was so obvious to any feminine eye that the tall brunette was the one wearing the designer 'original', both in the soft grey suit and high-necked silk blouse and even the general style of the matching shoes. Just one of the shoes would have paid for Vashti's outfit, costly as it had been on a working girl's budget.

Vashti's heart sank to join the leaden egg and bacon roll, helped on its way by the smug raising of one elegant dark eyebrow as Ms Gentry swept into the office murmuring a self-satisfied greeting.

If Phelan Keene, himself elegantly turned out in a perfectly tailored suit and a crisp white shirt that glistened against his tan, even noticed the similarity in the women's outfits, he gave no indication of it.

He greeted Vashti with a smile that was no more than polite, took the seat offered him, and leaned back in it as if to distance himself from the ensuing fireworks.

For her part, Vashti found herself merely taking a deep breath and plunging into discussion of the issues; delaying would accomplish nothing, she thought, so why not get it over with as soon as possible?

Janice Gentry countered almost immediately with a list of complaints—not one of them relevant—about the entire affair. With Phelan there, she was clearly playing to a captive audience, and her litany sounded—must have sounded, Vashti thought—quite valid and even logical. But there was no logic in it, and both girls knew it all too well.

Phelan Keene sat in silence, offering no explanations and being asked for none. He was doing, Vashti admitted beneath her growing frustration, exactly what she'd advised him to do—letting his adviser do what she was paid to do.

And throughout the performance—Vashti was certain it was no more than that, on Janice Gentry's part—lay a growing thread of accusation aimed not at the taxation office, but at herself.

She had missed it, at first, her attention admittedly divided by wondering just what part Phelan himself planned to take in all this. But as his silence continued, she found herself more and more aware that the elegant accountant was leading the discussion deliberately into the highly subjective field of simple harassment.

And Phelan was helping her, if only through his silence. He still took no active part in the verbal exchange, but where his eyes had held that element of distance, even of amusement, now they were icy and cold.

Vashti floundered, unsure of her ground now and not willing to let the arguments degenerate into something totally counter-productive. 'I think we're getting well off the subject here,' she finally said, starting to rise to her feet in a bid to end the interview somehow, anyhow.

She had to! With her attention divided between the Gentry woman's insidious, deliberate sniping and Phelan Keene's now almost threatening silence, she was in real danger of making what could be a serious professional mistake.

Help did come, however, if from the most surprising quarter.

'I think it's time we gave this a rest,' Phelan suddenly interjected, speaking virtually for the first time since he'd entered the room. 'We're starting to go round in circles now, and it's accomplishing damn-all.'

'But Phelan, *darling*.' Janice Gentry's voice was suddenly dove-soft, her mouth almost pouting as she turned her attention from Vashti to focus it upon Phelan.

But it was her words, not the change of attention, that captured Vashti, pinning her in her chair and stunning her to a silence that illogically roared in her ears.

'We are not just going in circles. It's just this kind of frivolous harassment, you know, that sent your father to his grave.'

The words seemed to zoom around the office, taking on a life of their own and increasing in volume. It was like a nightmare, a vortex of sound, a cyclone of accusation.

Vashti's breath seemed caught inside her chest; she felt as if she were gasping, drowning. Her own feelings of anger, surprise—indeed, astonishment—combined to keep her mute, to make it impossible to do anything except stare from Phelan Keene to his companion, hearing the accusation over and over again, but unable to really comprehend.

How could this woman *say* such a thing? Even *think* it? And how could Phelan Keene, the man who only yesterday, it seemed, had shared a meal with her, laughed with her, *kissed* her—how could he...?

'That's as it may be, but this isn't the time to get into it.' His voice echoed in Vashti's ears as if coming from some great distance. She forced herself to look at him, to meet those predatory eyes. He *couldn't* believe this... not possibly...

But he did! The belief fairly radiated in the chill look that met her pleading eyes. And suddenly she knew the reason behind his antagonism at their very first meeting, when he'd plundered her with his devilish wolf eyes in the bleak little churchyard on that lonely ridge.

This man truly *believed* she had harassed his father into the grave! Vashti's stomach churned just at the thought, and even as she tried to rise from her chair, tried to summon up the words of denial, she felt a curious light-headedness, knew she couldn't stand, much less speak. Her bottom seemed glued to the seat; her lips seemed glued to each other, despite being parted in what seemed a continual gasping for breath.

Phelan Keene was on his feet now, looking at her curiously while gesturing to Janice Gentry. He might even have been speaking, but Vashti couldn't hear the words through the roaring in her head, couldn't seem to see the expression in his eyes, because her own vision was swimming, blurred.

She could only sense the movement as her rival gathered up papers and moved in a blur of grey towards the office door. There was a change of light as the door opened and shut, closing off the sound of the accusation but not the horrible, gut-wrenching shock of it.

Vashti let her head sink into her hands, and allowed the new silence to wash over her as she gasped and gulped for air, in one second afraid she'd be ill, the next certain of it.

It all just seemed so impossible! She hadn't harassed Phelan's father; she had liked, perhaps even *loved* the old man, had certainly known and respected him as a person of great integrity. How anyone could even *think* otherwise—how *Phelan* could possibly think otherwise, close as he was to his brother and sister...

She didn't hear the door to her office open again, only sensed she was no longer alone when his voice, feather-soft, penetrated her shell of agony.

'I just wanted you to know that...that wasn't my idea,' he said. 'It was...nasty and uncalled-for.'

'Get out!'

Her own voice was as soft as his, almost a whisper in the quiet of the office. But it was tinged with steel, forged in the fires of her agony, her disgust. Phelan started to speak, indeed stepped further towards her as he did so.

'I said get out. Now!'

Vashti couldn't bear it. His very presence, despite his assurances, only served to add weight to the accusations, to the soul-destroying *evil* of the accusations. She hated it, hated it all—hated Janice Gentry, hated Phelan Keene, hated his words, his very existence.

'Out!'

Her voice was louder now, demanding, insisting. She half rose from her chair, fingers clenched around the bulk of her penholder, a solid obelisk of marble. The violence of her feelings had her shaking; she drew back her hand without any certainty of whether she might throw the penholder at him or simply bash him with it, but she would do something...something violent!

'We have to talk about——'

'I said *get out*.' Now her voice was ice itself, frozen as her feelings, brittle as her sudden feelings of loathing. Phelan met her eyes, ignoring the impromptu weapon in her hand. His own eyes were bleak, but it was a different bleakness from that of their first encounter, though Vashti couldn't have explained the difference, only knew it was so.

'Of course.' His words were almost self-defeating, caught by the barrier between them and hurled to nothingness. But he seemed not to notice as he turned and walked away, pausing in the doorway only to look back at Vashti, shaking his head in a tiny, silent gesture before he closed the door behind him.

Vashti didn't even try to continue working through the day. Pleading a migraine, something she had never had in her life and the mention of which drew a raised eyebrow from Ross Chandler, along with an unexpected acceptance, she left the office. She had no destination, no conscious desire to either go home, or anywhere else; she simply meandered her way through the downtown area, noticing nothing, seeing no one except as an obstacle to be avoided.

Images scampered through her mind as she walked, but they had no voices, made no sound. All they did was hurt, stabbing like knives, thudding like bludgeons. She didn't even notice when she finally, unthinkingly, arrived at home and flung herself on to her bed.

It was there, her tears staining the pillow even as her fists beat and thumped at it, that she heard again the accusations, saw the raw triumph in Janice Gentry's eyes.

Later, time no longer relevant, she stripped off her rumpled clothing and stood under the shower until the hot water ran out, scrubbing and scrubbing as if soap alone could remove the injustice, the hurt.

She was back at work by mid-afternoon, still hurt, still angry, but under total control. None of her colleagues, she felt, could detect the fragility of that control, and it didn't matter anyway.

CHAPTER FIVE

THE flowers arrived at four forty-five. Two dozen roses, all red.

It was such a surprise that Vashti had accepted the box and was watching the delivery girl walk away before she realised what was happening, what *had* happened.

She opened the box, then shut it again, wrinkling her nose as if she'd just smelled something rotten, laid it on her desk for a moment, then opened it again just enough to reach in and liberate the note that was tucked into the bouquet.

Without reading it, without even *looking* at it any more than absolutely necessary, she ripped it into small, then smaller pieces, and discarded those in her waste-basket. Then she went and washed her hands.

The girls in the general office downstairs thought the roses were lovely.

The letter arrived in the next morning's mail, and she had it half read before the contents became obvious. It was an apology from Janice Gentry—or what passed for an apology. Couched in the politest of terms, and brief to the point of ridiculousness, it was more insulting, Vashti thought, than apologetic.

What it really said, she thought, was, I'm glad I said what I did and I'm glad it hurt. This apology is only because *he* insisted I make it.

That, too, was ripped into infinitesimal pieces and consigned to the waste-basket, followed by its envelope.

Vashti's next step was to instruct the switchboard that she was involved in some critical work and absolutely *must* have as few interruptions as possible. And she *must* have the identity of any caller *before* she would accept the call. The roses paid for themselves twice over, there. She was, for the moment, quite popular downstairs.

By the end of the morning, having refused Phelan Keene's calls seven times, she could feel that popularity ebbing just slightly. That honeyed, chocolate-fudge voice was obviously working its wiles on the switchboard operators.

'I'm too busy to speak to him,' she instructed after returning from lunch to find notes of another *three* calls. 'I know what he wants and it isn't as important as he says it is, so for the rest of the day—for the rest of the *week*—just inform him I am not here.'

That got her through the rest of Tuesday. At work. At home it wasn't quite so simple; there was no obliging switchboard operator there to screen her calls. But there was, thank heaven, a telephone with a ringer that could be switched off, and, after hanging up on Phelan Keene for the second time in what seemed as many minutes, Vashti turned off the phone.

A few minutes later, having thought about it, she also turned out the lights, locked the door, and lay down on her bed in the dark. She'd had no dinner, but, with her stomach surging with the confusion of her emotions, wasn't sure she'd be able to keep anything down anyway. She finally drifted into a troubled slumber, only to wake shortly after midnight, hungry and no less troubled.

She felt a fool as she slunk through the flat, parting the lounge curtains ever so carefully so as to peer down on the street below, half certain she would see Phelan Keene's old utility crouched there, waiting, predatory as the man himself. She felt more of a fool when she found only the usual vehicles parked outside, yet couldn't quite summon the courage to turn on the lights and cook herself something to eat.

The refrigerator yielded three cheese slices and a carrot; her three remaining slices of bread were rock-hard and inedible, and she nearly scalded herself trying to pour boiling water into a coffee-cup in the dark. Not that it mattered; when she tried to drink the coffee she found she'd put in two spoons of coffee and one of sugar instead of the other way round, and had to pour it out and start over.

'This is idiocy,' she muttered, tiptoeing into the bedroom to stare at the clock's one-fifteen a.m. message. Then she stomped back to the kitchen, drank half the coffee before tossing away the other half in disgust, and returned to bed.

At first light she was busy making herself bacon and eggs and toast and jam and *proper* coffee, feeling even more a fool than she had the night before. Until she turned on the phone again and found it ringing almost immediately.

No prizes for guessing who it would be, she thought. At this hour? Nobody else that she knew would even be awake, much less have the nerve to ring anybody on the telephone.

'I won't answer it,' she said aloud. 'Damn you, Phelan Keene—I *won't*!'

And she didn't; instead she turned the ringer off and returned to a breakfast that had suddenly become inedible. She dressed, *drove* to the office, and within five minutes had organised herself a trip to Triabunna for the final tidying-up of an earlier job. There wasn't all that much to be done, but it would keep her out of the office and away from the telephone, she thought. Forgetting, until it was too late, that driving provided her with far too much time to think, when thinking was just what she wanted to avoid.

As she wound her way towards the coast, forced to concentrate on her driving by the constant presence of log trucks that loomed up behind her with fearsome determination when loaded and swayed alarmingly when approaching empty and headed back inland, she found the incident and all its ramifications flouncing through her mind like the aftermath of a pillow-fight.

Janice Gentry's involvement was the easiest to comprehend and—surprisingly—to simply ignore. It was nothing more or less than sheer bitchiness, so obvious a ploy that she ought to have expected it.

But the accountant's use of such a ploy in Phelan Keene's presence suggested, at the very least, that it was a subject she had already discussed with him. And if with Phelan, then logically also with his brother and sister. But when?

Surely, Vashti thought, it couldn't have been *before* the weekend; it was ludicrous, considering Alana Keene's warm and genuine attitude on Saturday, to assume Alana could even have been aware, at the time, of Janice Gentry's vindictive accusations.

Sunday? Possible, she thought. Probable, she ultimately decided, reviewing in her mind all that had happened. Phelan had obviously intended to see the Gentry woman on Saturday evening, probably *had* done so on Sunday.

Was the accusation linked to his earliest meeting with Vashti, when he'd been undeniably hostile, and quite clearly marked her as 'the enemy' and treated her as such?

That, she thought, made some modicum of sense, but only if she could ignore Saturday entirely. Surely no man could be so...so attentive, so charming, to a person he thought guilty of such behaviour?

It was *that*, she decided, that galled the most. Such behaviour was not only unthinkable to her personally, given her regard for old Bede Keene—it was damned well unprofessional!

And for him to have spent half of Saturday being deliberately nice to her, *more* than just nice. To have used his charm so blatantly, to have touched her, kissed her...when he felt like that. It was disgusting!

All these thoughts dashed helter-skelter through her mind as she drove mechanically, avoiding the log trucks, back to Hobart that afternoon, arriving at the office just at knock-off time.

She skimmed through the various telephone messages, mostly from Phelan Keene and automatically, therefore, discarded unread, than locked up her desk again and drove home.

She had parked and was halfway up the footpath when the decrepit old utility clanked to a halt behind her small sedan, and, although she did her best, Vashti couldn't reach her door and get herself safely behind it before Phelan Keene's strong fingers were clamped firmly around her wrist.

'Let go of me.' She growled the command without looking at him, twisting her body in a futile attempt to enforce her demand.

'Not a chance,' was the reply, soft and yet threatening in her ear. Long, tanned fingers reached out to pluck her keys from fingers too weak to resist, and he reached forward to unlock her apartment door while still holding her in an iron grip.

'In!' he commanded, his voice overriding her own squeal of protest. And in she went, thrust into her own home like a bag of groceries.

Vashti stumbled forward, almost tripping over her own coffee-table as Phelan slammed the door behind them. Even as she regained her balance and turned to cry out her objections to this invasion, he was flipping on the night-latch and turning to face her, eyes blazing.

'Now,' he said. 'No telephones, no lying little switchboard operators, no screaming hysterics.'

Vashti could have laughed at the last; her breath was coming in uneven gasps, her heart was thumping as if to batter its way out of her breast, and she thought her legs would collapse beneath her any instant.

'Get out. Leave me alone,' she gasped. 'Get out... get out...get out...'

'Not,' he said grimly, 'until we've talked this thing through.'

'There's nothing to talk about,' she snapped in reply, part-way back in control now. 'Nothing!'

'The hell there isn't.' And his voice was as fierce as her own was angry, the fierceness matched by the explosive expression in his ice-green eyes.

'There isn't.'

He was dressed as her mind always pictured him now, in faded jeans and a light checked shirt with the sleeves rolled up to reveal his powerful forearms. His hair was its usual curly crispness and, although he was clean-shaven and smelled of the unique aftershave he used, his face was drawn, the shadows under his eyes revealing . . . what?

Certainly they weren't revealing anything like a quiet, even temperament. He stalked towards her across the tiny battleground of her lounge, looming huge in the small room. Vashti backed away the few steps available to her, then squealed with alarm as he reached out one forefinger and quite literally *pushed* her backwards on to the sofa.

'Now listen,' he growled, shaking that same finger in admonishment, as if by the very action he could forestall any attempt to argue. He kicked aside Vashti's handbag, which she'd dropped as he pushed her, and stepped closer, so close that he had to bend to look directly into her eyes.

'No!' She shook her head, lifting both hands to cover her ears, knowing it appeared childish— probably, in fact, quite ridiculous—but doing it anyway. Just to be doing *something*, anything but just accepting his assault.

'Yes!'

He reached down and lifted her by the wrists, forcing her nose to nose with him, glaring into her eyes and shaking her so vigorously that it seemed her arms would be wrenched from their sockets.

'I had no idea Janice Gentry was going to say what she did.'

He made the statement in direct, forceful tones, keeping his voice flat, almost totally unemotional.

'Who . . . cares?'

Vashti's voice was far from flat; the two words burst from her gasping lips, pushed by the pain in her shoulders as much as by the emotional pain she felt and tried to disguise.

'I care. And you care, whether you want to admit it or not,' was the reply, not flat now, but growled from lips only inches from her own.

'I don't. Let me go! Damn you, let me go, I said.'

She might as well talk to the wall. His fingers never slackened for an instant, nor did he ease his grip to let her get where she wanted most to be—away from him. No breathing space, no thinking space.

She didn't have to think; the thrust of her knee was almost instinctive. And, considering her position, should have been effective as well. Only he turned his thigh, or twisted his body somehow; she didn't know just what, only that instead of the release she expected she gained only a grunt of effort, a quick shake of his head as he negated her assault.

'Naughty,' he growled then. 'Not at all nice.'

Vashti lashed out again, knowing it was a waste of time but unwilling to give in.

'Stop that, dammit!'

'Let me go.' She gasped out the command, but tried to level her voice into a firm insistence, rather than the panicky response she felt inside.

'Not likely,' was the response, and his fingers clenched briefly round her wrists as if to accentuate the remark.

Vashti lapsed into what she hoped would seem passive acceptance, then lashed out in a third attempt to destroy his manhood, both feet kicking now, both knees thrusting, and felt a sudden great surge of joy as one toe struck something firm and she felt him wince.

Then, without warning, she was lifted, tipped half upside-down, and found herself sprawled in his lap as he landed with a thump on the sofa. One hand miraculously maintained the grip of two on her wrists while the other casually removed her shoes and then clamped itself around her knees, locking her into a totally helpless position.

'Right,' he growled. 'Now about all you can do is go for the jugular, and, although I wouldn't put it past you, I'll take the chance that the taste of blood would put you off. So I shall talk, and you, Msssss Sinclair, will listen. OK?'

With her arms stretched above her head and the rest of her body firmly controlled by his strength, Vashti didn't bother to reply. Instead, she glared up at him, baring her teeth and curling her lip in a snarl. Irreverently, she had a mental picture of a farm kelpie she'd once seen edging up to a fight, its teeth fairly clattering as it threatened. In any other circumstance, it might have been funny, but she now thought she knew how the dog had felt.

'I *did not know* that woman was going to say what she did,' Phelan said, spacing each word out as if he were someone predicting the end of the world. 'If I *had* known, I wouldn't have allowed it. Is... that... clear?'

His eyes burned into hers, then, unccountably, broke the contact to move slowly, deliberately, across her face, down her throat, and along the cleft of her dishevelled blouse. Vashti squirmed, which only made her more aware of the heat of his groin against her hip, of the way her skirt was rucked up almost to her waist.

'I... don't... care,' she replied, spacing the words as deliberately as he had. It was a lie, but he'd never know that, she vowed. Sort of a lie. What she *did* care about, suddenly realised was *all* she cared about, was whether Phelan Keene had believed the accusation. Whether he'd have allowed it didn't matter a damn; whether he *believed* it . . .

'Of course you care; stop being so obtuse,' he snapped. 'You're not a fool and we both know it, so quit acting like one.'

The comment was punctuated by a slow, circling motion of his thumb against the back of her knee, a motion so light in its touch that for an instant she wasn't aware of it. Then she was!

'Damn you . . . Stop that!' Vashti snapped, wriggling to no real effect against the strength of his grip. He did stop, too, which served only to make her *more* aware of the warmth where their bodies touched, of the male strength of him growing now against her hip.

'Stop what?' And his face suddenly changed, sliding into a picture of such bland, total innocence that she almost laughed. Again that insidious thumb, moving against the thin, delicate skin behind her knee, moving in slow, deliberate circles as his elbow kept her from kicking free.

Vashti didn't answer; she just forced herself to meet his eyes, to deny the effect he was having on her, to maintain her rage, her sense of betrayal.

One dark eyebrow lifted in a sarcastic query; his teeth flashed in a sudden, wolfish grin that disappeared as quickly as it began. And always his eyes, those pale, pale eyes, maintained their grip on her. He was so close that she could see the tiny rays of colour up through his irises, minute rays of cold that shot like sunshine through the green ice.

'This?'

His voice was a whisper of warmth against her lips, but the question was for a firmer touch, the warmth that went with the exploration of his fingers along the length of her thigh.

Vashti could answer neither, because as she parted her lips to speak they were captured immediately by his mouth. And as she writhed against the arousing touch of his fingers, the movement only served to make their journey more erotic, more intimate.

More maddening!

'Damn you,' she muttered, wrenching her mouth from his, shaking her head furiously to avoid a continuation of his kiss. 'Damn you...'

The curse was muffled this time, because as she stopped shaking her head to speak his lips were there to claim her, to stifle her curse half-uttered as his tongue tasted her breath, fluttered against her fury. And his fingers never stopped their caressing exploration, moving always closer to an objective that would defeat her entirely.

'You don't want to damn me,' he whispered after an eternity.

'I do... I do...' she sighed, lying to both of them now in the last vestiges of her defence. His lips remained only a touch away from her own; his eyes were huge, encapsulating her vision.

'Pretty hard to damn someone with your glasses all skew-whiff,' he muttered, and, miraculously, freed her legs as he automatically reached up to push them into place. It was a gesture she had, Vashti realised, already come to think of as 'special', as something somehow intimate between them.

Something he probably did to Janice Gentry's glasses as well, she now thought with a driving, hurting anger. And before he could reposition that hand she was twisting, thrusting, driving her body into a furious bid for freedom.

Waste!

He laughed, a laugh that seemed to boom through the small flat, as he twisted his own position so that he could clamp her legs between his own now, holding her even more securely than before.

But this left him with one hand free, free to explore her body at his leisure, ignoring her attempts to twist free, ignoring her objections, by the simple expediency of closing her mouth with his own, easier now that he had that free hand to manipulate her as he pleased.

His fingers touched at her jawline, gently but firmly shifting her head to make her mouth more accessible. And as he kissed her, that hand traced its deliberate way down the length of her throat, pausing only briefly at the hollow where her breathing bubbled with a curious mixture of fear and anger and passion.

Then he stopped kissing her, just for an instant, and his hand lifted to take her glasses away, lifting them from her nose as gently as his lips returned to claim her mouth.

Vashti was silent during that interval, silent and still as the proverbial church mouse. Her glasses gone, she somehow felt suddenly more vulnerable—given that could be possible—than before. And again, it divided her attention, as she instinctively worried about the spectacles, and, instead of avoiding his touch, was concentrating on what he would do with them.

And through her head, ridiculous at such a moment, ran the hoary old saying: 'Men seldom make passes at girls who wear glasses.' Over and over and over, like white noise, blanking out both anger and the warmth that now spread along her thighs, rising like mercury in a thermometer from where his erect maleness thrust against her.

'Not to worry.'

Had he actually said that? she wondered, unsure despite seeing his hand reach back to place the glasses safely on a side-table, *feeling* the hand return to lift the hem of her skirt, *feeling* the fingers trace intricate intimacies along her thighs.

Now his eyes followed, and their gaze as her skirt rode high, exposing all of her hips and thighs, increased her vulnerability as she felt her body temperature soar in response to his visual caresses.

'Stop.'

Her voice sounded false in her own ears, and sounded so weak that she wasn't sure he'd even hear her, much less pay any attention.

'But we haven't hardly begun.'

His voice was a delicate whisper now against her throat, a whisper translated as if into Braille by fingers that followed his words, down into the cleft of her breasts, touching just ahead of his breath, his tongue, his kisses.

The buttons of her blouse, miraculously having survived the writhing and twisting of her futile defence, now fell to his gentler, yet more insistent assault. And his lips followed to let his tongue touch at the edges of her bra, to the soft hollow between her breasts.

Vashti felt her breath go ragged; her nipples throbbed against the fabric of the bra until his fingers dipped to free first one breast, then the other, to his touch, to his mouth.

Her mouth parted in an agony of sensual torment; she could only writhe in helplessness as his lips fluttered against the warm softness, plucked at her nipples, and teased them to a magic life of their own.

Vashti could only sigh her delight, moan her acceptance; their argument, her earlier fury, both were barely memories now, memories from a past that grew more distant with each touch of his lips, each probing lick of his tongue.

Part of her yearned for him to free her hands, to let her return his caresses, allow her the freedom to touch his mouth, his hair, his muscular shoulders. Her legs, trapped as they were, yearned to be free, to be able to shift and allow his touch greater access to the secrets of her body.

And within her, the tiny voice of logic, of reason, of *danger*, screamed almost silently against the winds of her passion, the roaring of her blood, as it surged to meet his touch, to carry the messages of his fingers, of his lips.

'This is madness.'

The voice plucked at her conscience, at first timidly, then with growing force as she realised it wasn't her own voice, but *his*!

And even as her fevered brain cried out for an explanation, ignoring the body that screamed only for more of his kisses, more of his caresses, his lips fled from her nipples, his fingers lifted from their journey up her thighs.

'It's no way to have a discussion,' he said, reaching up now to touch her cheek, to seek her gaze with eyes somehow soft and gentle beyond all logic. Vashti met his eyes blankly, her own unfocused grey eyes those of a zombie, a sleep-walker. His voice crept into her consciousness, but the words held almost no meaning, made almost no sense.

Until, 'Are you ready to stop fighting me now? Ready to listen without trying to unman me or scratch out my eyes?'

That question got through to her, if only enough to make her cognisant of Phelan's next words, which he uttered almost dreamily as he reached down to tug her skirt down against the place where his own leg still held her captive. 'Sometimes I really do feel it's a shame they invented these damned tights,' he muttered, and the words were, she thought, more for himself than for her. 'Proper stockings are just so much...'

She could hear the rest without him saying it, could *feel* what he meant, could feel his fingers against the heat of her near-submission without the scanty protection of tights.

And for whatever reason—Vashti was no more capable of considering reason than she was of flying, given the situation—his words touched her mind like a torch to a still, unseen pool of petrol.

'You rotten mongrel,' she squealed, angered that he could have so assaulted her senses while still *himself* having the control to think about their original argument, their *business* dealings, while *she* had become lost—almost irretrievably lost—in the mingling of their feelings. *Her* feelings! Which made her all the more angry.

'I'll give you *proper* stockings,' she raged, and somehow this time *did* manage to writhe free of his grip, sliding between his legs to land with a thump on the floor, leaving her poised with her cheek against the firm heat of his groin, her arms clasped instinctively around his thighs as she fought for balance.

One of Phelan's hands reached down to grasp her elbow, lifting her towards her feet, but Vashti's own flailing arm struck it away as she lurched back from him, somehow caught herself upright, and stood glaring down.

How could he *be* so damned calm? How could he sit there, eyes placid, lips quirked into what she could only see—her missing glasses making a difference even at that short distance—as a self-satisfied smirk?

'Get out!'

Even as she snapped the command her fingers were busy tucking herself back into her clothes, all too aware of the sensitivity of her nipples as she bent to thrust her heaving breasts back into the spurious safety of her bra, even more aware of how clumsy her fingers were in trying to button up her blouse, twist her skirt into place, while fumbling to tuck in the sheer fabric of the blouse at the same time.

Phelan met her accusing, furious eyes with such calm self-assurance that it made Vashti more infuriated than ever.

'All that and we're right back where we started?' he asked, voice soft, unchallenging, yet somehow so arrogant, so damned *smug*, that she could have screamed.

'We're *nowhere*!' she shouted. 'Nowhere; do you hear me? We never were anywhere and we are never going to be anywhere. Now get out!'

'We came very close indeed to being *everywhere*,' he replied with a pointed hitch of one eyebrow. 'You might just think about that before you go all *thing* and start screaming and shouting and carrying on like a pork chop.'

'I've every right to carry on however I like,' she cried. 'It's *my* home, after all. You've got damned cheek, talking about having a *discussion*! You're an animal!'

'We all are, at least by some theories,' he replied calmly. 'Some of us are just better-looking than others. You, for instance. I'm not surprised we never seem able to have a rational discussion, when it drives me half crazy just looking at you.'

'You're more than half crazy,' Vashti replied without thinking. 'And my looks have nothing to do with it.'

'And if they have, they shouldn't,' he agreed amicably. 'Except to a male chauvinist piglet like me, of course. Not that I've ever denied being one; you'd only have to read one of my books to know better.'

Vashti could only stand there, staring down at him and trying to maintain her rage against this curious turn of the conversation. What on earth was he on about now? she wondered.

'Please go and sit down—over there where you're well and truly out of reach,' he said then, almost wearily, she thought. 'I shall promise to at least try and keep my hands off you if you promise in turn to stop fighting me, stop trying to put your own interpretations on every single word I say, and just *listen*! OK?'

Vashti continued to stand over him, her mind racing in ridiculous circles, starting and going nowhere, until she finally managed to force a stop to the process.

'I want coffee,' she then said decisively, and turned away, without waiting for any reply, to pad silently across the carpet and on to the chill tiles of the kitchen floor.

Phelan sat silent, elbows resting on his knees and his chin resting in his cradled palms as he watched her boil the jug, measure the instant coffee, get the sugar, the milk. He was still in that identical position when she finally set a cup before him and moved over to sit opposite with her own coffee, silent herself and, now, expectant.

Their mutual silence wafted through the room with the aroma of the coffee, but although Vashti watched the tall, pale-eyed intruder he seemed lost in introspection. He looked across the room without really looking; his eyes weren't focused on her, on the wall behind her, on anything at all that she could determine.

He sipped at his coffee without a word, without looking down at the cup, without looking across at Vashti. Lost in his own mind, she thought, and wondered without being all that surprised.

'I had a book half done when I flew down here for the funeral and all,' he suddenly said, still not looking at her. 'It's still half done. Not a single, solitary page further along than on the day I arrived. Haven't been able to think straight, haven't been able to concentrate. Just sit and stare at the computer as if it was some strange machine I've never seen before.'

Now he looked at her, or appeared to. And the expression in his eyes was one Vashti had never seen before—totally unreadable, totally obscure, and yet somehow pleading.

'Part of it's this damned tax business, for sure,' he continued. 'The old man's been driving me mad; he's driven us *all* mad now that he's gone and can't explain what he was doing or how or why or...or whatever. I don't understand it, and neither does Bevan or Alana—and they were *here* while it was going on. I could only work from telephone conversations I had with him there towards the end, and some of that doesn't make a lot of sense even now.'

Vashti sat silent, her coffee forgotten as she listened, unable to make much sense out of what Phelan said, but certain it was important she at least listen.

'What Janice said in your office the other day...' he was very definitely focused now; his eyes held her, forced her to listen '...was totally uncalled-for. And if I'd had any idea she was going to take that track in all of this, I would have...it would have...it damned well wouldn't have been said!'

A fierce light blazed in his eyes as he made the statement, then faded as Vashti sat silent, unsure what, if anything, she ought to reply.

It shouldn't have been said? Of course it shouldn't have been said. It shouldn't even have been thought, much less said. But that wasn't the issue, and Phelan Keene seemed incapable or unwilling to see what *was* the issue—from her point of view.

Still silent, she rose and picked up both their coffee-cups, then walked back to the kitchen to refill them. There was, she decided, something to be said, something she *must* say, but she didn't have the faintest idea what it was. Certainly it was *not* to comment on how she could *feel* Phelan's eyes following her as she moved, how she could tangibly feel their exploration of her ankles, her calves, her hips. She had the strangest urge to spin round, to confront him with her knowledge, but she knew somehow that she would never catch him out. If she turned, he would be looking somewhere else, ostensibly innocent. Or, worse, he would be deliberately chauvinistic, not only letting her catch him, but planning for it, expecting it. She kept her attention on balancing the coffee-cups as she returned, not even trying to meet his eyes until she was seated again.

'I would be quite happy to turn this whole thing over to some other field auditor.'

The words were uttered even as she thought them, and only when it was too late did she realise her statement was less than totally honest. The examination of the old man's affairs was over and done with now, to all intents and purposes. But if she withdrew, even at this late stage, somebody might have to go right back to the beginning, creating more cost and more emotional turmoil for all concerned. *She* knew instinctively that the old man had been honest as the day was long, had made no deliberate attempt to evade tax. Just as she knew she hadn't harassed him into the grave because of it!

'What—so we can start all over again?' Phelan asked as if reading her thoughts. 'Waste of everybody's time.' And he picked up his second cup of coffee, lapsing into a silence that seemed to expand like smoke, filling the small flat, almost suffocating in its intensity.

'My car ought to be here on Friday,' he said then, not looking at Vashti, indeed looking at nothing in particular and making the statement as if to totally change the subject.

She nodded, but said nothing. Surely no comment was called for, she thought.

'And not before time, either. I'm getting awfully sick of driving that cranky old paddock ute the old man thought was so wonderful.'

Again, what to reply? She merely had another sip of her coffee and waited, until she was finally forced into some response simply by his silence.

'That's nice,' she replied. And wondered why she felt like a stray cat confronted by another stray cat, circling, cautious, ever ready to advance or retreat, ever ready to avoid any form of commitment until there was no choice left at all.

Now, she thought, might be the perfect time to be bold, to ask Phelan Keene straight out about this book he was writing, about this exposé of the tax office, about *her* role in all of this. Was he really, as he seemed to be implying, so taken with her that his writing was affected? The thought of his mooning about like a lovesick teenager was ludicrous, at best. Why couldn't she laugh? More likely, she thought, something she had said or done had put him off his original line of thinking. Was that it? Was she so different from his preconceptions that his entire script had come adrift?

Whatever, now was the time to ask. So why couldn't she utter the words that rolled around in her mouth like all black jelly beans, which she hated?

Because I...can't, she silently admitted. And hated herself for the cowardice.

'You're happy, then? It's finished now?'

His questions seemed innocuous enough; his voice showed no sign of aggression, no sign of anything, really. Vashti held off answering until she'd taken the time to listen—*really* listen, this time—to what he said and how he said it.

'I would certainly hope so,' she finally said, meeting his eyes, then looking away as she reached up to adjust glasses that weren't there and then cursed herelf for the mistake.

Phelan's generous mouth quirked just a bit as he reached to the side-table, picked up her glasses, and reared up out of the sofa to hand them across to her. The very movement was so swift, so wolfishly agile and quick, that Vashti found herself flinching away.

'Stop being so touchy; I've already proved that I can control myself,' he muttered, sitting back down as abruptly as he'd arisen. 'Not that I expect you to believe that.'

'I should certainly hope not,' she snapped, refusing to admit to either of them that it had, indeed, been *he* who had halted their encounter, not daring to admit to herself that she had been within seconds of total and absolute surrender.

'Do you really *need* those glasses?' he asked then, and, without waiting for a reply, 'Or do you just wear them as the business girl's first defence against roving male chauvinist pigs?'

'That's hardly worth bothering to answer.'

'Just as well; I think they're sexy as hell. They make your eyes look even bigger than they are,' he replied, leaning slightly towards her, his gaze snapping across the room like a lasso to capture her attention and hold it.

'Well, then, maybe you need glasses yourself,' Vashti replied, unaccountably flustered by the directness of the compliment, presuming it was intended to be a compliment at all!

'You wouldn't understand, but I'm inclined to agree with you,' was the curious reply. 'At any rate, I've said what I came to say, and——' with a mischievous grin '—perhaps just a bit more. What I'd like to know just now is whether you're going to accept it or not.'

'Accept what?' Vashti retorted. 'Being man-handled in my own home, being insulted, being——?'

'Accept that Janice's accusations weren't my idea and weren't made with my approval,' Phelan inter-rupted coldly. 'I don't mind if you can't or won't accept my apology; I just want the point made...that's all!'

'Consider it made.'

One dark eyebrow lifted in obvious scepticism, then lowered again, as did the temperature in the room, Vashti rather thought.

'Right,' he said, rising abruptly. 'I'll be off, then.' He had the door open and was halfway through it when he suddenly turned and said, 'And thanks for the coffee, by the way.' He was gone before she could reply.

Vashti sat there, staring at the now vacant doorway, only half aware of the sounds of the farm utility chugging to life, then rattling away down the street. Her mind whirled in a disjointed attempt to make sense of it all, to try and understand how Phelan Keene could be so damnably changeable, and, worse, so damnably capable of manipulating both her mind and her emotions until she hardly knew which end was up.

Eventually, none the wiser, she absently went through the routine of changing, cooking herself dinner and—far earlier than usual—showering and getting ready for bed.

As she stood under the soothing warmth of the shower, the encounter with Phelan replayed itself over and over in her mind.

As she soaped her breasts, it was to feel his touch, his lips so much warmer than the shower, so much more intimate than her own. It was as if her body had some unique memory bank of its own, one capable of endless memories of his kisses, of the ability his fingers had to rouse her, to lift her through layers of ecstasy, along paths of intimacy she could neither forget nor ignore.

If only, she thought as she drifted into sleep, she could somehow have met Phelan Keene without either of them being involved at a business level.

The thought remained with her through the night; it must have, she thought upon waking, to find it still on her mind. But with a new day came a more realistic outlook. Phelan Keene's involvement was, at best, purely physical, a simple matter of lust. At worst, he was deliberately manipulating her for his own advantage, or at least to *her* disadvantage.

A girl with any sense at all, she reasoned as she entered the office that morning, would march straight into the boss's office and have the entire Keene file transferred to somebody else—of course she would—but she didn't, for some reason or another.

A girl with any sense at all, she reasoned almost eight hours later, would not be idly browsing through the city's most exclusive hosiery salon, much less sending her bank card into orbit over shockingly expensive stockings and something astonishingly wispy and fragile to suspend them from.

CHAPTER SIX

THE exercise in extravagance seemed little short of ridiculous by Monday morning, and the morning's usual first exercise—reading the paper over coffee and a flaky croissant—did nothing to improve Vashti's sense of folly.

Once again the social pages affronted her with a photo of Phelan Keene being swarmed over by the sultry figure of Janice Gentry, this time wearing—what there was of it—something clinging, light-coloured and unquestionably expensive.

And slit so high along one—the photographic—side that the accountant's taste in frilly garter-belts left nothing to the imagination.

Phelan Keene, handsome in his own particularly understated fashion, seemed oblivious—or so Vashti thought from his expression—to the vivid display of feminine flesh that threatened to engulf him. Or was it, she wondered, her imagination? Certainly it wasn't important anyway.

Vashti used that section to wrap up the soggy, tasteless croissant. She was too busy to take time over the crossword puzzle on the next page anyway.

She took herself to dinner that evening at a new little restaurant about which she'd heard nothing but rave reviews, but didn't even bother to stay for dessert and coffee. This, she had decided by then, must be where her morning croissant had been made, probably by the head waiter doubling as an amateur pastry-cook. How everybody else in the place could so obviously be enjoying their meal was beyond all logic.

Every morning that week, her impromptu extravagance of the previous Thursday looked accusingly at her from her lingerie drawer; on Friday morning she tucked the minute parcel under an old jumper in the bottom drawer of her bureau and kicked the drawer shut.

'Are you as cranky as you sound?'

The voice of Alana Keene, irrepressibly and annoyingly cheerful, fairly bubbled through the telephone a few hours later.

'Worse. Why?'

'Because I was going to buy you lunch, but if you're like that I might change my mind.'

'You probably should; I'm not fit company even for myself,' Vashti replied honestly.

'Gone off your tucker?' Nothing if not direct, Vashti thought. Living with those two brothers had probably given Alana an unbreakable vivacity.

'A bit,' she admitted, glancing down at the remains of an apple Danish, half eaten and discarded, like every other that week.

'Hah! I never would have guessed. And I don't suppose my dear brother has anything to do with this?'

'Certainly not!'

'Shall I bring him, too, then?'

Alana waited through the silence, then giggled at the success of her gambit. 'I couldn't anyway,' she finally said. 'He's out at Dad's... gone all broody, or hermity or something. Even crankier than you sound. Probably off *his* tucker, too.'

Vashti kept silence, refusing to rise twice to the same bait. Not that it did her much good.

'I reckon it's PMT, myself. Him, that is; not you. Anyway, I'll come get you at noon and we'll walk down to the Mona Lisa. Unless you want to go really up-market, in which case you can phone for a booking and we'll go to Dear Friends,' Alana suggested.

'How about the take-away on the corner?' Vashti countered. 'Even that's beyond my budget this week, but I'd stretch it that final inch, seeing it's you.'

'That bad, eh? Maybe I ought to send Phelan instead, and the two of you could sit opposite and just depress the hell out of each other.'

Alana again waited through the silence that followed, then conceded, 'OK, it was a silly thing to say, and I'm sorry. Meet me outside at noon; we'll go to the Mona Lisa and I promise I won't so much as mention the mongrel.'

Whereupon she hung up before Vashti could say no, only to ring back thirty seconds later to announce, 'I forgot to tell you that the reason I'm doing this is because I sort of need a favour. See you at noon.'

And when Vashti emerged from the building at noon, Alana was there, her normal bright smile like a banner that sagged visibly when they were close enough for her to see Vashti's haggard expression.

'Not only off your tucker, you haven't been sleeping real good either, I see,' she said with a shake of her auburn hair. 'If I were you, I think I'd take a sickie for the afternoon, have a long and very liquid lunch, and then try and sleep until Monday. But I suppose that would be asking too much, eh? Hardly professional.'

'Hardly,' Vashti agreed, not bothering to admit that she'd been thinking the exact same thing.

She knew her eyes were hollow, knew she was as tired as she looked, if not more so, and knew also that she was not about to be led into any discussion at all about why she looked and felt so weary.

It wasn't that she didn't feel Alana could be trusted; it was that both girls knew Phelan's sister was blatantly matchmaking, which was the absolute last thing Vashti needed just at the moment.

Neither did she need the minor effort of introducing her companion to Ross Chandler, but it couldn't be avoided when the boss emerged while they were still standing there.

Chandler acknowledged the introduction gracefully, his shrewd, tiny eyes glinting with appreciation of Alana's youthful loveliness.

'Make it a long lunch,' he suggested upon being told their plans. 'In fact why not make it an executive-type Friday lunch, Vashti? And I'll see you Monday—hopefully looking a bit more rested.'

'You must be some kind of witch,' Vashti said after the man had departed with a beaming smile at Alana. 'I've never seen him react like that to...well... anybody. I'd have bet I could have been dying on the floor in front of his desk and he wouldn't have given me the afternoon off.'

'Sex appeal,' Alana replied with a flashing grin. 'Does it every time; you ought to try it some time.'

Vashti didn't bother to reply, merely raised one eyebrow. Alana took the hint. They walked down to Liverpool Street and their restaurant and began a lengthy lunch in which Alana did her very best not to mention her brother.

Not that her best was all that good; it seemed to Vashti that every second comment had to be amended or cut short because it might involve some mention of Phelan, where he was or what he was doing.

And when Alana finally gave up and changed the subject entirely, things only got worse. Vashti herself became the centre of discussion and, as usual, Alana was less than tactful.

'I invited you for lunch because I've been worried about you, for some reason,' she said. 'And now that I've seen you, I'm glad I did. You look like something the cat dragged in at midnight, if you don't mind me saying so.'

'Thank you so very much; just what my ego really needed,' Vashti replied with a weary smile and a shake of her head. 'Have you got any other compliments, or is that your best?'

'Better than you deserve, love. What on God's green earth have you been doing to yourself? Or I suppose I should ask what Phelan's been ... oh, sorry.' And Alana had the good grace to at least try to look contrite.

Only to blow it all, in total innocence, a moment later by trying to change the subject and embarking on a dissertation involving stockings and suspender belts.

'Absolutely stunning,' she was saying, 'except for the price, of course. You just wouldn't believe what you've got to pay for...'

And halted mid-sentence in astonishment as Vashti's face contorted with spasms of laughter she fought to contain within, lest she explode into either tears or laughs that would make their table the centre of attention in the crowded restaurant.

'Put my foot in it again, eh?' Alana quipped without showing the slightest remorse. 'And of course you wouldn't dream of telling me why that was so hilarious.'

'I...I...can't,' Vashti gasped, hardly able to speak at all through the emotions that bubbled up inside her. And hugged herself, eyes downcast. If she tried to explain she'd either burst into tears or scream with laughter, and she didn't want either. Not here; not now.

Instead, she gulped down the remains of her drink, kept her eyes averted as Alana ordered refills for both of them, and struggled to assemble control—at least *some* control—before the waitress returned with the drinks.

'It's not your fault,' she said after the refill arrived and she'd finished half of that, too. 'It's just that, well, I went out last week and blew my plastic absolutely into orbit on exactly that. And I don't even know *why*!'

'Well, I do, of course,' Alana replied matter-of-factly. 'And no, I won't mention the mongrel's name.'

'Good. Don't.'

'I said I wouldn't and I won't,' Alana replied almost snappily, conveniently forgetting that she already had and didn't—in any event—need to do it again to keep the conversation in troubled waters. 'But if that steak doesn't get here pretty damned soon, I'll mention a few others.'

'Having told the nice lady we were in no hurry at all,' Vashti remarked. 'Now who's being cranky?'

'I always am when I'm hungry,' was the reply. 'Or when I start dumping grog into an empty stomach. There are people who really shouldn't drink, and I think I'm one of them.'

'Just makes me sleepy,' Vashti replied, but was as pleased as her companion when their steaks arrived a moment later.

'You get stuck into that,' Alana said, suiting action to her own words. 'It's hard to say from looking at you which you need more—the food or the rest.'

They finished up with rich desserts and coffee with liqueurs, by which time Vashti could hardly keep her eyes open. Alana, by comparison, had returned to her usual brightness and was carrying the conversation virtually on her own.

'Which is a waste,' she concluded. 'I can stay home and talk to walls at far less expense and you *should* be home, before you go to sleep where you're sitting. So I'll be quick about asking this favour and then we're going to put you in a cab and send you home.'

Presuming Vashti's nod to mean she still had an audience, she reached into her handbag and pulled out a small tan-coloured envelope, from which she finally extracted a theatre ticket.

'Presuming you've wakened up by tomorrow night, and presuming you wouldn't knock back a chance to see the Chrissie Parrott Dance Collective from the front row of the dress circle, and presuming you're even listening to me—are you?'

Vashti managed another nod.

'Right. So here's your ticket. I'm probably going to be late, so don't wait for me; just get there on time yourself and I'll make it when I make it. See here? It says eight-fifteen, which as you know means you'll have to be there a bit early, because the old Theatre Royal can be slow filling up.'

'But...who...why...?'

'Because Ph...that mongrel who shall remain nameless was supposed to go with me and now he won't and I hate going alone, that's why. Now are you going to be in it or have I just wasted lunch and have to run around finding somebody else to join me?'

There was laughter in Alana's eyes, but a hint of something else, too. Maybe, Vashti thought, she really *did* hate going out alone.

'Thank you,' she said, reaching out for the ticket. 'For this and for lunch, which, no, was not wasted. I will join you, I promise, unless I somehow manage to sleep right through from the moment I get home today. And even *I* couldn't manage that, I don't think.'

'Good. Now let's go find you a cab. I'd drive you, although not after the liquid part of that lunch, except that I am without transportation until my *sane* brother, whose name I *can* mention, gets round to collecting me. Provided he remembers, of course. He may be saner than the other one, but he's a damned sight less reliable sometimes.'

It astonished Vashti when she wakened to find herself feeling so rested, so *totally* rested, and her bedroom still bright with daylight. Until she realised it was morning daylight, confirmed by the digital bedside clock-radio.

'Four in the afternoon until near as dammit eight o'clock in the morning,' she muttered aloud with considerable amazement. 'Well, I must have needed it.'

No lie there, and it would be something to tell Alana at the theatre that evening. On the way home in the taxi, she had wondered at the wisdom of accepting the ticket, had really not wanted to accept it in the first place. But this morning the idea seemed far more pleasant; she liked Alana and she liked modern dance and, well . . . why not?

Bouncing out of bed with a wondrous, unexpected feeling that, for once, all was right with her world, she climbed into her weekend housework clothes and rushed through the necessary chores—washing, ironing, even cleaning the oven.

Only then did she permit herself the usually earlier luxury of sprawling on the lounge floor to devour the weekend papers page by page, article by article. Two hours later she compounded the decadence by retiring to a hot, filled-to-the-brim bath with a jug of white wine and the latest novel.

Her buoyant mood persisted; when it came time to dress she had no difficulty making decisions. Out came the most flamboyant 'after five' outfit she owned. And with it, carrying a hint of apprehension small enough to be ignored, *the* lingerie.

'And to hell with you, Phelan Keene,' she muttered to a quite splendid image in the mirror. The stockings were, she decided, quite magnificent, and the fact that nobody was going to see what kept them up was ir- relevant. *She* would know; she *did* know, and that slight nuance of naughtiness almost made it worth the price.

The overall effect called for at least one drink at the Theatre Royal Hotel before the show, so Vashti left with plenty of time in hand and was lucky enough to secure a parking spot just over the road from the theatre.

Outside the theatre, people were already gathering, dressed in everything from jeans to evening wear; Hobart was nothing if not tolerant about what should be worn to the theatre. Vashti strolled across Campbell Street at the first opportunity, nodding to several acquaintances, but searching in vain for Alana.

Even knowing her friend had expected to be late, Vashti kept an eye open as she moved into the throng at the pub next door and fought her way to the serving bar. Here, again, were one or two acquaintances, along with a fair few men whose glances said they'd like to be.

It was, she decided, quite worth the price of quality clothes to deliver so many sops to the ego in a single evening. Nobody made an out-and-out pass at her, which was just as well, thank you, but there was sufficient interest to make her brief stay in the pub exceptionally enjoyable.

Alana still hadn't put in an appearance, however, when the ushers began ringing their bells and it came time to find her seat. Vashti kept looking for her as she made her way across to the theatre, and, once inside, upstairs and along to the front row of the dress circle. Only two seats there were vacant, by this time, and she automatically settled into the one furthest from the central aisles, still looking round for her friend. But even when the lights had dimmed, then focused on the stage and the vivid intricacy of the first dance number, there was no sign of Alana.

The vacant seat was taken, however, during the first fade between numbers, and as the tall, lean figure of Phelan Keene politely made his way to her side Vashti felt herself grow first hot then icy-cold with anger at the deceptions that had to be involved.

She visibly shrank away from him as he levered himself into the seat beside her, saying nothing, not even looking at her. Nor did he, during the second presentation, which began almost the instant he was seated. He sat like a grim spectre, only his profile visible in the dim lighting, with his eyes and attention apparently focused on the lithe, almost hypnotic movements on-stage.

Vashti couldn't ignore his presence. Had she been blind and deaf, she thought, she would have known it was him the instant he sat down. But she could force herself to emulate his indifference, and she tried her best to fixate on the dancing, to try and let the musical accompaniment drown out the roaring inside her.

The music was good, the dancing better, the seats, unfortunately, still the most uncomfortable in the known world of theatre. But even as she sat with a self-constructed mental wall of thorns between herself and Phelan, Vashti was eventually able to give herself over to the performance and enjoy it.

Until the interval!

She had planned for it, hoping against hope that the people on her left side were smokers, and would move quickly to get out to the foyer. That way she could be free to leave without having to move through the tiny space before Phelan's legs, without having to look at him, to speak to him.

They did move quickly; he was quicker still. A hand caught her elbow before she had a hope of moving, and he was there, leaning to force her attention. So close, almost kissing-close, she thought irrelevantly. But kissing appeared the last thing on his mind.

He spoke. So did she, and their words were so much the same that it would have been laughable under any other circumstance. 'I'm going to kill your...my... sister for this!'

But it was Phelan who continued.

'You'll have to stand in line,' he said grimly, then grinned, his teeth gleaming but his eyes like coals. 'Unless you'd like to help, of course. This being the first thing we've ever agreed on, maybe we should share the experience.'

'*You'll* only kill her in a book,' Vashti heard herself reply. '*I* am going to... to...' Possibilities occurred to her—shocking possibilities—but she couldn't put them into words she was game to say aloud.

Especially as she had suddenly realised he'd let go of her elbow; now he held her wrist, and it was anything but a confining grip, the way his thumb moved caressingly across her pulse.

'Come and I'll buy you a drink. We can discuss the gory details after the performance,' he said, rising to his feet and lifting her along with him.

Never so much as a thought that she might not *want* a drink, Vashti thought as she toddled along behind him. Much less that she might not want a drink with *him*. And if he'd given her half a chance she wouldn't have left her wrap there on the seat; she could have just walked out and left him!

'This is too good to waste by stomping off in a huff halfway through,' he said. Reading her mind again? 'So if you're planning that, tell me now, and I'll just fetch one glass of wine.'

This was all spoken with a straight face and eyes that danced with devilish laughter, daring her to make a scene, double-daring her to take up his offer and flee, much as they both knew she wanted to.

'*White* wine, please,' she replied, calmly and politely. 'Which I may very well dump down the front of you,' she added to his departing back, noting as she spoke how superbly the dinner suit fitted him, how easily he seemed to make his way through the throng at the bar.

And when he returned, casually carrying two glasses of wine in one hand while he used the other to fend his way through the crowd, she wondered how he could do that so easily and never take his eyes off her the whole time. Because he didn't. From the instant he'd made sufficient progress to be able to see her, his eyes roamed over the terrain of her body, climbing a breast here, descending a leg there.

Did he realise how much the stockings he appeared to be admiring had cost? she wondered. Not to mention the wispy suspender belt that now felt more fragile than *risqué*? For an instant, as she reached out to accept the glass from him, she had a ridiculous desire to ask him, to see if he thought the price justified. Vashti had to lower her head to hide the inner laugh that thought caused.

'I hope that chuckle was prompted by some suitable punishment for my almost departed sister,' Phelan said. And his own grin was far from humorous. It was wolfish, totally predatory, frightening.

But his eyes weren't. They met her own over the wine glass he raised in a mocking salute, then brushed across her face with a curious gentleness, touching her lips, her throat . . .

'What I'd like to do to her, well, there aren't suitable words to be used in public,' Vashti said, raising her own glass before gulping half the contents down in a futile bid to cool her sudden flush.

'I agree. It's a pity Dad didn't use his good old razor strap on my dear little sister while she was growing up!' Phelan said. 'It might've put her off pulling stunts like this one!'

Vashti replied, quietly and seriously, 'But really, I'm just astonished that she'd even think of doing a thing like this. It's just . . . just . . .'

'Totally in character. My darling baby sister is probably the world's greatest pure romantic. She's been trying to marry off both Bevan and me for years, although to be fair tonight's little performance was a bit off the wall even for her!'

'She's off her head, never mind being off the wall,' Vashti retorted.

Phelan laughed, a curt, low bark that offered only a glimpse of flashing teeth and no real sign of humour. But whatever he might have been going to say was cut off by the bells recalling them to their seats.

Vashti followed Phelan down the darkening aisle, and was all too conscious of his hand on her arm as he guided her along the row and into her seat. She was equally conscious that he didn't maintain his touch once she was in her seat and the house lights went down to announce the second performance.

Throughout the second half, he maintained his attention only on the stage and the dancers, while Vashti found her own attentions divided. She very much enjoyed the performance, but was also very much aware of the tall figure beside her, of the strong profile lurking in her side-vision and even, she fancied, of the man's very aura.

Because Phelan Keene did have an aura, she thought. Or perhaps it was easier described as a *presence*; the semantics weren't important. It was enough that she was strongly aware—too strongly, if anything—of the man beside her, despite his silence, despite his apparent attitude of ignoring her.

When the show was over, stimulating several well-deserved curtain calls, Vashti turned to bend down for her wrap, only to find it already in Phelan's hands. Without thinking, she turned to let him spread it over her shoulders, feeling the touch of his fingers on her bare skin as he did so, fancying that his fingertips lingered briefly, tantalising. Or was it only fancy? Certainly it was fact that he took her arm to guide her into the aisle, that he kept her elbow in the cup of his palm as they made their way downstairs and out on to the crowded footpath.

'Dare I suggest we adjourn to the casino for a drink while we scheme and plot a dastardly revenge on baby sister?' he asked. 'We can drop your car off on the way, unless you're set on maintaining your independence to the bitter end.'

'I'll see you at my place,' Vashti replied before she could change her mind, and skipped across the street to her car before he could move to accompany her.

'You're an idiot, girl,' she muttered as she drove home. 'You don't make a whit of sense; not even to yourself.' And then laughed. Did it matter? Did anything really matter? It was a nice night, she'd just enjoyed a splendid performance, and been invited for a drink at the Wrest Point casino. She was dressed for it, in the mood for it, and so indeed—why not?

The totally carefree atmosphere was less easy to maintain once she'd parked her own car and got out to find Phelan Keen waiting to hand her into his own—a magnificent Jaguar that reeked of luxury and comfort. As they drove through the city and south towards Sandy Bay and the casino, she found herself chattering almost non-stop, as if by noise alone she

could eliminate the feeling of luxurious intimacy
created by both man and automobile.

Keene drove with seemingly careless flair, yet on
several occasions during the journey she noticed how
he deftly slowed or switched lanes to avoid possible
problems, how he was totally alert to the traffic
around and ahead of him without appearing to be.
Was he equally alert to her, to her jangled feelings,
her forced spontaneity?

If so, he concealed it well, handing her out of the
big car at Wrest Point having said hardly a word since
they'd left her home, casually taking her arm for the
walk through the parking lot, but touching her only
with his fingertips. And his eyes.

Vashti wasn't so confused that she didn't notice the
admiring glances she attracted as they strolled through
the hotel's reception area, Phelan apparently seeking
a relatively quiet place where they could sit down with
their drinks. He, too, attracted a degree of attention,
she noticed, and wasn't a bit surprised.

He finally found a place for them, got Vashti seated
and then said, 'White wine for you, *Mssss*, or something a bit more...adventurous?' She shivered inwardly at the stretched-out Msssss, then noticed his
eyes were laughing; he was only being cheeky, she
hoped.

'Oh, definitely more adventurous,' she found
herself replying. 'A piña colada, I think.'

'The perfect choice,' he replied. 'I shall return quite
quickly, lest you succumb to the lecherous glances I
see all round the room.'

Gone before she could even smile at his phoney
pompous attitude, he was, indeed, back quite quickly

with an enormous goblet for her and what seemed an innocuous glass of something colourless for himself.

'Now what shall we drink to?' he mused as he handed over her drink. 'I'd say revenge, but that's far too general, much too simplistic. There really ought to be a twenty-dollar word that fits, don't you think?'

'You're the wordsmith,' Vashti replied, her mind blank, empty now even of simplistic synonyms to take his meaning.

Their glasses had yet to touch, and he was holding her glance over the rim of his, somehow making the toast frivolous and serious at the same time.

'Well,' he said, ' "vengeance" isn't bad, although I'm told it's the prerogative of the Bloke Upstairs. Some of our more primitive north-eastern neighbours call it "pe-bak"—in pidgin, of course. But that would mean all sorts of hard work, because we'd have to take her head and smoke it and shrink it, or eat her heart, or something equally gruesome. Too damned much trouble, say I. And "lex talionis", which is the Latin bit that requires punishment to fit the crime, wouldn't let us go quite that far, although I rather fancy the smoked head bit.'

'I just don't see myself as an avenging angel,' Vashti replied, smothering a grin and, still held by his pale eyes, suddenly dying of thirst, but unwilling to taste her drink without the formality of a toast. 'Couldn't we just let her off with a warning or something?'

'Not a chance!' And he clinked his glass firmly against hers. 'Here's to *retaliation*,' he said, stretching the syllables into, Vashti thought, a fifteen-dollar word, at least. But still . . .

'I'll drink to that,' she said dramatically. And did so, wishing she had the nerve to just come straight out and tell him that she was not, and would not be, a particularly vindictive person. Not, she supposed, that he would believe it anyway.

'And so you should,' he said with a grin that widened as he reached out with a napkin to dab ever so gently at the corner of her mouth. 'Froth in your moustache,' he said quite seriously. 'Should be more careful with frothy drinks.'

And laughed aloud at her instinctive gasp of surprise and the hand that flew to her mouth after his, leaving a curious feeling of intimacy, had gone.

Vashti could only laugh too then, but in her own ears it sounded false and contrived. Had she reacted too strongly? Certainly she'd been unprepared for such a gesture, was still having to force herself to be cautious with this man, to be *angry* with him, as she was supposed to be. But it was hard, indeed damned near impossible.

All he had done the other night, she was forced to admit, was make it very, very clear that he fancied her, that there was a strong sexual attraction. If she was going to deny vindictiveness, she could hardly lie even to herself about the fact that the attraction was mutual. But did she dare let herself relax?

'I know the classic line is something about you being so lovely when you're angry,' he said in that gentle, musing tone he sometimes used. 'But you're not. Or rather, you are, but it's nothing compared to how beautiful you are when you're not angry, when you're just being . . . well, you.'

Vashti giggled; she couldn't help it.

'Thus sayeth the great communicator, the master wordsmith,' she chuckled, inordinately pleased at having, for once, caught him flat-footed. Then even more pleased, somehow, to have him join her in laughter. No super-ego here, she thought; a man who could cheerfully laugh at himself couldn't be all bad.

'I may have to take you on as a collaborator,' he said. 'Or, better yet, as a fair-dinkum research assistant.'

Vashti couldn't resist the opportunity.

'I thought you already had,' she countered. Then added, hoping against hope, 'Or have you given up this mad idea of writing a book centred around the tax department?'

'Not on your life!' he replied vigorously. 'There's a wonderful book there if I can just get a handle on it. And I will—all it takes is time. And of course the right approach. Which is where you'll find yourself more involved than you might imagine.'

'You want me to rush around in my spare time investigating the various aspects of murder, sex and general mayhem? In the staid, conservative old tax office?' Vashti chuckled, couldn't help it, really. The idea seemed quite ridiculous.

'No, not exactly that either,' he replied, and now she saw the devilment in his eyes. It was no longer relevant who had started this little game; Phelan was also starting to enjoy himself.

'The mystery and intrigue part, then? No good. I'm hopeless at mysteries; sometimes I don't even know whodunit after it's been explained to me.'

Silence, but silence with a shake of his head and one lifted eyebrow.

'Well, it can't be the steamy bits, because I'm...'
She had to pause, realising only too late how easily
he'd trapped her—or she'd trapped herself.

'Off the boil? I never would have guessed.'

And now the devil laughed in his eyes, eyes that
forced her to laugh with him, to accept, as he had,
the joke on herself.

'*Right* off the boil,' Vashti replied sternly after
granting him hardly more than a smile. He was too
tricky, too devious by half, she thought. And she decided to be far more careful with what she might say.

Phelan didn't seem the least concerned. He
shrugged off her stern message and gazed thoughtfully for a moment.

'OK,' he finally said, 'we'll let that one go for a bit
and look at the practicalities of the matter. Is this
evening tax-deductible?'

'I...' She paused, eyes narrowed as she glared at
him for bringing business into what had been a lovely
evening despite its unusual beginning. Then decided
to hell with it. 'I couldn't imagine how,' she declared.
'Everybody knows by now, surely, that entertainment
expenses are no longer allowed.'

'Well, please don't take this wrong, because I'm
only being hypothetical,' he said, 'but what if I'm not
just "entertaining" you? What if what I'm doing is
research?'

'Hypothetical research?' Vashti definitely, she decided, did not like the direction this was going. But
she couldn't see an easy way out; nothing short of
a blunt refusal to play the *hypothetical* game
would work.

'*Research* research,' Phelan insisted. 'Now try and be objective about this; we're only speculating, after all.'

'OK,' she replied, feeling no assurance whatsoever.

'Right.' Phelan was enjoying this; she could see the glint of battle in his eyes. 'Now you remember at lunch that day when I insisted that if I'm awake I'm working?'

'I do. Was that luncheon "*research*" too?'

'Don't be cheeky,' he growled. 'You know damned well it wasn't.'

'That doesn't prohibit your presuming *your* portion was research,' she replied astutely. And nearly laughed at the expression on his face as he thought about that and was forced to accept her point.

'OK, I could have. Let's say I did. But it's to-night—hypothetically!—that we're looking at. Surely it's a legitimate business activity for a writer to bring a girl to a place like this to *research* how she reacts to the place, how she dresses, how the bar service works, how the drinks look, how...well...everything? After all, I can't very well put it in a book if I've never seen it, now, can I?'

Vashti thought about his theory long and hard, so long that he finally grinned hugely, then got up and went off to get fresh drinks. When he returned, she was ready.

'But you've been here before,' she submitted. 'And you've been here with a woman before, I'm sure.' She faltered only slightly as a vision of Janice Gentry intruded. 'How many times do you expect the tax office to accept that as research?'

'I've never been here before with *you*.'

'What does that have to do with anything, for goodness' sake?'

'Well, if you're going to be my . . . let's say heroine, then it's *your* reactions that I'm researching, surely. Not somebody else's.'

'But I'm not your heroine,' she protested. Feebly, because this was getting all too complicated, therefore dangerous. Phelan didn't laugh, but his eyes were ready to. She was on shaky ground here, and didn't know where to step.

'Hypothetical, don't forget.'

'All right. Hypothetically, I'm your heroine. But I think you're really stretching this a bit. Surely any woman would do?'

'Certainly not! After all, if I'm doing a book in which *you* are the heroine, then I have to know how *you* react to everything. I already know how . . . how some other women react, but if you're going to be the heroine, then *you're* the person whose reactions I have to research.'

And every time he stressed the *you*, something flickered in his eyes, something that Vashti felt could actually reach out and touch her, caress her. Dangerous!

'So tonight I'm a hypothetical woman being researched as a hypothetical heroine,' she finally charged. 'What happens tomorrow night if you bring me here again? There has to be a limit somewhere.'

'I accept.'

'Well, I'm pleased; I didn't think you'd give in that easily,' Vashti replied, honestly surprised.

'Who said anything about giving in? I just said I accept your invitation for tomorrow night; that's all.'

'Now who's being silly?' she replied lightly, hoping to divert him, to defuse the trap before she was hopelessly snared.

And it worked!

'Tomorrow night,' he said quite seriously, 'I could bring you in, let's say, grotty clothes, or clothes that didn't fit, didn't suit you. Still the heroine, but I reckon the research element is still there.'

'And so on and so on,' Vashti mused, intrigued by his logic and ninety-nine per cent certain of how Ross Chandler would react to it. Then she thought about how close to the wind she might be sailing from a purely ethical basis.

'I think . . . I think we'd better let this go,' she said.

'A bit too close to home? Don't forget it's only hypothetical,' Phelan replied directly. 'And don't forget too that you, personally, are never going to have to find yourself having to deal with it professionally.'

'You're aiming to put me in a terribly compromising position, but it's all right because it's only hypothetical? Thank you so very much, I think.'

'I am indeed, and it's got nothing to do with taxes.'

He was only half joking, if that. His eyes told her that, his glance reaching out to stroke her cheek, to touch her lips, run a line of fire down her throat.

'I can't be a heroine and a tax auditor too,' she stressed, trying to hide her confusion.

'Ah, but that's where you're wrong,' he said. 'I've got it all worked out. What I'll do is a romance: female tax auditor—make that *beautiful* female tax auditor—gets all involved with the tax affairs of handsome, charming, debonair writer who has strange but firm ideas about how his tax should be assessed . . .'

He was looking at her quite strangely now, she thought, his words rocketing directionless through her mind.

'They could meet for the first time, let's say, in a remote little country cemetery, maybe, some place really dark and spooky and vivid with atmosphere. What do you reckon?'

Vashti didn't reply. She felt suddenly cold, as if someone had abruptly taken away all the heat in the room. She reached out for her glass, realising only then that it was once again empty.

'Another?' Phelan was on his feet, reaching out to take the glass from her. She nodded, still silent. He moved off into the crowd and Vashti unfolded her wrap and threw it over her shoulders.

What kind of game was he playing? For an instant, she found her mind clouded with stark terror. She was halfway to her feet, ready to run, before she managed to take a deep breath and regain control, or at least some semblance of control. By then it was too late to run.

'I don't think you fancy being my heroine, some-how,' Phelan was saying as he set her drink in front of her, then reached out to take her hand in his. 'And you're cold. Are you feeling all right?'

'Yes. Just . . . cold,' she replied. Worse than cold now. Freezing. Except that one hand, burning in his grasp as if both their hands were on fire.

Vashti felt like a mouse trapped by a cat. Not a hungry cat, which would at least perhaps ensure a quick and certain death. A cruel cat, a cat that would toy with its prey, tease, torment. Just, she thought, for the fun of it.

'Would you rather collaborate on retribution?' he was asking. 'You seemed to enjoy that more, I think.'

No, she wanted to shout. I don't want to collaborate on anything. I just want this to end. It was too dangerous, too risky by half—emotionally and ethically and personally and professionally.

She wasn't even aware of shaking her head, but she *was* aware of him lifting his eyes to look beyond her, of him suddenly releasing her hand, of his glance changing, evolving from what had seemed vaguely concerned to that tense, predatory alertness.

'Too late, I fancy. Best you gird up your lovely loins for battle, darling Vashti. And if you can't help, for God's sake don't get in the way.'

And before she could reply he was on his feet, grinning broadly, warmly, welcoming.

'Alana! Well, well. This is a surprise. Bit late for you to be out, isn't it, dear sister?'

CHAPTER SEVEN

VASHTI came to her feet so quickly, trying to turn at the same time, that she stumbled, saved only by Phelan's hand catching her arm, pulling her against him, and then reaching round to hold her that way.

Her eyes seemed out of focus for just that instant; she opened them to see Alana, dressed resplendently in the palest mauve, on the arm of a tall, strikingly attractive man about Vashti's own age.

Alana was open-mouthed, staring at her brother with the haunted, enormous eyes of a trapped animal. Poised to flee, but held by her unwitting companion, Alana seemed caught in a pool of silence; she stood there, eyes whipping back and forth from Phelan to Vashti, at first with pleading, then a sort of resigned acceptance.

Vashti couldn't speak. All her anger at the girl's deception had frothed up to lodge in her throat then dissipate as she emphathised with Alana's plight.

The freezing moment thawed, melted by Phelan's gentle voice as he smiled at his sister and reached a hand out to her companion. Introductions were made; Vashti forgot the young man's name as quickly as she heard it. It was, she knew, irrelevant in the face of the explosion to come.

Only it didn't. Phelan insisted Alana and her friend must join them for a drink, noted their preference, and walked off to leave the girls and Alana's unknowing companion. Vashti was numb, unsure of what to say, what to do. Alana, she fancied, was worse.

Someone's voice—Vashti realised after an instant that it was her own—chopped the silence into appropriate slices of small talk, forcing a response from Alana, coaxing one from her companion. Phelan was gone for minutes—hours, it seemed.

Then he was there, materialising from the crowd like a magician from a puff of smoke, an enigmatic smile on his lips and a tray of drinks on the cupped fingers of one hand. But his eyes! Alana's companion—what *was* his name?—had never met Phelan before, obviously. Or else he was just thick. Maybe both; surely nobody, Vashti thought, could miss the fire in those eyes, the explosive, wild madness.

Certainly Alana didn't. She accepted her drink, then sat there, staring at it as if it might leap up and take her by the throat. Occasionally she shot a look of pure panic at her brother, or at Vashti, who held on to her own glass as if to maintain her balance.

And Phelan dominated the situation. His rich voice purred like that of a hunting cat; his personality held all of them as if in a cage. Skilfully, using words like fencing foils, he drew out Alana's young man—who he was, what he did for a living, and did he ride? Of course, Alana wouldn't even *talk* to a man who didn't ride. Within minutes, it seemed, he knew more about the man than his mother did; Vashti still couldn't remember his name!

Then it was time for another round, and of course it was Alana's friend's turn to buy. He was gone for what seemed like days, *silent* days in which Phelan sat with a warm smile and ice-bleak eyes, pinning his

sister in place, forestalling so much as a word from
her by sheer will-power.

Alana seemed incapable of countering his silent assault, and Vashti was equally impotent. She wanted
to cry out to Phelan, to somehow make him stop this
torture, but it was as if she were locked out of the
tableau, despite being a part of it.

Why didn't he say something? Why no accusation,
no yelling or screaming or whatever it was that
brothers and sisters did under such duress? Vashti
merely wanted to get away, to go and hide under a
table, if nothing else. The atmosphere was so alive
with tension that she could hardly breathe; she was
freezing and stifling at the same time.

Alana sat like a mannequin, so still that she didn't
appear to breathe at all. Her eyes were wounded, her
lips parted as if to gasp, or speak, or scream. Phelan
smiled.

The boyfriend returned. Phelan turned the sound
back on and conversation returned, but the tension
remained—tangible, it seemed, to only three of the
four.

Then Phelan began applying the pressure, *forcing*
his sister to take an active role in the conversation,
making her respond. He was truly a master mani-
pulator, somehow engendering not only conversation
but smiles, once even a laugh. Ghostly hollow, it was,
but a laugh.

And he kept twisting the conversation, working it
like potters' clay to find places for words like 'vengeance', 'vendetta', and a host of other synonyms.
Each one seemed to strike his sister like a lash. Most
had a similar effect on Vashti, but he couldn't realise

that; seated beside him, she was on the periphery of his attention, she thought.

Wrong. He finished up with a line that allowed him to exhibit 'retaliation', then turned to favour Vashti with a smile so huge, so obviously genuine, that she couldn't believe it.

'Of course you're not a vengeful person, dear Vashti,' he grinned, but it was a false grin now. Then he rose to his feet and turned to his sister with an even broader, more false grin. 'Anyway, we have to go now,' he said to Alana, reaching out to her friend with an outstretched hand to be shaken.

Alana got a kiss on the cheek, then Phelan quietly said, 'You know...you've kept your figure really well. Must be all the riding. Give all the children a kiss for me when you get home, eh?'

And to Vashti, who simply didn't *believe* what she'd just heard, 'Come along, darling.'

Come along she must, because he had taken her wrist and was already turning away, leaving Alana standing there with a stunned expression and her companion looking like a man who'd just got his tax assessment.

Vashti would have been pulled along like the tail on a kite, except that as soon as they were out of the young couple's sight Phelan tugged her close to him and put his arm companionably around her waist. And the fingers there trembled, as did, she quickly realised, the hip she was being bounced against as they walked. A few steps more and he stopped, his entire body shaking.

The bastard was laughing! And so, despite the turmoil of emotion that threatened to blow her head off, was Vashti. Phelan turned her to face him, loomed over her with tears brightening his eyes as he chortled at the success of his gambit, and Vashti simply couldn't help but join in. They stood there, oblivious to the passing throng, and fairly howled with laughter.

'You were magnificent; the perfect foil,' he said after a minute, and leaned down to kiss her, almost chastely, on the lips.

'I wasn't being your damned foil,' she replied. 'I was just as dumbstruck by the whole performance as everybody else.' And somehow the humour had gone out of it, for her. 'You really are a cruel man,' she said bluntly.

'Fiddlesticks! The bloke was a nerd and she'll thank me in the morning,' he retorted. 'That's if she doesn't come blazing out to the farm and slaughter me in my bed. I don't suppose you'd let me stay with you to-night, where it's safe?'

Vashti ignored him. 'I really ought to go to her,' she mused. 'You had her absolutely terrified, you know? And that poor young man...'

'He probably won't figure it all out for a week,' Phelan replied. 'Stop fussing. When you've had a chance to think it all through, you'll realise it wasn't anywhere near as depraved as it sounded. Besides, it was *your* revenge too—or had you forgotten that?'

'I'm not a vengeful person,' she replied, throwing his words back at him, then suddenly aware that they were standing in the middle of the Wrest Point lobby, dividing the throngs of late-night gamblers and diners that flowed past them, and Phelan Keene was still holding her disturbingly close against him while he stared down into her eyes. One hand was acceptably enough placed on her hip, but the other...

'And all the prettier for it,' he replied, and for an instant she thought he was going to kiss her again. Vashti backed away the inch his hands would allow, only to have him whisper, 'And you've kept your figure well, too.'

Which brought an immediate vision of Alana's gentleman friend, rigid with astonishment. It was enough to break the spell that had been forming; Vashti couldn't stop herself smiling.

'It's the riding that does it,' she chuckled, and carefully kicked Phelan in the shin, just enough to make him release her. The gentle kick was rewarded with a grimace, but he *did* release her, only to take her arm immediately in a gentle but proprietorial grip.

'I don't know about you,' he said with a grin, 'but all this vengeance has me fair starving. Fancy a snack before we retire to plot some more?'

'No more! If I were your sister I'd shoot you for what you've done already,' Vashti cried. 'And no, I'm not hungry. Or rather, I'm not sure. I don't know whether to laugh—because it *was* funny, I suppose—or to be just as angry with you as your sister is.'

'If *I* were my sister, I'd be scampering for the nearest hills, rightfully fearful of more to come,' he replied grimly. 'That was just a taste of her own medicine; there's the rest of the bottle to come—and it's a big, big bottle that won't taste one bit good. I'm certainly glad that you're not my sister, by the way. It would make things very difficult indeed.' And his eyes made very clear what he meant by that; they literally devoured her. 'Do you gamble, by the way?'

'The way they do here? Hardly. I'm just a working girl, remember.'

'How could I forget? Actually, I'm not much of a punter either, just in case it worries you. But I do have my moments and tonight I feel rather specially lucky. Must be the company I keep. Let's take a stroll through the gaming rooms and see if you're as lucky for me as I'd expect.'

To which there was no rational answer, much less a safe one. Vashti allowed herself to be guided down to the glitz and glitter of the gaming rooms, thinking as they went that she must be out of her mind even *trying* to keep up with this man.

I am well and truly out of my league, she thought, only to compare that intellectual rationale with how pleasant she found Phelan's company, how much she actually enjoyed being with him.

Waiting while he exchanged money for chips, she idly glanced at the crowds which surrounded the various roulette and blackjack tables, their faces an education in itself. Most seemed to take their gambling seriously; it was the locals at the poker machines who radiated elation or dejection with each small win or loss. The serious gamblers didn't, she thought, seem to have much fun at all.

Phelan, she quickly discovered, could never be described as a serious gambler. Within ten minutes at a roulette table he quadrupled his stake, only to be down to a single chip five minutes later.

'A kiss for luck,' he said then, and plundered her mouth before she could even think to object. Taking the longest possible odds, his chip multiplied as if by magic into stacks and stacks that grew like mushrooms.

'You *are* lucky for me,' he said, removing his winings with a delighted grin. 'Now let's see how lucky you can be for yourself.'

'But I don't even know what's going on,' she protested. 'And I can't gamble with ... well, you know.'

'With my money? Course you can. You just take a chip like this——' and he put one in her hand, then guided it over the betting zone '—and put it where you fancy.' The chip dropped from nerveless fingers as he put his other arm around her, his touch moving gently at her waist, his hip against hers and his breath warm in her ear as he whispered instructions.

She lost. Lost again. And again. No third time lucky, nor fourth nor fifth nor sixth.

'This is crazy,' she said aloud, turning to Phelan, urging him. 'I've got to stop. I can't keep this up.'

'It's 'cause you've got no faith,' he smiled. 'Or maybe because I haven't kissed *you* for luck.'

It was a shortcoming he proceeded to rectify with a thoroughness that left Vashti gasping and flushed with a sudden shyness. She'd have been embarrassed beyond belief, except that nobody noticed! And it was time to bet, which she did with all she had left, at Phelan's insistence.

'You can't test kissing luck by being a piker,' he said.

'You only used one chip,' she protested, horrified at the thought of losing everything in one go.

'I only had one left,' he said with a shrug. 'And besides, I trusted you for luck.'

I don't have your faith, she was about to say. Only suddenly she did—because she won! The pile of chips was magically cloned over and over and over.

'I won!' she cried. And again. Her eyes were wide with delight, her breath coming in gasps of excitement.

'Again?' Phelan smiled indulgently, helped rake in her winnings—*their* winnings.

'Not on your life,' Vashti said. 'I'd have to be mad! There's nearly a week's salary there.'

Phelan reached out and retrieved a handful of chips. 'Minus our original stake. What's left here now is just play money; it doesn't matter if you win with it, lose it or burn it.'

'No,' she said firmly, raking in the remainder and pouring the chips into his dinner-jacket pocket before he could move to object. The gloss was gone now. The heady feeling of excitement had ebbed to become common sense. Or, at least, as much common sense as Vashti felt capable of in this man's presence.

Suddenly she was exhausted, sagging. And it must have been obvious, because he didn't argue, didn't protest, merely looked down into her eyes, his gaze warm and gentle and...sharing.

'Time I took you home,' he said quietly. 'You've had a busy day for a little girl.'

Ten minutes later they were again in his luxurious car, moving smoothly through the scant traffic along Sandy Bay Road. Vashti lounged against the leather of her seat, her mind coasting, revelling in the silence and the car's super-smooth ride.

When they reached her flat, Phelan walked her to the door, his fingers warm on her arm. She ought to ask him in, she thought, but tiredness combined with caution to hold back the invitation. If she'd been vulnerable the other night, tonight was doubly so, dangerously so.

And he seemed to know it, even expect it.

'I've enjoyed this evening very much,' he said, lifting her hand to press his lips against it, then, startling, to press a wad of paper into it.

'What?'

'Your share,' he said, voice very soft now. 'And don't spoil it by arguing. Use it to buy something sexy—not that you need it.'

'But I can't take this,' she protested, ignoring him, forcing the money back into his hand.

'You just did.' And he deftly reached out to tuck the wad down the front of her dress, his fingers tracing a seductive retreat after he'd done so, his eyes claiming her, his lips ready to forestall any further argument.

'We'll do this again some time,' he said, 'if my sister survives long enough to arrange it. Now take yourself to bed, because if I have to do it for you I'd end up putting all my good luck at risk. Goodnight.'

And he left her, leaving the warmth of his lips against her throat, the feel of his fingers along her breast, along the length of her back. Warm feelings . . . right feelings. But . . .

Vashti stood in the doorway as he walked back to his car, knowing she wanted to call out to him, to invite him inside, despite the certainty of what that would mean. Knowing exactly what it would mean, and hating herself for not having the nerve to find out.

'No guts,' she told herself as he slid into the big car, closing the door with an over-casual wave in her direction. Vashti stepped into the flat, resisting the temptation to slam the door behind her, to display her temper and frustration in some physical, angry gesture.

'No guts,' she said again, flinging her wrap to land on the sofa, flinging her purse to join it, and kicking off her shoes to let them sleep where they landed.

The dress she hung up. Even childish temper tantrums had their limits, she told herself. And the frothy-frilly underwear, the ever so sexy stockings and minuscule suspender belt that had promised so much and delivered so little went into the laundry hamper to live with fair-dinkum working clothes until next wash-day.

Phelan's money she flung on her dressing-table, then retrieved it and carefully tucked it beneath the old sweater in her drawer. Then she retrieved the lingerie and tenderly tucked that away too.

'Not your fault,' she found herself muttering, and ended the performance by flinging *herself* into a bed that somehow seemed too big, too... something. She tried to take herself into sleep with thoughts of even sexier lingerie, of Phelan Keene's response to it. Of how she *thought* he'd respond to it, of how she wanted him to respond.

Why hadn't he? He surely would have sensed her readiness, her wanting him. And, she thought, he'd have sensed just as thoroughly how tired she was... had been! Angry now and wide awake, she walked naked through her flat, picking up the shoes and putting them away, carefully folding the evening wrap.

Then she discovered she was hungry. *His* fault; if he hadn't mentioned it, she wouldn't be. She made herself a sandwich, forced herself to eat it; heated some milk, forced herself to drink it. Went back to bed, got up again, made some more warm milk, and took a long shower that became a short one when she found herself scrubbing her body and hating it, not wanting to see it, not wanting to touch it. Wanting *him* to touch it.

She finally tumbled into sleep through sheer exhaustion, her body driven to it despite the confusion in her head, only to find herself waking with the sun and the alarm clock she must have set without thinking about it.

'No...no...nooo,' she groaned, turning off the alarm and plunging back into the safety of sleep, only to be wakened five seconds later, it seemed, by the telephone.

'I'm going to apologise to you,' said a familiar voice. 'Because *you* deserve an apology. For everything. Especially for involving you with him. *Him*, I'm going to kill. Slowly.'

'Alana? Is this really necessary at this ungodly hour of the morning?'

'It's one o'clock in the afternoon. I've been wanting to ring since...well, since very early. *He* won't answer his phone, or has it turned off, or isn't there at all.'

There was a long pause while the implications, Vashti thought, rattled round like peas in Alana's questionable brain.

'Oh. Oh...oh! He's not...not there, not there with you? I never thought of that. Oh, dear.'

'You never thought at all,' Vashti replied, trying to keep her voice firm, but failing. The younger girl's confusion had brought back memories of the night before, and with them the giggles. There was no sense trying to be stern; already she could feel herself wanting to laugh. Then had a better idea.

'Would you like to speak to him?'

She listened to the silence, then rushed into it, suddenly alive with the idiocy of it all. 'I'll have to wake him; he's had a rather hard night of it, poor love. How are the children, by the way? You did give them all a kiss, I hope. Ah, there's the handle bit; he'll wake up now, I reckon...'

An explosion of laughter cut her off, then both girls dissolved into laughter together. But it was Alana who recovered first.

'Full marks for that,' she gasped. 'And I deserved it. Deserved last night, too, I have to admit. Damn Phelan! That's the first time ever he's caught me that flustered that I couldn't even defend myself. I've never *been* so embarrassed.'

'You deserved all of it, and more,' Vashti replied. 'As he'd tell you himself if he were here, which of course he isn't. You're damned lucky either one of us is speaking to you, or ever will again.'

'You didn't enjoy yourself? You must have, or you wouldn't have ended up at the casino with him, would you?'

'That,' Vashti replied hotly, 'is not the point.'

'Course it is.' Alana seemed suddenly totally recovered from her apology mode. And that, for whatever reasons, served only to make Vashti angry about the whole situation. She really hadn't been, before. She'd been too involved, she realised, in Phelan Keene—just as Alana had intended! Which now made her even more angry.

'It's not! The point is that you've been messing round with other people's lives like...like some damned teenager. Which you're not, although nobody could ever tell, the way you act sometimes.'

Silence.

'Well?'

'I said I was sorry.'

'Not good enough.'

'Didn't you even enjoy the dancing? It should have been wonderful, what it cost me for the tickets.'

'I'm surprised you don't expect me to pay you back.'

Silence.

Cruel, that. Vashti felt the first flutterings of unease. Perhaps, she thought, she was making too much of this entirely. Except that she was still angry!

'You probably should; you'll thank me for this one day.'

'Well, if that ever happens, which I doubt, I will indeed pay you for the tickets,' she snapped, only to find that remark the final flurry of her anger. She wanted to maintain the rage, even though she probably *should*, but couldn't do it.

'Look, Alana,' she said, 'this isn't the time or the place to even be discussing this. I'm angry and you're upset and neither of us is making much sense any more. How about I accept your apology and we'll just let it go for now. OK?'

Alana sighed, the sound forlorn through the emptiness of the telephone wires. 'You're right, of course. And I *do* apologise, honestly. Not much wonder I'm off the wall; I barely slept all night. Probably,' she added grimly, 'the children. See you.'

And she was gone, hanging up quietly without waiting for Vashti's farewell.

Vashti hung up her own phone, but sat there, half expecting it to ring again, half tempted to ring Alana herself. It was ludicrous, she thought, for both of them to be feeling badly over what had been really no more than a childish prank, committed with the best of intentions.

'The road to hell is paved with good intentions,' she muttered at the silent telephone, then wished Alana a different path.

Vengeance, she thought, was fine for some people, but she wasn't one of them and didn't want to be. Then she found herself wondering about why Phelan hadn't answered *his* telephone when his sister rang. Any number of logical reasons filtered through her mind, but the only one that stuck was Alana's suggestion that perhaps he hadn't been there at all.

She had a mental flash of a leech with Janice Gentry's face, then forcibly ejected the image as unworthy. There had to be five thousand better reasons he hadn't answered his phone.

At least half of them rattled around like marbles in her skull, only to fly out of the window when he rapped on her door an hour later and she opened it to find him still in his clothes from the night before, looking just as he had at the start of the evening, except for his eyes.

'Don't even bother to say it; they look even worse from this side,' he said, ignoring a more conventional greeting. Vashti, wearing only faded jeans and a T-shirt, her hair crudely twisted up to keep it out of the way, could only stare at him.

'You look like death,' she said uncharitably. 'Are you sober?'

'As the proverbial judge,' he replied, and his grin was the same, flashing teeth that seemed rather at odds with those red-rimmed, ravaged eyes. 'I am prepared to swear that I've only had one alcoholic drink since I saw you last.'

'One drink, but no sleep, I presume,' she said, waving him inside, then rushing to steady him as he lurched across the lounge, collapsing on to the sofa, where he sprawled as if boneless.

'What *have* you been doing?' Vashti demanded. And had a flash of intuition. 'Surely not going off on the world's biggest ever guilt trip over the way you treated Alana last night? She phoned this morning—no, earlier this afternoon—worrying about you because she couldn't reach you.'

'Let her worry,' he sighed. 'Not that she was. All she was doing was checking to see where...no, whether...we were...if you know what I mean. Probably apologised profusely, as she ought. Knows she's still in deep trouble. Terrible child, my sister. Best of intentions, but a terrible child. Wants her bottom smacked.'

'She sounded reasonably contrite when she phoned,' Vashti said. 'And I think she was genuinely worried about you.'

'For goodness' sake, woman. I'm not a child—not even one of *her* children,' he said with a half-awake grin that didn't quite make it. 'Why in God's name should she be worried about my staying out all night? I don't live with her. I haven't even lived in the same house for about half her lifetime. She's never worried before; why should she start now?'

'Well, from the look of you, somebody should worry,' Vashti retorted. 'Do you want some coffee?'

'No coffee. Definitely no coffee. I've drunk enough coffee to float the QEII,' he muttered, somehow managing to sway even in his boneless, sagging slump. 'Just came to show you something. Unbelievable. All your fault, too, by the way. If anybody should be worried about me, it's you.'

Reaching, fumbling, he managed to get a hand into the inside pocket of his dinner-jacket. The hand stayed there; his eyelids slumped like empty sacks, then fluttered half open as his hand emerged with a piece of paper which he then waved expansively.

Vashti leaned down to pluck the paper from the air as he let it go, and straightened up to find herself holding a Wrest Point casino cheque for a quite incredible amount.

'Gambling? You've been up all night and half the day *gambling*?' She looked at Phelan, whose eyes had fallen closed again, then back at the cheque, which hadn't altered.

'Better than a cold shower,' he replied with what could have been a cheeky grin if he'd been awake enough to manage it. 'Takes longer, but——'

'You're mad as a meat axe,' she cried. And meant it. To have won this much, he must have risked, well, half that anyway. No sane person, she thought, could do that.

'Frustrated.' The word mumbled out of him as he slumped sideways to lie half sprawled on the sofa with his head hanging over the arm and his feet still on the floor.

Vashti looked at him, then found herself glancing wildly around the room and up to the ceiling as if there might be some deity to offer help. Fat chance!

'You can't go to sleep like that; you'll wake up as a pretzel,' she muttered, yanking at Phelan's arm to try to get him upright. Eyes like road-maps stared at her, unfocused, then he wobbled to his feet with her assistance and placidly allowed himself to be led into the bedroom, even to be propped against the wardrobe while she struggled to get his jacket off, then gripped him by the shoulders and swung him round to end up sitting on the edge of the bed.

'Nice,' he whispered as she knelt to unlace his shoes and remove them. Then was, thankfully, silent as she fumbled with his tie, irrelevantly noticing the crisp stubble on his chin as she did so.

And now? She drew a deep breath and started on the shirt studs, angrily slapping aside his fingers as he tried to manage them himself. She just couldn't give him a little push, topple him into her bed still wearing his clothes. But she wanted to; it would be safer.

He helped by falling over by himself once she had his shirt off, though it didn't make it much easier for her to relieve him of the trousers. She managed, finally, only too aware of the enforced intimacy involved.

'You're a worse nuisance than your sister,' she snarled, fighting the reaction she had to just lean down then and touch him. He was, she thought, quite splendid, his body muscular, lean almost to the point of gauntness. Crisp dark hair, not as coarse as that on his head, curled up from his groin to fan itself across his chest.

Just to look at him caused a *frisson* of emotion to run through her body, but it wasn't, Vashti realised, entirely sexual. Asleep now, his facial features had softened, regressed to the patterns of boyhood. He must, she thought, have been a happy child; even in sleep the lines around his eyes were laugh lines, and those surrounding his generous mouth were made by smiling.

Impulsively, she bent to touch his cheek, to kiss him ever so gently on the forehead. Then she carefully spread the feather quilt over him, picked up his clothes, and slipped out of the room. She hung up the dinner suit, suddenly totally embarrassed, incredibly aware of how he had looked, how he had felt, and the scent of him that still lingered on his shirt. She put the cheque back in the pocket from where he'd taken it, tucked his socks into his shoes and placed them neatly in the hall closet, then yielded to a sudden panic and rushed over to turn off the ringer on her phone.

For a moment she felt exhausted herself, though it had to be impossible since she'd slept most of the dozen hours that Phelan had spent gambling. Gambling! And this the man who'd told her he hardly ever gambled.

The man she now had to admit she wanted in her bed and had wanted there for some time. For all the good it does me, she thought, and wondered for a second if she was going to laugh or cry.

She frittered away most of the afternoon, dusting needlessly, tidying the already tidy, tiptoeing around like a little mouse to avoid making noise, and wondering quite astonishing things, like how Phelan Keene might react if he woke to find her beside him, or waiting here in the lounge in the lingerie she had to admit to herself she'd bought for *him* and which he'd never seen. She tried to read a book and failed, tried to do the *Sunday Tasmanian* crossword and failed even worse.

When would he wake up? And what would he do when he did? What would *she* do? What would they say? In the end, she gave it up, slipped out to her car, and drove over into Lenah Valley to the *Wursthaus*, where she spent half an hour in conversation with the butcher before finally choosing a selection of sausages—wallaby, hot Greek pork, various others—and a two-person leg of lamb. Over the road she found potatoes and other vegetables, buying an assortment, because she realised she had no idea of Phelan's taste in food. She struggled to remember what he'd eaten at the botanical gardens that time, but found the picture erased from her mind.

Ah, well, she thought, beggars can't be choosers, and laughed at the suggestion that a man with *that* cheque in his pocket might be considered a beggar. She drove home with the refrain of an old television commercial repeating in her mind—feed the man meat!

Her guest was still dead to the world when she peeked into the bedroom on her return, and she forced herself to work quietly as she prepared the meal, determined that the roast would be ready at seven, and, if he wasn't awake by then, he *would* be!

The simple, homely acts of cooking and setting the small kitchen table left her mind free to roam uninhibited, and Vashti was occasionally shocked and surprised with herself at the surprises she encountered while chilling the wine, while sneaking round to her neighbour's herb garden to pinch some fresh rosemary. She was not surprised, however, at the face she made when she went past the open bathroom and caught a glimpse of herself.

'Grotty,' she murmured, then had to stifle the laugh that came with her next thoughts. Sneaking into the bedroom, moving with the savage determination of a predator, she managed to emerge with what she'd gone for without Phelan even stirring.

Twenty minutes later, staring at her image in the mirror, she had second thoughts, but forced them away, thinking that Alana would have a fit if she could see Vashti, knowing Phelan's sister might have a fit anyway, if she knew where he was.

The old miniskirt, allegedly soon to become fashionable again, only just covered the tops of her stockings, and if she wasn't careful how she sat down the flimsy, frilly, *decadent* suspender belt was due for the exhibition she thought it had been intended for. Her blouse, this one neither old nor out of fashion, was of the softest jersey, and hugged her breasts with provocative innuendo, rather than being blatant. Just as well, she thought, having summoned up the courage—though only just!—to wear it without a bra.

Not wanting to risk the noise of a shower, she hadn't been able to wash her hair, hadn't really needed to since she'd done it during the sleepless hours of the night before, but she'd practically worn out her hairbrush to create a glossy, deliberately careless effect. A little make-up, but only a little, and dangly earrings completed the picture—just right, she thought, for the job of waking a slumbering prince.

She poured herself a glass of wine at six, another when the clock lied and said only ten minutes had passed. She checked the roast, checked it again, and argued with herself about whether to chicken out and put her bra on after all. Won. Or maybe lost, she thought with a self-satisfied grin, but left things as they were.

And at six-thirty precisely, she marched towards the bedroom, having liquefied her courage with a third glass of wine and still not sure it would be enough. She was standing there, hand raised to knock, her eyes closed as she summoned that last, vital bit of nerve, when the door opened a crack and one pale, still bloodshot eye peered out at her.

It looked her up and down; then a disembodied voice said, 'I see you're not wearing any trousers. Does that mean I can have them back? Or is this a come-as-you-are party?'

Flustered, she realised all his clothes were hung up in the hall closet, and if he emerged from the bedroom wearing what she left him in...

'Wait! Wait right there,' she cried. And rushed to grab up trousers and shirt, thrusting them through the crack in the door as if they were hot enough to burn her fingers. Maybe she only thought she heard a growl of laughter as the door closed. When it opened again she had her back turned, was kneeling to examine the roast, afraid to turn around, almost afraid to speak.

'Smells wonderful. Would there be time for me to steal a shower before we...?' The voice oozed chocolate fudge down her back; she could feel the warmth of it, tingled beneath the caress.

'Of course,' she said, rising easily to her full height without so much as a wobble of her stiletto heels. 'There are fresh towels in the cupboard and some of those throw-away razors in the medicine chest.'

She didn't dare turn around, poised as if for flight until she heard the bathroom door close and the sound of running water.

When he padded out to join her a few minutes later, hair close-kinked with moisture, and wearing only his trousers and shirt, sleeves casually rolled up, the first thing Vashti was aware of was how he looked at her.

It wasn't, as she had somehow expected—wanted?—a survey of her provocative dress, nor even a glance along the expanse of leg not covered by her choice of skirt. He looked her square in the eye, his own eyes still tired, but warm, friendly, comfortable.

'I'm not only a worse nuisance than my sister,' he said, revealing he hadn't been *quite* asleep when she'd removed his trousers, 'but I'm ruder as well. If I've presumed by thinking I was invited to the feast you're preparing, please just tell me to disappear and I'll try to manage it as gracefully as I can.'

'You're invited,' Vashti replied, not quite sure how to take *this* Phelan Keene. Did he think she'd be planning a dinner party with him sleeping nearly naked in her bed? Didn't he even notice the way she was dressed? Was he even awake yet?

'I'll just put some shoes on, then,' he said. 'Can't attend Sunday dinner barefoot, not with you looking so delectable.'

Vashti poured him a glass of wine without asking while he sank on to the sofa and put his socks and shoes on, but suddenly found herself totally bereft of any other social graces. She could only stand there watching him, her mind empty of words, her uncertainty growing.

'Thank you,' he said when she handed him the glass. 'And for the use of your bed, too. I have this vague memory of just flaking out, but I imagine I showed you that bloody great cheque, told you what happened?'

'It's in the pocket of your jacket,' she said. 'And no, you did *not* tell me what happened. Except that you were gambling, which seemed obvious enough.

And gambling rather heavily, for somebody who claims not to indulge very often.'

'I wish you'd been there,' he replied with a grin. 'Although of course if you had been I wouldn't have dared punt like that, wouldn't even have been there, I suppose.'

'You're making no sense,' she replied. 'And please, sit down. You're making me nervous, hovering like that.'

'Do I recall you accusing me of getting a world-class guilt complex over how we messed with Alana?' he said, changing the subject as he turned a kitchen chair round and sat leaning on the back of it.

'I . . . may have said something like that,' Vashti replied, cautious now. Half asleep, Phelan was manageable; fresh from the shower, alert and wide awake, he was dangerous. 'I told you that she'd phoned here, looking for you, when she couldn't raise you at home.'

'I'll bet *that* impressed you,' he replied with a boyish grin. 'Bet you lied to her.'

'I did not. Why should I have? It was the middle of the day, for goodness' sake, no reason for you *not* to be here. And I wouldn't have lied anyway,' she said, doing exactly that. Then compounded it by adding, 'Not that it would have been necessary.'

'It should have been,' he said with a grin that was now positively wicked. 'Only my splendid sense of propriety saved you from being ravished last night. I'd give you a wonderful song and dance about how tragic it is to be so saintly and pure, except that I've already proved how lucrative it can be. And here I always thought virtue was its own reward.'

Vashti leaned back against the sink, twiddling her wine glass between her fingers. Carefully. The man was as egocentric as his sister, she told herself. Impossible.

'And what if you'd lost? I suppose you'd have just tried to write it off as research expenses?'

'Why,' he said, rising slowly from the chair and stalking over to stand in front of her, fencing her in with his arms after first setting down his own glass, then taking hers and doing the same, 'do I get the distinct impression you'd rather be a sex object than a research object?'

'Probably because that's all you ever have on your mind,' she snapped, ducking beneath his arm to the questionable freedom of a flat that suddenly seemed to shrink round the two of them. Phelan didn't pursue her; he assumed her earlier stance, leaning back comfortably as his eyes ranged over Vashti's tense figure.

'I'll bet you'd taste better than whatever it is you're cooking,' he said, licking his lips, already devouring her with his eyes. 'If you'd looked like that when I arrived, I wouldn't have been able to stay tired.'

'I've known teddy bears more dangerous than you were when you arrived,' she protested. 'And now, if you wouldn't mind getting out of the way, we might *both* have a chance to eat something tasty.'

'And if not?' He was being deliberately provocative now, but Vashti was getting wise to it.

'If not, the potatoes beside you will start boiling over and dinner will be ruined and it will all... be...your...fault,' she said sternly. 'Now shift it! Go pour us some more wine while I finish up here.'

Phelan laughed, then turned and deftly shifted the pan of potatoes off to one side, lifting the lid as soon as the boil-over stopped. 'Another five minutes, at least,' he said. 'Would you like me to check the roast for you while I'm at it?'

'You can dish up, too, if you like,' she replied stubbornly, aware that if he so much as touched her, even if he was allowed to continue ravishing her with his eyes, dinner might as well go hang.

'I'd rather wash up, seeing I've managed to be so well behaved so far,' he said with a deprecating laugh. And moved aside, picking up the wine glasses as he did so.

Vashti poked at the potatoes with a long-handled fork, grudgingly admitting to herself that he'd been spot-on about the timing and equally aware that he'd hardly taken his eyes off her. She didn't have to turn and look; she *knew* he was watching, could actually feel him caressing her without even touching her.

And then he *was* touching her, and somehow she'd expected it, because she didn't drop the pan lid, didn't fly apart in a thousand pieces, or scream, or faint.

She merely turned under the guidance of his hands at her waist, turning to meet his descending lips with her own parted, welcoming, needing.

His fingers laced together round the small of her back, pulling her against him, fitting her to him as if she had been designed to fit just . . . so. Her own arms lifted, hands gathering behind his neck to hold him, to adjust the fit of his mouth against hers, feeling the coarse curls beneath her fingers, the warmth of his firm shoulder muscles against her wrists.

And it went on . . . and on . . . their breaths merging, the very flavours of them merging. She could smell him, the spicy, fresh-clean smell rich in her nostrils. As their tongues coiled together she tasted him, loving the taste, drinking it.

'Dinner later? Dinner now?' His voice was whisper-soft; he knew the answer, but was forcing her to say it, to admit it, to agree.

'Now,' she sighed into his mouth. But she *meant* later, and he knew that too. Keeping her prisoner with his lips, with one hand at her waist, he somehow reached out to turn knobs on the stove, to shut things off while he was turning her on.

'Now...dessert,' he whispered after a lifetime. And still claiming her mouth he lifted her, twisted her into the cradle of his arms, and carried her away from the kitchen and through the door to where the bed was still warm from his body.

CHAPTER EIGHT

VASHTI had to force herself at first. Her body screamed out for Phelan's caresses, seemed to fit itself so perfectly to him, to his touch. But her mind fitted the situation less well; it kept trying to interfere, to establish some sense, some order, some caution.

It would have been so easy to submit entirely, to simply abandon herself to the sensation that was heightened with his every caress. But she couldn't... quite. It was easy to have abandoned dinner, less easy to stop thinking about it. As his fingers raced patterns of delight along her spine, playing a sensuous symphony from buttocks to shoulders, as her own fingers explored his cheek, his neck, the touch of his lips against her own, she felt like a person divided.

And he didn't help. She wanted a swift and un-thinking plunge into this unknown realm of their lovemaking, but Phelan by his slow, tortuous path forced her to take it step by step, touch by touch, sensation by sensation.

He plundered her mouth, but slowly, delicately, his kisses at times insistent, at times so teasing, so tantalisingly gentle, that she wanted to take the initiative herself, to roll him over so that she could dominate their lovemaking, force the pace herself.

His fingers touched her everywhere, moving across her cheeks like butterfly wings, spilling down across her neck and shoulders like warm water; his lips followed, flooding her breasts with kisses, making the undoing of every blouse button a slow, deliberate adventure of delight. His fluttering touch along her ribcage only added to the wonder as he took each nipple in turn between his lips, making them firm, tender beyond all imagining.

Vashti twisted in his arms, wanting herself free of the now open blouse, wanting him free of his shirt, uanble to say what she wanted, unable to *say* anything. Her lips were buried in the hollow of his shoulder, her nostrils filled with the scent of him, her tongue flicking out like a snake's to taste him, to feel the texture of his skin, the bristling of beard at his throat.

Then she felt his mouth returning along her body, softly exploring between her breasts, laying tracks of kisses along her throat, returning to the home of her mouth, which awaited him desperately, eagerly.

His fingers lifted to free her of the constraining blouse; she had a half-felt sensation of it being stripped from her shoulders, flung away from them to sprawl unwanted, unneeded, somewhere beyond the world of the bed.

And as if guided by that action, her own hands lifted now to unravel the mystery of his shirt studs, so similar to buttons but so different. Her mind intruded, making pictures of how they worked, guiding her fingers so that the studs came free as easily as they had when she had taken the shirt from him earlier that day.

Her fingers now had freedom; they roved across the contours of muscle, the twisting patterns of the hair on his chest. Beneath them, his nipples hardened, firmed. She caught the soft gasp he uttered as her lips followed that path of exploration, and something inside her exulted at the reaction.

The tempo of their lovemaking quickened then. Their lips found each other to become the focus of the fusion that turned Vashti's entire body into a vessel of sensation. His fingers touched her spine and she quivered; they moved down along the line of her bottom, beyond the hampering fabric of the skirt to where those ever so expensive stockings only added to the smoothness of his caress.

Then back, blindly but quickly fumbling loose the fastenings of the skirt; her hips lifted, twisted, thrust against his manipulations. Her hand flew down to assist—was rejected, lifted away to find its own path along his chest and stomach.

Then the skirt was in flight, soaring after the blouse, to the sound of Phelan's appreciative groan, and her own gasp of delight as his lips fled from her mouth to scamper along the line of her breast, flickering across her stomach like swamp-fire, touching, branding, turning her body to jelly.

His fingers touched at her ankle, then she could *hear* the feel of them moving along her leg, their touch enhanced by the fine hosiery between his fingers and her skin. Until he reached to the top of the stocking; until his fingers and his lips met to ravage the warm softness of her inner thighs.

Vashti was contorted by the ecstasy of it. Her back arched; her hands flew to tangle themselves in his hair, holding his mouth against her, wanting the branding of his lips, hating the teasing of his tongue as it moved closer to the centre of her passion, then maddeningly away again.

'Beautiful . . . soooo beautiful.' His voice, whisper-soft, became a litany that sang its way along her body, making her the instrument that accompanied the song. His fingertips lifted the music from her; his lips took the notes and shaped them, built them towards a crescendo, then slid away down the scale before she could catch up, teasing, tickling, tantalising.

She couldn't breathe, felt as if she never would again, gasped with each new sensation, each new and somehow different place his lips enlightened, each new part of her his knowing fingers explored. To the edge of oblivion and then away, back and forth and back again.

His mouth trekked across her body, climbing the hills and peaks, descending into secret valleys, finding oases of delight and leaving magic everywhere. His fingers found routes of their own, and they, also, dispersed magic. If she closed her eyes, it was to find sunbursts of sensation in her mind; open, it seemed the room was bathed in a wondrous light.

Vashti thought she might faint, was sure she could take no more, but wanted more and more and more. Wanted everything. Her hands crept along the muscles of his back and shoulders, the flat, hard planes of his hips, moving without conscious volition to fumble at the waistband of his trousers, to explore the throbbing warmth of him, touching, wondering, wanting him, all of him. Now.

Her flimsy knickers slid like oil from her body, giving way to his hands, his lips, as he stirred her body to a new awareness, yet another plateau of sensation. She gasped, heard herself moaning with pleasure beyond anything she had ever known, heard also his litany of compliments, of loving; she felt his body tense as if in agony, felt her own body writhing beneath his touch, crying out for his lips, his tongue.

His entrance was slow, almost teasingly so. She writhed beneath him, instictively trying to force the pace, to merge with him in totality. But he was stronger; he used his body, his hands, his lips in a symphony that took her to the brink of abandonment, held her there, teetering, until she could take no more. Then they plunged together into a time of magical union, melting into a single pool of sensation where it felt she could float forever.

And then she was in his arms, their bodies still united but her mind fuzzily seeking its way back to the real world, no longer conscious only of sensation, but able to see the man above her, to focus on his pale, strangely gentle eyes, able to feel his fingers as they touched her cheek, traced a pattern of love up the side of her nose, making that loving gesture of pushing up her non-existent glasses.

'My . . . God!' she sighed, staring up into those incredible eyes. And then, giving way to a sudden fit of shyness, she tucked her face in against his neck and was mute.

Phelan's hands moved along her back, holding her against him, holding them together, united now in a strangely peaceful union of both body and spirit.

As Vashti felt herself relaxing, his caresses slowly began to quicken, and she felt her body quicken in response even as her mind denied the possibility. Within her, he moved, filling her even further, rousing her slowly again to heights beyond belief, beyond even what they had shared before. This time they were together from the very moment of beginning, and Vashti's body seemed totally attuned to his rhythms,

to the way he filled her, the way he moved within her,
to his every touch, his every kiss.

This time when they plunged together it was as if
they were a sky-diving team, but without parachutes,
with no way to slow their descent into ecstasy, no
need—because they were hand in hand, mouth to
mouth, soul to soul. And at the end, no crashing arrival; it was light as the landing of a butterfly, and
equally graceful.

'You are just sooo amazing,' he whispered, this time
holding her gaze, banishing her need for shyness. 'I
knew it would be like this.'

'How could you?' She met his eyes, reached up to
touch his cheek, to move her fingers wonderingly
along his lips. 'I . . . certainly didn't know.'

'I would have told you. Only we . . . sort of got off
on the wrong foot.'

'I thought you hated me.' It had to come out; she
had to *know*.

'Never that, but I did have some bloody awful
mixed feelings,' he admitted. Still holding her, still
meeting her eyes, still united.

'You thought I drove your father to the grave.' No
question, this. She knew it; he knew it. Now it needed
only an admission by both of them.

'I did, and the funny part is that I knew better, I
think, right from the beginning. Only that was on an
emotional basis, and you've had me so confused from
the very beginning that I couldn't manage to think
straight about it for the longest time.'

He kissed her then, his kiss a whisper of security,
of promise, then eased himself gently away so that he
was able to prop himself on one elbow, looking down
at her while his fingers moved to caress her breasts.

'Writers sometimes aren't the most rational of people,' he said. 'Too much emotion and not enough plain common sense.'

Vashti wriggled under his touch, feeling like a puppy being stroked. And loving every instant, every sensation.

'I talked to the old man a few days before he died,' Phelan explained, 'and he mentioned the audit, said it was shaping up to be a proper mishmash, and that he was really worried about it, because he wasn't a tax cheat, never had been, but was afraid he was going to come out looking like one.'

'He wasn't,' Vashti said, reaching down to halt the progress of his insidious fingers. 'He wasn't any sort of tax cheat, and I knew it and he knew I knew it. I can't imagine why he'd say such a thing.'

'He'd been drinking a bit, and he was just upset enough that he rambled, couldn't seem to keep all the bits and pieces of the story in any logical order,' Phelan said. 'And not knowing it all from the beginning, I had a lot of trouble following the thread.'

Disentangling her fingers, he returned his hand to her breast, then moved it lower, slowly tracing circles until he reached where his touch could destroy any hope of concentration. Vashti moved to stop him, then gasped and thrust herself against the pressure, yielding to his touch, all thought gone except that of the sensations he roused in her body.

'Not . . . fair,' she sighed some time later. 'How can you expect me to pay attention when you're doing that?'

'It's a long explanation,' he replied with a truly wicked grin. 'I wouldn't want you to get bored.'

Vashti matched his grin, her hand lifting to touch his lips, then moving down along the length of his body, tweaking at his nipples, then seeking the most obvious form of retaliation, revelling in her power as he stiffened in reply.

'You were saying?'

His answer now was to loom over her, seeking her mouth with his own, letting her guide him to his goal, then taking control so that she had no choice but to follow him back to the edge of ecstasy, her body his to plunder, to pleasure, to possess.

'I was saying,' he continued much, much later, 'that Dad ended up pretty upset, and the last thing he said was something about "that damned woman". Then the line dropped out, for some reason, and . . . I never talked to him again.'

Sadness flowed in to replace the loving in his eyes, and Vashti reached up to touch his face, to somehow comfort him. He smiled his acceptance, fingers reaching to hold her own.

'But of course when I got to the funeral and saw you, I thought . . . well, you can imagine what I thought. I hadn't talked to Bevan or Alana about you at that point, and even when we did discuss the whole issue of your audit . . . I was already blind and I stayed that way. Even though it was obvious both of them liked you.'

He reached down and shifted the down coverlet over them, using the gesture to let him then hide from view the movements of his hand as he returned it to caress her thighs above the stockings. Vashti tightened against his probing fingers, holding him still between her thighs, shaking her finger in a 'halt' gesture they both knew to be powerless.

'I knew that,' she said, 'although I didn't realise it until...until...'

'Until *that* woman—the one the old man really meant when he said it—accused you. That's when I took a good look at myself and realised what an utter fool I'd been,' Phelan said. 'Worse than a fool—a damned, blind idiot. I could have killed the bitch, right there on the spot. Except that I was just so...so angry with *myself* as well, that I didn't know which to do first—murder her or come grovelling to you.'

'It wouldn't have mattered,' Vashti said. 'I was just so stunned, so *hurt*, that I wouldn't have listened. I *didn't* listen.'

'Well, you didn't make it easy for me to explain; that's for sure. And I was so damned confused myself about it all that I was probably coming on a bit heavy. I won't even apologise for that, although probably I should. You just got under my skin from the very first moment I saw you. Even the way I felt then, I could barely keep my hands off you.'

'It's called "lust" in some books by authors who shall remain nameless,' she replied cheekily. 'And keep that hand still if you want to continue this conversation.'

'Plenty of time,' he grinned. 'It isn't as if we have to leap out of this bed and go anywhere. We could, indeed, stay here for days and days. We've got food, wine...'

'Even a loaf of bed. Stop that!' she cried, then joined him in laughing at the Freudian slip. 'And I have a job to go to tomorrow, in case you've forgotten. My boss—by some miracle I shall never understand—gave me half of Friday off; he'd be just a bit hostile if I didn't make it in on time tomorrow.'

'Phone him first thing in the morning and say you're still in bed,' Phelan chuckled, moving *that* hand just enough to divert her attention. 'I'll make damned sure it won't be a lie.'

'You will not!'

'I probably wouldn't have the strength,' he said. 'All this *lust* has made that lamb roast look better than you do, almost. I don't suppose you'd like to stop fondling my body long enough to get back in the kitchen?'

'Wearing just what I'm wearing, I suppose?' she replied with a grin, all thought of shyness long gone. 'Or do I at least get to put on an apron?'

'I should certainly hope so,' he said, swinging out of the bed and reaching down to lift her to stand beside him. 'No way am I going to let you put this body at risk. It has a lot of years of good value left in it.'

Twenty minutes later—both wearing at least *something*—they sat across from each other at the kitchen table, demolishing Vashti's roast dinner as if neither had eaten for weeks.

'I'm pleased you're a good cook,' Phelan said, teasingly. 'Being sexy and decorative is all right in its place, but when all is said and done...'

'You mean that's all there was?' Vashti could tease too, she found, and revelled in it. 'I'd have thought your hero's abilities were more than just wishful thinking.'

'You're starting to sound like my sister,' he cautioned. 'Keep it up and I won't help with the dishes, much less phone in your excuses in the morning.'

'No such thing,' she said, eyes widening at what she imagined Ross Chandler's reaction would be to a telephone call from one of her clients saying she was in bed and couldn't come to work. Then she giggled, unable not to at the mental picture she'd created.

'All right, I suppose it wouldn't be the best idea,' he admitted with a chuckle of his own. 'I will do the dishes, though, provided you promise to keep your hands off my body. Any fondling and you'll be picking up broken crockery for the next fortnight.'

'You can dry,' she said. 'No, on second thoughts, *I'll* dry. You'd only take advantage of me while I had both hands in the sink. This way, I keep control, and besides, I know where everything goes. You can tell me all about your gambling foray while you're at it.'

Which he proceeded to do in great detail, creating for Vashti a wonderful, hilarious story; she howled so much at one point that she almost started dropping dishes herself.

'Oh, I wish I'd been there,' she cried, only to have Phelan flick a fistful of suds at her.

'I've already told you—if you'd been there I wouldn't have done it,' he said with a mock-scowl. 'Because if we'd been together, we'd have been *here*, and there'd have been other things on my mind besides gambling, I can tell you that!'

'We were here,' she said, serious for a moment. 'And you did have other things on your mind. But you didn't stay.'

'I did not!'

'Why not?'

'Because it wouldn't have been right.'

'You can say that, now? I...don't think I understand.'

'You were too tired to understand anything,' he replied, 'which is why I didn't stay. And, I suppose, why I came back today, if you want the truth.'

'Of course I do. This isn't one of your books, for goodness' sake.'

'Sometimes I wonder. When life starts getting stranger than my own fiction, well . . .'

'I . . . I really would like to know,' she said hesitantly, afraid now she was about to get an answer she didn't want to hear.

Phelan grinned, the sheer magic of his grin dispelling the worst of her fears.

'You were too tired,' he said again. 'The timing was wrong, the circumstances were wrong, everything was wrong. It would have been a disaster. And—you would have hated me in the morning.'

'I wouldn't!'

'You might have. *I* might have.' His eyes flashed for an instant, radiating something Vashti couldn't quite discern.

'And besides,' he said in a tone of voice just a tinge different somehow, 'when I left here last night I was broke, or near as damn it.' His eyes were on what he was doing in the sink now; Vashti could only hear what he was saying, not see his expression.

'And you thought that would matter to me?'

Her voice must have registered some of the confusion she felt, the astonishment.

'It would have mattered to me. One doesn't take advantage of a beautiful woman when one can't even afford to offer to buy her breakfast afterwards.'

Vashti could only laugh.

'And last night I was feeling . . . lucky,' he continued, pretending not to notice. 'Probably because of what I *now* think might have been misplaced feelings about being virtuous and honourable and all that stuff. Not realising what a wanton you really are, I had myself convinced that it would have been wrong to take advantage, so even before we left the casino I was busy talking myself out of my lustful ideas. Which I did, and I left here feeling quite pleased with myself.

'Now, of course,' he said with a mischievous grin, 'I realise I was only lucky you didn't trip me and beat me to the floor. But I couldn't have known that then, could I? Not when I was busy convincing myself not to work my wicked way with you because . . . I wanted it to be right. More than right, damn it! Perfect!'

'You're not making a lot of sense,' Vashti said, picking up the cutlery all in a bunch and drying the bits as they came to hand.

'More than you do, sometimes,' he said, reaching down to stop her. 'Are you trying to cut off a finger or something?'

'Don't be silly,' she replied. 'I do this all the time.'

'Well, don't do it when I'm around, OK? I don't want the body damaged; it's far too valuable.'

'Just get on with your story,' she said. 'I'm still waiting for the full explanation. And...I have a knife in my hand now. So be truthful.'

'I was afraid you'd insist on that,' he replied. 'Anyway, knowing I was going to be virtuous—presuming I got the chance to have a choice—I saved out one chip from the lot I cashed in to give me an excuse.'

'An excuse for what?'

'For not taking advantage, of course. That way I could convince myself I ought to be virtuous because you'd brought me luck and I still had *your* chip in my pocket, so I'd have to go back and finish up that run of luck.'

'Have you been reading your own books or something?' Vashti cried. 'That's the most convoluted, nonsensical load of old cobblers I've ever heard.'

'I was looking after your best interests,' he replied, totally unabashed. Except for that wicked gleam in his eyes.

'And what would you have done, pray tell, if I'd come on all frisky? What if I *had* tripped you and beaten you to the floor, as you so politely put it?'

'I'd have helped!'

'And then what?'

'Probably borrowed the money from you to buy you breakfast—is that what you want to hear?' His scowl was fierce, but his eyes were warm, laughing.

I want to hear you say you love me! The words flashed through her mind in huge, blazing capital letters. But went unsaid. Instead, she resorted to cheekiness, taking solace from the fact that she was comfortable enough with Phelan to allow that much.

'Maybe I just want to hear you say you've finished the washing-up,' she said. 'It would be awfully hard to trip you while you can grab the sink for support.'

'You're insatiable, woman,' he accused with a grin. 'I'm going as fast as I can and it still isn't good enough for you. I might have to change my mind about this whole arrangement; I can't have a heroine with such lustful ideas in a romance. The research would kill me before I could manage to finish the damned thing.'

'And that's what I am? A heroine for one of your books?' Vashti couldn't meet his eyes, could hardly credit her own daring, didn't *want* to. Nor did she want to hear the answer, but it was too late now!

'Is that what you think?'

He smiled, but it was a false smile, a liar's smile. She *knew* it was, suddenly hated him. Hated herself more. Wanted to run, but couldn't, of course. This was her home; this was where she ought to be running to, not from. And in that burning instant the wonder of the afternoon seemed to collapse around her. Impossible, she thought, but she tasted deception where she'd only tasted love, caring.

'For the book you're working on now? The one about the tax office? That's what it's all been about, isn't it? You've just been *using* me.' She was becoming hysterical, could hear it in her own voice, could see it in the strange look on Phelan's face, the stranger light in his eyes.

'Well? Is that it? It is—isn't it? *Isn't* it?'

She was screaming at him now, waving the knife she'd forgotten she even held until just that instant. '*Isn't it*? This whole damned thing has been nothing more than a...a charade, a game, to you. You've been orchestrating it all with that...*that* woman, *just for a lousy book*!'

'I don't believe this.'

He was reaching out, braving the knife to lift the tea-towel from her other hand, using it to wipe the soap suds from his hands. And all the while looking at her, shaking his head in tiny, abrupt motions.

'Answer me!'

He reached out, plucked the knife from her fingers, and flung it into the sink. The gesture was swift, angry.

But his eyes weren't angry. Only... different, somehow.

'Will you please come and sit down?'

'*No*! I want an answer and I want it *now*!'

Phelan sighed, looking down at the floor for an
instant, his shoulders drooping.

'Please?'

'*Now*, damn you.'

'All right,' he said, voice quiet, resigned. 'Yes, I'm
writing a book. That *is* what I do...write books. And
yes, it's about the tax office, sort of. But I am not—
repeat *not*—using you. Nor am I *using* whatever tax
affairs were between us.'

He paused, looked in her eyes and saw the fury,
the hurt, the total disbelief, and sighed again.

'And I don't know how you could think I would.'

Not one word about Janice Gentry, not even a
suggestion of denial about his involvement with her,
their pictures together in the paper, her obvious attitude to him.

'You're lying.' She fought to control her growing
hysteria, made the statement flat, emotionless.

Phelan just looked at her, eyes weary, but cold now.
He shook his head.

'OK,' he said then, 'I guess you're entitled to your
opinion, no matter how ridiculous it is.'

Without waiting for a reply, he stepped around her,
quickly gathering up shoes and socks, and shrugging
into his shirt. He took his dinner-jacket from the hall
closet as he passed it, and walked out of the door.

He didn't slam it, didn't even look back as he
slouched down the footpath in his bare feet, climbed

into his luxury motor car, and drove slowly, almost sedately, out of her life.

Vashti watched him go without a tear, then plunged into the shower and stayed there, trembling and shivering in the steam, scrubbing him away. Obsessively, compulsively, angrily. Fruitlessly. Until the hot water turned cold.

CHAPTER NINE

'The Keene file is closed!'

Vashti blurted out the words and could have kicked herself for how she knew they sounded. Ross Chandler didn't appear to notice, any more than he'd noticed that she was half an hour late for work.

'All right,' he said, lifting his small, shrewd eyes from the mountain of paperwork on his desk only long enough to utter those two words.

'I've ... I ... it just shouldn't have been me,' Vashti stammered, then plunged on. 'The audit is complete now anyway and there's no evidence against ... Mr Keene.'

'I said it was all right.' He didn't even bother to look up this time. He'd seen her come into his office, dressed appropriately for a businesswoman, hair neatly spun into a chignon, tailored skirt and jacket, sensible shoes. If he'd noticed the vain attempt to disguise reddened eyes and a complexion pale as death, he didn't bother to say.

'I'm ... sorry. It's the first time ...' Vashti couldn't just accept *his* acceptance; she felt she must try and explain, *had* to somehow explain. Only she couldn't, couldn't even get the words together sufficiently to make a coherent sentence.

He looked up again, impatient now. She knew the signs, had seen them often enough before. And now, she realised, he was noticing her appearance.

'I said it didn't matter, Vashti,' he said, unusually gentle for the mood she could see he was in. 'Why don't you go home? You look worse than you did on Friday.'

I looked *fine* on Friday, she wanted to scream. Infinitely better than now! A million times better than now! And I felt better, too.

'I'm fine,' was all she could manage. 'Just... tired, a bit. But I didn't sleep in or anything; I was late because my car played up and wouldn't start, so I had to walk.'

'If you're so fine, you might explain why you charged into the building—admittedly late, but let's ignore that—and promptly went off to be sick?'

'How...?' She had to stop, or risk being sick again.

'I know everything. That's why I'm the boss.' And he bent again to his paperwork. 'Now either go on back to work or book yourself off sick, but stop standing around my office like a dog waiting to be shot.'

He didn't know everything, *couldn't* know everything, thank God, she thought as she fled back to the relative sanctuary of her own office, moving fairly stiffly, as if all her muscles were sore, knowing why and hating it, hating even more the way all her nerve-endings seemed exposed, tender. It was like the worst of hangovers without the headache.

Only hangovers, she decided a week later, didn't go on and on, *ad infinitum*, didn't renew themselves without a fresh infusion of what started them, didn't creep up unseen to leap out of the bushes at one with no warning, no chance of defence.

She had read something once about the so-called 'drinker's hour', that apparently horrific time in the wee small hours when alcoholics woke to sweats and nightmares and unknown, unseen, indescribable fears. Did they also, she wondered, have insanely erotic nightmares?

Worse, did they have them in the middle of the day, in the middle of walking down a city street where a glint of glossy dark hair, a certain type of masculine posture, a certain type of walk, could make one go weak at the knees, could create a dryness in the mouth, a moist, spongy feeling in the tummy?

By the end of another week, she had generally stopped finding herself assaulted by such feelings while at work, where it was damnably embarrassing to be recalled to the present and find herself squirming in her seat, her body burning, her clothing insanely constricting.

But it was done now. Finished. Over. Had been for days when Vashti got the call from downstairs asking if a Miss Alana Keene might be allowed to see her without an appointment.

'No,' she replied instinctively, only to relent within the space of a heartbeat. Her calendar was a desert; she could spare three hours without any appointment if she wanted to. Which she damned well didn't, but couldn't in all conscience find a single excuse even *she* would think worthy. And she liked Alana, despite the girl's propensity for meddling, despite her...relatives.

Alana walked through the door a few moments later, granting Vashti a fleeting smile, but having little else in her demeanour that indicated friendliness.

'I am instructed,' she said gravely, 'to deliver this to you personally, by hand, and—if possible—to obtain a receipt.'

'This' was a fat, large *Jiffy bag* which Alana was holding as if it contained live tiger-snakes. She plunked the parcel down on Vashti's desk with obvious relief, took a deep breath, and announced dramatically, 'And I am instructed to sit here while you read it.'

'Alana, the audit is over, all done, finished,' Vashti said. 'I don't see——'

'Exactly my point,' Alana interrupted. 'You don't see, and without a bit of help you probably never will. Now will you please just humour me and read this so I can finish my penance and get back to what passes for a normal life again?' The girl's tension was unnerving, and it forced her voice up and up and up with every word. She was almost screaming at the end.

'Must I?' Stupid question, Vashti realised, as Alana stomped over to sit down beside the window, glaring at her, tense, angry, defensive. It would have something to do with Phelan; Vashti was certain of it, and even more certain when Alana snapped,

'Too right you do!'

'You wouldn't like to leave it with me and we can talk about it over lunch?' Vashti ventured, seeking some semblance of sweet reason, some escape valve for the naked hostility that filled the office like smoke.

'I am instructed to *watch* you read it. Every...single...word! If possible,' she added, making it obvious she wasn't impressed with even that concession.

'Dare I ask what penance you're talking about?' Vashti asked gently. Very gently! Alana was clearly upset, and Vashti didn't want to make it any worse.

'That,' her visitor replied, 'is a very, very silly question. Please, Vashti...will you just *read* the damned thing and stop harassing me? I've been harassed quite enough over this already and I'm getting intensely sick of it.'

Alana sighed as if she could see the end of the world, then leaped to her feet and rushed forward. 'Please,' she pleaded, hostility exchanged now for concern. 'I'm sorry I played at being a matchmaker; I'll never do it again as long as I live, I swear it! All I wanted was for you and Phelan to stop being stupid and get it together; it isn't *my* fault that ... whatever happened.' And she sighed hopelessly. 'But I can't handle this being an ... an intermediary, either. I *told* him that, but *he* said I owed him—owed *both of you*. Please.'

The final plea was so genuine, so heart-breaking, that Vashti couldn't refuse, despite her better judgement.

'All right,' she said. 'But I'd rather be alone.'

Alana closed her eyes, obviously on the brink of agreeing, but her courage failed her. Shaking her head, she walked slowly back to her chair and slumped in it, quite obviously prepared to sit and stare at the floor, if necessary, until Vashti had read whatever it was she was supposed to read.

'At least take this,' Vashti sighed, reaching into her bottom drawer for the Dick Francis novel she was currently involved in. 'I won't be able to concentrate on anything with you sitting there sighing like some spectre of doom.' She tossed the paperback over to Alana, who looked at it as if it were a cheese sandwich or something, sighed again, and nodded some vague form of agreement.

There was a note attached to the bulky manuscript that emerged from the Jiffy bag.

I wanted to be sure you'd read this, and couldn't wait a year or more for it to be published first. So I'm sending it in manuscript form—at great cost for the photocopying of same. My sister the former matchmaker has strict instructions to *watch* you read it, and if you refuse she is to knock you down, sit on you, and *read it aloud*, if necessary. I suggest you take the easy way out.

Vashti snarled aloud and glared over to where Alana was peeeping over the top of the paperback, so alert that she *almost* managed to duck her head without Vashti catching her at it.

It was an incident that occurred and recurred with ludicrous regularity over the next hour and a half as Vashti forced her way through the manuscript, at first skimming quickly, then making heavier work of it as she became lost—at least occasionally—in the story itself.

Phelan Keene's tax book. His tax *romance*. And yes, the heroine was blonde, small, with grey eyes . . . and *glasses* . . . and a tiny mole where the author shouldn't have known it was! Her involuntary gasp at that disclosure brought, she was sure, a muffled giggle from behind the paperback, but her stern glance revealed no eyes peeping over the top.

And yes, the owner of those eyes was in the book, too, fat ankles and all. That brought a chuckle from Vashti herself, but she must have stifled it well because once again she failed to catch Alana out.

And, Vashti had to admit, there wasn't one thing about the tax office or its workings that Phelan couldn't have found out just by picking up a phone and asking. Much less was there anything he might have gained through *using* her.

The romance part, however, was something else again. As was the entire interplay between hero and heroine. All of that, she recognised. Every word, every nuance, every touch, every kiss, every emotion. Even the kitchen knife.

As she read, she felt at first as if her entire relationship with Phelan had been conducted in a glasshouse, or in front of a movie camera, to be exhibited to the world. Her stomach churned; she had to swallow several times to keep from being physically sick. But gradually she realised that *his* emotions, too, were just as revealed, just as obvious. To everybody, it seemed, but her!

And his heroine, to her astonishment, emerged as a wonderfully well-rounded person—a private person, to be sure, but a true *heroine*, who faced problems and conquered them, who was anything but the sex-object doormats he'd portrayed in his other books.

When she finally reached the dénouement, the part where hero and heroine resolved their differences and figuratively rode off into the sunset together, she had to stop. She was certain for a long, eyes-closed moment that she couldn't go on. Didn't dare.

Forgotten were her divided feelings at finding it all there, all written down for her to review—the love-making, the Japanese bridge, the roast lamb dinner!—all there to be forced upon her, to *make* her see his side of it, to see aspects of her *own* side of it that she hadn't been aware of.

She wanted to know how it ended, but didn't dare keep reading. Stop at the end of chapter eight. Stop and don't ever dare read further, she vowed. It will surely destroy you, destroy everything!

Slyly glancing up to make sure Alana was still in hiding behind the book, Vashti turned over the last chapter unread, and gathered the manuscript together with what she hoped would give an appearance of having finished it. Then she grabbed up a piece of scrap paper and scrawled a receipt, dashing off the words in an almost unreadable flurry of chicken-tracks.

'You can come out now,' she said, knowing her voice was furry, trembling. Like her body. 'I'm done and I haven't exploded yet.'

Violet eyes, moist with concern, peered over the top of the book. Then a face emerged, but there was no smile, only a rather grimly determined stare. Alana got up and moved cautiously over to exchange the paperback for the receipt, then walked with equal caution over to the door.

'You didn't finish,' she called back over her shoulder. 'You didn't read the final chapter.'

Vashti couldn't lie, but couldn't admit it, either. Alana didn't even wait for a reply.

'I know because you're still here, dummy!' she cried. 'Damn it, Vashti. He loves you. L.O.V.E.S. What do you want him to do—grovel?'

She swung open the office door and stepped out, then back, holding the door open as she scowled fiercely. 'If we weren't friends I wouldn't say this,' she snarled. 'But sometimes you are just too...*strong* for your own good.' And she slammed the door behind her.

Vashti hardly noticed. She sat there, staring into space, into memory and the past and the future at the same time, for the longest time. Then she turned over the manuscript and started again from the beginning, not skimming this time but reading each and every word, right through to the end of chapter eight, and then, before she could talk herself out of it, on into the unknown.

On to where he ripped up the cheque for his gambling winnings, took the heroine in his arms, and declared, 'The best things in life aren't free—they're shared. I love you, and if I can't share my life with you it isn't hardly worth bothering with. I love you, and I'll wait forever if I have to.'

Ross Chandler looked up in surprise when she knocked on his door and strode into the office without waiting for his bark of admittance.

'I'm taking the rest of the day off,' she declared. 'I'll make it up some time later.'

She didn't wait for his answer either. The taxi she'd called would be downstairs by now.

Twenty minutes later she was on the road in her own car, crossing the Bridgewater causeway, and turning up the Boyer Road with all her senses alert; this was no time to be taking risks. Not now.

She held to the speed limit, only too aware it was far slower than the screaming pace in her heart and mind. New Norfolk, Hamilton, Ouse, all passed in a haze as she concentrated only on the ribbon of highway in front of her. What she passed was irrelevant; her destination was the only thing of importance now.

The tiny church was in sunshine, this day, crouched snugly beneath its sentry pines in a quiet that held its own sound. He rose from the stoop as she skidded to a halt in the gravel turnaround, was smiling, arms outstretched to gather her in as she flew through the gate.

His auburn hair blazed in the sunshine, and his eyes held a special glow of their own, a glow that not even sunshine could produce, because it came from within.

Vashti stepped from her car, feeling an instant's hesitation, a flicker of caution that she flung from her like an intruding insect. Irrelevant!

She had her priorities right now, and she knew it as she marched straight into arms that closed round her slender waist, lifting her to meet his smiling lips.

'If you tore up that cheque, I'll kill you,' she cried when he finally released her mouth, when her heart had slowed down enough to allow speech of any kind. 'I'm going to have to borrow from it to pay Alana for the tickets.'

'What tickets?' he asked after kissing her again so thoroughly that she was sure he hadn't heard.

'The theatre tickets, the night ... you know!'

'Ah ... *that* night.' And his grin was infectious. 'The night of the second-biggest gambling win of my life. You don't *really* think I'd have ripped up that cheque? Not really?'

'What do you mean, second-biggest win?' she countered, visibly sighing with relief not because she cared about the money—it was irrelevant despite the amount—but because she didn't, *couldn't* accept herself as the cause of throwing that much away, like in the book. Damned book, wonderful, wonderful book! The best book, the most important book she would ever read, Vashti knew. And was glad of it.

Phelan's first answer was silent, his mouth capturing hers in a reply that was none the less clear.

Vashti could only accept, her nostrils filled with the scent of him, his touch like lightning wherever his fingers traced intricate, intimate designs along her body. She reached up to touch his face, to run her fingers along the strong column of his neck, into the thatch of hair at his nape. Her toes still touched the ground, although only just, but that was enough; elsewhere their bodies seemed to meld into one, each part fitting against the other in a splendid blend of rightness.

'I love you, you know?' was his second reply. 'But I'd never make it as a writer if I couldn't tell the difference between fiction and real life.

'Today was the biggest gamble, by far. And *this* is the biggest win.' His fingers crept along her spine, playing an ancient tune that sent music right to her soul.

'For both of us,' she sighed, trying to move closer into his arms and knowing it wasn't possible here. Having to let go of him, to have him let go of *her*, so they could get into separate vehicles just to remedy that situation was like walking into winter. Thankfully, it was short-lived.

They were considerably closer in the bed at the ancient farmhouse when he finished kissing her for the thousandth time and said, 'I may give up gambling now. I think I've found a much more pleasant pastime.'

'Good,' she said. 'This is much healthier for you.' And her exploring fingers revealed just how *much* healthier. Phelan seemed suitably impressed.

'Just as addictive. Maybe more,' he sighed as she reached a particularly sensitive spot.

'I should hope so.'

The conversation lapsed for a time, at least in verbal terms, but eventually Phelan slowed the pace sufficiently to allow him breath to speak.

'You can't pay Alana for those tickets, by the way. Did she *really* ask you to?'

'Sort of,' Vashti replied, her mind barely on the conversation, far too engrossed in what his hands were doing while he spoke. 'Why can't I pay her?'

'Because you have to pay *me*. *I'm* the one who bought them; she shouldn't benefit just because I didn't ask you, didn't think you'd go. So I gave them to her—*gave*—and only agreed to go myself when she rang at the last minute and said she couldn't find anybody to go with and didn't want to go alone. All trickery, and now she expects to be paid, the devious little bitch. I'll put her in a book—that'll fix her!'

'Just don't forget the fat ankles,' Vashti sighed, then gave herself to the magic of his fingers. Literally.

Accept 4 FREE Romances and 2 FREE gifts

FROM READER SERVICE

Here's an irresistible invitation from Mills & Boon. Please accept our offer of 4 FREE Romances, a CUDDLY TEDDY and a special MYSTERY GIFT! Then, if you choose, go on to enjoy 6 captivating Romances every month for just £1.80 each, postage and packing FREE. Plus our FREE Newsletter with author news, competitions and much more.

Send the coupon below to: Mills & Boon Reader Service, FREEPOST, PO Box 236, Croydon, Surrey CR9 9EL.

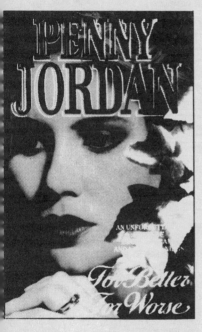

Next Month's Romances

Each month you can choose from a wide variety of romance with Mills & Boon. Below are the new titles to look out for next month, why not ask either Mills & Boon Reader Service or your Newsagent to reserve you a copy of the titles you want to buy – just tick the titles you would like and either post to Reader Service or take it to any Newsagent and ask them to order your books.

Please save me the following titles:	**Please tick**	✓
HEART OF THE OUTBACK	Emma Darcy	
DARK FIRE	Robyn Donald	
SEPARATE ROOMS	Diana Hamilton	
GUILTY LOVE	Charlotte Lamb	
GAMBLE ON PASSION	Jacqueline Baird	
LAIR OF THE DRAGON	Catherine George	
SCENT OF BETRAYAL	Kathryn Ross	
A LOVE UNTAMED	Karen van der Zee	
TRIUMPH OF THE DAWN	Sophie Weston	
THE DARK EDGE OF LOVE	Sara Wood	
A PERFECT ARRANGEMENT	Kay Gregory	
RELUCTANT ENCHANTRESS	Lucy Keane	
DEVIL'S QUEST	Joanna Neil	
UNWILLING SURRENDER	Cathy Williams	
ALMOST AN ANGEL	Debbie Macomber	
THE MARRIAGE BRACELET	Rebecca Winters	

If you would like to order these books in addition to your regular subscription from Mills & Boon Reader Service please send £1.90 per title to: Mills & Boon Reader Service, Freepost, P.O. Box 236, Croydon, Surrey, CR9 9EL, quote your Subscriber No:................................... (If applicable) and complete the name and address details below. Alternatively, these books are available from many local Newsagents including W.H.Smith, J.Menzies, Martins and other paperback stockists from 12 March 1994.

Name:..

Address:...

....Post Code:....................

To Retailer: If you would like to stock M&B books please contact your regular book/magazine wholesaler for details.

You may be mailed with offers from other reputable companies as a result of this application. If you would rather not take advantage of these opportunities please tick box ☐

'How are our children? What are their names again?'

'Just how long do you intend to go on teasing me?' Caitlin snapped.

Joe grinned. 'I just wanted to see if I could get a rise out of you. It never worked when we were kids. You were always so prim and proper.'

'Look, you didn't like me then, and I see no reason for you to——'

'Not *like* you?' he countered. 'I married you, didn't I?'

Dear Reader

As the dark winter nights unfold, what better to turn to than a heart-warming Mills & Boon! As usual, we bring you a selection of books which take you all over the world, with heroines you like and heroes you would love to be with! So take a flight of fancy away from everyday life to the wonderful world of Mills & Boon—you'll be glad you did.

The Editor

Debbie Macomber is an American writer living in the state of Washington. She and her electrician husband have four teenage children, as well as horses, cats, a dog and some guinea pigs. Debbie's successful writing career actually started in childhood, when her brother copied— and sold!—her diary. She's gone on to a considerably wider readership as a prolific and popular author who says she wrote her first book after falling in love with romance novels.

Recent titles by the same author:

HERE COMES TROUBLE

THE FORGETFUL BRIDE

BY

DEBBIE MACOMBER

MILLS & BOON LIMITED
ETON HOUSE, 18-24 PARADISE ROAD
RICHMOND, SURREY TW9 1SR

*Original edition published in 1991
by Harlequin Romances*

*First published in Great Britain 1993
by Mills & Boon Limited*

© Debbie Macomber 1991

*Australian copyright 1993
Philippine copyright 1994
This edition 1994*

ISBN 0 263 78307 3

*Set in Times Roman 10 on 12¼ pt.
91-9402-46686 C*

Made and printed in Great Britain

PROLOGUE

"NOT UNLESS we're married."

Ten-year-old Martin Marshall slapped his hands against his thighs in disgust. "I told you she was going to be unreasonable about this."

Caitlin watched as her brother's best friend withdrew a second baseball card from his shirt pocket. If Joseph Rockwell wanted to kiss her, then he was going to have to do it the right way. She might be only eight, but Caitlin knew about these things. Glancing down at the doll held tightly in her arms, she realised instinctively that Barbie wouldn't approve of kissing a boy unless he married you first.

Martin approached her again. "Joe says he'll throw in his Don Drysdale baseball card."

"Not unless we're married," she repeated, smoothing the front of her sundress with a haughty air.

"All right, all right, I'll marry her," Joe muttered as he stalked across the backyard.

"How you gonna do that?" Martin demanded.

"Get your Bible."

For someone who wanted to kiss her so badly, Joseph didn't look very pleased. Caitlin decided to press her luck. "In the fort."

"The fort?" Joe exploded. "No girls are allowed in there and you know it."

"I refuse to get married to a boy who won't allow me into his fort."

"Call it off," Martin demanded. "She's asking too much."

"You don't have to give me the second baseball card," she said. The idea of being the first girl ever to view their precious fort had a certain appeal. For one thing, she'd probably get invited to Betsy McDonald's birthday party.

The boys exchanged glances and started whispering to each other, but Caitlin heard only snatches of their conversation. Martin clearly wasn't thrilled with Joseph's concessions, and he kept shaking his head as though he couldn't believe his friend might actually go through with this. For her part, Caitlin didn't know whether to trust Joseph. He liked playing practical jokes and everyone in the neighbourhood knew it.

"It's time to feed my baby," she announced, preparing to leave.

"All right, all right," Joseph said with obvious reluctance. "I'll marry you in the fort. Martin'll say the words, only you can't tell anyone about going inside, understand?"

"If you do," Martin threatened, glaring at his sister, "you'll be sorry."

"I won't tell," Caitlin promised. It would have to be a secret, but that was fine because she liked keeping secrets.

"You ready?" Joseph demanded. Now that the terms were set, he seemed to be in a rush, which rather annoyed Caitlin. The frown on his face didn't please her, either. A bridegroom should at least *look* happy. She was about to say so, but decided not to.

"You'll have to change clothes, of course. The suit you wore on Easter Sunday will do nicely."

"What?" Joseph shrieked. "I'm not wearing any suit. Listen, Caitlin, you've gone about as far as you can with this. I get married exactly the way I am or we call it off."

She sighed, rolling her eyes expressively. "Oh, all right, but I'll need to get a few things first."

"Just hurry up, would you?"

Martin followed her into the house, letting the screen door slam behind him. He took his Bible off the hallway table and rushed back outside.

Caitlin hurried up to her room, where she grabbed a brush to run through her hair and straightened the two pink ribbons tied around her pigtails. She always insisted on pink ribbons because pink was a colour for girls. Boys were supposed to wear blue and brown and boring colours like that. Boys were okay sometimes, but mostly they did disgusting things.

Her four dolls accompanied her across the backyard and into the wooded acre behind. She hated getting her Mary Janes dusty, but that couldn't be helped.

With a good deal of ceremony, she opened the rickety door and then slowly, the way she'd seen it done at her older cousin's wedding, Caitlin marched into the boys' packing-crate-and-cardboard fort.

Pausing inside the narrow entry, she glanced around. It wasn't anything to brag about. Martin had made it sound like a palace with marble floors and crystal chandeliers. She couldn't help feeling disillusioned. If she hadn't been so eager to see the fort, she would have insisted they do this properly, in church.

Her brother stood tall and proud on an upturned apple crate, the Bible clutched to his chest. His face was dutifully sombre Caitlin smiled approvingly. He, at least, was taking this seriously.

"You can't bring those dolls in here," Joseph said loudly.

"I most certainly can. Barbie and Ken and Paula and Jane are our children."

"Our children?"

"Naturally they haven't been born yet, so they're really just a glint in your eye." She'd heard her father say that once and it sounded special. "They're angels for now, but I thought they should be here so you could meet them." She was busily arranging her dolls in a tidy row behind Martin on another apple crate.

Joseph covered his face with his hands and it looked for a moment like he might actually change his mind.

"Are we going to get married or not?" she asked.

"All right, all right." Joseph sighed heavily and pulled her forward, a little more roughly than necessary, in Caitlin's opinion.

The two of them stood in front of Martin, who randomly opened his Bible. He gazed down at the leather-bound book and then at Caitlin and his best friend. He nodded solemnly. "Do you, Joseph James Rockwell take Caitlin Rose Marshall for your wife?"

"Lawfully wedded," Caitlin corrected. She remembered this part from a television show.

"Lawfully wedded wife," Martin amended grudgingly.

"I do." Caitlin noticed that he didn't say it with any real enthusiasm. "I think there's supposed to be something about richer or poorer and sickness and health," Joseph said, smirking at Caitlin as if to say she wasn't the only one who knew the proper words.

Martin nodded and continued. "Do you, Caitlin Rose Marshall, hereby take Joseph James Rockwell in sickness and health and in riches and in poorness?"

"I'll only marry a man who's healthy and rich."

"You can't go putting conditions on this now," Joseph argued. "We already agreed."

"Just say 'I do,'" Martin urged, his voice tight with annoyance. Caitlin suspected that only the seriousness of the occasion prevented him from adding, "You pest."

She wasn't sure if she should go through with this or not. She was old enough to know she liked pretty things and that when she married, her husband would build her a castle at the edge of the forest. He would love her so much, he'd bring home silk ribbons for her hair, and bottles and bottles of expensive perfume. So many that there wouldn't be room for them all on her makeup table.

"Caitlin," Martin said through clenched teeth.

"I do," she answered solemnly.

"I hereby pronounce you married," Martin proclaimed, closing the Bible with a resounding thud. "You may kiss the bride."

Joseph turned to face Caitlin. He was several inches taller than she was. His eyes were a pretty shade of blue that reminded her of the way the sky looked the morning after a bad rainstorm. She liked Joseph's eyes.

"You ready?" he asked.

She nodded, closed her eyes and pressed her lips tightly together as she angled her head to the left. If the truth be known, she wasn't all that opposed to having Joseph kiss her, but she'd never let him know that because...well, because kissing wasn't something ladies talked about.

A long time passed before she felt his mouth touch hers. Actually his lips sort of bounced against hers. Gee, she thought. What a bunch of hullabaloo over nothing.

"Well?" Martin demanded of his friend.

Caitlin opened her eyes to discover Joseph frowning down at her. "It wasn't anything like Pete said it would be," he grumbled.

"Caitlin might be doing it wrong," Martin offered, glaring accusingly at his sister.

"If anyone did anything wrong, it's Joseph." They were making it sound like she'd purposely cheated them. If anyone was being cheated, it was Caitlin, because she couldn't tell Betsy McDonald about going inside their precious fort.

Joseph didn't say anything for a long moment. Then he slowly withdrew his prized baseball card from his shirt pocket. He gazed at it lovingly, then reluctantly held it out to her. "Here," he said, "this is yours now."

"You aren't going to *give* it to her, are you? Not when she flubbed up!" Martin cried. "Kissing a girl wasn't like Pete said, and that's got to be Caitlin's fault. I told you she's not really a girl, anyway. She's a pest."

"A deal's a deal," Joseph said sadly.

"You can keep your silly old baseball card." Head held high, Caitlin gathered up her dolls in a huff, prepared to make a proper exit.

"You won't tell anyone about us letting you into the fort, will you?" Martin shouted after her.

"No." She'd keep that promise.

But neither of them had said a word about telling everyone in school that she and Joseph Rockwell had got married.

CHAPTER ONE

FOR THE THIRD TIME that afternoon, Cait indignantly wiped sawdust from the top of her desk. If this remodelling mess got much worse, the particles were going to get into her computer, destroying her vital link with the New York Stock Exchange.

"We'll have to move her out," a gruff male voice said from behind her.

"I beg your pardon?" Cait demanded, rising abruptly and whirling towards the doorway. She clapped the dust from her hands, preparing to do battle. So much for this being the season of peace and goodwill. All these men in hard hats strolling through the office, moving things about, was inconvenient enough. But at least she'd been able to close her door to reduce the noise. Now, it seemed, even that would be impossible.

"We're going to have to pull some electrical wires through there," the same brusque voice explained. She couldn't see the man's face, since he stood just outside her doorway, but she had an impression of broadshouldered height. "We'll have everything back to normal within a week."

"A week!" She wouldn't be able to service her customers, let alone function, without her desk and phone. And just exactly where did they intend to put her? Certainly not in a hallway! She wouldn't stand for it.

The mess this simple remodelling project had created was one thing, but transplanting her entire office as if she were nothing more than a . . . a tulip bulb was something else again.

"I'm sorry about this, Cait," Paul Jamison said, slipping past the crew foreman to her side.

The wind went out of her argument at the merest hint of his devastating smile. "Don't worry about it," she said, the picture of meekness and tolerance. "Things like this happen when a company grows as quickly as ours."

She glanced across the hallway to her best friend's office, shrugging slightly as if to ask, *Is Paul ever going to notice me?* Lindy shot her a crooked grin and a quick nod that suggested Cait stop being so negative. Her friend's confidence didn't help. Paul was a wonderful district manager and she was fortunate to have the opportunity to work with him. He was both talented and resourceful. The brokerage firm of Webster, Rodale and Missen was an affiliate of the fastest-growing firm in the country. This branch had been open for less than two years and already they were breaking sales records all across the country. Due mainly, Cait believed, to Paul's administrative skills.

Paul was slender, dark-haired and handsome in an urbane, sophisticated way—every woman's dream man. Certainly Cait's. But as far as she could determine, he didn't see her in a similar romantic light. He thought of her as an important team member. One of the staff. At most, a friend.

Cait knew that friendship was often fertile ground for romance, and she hoped for an opportunity to cultivate it. Willingly surrendering her office to an irritating crew of carpenters and electricians was sure to gain her a few points with her boss.

"Where would you like me to set up my desk in the interval?" she asked, smiling warmly at Paul. From habit, she lifted her hand to push back a stray lock of hair, forgetting she'd recently had it cut. That had been another futile attempt to attract Paul's affections—or at least his attention. Her shoulder-length chestnut-brown hair had been trimmed and permed into a pixie style with a halo of soft curls.

The difference from the tightly styled chignon she'd always worn to work was striking, or so everyone said. Everyone, except Paul. The hairdresser had claimed it changed Cait's coolly polished look into one of warmth and enthusiasm. It was exactly the image Cait wanted Paul to have of her.

Unfortunately he didn't seem to detect the slightest difference in her appearance. At least not until Lindy had pointedly commented on the change within earshot of their absentminded employer. Then, and only then, had Paul made a remark about noticing something different; he just hadn't been sure what it was, he'd said.

"I suppose we could move you . . ." Paul hesitated.

"Your office seems to be the best choice," the foreman said.

Cait resisted the urge to hug the man. He was tall, easily six three, and as solid as Mount Rainier, the majestic mountain she could see from her office window. She hadn't paid much attention to him until this moment and was surprised to note something vaguely familiar about him. She'd assumed he was the foreman, but she wasn't certain. He seemed to be around the office fairly often, although not on a predictable schedule. Every time he did show up, the level of activity rose dramatically.

"Ah...I suppose Cait could move in with me for the time being," Paul agreed. In her daydreams, Cait would play back this moment; her version had Paul looking at her with surprise and wonder, his mouth moving towards hers and—

"Miss?"

Cait broke out of her reverie and glanced towards the foreman—the man who'd suggested she share Paul's office. "Yes?"

"Would you show us exactly what you need moved?"

"Of course," she returned crisply. This romantic heart of hers was always getting her into trouble. She'd look at Paul and her head would start to spin with hopes and fantasies and she'd be lost....

Cait's arms were loaded with files as she followed the carpenters who hauled her desk into a corner of Paul's much larger office. Her computer and phone followed, and within fifteen minutes she was back in business.

She was on the phone, talking with one of her most important clients, when the same man walked back, unannounced, into the room. At first Caitlin assumed he was looking for Paul, who'd stepped out of the office. The foreman—or whatever he was—hesitated, then, scooping up her nameplate, he grinned at her as if he found something highly entertaining. Cait did her best to ignore him, flipping needlessly through the pages of the file.

Not taking the hint, he stepped forward and plunked the nameplate on the edge of her desk. As she glanced up in annoyance, he boldly winked at her.

Cait was not amused. How dare this...this... redneck flirt with her!

She glared at him, hoping he'd have the good manners and good sense to leave—which, of course, he didn't. In fact, he seemed downright stubborn about staying and making her as uncomfortable as possible. Her phone conversation ran its natural course and after making several notations, she replaced the receiver.

"You wanted something?" she demanded, her eyes finding his. Once more she noted his apparent amusement. It didn't make sense.

"No," he answered, grinning. "Sorry to have bothered you."

For the second time, Cait was struck by a twinge of something familiar. He strolled out of her makeshift office as if he owned the building.

Cait waited a few minutes, then approached Lindy. "Did you happen to catch his name?"

"Whose name?"

"The...man who insisted I vacate my office. I don't know who he is. I thought he was the foreman, but..." She crossed her arms and furrowed her brow, trying to remember if she'd heard anyone say his name.

"I have no idea." Lindy pushed back her chair and rolled a pencil between her palms. "He is kinda cute, though, don't you think?"

A smile softened Cait's lips. "There's only one man for me and you know it."

"Then why are you asking questions about one of the construction crew?"

"I...don't know. He seems familiar for some reason, and he keeps grinning at me as if he knows something I don't. I hate it when men do that."

"Then ask one of the others what his name is. They'll tell you."

"I can't do that."

"Why not?"

"He might think I'm interested in him."

"And we both know how impossible that would be," Lindy said with mild sarcasm.

"Exactly." Lindy and probably everyone else in the office complex knew how Cait felt about Paul. The district manager himself, however, seemed to be completely oblivious. Other than throwing herself at him, which she'd seriously considered more than once, there was little she could do but be patient. One day when she was least expecting it, Cupid was going to let fly an arrow and hit her lovable boss directly between the eyes.

When it happened—and it would!—Cait planned to be ready.

"You want to go for lunch now?" Lindy asked.

Cait nodded. It was nearly two and she hadn't eaten since breakfast, which had consisted of a banana and a cup of coffee. A West Coast stockbroker's day started before dawn. Cait was generally in the office well before six and didn't stop work until the market closed at one-thirty, Seattle time. Only then did she break for something to eat.

Somewhere in the middle of her turkey on whole wheat, Cait convinced herself she was imagining things when it came to that construction worker. He'd probably been waiting around to ask her where Paul was and then changed his mind. He did say he was sorry for bothering her.

If only he hadn't winked.

HE WAS BACK the following day, a tool pouch riding on his hip like a six-shooter, hard hat in place. He was issuing orders like a drill sergeant, and Cait found herself gazing after him with reluctant fascination. She'd heard he owned the construction company, and she wasn't surprised.

As she studied him, she noted once again how striking he was. Not because he was extraordinarily handsome, but because he was somehow commanding. He possessed an authority, a presence, that attracted attention wherever he went. Cait was as drawn to it as those around her. She observed how the crew instinctively turned to him for directions and approval.

The more she analysed him, the more she recognised that he was a man who had an appetite for life. Which meant excitement, adventure and probably women, and that confused her even more because she couldn't recall ever knowing anyone quite like him. Then why did she find him so...familiar?

Cait herself had a quiet nature. She rarely ventured out of the comfortable, compact world she'd built. She had her job, a nice apartment in Seattle's university district, and a few close friends. Excitement to her was growing herbs and participating in nature walks.

The following day while she was studying the construction worker, he'd unexpectedly turned and smiled at something one of his men had said. His smile, she decided, intrigued her most. It was slightly off centre and seemed to tease the corners of his mouth. He looked her way more than once and each time she thought she detected a touch of humour, an amused knowledge that lurked just beneath the surface.

"It's driving me crazy," Cait confessed to Lindy over lunch.

"What is?"

"That I can't place him."

Lindy set her elbows on the table, holding her sandwich poised in front of her mouth. She nodded slowly, her eyes distant. "When you figure it out, introduce me, will you? I could go for a guy this sexy."

So Lindy had noticed that earthy sensuality about him, too. Well, of course she had—any woman would.

After lunch, Cait returned to the office to make a few calls. He was there again.

No matter how hard she tried, she couldn't place him. Work became a pretence as she continued to scrutinise him, racking her brain. Then, when she least expected it, he strolled past her and brazenly winked a second time.

As the colour clawed up her neck, Cait flashed her attention back to her computer screen.

"His name is Joe," Lindy rushed in to tell her ten minutes later. "I heard one of the men call him that."

"Joe," Cait repeated slowly. She couldn't remember ever knowing anyone named Joe.

"Does that help?"

"No," Cait said, shaking her head regretfully. If she'd ever met this man, she wasn't likely to have overlooked the experience. He wasn't someone a woman easily forgot.

"Ask him," Lindy insisted. "It's ridiculous not to. It's driving you bananas. Then," she added with infuriating logic, "when you find out, you can nonchalantly introduce me."

"I can't just waltz up and start quizzing him," Cait argued. The idea was preposterous. "He'll think I'm trying to pick him up."

"You'll go crazy if you don't."

Cait sighed. "You're right. I'm not going to sleep tonight if I don't settle this."

With Lindy waiting expectantly in her office, Cait approached him. He was talking to another one of the crew and once he'd finished, he turned to her with one of his devastating lazy smiles.

"Hello," she said, and her voice shook slightly. "Do I know you?"

"You mean you've forgotten?" he asked, sounding shocked and insulted.

"Apparently. Though I'll admit you look somewhat familiar."

"I should certainly hope so. We shared something very special a few years back."

"We did?" Cait was more confused than ever.

"Hey, Joe, there's a problem over here," a male voice shouted. "Could you come look at this?"

"I'll be with you in a minute," he answered brusquely over his shoulder. "Sorry, we'll have to talk later."

"But—"

"Say hello to Martin for me, would you?" he asked as he stalked past her and into the room that had once been Cait's office.

Martin, her brother. Cait hadn't a clue what her brother could possibly have to do with this. Mentally she ran through a list of his teenage friends and came up blank.

Then it hit her. Bull's-eye. Her heart started to pound until it roared like a tropical storm in her ears. Mechanically Cait made her way back to Lindy's office. She sank into a chair beside the desk and stared into space.

"Well?" Lindy pressed. "Don't keep me in suspense."

"Um, it's not that easy to explain."

"You remember him, then?"

She nodded. Oh, lord, did she ever.

"Good grief, what's wrong? You've gone so pale!"

Cait tried to come up with an explanation that wouldn't sound . . . ridiculous.

"Tell me," Lindy insisted. "Don't just sit there wearing a silly grin and looking like you're about to faint."

"Um, it goes back a few years."

"All right. Start there."

"Remember how kids sometimes do silly things? Like when you're young and foolish and don't know any better?"

"Me, yes, but not you," Lindy said calmly. "You're perfect. In all the time we've been friends, I haven't seen you do one impulsive thing. Not one. You analyse everything before you act. I can't imagine you ever doing anything silly."

"I did once," Cait corrected, "but I was only eight."

"What could you have possibly done at age eight?"

"I . . . I got married."

"Married?" Lindy half rose from her chair. "You've got to be kidding."

"I wish I was."

"I'll bet a week's commissions that your husband's name is Joe." Lindy was smiling now, smiling widely.

Cait nodded and tried to smile in return.

"What's there to worry about? Good grief, kids do that sort of thing all the time! It doesn't mean anything."

"But I was a real brat about it. Joe and my brother, Martin, were best friends. Joe wanted to know what it felt like to kiss a girl, and I insisted he marry me first. If that wasn't bad enough, I pressured them into performing the ceremony inside their boys-only fort."

"So, you were a bit of pain—most eight-year-old girls are when it comes to dealing with their brothers. He got what he wanted, didn't he?"

Cait took a deep breath and nodded again.

"What was kissing him like?" Lindy asked in a curiously throaty voice.

"Good heavens, I don't remember," Cait answered shortly, then reconsidered. "I take that back. As I recall, it wasn't so bad, though obviously neither one of us had a clue what we were doing."

"Lindy, you're still here," Paul said as he strolled into the office. He nodded briefly in Cait's direction, but she had the impression he barely saw her. He'd hardly been around in the past couple of days—almost as if he was purposely avoiding her, she mused, but that thought was too painful to consider.

"I was just finishing up," Lindy said, glancing guiltily towards Cait. "We both were."

"Fine, fine, I didn't mean to disturb you. I'll see you two in the morning." With that he was gone.

Cait gazed after him with thinly disguised emotion. She waited until Paul was out of earshot before she spoke. "He's so blind. What do I have to do, hit him over the head?"

"Quit being so negative," Lindy admonished. "You're going to be sharing an office with him for another five days. Do whatever you need to make darn sure he notices you."

"I've tried," Cait murmured, discouraged. And she had. She'd tried every trick known to woman, with little success.

Lindy left the office before her. Cait gathered up some stock reports to read that evening and stacked them neatly inside her leather briefcase. What Lindy had said about her being methodical and careful was true. It was also a source of pride; those traits had served her clients well.

To Cait's dismay, Joe followed her. "So," he said, smiling down at her, apparently oblivious to the other people clustering around the lift. "Who have you been kissing these days?"

Hot colour rose instantly to her face. Did he have to humiliate her in public?

"I could find myself jealous, you know."

"Would you kindly stop," she whispered furiously, glaring at him. Her hand tightened around the handle of her briefcase so hard her fingers ached.

"You figured it out?"

She nodded, her eyes darting to the lighted numbers above the lift door, praying it would make its descent in record time instead of pausing on each floor.

"The years have been good to you."

"Thank you." *Please hurry,* she urged the lift.

"I never would've believed Martin's little sister would turn out to be such a beauty."

If he was making fun of her, she didn't appreciate it. She was attractive, she knew that, but she certainly wasn't waiting for anyone to place a tiara on her head. "Thank you," she repeated grudgingly.

He gave an exaggerated sigh. "How are our children doing? What were their names again?" When she didn't answer right away, he added, "Don't tell me you've forgotten."

"Barbie and Ken," she muttered under her breath.

"That's right. I remember now."

If Joe hadn't drawn the attention of her co-workers before, he had now. Cait could have sworn every single person standing by the lift turned to stare at her. The hope that no one was interested in their conversation was forever lost.

"Just how long do you intend to tease me about this?" she snapped.

"That depends," Joe responded with a chuckle Cait could only describe as sadistic. She gritted her teeth. He might have found the situation amusing, but she derived little enjoyment from being the office laughingstock.

Just then the lift arrived, and not a moment too soon to suit Cait. The instant the doors slid open, she stepped towards it, determined to get as far away from this irritating man as possible.

He quickly caught up with her and she whirled around to face him, her back ramrod-stiff. "Is this really necessary?" she hissed, painfully conscious of the other people crowding into the lift ahead of her.

He grinned. "I suppose not. I just wanted to see if I could get a rise out of you. It never worked when we were kids, you know. You were always so prim and proper."

"Look, you didn't like me then and I see no reason for you to—"

"Not *like* you?" he countered loud enough for everyone in the building to hear. "I married you, didn't I?"

CHAPTER TWO

CAIT'S HEART seemed to stop. She realised that not only the people in the lift but everyone left in the office was staring at her with unconcealed interest. The lift was about to close and she quickly stepped forward, straightening her arms to hold the doors open. She felt like Samson balanced between two marble columns.

"It's not like it sounds," she felt obliged to explain in a loud voice, her gaze pleading.

No one made eye contact with her and, desperate, she turned to glare at Joe, issuing him a silent challenge to retract his words. His eyes were sparkling with mischief. If he did say anything, Cait thought in sudden horror, it was bound to make things even worse.

There didn't seem to be anything to do but tell the truth. "In case anyone has the wrong impression, this man and I are not married," she shouted. "Good grief, I was only eight!"

There was no reaction. It was as if she'd vanished into thin air. Defeated, she dropped her arms and stepped back, freeing the doors, which promptly closed.

Ignoring the other people in the lift—who were carefully ignoring her—Cait clenched her hands into hard fists and glared up at Joe. Her face tightened with anger. "That was a rotten thing to do," she whispered hoarsely.

"What? It's true, isn't it?" he whispered back.

"You're being ridiculous to talk as though we're married!"

"We were once. It wounds me that you treat our marriage so lightly."

"I . . . it wasn't legal." The fact that they were even discussing this was preposterous. "You can't possibly hold me responsible for something that happened so long ago. To play this game now is . . . is infantile, and I refuse to be part of it."

The lift finally came to a halt on the ground floor and, eager to make her escape, Cait rushed out. Straightening to keep her dignity intact, she headed through the crowded foyer towards the front doors. Although it was mid-afternoon, dusk was already settling, casting dark shadows between the towering office buildings.

Cait reached the first intersection and sighed in relief as she glanced around her. Good. No sign of Joseph Rockwell. The light was red and she paused, although others hurried across the street after checking for traffic; Cait always felt obliged to obey the signal.

"What do you think Paul's going to say when he hears about this?" Joe asked behind her.

Cait gave a start, then turned to look at her tormentor. She hadn't thought about Paul's reaction. Her throat seemed to constrict, rendering her speechless, otherwise she would have demanded Joe leave her alone. But he'd raised a question she dared not ignore. Paul might hear about her former relationship

with Joe and might even think there was something
between them.

"You're in love with him, aren't you?"

She nodded. At the very mention of Paul's name,
her knees went weak. He was everything she wanted in
a man and more. She'd been crazy about him for
months and now it was all about to be ruined by this
irritating, unreasonable ghost from her past.

"Who told you?" Cait snapped. She couldn't
imagine Lindy betraying her confidence, but Cait
hadn't told anyone else.

"No one had to tell me," Joe explained. "It's written all over you."

Shocked, Cait stared at Joe, her heart sinking.
"Do... do you think Paul knows how I feel?"

Joe shrugged. "Maybe."

"But Lindy said . . ."

The light changed and, clasping her elbow, Joe
urged her into the street. "What was it Lindy said?"
he prompted when they'd crossed.

Cait glanced up, about to tell him, when she realised exactly what she was doing—conversing with her
antagonist. This was the very man who'd gone out of
his way to embarrass and humiliate her in front of the
entire office staff. Not to mention assorted clients and
carpenters.

She stiffened. "Never mind what Lindy said. Now
if you'll kindly excuse me..." With her head held high,
she marched down the street. She hadn't gone more
than a few feet when the hearty sound of Joe's laughter caught up with her.

"You haven't changed in twenty years, Caitlin
Marshall. Not a single bit."

Gritting her teeth, she marched on.

"DO YOU THINK Paul's heard?" Cait asked Lindy the instant she had a free moment the following afternoon. The New York Stock Exchange had closed for the day and Cait hadn't seen Paul since morning. It looked like he really *was* avoiding her.

"I wouldn't know," Lindy said as she typed some figures into her computer. "But the word about your childhood marriage has spread like wildfire everywhere else. It's the joke of the day. What did you and Joe do? Make a public announcement before you left the office yesterday afternoon?"

It was so nearly the truth that Cait guiltily looked away. "I didn't say a word," she defended herself. "Joe was the one."

"He told everyone you were married?" A suspicious tilt at the corner of her mouth betrayed Lindy's amusement.

"Not exactly. He started asking about our children in front of everyone."

"There were children?"

Cait resisted the urge to close her eyes and count to ten. "No. I brought my dolls to the wedding. Listen, I don't want to rehash a silly incident that happened years ago. I'm more afraid Paul's going to hear about it and put the wrong connotation on the whole thing. There's absolutely nothing between me and Joseph Rockwell. More than likely Paul won't give the matter a second thought, but I don't want there to be any...doubts between us, if you know what I mean."

"If you're so worried about it, talk to him," Lindy advised without lifting her eyes from the screen. "Honesty is the best policy, you know that."

"Yes, but it could prove to be a bit embarrassing, don't you think?"

"Paul will respect you for telling him the truth before he hears the rumours from someone else. Frankly, Cait, I think you're making a fuss over nothing. It isn't like you've committed a felony, you know."

"I realise that."

"Paul will probably be amused, like everyone else. He's not going to say anything." She looked up quickly, as though she expected Cait to try yet another argument.

Cait didn't. Instead she mulled over her friend's advice, gnawing on her lower lip. "I think you might be right. Paul will respect me for explaining the situation myself, instead of ignoring everything." Telling him the truth could be helpful in other respects, too, now that she thought about it.

If Paul had any feeling for her whatsoever, and oh, how she prayed he did, then he might become just a little jealous of her relationship with Joseph Rockwell. After all, Joe was an attractive man in a rugged outdoor sort of way. He was tall and muscular and, well, good-looking. The kind of good-looking that appealed to women—not Cait, of course, but other women. Hadn't Lindy commented almost immediately on how attractive he was?

"You're right," Cait said, walking resolutely towards the office she was temporarily sharing with Paul. Although she'd felt annoyed, at first, about being shuffled out of her own space, she'd come to think of this inconvenience as a blessing in disguise. However, she had to admit she'd been disappointed thus far. She had assumed she'd be spending a lot of time alone with him. That hadn't happened yet.

The more Cait considered the idea of a heart-to-heart talk with her boss, the more appealing it became. As was her habit, she mentally rehearsed what she wanted to say to him, then gave herself a small pep talk.

"I don't remember that you talked to yourself." The male voice booming behind her startled Cait. "But then there's a great deal I've missed over the years, isn't there, Caitlin?"

Cait was so rattled she nearly stumbled. "What are you doing here?" she demanded. "Why do you insist on following me around? Can't you see I'm busy?" He was the last person she wanted to confront just now.

"Sorry." He raised both hands in a gesture of apology contradicted by his twinkling blue eyes. "How about lunch later?"

He was teasing. He had to be. Besides, it would be insane for her to have anything to do with Joseph Rockwell. Heaven only knew what would happen if she gave him the least bit of encouragement. He'd probably hire a skywriter and announce to the entire city that they'd married as children.

"It shouldn't be that difficult to agree to a luncheon date," he informed her coolly.

"You're serious about this?"

"Of course I'm serious. We have a lot of years to catch up on." His hand rested on his leather pouch, giving him a rakish air of indifference.

"I've got an appointment this afternoon..." She offered the first plausible excuse she could think of; it might be uninspired but it also happened to be true. She'd made plans to eat lunch with Lindy.

"Dinner, then. I'm anxious to hear what Martin's been up to."

"Martin," she repeated, stalling for time while she invented another excuse. This wasn't a situation she had much experience with. She did date, but infrequently.

"Listen, bright eyes, no need to look so concerned. This isn't an invitation to the senior prom. It's one friend to another. Strictly platonic."

"You won't mention ... our wedding to the waiter? Or anyone else?"

"I promise." As if to offer proof of his intent, he licked the end of his index finger and crossed his heart. "That was Martin's and my secret pledge sign. If either of us broke our word, the other was entitled to come up with a punishment. We both understood it would be a fate worse than death."

"I don't need any broken pledge to torture you, Joseph Rockwell. In two days you've managed to turn my life into..." She paused mid-sentence as Paul Jamison casually strolled past. He glanced in Cait's direction and smiled benignly.

"Hello, Paul," she called out, weakly raising her right hand. He looked exceptionally handsome this morning in a three-piece dark blue suit. The contrast between him and Joe, who was wearing dust-covered jeans, heavy boots and a tool pouch, was so striking that Cait had to force herself not to stare at her boss.

If only Paul had been the one to invite her to dinner . . .

"If you'll excuse me," she said politely, edging her way around Joe and towards Paul, who'd gone into his office. Their office. The need to talk to him burned within her. Words of explanation began to form themselves in her mind.

Joe caught her by the shoulders, bringing her up short. Cait gasped and raised shocked eyes to his.

"Dinner," he reminded her.

She blinked, hardly knowing what to say. "All right," she mumbled distractedly and recited her address, eager to have him gone.

"Good. I'll pick you up tonight at six." With that he released her and stalked away.

After taking a couple of moments to compose herself, Cait headed towards the office. "Hello, Paul," she said, standing just inside the doorway. "Do you have a moment to talk?"

He glanced up from a file on his desk and grinned warmly. "Of course, Cait. Sit down and make yourself comfortable."

She moved into the room and closed the door behind her. When she looked back to Paul, he'd cocked his eyebrows in surprise. "Problems?" he asked.

"Not exactly." She pulled out the chair opposite his desk and slowly sat down. Now that she had his full attention, she was at a loss. All her prepared explanations and witticisms had flown out of her head. "The rate on municipal bonds has been exceptionally high lately," she commented nervously.

Paul agreed with a quick nod. "They have been for several months now."

"Yes, I know. That's what makes them such excellent value." Cait had been selling bonds heavily in the past few weeks.

"You didn't close the door to talk to me about bonds," Paul said softly. "What's troubling you, Cait?"

She laughed uncomfortably, wondering how a man could be so astute in one area and blind in another. If only he would reveal some emotion towards her. Anything. All he did was sit across from her and wait. He was cordial enough, gracious even, but there was no hint of more. Nothing to give Cait any hope that he was starting to care for her.

"It's about Joseph Rockwell."

"The contractor who's handling the remodelling?"

Cait nodded. "I knew him years ago when we were just children." She glanced at Paul, whose face remained blank. "We were neighbours. In fact Joe and my brother, Martin, were best friends. Joe moved out to the suburbs when he and Martin were in the sixth grade and I hadn't heard anything from him since."

"It's a small world, isn't it?" Paul remarked affably enough.

"Joe and Martin were typical young boys," she said, rushing her words a little in her eagerness to have this out in the open. "Full of tomfoolery and pranks."

"Boys will be boys," Paul said without any real enthusiasm.

"Yes, I know. Once—" she forced a light laugh "—they actually involved me in one of their crazy schemes."

"What did they put you up to? Robbing a bank?"

She somehow managed a smile. "Not exactly. Joe—
I always called him Joseph back then, because it irritated him. Anyway, Joe and Martin had this friend
named Pete who was a year older and he'd spent part
of his summer vacation visiting his aunt in Peoria, at
least I think it was Peoria ... Anyway he came back
bragging about having kissed a girl. Naturally Martin
and Joe were jealous and as you said, boys will be
boys, so they decided that one of them should test it
out and see if kissing a girl was everything Pete
claimed it was."

"I take it they decided to make you their guinea
pig."

"Exactly." Cait slid to the edge of the chair, delighted that Paul was following this rather convoluted
explanation. "I was eight and considered something
of a ... pest." She paused, hoping Paul would make
some comment about how impossible that was. When
he didn't, she continued, a little disappointed at his
restraint. "Apparently I was more of one than I remembered," she said, with another forced laugh. "At
eight, I didn't think kissing was something nice girls
did, at least not without a wedding band on their finger."

"So you kissed Joseph Rockwell," Paul said absently.

"Yes, but there was a tiny bit more than that. I
made him marry me."

Paul's eyebrows shot to the ceiling.

"Now, almost twenty years later, he's getting his
revenge by going around telling everyone within earshot that we're actually married. Which of course
is ridiculous."

A couple of strained seconds followed her announcement.

"I'm not sure what to say," Paul murmured.

"Oh, I wasn't expecting you to say anything. I thought it was important to clear the air, that's all."

"I see."

"He's only doing it because . . . well, because that's Joe. Even when we were kids he enjoyed playing these little games. No one really minded, though, at least not the girls, because he was so cute." She certainly had Paul's attention now.

"I thought you should know," she added, "in case you happened to hear a rumour or something. I didn't want you thinking Joe and I were involved or even considering a relationship. I was fairly certain you wouldn't, but one never knows and I'm a firm believer in being forthright and honest."

Paul blinked. Wanting to fill the awkward silence, Cait chattered on. "Apparently Joe recognised my name when he and his men moved my office in here with yours. He was delighted when I didn't recognise him. In fact, he caused something of a commotion by asking me about our children in front of everyone."

"Children?"

"My dolls," Cait was quick to explain.

"Joe Rockwell's an excellent man. I couldn't fault your taste, Cait."

"The two of us aren't involved," she protested. "Good grief, I haven't seen him in nearly twenty years."

"I see," Paul said slowly. He sounded . . . disappointed, Cait thought. But she must have misread his tone because there wasn't a single, solitary reason for him to be disappointed. Cait felt foolish now for even trying to explain this fiasco. Paul was so blind when it came to her feelings that there was nothing she could say or do to make him understand.

"I just wanted you to know," she repeated, "in case you heard the rumours and were wondering if there was anything between me and Joseph Rockwell. I wanted to assure you there isn't."

"I see," he said again. "Don't worry about it, Cait. What happened between you and Rockwell isn't going to affect your job."

She stood up to leave, praying she would detect a suggestion of jealousy. A hint of rivalry. Anything to show he cared. There was nothing, so she tried again. "I agreed to have dinner with him, though."

Paul had returned his attention to the papers he'd been reading when she'd interrupted him.

"For old times' sake," she added in a reassuring voice—to fend off any violent display of resentment, she told herself. "I certainly don't have any intention of dating him on a regular basis."

Paul grinned. "Have a good time."

"Yes, I will, thanks." Her heart felt as heavy as a sinking battleship. Without thought of where she was headed or who she would talk to, Cait wandered out of Paul's office, forgetting for a second that she had no office of her own. The area where her desk once sat was cluttered with wire reels, ladders and men. Joe must have left, a fact for which Cait was grateful.

She walked into Lindy's small office across the aisle. Her friend glanced up. "So?" she murmured. "Did you talk to Paul?"

Cait nodded.

"How'd it go?"

"Fine, I guess." She perched on the corner of Lindy's desk, crossing her arms around her waist as her left leg swung rhythmically, keeping time with her discouraged heart. She should be accustomed to disappointment when it came to dealing with Paul, but somehow each rejection inflicted a fresh wound on her already battered ego. "I was hoping Paul might be jealous."

"And he wasn't?"

"Not that I could tell."

"It isn't as though you and Joe have anything to do with each other now," Lindy sensibly pointed out. "Marrying him was a childhood prank. It isn't likely to concern Paul."

"I even mentioned that I was going out to dinner with Joe," Cait said morosely.

"You are? When?" Lindy asked, her eyes lighting up. "Where?"

If only Paul had revealed half as much interest. "Tonight. And I don't know where."

"You are going, aren't you?"

"I guess. I can't see any way of avoiding it. No doubt he'll pester me until I give in. If I ever marry and have daughters, Lindy, I'm going to warn them about boys from the time they're old enough to understand."

"Don't you think you should follow your own advice?" Lindy asked, glancing pointedly in the direction of Paul's office.

"Not if I were to have Paul's children," Cait said, eager to defend her boss. "Our daughter would be so intelligent and perceptive she wouldn't need to be warned."

Lindy's returning smile was distracted. "Listen, I've got a few things to finish up here. Why don't you go over to the deli and grab us a table? I'll meet you there in fifteen minutes."

"Sure," Cait agreed. "Do you want me to order for you?"

"No. I don't know what I want yet."

"Okay, I'll see you in a few minutes."

They often ate at the deli across the street from their office complex. The food was good, the service fast, and generally by three in the afternoon, Cait was famished.

She was so wrapped up in her thoughts, which were muddled and gloomy following her talk with Paul, that she didn't notice how late Lindy was. Her friend rushed into the restaurant more than half an hour after Cait had arrived.

"I'm sorry," she said, sounding flustered and oddly shaken. "I had no idea those last odds and ends would take me so long. Oh, you must be starved. I hope you've ordered." Lindy removed her coat and stuffed it into the booth before sliding onto the red upholstered seat herself.

"Actually, no, I didn't." Cait sighed. "Just tea." Her spirits were at an all-time low. It was becoming painfully clear that Paul didn't harbour a single romantic feeling towards her. She was wasting her time and her emotional energy on him. If only she'd had more experience with the opposite sex. It seemed her whole love life had gone into neutral the moment she'd graduated from college. At the rate matters were developing, she'd still be single by the time she turned thirty—a possibility too dismal to contemplate. She hadn't given much thought to marriage and children, always assuming they'd become part of her life; now she wasn't so sure. Even as a child, she'd pictured her grown-up self with a career *and* a family. Behind the business exterior was a woman traditional enough to hunger for that most special of relationships.

She had to face the fact that marriage would never happen if she continued to love a man who didn't return her feelings. She gave a low groan, then noticed that Lindy was gazing at her in concern.

"Let's order something," Lindy said quickly, reaching for the menu tucked behind the napkin holder. "I'm starved."

"I was thinking I'd skip lunch today," Cait mumbled. She sipped her lukewarm tea and frowned. "Joe will be taking me out to dinner soon. And frankly, I don't have much of an appetite."

"This is all my fault, isn't it?" Lindy asked, looking guilty.

"Of course not. I'm just being practical." If Cait was anything, it was practical—except about Paul. "Go ahead and order."

"You're sure you don't mind?"

Cait gestured nonchalantly. "Heavens, no."

"If you're sure, then I'll have the turkey on wholewheat," Lindy said after a moment. "You know how I like turkey, though you'd think I'd have gotten enough over Thanksgiving."

"I'll just have a refill on my tea," Cait said.

"You're still flying to Minnesota for the holidays, aren't you?" Lindy asked, fidgeting with the menu.

"Mmm-hmm." Cait had purchased her ticket several months earlier. Martin and his family lived near Minneapolis. When their father had died several years earlier, Cait's mother moved to Minnesota, settling down in a new subdivision not far from Martin, his wife and their four children. Cait tried to visit at least once a year. However, she'd been there in August, stopping off on her way home from a business trip. Usually she made a point of visiting her brother and his family over the Christmas holidays. It was generally a slow week on the stock market, anyway. And if she was going to travel halfway across the country, she wanted to make it worth her while.

"When will you be leaving?" Lindy asked, although Cait was sure she'd already told her friend more than once.

"The twenty-third." For the past few years, Cait had used one week of her vacation at Christmas time, usually starting the weekend before.

But this year Paul was having a Christmas party and Cait didn't want to miss that, so she'd booked her flight closer to the holiday.

The waitress came to take Lindy's order and replenish the hot water for Cait's tea. The instant she moved away from their booth, Lindy launched into a lengthy tirade about how she hated Christmas shopping and how busy the malls were this time of year. Cait stared at her, bewildered. It wasn't like her friend to chat nonstop.

"Lindy," she interrupted, "is something wrong?"

"Wrong? What could possibly be wrong?"

"I don't know. You haven't stopped talking for the last ten minutes."

"I haven't?" There was an abrupt, uncomfortable silence.

Cait decided it was her turn to say something. "I think I'll wear my red velvet dress," she mused.

"To dinner with Joe?"

"No," she said, shaking her head. "To Paul's Christmas party."

Lindy sighed. "But what are you wearing tonight?"

The question took Cait by surprise. She didn't consider this dinner with Joe a real date. He just wanted to talk over old times, which was fine with Cait as long as he behaved himself. Suddenly she glanced up and frowned, then closed her eyes. "Martin's a Methodist minister," she said softly.

"Yes, I know," Lindy reminded her. "I've known that since I first met you, which was what? Three years ago now."

"Four last month."

"So what does Martin's occupation have to do with anything?" Lindy wanted to know.

"Joe Rockwell can't find out," Cait whispered.

"I didn't plan on telling him," Lindy whispered back.

"I've got to make up some other occupation like..."

"Counsellor," Lindy suggested. "I'm curious, though. Why can't you tell Joe about Martin?"

"Think about it!"

"I am thinking. I really doubt Joe would care one way or the other."

"He might put some connotation on it. You don't know Joe the way I do. He'd razz me about it all evening, claiming the marriage was valid. You know, because Martin really *is* a minister, and since Martin performed the ceremony, we must really be married—that kind of nonsense.''

''I didn't think of that.''

But then, Lindy didn't seem to be thinking much about anything of late. It was as if she was walking about in a perpetual daydream. Cait couldn't remember Lindy's ever being so scatterbrained. If she didn't know better she'd think there was a man involved.

CHAPTER THREE

AT TEN TO SIX, Cait was blow-drying her hair in a haphazard fashion, regretting that she'd ever had it cut. She was looking forward to this dinner date about as much as a trip to the dentist. All she wanted was to get it over with, come home and bury her head under a pillow while she sorted out how she was going to get Paul to notice her.

Restyling her hair hadn't done the trick. Putting in extra hours at the office hadn't impressed him, either. Cait was beginning to think she could stand on top of his desk naked and not attract his attention.

She walked into her compact living room and smoothed the bulky-knit sweater over her slim hips. She hadn't dressed for the occasion, although the sweater was new and expensive. Grey wool trousers and a powder-blue turtleneck with a silver heart-shaped necklace dangling from her neck were about as dressy as she cared to get with someone like Joe. He'd probably be wearing cowboy boots and jeans, if not his hard hat and tool pouch.

Oh, yes, Cait had recognised his type when she'd first seen him. Joe Rockwell was a man's man. He walked and talked macho. No doubt he drove a truck with tyres so high off the ground she'd need a step-ladder to climb inside. He was tough and gruff and liked his women meek and submissive. In that case, of course, she had nothing to worry about.

He arrived right on time, which surprised Cait. Being prompt didn't fit the image she had of Joe Rockwell, redneck contractor. She sighed and painted on a smile, then walked slowly to the door.

The smile faded. Joe stood before her, tall and debonair, dressed in a dark grey pin-striped suit. His grey silk tie had *pink* stripes. He was the picture of smooth sophistication. She knew that Joe was the same man she'd seen earlier in dusty work clothes—yet he was different. He was nothing like Paul, of course. But Joseph Rockwell was a devastatingly handsome man. With a devastating charm. Rarely had she seen a man smile the way he did. His eyes twinkled with warmth and life and mischief. It wasn't difficult to imagine Joe with a little boy whose eyes mirrored his. Cait didn't know where that thought came from, but she pushed it aside before it could linger and take root.

"Hello," he said, flashing her that smile.

"Hi." She couldn't stop looking at him.

"May I come in?"

"Oh . . . of course. I'm sorry," she faltered, stumbling in her haste to step aside. He'd caught her completely off guard. "I was about to change clothes," she said quickly.

"You look fine."

"These old things?" She feigned a laugh. "If you'll excuse me, I'll only be a minute." She poured him a cup of coffee, then dashed into her bedroom, ripping the sweater over her head and closing the door with one foot. Her shoes went flying as she ran to her wardrobe. Jerking aside the orderly row of business jackets and skirts, she pulled clothes off their hangers, considered them, then tossed them on the bed. Nearly everything she owned was more suitable for the office than a dinner date.

The only really special dress she owned was the red velvet one she'd purchased for Paul's Christmas party. The temptation to slip into that was strong but she resisted, wanting to save it for her boss, though heaven knew he probably wouldn't notice.

Deciding on a skirt and blazer, she hopped frantically around her bedroom as she pulled on her tights. Next she threw on a rose-coloured silk blouse and managed to button it while stepping into her skirt. She tucked the blouse into the waistband and her feet into a pair of medium-heeled pumps. Finally, her velvet blazer and she was ready. Taking a deep breath, she returned to the living room in three minutes flat.

"That was fast," Joe commented, standing by the fireplace, hands clasped behind his back. He was examining a framed photograph that sat on the mantel. "Is this Martin's family?"

"Martin...why, yes, that's Martin, his wife and their children." She hoped he didn't detect the breathless catch in her voice.

"Four children."

"Yes, he and Rebecca decided they wanted a large family." Her heartbeat was slowly returning to normal though Cait still felt light-headed. She had a sneaking suspicion that she was suffering from the effects of unleashed male charm.

She realised with surprise that Joe hadn't once said or done anything to embarrass or fluster her. She'd expected him to arrive with a whole series of remarks designed to disconcert her.

"Timmy's ten, Kurt's eight, Jenny's six and Clay's four." She introduced the freckle-faced youngsters, pointing each one out.

"They're handsome children."

"They are, aren't they?"

Cait experienced a twinge of pride. The main reason she went to Minneapolis every year was Martin's children. They adored her and she was crazy about them. Christmas wouldn't be Christmas without Jenny and Clay snuggling on her lap while their father read them the Nativity story. Christmas was singing carols in front of a crackling wood fire, accompanied by Martin's guitar. It meant stringing popcorn and cranberries for the seven-foot-tall tree that always adorned the living room. It was having the children take turns licking fudge from the sides of the copper kettle, and supervising the decorating of sugar cookies with all four crowded around the kitchen table. Caitlin Marshall might be a dedicated stockbroker with an impressive clientele, but when it came to Martin's children, she was Aunty Cait.

"It's difficult to think of Martin with kids," Joe said, carefully placing the family photo back on the mantel.

"He met Rebecca his first year of college and the rest, as they say, is history."

"What about you?" Joe asked, turning unexpectedly to face her.

"What about me?"

"Why haven't you married?"

"Uh..." Cait wasn't sure how to answer him. She had a glib reply she usually gave when anyone asked, but somehow she knew Joe wouldn't accept that. "I...I've never really fallen in love."

"What about Paul?"

"Until Paul," she corrected, stunned that she'd forgotten the strong feelings she held for her employer. She'd been so concerned with being honest that she'd overlooked the obvious. "I am deeply in love with Paul," she said defiantly, wanting there to be no misunderstanding.

"There's no need to convince me, Caitlin."

"I'm not trying to convince you of anything. I've been in love with Paul for nearly a year. Once he realises he loves me too, we'll be married."

Joe's mouth slanted in a wry line and he seemed about to argue with her. Cait waylaid any attempt by glancing pointedly at her watch. "Shouldn't we be leaving?"

After a long moment, Joe said, "Yes, I suppose we should," in a mild, neutral voice.

Cait went to the hall cupboard for her coat, aware with every step she took that Joe was watching her. She turned back to smile at him, but somehow the smile didn't materialise. His blue eyes met hers, and she found his look disturbing—caressing, somehow, and intimate.

Joe helped her on with her coat and led her to the car park, where he'd left his car. Another surprise awaited her. It wasn't a four-wheel-drive truck, but a late sixties black convertible in mint condition.

The restaurant was one of the most respected in Seattle, with a noted chef and a reputation for excellent seafood. Cait chose grilled salmon and Joe ordered Cajun shrimp.

"Do you remember the time Martin and I decided to open our own business?" Joe asked, as they sipped a pre-dinner glass of wine.

Cait did indeed recall that summer. "You might have been a bit more ingenious. A lemonade stand wasn't the world's most creative enterprise."

"Perhaps not, but we were doing a brisk business until an annoying eight-year-old girl ruined everything."

Cait wasn't about to let that comment pass. "You were using mouldy lemons and covering the taste with too much sugar. Besides, it's unhealthy to share paper cups."

Joe chuckled, the sound deep and rich. "I should have known then you were nothing but trouble."

"It seems to me that the whole mess was your own fault. You boys wouldn't listen to me. I had to do something before someone got sick on those lemons."

"Carrying a picket sign that read 'Talk to me before you buy this lemonade' was a bit drastic even for you, don't you think?"

"If anything, it brought you more business." Cait said drily, recalling how her plan had backfired. "All the boys in the neighbourhood wanted to see what contaminated lemonade tasted like."

"You were a damn nuisance, Cait. Own up to it." He smiled and Cait sincerely doubted that any woman could argue with him when he smiled full-force.

"I most certainly was not! If anything you two were—"

"Disgusting, I believe, was your favourite word for Martin and me."

"And you did your level best to live up to it," she said, struggling to hold back a smile. She reached for a breadstick and bit into it to disguise her amusement. She'd always enjoyed rankling Martin and Joe, though she'd never have admitted it, especially at the age of eight.

"Picketing our lemonade stand wasn't the worst trick you ever pulled, either," Joe said mischievously.

Cait had trouble swallowing. She should have been prepared for this. If he remembered her complaints about the lemonade stand, he was sure to remember what had happened once Betsy McDonald found out about the kissing incident.

"It wasn't a trick," Cait protested.

"But you told everyone at school that I'd kissed you—even though you'd promised not to."

"Not exactly." There was a small discrepancy that needed clarification. "If you think back you'll remember you said I couldn't tell anyone I'd been inside the fort. You didn't say anything about the kiss."

Joe frowned darkly as if attempting to jog his memory. "How can you remember details like that? All this happened years ago."

"I remember everything," Cait said grandly—a gross exaggeration. She hadn't recognised Joe, after all. But on this one point she was absolutely clear. "You and Martin were far more concerned that I not tell anyone about going inside the fort. You didn't say a word about keeping the kiss a secret."

"But did you have to tell Betsy McDonald? That girl had been making eyes at me for weeks. As soon as she learned I'd kissed you instead of her, she was furious."

"Betsy was the most popular girl in school. I wanted her for my friend, so I told."

"And sold me down the river."

"Would an apology help?" Confident he was teasing her once again, Cait gave him her most charming smile.

"An apology just might do it." Joe grinned back, a grin that brightened his eyes to a deeper, more tantalising shade of blue. It was with some difficulty that Cait pulled her gaze away from his.

"If Betsy liked you," she asked, smoothing the linen napkin across her lap, "then why didn't you kiss her? She'd probably have let you. You wouldn't have had to bribe her with your precious baseball cards, either."

"You're kidding. If I kissed Betsy McDonald I might as well have signed over my soul," Joe said, continuing the joke.

"Even as mere children, men are afraid of commitment," Cait said solemnly.

Joe ignored her comment.

"Your memory's not as sharp as you think," Cait felt obliged to tell him, enjoying herself more than she'd thought possible.

Once again, Joe overlooked her comment. "I can remember Martin complaining about how you'd line up your dolls in a row and teach them school. Once you even got him to come in as a guest lecturer. Heaven knew what you had to do to get him to play professor to a bunch of dolls."

"I found a pair of dirty jeans stuffed under the sofa with something dead in the pocket. Mom would have tanned his hide if she'd found them, so Martin owed me a favour. Then he got all bent out of shape when I collected it. He didn't seem the least bit appreciative that I'd saved him."

"Good old Martin," Joe said, shaking his head. "I swear he was as big on ceremony as you were. Marrying us was a turning point in his life. From that point on, he started carting a Bible around with him the way some kids do a slingshot. Right in his hip pocket. If he wasn't burying something, he was holding revival meetings. Remember how he got in a pack of trouble at school for writing 'God loves you, ask Martin' on the back wall of the school?"

"I remember."

"I half expected him to become a missionary."

"Martin?" She gave an abrupt laugh. "Never. He likes his conveniences. He doesn't even go camping. Martin's idea of roughing it is doing without valet service."

She expected Joe to chuckle. He did smile at her attempted joke, but that was all. He seemed to be studying her the same way she'd been studying him.

"You surprise me," Joe announced suddenly.

"I do? Am I a disappointment to you?"

"Not in the least. I always thought you'd grow up and have a passel of children yourself. You used to haul those dolls of yours around with you everywhere. If Martin and I were too noisy, you'd shush us, saying the babies were asleep. If we wanted to play in the backyard, we couldn't because you were having a tea party with your dolls. It was enough to drive a ten-year-old boy crazy. But if we ever dared complain, you'd look at us serenely and with the sweetest smile tell us we had to be patient because it was for the children."

"I did get carried away with all that motherhood business, didn't I?" Joe's words stirred up uncomfortable memories, the same ones she'd entertained earlier that afternoon. She really did love children. Yet, somehow, without her quite knowing how it had happened, the years had passed and she'd buried the dream. Nowadays she didn't like to think too much about a husband and family—the life that hadn't happened. It haunted her at odd moments.

"I should have known you'd end up in construction," she said, switching the subject away from herself.

"How's that?" Joe asked.

"Wasn't it you who built the fort?"

"Martin helped."

"Sure, by staying out of the way." She grinned. "I know my brother. He's a marvel with people, but please don't ever give him a hammer."

Their dinner arrived, and it was as delicious as Cait had expected, although by then she was enjoying herself so much that even a plateful of dry toast would have tasted good. They drank two cups of cappuccino after their meal, and talked and laughed as the hours melted away. Cait couldn't remember the last time she'd laughed so much.

When at last she happened to glance at her watch, she was shocked to realise it was well past ten. "I had no idea it was so late!" she said. "I should probably get home." She had to be up by five.

Joe took care of the bill and collected her coat. When they walked outside, the December night was clear and chilly, with a multitude of stars twinkling brightly above.

"Are you cold?" he asked as they waited for the valet to deliver the car.

"Not at all." Nevertheless, he placed his arm around her shoulders, drawing her close.

Cait didn't protest. It felt natural for this man to hold her close.

His car arrived and they drove back to her apartment building in silence. When he pulled into the car park, she considered inviting him inside for coffee, then decided against it. They'd already drunk enough coffee, and besides, they both had to work the following morning. But more important, Joe might read something else into the invitation. He was an old friend. Nothing more. And she wanted to keep it that way.

She turned to him and smiled softly. "I had a lovely time. Thank you so much."

"You're welcome, Cait. We'll do it again."

Cait was astonished to realise how appealing another evening with Joseph Rockwell was. She'd underestimated him.

Or had she?

"There's something else I'd like to try again," he was saying, his eyes filled with devilry.

"Try again?"

He slid his arm behind her and for a breathless moment they looked at each other. "I don't know if I've got a chance without trading a few baseball cards, though."

Cait swallowed. "You want to kiss me?"

He nodded. His eyes seemed to grow darker, more intense. "For old times' sake." His hand caressed the curve of her neck, his thumb moving slowly towards the scented hollow of her throat.

"Well, sure. For old times' sake." She was amazed at the way her heart was reacting to the thought of Joe holding her ... kissing her.

His mouth began a slow descent towards hers, his warm breath nuzzling her skin.

"Just remember," she whispered when his mouth was about to settle over hers. Her hands gripped his lapels. "Old times'..."

"I'll remember," he said as his lips came down on hers.

She sighed and slid her hands up his solid chest to link her fingers at the base of his neck. The kiss was slow and thorough. When it was over, Cait's hands were clenching his collar.

Joe's fingers were in her hair, tangled in the short, soft curls, cradling the back of her head.

A sweet rush of joy coursed through her veins. Cait felt a bubbling excitement, a burst of warmth, unlike anything she'd ever known before.

Then he kissed her a second time ...

"Just remember..." she repeated when he pulled his mouth from hers and buried it in the delicate curve of her neck.

He drew in several ragged breaths before asking, "What is it I'm supposed to remember?"

"Yes, oh, please, remember."

He lifted his head and rested his hands lightly on her shoulders, his face only inches from hers. "What's so important you don't want me to forget?'' he whispered.

It wasn't Joe who was supposed to remember; it was Cait. She didn't realise she'd spoken out loud. She blinked, uncertain, then tilted her head to gaze down at her hands, anywhere but at him. ''Oh...that I'm in love with Paul.''

There was a moment of silence. An awkward moment. ''Right,'' he answered shortly. ''You're in love with Paul.'' His arms fell away and he released her.

Cait hesitated, uneasy. ''Thanks again for a wonderful dinner.'' Her hand closed around the door handle. She was eager now to make her escape.

''Any time,'' he said flippantly. His own hands gripped the steering wheel.

''I'll see you soon.''

''Soon,'' he repeated. She climbed out of the car, not giving Joe a chance to come around and open the door for her. She was aware of him sitting in the car, waiting until she'd unlocked the lobby door and stepped inside. She hurried down the first-floor hall and into her apartment, turning on the lights so he'd know she'd made it safely home.

Then she slowly removed her coat and carefully hung it in the cupboard. When she peeked out of the window, she noticed that Joe had already left.

LINDY WAS AT HER DESK working when Cait arrived the next morning. Cait smiled at her as she hurried past, but didn't stop to indulge in conversation.

Cait could feel Lindy's gaze trailing after her and she knew her friend was disappointed that she hadn't told her about the dinner date with Joe Rockwell.

Cait didn't want to talk about it. She was afraid that if she said anything to Lindy, she wouldn't be able to avoid mentioning the kiss, which was a subject she wanted to avoid at all costs. She wouldn't be able to delay her friend's questions forever, but Cait wanted to put them off until at least the end of the day. Longer, if possible.

What a fool she'd been to let Joe kiss her. It had seemed so right at the time, a natural conclusion to a delightful evening.

The fact that she'd let him do it without even making a token protest still confused her. If Paul was to hear of it, he might think she really *was* interested in Joe. Which, of course, she wasn't.

Her boss was a man of principle and integrity—and altogether a frustrating person to fall in love with. Judging by his reaction to her dinner with Joe, he seemed immune to jealousy. Now if only she could discover a way of letting him know how she felt...and spark his interest in the process!

The morning was hectic. Out of the corner of her eye, Cait saw Joe arrive. Although she was speaking to an important client on the phone, she stared after him as he approached the burly foreman. She watched Joe remove a blueprint from a long, narrow tube and roll it open so two other men could study it. There seemed to be some discussion, then the foreman nodded and Joe left, without so much as glancing in Cait's direction.

That stung.

At least he could have waved hello. But if he wanted to ignore her, well, fine. She'd do the same.

The market closed on the up side, the Dow Jones industrial average at 2600 points after brisk trading. The day's work was over.

As Cait had predicted, Lindy sought her out almost immediately.

"So how'd your dinner date go?"

"It was fun."

"Where'd he take you? Sam's Bar and Grill, the way you thought?"

"Actually, no," she said, clearing her throat, feeling more than a little foolish for having suggested such a thing.' "He took me to Henry's." She announced it louder than necessary, since Paul was strolling into the office just then. But for all the notice he gave her, she might as well have been fresh paint drying on the company wall.

"Henry's," Lindy echoed. "He took you to Henry's? Why, that's one of the best restaurants in town. It must have cost him a small fortune."

"I wouldn't know. My menu didn't list any prices."

"You're joking. No one's ever taken me anyplace so fancy. What did you order?"

"Grilled salmon." She continued to study Paul for some clue that he was listening in on her and Lindy's conversation. He was seated at his desk, reading a report on short-term partnerships as a tax advantage. Cait had read it earlier in the week and had recommended it to him.

"Was it wonderful?" Lindy pressed.

It took Cait a moment to realise her friend was quizzing her about the dinner. "Excellent. The best fish I've had in years."

"What did you do afterward?"

Cait looked back at her friend. "What makes you think we did anything? We had dinner, talked, and then he drove me home. Nothing more happened. Understand? Nothing."

"If you say so," Lindy said, eyeing her suspiciously. "But you're certainly defensive about it."

"I just want you to know that nothing happened. Joseph Rockwell is an old friend. That's all."

Paul glanced up from the report, but his gaze connected with Lindy's before slowly progressing to Cait.

"Hello, Paul," Cait greeted him cheerfully. "Are Lindy and I disturbing you? We'd be happy to go into the hallway if you'd like."

"No, no, you're fine. Don't worry about it." He glanced past them to the doorway and got to his feet. "Hello, Rockwell."

"Am I interrupting a meeting?" Joe asked, stepping into the office as if it didn't really matter whether he was or not. His hard hat was back in place, along with the dusty jeans and the tool pouch. And yet Cait had no difficulty remembering last night's sophisticated dinner companion when she looked at him.

"No, no," Paul answered, "we were just chatting. Come on in. Problems?"

"Not really. But there's something I'd like you to take a look at in the other room."

"I'll be right there."

Joe threw Cait a cool smile as he strolled past. "Hello, Cait."

"Joe." Her heart was pounding hard, and that was ridiculous. It must have been due to embarrassment, she told herself. Joe was a friend, a boy from the old neighbourhood; just because she'd allowed him to kiss her, it didn't mean there was—or ever would be—anything romantic between them. The sooner she made him understand this, the better.

"Joe and Cait went out to dinner last night," Lindy said pointedly to Paul. "He took her to Henry's."

"How nice," Paul commented, clearly more interested in troubleshooting with Joe than discussing Cait's dating history.

"We had a good time, didn't we?" Joe asked Cait.

"Yes, very nice," she responded stiffly.

Joe waited until Paul was out of the room before he stepped back and dropped a kiss on her cheek. Then he announced loudly enough for everyone in the vicinity to hear, "You were incredible last night."

CHAPTER FOUR

"I THOUGHT YOU SAID nothing happened," Lindy said, looking intently at a red-faced Cait.

"Nothing did happen." Cait was furious enough to kick Joe Rockwell in the shins the way he deserved. How dared he say something so... so embarrassing in front of Lindy! And probably within earshot of Paul!

"But why would he say something like that?"

"How should I know?" Cait snapped. "One little kiss and he makes it sound like—"

"He kissed you?" Lindy asked sharply, her eyes narrowing. "You just got done telling me there's nothing between the two of you."

"Good grief, the kiss didn't mean anything. It was for old times' sake. Just a platonic little kiss." All right, she was exaggerating a bit, but it couldn't be helped.

While Cait was speaking, she gathered her things and shoved them in her briefcase. Then she slammed the lid closed and reached for her coat, thrusting her arms into the sleeves, her movements abrupt and ungraceful.

"Have a nice weekend," she said tightly, not completely understanding why she felt so annoyed with Lindy. "I'll see you Monday." She marched through the office, but paused in front of Joe.

"You wanted something, sweetheart?' he asked in a cajoling voice.

"You're despicable!"

Joe looked downright disappointed. "Not low and disgusting?"

"That, too."

He grinned ear to ear just the way she knew he would. "I'm glad to hear it."

Cait bit back an angry retort. It wouldn't do any good to engage in a verbal battle with Joe Rockwell. He'd have a comeback for any insult she could hurl. Seething, Cait marched to the lift and jabbed the button impatiently.

"I'll be by later tonight, darling," Joe called to her just as the doors were closing, effectively cutting off any protest from her.

He was joking. He had to be joking. No man in his right mind could possibly expect her to invite him into her home after this latest stunt. Not even the impertinent Joe Rockwell.

Once home, Cait took a long, soothing shower, dried her hair and changed into jeans and a sweater. Friday nights were generally quiet ones for her. She was munching on pretzels and surveying the bleak contents of her refrigerator when there was a knock on the door.

It couldn't possibly be Joe, she told herself.

It was Joe, balancing a large pizza on the palm of one hand and clutching a bottle of red wine in the other.

Cait stared at him, too dumbfounded at his audacity to speak.

"I come bearing gifts," he said, presenting the pizza to her with more than a little ceremony.

"Listen here, you . . . you fool, it's going to take a whole lot more than pizza to make up for that stunt you pulled this afternoon."

"Come on, Cait, lighten up a little."

"Lighten up! You . . . you . . ."

"I believe the word you're looking for is fool."

"You have your nerve." She dug her fists into her hips, knowing she should slam the door in his face. She would have, too, but the pizza smelled *so* good it was difficult to maintain her indignation.

"Okay, I'll admit it," Joe said, his deep blue eyes revealing genuine contrition. "I got carried away. You're right, I am an idiot. All I can do is ask your forgiveness." He lifted the lid of the pizza box and Cait was confronted by the thickest, most mouth-watering masterpiece she'd ever seen. The top was crowded with no less than ten tempting toppings, all covered with a thick layer of hot melted cheese.

"Do you accept my humble apology?" Joe pressed, waving the pizza under her nose.

"Are there any anchovies on that thing?"

"Only on half."

"You're forgiven." She took him by the elbow and dragged him inside her apartment.

Cait led the way into the kitchen. She got two plates from the cupboard and collected knives, forks and napkins as she mentally reviewed his crimes. "I couldn't believe you actually said that," she mumbled, shaking her head. She set the kitchen table, neatly positioning the napkins after shoving the day's mail to one side. "The least you could do is tell me why you found it necessary to say that in front of Paul. Lindy had already started grilling me. Can you imagine what she and Paul must think now?" She retrieved two wineglasses from the cupboard and set them by the plates. "I've never been more embarrassed in my life."

"Never?" he prompted, opening and closing her kitchen drawers until he located a corkscrew.

"Never," she repeated. "And don't think a pizza's going to ensure lasting peace."

"I wouldn't dream of it."

"It's a start, but you're going to owe me a good long time for this prank, Joseph Rockwell."

"I'll be good," he promised, his eyes twinkling. He agilely removed the cork, tested the wine and then filled both glasses.

Cait jerked out a wicker-back chair and threw herself down. "Did Paul say anything after I left?"

"About what?" Joe slid out a chair and joined her.

Cait had already dished up a thick slice for each of them, fastidiously using a knife to disconnect the strings of melted cheese that stretched from the box to their plates.

"About me, of course," she growled.

Joe handed her a glass of wine. "Not really."

Cait paused and lifted her eyes to his. "Not really? What does that mean?"

"Only that he didn't say much about you."

Joe was taunting her, dangling bits and pieces of information, waiting for her reaction. She should have known better than to trust him, but she was so anxious to find out what Paul had said that she ignored her pride. "Tell me everything he said," she demanded, "word for word."

Joe had a mouthful of pizza and Cait was left to wait several moments until he swallowed. "I seem to recall he said something about your explaining that the two of us go back a long way."

Cait straightened, too curious to hide her interest. "Did he look concerned? Jealous?"

"Paul? No, if anything, he looked bored."

"Bored," Cait repeated. Her shoulders sagged with defeat. "I swear that man wouldn't notice me if I pranced around his office naked."

"That's a clever idea, and one that just might work. Maybe you should practice around the house first, get the hang of it. I'd be willing to help you out if you're really serious about this." He sounded utterly nonchalant, as though she'd suggested subscribing to cable television. "This is what friends are for. Do you need help undressing?"

Cait took a sip from her wine to hide a smile. Joe hadn't changed in twenty years. He was still witty and fun-loving and a terrible tease. "Very funny."

"Hey, I wasn't kidding. I'll pretend I'm Paul and—"

"You promised you were going to be good."

He wiggled his eyebrows suggestively. "I will be. Just you wait."

Cait could feel the tide of colour flow into her cheeks. She quickly lowered her eyes to her plate. "Joe, cut it out. You're making me blush and I hate to blush. My face looks like a ripe tomato." She lifted her slice of pizza and bit into it, chewing thoughtfully. "I don't understand you. Every time I think I have you figured out you do something to surprise me.''

"Like what?"

"Like yesterday. You invited me to dinner, but I never dreamed you'd take me someplace as elegant as Henry's. You were the perfect gentleman all evening and then today, you were so . . ."

"Low and disgusting."

"Exactly." She nodded righteously. "One minute you're the picture of charm and culture and the next you're badgering me with your wisecracks."

"I'm a tease, remember?"

"The problem is that I can't deal with you when I don't know what to expect."

"That's my charm." He reached for a second piece of pizza. "Women are said to adore the unexpected in a man."

"Not this woman," she informed him promptly. "I need to know where I stand with you."

"A little to the left."

"Joe, please, I'm not joking. I can't have you pulling stunts like you did today. I've lived a good, clean life for the past twenty-eight years. Two days with you has ruined my reputation with the company. I can't walk into the office and hold my head up any longer. I hear people whispering and I know they're talking about me."

"Us," he corrected. "They're talking about us."

"That's even worse. If they want to talk about me and a man, I'd rather it was Paul. Just how much longer is this remodelling project going to take, anyway?" As far as Cait was concerned, the sooner Joe and his renegade crew were out of her office, the sooner her life would settle back to normal.

"Not too much longer."

"At the rate you're progressing, Webster, Rodale and Missen will have offices on the moon."

"Before the end of the year, I promise."

"Yes, but just how reliable are your promises?"

"I'm being good, aren't I?"

"I suppose," she conceded ungraciously, jerking a stack of mail away from Joe as he started to sort through it.

"What's this?" Joe asked, rescuing a single piece of paper before it fluttered to the floor.

"A Christmas list. I'm going shopping tomorrow."

"I should have known you'd be organised about that, too." He sounded vaguely insulting.

"I've been organised all my life. It isn't likely to change now."

"That's why I want you to lighten up a little." He continued studying her list. "What time are you going?"

"The stores open at eight and I plan to be there then."

"I suppose you've written down everything you need to buy so you won't forget anything."

"Of course."

"Sounds sensible." His remark surprised her. He scanned her list, then yelped, "Hey, I'm not on here!" He withdrew a pen from his shirt pocket and added his own name. "Do you want me to give you a few suggestions on what I'd like?"

"I already know what I'm getting you."

Joe arched his brows. "You do? And please don't say 'nothing.'"

"No, but it'll be something appropriate—like a muzzle."

"Oh, Caitlin, darling, you injure me." He gave her one of his devilishly handsome smiles, and Cait could feel herself weakening. Just what she didn't want! She had every right to be angry with Joe. If he hadn't brought that pizza, she'd have slammed the door in his face. Wouldn't she? Sure, she would! But she'd always been susceptible to Italian food. Her only other fault was Paul. She did love him. No one seemed to believe that, but she'd known almost from the moment they'd met that she was destined to spend the rest of her life loving Paul Jamison. Only she'd rather do it as his wife than his employee!

"Have you finished your shopping?" she asked idly, making small talk with Joe since he seemed determined to hang around.

"I haven't started. I have good intentions every year, you know, like I'll get a head start on finding the perfect gifts for my nieces and nephews, but they never work out. Usually panic sets in Christmas Eve and I tear around the stores like mad and buy everything in sight. Last year I forgot wrapping paper. My mother saved the day."

"I doubt it'd do any good to suggest you get organised."

"I haven't got the time."

"What are you doing right now? Write out your list, stick to it and make the time to go shopping."

"My darling Cait, is this an invitation for me to join you tomorrow?"

"Uh . . ." Cait hadn't intended it to be, but she supposed she couldn't object as long as he behaved himself. "You're welcome on one condition."

"Name it."

"No jokes, no stunts like you pulled today and absolutely no teasing. If you announce to a single person that we're married, I'm walking away from you and that's a promise."

"You've got it." He raised his hand, then ceremoniously crossed his heart.

"Lick your fingertips first," Cait demanded. The instant the words were out of her mouth, she realised how ridiculous she sounded, as if they were eight and ten all over again. "Forget I said that."

His eyes were twinkling as he stood to deliver his plate to the sink. "I swear it's a shame you're so in love with Paul," he told her. "If I'm not careful, I could fall for you myself." With that, he kissed her on the cheek and let himself out of the door.

Pressing her fingers to her cheek, Cait drew in a deep, shuddering breath and held it until she heard the door close. Then and only then did it seep out in ragged bursts, as if she'd forgotten how to breathe normally.

"Oh, Joe," she whispered. The last thing she wanted was for Joe to fall in love with her. Not that he wasn't handsome and sweet and wonderful. He was. He always had been. He just wasn't for her. Their personalities were poles apart. Joe was unpredictable, always doing the unexpected, whereas Cait's life ran like clockwork.

She liked Joe. She almost wished she didn't, but she couldn't help herself. However, a steady diet of his pranks would soon drive her into the nearest asylum.

Standing, Cait closed the pizza box and tucked the uneaten portion into the top shelf of her refrigerator. She was putting the dirty plates in her dishwasher when the phone rang. She quickly washed her hands and reached for it.

"Hello."

"Cait, it's Paul."

Cait was so startled that the receiver slipped out of her hand. Grabbing for it, she nearly stumbled over the open dishwasher door, knocking her shin against the sharp edge. She yelped and swallowed a cry as she jerked the dangling phone cord towards her.

"Sorry, sorry," she cried, once she'd rescued the telephone receiver. "Paul? Are you still there?"

"Yes, I'm here. Is this a bad time? I could call back later if this is inconvenient. You don't have company, do you? I wouldn't want to interrupt a party or anything."

"Oh, no, now is perfect. I didn't realise you had my home number...but obviously you do. After all, we've been working together for nearly a year now." Eleven months and four days, not that she was counting or anything. "Naturally my number would be in the personnel file."

He hesitated and Cait bent over to rub her shin where it had collided with the dishwasher door. She was sure to have an ugly bruise, but a bruised leg was a small price to pay. Paul had phoned her!

"The reason I'm calling..."

"Yes, Paul," she prompted when he didn't immediately continue.

The silence lengthened before he blurted out, "I just wanted to thank you for passing on that article on the tax advantages of limited partnerships. It was thoughtful of you and I appreciate it."

"Any time. I read quite a lot in that area, you know. There are several recent articles on the same subject. If you'd like, I could bring them in next week."

"Sure. That would be fine. Thanks again, Cait. Goodbye."

The line was disconnected before Cait could say anything else and she was left holding the receiver. A smile came, slow and confident, and with a small cry of triumph, she tossed the telephone receiver into the air, caught it behind her back and replaced it with a flourish.

CAIT WAS DRESSED and waiting for Joe early the next morning. "Joe," she cried, throwing open her apartment door, "I could just kiss you."

He was dressed in faded jeans and a hip-length bronze-coloured leather jacket. "Hey, I'm not stopping you," he said, opening his arms.

Cait ignored the invitation. "Paul phoned me last night." She didn't even try to contain her excitement; she felt like leaping and skipping and singing out loud.

"Paul did?" Joe sounded surprised.

"Yes. It was shortly after you left. He thanked me for giving him an interesting article I found in one of the business journals and—this is the good part—he asked if I was alone...as if it really mattered to him."

"If you were alone?" Joe repeated, and frowned. "What's that got to do with anything?"

"Don't you understand?" For all his intelligence Joe could be pretty obtuse, sometimes. "He wanted to know if *you* were here with me. I makes sense, doesn't it? Paul's jealous, only he doesn't realise it yet. Oh, Joe, I can't remember ever being this happy. Not in years and years and years."

"Because Paul Jamison phoned?"

"Don't sound so sceptical. It's exactly the break I've been looking for all these months. Paul's finally noticed me and it's all thanks to you."

"At least you're willing to give credit where credit is due." But he still didn't seem particularly thrilled.

"It's just so incredible," she continued. "I don't think I slept a wink last night. There was something in his voice that I've never heard before. Something...deep and personal. I don't know how to explain it. For the first time in a whole year, Paul knows I'm alive!"

"Are we going Christmas shopping or not?" Joe demanded brusquely. "Damn it all, Cait, I never expected you to go soft over a stupid phone call."

"But this wasn't just any call," she reminded him. She reached for her purse and her coat in one sweeping motion. "This call was from *Paul.*"

"You sound like a silly schoolgirl." Joe frowned, but Cait wasn't about to let his short temper destroy her mood. Paul had phoned her at home and she was sure that this was the beginning of a *real* relationship. Next he'd ask her out for lunch, and then...

They left her apartment and walked down the hall, Cait grinning all the way. Standing just outside the front doors was a huge truck with gigantic wheels. Just the type of vehicle she'd expected him to drive the night he'd taken her to Henry's.

"This is your truck?" she asked when they were outside. She was unable to keep the laughter out of her voice.

"Is there something wrong with it?"

"Not a single thing, but Joe, honestly, you are so predictable."

"That's not what you said yesterday."

She grinned as he opened the truck door, set down a stool for her and helped her climb into the cab. The seat was cluttered, but so wide she was able to shove everything to one side. When she'd made room for herself, she fastened the seatbelt, snapping it jauntily in place. She was so happy, the whole world seemed delightful this morning.

"Will you quit smiling before someone suggests you've been overdosing on vitamins?" Joe grumbled.

"My, aren't we testy this morning."

"Where to?" he asked, starting the engine.

"Any of the big shopping malls will do. You decide. Do you have your list all made out?"

Joe patted his heart. "It's in my shirt pocket."

"Good."

"Have you decided what you're going to buy for whom?"

His smile was slightly off kilter. "Not exactly. I thought I'd follow you around and buy whatever you did. Do you know what you're getting your mother? Mine's damn difficult to buy for. Last year I ended up getting her cat food. She's got five cats of her own and God only knows how many strays she's feeding."

"At least your idea was practical."

"Well, there's that, and the fact that by the time I started my Christmas shopping the only store open was a supermarket."

Cait laughed. "Honestly, Joe!"

"Hey, I was desperate and before you get all righteous on me, Mom thought the cat food and the two rib roasts were great gifts."

"I'm sure she did," Cait returned, grinning. She found herself doing a lot of that when she was with Joe. Imagine buying his mother rib roasts for Christmas!

"Give me some ideas, would you? Mom's a hard case."

"To be honest, I'm not all that imaginative myself. I buy my mother the same thing every year."

"What is it?"

"Long-distance phone coupons. That way she can phone her sister in Dubuque and her high-school friend in Olathe, Kansas. Of course she calls me every now and again, too."

"Okay, that takes care of Mom. What about Martin? What are you buying him?"

"A bronze eagle." She'd decided on that gift last summer when she'd attended Sunday services at Martin's church. In the opening part of his sermon, Martin had used eagles to illustrate a point of faith.

"An eagle," Joe repeated. "Any special reason?"

"Y-yes," she said, not wanting to explain. "It's a long story, but I happen to be partial to eagles myself."

"Any other hints you'd care to pass on?"

"Buy wrapping paper in the after-Christmas sales. It's about half the price and it stores easily under the bed."

"Great idea. I'll have to remember that for next year."

Joe chose Northgate, the shopping mall closest to Cait's apartment. The car park was already beginning to fill up and it was only a few minutes after eight.

Joe managed to park fairly close to the entrance and came around to help Cait out of the truck. This time he didn't bother with the step stool, but gripped her around the waist to lift her down. "What did you mean when you said I was so predictable?" he asked, giving her a reproachful look.

With her hands resting on his shoulders and her feet dangling in mid-air, she felt vulnerable and small. "Nothing. It was just that I assumed you drove one of those Sherman-tank trucks, and I was right. I just hadn't seen it before."

"The kind of truck I drive bothers you?" His brow furrowed in a scowl.

"Not at all. What's the matter with you today, Joe? You're so touchy."

"I am not touchy," he snapped.

"Fine. Would you mind putting me down, then?" His large hands were squeezing her waist almost painfully, though she doubted he was aware of it. She couldn't imagine what had angered him. Unless it was the fact that Paul had called her—which didn't make sense. Maybe, like most men, he just hated shopping.

He lowered her slowly to the asphalt and released her with seeming reluctance. "I need a coffee break," he announced grimly.

"But we just arrived."

Joe forcefully expelled his breath. "It doesn't matter. I need something to calm my nerves."

If he needed a caffeine fix so early in the day, Cait wondered how he'd manage during the next few hours. The shops became quickly crowded this time of year, especially on a Saturday. By ten it would be nearly impossible to get from one aisle to the next.

By twelve, she knew: Joe disliked Christmas shopping every bit as much as she'd expected.

"I've had it," Joe complained after making three separate trips back to the truck to deposit their spoils.

"Me, too," Cait agreed laughingly. "This place is turning into a madhouse."

"How about some lunch?" Joe suggested. "Some place far away from here. Like Tibet."

Cait laughed again and tucked her arm in his. "That sounds like a great idea."

Outside, they noticed several cars circling the car park looking for a parking space and three of them rushed to fill the one Joe vacated. Two cars nearly collided in their eagerness. One man leapt out of his and shook an angry fist at the other driver.

"So much for peace and goodwill," Joe commented. "I swear Christmas brings out the worst in everyone."

"And the best," Cait reminded him.

"To be honest, I don't know what crammed shopping malls and fighting the crowds and all this commercialism have to do with Christmas in the first place," he grumbled. A car cut in front of him, and Joe blared his horn.

"Quite a lot when you think about it," Cait said softly. "Imagine the streets of Bethlehem, the crowds and the noise..." The Christmas before, fresh from a shopping expedition, Cait had asked herself the same question. Christmas seemed so commercial. The crowds had been unbearable. First at Northgate, where she did most of her shopping and then at the airport. Sea-Tac had been filled with activity and noise, everyone in a hurry to get someplace or another. There seemed to be little peace or good cheer and a whole lot of selfish concern and rudeness. Then, in the tranquillity of church on Christmas Eve, everything had come into perspective for Cait. There had been crowds and rudeness that first Christmas, too, she reasoned. Yet in the midst of that confusion had come joy and peace and love. For most people, it was still the same. Christmas gifts and decorations and dinners were, after all, expressions of the love you felt for your family and friends. And if the preparations sometimes got a bit chaotic, well, that no longer bothered Cait.

"Where should we go to eat?" Joe asked, breaking into her thoughts. They were barely moving, stuck in heavy traffic.

She looked over at him and smiled serenely. "Any place will do. There're several excellent restaurants close by. You choose, only let it be my treat this time."

"We'll talk about who pays later. Right now, I'm more concerned with getting out of this traffic sometime within my life span."

Still smiling, Cait said, "I don't think it'll take much longer."

He returned her smile. "I don't, either." His eyes held hers for what seemed an eternity—until someone behind them honked irritably. Joe glanced up and saw that traffic ahead of them had started to move. He immediately stepped on the accelerator.

Cait didn't know what Joe had found so fascinating about her unless it was her unruly hair. She hadn't combed it since leaving the house; it was probably a mass of tight, disorderly curls. She'd been so concerned with finding the right gift for her nephews and niece that she hadn't given it a thought.

"What's wrong?" she asked, feeling self-conscious.

"What makes you think anything's wrong?"

"The way you were looking at me a few minutes ago."

"Oh, that," he said easing, into a restaurant car park. "I don't think I've ever fully appreciated how lovely you are," he answered in a calm, matter-of-fact voice.

Cait blushed and looked away. "I'm sure you're mistaken. I'm really not all that pretty. I sometimes wondered if Paul would have noticed me sooner if I was a little more attractive."

"Trust me, Bright Eyes," he said, turning off the engine. "You're pretty enough."

"For what?"

"For this." And he leaned across the seat and captured her mouth with his.

CHAPTER FIVE

"I . . . WISH YOU HADN'T done that," Cait whispered, slowly opening her eyes in an effort to pull herself back to reality.

As far as kisses went, Joe's were good. Very good. He kissed better than just about anyone she'd ever kissed before—but that didn't alter the fact that she was in love with Paul.

"You're right," he muttered, opening the door and climbing out of the cab. "I shouldn't have done that." He walked around to her side and yanked the door open with more force than necessary.

Cait frowned, wondering at his strange mood. One minute he was holding her in his arms, kissing her tenderly; the next he was short-tempered and irritable.

"I'm hungry," he barked, lifting her abruptly down onto the pavement. "I sometimes do irrational things when I haven't eaten."

"I see." The next time she went anywhere with Joseph Rockwell, she'd have to be certain he ate a good meal first.

The restaurant was crowded and Joe gave the receptionist their names to add to the growing waiting list. Sitting on the last empty chair in the foyer, Cait set her large black leather bag on her lap and started rooting through it.

"What are you looking for? Uranium?" Joe teased, watching her.

"Crackers," she answered, shifting the bulky bag and handing him several items to hold while she continued digging.

"You're looking for crackers? Whatever for?"

She glanced up long enough to give him a look that questioned his intelligence. "For obvious reasons. If you're irrational when you're hungry, you might do something stupid while we're here. Frankly, I don't want you to embarrass me." She returned to the task with renewed vigour. "I can just see you standing on top of the table tap-dancing."

"That's one way to gain the waiter's attention. Thanks for suggesting it."

"Aha!" Triumphantly Cait pulled two miniature bread sticks wrapped in cellophane from the bottom of her bag. "Eat," she instructed. "Before you're overcome by some other craziness."

"You mean before I kiss you again," he said in a low voice, bending his head towards hers.

She leaned back quickly, not giving him any chance of following through on that. "Exactly. Or waltz with the waitress or any of the other loony things you do."

"You have to admit I've been good all morning."

"With one minor slip," she reminded him, pressing the bread sticks into his hand. "Now eat."

Before Joe had a chance to open the package, the hostess approached then with two menus tucked under her arm. "Mr. and Mrs. Rockwell. Your table is ready."

"Mr. and Mrs. Rockwell," Cait muttered under her breath, glaring at Joe. She should have known she couldn't trust him.

"Excuse me, miss," Cait said, standing abruptly and raising her index finger. "His name is Rockwell, mine is Marshall," she explained patiently. She was not about to let Joe continue his silly games. "We're just friends here for lunch." Her narrowed eyes caught Joe's, which looked as innocent as freshly fallen snow. He shrugged as though to say any misunderstanding hadn't been *his* fault.

"I see," the hostess replied. "I'm sorry for the confusion."

"No problem." Cait hadn't wanted to make a big issue of this, but on the other hand she didn't want Joe to think he was going to get away with it, either.

The woman led them to a linen-covered table in the middle of the room. Joe held out Cait's chair for her and then whispered something to the hostess who immediately cast Cait a sympathetic glance. Joe's own gaze rested momentarily on Cait before he pulled out his chair and sat across from her.

"All right, what did you say to her?" she hissed.

The menu seemed to command his complete interest for a couple of minutes. "What makes you think I said anything?"

"I heard you whispering and then she gave me this pathetic look like she wanted to hug me and tell me everything was going to be all right."

"Then you know."

"Joe, don't play games with me," Cait warned.

"All right, if you must know, I explained that you'd suffered a head injury and developed amnesia."

"Amnesia," she repeated loudly enough to attract the attention of the diners at the next table. Gritting her teeth, Cait snatched up her menu, gripping it tightly enough to curl the edges. It didn't do any good to argue with Joe. The man was impossible. Every time she tried to reason with him, he did something to make her regret it.

"How else was I supposed to explain the fact you'd forgotten our marriage?" he asked reasonably.

"I did not forget our marriage," she informed him from between clenched teeth, reviewing the menu and quickly making her selection. "Good grief, it wasn't even legal."

She realised that the waitress was standing by their table, pen and pad in hand. The woman's ready smile faded as she looked from Cait to Joe and back again. Her mouth tightened as if she strongly suspected they really were involved in something illegal.

"Uh..." Cait hedged, feeling like even more of an idiot. The urge to explain was overwhelming, but every time she tried, she only made matters worse. "I'll have the club sandwich," she said, glaring across the table at Joe.

"That sounds good. I'll have the same," he said, closing his menu.

The woman scribbled down their order, then hurried away, pausing to glance over her shoulder as if she wanted to be able to identify them later in a police lineup.

"Now look what you've done," Cait whispered heatedly once the waitress was far enough away from their table not to overhear.

"Me?"

Maybe she was being unreasonable, but Joe was the one who'd started this nonsense in the first place. No one had ever got a rise out of her the way Joe did. No one could rattle her so effectively. And worse, she let him.

This shopping trip was a good example, and so was the pizza that led up to it. No woman in her right mind should have allowed Joe into her apartment after what he'd said to her in front of Lindy. Not only had she invited him inside her home, she'd agreed to let him accompany her Christmas shopping. She ought to have her head examined!

"What's wrong?" Joe asked, tearing open the package of bread sticks. Rather pointless in Cait's opinion, since their lunch would be served any minute.

"What's wrong?" she cried, dumbfounded that he had to ask. "You mean other than the hostess believing I've suffered a head injury and the waitress thinking that we're drug dealers or something equally disgusting?"

"Here." He handed her one of the miniature breadsticks. "Eat this and you'll feel better."

Cait sincerely doubted that, but she took it, anyway, muttering under her breath.

"Relax," he urged.

"Relax," she mocked. "How can I possibly relax when you're doing and saying things I find excruciatingly embarrassing?"

"I'm sorry, Cait. Really, I am." To his credit, he did look contrite. "But you're so easy to fluster and I can't seem to stop myself."

Their sandwiches arrived, thick with slices of turkey, ham and a variety of cheeses. Cait was reluctant to admit how much better she felt after she'd eaten. Joe's spirits had apparently improved, as well.

"So," he said, his hands resting on his abdomen. "What do you have planned for the rest of the afternoon?"

Cait hadn't given it much thought. "I suppose I should wrap the gifts I bought this morning." But the thought didn't particularly excite her. Good grief, after the adventures she'd had with Joe, it wasn't any wonder.

"You mean you actually wrap gifts before Christmas Eve?" Joe asked. "Doesn't that take all the fun out of it? I mean, for me it's a game just to see if I can get the presents bought."

She grinned, trying to imagine herself in such a disorganised race to the deadline. Definitely not her style.

"How about a movie?" he suggested out of the blue. "I have the feeling you don't get out enough."

"A movie?" Cait ignored the comment about her social life, mainly because he was right. She rarely took the time to go to a show.

"We're both exhausted from fighting the crowds," Joe added. "There's a six-cinema theatre next to the restaurant. I'll even let you choose."

"I suppose you'd object to a love story?"

"We can see one if you insist, only..."

"Only what?"

"Only promise me you won't ever expect a man to say the things those guys on the screen do."

"I beg your pardon?"

"You heard me. Women hear actors say this incredible drivel and then they're disappointed when real men don't."

"Real men like you, I suppose?"

"Right." He looked smug, then suddenly he frowned. "Does Paul like romances?"

Cait hadn't a clue, since she'd never gone on a date with Paul and the subject wasn't one they'd ever discussed at the office. "I imagine he does," she said, dabbing her mouth with her napkin. "He isn't the type of man to be intimidated by such things."

Joe's deep blue eyes widened with surprise and a touch of respect. "Ouch. So Martin's little sister reveals her claws."

"I don't have claws. I just happen to have strong opinions on certain subjects." She reached for her bag while she was speaking and removed her wallet.

"What are you doing now?" Joe demanded.

"Paying for lunch." She sorted through the bills and withdrew a twenty. "It's my turn and I insist on paying . . ." She hesitated when she saw Joe's deepening frown. "Or don't real men allow women friends to buy their lunch?"

"Sure, go ahead," he returned flippantly.

It was all Cait could do to hide a smile. She guessed that her gesture in paying for their sandwiches would somehow be seen as compromising his male pride.

Apparently she was right. As they were walking towards the cashier, Joe stepped up his pace, grabbed the bill from her hand and slapped some money on the counter. He glared at her as if he expected a drawn-out public argument. After the fuss they'd already caused in the restaurant, Cait was darned if she was going to let that happen.

"Joe," she argued, the minute they were out the door. "What was that all about?"

"All right, you win. Tell me my views are outdated, but when a woman goes out with me I pick up the tab, no matter how liberated she is."

"But this isn't a real date. We're only friends, and even that's—"

"I don't give a damn. Consider it an apology for the embarrassment I caused you earlier."

"You're a chauvinist, aren't you?"

"I'm not! I just have certain...standards."

"So I see." His attitude shouldn't have come as any big surprise. Just as Cait had told him earlier, he was shockingly predictable.

Hand at her elbow, Joe led the way across the car-filled car park towards the sprawling theatre complex. The movies appealed to a wide audience. There was a Disney classic showing, along with a horror flick and a couple of adventure movies and last, but not least, a well-publicised love story.

As they stood in line, Cait caught Joe's gaze lingering on the poster for one of the adventure films, yet another story about a law-and-order cop with renegade ideas.

"I suppose you're more interested in seeing that than the romance."

"I already promised you could choose the show, and I'm a man of my word. If, however, you were to pick another movie—" he buried his hands in his pockets as he grinned at her appealingly "—I wouldn't complain."

"I'm willing to pick another movie, but on one condition."

"Name it." His eyes lit up.

"I pay."

"Those claws of yours are out again."

She raised her hands and flexed her fingers in a cat-like motion. "It's your decision."

"What about popcorn?"

"You can buy that if you insist."

"All right," he said, "you've got yourself a deal."

When it was Cait's turn at the ticket window, she purchased two for the Disney classic.

"Disney?" Joe repeated, shocked when Cait handed him his ticket.

"It seemed like a good compromise," she answered.

For a moment it looked as if he was going to argue with her, then a slow grin spread across his face. "Disney," he said again. "You're right, it does sound like fun. Only I hope we're not the only ones there over the age of ten."

They sat towards the back of the theatre, sharing a large bucket of buttered popcorn. The theatre was crowded and several kids seemed to be taking turns running up and down the aisles. Joe needn't have worried; there were plenty of adults in attendance, but of course most of them were accompanying children.

The lights dimmed and Cait reached for a handful of popcorn, relaxing in her seat. "I love this movie."

"How many times have you seen it?"

"Five or six. But it's been several years now."

"Me, too." Joe relaxed beside her, crossing his long legs and leaning back.

The credits started to roll, but the noise level hadn't decreased much. "Will the kids bother you?" Joe wanted to know.

"Heavens, no. I love kids."

"You do?" The fact that he was so surprised seemed vaguely insulting and Cait stiffened.

"We've already had this discussion," she responded, licking the salt from her fingertips.

"We did? When?"

"The other day. You commented on how much I used to enjoy playing with my dolls and how you'd expected me to be married with a house full of children." His words had troubled her then, because "a house full of children" was exactly what Cait would have liked, and she seemed a long way from realising her dream.

"Ah, yes, I remember our conversation about that now." He scooped up a large handful of popcorn. "You'd be a very good mother, you know."

That Joe would say this was enough to bring an unexpected rush of tears to her eyes. She blinked them back, surprised that she'd get weepy over something so silly.

The previews were over and the audience settled down as the movie started. Cait focused her attention on the screen, munching popcorn every now and then, reaching blindly for the bucket. Their hands collided more than once and almost before she was aware of it, their fingers were entwined. It was a peaceful sort of feeling, being linked to Joe this way. There was a *rightness* about it that she didn't want to explore just yet. He hadn't really changed; he was still lovable and funny and fun. For that matter, she hadn't changed very much, either. . . .

The movie was as good as Cait remembered, better, even—perhaps because Joe was there to share it with her. She half expected him to make the occasional wisecrack, but he seemed to respect the artistic value of the classic animation and, judging by his wholehearted laughter, he enjoyed the story.

When the show was over, he released Cait's hand. Hurriedly she gathered her bag and coat. As they walked out of the noisy, crowded theatre, it seemed only natural to hold hands again.

Joe opened the truck, lifted down the step stool and helped her inside. Dusk came early these days, and bright, cheery lights were ablaze on every street. A vacant lot across the street was now filled with Christmas trees. A row of red lights was strung between two posts, sagging in the middle, and a portable tape player sent forth saccharine versions of better-known Christmas carols.

"Have you bought your tree yet?" Joe asked, nodding in the direction of the lot after he'd climbed into the driver's seat and started the engine.

"No. I don't usually put one up since I spend the holidays with Martin and his family."

"Ah."

"What about you? Or is that something else you save for Christmas Eve?" she joked. It warmed her a little to imagine Joe staying up past midnight to decorate a Christmas tree for his nieces and nephews.

"Finding time to do the shopping is bad enough."

"Your construction projects keep you that busy?" She hadn't given much thought to Joe's business. She knew from little remarks Paul had made that Joe was very successful. It wasn't logical that she should feel pride in his accomplishments, but she did.

"Owning a business isn't like being in a nine-to-five job. I'm on call twenty-four hours a day, but I wouldn't have it any other way. I love what I do."

"I'm happy for you, Joe. I really am."

"Happy enough to decorate my Christmas tree with me?"

"When?"

"Next weekend."

"I'd like to," she told him, touched by the invitation, "but I'll have left for Minnesota by then."

"That's all right," Joe said, grinning at her. "Maybe next time."

She turned, frowning, to hide her blush.

They remained silent as he concentrated on easing the truck into the heavy late-afternoon traffic.

"I enjoyed the movie," she said some time later, resisting the urge to rest her head on his shoulder. The impulse to do that arose from her exhaustion, she told herself. Nothing else!

"So did I," he said softly. "Only next time, I'll be the one to pay. Understand?"

Next time. There it was again. She suspected Joe was beginning to take their relationship, such as it was, far too seriously. Already he was suggesting they'd be seeing each other soon, matter-of-factly discussing dates as if they were long-time companions. Almost as if they were married . . .

She was mulling over this realisation when Joe pulled into the parking area in front of her building. He climbed out and began to gather her packages, bundling them in his arms. She managed to scramble down by herself, not giving him a chance to help her, then she led the way into the building and unlocked her door.

Cait stood just inside the doorway and turned slightly to take a couple of the larger packages from Joe's arms.

"I had a great time," she told him briskly.

"Me, too." He nudged her, forcing her to enter the living room. He followed close behind and unloaded her remaining things onto the sofa. His presence seemed to reach out and fill every corner of the room.

Neither of them spoke for several minutes, but Cait sensed Joe wanted her to invite him to stay for coffee. The idea was tempting but dangerous. She mustn't let him think there might ever be anything romantic between them. Not when she was in love with Paul. For the first time in nearly a year, Paul was actually beginning to notice her. She refused to ruin everything now by becoming involved with Joe.

"Thank you for...today," she said, returning to the door, intending to open it for him. Instead, Joe caught her by the wrist and pulled her against him. She was in his arms before she could voice a protest.

"I'm going to kiss you," he told her, his voice rough yet oddly tender.

"You are?" She'd never been more aware of a man, of his hard, muscular body against hers, his clean, masculine scent. Her own body reacted in a chaotic scramble of mixed sensations. Above all, though, it felt *good* to be in his arms. She wasn't sure why and dared not examine the feeling.

Slowly, leisurely, he lowered his head. She made a soft weak sound as his mouth touched hers.

Cait sighed, forgetting for a moment that she meant to free herself before his kiss deepened. Before things went any further . . .

Joe must have sensed her resolve because his hands slid down her spine in a gentle caress, drawing her even closer. His mouth began a sensuous journey along her jaw, and down her throat—

"Joe!" She moaned his name, uncertain of what she wanted to say.

"Hmm?"

"Are you hungry again?" She wondered desperately if there were any more bread sticks in the bottom of her bag. Maybe that would convince him to stop.

"Very hungry," he told her, his voice low and solemn. "I've never been hungrier."

"But you had lunch and then you ate nearly all the popcorn."

He hesitated, then slowly raised his head. "Cait, are we talking about the same things here? Oh, hell, what does it matter? The only thing that matters is this." He covered her parted lips with his.

Cait felt her knees go weak and sagged against him, her fingers gripping his jacket as though she expected to collapse any moment. Which was becoming a distinct possibility as he continued to kiss her. . . .

"Joe, no more, please." But she was the one clinging to him. She had to do something, and fast, before her ability to reason was lost entirely.

He drew an unsteady breath and muttered something she couldn't decipher as his lips grazed the delicate line of her jaw.

"We . . . need to talk," she announced, keeping her eyes tightly closed. If she didn't look at Joe, then she could concentrate on what she had to do.

"All right," he agreed.

"I'll make a pot of coffee."

With a heavy sigh, Joe abruptly released her. Cait half fell against the sofa arm, requiring its support while she collected herself enough to walk into the kitchen. She unconsciously reached up and brushed her lips, as if she wasn't completely sure even now that he'd taken her in his arms and kissed her.

He hadn't been joking this time, or teasing. The kisses they'd shared were serious kisses. The type a man gives a woman he's strongly attracted to. A woman he's interested in developing a relationship with. Cait found herself shaking, unable to move.

"You want me to make that coffee?" he suggested.

She nodded and sank down on the couch. She could scarcely stand, let alone prepare a pot of coffee.

Joe returned a few minutes later, carrying two steaming mugs. Carefully he handed her one, then sat across from her on the blue velvet ottoman.

"You wanted to talk?"

Cait nodded. "Yes." Her throat felt thick, clogged with confused emotion, and forming coherent words suddenly seemed beyond her means. She tried gesturing with her free hand, but that only served to frustrate Joe.

"Cait," he asked, "what's wrong?"

"Paul." The name came out in an eerie squeak.

"What about him?"

"He phoned me."

"Yes, I know. You already told me that."

"Don't you understand?" she cried, her throat unexpectedly clearing. "Paul is finally showing some interest in me and now you're kissing me and telling anyone who'll listen that the two of us are married and you're doing ridiculous things like..." She paused to draw in a deep breath. "Joe, oh, please, Joe, don't fall in love with me."

"Fall in love with you?" he echoed incredulously. "Caitlin, you can't be serious. It won't happen. No chance."

CHAPTER SIX

"NO CHANCE?" Cait repeated, convinced she'd misunderstood him. She blinked a couple of times as if that would correct her hearing. Either Joe was underestimating her intelligence, or he was more of a . . . a cad than she'd realised.

"You have nothing to worry about." He sipped coffee, his gaze steady, and emotionless. "I'm not falling in love with you."

"In other words you make a habit of kissing unsuspecting women."

"It isn't a habit," he answered thoughtfully. "It's more of a pastime."

"You certainly seem to be making a habit of it with me." Her anger was quickly gaining momentum and she was at odds to understand why she found his casual attitude so offensive. He was telling her exactly what she wanted to hear. But she hadn't expected her ego to take such a beating in the process. The fact that he wasn't the least bit tempted to fall in love with her should have pleased her.

It didn't.

It was as if their brief kisses were little more than a pleasant interlude for him. Something to occupy his time and keep him from growing bored with her company.

"This may come as something of a shock to you," Joe continued indifferently, "but a man doesn't have to be in love with a woman to kiss her."

"I know that," Cait snapped, fighting to hold back her temper, which was threatening to break free at any moment. "But you don't have to be so...so casual about it, either. If I wasn't involved with Paul, I might have taken you seriously."

"I didn't know you were involved with Paul," he returned with mild sarcasm. He leaned forward and rested his elbows on his knees, his pose infuriatingly relaxed. "If that was true I'd never have taken you out. The way I see it, the involvement is all on your part. Am I wrong?"

"No," she admitted reluctantly. How like a man to talk about semantics in the middle of an argument!

"So," he said, leaning back again and crossing his legs. "Are you enjoying the kisses? I take it I've improved from the first go-around."

"You honestly want me to rate you?" she sputtered.

"Obviously I'm much better than I was as a kid, otherwise you wouldn't be so worried." He took another drink of his coffee, smiling pleasantly all the while.

"Believe me, I'm not worried."

He arched his brows. "Really?"

"No doubt you expect me to fall at your feet, overcome by your masculine charm. Well, if that's what you're waiting for, you have one hell of a long wait!"

His grin was slightly off centre, as if he was picturing her arrayed at his feet—and enjoying the sight. "I think the problem here is that *you* might be falling in love with *me* and just don't know it."

"Falling in love with you and not know it?" she repeated with a loud disbelieving snort. "You've gone completely out of your mind. There's no chance of that."

"Why not? Plenty of women have told me I'm a handsome son of a gun. Plus, I'm said to possess a certain amount of charm. Heaven knows, I'm generous enough and rather—"

"Who told you that? Your mother?" She made it sound like the most ludicrous thing she'd heard in years.

"You might be surprised to learn that I do have admirers."

Why this news should add fuel to the fire of her temper was beyond Cait, but she was so furious with him she could barely sit still. "I don't doubt it, but if I fall in love with a man you can believe it won't be just because he's 'a handsome son of a gun,'" she quoted sarcastically. "Look at Paul— He's the type of man I'm attracted to. What's on the inside matters more than outward appearances."

"Then why are you so worried about falling in love with me?"

"I'm not worried! You've got it the wrong way around. The only reason I mentioned anything was because I thought *you* were beginning to take our times together much too seriously."

"I already explained that wasn't a problem."

"So I heard." Cait set her coffee aside. Joe was upsetting her so much that her hand was shaking hard enough to spill it.

"Well," Joe murmured, glancing at her. "You never did answer my question."

"Which one?" she asked irritably.

"About how I rated as a kisser."

"You weren't serious!"

"On the contrary." He set his own coffee down and raised himself off the ottoman far enough to clasp her by the waist and pull her into his lap.

Caught off balance, Cait fell onto his thighs, too astonished to struggle.

"Let's try it again," he whispered in a rough undertone.

"Ah..." A frightening excitement took hold of Cait. Her mind commanded her to leap away from this man, but some emotion, far stronger than common sense or prudence, urged the opposite.

Before she could form a protest, Joe bent towards her and covered her mouth with his. She'd hold herself stiff in his arms, that was what she'd do, teach him the lesson he deserved. How dared he assume she'd automatically fall in love with him? How dared he insinuate he was some...some Greek god women adored? But the instant his lips met hers, Cait trembled with a mixture of shock and profound pleasure.

Everything within her longed to cry out at the unfairness of it all. It shouldn't be this good with Joe. They were friends, nothing more. This was the kind of response she expected when Paul kissed her. If he ever did.

She meant to pull away, but instead, Cait moaned softly. It felt so incredibly wonderful. So incredibly right. At that moment, there didn't seem to be anything to worry about—except the likelihood of dissolving in his arms then and there.

Suddenly Joe broke the contact. Her instinctive disappointment, even more than the unexpectedness of the action, sent her eyes flying open. Her own dark eyes met his blue ones, which now seemed almost aquamarine.

"So, how do I rate?" he murmured thickly, as though he was having trouble speaking himself.

"Good." A one-word reply was all she could manage, although she was furious with him for asking.

"Just good?"

She nodded forcefully.

"I thought we were better than that."

"We?"

"Naturally I'm only as good as my partner."

"Th-then how do you rate me?" She had to ask. Like a fool she handed him the axe and laid her neck on the chopping board. Joe was sure to use the opportunity to trample all over her ego, to turn the whole bewildering experience into a joke. She couldn't take that right now. She dropped her gaze, waiting for him to devastate her.

"Much improved."

She cocked one brow in surprise. She had no idea what to say next.

They were both silent. Then he said softly, "You know, Cait, we're getting better at this. Much, much better." He pressed his forehead to hers. "If we're not careful, you just might fall in love with me, after all."

"WHERE WERE YOU all day Saturday?" Lindy asked early Monday morning, walking into Cait's office.

The renovations to it had just been completed late Friday and Cait had moved everything back into her office first thing this morning. "I must have tried calling you ten times."

"I told you I was going Christmas shopping. In fact, I bought some decorations for my office."

Lindy nodded. "But all day?" Her eyes narrowed suspiciously as she set down her briefcase and leaned against Cait's desk, crossing her arms. "You didn't happen to be with Joe Rockwell, did you?"

Cait could feel a telltale shade of pink creep up her neck. She lowered her gaze to the list of current Dow Jones stock prices and took a moment to compose herself. She couldn't admit the truth. "I said I was shopping," she said somewhat defensively. Then, in an effort to change the topic, she reached for a thick folder with Paul's name inked across the top and said, "You wouldn't happen to know what Paul's schedule is for the day, would you?"

"N-no, I haven't seen him yet. Why do you ask?"

Cait flashed her friend a bright smile. "He phoned me Friday night. Oh, Lindy, I was so excited I nearly fell all over myself." She dropped her voice as she glanced around to make sure none of the others could hear her. "I honestly think he intends to ask me out."

"Did he say so?"

"Not exactly." Cait frowned. Lindy wasn't revealing any of the enthusiasm she expected.

"Then why did he phone?"

Cait rolled her chair away from the desk and glanced around once again. "I think he might be jealous," she whispered.

"Really?" Lindy's eyes widened.

"Don't look so surprised." Cait, however, was much too excited recounting Paul's phone call to be offended by Lindy's attitude.

"What makes you think Paul would be jealous?" Lindy asked next.

"Maybe I'm magnifying everything in my own mind because it's what I so badly want to believe. But he did phone..."

"What did he say?" Lindy pressed, sounding more curious now. "It seems to me he must have had a reason."

"Oh, he did. He mentioned something about appreciating an article I'd given him, but we both know that was just an excuse. What clued me in to his jealousy was the way he kept asking if I was alone."

"But that could have several connotations, don't you think?" Lindy suggested.

"Yes, I know, but it made sense that he'd want to know if Joe was at the apartment or not."

"And was he?"

"Of course not," Cait said righteously. She didn't feel guilty about hiding the fact that he'd been there earlier, or that they'd spent nearly all of Saturday together. "I'm sure Joe's ridiculous remark when I left the office Friday is what convinced Paul to phone me. If I wasn't so furious with Joe, I might even be grateful."

"What's that?" Lindy asked abruptly, pointing to the thick folder in front of Cait. Her lips had thinned slightly as if she was confused or annoyed—about what, Cait couldn't figure out.

"This, my friend," she began, holding up the folder, "is the key to my future with our dedicated manager."

Lindy didn't immediately respond and looked more puzzled then before. "How do you mean?"

Cait couldn't get over the feeling that things weren't quite right with her best friend; she seemed to be holding something back. But Cait realised Lindy would tell her when she was ready. Lindy always hated being pushed or prodded.

"The folder?" Lindy prompted when Cait didn't answer.

Cait flipped it open. "I spent all day Sunday reading through old business journals looking for additional articles that might interest Paul. I must have gone back five years. I copied the articles I consider the most valuable and added a brief analysis of my own. I was hoping to give it to him sometime today. That's why I was asking if you knew his schedule."

"Unfortunately I don't," Lindy murmured. She straightened, reached for her briefcase and made a show of checking her watch. Then she looked up to smile reassuringly at Cait. "I'd better get to work. I'll come by later to help you put up your decorations, okay?"

"Thanks," Cait said, then added, "Wish me luck with Paul."

"You know I do," Lindy mumbled on her way out of the door.

Mondays were generally slow for the stock market, slow, that is, unless there was a crisis. World events and financial reports had a significant impact on the market. However, as the day progressed, everything ran smoothly.

Cait glanced up every now and again, half expecting to see Joe lounging in her doorway. His men had started early that morning, but by noon, Joe hadn't arrived.

Not until much later did she realise it was Paul she should be anticipating, not Joe. Paul was the romantic interest of her life and it irritated her that Joe seemed to preoccupy her thoughts.

As it happened, Paul did stroll past her office shortly after the New York market closed. Grabbing the folder, Cait raced towards his office, not hesitating for an instant. This was her golden opportunity and she was taking hold of it with both hands.

"Good afternoon, Paul," she said cordially as she stood in his doorway, clutching the folder. "Do you have a moment or would you rather I came back later?"

He looked tired, as if the day had already been a gruelling one. It was all Cait could do not to offer to massage away the stress and worry that complicated his life. Her heart swelled with a renewed wave of love. For a wild, impetuous moment, it was true, she'd suffered her doubts. Any woman would have when a man like Joe took her in his arms. He might be arrogant in the extreme and one of the worst pranksters she'd ever met, but despite all that, he had a certain charm. But now that she was with Paul, Cait remembered sharply who it was she really loved.

"I don't want to be a bother," she added softly.

He offered her a listless smile. "Come in, Cait. Now is fine." He gestured towards a chair.

She hurried into the office, trying to keep the bounce out of her step. Knowing she'd be spending a few extra minutes alone with Paul, Cait had taken special care with her appearance that morning.

He glanced up and smiled at her again, but this time Cait thought she could see a glimmer of appreciation in his eyes. "What can I do for you? I hope you're pleased with your office." He frowned slightly.

For a second, she forgot what she was doing in Paul's office and stared at him blankly until his own gaze fell to the folder. "The office looks great," she said quickly. "Um, the reason I'm here..." She faltered, then gulped in a quick breath and continued, "I went through some of the business journals I have at home and found several I felt would interest you." She extended the folder to him, like a ceremonial offering.

He took it from her and opened it gingerly. "Gracious," he said, flipping through the pages and scanning her written comments, "you must have spent hours on this."

"It was...nothing." She'd willingly have done a good deal more to gain his appreciation and eventually his love.

"I won't have a chance to look at this for a few days," he said.

"Oh, please, there's no rush. You happened to mention you got some useful insights from the previous article I gave you. So I thought I'd share a few others that seem relevant to what's happening with the market now."

"It's very thoughtful of you."

"I was happy to do it. More than happy," she amended with her most brilliant smile. When he didn't say anything more, Cait rose reluctantly to her feet. "You must be swamped after being in meetings most of the day, so I'll leave you for now."

She was almost at the door when he spoke. "Actually I only dropped into the office to collect a few things before heading out again. I've got an important date this evening."

Cait felt as if the floor had suddenly disappeared and she was plummeting through empty space. "Date?" she repeated before she could stop herself. It was a struggle to keep smiling.

Paul's grin was downright boyish. "Yes, I'm meeting her for dinner."

"In that case, have a good time."

"Thanks, I will," he returned confidently, his eyes alight with excitement. "Oh, and by the way," he added, indicating the folder she'd worked so hard on, "thanks for all the effort you put into this."

"You're . . . welcome."

By the time Cait returned to her office she felt numb. Paul had an important date. It wasn't as though she'd expected him to live the life of a hermit, but before today, he'd never mentioned going out with anyone. She might have suspected he'd thrown out the information hoping to make her jealous if it hadn't been for one thing. He seemed genuinely thrilled about this date. Besides, Paul wasn't the kind of man to resort to pretence.

"Cait, my goodness," Lindy said, strolling into her office a while later, "what's wrong? You look dreadful."

Cait swallowed against the lump in her throat and managed a shaky smile. "I talked to Paul and gave him the research I'd done."

"He didn't appreciate it?" Lindy picked up the wreath that lay on Cait's desk and pinned it to the door.

"I'm sure he did," she replied. "What he doesn't appreciate is me. I might as well be invisible to that man." She pushed the hair away from her forehead and braced both elbows on her desk, feeling totally disheartened. Unless she acted quickly, she was going to lose Paul to some faceless, nameless woman.

"You've been invisible to him before. What's different about this time?" She fastened a silver bell to the window as Cait abstractedly fingered her three ceramic Wise Men.

"Paul's got a date, and from the way he said it, this isn't with just any woman, either. Whoever she is must be important, otherwise he wouldn't have mentioned her. He looked like a little kid who's been given the keys to a candy store."

The information seemed to surprise Lindy as much as it had Cait. She was quiet for a few minutes before she asked quietly, "What are you going to do about it?"

"Heavens, I don't know," Cait cried, hiding her face in her hands. She'd once jokingly suggested to Joe that she parade around naked in an effort to gain Paul's attention. Of course she'd been exaggerating, but some form of drastic action was obviously needed. If only she knew what.

Lindy mumbled an excuse and left. It wasn't until Cait looked up that she realised her friend was gone.

She sighed wearily. She'd arrived at work this morning with such bright expectations, and now everything had gone wrong. She felt more depressed than she'd been in a long time. She knew the best remedy would be to force herself into some physical activity. Anything. The worst possible thing she could do was sit home alone and mope. Maybe she should plan to buy herself a Christmas tree and some ornaments. Her spirits couldn't help being at least a little improved by that; it would get her out of the house, if nothing else. And then she'd have something to entertain herself with, instead of brooding about this unexpected turn of events. Getting out of the house had an added advantage. If Joe phoned, she wouldn't be there to answer.

No sooner had that thought passed through her mind when a large form filled her doorway.

Joe.

A bright orange hard hat was pushed back on his head, the way movie cowboys wore their Stetsons. His boots were dusty and his tool pouch rode low on his hip, completing the gunslinger image. Even the way he stood with his thumbs tucked in his belt suggested he was expecting a showdown.

"Hi, beautiful," he drawled, giving her that lazy, intimate smile of his. The one designed, Cait swore, just to unnerve her. But it wasn't going to work, not in her present state of mind.

"Don't you have anyone else to pester?" she snapped.

"My, my," Joe said, shaking his head in mock chagrin. Disregarding her lack of welcome, he strode into the office and threw himself down in the chair beside her desk. "You're in a rare mood."

"You would be too after the day I've had. Listen, Joe, as you can see, I'm poor company. Go flirt with the receptionist if you're looking to make someone miserable."

"Those claws are certainly sharp this afternoon." He ran his hands down the front of his shirt, pretending to inspect the damage inflicted. "What's wrong?" Some of the teasing light faded from his eyes as he studied her.

She sent him a look meant to blister his ego, but as always Joe seemed invincible against her practised glares.

"How do you know I'm not here to invest fifty thousand dollars?" he demanded, making himself at home by reaching across her desk for a pen. He rolled it casually between his palms.

Cait wasn't about to fall for this little game. "Are you here to invest money?"

"Not exactly. I wanted to ask you to—"

"Then come back when you are." She grabbed a stack of papers and slapped them down on her desk. But being rude, even to Joe, went against her nature. She was battling tears and the growing need to explain her behaviour, apologise for it, when he slowly rose to his feet. He tossed the pen carelessly onto her desk.

"Have it your way. If asking you to join me to look for a Christmas tree is such a terrible crime, then—"

"You're going to buy a Christmas tree?"

"That's what I just said." He flung the words over his shoulder on his way out of the door.

In that moment, Cait felt as though the whole world was tumbling down around her shoulders. She felt like such a shrew. He'd come here wanting to include her in his Christmas preparations and she'd driven him away with a spiteful tongue and a haughty attitude.

Cait wasn't a woman easily given to tears, but she struggled with them now. Her lower lip started to quiver. She might have been eight years old all over again—this was like the day she found out she wasn't invited to Betsy McDonald's birthday party. Only now it was Paul doing the excluding. He and this important woman of his were going out to have the time of their lives while she stayed home in her lonely apartment, suffering from a serious bout of self-pity.

Gathering up her things, Cait thrust the papers into her briefcase with uncharacteristic negligence. She put on her coat, buttoned it quickly and wrapped the scarf around her neck as though it was a hangman's noose.

Joe was talking to the foreman of the crew who'd been unobtrusively working around the office all day. He hesitated when he saw her, halting the conversation. Cait's eyes briefly met his and although she tried to disguise how regretful she felt, she obviously did a poor job of it. He took a step towards her, but she raised her chin a notch, too proud to admit her feelings.

She had to walk directly past Joe on her way to the lift and forced herself to look anywhere but at him.

The stocky foreman clearly wanted to resume the discussion, but Joe ignored him and stared at Cait instead, with narrowed, assessing eyes. She could feel his questioning concern as profoundly as if he'd touched her. When she could bear it no longer, she turned to face him, her lower lip quivering uncontrollably.

"Cait," he called out.

She raced for the lift, fearing she'd burst into tears before she could make her grand exit. She didn't bother to respond, knowing that if she said anything she'd make an even greater fool of herself than usual. She wasn't even sure what had prompted her to say the atrocious things to Joe that she had. He wasn't the one who'd upset her, yet she'd unfairly taken her frustrations out on him.

She should have known it would be impossible to make a clean getaway. She almost ran through the office, past the reception desk, towards the lift.

"Aren't you going to answer me?" Joe demanded, following on her heels like a Mississippi hound.

"No." She concentrated on the lighted numbers above the lift, which moved with painstaking slowness. Three more floors and she could make good her escape.

"What's so insulting about inviting you to go Christmas-tree shopping?" he asked.

Close to weeping, she waved her free hand, hoping he'd understand that she was incapable of explaining just then. Her throat was clogged up and it hurt to breathe, let alone talk. Her eyes filled with tears, and everything started to blur.

"Tell me," he commanded a second time.

Cait gulped at the tightness in her throat. "Y-you wouldn't understand." Why, oh, why, wouldn't that lift hurry?

"Try me."

It was either give in and explain, or stand there and argue. The first choice was easier; frankly, Cait hadn't the energy to fight with him. Sighing deeply, she began, "It—it all started when I made up this folder of business articles for Paul..."

"I might have known Paul had something to do with this," Joe muttered under his breath.

"I spent hours putting it together for him, adding little comments, and... and... I don't know what I expected but it wasn't..."

"What happened? What did Paul do?"

Cait rubbed her eyes with the back of her hand. "If you're going to interrupt me, then I can't see any reason to explain."

"Boss?" the foreman called out, sounding impatient.

Just then the lift arrived and the doors opened, revealing half a dozen men and women. They stared out at Cait and Joe while he blocked the entrance, gripping her by the elbow.

"Joseph," she hissed, "let me go!" Recognising her advantage, she called out, "This man refuses to release my arm." If she expected a knight in shining armor to leap to her rescue, Cait was to be sorely disappointed. It was as if no one had heard her.

"Don't worry, folks, we're married." Joe charmed them with another of his lazy, lopsided grins.

"Boss?" the foreman pleaded again.

"Take the rest of the day off," Joe shouted. "Tell the crew to go out and buy Christmas gifts for their wives."

"You want me to do what?" the foreman shouted back. Joe moved into the lift with Cait.

"You heard me."

"Let me make sure I understand you right. You want the men to go Christmas shopping for their wives? I thought you just said we're on a tight schedule?"

"That's right," Joe said loudly as the lift doors closed.

Cait had never felt more conspicuous in her life. Every eye was focused on her and Joe, and it was all she could do to keep her head held high.

When the tension became intolerable, Cait turned to face her fellow passengers. "We are not married," she announced.

"Yes, we are," Joe insisted. "She's simply forgotten."

"I did not forget our marriage and don't you dare tell them that cock-and-bull story about amnesia."

"But, darling—"

"Stop it right now, Joseph Rockwell! No one believes you. These people can take one look at us and determine that I'm the one who's telling the truth."

The lift finally stopped on the ground floor, a fact for which Cait was deeply grateful. The doors glided open and two women stepped out first, but not before pausing to get a good appreciative look at Joe.

"Does she do this often?" one of the men asked, directing his question to Joe, his amusement obvious.

"Unfortunately, yes," he answered, chuckling as he tucked his hand under Cait's elbow and led her into the foyer. She tried to jerk her arm away, but he wouldn't allow it. "You see, I married a forgetful bride."

CHAPTER SEVEN

PACING THE CARPET in the living room, Cait nervously smoothed the front of her red satin dress, her heart pumping a mile a second while she waited impatiently for Joe to arrive. She'd spent hours preparing for this Christmas party, which was being held in Paul's home. Her stomach was in knots and had been for hours.

She, the mysterious woman Paul was dating, would surely be there. Cait would have her first opportunity to size up the competition. Cait had studied her reflection countless times, trying to be objective about her chances with Paul based on looks alone. The dress was gorgeous. Her hair flawless. Everything else was as perfect as she could make it.

The doorbell sounded and Cait hurried across the room, throwing open the door. "You know what you are, Joseph Rockwell?"

"Late?" he suggested.

Cait pretended not to hear him. "A bully," she furnished. "A badgering bully, no less. I'm sorry I ever agreed to let you take me to Paul's party. I don't know what I was thinking of."

"No doubt you were hoping to corner me under the mistletoe," he remarked, with a wink that implied he wouldn't be difficult to persuade.

"First you practically kidnap me into going Christmas-tree shopping with you," she raged on. "Then—"

"Come on, Cait, admit it, you had fun." He lounged indolently on her sofa while she got her coat and bag.

She hesitated, her mouth twitching with a smile. "Who'd ever believe that a man who bought his mother a rib roast and a case of cat food for Christmas last year would be so particular about a silly tree?" Joe had dragged her to no less than four lots, searching for the perfect tree.

"I took you to dinner afterward, didn't I?" he reminded her.

Cait nodded. She had to admit it: Joe had gone out of his way to help her forget her troubles. Although she'd made the tree-shopping expedition sound like a chore, he'd turned the evening into an enjoyable and, yes, a memorable one.

His good mood had been infectious and after a while she'd completely forgotten Paul was out with another woman—someone so special that his enthusiasm about her had overcome his normal restraint.

"I've changed my mind," Cait decided suddenly, clasping her hands over her stomach, which was in turmoil. "I don't want to go to this Christmas party, after all." The evening was already doomed. She couldn't possibly have a good time watching the man she loved entertain the woman *he* loved. Cait couldn't think of a single reason to expose herself to that kind of misery.

"Not go to the party?' Joe repeated. "But I thought you'd arranged your flight schedule just so you could."

"I did, but that was before." Cait stubbornly squared her shoulders and elevated her chin just enough to convince Joe she meant business. He might be able to bully her into going shopping with him for a Christmas tree, but this was something entirely different. "*She'll* be there," Cait added as an explanation.

"She?" Joe repeated slowly, burying his hands in his suit pockets. He was devilishly handsome in his dark blue suit and no doubt knew it. He was no less comfortable in tailored trousers than he was in dirty jeans.

A lock of thick hair slanted across his forehead; Cait managed—it was an effort—to resist brushing it back. An effort not because it disrupted his polished appearance, but because she had the strangest desire to run her fingers through his hair. Why she would think such a thing now was beyond her. She'd long since stopped trying to figure out her feelings for Joe. He was a friend and a confidant even if, at odd moments, he behaved like a lunatic. Just remembering some of the comments he'd made to embarrass her was enough to bring colour to her cheeks.

"I'd think you'd want to meet her," Joe challenged. "That way you can size her up."

"I don't even want to know what she looks like," Cait countered sharply. She didn't need to. Cait already knew everything she cared to about Paul's hot date. "She's beautiful."

"So are you."

Cait gave a short, derisive laugh. She wasn't discounting her own homespun appeal. She was reasonably attractive, and never more so than this evening. Catching a glimpse of herself in the mirror, she was pleased to note how nice her hair looked, with the froth of curls circling her head. But she wasn't going to kid herself, either. Her allure wasn't extraordinary by any stretch of the imagination. Her eyes were a nice warm shade of brown, though, and her nose was kind of cute. Perky, Lindy had once called it. But none of that mattered. Measuring herself against Paul's sure-to-be-gorgeous, nameless date was like comparing bulky sweat socks with a silk stocking. She'd already spent hours picturing her as a classic beauty... tall... sophisticated.

"I've never taken you for a coward," Joe said in a flat tone as he headed towards the door.

Apparently he wasn't even going to argue with her. Cait almost wished he would, just so she could show him how strong her will was. Nothing he could say or do would convince her to attend this party. Besides, her feet hurt. She was wearing new heels and hadn't broken them in yet, and if she did go to the party, she'd probably be limping for days afterwards.

"I'm not a coward," she insisted, schooling her face to remain as emotionless as possible. "All I'm doing is exercising a little common sense. Why depress myself over the holidays? This is the last time I'll see Paul before Christmas. I leave for Minnesota in the morning."

"Yes, I know." Joe frowned as he said it, hesitating before he opened her door. "You're sure about this?"

"Positive." She was mildly surprised Joe wasn't putting up more of a fuss. From past experience, she'd expected a full-scale verbal battle.

"The choice is yours of course," he granted, shrugging. "But if it was me, I know I'd spend the whole time I was away regretting it." He studied her when he'd finished, then smiled in a way Cait could only describe as crafty.

She groaned inwardly. If there was one thing that drove her crazy about Joe it was the way he made the most outrageous statements. Then every once in a while he'd say something so wise it caused her to doubt her own conclusions and beliefs. This was one of those times. He was right: if she didn't go to Paul's, she'd regret it. Since she was leaving the following day for Minnesota, she wouldn't be able to ask anyone about the party, either.

"Are you coming or not?" he demanded.

Grumbling under her breath, Cait let him help her on with her coat. "I'm coming, but I don't like it. Not one darn bit."

"You're going to do just fine."

"They probably said that to Joan of Arc."

CAIT CLUTCHED the punch glass in both hands, as though terrified someone might try to take it back. Standing next to the fireplace, with its garlanded mantel and cheerful blaze, she hadn't moved since they'd arrived a half hour earlier.

"Is *she* here yet?" she whispered to Lindy when her friend strolled past carrying in a tray of canapés.

"Who?"

"Paul's woman friend," Cait said pointedly. Both Joe and Lindy were beginning to exasperate her. "I've been standing here for the past thirty minutes hoping to catch a glimpse of her."

Lindy looked away. "I...I don't know if she's here or not."

"Stay with me, for heaven's sake," Cait requested, feeling shaky inside and out. Joe had deserted her almost as soon as they'd arrived. Oh, he'd stuck around long enough to bring her a cup of punch, but then he'd drifted away, leaving Cait to deal with the situation on her own. This was the very man who'd insisted she attend this Christmas party, claiming he'd be right by her side the entire evening in case she needed him.

"I'm helping Paul with the hors d'oeuvres," Lindy explained, "otherwise I'd be happy to stay and chat."

"See if you can find Joe for me, would you?" She'd do it herself, but her feet were killing her.

"Sure."

Once Lindy was gone, Cait scanned the crowded living room. Many of the guests were business associates and clients Paul had worked with over the years. Naturally everyone from the office was there, as well.

"You wanted to see me?" Joe asked, reaching her side.

"Thank you very much," she hissed, doing her best to sound sarcastic and keep a smile on her face at the same time.

"You're welcome." He leaned one elbow on the fireplace mantel and grinned boyishly at her. "Might I ask what you're thanking me for?"

"Don't play games with me, Joe. Not now, please."
She shifted her weight from one foot to the other,
drawing his attention to her shoes.

"Your feet hurt?" he asked, frowning.

"Walking across hot coals would be less painful
than these stupid high heels."

"Then why did you wear them?"

"Because they go with the dress. Listen, would you
mind very much if we got off the subject of my shoes
and discussed the matter at hand?"

"Which is?"

Joe was being as obtuse as Lindy had been. Surely
he was doing it deliberately, just to get a rise out of
her. Well, it was working.

"Did you see her?" she asked with exaggerated patience.

"Not yet," he whispered back as though they were
exchanging top-secret information. "She doesn't seem
to have arrived."

"Have you talked to Paul?"

"No. Have you?"

"Not really." Paul had greeted them at the door, but
other than that, Cait hadn't had a chance to do anything but watch him mingle with his guests. The day
at the office hadn't been any help, either. Paul had
breezed in and out without giving Cait more than a
friendly wave. Since they hadn't exchanged a single
word, it was impossible for her to determine how his
date had gone.

It must have been a busy day for Lindy, as well, because Cait hadn't had a chance to talk to her, either.
They'd met on their way out the door late in the af-

ternoon and Lindy had hurried past, muttering that
she'd see Cait at Paul's party.

"I think I'll go help Lindy with the hors d'oeuvres,"
Cait said now. "Do you want me to get you anything?"

"Nothing, thanks." He was grinning as he strolled
away, leaving Cait to wonder what he found so amusing.

Cait limped into the kitchen, leaving the polished
wooden door swinging in her wake. She stopped
abruptly when she encountered Paul and Lindy in the
middle of a heated discussion.

"Oh, sorry," Cait apologised automatically.

Paul's gaze darted to Cait's. "No problem," he said
pointedly. "I was just leaving." He stalked past her,
shoving the door open with the palm of his hand.
Once again the door swung back and forth.

"What was that all about?" Cait wanted to know.

Lindy continued transferring the small cheese-
dotted crackers from the cookie sheet onto the serving platter. "Nothing."

"It sounded as if you and Paul were arguing."

Lindy straightened and bit her lip. She avoided
looking at Cait, concentrating on her task as if it was
of vital importance to properly arrange the crackers on
the plate.

"You were arguing, weren't you?" Cait pressed.

"Yes."

As far as she knew, Lindy and Paul had always got
along. The fact that they were at odds with each other
surprised her. "About what?"

"I—I gave Paul my two-week notice
this afternoon."

Cait was so shocked, she pulled out a kitchen chair and sank down on it. "You did what?" Removing her high heels, she massaged her pinched toes.

"You heard me."

"But why? Good grief, Lindy, you never said a word to anyone. Not even me. The least you could have done was talk to me about it first." No wonder Paul was angry. If Lindy left, it would mean bringing in someone new when the office was short-staffed. With Cait and a number of other people away for the holidays, the place would be a madhouse.

"Did you receive an offer you couldn't refuse?" Cait hadn't had any idea her friend was unhappy at Webster, Rodale and Missen. That didn't shock her nearly as much as Lindy's remaining tight-lipped about it all.

"It wasn't exactly an offer—but it was something like that," Lindy replied vaguely. With that, she set aside the cookie sheet, smiled at Cait and then carried the platter into the living room.

For the past couple of weeks Cait had noticed that something was troubling her friend. It hadn't been anything she could readily name. Just that Lindy hadn't been her usual high-spirited self. Cait had meant to ask her about it, but she'd been so busy herself, so involved with her own problems, that she'd never brought it up.

She was still sitting there rubbing her feet when Joe sauntered into the kitchen, nibbling on a cheese cracker. "I thought I'd find you in here." He pulled out the chair across from her and sat down.

"Has she arrived yet?"

"Apparently so."

Cait dropped her foot and frantically worked the shoe back and forth until she'd managed to squeeze her toes inside. Then she forced her other foot into its shoe. "Well, for heaven's sake, why didn't you say something sooner?" she chastised. She straightened, ran her hands down the satin skirt and drew a shaky breath. "How do I look?"

"Like your feet hurt."

She sent him a scalding look. "Thank you very much," she muttered sarcastically. Hobbling to the door, she opened it a crack and peeked out, hoping to catch sight of the mystery woman. From what she could see, there weren't any new arrivals.

"What does she look like?" Cait demanded and whirled around to discover Joe standing directly behind her. She nearly collided with him and gave a small cry of surprise. Joe caught her by the shoulders to keep her from stumbling. Eager to question him about Paul's date, she didn't take the time to analyse why her heartrate soared when his hands made contact with her bare skin.

"What does she look like?" Cait demanded again.

"I don't know," Joe returned flippantly.

"What do you mean you don't know? You just said she'd arrived."

"Unfortunately she doesn't have a tattoo across her forehead announcing that she's the woman Paul's dating."

"Then how do you know she's here?" If Joe was playing games with her, she'd make damn sure he'd regret it. Her love for Paul was no joking matter.

"It's more a feeling I have."

"You had me stuff my feet back into these shoes for a stupid feeling?" It was all she could do not to slap him silly. "You are no friend of mine, Joseph Rockwell. No friend whatsoever." Having said that, she limped back into the living room.

Obviously unscathed by her remark, Joe strolled out of the kitchen behind her. He walked over to the tray of canapés and helped himself to three or four while Cait did her best to ignore him.

Since the punch bowl was close by, she poured herself a second glass. The taste was sweet and cold, but Cait noticed that she felt a bit light-headed afterwards. Potent drinks didn't sit well on an empty stomach, so she scooped up a handful of mixed nuts.

"I remember a time when you used to line up all the Spanish peanuts and eat those first," Joe said from behind her. "Then it was the hazelnuts, followed by the—"

"Almonds." Leave it to him to bring up her foolish past. "I haven't done that since I was—"

"Twenty," he guessed.

"Twenty-five," she corrected.

Joe laughed, and despite her aching feet and the certainty that she should never have come to this party, Cait laughed, too.

Refilling her punch glass, she downed it all in a single drink. Once more, it tasted cool and refreshing.

"Cait," Joe warned, "how much punch have you had?"

"Not enough." She filled the crystal cup a third time—or was it the fourth?—squared her shoulders and gulped it down. When she'd finished, she wiped the back of her hand across her mouth and smiled bravely.

"Are you purposely trying to get drunk?" he demanded.

"No." She reached for another handful of nuts. "All I'm looking for is a little courage."

"Courage?"

"Yes," she said with a sigh. "The way I figure it..." She paused, smiling giddily, then twisted around in a full circle. "There *is* some mistletoe here, isn't there?"

"I think so," Joe said, frowning. "What makes you ask?"

"I'm going to kiss Paul," she announced proudly. "All I have to do is wait until he strolls past. Then I'll grab him by the hand, wish him a merry Christmas and give him a kiss he won't soon forget." If the fantasy fulfilled itself, Paul would then realise he'd met the woman of his dreams, and then and there propose marriage....

"What is kissing Paul supposed to prove?"

She returned to reality. "Well, this is where you come in. I want you to look around and watch the faces of the other women. If any one of them shows signs of jealousy, then we'll know who it is."

"I'm not sure this plan of yours will work."

"It's better than trusting those feelings of yours," she countered.

She spied the mistletoe hanging from the archway between the formal dining room and the living room. Slouched against the wall, hands tucked behind her back, Cait waited patiently for Paul to stroll past.

Ten minutes passed or maybe it was fifteen—Cait couldn't tell. Yawning, she covered her mouth. "I think we should leave," Joe suggested as he casually walked by. "You're ready to drop on your feet."

"I haven't kissed Paul yet," she reminded him.

"He seems to be involved in a lengthy discussion. This could take a while."

"I'm in no hurry." Her throat felt unusually dry. She would have preferred something nonalcoholic, but the only drink nearby was the punch.

"Cait," Joe warned when he saw her helping herself to yet another glass.

"Don't worry, I know what I'm doing."

"So did the captain of the *Titanic*."

"Don't get cute with me, Joseph Rockwell. I'm in no mood to deal with someone amusing." Finding herself hilariously funny, she smothered a round of giggles.

"Oh, no," Joe groaned. "I was afraid of this."

"Afraid of what?"

"You're drunk!"

She gave him a sour look. "That's ridiculous. All I had is four little, bitty glasses of punch." To prove she knew exactly what she was doing, she held up three fingers, recognised her mistake and promptly corrected herself. At least she tried to do it promptly; figuring out how many fingers equalled four seemed to take an inordinate amount of time. She finally held up two from each hand.

Expelling her breath, she leaned back against the wall and closed her eyes. That was her second mistake. The world took a sharp and unexpected nosedive. Snapping open her eyes, Cait looked to Joe as the anchor that would keep her afloat. He must have read the panic in her expression because he walked over to her and slowly shook his head.

"That does it, Miss Singapore Sling. I'm getting you out of here."

"But I haven't been under the mistletoe yet."

"If you want anyone to kiss you, it'll be me."

The offer sounded tempting, but it was her stubborn boss Cait wanted to kiss, not Joe. "I'd rather dance with you."

"Unfortunately there isn't any music at the moment."

"You need music to dance?" It sounded like the saddest thing she'd ever heard, and her bottom lip started to tremble at the tragedy of it all. "Oh, dear, Joe," she whispered, placing both hands on the sides of her head. "I think you might be right. The liquor seems to be affecting me...."

"It's that bad, is it?"

"Uh, yes... The whole room's just started to pitch and heave. We're not having an earthquake, are we?"

"No." His hand was on her forearm, guiding her towards the front door.

"Wait," she said dramatically, raising her index finger. "I have a coat."

"I know. Wait here and I'll get it for you." He seemed worried about leaving her. Cait smiled at him, trying to reassure him she'd be perfectly fine, but she seemed unable to keep her balance. He urged her against the wall, stepped back a couple of paces as though he expected her to slip sideways, then hurriedly located her coat.

"What's wrong?" he asked when he returned.

"What makes you think anything's wrong?"

"Other than the fact that you're crying?"

"My feet hurt."

Joe rolled his eyes. "Why did you wear those stupid shoes in the first place?"

"I already told you," she whimpered. "Don't be mad at me." She held out her arms to him, needing his comfort. "Would you carry me to the car?"

Joe hesitated. "You want me to carry you?" He sounded as though it was a task of Herculean proportions.

"I can't walk." She'd taken the shoes off, and it would take God's own army to get them back on. She couldn't very well traipse outside in her stockinged feet.

"If I carry you, we'd better find another way out of the house."

"All right." She agreed just to prove what an amicable person she actually was. When she was a child, she'd been a pest, but she wasn't anymore and she wanted to be sure Joe understood that.

Grasping Cait's hand, he led her into the kitchen.

"Don't you think we should make our farewells?" she asked. It seemed the polite thing to do.

"No," he answered sharply. "With the mood you're in you're likely to throw yourself in Paul's arms and demand that he make mad passionate love to you there on the spot."

Cait's face went fire-engine red. "That's ridiculous."

Joe mumbled something she couldn't hear while he lifted her hand and slipped one arm, then the other, into the satin-lined sleeves of her full-length coat.

When he'd finished, Cait climbed on top of the kitchen chair, stretching out her arms to him. Joe stared at her as though she'd suddenly turned into a werewolf.

"What are you doing now?" he demanded in an exasperated voice.

"You're going to carry me, aren't you?"

"I was considering it."

"I want a piggyback ride. You gave Betsy McDonald a piggyback ride once and not me."

"Cait," Joe groaned. He jerked his fingers through his hair, and offered her his hand, wanting her to climb down from the chair. "Get down before you fall. Good lord, I swear you'd try the patience of a saint."

"I want you to carry me piggyback," she insisted. "Oh, please, Joe. My toes hurt so bad."

Once again her hero grumbled under his breath. She couldn't make out everything he said, but what she did hear was enough to curl her hair. With obvious reluctance, he walked to the chair, and giving a sigh of pure bliss, Cait wrapped her arms around his neck and hugged his lean hips with her legs. She laid her head on his shoulder and sighed again.

Still grumbling, Joe moved towards the back door.

Just then the kitchen door opened and Paul and Lindy walked in. Lindy gasped. Paul just stared.

"It's all right," Cait was quick to assure them. "Really it is. I was waiting under the mistletoe and you—"

"She downed four glasses of punch nonstop," Joe inserted before Cait could admit she'd been waiting there for Paul.

"Do you need any help?" Paul asked.

"None, thanks," Joe returned. "There's nothing to worry about."

"But..." Lindy looked concerned.

"She ain't heavy," Joe teased. "She's my wife."

THE PHONE RANG, waking Cait from a sound sleep. Her head began throbbing in time to the painful noise and she groped for the telephone receiver.

"Hello," she barked, instantly regretting that she'd spoken loudly.

"How are you feeling?" Joe asked.

"About like you'd expect," she whispered, keeping her eyes closed and gently massaging one temple. It felt as though tiny men had taken up residence in her head and were pounding away, hoping to attract her attention.

"What time does your flight leave?" he asked.

"It's okay. I'm not scheduled to leave until afternoon."

"It is afternoon."

Her eyes flew open. "What?"

"Do you still need me to take you to the airport?"

"Yes...please." She tossed aside the covers and reached for her clock, stunned to realise Joe was right. "I'm already packed. I'll be dressed by the time you arrive. Oh, thank goodness you phoned."

Cait didn't have time to listen to the pounding of the tiny men in her head. She showered and dressed in record time, swallowed a cup of coffee and a couple of aspirin, and was just shrugging into her coat when Joe arrived at the door.

She let him in, despite the suspiciously wide grin he wore.

"What's so amusing?"

"What makes you think I'm amused?" He strolled into the room, hands behind his back, as if he owned the place.

"Joe, we don't have time for your little games. Come on, or I'm going to miss my plane. What's with you, anyway?"

"Nothing." He circled her living room, still wearing that silly grin. "I don't suppose you realise it, but liquor has a peculiar effect on you."

Cait stiffened. "It does?" She remembered most of the party with great clarity. Good thing Joe had taken her home when he had.

"Liquor loosens your tongue."

"So?" She picked up two shopping bags filled with wrapped packages, leaving the lone suitcase for him. "Did I say anything of interest?"

"Oh, my, yes."

"Joe," she groaned, glancing quickly at her watch. They needed to get moving if she was to catch her flight. "Discount whatever I said—I'm sure I didn't mean it. If I insulted you, I apologise. If I told any family secrets, kindly forget I mentioned them."

He strolled to her side and tucked his finger under her chin. "This was a secret all right," he informed her in a lazy drawl.

"Are you sure it's true?"

"Relatively sure."

"What did I do? Declare undying love for you? Because if I did—"

"No, no, nothing like that."

"Just how long do you intend to torment me like this?" She was rapidly losing interest in his little game.

"Not much longer." He looked exceptionally pleased with himself. "So Martin's a minister now. Funny you never thought to mention that before."

"Ah..." Cait set aside the two bags and lowered herself to the sofa. So he'd found out. Worse, she'd been the one to tell him.

"That may well have some interesting ramifications, my dear. Have you ever stopped to think about them?"

CHAPTER EIGHT

"THIS IS EXACTLY why I didn't tell you about Martin," Cait informed Joe as he tossed her suitcase into the back seat of his car. She checked her watch again and groaned. They had barely an hour and a half before her flight was scheduled to leave. Cait was never late. Never—at least not when it was her own fault.

"It seems to me," Joe continued, his face deadpan, "there could very well be some legal grounds to our marriage."

Joe was saying that just to annoy her, and unfortunately it was working. "I've never heard anything more ridiculous in my life."

"Think about it, Cait," he said, ignoring her protest. "We could be celebrating our anniversary this spring. How many years is it now? Eighteen? My, how the years fly."

"Listen, Joe, I don't find this amusing." Again she glanced at her watch. If only she hadn't slept so late. Never again would she sample Christmas punch. Briefly she wondered what else she'd said to Joe, then decided it was better not to know.

"I heard a news report of a three-car pileup on the freeway, so we'd better take the side streets."

"Just hurry," Cait urged in an anxious voice.

"I'll do the best I can," Joe said, "but worrying about it isn't going to get us there any faster."

She glared at him. She couldn't help it. He wasn't the one who'd been planning this trip for months. If she missed this flight, her nephews and niece wouldn't have their Christmas presents from their Aunty Cait. Nor would she share in the family traditions that were so much a part of her Christmas. It was vital she get to the airport on time.

Everyone else had apparently heard about the accident on the freeway, too, and the downtown area was crowded with the overflow. Cait and Joe were delayed at every intersection and twice were forced to sit through two changes of the traffic signal.

Cait was growing more panicky by the moment. She just had to make this flight. But it almost seemed that she'd get to the airport faster if she simply jumped out of the car and ran there.

Joe stopped for another red light, but when the signal turned green, they still couldn't move—a delivery truck in front of them had stalled. Furious, Cait rolled down the window and stuck out her head. "Listen here, buster, get this show on the road," she shouted at the top of her lungs.

Her head was pounding and she prayed the aspirin would soon take effect.

"Quite the Christmas spirit," Joe muttered drily under his breath.

"I can't help it. I have to catch this plane."

"You'll be there in plenty of time."

"At this rate we won't make it to Sea-Tac Airport before Easter!"

"Relax, will you?" Joe suggested gently. He turned on the radio and a medley of Christmas carols filled the air. Normally the music would have had a calming effect on Cait, but she was suffering from a hangover, depression and severe anxiety, all at the same time. Her fingernails found their way into her mouth.

Suddenly she straightened. "Darn! I forgot to give you your Christmas gift. I left it at home."

"Don't worry about it."

"I didn't get you a gag gift the way I said." Actually she was pleased with the book she'd managed to find—an attractive coffee-table volume about the history of baseball.

Cait waited for Joe to mention *her* gift. Surely he'd bought her one. At least she fervently hoped he had, otherwise she'd feel like a fool. Though, admittedly, that was a feeling she'd grown accustomed to in the past few weeks.

"I think we might be able to get back on the freeway here," Joe said, as he made a sharp lefthand turn. They crossed the overpass, and from their vantage point, Cait could see that the freeway was unclogged and running smoothly.

"Thank God," she whispered, relaxing against the back of the thickly cushioned seat as Joe drove quickly ahead.

Her chauffeur chuckled. "I seem to remember you lecturing me—"

"I never lecture," she said testily. "I may have a strong opinion on certain subjects, but let me assure you, I never lecture."

"You were right, though. The streets of Bethlehem must have been crowded and bustling with activity at the time of that first Christmas. I can see it all now, can't you? A rug dealer is held up by a shepherd driving his flock through the middle of town."

Cait smiled for the first time that morning, because she could easily picture the scene Joe was describing.

"Then some furious woman, impatient to make it to the local camel merchant on time, sticks her nose in the middle of everything and shouts at the rug dealer to get his show on the road." He paused to chuckle at his own wit. "I'm convinced she wouldn't have been so testy except that she was suffering from one whopper of a hangover."

"Very funny," Cait grumbled, smiling despite herself.

He took the exit for the airport and Cait was gratified to note that her flight wasn't scheduled to leave for another thirty minutes. She was cutting it close, closer than she ever had before, but she'd confirmed her ticket two days earlier and had already been assigned her seat.

Joe pulled up at the drop-off point for her airline and gave her suitcase to a porter while Cait rummaged around in her bag for her ticket.

"I suppose this is goodbye for now," he said with an endearingly crooked grin that sent her pulses racing.

"I'll be back in less than two weeks," she reminded him, trying to keep her tone light and casual.

"You'll phone once you arrive?"

She nodded. For all her earlier panic, Cait now felt oddly unwilling to part company with Joe. She should be rushing through the airport to her departure gate, but she lingered, her heart overflowing with emotions she couldn't name.

"Have a safe trip," he said quietly.

"I will. Thanks so much . . . for everything."

"You're welcome." His expression sobered and the ever-ready mirth drained from his eyes. Cait wasn't sure who moved first. All she knew was that she was in Joe's arms, his thumb caressing the softness of her cheek as they gazed hungrily into each other's eyes.

Slowly he leaned forward to kiss her. Cait's eyes drifted shut as his mouth met hers.

Joe's kiss was heart-stoppingly tender. The noise and activity around them seemed to fade into the distance. Cait could feel herself dissolving. She moaned and arched closer, not wanting to leave the protective haven of his arms. Joe shuddered and hugged her tight, as if he, too, found it difficult to part.

"Merry Christmas, love," he whispered, releasing her with a reluctance that made her heart sing.

"Merry Christmas," she echoed, but she didn't move.

Joe gave her the gentlest of nudges. "You'd better hurry, Cait."

"Oh, right," she said, momentarily forgetting why she was at the airport. Reaching for the bags filled with gaily wrapped Christmas packages, she took two steps backward. "I'll phone when I arrive."

"Do. I'll be waiting to hear from you." He thrust his hands into his pockets and Cait had the distinct impression he did it to stop himself from reaching out for her again. The thought was a romantic one, a certainty straight from her heart.

Her heart . . . Her heart was full of feeling for Joe. More than she'd ever realised. He'd dominated her life these past few weeks—taking her to dinner, bribing his way back into her good graces with a pizza, taking her on a Christmas shopping expedition, escorting her to Paul's party. Joe had become her whole world. Joe, not Paul. Joe.

Given no other choice, Cait abruptly turned and hurried into the airport, through the security check and down the concourse to the proper gate.

The flight had already been called and only a handful of passengers had yet to board. Several were making lingering farewells to loved ones.

Cait dashed to the ticket counter to check in. A young soldier stood just ahead of her. "But you don't understand," the tall marine was saying to the airline employee. "I booked this flight over a month ago. I've got to be on that plane!"

"I couldn't be more sorry," the woman apologised, her dark eyes filled with regret. "This sort of thing happens, especially during holidays, but your ticket's for standby. I wish I could do something for you, but there isn't a single seat available."

"But I haven't seen my family in over a year. My Uncle Harvey is driving from Duluth to visit. He was in the marines, too. My mom's been baking for three weeks. Don't you see? I can't disappoint them now!"

Cait watched as the ticket agent rechecked her computer. "If I could magically create a seat for you, I would," she said sympathetically. "But there just isn't one."

"But when I bought the ticket, the woman told me I wouldn't have a problem getting on the flight. She said there're always no-shows. She sounded so sure."

"I couldn't be more sorry," the agent repeated, looking past the young marine to Cait.

"All right," he said, forcefully expelling his breath. "When's the next flight with available space? Any flight within a hundred miles of Minneapolis. I'll walk the rest of the way if I have to."

Once again, the woman consulted her computer. "We have space available the evening of the twenty-sixth."

"The twenty-sixth!" the young man shouted. "But that's after Christmas and eats up nearly all my leave. I'd be home less than a week."

"May I help you?" the airline employee said to Cait. She looked almost as unhappy as the marine, but apparently there wasn't anything she could do to help him.

Cait stepped forward and handed the woman her ticket. The soldier gazed at it longingly, then moved dejectedly from the counter and lowered himself into one of the moulded plastic chairs.

Cait hesitated, remembering how she'd stuck her head out of the window of Joe's truck that morning and shouted impatiently at the truck driver who was holding up traffic. A conversation she'd had with Joe earlier returned to haunt her. She'd argued that Christmas was a time filled with love and good cheer, the one time of year that brought out the very best in everyone. And sometimes, Joe had insisted, the very worst.

"Since you already have your seat assignment, you may board the flight now."

Cait grabbed the ticket with both hands, the urge to hurry nearly overwhelming her. Yet she hesitated.

"Excuse me," Cait said, drawing a breath and making her decision. She approached the soldier. He seemed impossibly young now that she had a good look at him. No more than eighteen, maybe nineteen. He'd probably joined the service right out of high school. His hair was cropped close to his head and his combat boots were so shiny Cait could see her reflection in them.

The marine glanced up at her, his face heavy with defeat. "Yes?"

"Did I hear you say you needed a ticket for this plane?"

"I have a ticket, ma'am. But it's standby and there aren't any seats."

"Here," she said, giving him her ticket. "Take mine."

The way his face lit up was enough to blot out her own disappointment at missing Christmas with Martin and her sister-in-law. The kids. Her mother... "My family's in Minneapolis, too, but I was there this summer."

"Ma'am, I can't let you do this."

"Don't cheat me out of the pleasure."

The last call for their flight was announced. The marine stood, his eyes wide with disbelief. "I insist," Cait said, her throat growing thick. "Here." She handed him the two bags full of gifts for her nephews and nieces. "There'll be a man waiting on the other end. A tall minister—he'll have on a collar. Give him these. I'll phone so he'll know to look for you."

"But, ma'am—"

"We don't have time to argue. Just do it."

"Thank you . . . I can't believe you're doing this." He reached inside his jacket and gave her his ticket. "Here. At least you'll be able to get a refund."

Cait smiled and nodded. Impulsively the marine hugged her, then swinging his duffel bag over his shoulder, he picked up the two bags of gifts and jogged down the ramp.

Cait waited for a couple of minutes, then wiped the tears from her eyes. She wasn't completely sure why she was crying. She'd never felt better in her life.

IT WAS AROUND SIX when she awoke. The apartment was dark and silent. Sighing, she picked up the phone, dragged it onto the bed with her and punched out Joe's number.

He answered on the first ring, as if he'd been waiting for her call. "How was the flight?" he asked immediately.

"I wouldn't know. I wasn't on it."

"You missed the plane!" he shouted incredulously. "But you were there in plenty of time."

"I know. It's a long story, but basically, I gave my seat to someone who needed it more than I did." She smiled dreamily, remembering how the young marine's face had lit up. "I'll tell you about it sometime."

"Where are you now?"

"Home."

He exhaled sharply, then said, "I'll be over in fifteen minutes."

Actually it took him twelve. By then Cait had brewed a pot of coffee and made herself a peanut-butter-and-jelly sandwich. She hadn't eaten all day and was starved. She'd just finished the sandwich when Joe arrived.

"What about your luggage?" Joe asked, looking concerned. He didn't give her a chance to respond. "Exactly what do you mean, you gave your seat away?"

Cait explained as best she could. Even now she found herself surprised by her actions. Cait rarely behaved spontaneously. But something about that young soldier had reached deep within her heart and she'd reacted instinctively.

"The airline is sending my suitcase back to Seattle on the next available flight, so there's no need to worry," Cait explained. "I talked to Martin, who was quick to tell me the Lord would reward my generosity."

"Are you going to catch a later flight, then?" Joe asked. He helped himself to a cup of coffee and pulled out the chair across from hers.

"There aren't any seats," Cait said. She leaned back, yawning, and covered her mouth. Why she should be so tired after sleeping away most of the afternoon was beyond her. "Besides, the office is short-staffed. Lindy gave Paul her notice and a trainee is coming in, which makes everything even more difficult. They can use me."

Joe frowned. "Giving up your vacation is one way to impress Paul."

Words of explanation crowded on the end of her tongue. She realised Joe wasn't insulting her; he was only stating a fact. What he didn't understand was that Cait hadn't thought of Paul once the entire day. Her staying or leaving had absolutely nothing to do with him.

If she'd been thinking of anyone, it was Joe. She knew now that giving up her seat to the marine hadn't been entirely unselfish. When Joe kissed her good-bye, her heart had started telegraphing messages she had yet to fully decode. The plain and honest truth was that she hadn't wanted to leave him. It was as if she really did belong to him....

That perception had been with her from the moment they'd parted at the airport. It had followed her in the taxi on the ride back to the apartment. Joe was the last person she thought of when she'd fallen asleep, and the first person she remembered when she awoke.

It was the most amazing thing.

"What are you going to do for Christmas?" Joe asked, still frowning into his coffee cup. For someone who'd seemed downright regretful that she was flying halfway across the country, he didn't seem all that pleased to be sharing her company now.

"I...haven't decided yet. I suppose I'll spend a quiet day by myself." She'd wake up late, indulge in a lazy scented bath, find something sinful for breakfast. Ice cream, maybe. Then she'd paint her toenails and settle down with a good book. The day would be lonely, true, but certainly not wasted.

"It'll be anything but quiet," Joe challenged.

"Oh?"

"You'll be spending it with me and my family."

"THIS IS THE FIRST TIME Joe has ever brought a girl to join us for Christmas," Virginia Rockwell said as she set a large tray of freshly baked cinnamon rolls in the centre of the huge kitchen table. She wiped her hands clean on the apron that was secured around her thick waist.

Cait felt she should explain. She was a little uncomfortable arriving unannounced with Joe this way. "Joe and I are just friends."

Mrs. Rockwell shook her head, which set the white curls bobbing. "I saw my son's eyes when he brought you into the house." She grinned knowingly. "I remember you from the old neighbourhood, with your starched dresses and the pigtails with those bright pink ribbons. You were a pretty girl then and you're even prettier now."

"The starched dresses were me all right," Cait confirmed. She'd been the only girl for blocks around who always wore dresses to school.

Joe's mother chuckled again. "I remember the sensation you caused in the neighbourhood when you revealed that Joe had kissed you." She chuckled, her eyes shining. "His father and I got quite a kick out of that. I still remember how furious Joe was when he learned his secret was out."

"I only told one person," Cait protested. But Betsy had told plenty of others, and the news had spread with alarming speed. However, Cait figured she'd since paid for her sins tenfold. Joe had made sure of that in the past few weeks.

"It's so good to see you again, Caitlin. When we've got a minute I want you to sit down and tell me all about your mother. We lost contact years ago, but I always thought she was a darling.''

"I think so, too," Cait agreed, carrying a platter of scrambled eggs to the table. She did miss being with her family, but Joe's mother made it almost as good as being home. "I know that's how Mom feels about you, too. She'll want to thank you for being kind enough to invite me into your home for Christmas."

"I wouldn't have it any other way."

"I know." She glanced into the other room where Joe was sitting with his brother and sister-in-law. Her heart throbbed at the sight of him with his family. But these newfound feelings for Joe left her at a complete loss. What she'd told Mrs. Rockwell was true. Joe was her friend. The very best friend she'd ever had. She was grateful for everything he'd done for her since they'd chanced upon each other, just weeks ago, really. But their friendship was developing into something much stronger. If only she didn't feel so...so ardent about Paul. If only she didn't feel so confused!

Joe laughed at something one of his nephews said and Cait couldn't help smiling. She loved the sound of his laughter. It was vigorous and robust and lively— just like his personality.

"Joe says you're working as a stockbroker right here in Seattle."

"Yes. I've been with Webster, Rodale and Missen for over a year now. My degree was in accounting but—"

"Accounting?" Mrs. Rockwell nodded approvingly. "My Joe has his own accountant now. Good thing, too. His books were in a terrible mess. He's a builder, not a pencil pusher, that boy."

"Are you telling tales on me, Mom?" Joe asked as he sauntered into the kitchen. He picked up a piece of bacon and bit off the end. "When are we going to open the gifts? The kids are getting restless."

"The kids, nothing. You're the one who's eager to tear into those packages," his mother admonished. "We'll open them after breakfast, the way we do every Christmas."

Joe winked at Cait and disappeared into the living room once more.

Mrs. Rockwell watched her son affectionately. "Last year he shows up on my doorstep bright and early Christmas morning needing gift wrap. Then, once he's got all his presents wrapped, he walks into my kitchen—" her face crinkled in a wide grin "—and he sticks all those presents in my refrigerator." She chuckled at the memory. "For his brother, he bought two canned hams and three gallons of ice cream. For me it was canned cat food and a couple of rib roasts."

Breakfast was a bustling affair, with Joe's younger brother, his wife and their children gathered around the table. Joe sat next to Cait and held her hand while his mother offered the blessing. Although she wasn't home with her own family, Cait felt she had a good deal for which to be thankful.

Conversation was pleasant and relaxed, but foremost on the children's minds was opening the gifts. The table was cleared and the dishes washed in record time.

Cait sat beside Joe, holding a cup of coffee, as the oldest grandchild gave out the presents. Christmas music played softly in the background as the children tore into their packages. The youngest, a two-year-old girl, was more interested in the box than in the gift itself.

When Joe came to the square package Cait had given him, he shook it enthusiastically.

"Be careful, it might break," she warned, knowing there was no chance of that happening.

Carefully he removed the bows, then slowly unwrapped his gift. Cait watched expectantly as he lifted the book from the layers of bright paper. "A book on baseball?"

Cait nodded, smiling. "As I recall, you used to collect baseball cards."

"I ended up trading away my two favourites."

"I'm sure it was for a very good reason."

"Of course."

Their eyes held until it became apparent that everyone in the room was watching them. Cait glanced self-consciously away.

Joe cleared his throat. "This is a great gift, Cait. Thank you, very much."

"You're welcome very much."

He leaned over and kissed her as if it was the most natural thing in the world. It felt right, their kiss. If anything Cait was sorry to stop at one.

"Surely you have something for Cait," Virginia Rockwell prompted her son.

"Of course I do."

"He's probably keeping it in the refrigerator," Cait suggested, to the delight of Joe's family.

"Oh, ye of little faith," he said, removing a box from his shirt pocket.

"I recognise that paper," Sally, Joe's sister-in-law, murmured to Cait. "It's from Stanley's."

Cait's eyes widened at the name of an expensive local jeweller's. "Joe?"

"Go ahead and open it," he urged.

Cait did as he suggested, hands fumbling in her eagerness. She slipped off the ribbon and peeled away the gold textured wrap to reveal a white jeweller's box. It contained a second box, a small black velvet one, which she opened very slowly. She gasped at the lovely cameo brooch inside.

"Oh, Joe," she whispered. It was a lovely piece carved in onyx and overlaid with ivory. She'd longed for a cameo, a really nice one, for years and wondered how Joe could possibly have known.

"You gonna kiss Uncle Joe?" his nephew asked. "'Cause if you are, I'm hiding my eyes."

"Of course she's going to kiss me," Joe answered for her. "Only she can do it later when there aren't so many curious people watching her." He glanced swiftly at his mother. "Just the way Mom used to thank Dad for her Christmas gift. Isn't that right, Mom?"

"I'm sure Cait...will," Virginia answered, clearly flustered. She patted her hand against the side of her head as though she feared the pins had fallen from her hair, her gaze skirting around the room.

Cait didn't blame the older woman for being embarrassed, but one look at the cameo and she was willing to forgive him anything.

The day flew past. After the gifts were opened—
with everyone exclaiming in surprised delight over the
gifts Joe had bought, with Cait's help—the family
gathered around the piano. Mrs. Rockwell played as
they sang a variety of Christmas carols, their voices
loud and cheerful. Joe's father had died several years
earlier, but often throughout the day he was mentioned with affection and love. Cait hadn't known
Joe's father well. She barely remembered his mother,
but the family obviously felt Andrew Rockwell's
presence far more than his absence on this festive day.

Joe drove Cait back to her apartment late that
night. Mrs. Rockwell had insisted on sending a plate
of cookies and candy home with her, and Cait swore
it was enough goodies to last her a month of Sundays.
Now she felt sleepy and warm; leaning her head
against the seat, she closed her eyes.

"We're here," Joe whispered close to her ear.

Reluctantly Cait opened her eyes and sighed. "I had
such a wonderful day. Thank you, Joe." She couldn't
quite stifle a yawn as she reached for the door handle,
thinking longingly of bed.

"That's it?" He sounded disappointed.

"What do you mean, that's it?"

"I seem to remember a certain promise you made
this morning."

Cait frowned, not sure she understood what he
meant. "When?"

"When we were opening the gifts," he reminded
her.

"Oh," Cait said, straightening. "You mean when I
opened your gift to me and saw the brooch."

Joe nodded with slow, exaggerated emphasis. "Right. Now do you remember?"

"Of course." The kiss. He planned to claim the kiss she'd promised him. She brushed her mouth quickly over his and grinned. "There."

"If that's the best you can do, you should have kissed me in front of Charlie."

"You're faulting my kissing ability?"

"Charlie's dog gives better kisses than that."

Cait felt more than a little insulted. "Is this a challenge, Joseph Rockwell?"

"Yes," he returned archly. "You're darn right it is."

"All right, then you're on." She set the plate of cookies aside, slid over on the wide seat and slipped her arms around Joe's neck. Next she wove her fingers into his thick hair.

"This is more like it," Joe murmured contentedly.

Cait paused. She wasn't entirely sure why. Perhaps it was because she'd suddenly lost all interest in making fun out of something that had always been so wonderful between them.

Joe's eyes met hers, and the laughter and fun seemed to empty out of them. Slowly he expelled his breath and brushed his lips along her jaw. The warmth of his breath was exciting as his mouth skimmed towards her temple. His arms closed around her waist and pulled her tight against him.

Impatiently he began to kiss her, introducing her to a world of warm, thrilling sensations. His moist mouth then explored the curve of her neck. It felt so good that Cait closed her eyes and experienced a curious weightlessness she'd never known—a heightened awareness of physical longing.

"Oh, Cait..." He broke away from her, his breathing laboured and heavy. She knew instinctively that he wanted to say more, but he changed his mind and buried his face in her hair, exhaling sharply.

"How am I doing?" she whispered once she found her voice.

"Just fine."

"Are you ready to retract your statement?"

He hesitated. "I don't know. Convince me again." So she did, her kiss moist and gentle, her heart fluttering hard against her ribs.

"Is that good enough?" she asked when she'd recovered her breath.

Joe nodded, as though he didn't quite trust his own voice. "Excellent."

"I had a wonderful day," she whispered. "I can't thank you enough for including me."

Joe shook his head lightly as though there was so much more he wanted to say to her and couldn't. Cait slipped out of the car and walked into her building, turning on the lights when she reached her apartment. She slowly put away her things, wanting to wrap this feeling around her like a warm quilt. Minutes later, she glanced out of her window to see Joe still sitting in his car, his hands gripping the steering wheel and his head bent over. It looked to Cait as though he was battling with himself to keep from following her inside. And she would have welcomed him if he had.

CHAPTER NINE

CAIT STARED at the computer screen for several minutes, blind to the information in front of her. Deep in thought, she released a long, slow breath.

Paul had seemed grateful to see her when she'd shown up at the office that morning. The week between Christmas and New Year's could be a harried one. Lindy had looked surprised, then quickly retreated into her own office after exchanging a brief good-morning and little else. Her friend's behaviour continued to baffle Cait, but she couldn't concentrate on Lindy's problems just now, or even on her work.

No matter what she did, Cait couldn't stop thinking about Joe and the kisses they'd exchanged Christmas evening. Nor could she forget his tortured look as he'd sat in his car after she'd gone into her apartment. Even now she wasn't certain why she hadn't immediately run back outside. And by the time she'd decided to do that, he was gone.

Cait was so absorbed in her musings that she barely heard the knock at her office door. Guiltily she glanced up to find Paul standing just inside her doorway, his hands in his pockets, his eyes weary.

"Paul!" Cait waited for her heart to trip into double time the way it usually did whenever she was anywhere near him. It didn't, which was a relief but no longer much of a surprise.

"Hello, Cait." His smile was uneven, his face tight. He seemed ill at ease and struggling to disguise it. "Have you got a moment?"

"Sure. Come on in." She stood and motioned towards her client chair. "This is a pleasant surprise. What can I do for you?"

"Nothing much," he said vaguely, sitting down. "Uh, I just wanted you to know how pleased I am that you're here. I'm sorry you cancelled your vacation, but I appreciate your coming in today. Especially in light of the fact that Lindy will be leaving." His mouth thinned briefly.

No one, other than Joe and Martin, was aware of the real reason Cait wasn't in Minnesota the way she'd planned. Nor had she suggested to Paul that she'd changed her plans to help him out because they'd be short-staffed; apparently he'd drawn his own conclusions.

"So Lindy's decided to follow through with her resignation?"

Paul nodded, then frowned anew. "Nothing I say will change her mind. That woman's got a stubborn streak as wide as a..." He shrugged, apparently unable to come up with an appropriate comparison.

"The construction project's nearly finished," Cait offered, making small talk rather than joining in his criticism of Lindy. Absently she stood up and wandered around her office, stopping to straighten the large Christmas wreath on her door, the one she and Lindy had put up earlier in the month. Lindy was her friend and she wasn't about to agree with Paul, or argue with him, for that matter. Actually she should have been pleased that Paul had sought her out this way, but she felt curiously indifferent. And she did have several things that needed to be done.

"Yes, I'm delighted with the way everything's turned out," Paul said. "Joe Rockwell's done a fine job. His reputation is excellent and I imagine he'll be one of the big-time contractors in the area within the next few years."

Cait nodded casually, hoping she'd concealed the thrill of excitement that had surged through her at the mention of Joe's name. She didn't need Paul to tell her Joe's future was bright; she could see that for herself. At Christmas, his mother had boasted freely about his success. Joe had recently received a contract for a large government project—his most important to date—and she was exceptionally proud of him. He might have trouble keeping his books straight, but he left his customers satisfied. If he worked as hard at satisfying them as he did at finding the right Christmas tree, Cait could well believe that he was gaining a reputation for excellence.

"Well, listen," Paul said, drawing in a deep breath, "I won't keep you." His eyes were clouded as he stood and headed towards the door. He hesitated, turning back to face her. "I don't suppose you'd be free for dinner tonight, would you?"

"Dinner," Cait repeated as though she'd never heard the word before. Paul was inviting her to dinner? After all these months? Now, when she least expected it? Now, when it no longer mattered? After all the times she'd ached to the bottom of her heart for

some attention from him, he was finally asking her out
on a date? Now?

"That is, if you're free."

"Uh...yes, sure...that would be nice."

"Great. How about if I pick you up around five-
thirty? Unless that's too early for you?"

"Five-thirty will be fine."

"I'll see you then."

"Thanks, Paul." Cait felt numb. There wasn't any
other way to describe it. It was as if her dreams were
finally beginning to play themselves out—too late.
Paul, whom she'd loved from afar for so long, wanted
to take her to dinner. She should be dancing around
the office with glee, or at least feeling something other
than this peculiar dull sensation in the pit of her
stomach. If this was such a significant, exciting,
hoped-for event, why didn't she feel any of the exhil-
aration she'd expected?

After taking a moment to collect her thoughts, Cait
walked down the hallway to Lindy's office and found
her friend on the phone. Lindy glanced up, smiled
feebly in Cait's direction, then abruptly dropped her
gaze as if the call demanded her full attention.

Cait waited a couple of minutes, then decided to
return later when Lindy wasn't so busy. She needed to
talk to her friend, needed her counsel. Lindy had always encouraged Cait in her dreams of a relationship
with Paul. When she was discouraged, it was Lindy
who cheered her sagging spirits. Yes, it was definitely
time for a talk. She'd try to get Lindy to confide in her,
too. Cait valued Lindy's friendship; true, she couldn't
help being hurt that the person she considered one of
her best friends would give notice to leave the firm

without so much as discussing it with her. But Lindy must have had her reasons. And maybe she, too, needed some support just about now.

Hearing her own phone ring, Cait hurried back to her office. She was busy for the remainder of the day. The New York Stock Exchange was due to close in a matter of minutes when Joe happened by.

"Hi," Cait greeted, her smile wide and welcoming. Her gaze connected with Joe's and he returned her smile. Her heart reacted automatically, leaping with sheer happiness.

"Hi, yourself." He sauntered into her office and threw himself down in the same chair Paul had taken earlier, stretching out his long legs in front of him and folding his hands over his stomach. "So how's the world of finance this fine day?"

"About as well as always."

"Then we're in deep trouble," he joked.

His smile was infectious. It always had been, but Cait had initially resisted him. Her defences had weakened long before, though, and she responded readily with a smile of her own.

"You done for the day?"

"Just about." She checked the time. In another five minutes, New York would be closing down. There were several items she needed to clear from her desk, but nothing pressing. "Why?"

"Why?" It was little short of astonishing how far Joe's eyebrows could reach, Cait noted, all but disappearing into his hairline.

"Can't a man ask a simple question?" Joe asked.

"Of course." The banter between them was like a well-rehearsed play. Never had Cait been more at ease with a man—or had more fun with a man. Or with anyone, really. "What I want to know is whether 'simple' refers to the question or to the man asking it."

"Ouch," Joe said, grinning broadly. "Those claws are sharp this afternoon."

"Actually today's been good." Or at least it had since he'd arrived.

"I'm glad to hear it. How about dinner?" He jumped to his feet and pretended to waltz around her office, playing a violin. "You and me. Wine and moonlight and music. Romance and roses." He wiggled his eyebrows at her suggestively. "You work too hard. You always have. I want you to enjoy life a little more. It would be good for both of us."

Joe didn't need to give her an incentive to go out with him. Cait's heart soared at the mere idea. Joe made her laugh, made her feel good about herself and the world. Of course, he possessed a remarkable talent for driving her crazy, too. But she supposed a little craziness was good for the spirit.

"Only promise me you won't wear those high heels of yours," he chided, pressing his hand to the small of her back. "I've suffered excruciating back pains ever since Paul's Christmas party."

Paul's name seemed to leap out and grab Cait by the throat. "Paul," she repeated, sagging against the back of her chair. "Oh, dear."

"I know you consider him a dear," Joe teased. "What has your stalwart employer done this time?"

"He asked me out to dinner," Cait admitted, frowning. "Out of the blue this morning he popped into my office and invited me to dinner as if we'd been dating for months. I was so stunned, I didn't know what to think.''

"What did you tell him?'' Joe seemed to consider the whole thing a huge joke. "Wait—'' he held up his hand "—you don't need to answer that. I already know. You sprang at the offer.''

"I didn't exactly spring,'' she contended, somewhat offended by Joe's attitude. The least he could do was show a little concern. She'd spent Christmas with him, and according to his own mother this was the first time he'd ever brought a woman home for the holiday. Furthermore, despite his insisting to all and sundry that they were married, he certainly didn't seem to mind her seeing another man.

"I'll bet you nearly went into shock.'' A smile trembled at the edges of his mouth as if he was picturing her reaction to Paul's invitation and finding it all terribly amusing.

"I did not go into shock,'' she defended herself heatedly. She'd been taken by surprise, that was all.

"Listen,'' he said, walking towards the door, "have a great time. I'll catch you later.'' With that he was gone.

Cait couldn't believe it. Her mouth dropped open and she paced frantically, clenching and unclenching her fists. It took her a full minute to recover enough to run after him.

Joe was talking to his foreman, the same stocky man he'd been with the day he followed Cait into the lift.

"Excuse me,'' she said, interrupting their conversation, "but when you're finished I'd like a few words with you, Joe.'' Her back was ramrod-stiff and she kept flexing her hands as though preparing for a fight.

Joe glanced at his watch. "It might be a while."

"Then might I have a few minutes of your time now?"

The foreman stepped away, his step cocky. "You want me to dismiss the crew again, boss? I can tell them to go out and buy a New Year's present for their wives, if you like."

The man was rewarded with a look that was hot enough to barbecue spareribs. "That won't be necessary, thanks, anyway, Harry."

"You're welcome, boss. We only serve tớ please."

"Then please me by kindly shutting up."

Harry chuckled and returned to another section of the office.

"You wanted something?" Joe demanded of Cait.

Boy, did she. "Is that all you're going to say?"

"About what?"

"About my going to dinner with Paul? I expected you to be ... I don't know, upset or something."

"Why should I be upset? Is he going to have his way with you? I sincerely doubt it, but if you're worried, invite me along and I'll be more than happy to protect your honour."

"What's the matter with you?" she demanded, not bothering to disguise her fury and disappointment. She stared at Joe, waiting for him to mock her again, but once more he surprised her. His gaze sobered.

"You honestly expect me to be jealous?"

"Not jealous exactly," she corrected, although he wasn't far from the truth. "Concerned."

"I'm not. Paul's a good man."

"I know, but—"

"You've been in love with him for months—"

"I think it was more of an infatuation."

"True. But he's finally asked you out, and you've accepted."

"Yes, but—"

"We know each other well, Cait. We were married, remember?"

"I'm not likely to forget it." Especially when Joe took pains to point it out at every opportunity. "Shouldn't that mean...something?" Cait couldn't believe she'd said that. For weeks she'd suffered acute mortification every time Joe mentioned the childhood stunt. Now she was using it to suit her own purposes.

Joe reached out and took hold of her shoulders. "As a matter of fact, our marriage does mean a good deal."

Hearing Joe admit as much was gratifying.

"I want only the best for you," he continued. "It's what you deserve. All I can say is that I'd be more than pleased if everything works out between you and Paul. Now if you'll excuse me, I need to talk over some matters with Harry."

"Oh, right, sure, go ahead." She couldn't seem to get the words out fast enough. When she'd called Martin to explain why she wouldn't be in Minnesota for Christmas, he'd claimed that God would reward her sacrifice. If Paul's invitation to dinner was God's reward, she wanted her airline ticket back.

The numb feeling returned as Cait walked back to her office. She didn't know what to think. She'd believed...she'd hoped she and Joe shared something very special. Clearly their times together meant something entirely different to him than they had to her. Otherwise he wouldn't behave so casually about her going out with Paul. And he certainly wouldn't seem so pleased about it!

That was what hurt Cait the most, and yes, she was hurt. It had taken her several minutes to identify her feelings, but now she did.

More by accident than design, Cait walked into Lindy's office. Her friend had already put on her coat and was carrying her briefcase, ready to leave the office.

"Paul asked me out to dinner," Cait blurted out.

"He did?" Lindy's eyes widened with surprise. But she didn't turn it into a joke, the way Joe had.

Cait nodded. "He just strolled in as if it was something he did every day and asked me out."

"Are you happy about it?"

"I don't know," Cait answered honestly. "I suppose I should be pleased. It's what I'd prayed would happen for months."

"Then what's the problem?" Lindy asked.

"Joe doesn't seem to care. He said he hopes everything works out the way I want it to."

"Which is?" Lindy pressed.

Cait had to think about that a moment, her heart in her throat. "Honest to heaven, Lindy, I don't know anymore."

"I UNDERSTAND the salmon here is superb," Paul was saying, reading over the Boathouse menu. It was a well-known restaurant on Lake Union.

Cait scanned the list of entrées, which featured fresh seafood, then chose the grilled salmon—the same dish she'd ordered that night with Joe. Tonight, though, she wasn't sure why she was even bothering. She wasn't hungry, and Paul was going to be wasting good money while she made a pretence of enjoying her meal.

"I understand you've been seeing a lot of Joe Rockwell," he said conversationally.

That Paul should mention Joe's name right now was ironic. Cait hadn't stopped thinking about him from the moment he'd dropped into her office earlier that afternoon. Their conversation had left a bitter taste in her mouth. She'd sincerely believed their relationship was developing into something...special. Yet Joe had gone out of his way to give her the opposite impression.

"Cait?" Paul stared at her.

"I'm sorry, what were you saying?"

"Simply that you and Joe Rockwell have been seeing a lot of each other recently."

"Uh, yes. As you know, we were childhood friends," she murmured. "Actually Joe and my older brother were best friends. Then Joe's family moved to the suburbs and our families lost contact."

"Yes, I remember you mentioned that."

The waitress came for their order, and Paul requested a bottle of white wine. Then he chatted amicably for several minutes, mentioning subjects of shared interest from the office.

Cait listened attentively, nodding from time to time or adding the occasional comment. Now that she had his undivided attention, Cait wondered what it was about Paul that she'd found so extraordinary. He was attractive, but not nearly as dynamic or exciting as she found Joe. True, Paul possessed a certain charm, but compared to Joe, he was subdued and perhaps even a little dull. Cait couldn't imagine her stalwart boss carrying her piggyback out the back door because her high heels were too tight. Nor could she see Paul bantering with her the way Joe did.

The waitress delivered the wine bottle, opened it and poured them each a glass, after Paul had given his approval. Their dinners followed shortly afterwards. After taking a bite or two of her delicious salmon, Cait noticed that Paul hadn't touched his meal. If anything, he seemed restless.

He rolled the stem of the wineglass between his fingers, watching the wine swirl inside. Then he suddenly blurted out, "What do you think of Lindy's leaving the firm?"

Cait was taken aback by the fervour in his voice when he mentioned Lindy's name. "Frankly I was shocked," Cait said. "Lindy and I have been good friends for a couple of years now." There'd been a time when the two had done nearly everything together. The summer before, they'd holidayed in Mexico and returned to Seattle with enough handwoven baskets and bulky blankets to set up shop themselves.

"Lindy's resigning came as a surprise to you, then?"

"Yes, this whole thing caught me completely unaware. Lindy didn't even mention the other job offer to me. I always thought we were good friends."

"Lindy *is* your friend," Paul said with enough conviction to persuade the patrons at the nearby tables. "You wouldn't believe what a good friend she is."

"I . . . know that." But friends sometimes had surprises up their sleeves. Lindy was a good example of that, and apparently so was Joe.

"I find Lindy an exceptional woman," Paul commented, watching Cait closely.

"She's probably one of the best stockbrokers in the business," Cait said, taking a sip of her wine.

"My . . . admiration for her goes beyond her keen business mind."

"Oh, mine, too," Cait was quick to agree. Lindy was the kind of friend who would traipse through the blazing sun of Mexico looking for a conch shell because she knew Cait really wanted to take one home with her. And Lindy had listened to countless hours of Cait's bemoaning her sorry fate of unrequited love for Paul.

"She's a wonderful woman."

Joe was wonderful, too, Cait thought. So wonderful her heart ached at his indifference when she'd announced she would be dining with Paul.

"Lindy's the kind of woman a man could treasure all his life," Paul went on.

"I couldn't agree with you more," Cait said. Now, if only Joe would realise what a treasure *she* was. He'd married her once—well, sort of—and surely the thought of spending their lives together had crossed his mind in the past few weeks.

Paul hesitated as though he were at a loss for words. "I don't suppose you've given any thought to the reason Lindy made this unexpected decision to resign?"

Frankly Cait hadn't. Her mind and her heart had been so full of Joe that deciphering her friend's actions had somehow escaped her. "She received a better offer, didn't she?" Which was understandable. Lindy would be an asset to any firm.

It was then that Cait understood. Paul hadn't asked her to dinner out of any desire to develop a romantic relationship with her. He saw her as a means of discovering what had prompted Lindy to resign. This new awareness came as a relief, a burden lifted from her shoulders. Paul wasn't interested in her. He never had been and probably never would be. A few weeks ago, that realisation would have been a crushing defeat, but all Cait experienced now was an overwhelming sense of gratitude.

"I'm sure if you talk to Lindy, she might reconsider," Cait suggested.

"I've tried, trust me. But there's a problem."

"Oh?" Now that Cait had sampled the salmon, she discovered it to be truly delicious. She hadn't realised how hungry she was.

"Cait, look at me," Paul said, raising his voice slightly. His face was pinched, his eyes intense. "Damn, but you've made this nearly impossible."

She looked up at him, her face puzzled. "What is it, Paul?"

"You have no idea, do you? I swear you've got to be the most obtuse woman in the world." He pushed aside his plate and briefly closed his eyes, shaking his head. "I'm in love with Lindy. I have been for weeks...months. But for the life of me I couldn't get her to notice me. I swear I did everything but turn cartwheels in her office. It finally dawned on me why she wasn't responding.''

"Me?" Cait asked in a feeble, mouselike squeak.

"Exactly. She didn't want to betray your friendship. Then one afternoon—I think it was the day you first recognised Joe—we, Lindy and I, were in my office alone together and— Oh, hell, I don't know how it happened, but Lindy was looking something up for me and she stumbled over one of the cords the construction crew was using. Fortunately I was able to catch her before she fell to the floor. I know it wasn't her fault, but I was so angry, afraid she might have been hurt. Lindy was just as angry with me for being angry with her, and it seemed the only way to shut her up was to kiss her. That was the beginning and I swear to you everything exploded in our faces at that moment.''

Cait swallowed, fascinated by the story. "Go on.''

"I tried for days to get her to agree to go out with me. But she kept refusing until I demanded to know why."

"She told you...how I felt about you?" The thought was mortifying.

"Of course not. Lindy's too good a friend to divulge your confidence. Besides, she didn't need to tell me. I've known all along. Good grief, Cait, what did I have to do to discourage you? Hire a skywriter?''

"I don't think anything that drastic was necessary," she muttered, humiliated to the very marrow of her bones.

"I repeatedly told Lindy I wasn't attracted to you, but she wouldn't listen. Finally she told me if I'd talk to you, explain everything myself, she'd agree to go out with me."

"The phone call," Cait said on a stroke of genius. "That was the reason you called me, wasn't it? You wanted to talk about Lindy, not that business article."

"Yes." He looked deeply grateful for her insight, late though it was.

"Well, for heaven's sake, why didn't you?"

"Believe me, I've kicked myself a dozen times since. I wish I knew. At the time, it seemed so heartless to have such a frank discussion over the phone. Again and again, I promised myself I'd say something. Lord knows I dropped enough hints, but you weren't exactly receptive."

She winced. "But why is Lindy resigning?"

"Isn't it obvious?" Paul demanded. "It was becoming increasingly difficult for us to work together. She didn't want to betray her best friend, but at the same time..."

"But at the same time you two were falling in love."

"Exactly. I can't lose her, Cait. I don't want to hurt your feelings, and believe me, it's nothing personal— you're a trustworthy employee and a decent person— but I'm simply not attracted to you."

Paul didn't seem to be the only one. Other than treating their relationship like one big joke, Joe hadn't ever claimed any romantic feelings for her, either.

"I had to do something before I lost Lindy."

"I couldn't agree more."

"You're not angry with her, are you?"

"Good heavens, no," Cait said, offering him a brave smile.

"We both thought something was developing between you and Joe Rockwell. You seemed to be seeing quite a bit of each other, and then at the Christmas party—"

"Don't remind me," Cait said with a low groan.

Paul's face creased in a spontaneous smile. "Joe certainly has a wit about him, doesn't he?"

Cait gave a resigned nod.

Now that Paul had cleared the air, he seemed to develop an appetite. He reached for his dinner and ate heartily. By contrast, Cait's salmon had lost its appeal. She stared down at her plate, wondering how she could possibly make it through the rest of the evening.

She did, though, quite nicely. Paul didn't even seem to notice that anything was amiss. It wasn't that Cait was distressed by his confession. If anything, she was relieved at this turn of events and delighted that Lindy had fallen in love. Paul was obviously crazy about her; she'd never seen him more animated than when he was discussing Lindy. It still amazed Cait that she'd been so unperceptive about Lindy's real feelings. Not to mention Paul's...

Paul dropped her off at her building and saw her to the front door. "I can't thank you enough," he said, his voice warm. Impulsively he hugged her, then hurried back to his sports car.

Although she was certainly guilty of being obtuse, Cait knew exactly where Paul was headed. No doubt Lindy would be waiting for him, eager to hear the details of their conversation. Cait planned to talk to her friend herself first thing in the morning.

Cait's apartment was dark and lonely. So lonely the silence seemed to echo off the walls. She hung up her coat before turning on the lights, her thoughts as dark as the room had been.

She made herself a cup of tea. Then she sat on the sofa, tucking her feet beneath her as she stared unseeingly at the walls, assessing her options. They seemed terribly limited.

Paul was in love with Lindy. And Joe... Cait had no idea where she stood with him. For all she knew—

Her thoughts were interrupted by the phone. She answered on the second ring.

"Cait?" It was Joe and he seemed surprised to find her back so early. "When did you get in?"

"A few minutes ago."

"You don't sound right. Is something wrong?"

"My goodness," she said, breaking into sobs. "What could possibly be wrong?"

CHAPTER TEN

THE FLOW OF EMOTION took Cait by storm. She'd had no intention of crying; in fact, the thought hadn't even entered her mind. One moment she was sitting there, contemplating the evening's revelations, and the next she was sobbing hysterically into the phone.

"Cait?"

"Oh," she wailed. "This is all your fault in the first place." Cait didn't know what made her say that. The words had slipped out before she'd realised it.

"What happened?"

"Nothing. I...I can't talk to you now. I'm going to bed." With that, she gently replaced the receiver. Part of her hoped Joe would call back, but the telephone remained stubbornly silent. She stared at it for several minutes. Apparently Joe didn't care if he talked to her or not.

The tears continued to flow. They remained a mystery to Cait. She wasn't a woman given to bouts of crying, but now that she'd started she couldn't seem to stop.

She changed out of her dress and into a tracksuit, pausing halfway through to wash her face.

Sniffling and hiccuping, she sat on the end of her bed and dragged a shuddering breath through her lungs. Crying like this made absolutely no sense whatsoever.

Paul was in love with Lindy. At one time, the news would have devastated her, but not now. Cait felt a tingling happiness that her best friend had found a man to love. And the infatuation she'd held for Paul couldn't compare with the strength of her love for Joe.

Love.

There, she'd admitted it. She was in love with Joe. The man who told restaurant employees that she was suffering from amnesia. The man who walked into lifts and announced to total strangers that they were married. Yet this was the same man who hadn't revealed a minute's concern about her dating Paul Jamison.

Joe was also the man who'd gently held her hand through a children's film. The man who made a practice of kissing her senseless. The man who'd held her in his arms Christmas night as though he never intended to let her go.

Joseph Rockwell was a fun-loving jokester who took delight in teasing her. He was also tender and thoughtful and loving—the man who'd captured her heart only to drop it carelessly.

Her doorbell chimed and she didn't need to look in the peephole to know it was Joe. But she felt panicky all of a sudden, too confused and vulnerable to see him now.

She walked slowly to the door and opened it a crack.

"What the hell is going on?" Joe demanded, not waiting for an invitation to march inside.

Cait wiped her eyes on her sleeve and shut the door. "Nothing."

"Did Paul try anything?"

She rolled her eyes. "Of course not."

"Then why are you crying?" He stood in the middle of her living room, fists planted on his hips as if he'd welcome the opportunity to punch out her boss.

If Cait knew why it was necessary to cry nonstop like this, she would have answered him. She opened her mouth, hoping some intelligent reason would emerge, but the only thing that came out was a low-pitched squeak. Joe was gazing at her in complete confusion. "I . . . Paul's in love."

"With you?" His voice rose half an octave with disbelief.

"Don't make it sound like such an impossibility," she said crossly. "I'm reasonably attractive, you know." If she was expecting Joe to list her myriad charms, Cait was disappointed.

Instead, his frown darkened. "So what's Paul being in love got to do with anything?"

"Absolutely nothing. I wished him and Lindy the very best."

"So it is Lindy?" Joe murmured as though he'd known it all along.

"You didn't honestly think it was me, did you?"

"Hell, how was I supposed to know? I *thought* it was Lindy, but it was you he was taking to dinner. Frankly it didn't make a whole lot of sense to me."

"Which is something else," Cait grumbled, standing so close to him, their faces were only inches apart. Her hands were planted on her hips, her pose mirroring his. They resembled a pair of gunslingers ready for a shootout, Cait thought absently. "I want to know one thing. Every time I turn around, you're telling anyone and everyone who'll listen that we're married. But when it really matters you—"

"When did it really matter?"

Cait ignored the question, thinking the answer was obvious. "You casually turn me over to Paul as if you couldn't wait to be rid of me. Obviously you couldn't have cared less."

"I cared," he shouted.

"Oh, right," she shouted back, "but if that was the case, you certainly didn't bother to show it!"

"What was I supposed to do, challenge him to a duel?"

He was being ridiculous, Cait decided, and she refused to take the bait. The more they talked, the more unreasonable they were both becoming.

"I thought dating Paul was what you wanted," he complained. "You talked about it long enough. Paul this and Paul that. He'd walk past and you'd all but swoon."

"That's not the least bit true." Maybe it had been at one time, but not now and not for weeks. "If you'd taken the trouble to ask me, you might have learned the truth."

"You mean you don't love Paul?"

Cait rolled her eyes again. "Bingo."

"It isn't like you to be so sarcastic."

"It isn't like you to be so... awful."

He seemed to mull that over for a moment. "If we're going to be throwing out accusations," he said tightly, "then maybe you should take a look at yourself."

"What exactly do you mean by that?" As usual, no one could get a reaction out of Cait more effectively than Joe. "Never mind," she answered, walking to the door. "This discussion isn't getting us anywhere. All we seem capable of doing is hurling insults at each other."

"I disagree," Joe answered calmly. "I think it's time we cleared the air."

She took a deep breath, feeling physically and emotionally deflated.

"Joe, it'll have to wait. I'm in no condition to be rational right now and I don't want either of us saying things we'll regret." She held open her door for him. "Please?"

He seemed about to argue with her, then he sighed and dropped a quick kiss on her mouth. Wide-eyed, she watched him leave.

LINDY WAS WAITING in Cait's office early the following morning, holding two plastic cups of freshly brewed coffee. Her eyes were wide and expectant as Cait entered the office. They stared at each other for several moments.

"Are you angry with me?" Lindy whispered. She handed Cait one of the cups in an apparent peace offering.

"Of course not," Cait murmured. She put down her briefcase and accepted the cup, which she placed carefully on her desk. Then she gave Lindy a reassur-

174   THE FORGETFUL BRIDE

ing hug, and the two of them sat down for their much postponed talk.

"Why didn't you tell me?" Cait burst out.

"I wanted to," Lindy said earnestly. "I had to stop myself a hundred times. The worst part of it was the guilt—knowing you were in love with Paul, and loving him myself."

Cait wasn't sure how she would have reacted to the truth, but she preferred to think she would've understood, and wished Lindy well. It wasn't as though Lindy had stolen Paul away from her.

"I don't think I realised how I felt," Lindy continued, "until one afternoon when I tripped over a stupid cord and fell into Paul's arms. From there, everything sort of snowballed."

"Paul told me."

"He . . . told you about that afternoon?"

Cait grinned and nodded. "I found the story wildly romantic."

"You don't mind?" Lindy watched her closely as if half-afraid of Cait's reaction even now.

"I think it's wonderful."

Lindy's smile was filled with warmth and excitement. "I never knew being in love could be so delightful, but at the same time cause so much pain."

"Amen to that," Cait stated emphatically.

Her words shot like live bullets into the room. If Cait could have reached out and pulled them back, she would have.

"Is it Joe Rockwell?" Lindy asked quietly.

Cait nodded, then shook her head. "See how much he's confused me?" She made a sound that was half sob, half giggle. "That man infuriates me so much I want to scream. Or cry." Cait had always thought of herself as a sane and sensible person. She lived a quiet life, worked hard at her job, enjoyed travelling and crossword puzzles. Then she'd bumped into Joe. Suddenly she found herself demanding piggyback rides, talking to strangers in lifts and seeking out phantom women at Christmas parties while downing spiked punch like it was soda pop.

"But then at other times?" Lindy prompted.

"At other times I love him so much I hurt all the way through. I love everything about him. Even those loony stunts of his. In fact, I usually laugh as hard as everyone else does. Even if I don't always want him to know it."

"So what's going to happen with you two?" Lindy asked. She took a sip of coffee and as she did so, Cait caught a flash of diamond.

"Lindy?" Cait demanded, jumping out of her seat. "What's that on your finger?"

Lindy's face broke into a smile so wide Cait was nearly blinded. "You noticed."

"Of course I did."

"It's from Paul. After he had dinner with you, he stopped over at my apartment. We talked for the longest time and then after a while he asked me to marry him. At first I didn't know what to say. It seems so soon. We . . . we hardly know each other."

"Good grief, you've worked together for months."

"I know," Lindy said with a shy smile. "That was what Paul told me. It didn't take him long to convince me. He had the ring all picked out. Isn't it beautiful?''

"Oh, Lindy." The diamond was a lovely solitaire set in a wide band of gold. The style and shape were perfect for Lindy's long, elegant finger.

"I didn't know if I should wear it until you and I had talked, but I couldn't make myself take it off this morning."

"Of course you should wear it!" The fact that Paul had been carting it around when he'd had dinner with her didn't exactly flatter her ego, but she was so thrilled for Lindy that seemed a minor concern.

Lindy splayed her fingers out in front of her to better show off the ring. "When he slipped it on my finger, I swear it was the most romantic moment of my life. Before I knew it, tears were streaming down my face. I still don't understand why I felt like crying. I think Paul was as surprised as I was."

There must have been something in the air that reduced susceptible females to tears, Cait decided. Whatever it was had certainly affected her.

"Now you've sidetracked me," Lindy said, looking up from her diamond, her gaze dreamy and warm. "You were telling me about you and Joe."

"I was?"

"Yes, you were," Lindy insisted.

"There's nothing to tell. If there was you'd be the first person to hear. I know," she admitted before her friend could bring up the point, "we have seen a lot of each other recently, but I don't think it meant anything to him. When he found out Paul had invited me to dinner, he seemed downright delighted."

"I'm sure it was all an act."

Cait wished she could believe that. Oh, how she wished it.

"You're in love with him?" Lindy asked softly, hesitantly.

Cait nodded and lowered her eyes. It hurt to think about Joe. Everything was a game to him—one big joke. Lindy had been right about one thing, though. Love was the most wonderful experience of her life. And the most painful.

THE NEW YORK Stock Exchange had closed and Cait was punching some figures into her computer when Joe strode into her office and closed the door.

"Feel free to come in," she muttered, continuing her work. Her heart was pounding but she dared not let him know the effect he had on her.

"I will make myself at home, thank you," he answered cheerfully, ignoring her sarcasm. He pulled out a chair and sat down expansively, resting one ankle on the opposite knee and relaxing as if he was in a cinema, waiting for the main feature to begin.

"If you're here to discuss business, might I suggest investing in blue-chip stocks? They're always a safe bet." Cait went on typing, doing her best to ignore Joe—which was nearly impossible, although she gave an Oscar-winning performance, if she did say so herself.

"I'm here to talk business all right," Joe said, "but it has nothing to do with the stock market."

"What business could the two of us possibly have?" she asked, her voice deliberately ironic.

"I want to continue the discussion we were having last night."

"Perhaps you do, but unfortunately that was last night and this is now." How confident she sounded, Cait thought, mildly pleased with herself. "I can do without hearing you list my no doubt numerous flaws."

"It's your being my wife I want to discuss."

"Your wife?" She wished he'd quit throwing the subject at her as if it meant something to him. Something other than a joke.

"Yes, my wife." He gave a short laugh. "Believe me, it isn't your flaws I'm here to discuss."

Despite everything, Cait's heart raced. She reached for a stack of papers and switched them from one basket to another. Her entire filing system was probably in jeopardy, but she had to do something with her hands before she stood up and reached out to Joe. She did stand then, but it was to remove a large silver bell strung from a red velvet ribbon hanging in her office window.

"Paul and Lindy are getting married," he supplied next.

"Yes, I know. Lindy and I had a long talk this morning." She took the wreath off her door next.

"I take it the two of you are friends again?"

"We were never not friends," Cait answered stiffly, stuffing the wreath, the bell and the three ceramic Wise Men into the bottom drawer of her filing cabinet. Hard as she tried not to, she could feel her defences crumbling. "Lindy's asked me to be her maid of honour and I've agreed."

"Will you return the favour?"

It took a moment for the implication to sink in, and even then Cait wasn't sure she should follow the trail Joe seemed to be forging through this conversation. She leaned forward and rested her hands on the edge of the desk.

"I'm destined to be an old maid," she said flippantly, although she couldn't help feeling a sliver of real hope.

"You'll never be that."

Cait was hoping he'd say her beauty would make her irresistible, or that her warmth and wit and intelligence was sure to attract a dozen suitors. Instead he said the very thing she could have predicted. "We're already married, so you don't need to worry about being a spinster."

Cait released a sigh of impatience. "I wish you'd give up on that, Joe. It's growing increasingly old."

"As I recall, we celebrated our eighteenth wedding anniversary not long ago."

"Don't be ridiculous. All right," she said, straightening abruptly. If he wanted to play games, then she'd respond in kind. "Since we're married, I want a family."

"Hey, sweetheart," he cried, tossing his arms in the air, "that's music to my ears. I'm willing."

Cait prepared to leave the office, if not the building. "Somehow I knew you would be."

"Two or three," he interjected, then chuckled and added, "I suppose we should name the first two Barbie and Ken."

Cait sent him a scalding look that made him chuckle even louder.

"If you prefer, we'll leave the names open to negotiation," he said.

"Of all the colossal nerve..." Cait muttered, moving to the window and gazing out.

"If you want daughters, I've got no objection, but from what I understand that's not left up to us."

Cait turned around, folding her arms across her chest. "Correct me if I'm wrong," she said coldly, certain he'd delight in doing so. "But you did just ask me to marry you. Could you confirm that?"

"All I'm looking to do is make legal what's already been done."

Cait frowned. Was he serious, or wasn't he? He was talking about marriage, about joining their lives as if he were planning a bid on a construction project.

"When Paul asked Lindy to marry him, he had a diamond ring with him."

"I was going to buy you a ring," Joe said emphatically. "I still am. But I thought you'd want to pick it out yourself. If you wanted a diamond, why didn't you say so? I'll buy you the whole store if that'll make you happy."

"One ring will suffice, thank you."

"Pick out two or three. I understand diamonds are an excellent investment."

Cait frowned. "Not so fast," she said, holding out her arm. It was vital she maintain some distance between them. If Joe kissed her or started talking about having children again, they might never get the facts clear.

"Not so fast?" he repeated incredulously. "Honey, I've been waiting eighteen years to discuss this. You're not going to ruin everything now, are you?" He advanced a couple of steps towards her.

"I'm not agreeing to anything until you explain yourself." For every step he took towards her, Cait retreated two.

"About what?" Joe was frowning, which wasn't a good sign.

"Paul."

His eyelids slammed shut, then slowly raised. "I don't understand why that man's name has to come into every conversation you and I have."

Cait decided it was better to ignore that comment. "You haven't even told me you love me."

"I love you." He actually sounded annoyed, as if she'd insisted on having the obvious reiterated.

"You might say it with a little more feeling," Cait suggested.

"If you want feeling, come here and let me kiss you."

"No."

"Why not?" By now they'd completely circled her desk. "We're talking serious things here. Trust me, sweetheart, a man doesn't bring up marriage and babies with just any woman. I love you. I've loved you for years, only I didn't know it."

"Then why did you let Paul take me out to dinner?"

"You mean I could have stopped you?"

"Of course. I didn't want to go out with him! I was sick about having to turn down your offer for dinner, and you didn't even seem to care that I was going out with another man. And as far as you were concerned, he was your main competition.''

''I wasn't worried.''

''That wasn't the impression I got later.''

''All right, all right,'' Joe said, rifling his fingers through his hair. ''I didn't think Paul was interested in you. I saw him and Lindy together one night at the office and the electricity between them was so thick it could have lit up Seattle.''

''You knew about Lindy and Paul?''

Joe shrugged. ''Let me put it this way. I had a sneaking suspicion. But when you started talking about Paul as though you were in love with him, I got worried.''

''You should have been.'' Which was a bold-faced lie.

Somehow without her being quite sure how it happened, Joe manoeuvred himself so only a few inches separated them.

''Are you ever going to kiss me?'' he demanded.

Meekly Cait nodded and walked into his arms like a child opening the gate and skipping up the path to home. This was the place she belonged. With Joe. This was home and she need never doubt his love again.

With a sigh that seemed to come from the deepest part of him, Joe swept her close. For a breathless moment they looked into each other's eyes. He was about to kiss her when there was a knock at her door.

Harry, Joe's foreman, walked in without waiting for a response. ''I don't suppose you've seen Joe—'' He stopped abruptly. "Oh, sorry," he said, flustered and eager to make his escape.

"No problem," Cait assured him. "We're married. We have been for years and years."

Joe was chuckling as his mouth settled over hers, and in a single kiss he wiped out all the doubts and misgivings, replacing them with promises and thrills.

EPILOGUE

THE ROBUST SOUND of organ music filled the Seattle church as Cait slowly stepped down the centre aisle, her feet moving in time to the traditional music. As the maid of honour, Lindy stood to one side of the altar while Joe and his brother, who was serving as the best man, waited on the other.

Cait's brother, Martin, stood directly ahead of her. He smiled at Cait as the assembly rose and she came down the aisle, her heart overflowing with happiness.

Cait and Joe had planned this day for months. If there'd been any lingering doubts that Joe really loved her, they were long gone. He wasn't the type of man who expressed his love with flowery words and gifts. But Cait had known that from the first. He'd insisted on building their home before the wedding and they'd spent countless hours going over the plans. Cait was helping him with his accounting and would be taking over the task full-time as soon as they started their family. Which would be soon, very soon. The way Cait figured it, she'd be pregnant by next Christmas.

But before they began their real life together, they'd enjoy a perfect honeymoon in New Zealand. He'd wanted to surprise her with the trip, but Cait had needed a passport. They'd only be gone two weeks, which was all the time Joe could afford to take, since he had several large projects coming up.

As the organ concluded the ''Wedding March,'' Cait handed her bouquet to Lindy and placed her hands in Joe's. He smiled down on her as if he'd never seen a more beautiful woman in his life. From the look on his face, Cait knew he could hardly keep from kissing her right then and there.

''Dearly beloved,'' Martin said, stepping forward, ''we are gathered here today in the sight of God and man to celebrate the love of Joseph James Rockwell and Caitlin Rose Marshall.''

Cait's eyes locked with Joe's. She did love him, so much her heart felt close to bursting. After all these months of waiting for this moment, Cait was sure she'd be so nervous her voice would falter. That didn't happen. She'd never felt more confident of anything than her feelings for Joe and his for her. Cait's voice rang out strong and clear, as did Joe's.

As they exchanged the rings, Cait could hear her mother and Joe's weeping softly in the background. But these were tears of shared happiness. The two women had renewed their friendship and were excited about the prospect of grandchildren.

Cait waited for the moment when Martin would tell Joe he could kiss his bride. Instead he closed his Bible, reverently set it aside, and said, ''Joseph James Rockwell, do you have the baseball cards with you?''

''I do.''

Cait looked at them as if they'd both lost their minds. Joe reached inside his tuxedo jacket and produced two flashy baseball cards.

"You may give them to your bride."

With a dramatic flourish, Joe did as Martin instructed. Cait stared down at the two cards and grinned broadly.

"You may now kiss the bride," Martin declared.

Joe was more than happy to comply.

TASTY FOOD COMPETITION!

How would you like a years supply of Mills & Boon Romances ABSOLUTELY FREE? Well, you can win them! All you have to do is complete the word puzzle below and send it in to us by 30th June 1994. The first 5 correct entries picked out of the bag after that date will win a years supply of Mills & Boon Romances (*four books every month - worth over £90*) What could be easier?

```
H O L L A N D A I S E R
E Y E G G O W H A O H A
R S E E C L A I R U C T
B T K K A E T S I F I A
E E T I S M A L C F U T
U R C M T L H E E L Q O
G S I U T F O N O E D U
N H L T A S O T O N E F M I
I S R S O M A C W A A L
R I A E E T I R J A E L
E F G L L P T O T V R E
M O U S S E E O D O C P
```

CLAM	HOLLANDAISE	OYSTERS	SPICE
COD	JAM	PRAWN	STEAK
CREAM	LEEK	QUICHE	TART
ECLAIR	LEMON	RATATOUILLE	
EGG	MELON	RICE	**PLEASE TURN**
FISH	MERINGUE	RISOTTO	**OVER FOR**
GARLIC	MOUSSE	SALT	**DETAILS**
HERB	MUSSELS	SOUFFLE	**ON HOW**
			TO ENTER ➡

HOW TO ENTER

All the words listed overleaf, below the word puzzle, are hidden in the grid. You can find them by reading the letters forward, backwards, up or down, or diagonally. When you find a word, circle it or put a line through it, the remaining letters (which you can read from left to right, from the top of the puzzle through to the bottom) will ask a romantic question.

After you have filled in all the words, don't forget to fill in your name and address in the space provided and pop this page in an envelope (you don't need a stamp) and post it today. Hurry – competition ends 30th June 1994.

Mills & Boon Tasty Food Competition,
FREEPOST,
P.O. Box 236,
Croydon,
Surrey. CR9 9EL

Hidden Question _____

_____

Are you a Reader Service Subscriber?   Yes ☐   No ☐

Ms/Mrs/Miss/Mr _____

Address _____

_____

_____ Postcode _____

mps MAILING PREFERENCE SERVICE   COMTF

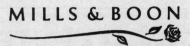

MILLS & BOON

NEW LOOK MILLS & BOON ROMANCES

A few months ago we introduced new look covers on our Romance series and we'd like to hear just how much you like them.

Please spare a few minutes to answer the questions below and we will send you a **FREE** Mills & Boon novel as a thank you. Just send the completed questionnaire back to us today - **NO STAMP NEEDED.**

Don't forget to fill in your name and address, so that we know where to send your **FREE** book!

Please tick the appropriate box to indicate your answers. ✔

1. For how long have you been a Mills & Boon Romance reader?

Since the new covers ☐	1 to 2 years ☐	6 to 10 years ☐
Less than 1 year ☐	3 to 5 years ☐	Over 10 years ☐

2. How frequently do you read Mills & Boon Romances?

Every Month ☐   Every 2 to 3 Months ☐   Less Often ☐

3. From where do you usually obtain your Romances?

Mills & Boon Reader Service ☐   Supermarket ☐

W H Smith/John Menzies/Other Newsagent ☐

Boots/Woolworths/Department Store ☐

Other (please specify:) _____

4. Please let us know how much you like the new covers:

Like very much ☐ Don't like very much ☐

Like quite a lot ☐ Don't like at all ☐

5. What do you like most about the design of the covers? _____

_____

_____

6. What do you like least about the design of the covers? _____

_____

_____

7. Do you have any additional comments you'd like to make about our new look Romances? _____

_____

_____

8. Do you read any other Mills & Boon series? (Please tick each series you read).

Love on Call (Medical Romances) ☐ Temptation ☐

Legacy of Love (Masquerade) ☐ Duet ☐

Favourites (Best Sellers) ☐ Don't read any others ☐

9. Are you a Reader Service subscriber?

Yes ☐   No ☐

If Yes, what is your subscriber number? _____

10. What is your age group?

16-24 ☐ 25-34 ☐ 35-44 ☐ 45-54 ☐ 55-64 ☐ 65+ ☐

THANK YOU FOR YOUR HELP

✉   Please send your completed questionnaire to: ✉

Mills & Boon Reader Service, FREEPOST,
P O Box 236, Croydon, Surrey CR9 9EL

NO STAMP NEEDED

Ms/Mrs/Miss/Mr: _____ NR

Address: _____

_____

_____ Postcode: _____

You may be mailed with offers from other reputable companies as a result of this application. Please tick box if you would prefer not to receive such offers. ☐
One application per household.

mps MAILING PREFERENCE SERVICE

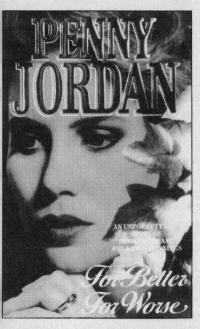

Next Month's Romances

Each month you can choose from a wide variety of romance with Mills & Boon. Below are the new titles to look out for next month, why not ask either Mills & Boon Reader Service or your Newsagent to reserve you a copy of the titles you want to buy – just tick the titles you would like and either post to Reader Service or take it to any Newsagent and ask them to order your books.

Please save me the following titles: Please tick ✓

HEART OF THE OUTBACK	Emma Darcy	
DARK FIRE	Robyn Donald	
SEPARATE ROOMS	Diana Hamilton	
GUILTY LOVE	Charlotte Lamb	
GAMBLE ON PASSION	Jacqueline Baird	
LAIR OF THE DRAGON	Catherine George	
SCENT OF BETRAYAL	Kathryn Ross	
A LOVE UNTAMED	Karen van der Zee	
TRIUMPH OF THE DAWN	Sophie Weston	
THE DARK EDGE OF LOVE	Sara Wood	
A PERFECT ARRANGEMENT	Kay Gregory	
RELUCTANT ENCHANTRESS	Lucy Keane	
DEVIL'S QUEST	Joanna Neil	
UNWILLING SURRENDER	Cathy Williams	
ALMOST AN ANGEL	Debbie Macomber	
THE MARRIAGE BRACELET	Rebecca Winters	

If you would like to order these books in addition to your regular subscription from Mills & Boon Reader Service please send £1.90 per title to: Mills & Boon Reader Service, Freepost, P.O. Box 236, Croydon, Surrey, CR9 9EL, quote your Subscriber No:.................................... (If applicable) and complete the name and address details below. Alternatively, these books are available from many local Newsagents including W.H.Smith, J.Menzies, Martins and other paperback stockists from 12 March 1994.

Name:...

Address:...

....Post Code:.........................

To Retailer: If you would like to stock M&B books please contact your regular book/magazine wholesaler for details.

You may be mailed with offers from other reputable companies as a result of this application.
If you would rather not take advantage of these opportunities please tick box ☐

'Go back, Cassie.'

There was a harsh, mocking inflexion in Ryker's voice as he moved away from her. She was bereft, stunned. 'Tell Jim Harker that there's no deal. No story.'

Cassie closed her eyes, absorbing the impact of the shock on her bewildered senses. When would she ever learn the lesson he had been trying to teach her throughout all those long, empty years? He did not want her. He would never want her.

Dear Reader

As the dark winter nights unfold, what better to turn to than a heart-warming Mills & Boon! As usual, we bring you a selection of books which take you all over the world, with heroines you like and heroes you would love to be with! So take a flight of fancy away from everyday life to the wonderful world of Mills & Boon—you'll be glad you did.

The Editor

When **Joanna Neil** discovered Mills & Boon, her lifelong addiction to reading crystallised into an exciting new career—writing romances. Always prey to a self-indulgent imagination, she loved to give free rein to her characters, who were probably the outcome of her varied lifestyle. She has been a clerk, telephonist, typist, nurse and infant teacher. She enjoys dressmaking and cooking at her Leicestershire home. Her family includes a husband, son and daughter, an exuberant yellow Labrador, and two slightly crazed cockatiels.

FLAME OF
LOVE

BY

JOANNA NEIL

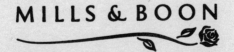

MILLS & BOON

MILLS & BOON LIMITED
ETON HOUSE, 18-24 PARADISE ROAD
RICHMOND, SURREY TW9 1SR

*First published in Great Britain 1993
by Mills & Boon Limited*

© Joanna Neil 1993

*Australian copyright 1993
Philippine copyright 1994
This edition 1994*

ISBN 0 263 78308 1

*Set in Times Roman 11 on 12 pt.
91-9402-48091 C*

Made and printed in Great Britain

CHAPTER ONE

'I WANT to come in. Open up.'

The voice was strong and deep, and even though it was distorted by the heavy wood panelling of the front door the sound of it floated upwards and filtered through to the room where Cassie sat, bare feet curled up beneath her on the makeshift bed.

Someone would deal with it, she decided, going back to her writing.

'I have to talk to you, all of you,' the man insisted.

A commotion had started up downstairs, and through it she strained to hear the muffled reply. Some kind of heated exchange was going on, but they wouldn't let him in; whoever he was, he was wasting his time.

They were worried about the bailiffs for a start, and, with one thing and another, there had been enough trouble over the last few days. They simply weren't taking any risks.

She stretched her legs, easing them into a more comfortable position on the mattress, and settled back, her spine resting against the hard wall, the notepad lying open across her knees. Chewing on the end of her pencil, she idly studied her pink-enamelled toes.

The desire for realism and authenticity was all very well, but she hadn't counted on quite so many disturbances when she had set out to write this article.

A loud hammering started up, the sound of a steel-hard fist meeting up with resistant wood. She could almost feel the reverberations echoing through the house.

'You needn't imagine that I'll go away.' The rumbling tones came again, and she frowned, scoring through the last phrase she had written before checking the watch on her slim wrist.

It was late in the afternoon, so it couldn't be the bailiffs, could it? Anyway, it wasn't likely that they'd be back again, not if Nick's information was right and the police were going to arrive hotfoot in the morning.

The sun streamed in relentlessly through the window and she pushed her fingers through the errant black curls that had escaped from her untidy topknot. Pinning up her long hair made her feel much cooler in this summer heat. It had been just her luck to finish up with the smallest room in the place. If she hadn't been made of sterner stuff, she might almost have begun to feel claustrophobic.

The pounding started up again. 'I know she's in there. I want to talk to her.'

Cassie grinned. It was probably one of Steph's admirers. It wasn't the first time there had been angry spats. He was determined, too, from the sound of him. She opened up the window a notch, allowing the faint breeze to fan her cheeks and throat.

'Patience is not my strong point. You'd do well to think on that.' The gravelled intonation wafted on the air, muted by the clamour that was going on below her in the hall, and a ragged line etched its way into her brow. Wasn't there something vaguely familiar about that voice?

She shrugged dismissively and her oversized T-shirt slid precariously down over her shoulder. Hitching it back into place, she decided that it was times like these when she longed for the privacy of her own flat. The first thing she would do when she went back would be to indulge herself in a long, long soak in the bath.

But work came first. She sighed. Nick was convinced he already had some good photos to send in for the feature. Her mouth quirked wryly. She'd hardly seen him since he'd turned the loft into a dark-room.

'OK, that's it. I'm giving you just five more seconds. One...'

There was a silence.

'Two...'

She held her breath. This man meant business, and he was in a hurry.

'Three...four...'

He wouldn't get through the barricades, would he? She shook her head. Of course he wouldn't.

'Five—stand clear.'

Her mouth gaped a little as the noise of splintering wood gave way to the almighty crash of planking hurling itself to the floor.

'Where is she?' Cold purpose penetrated every syllable, and Cassie's fingers froze on the pencil. She sat up very straight, her face paling with shock. She knew that voice.

Her eyes widened. It couldn't be him, could it? Hadn't he gone over to France just a few weeks ago? He'd said he had some business to sort out over there, that he might extend it to a short holiday. And anyway, he didn't know she was here, did he? How on earth would he have tracked her down? Why would he have wanted to?

Even as she thought it, the knowledge came that anything was possible where he was concerned. The man had his own in-built radar system, didn't he? She flipped her notebook closed and rammed it into her bag on the floor. Pushing her feet into her shoes, she went out on to the landing and surreptitiously peered down over the stair rail.

Studying the newcomer who had erupted with such shattering force into the cramped hallway, she was all too aware that her heart had begun a heavy, discordant pounding against her ribcage, and that her palms were slowly clenching on the wooden rail. It was him all right. Even though he had his back to her, there could be no mistaking him.

Ryker. Six feet two of pure trouble.

There was a clatter in the hall below as someone tripped over what was left of the rough barricade, and Ryker's wide shoulders moved, his unyielding frame tensed, at the ready. The sun's rays lanced through the open doorway, marking him out, touching his crisp black hair with an iridescent gleam.

For a few unguarded moments, Cassie felt the slow, familiar melt of her limbs, the undermining lap at the edges of her resistance. It wasn't fair, this magnetic pull he seemed to exert over her emotions, this way he had of drawing her to him with his own irresistible brand of sorcery. She closed her eyes briefly, fiercely, trying to shut him out. There was no future in loving Ryker. He would never return her feelings.

It was ironic—wasn't it?—that she had spent three years at university trying to get him out of her system—what a futile hope that had been. Her brow furrowed as she tried to clamp down on her wavering thoughts. She wouldn't let his presence cloud her thinking. She had work to do, a feature to write.

Why did he have to turn up here now, when she was in the middle of a scoop? He couldn't just come along and disrupt everything. She hated the thought that he might jeopardise the stand her companions were taking. That was why his sudden arrival had unnerved her, wasn't it? Her inner shakiness had nothing at all to do with fragmented hopes and reckless longings.

Her glance skimmed the small group of men who had assembled in the hallway, and her frown deepened. What were they thinking of, anyway, standing back and letting him through? What was the matter with them? Were their brains completely addled?

All right, so he was a tough-looking proposition, but they didn't know about the black belt in karate, did they? And they outnumbered him three to one, for heaven's sake. They might at least put up some kind of a fight, instead of letting him force his way into the building.

Nick was the first to find his tongue. 'We don't want any trouble, Ryker.'

'Nor do I. If you had let me in I wouldn't have had to resort to force. I have something to say to all of you when I've finished.'

Nick said, 'Couldn't you have waited till tomorrow? Your timing's way out, you know.'

Ryker's impatience showed. 'No, I couldn't.'

He turned to Steph, and Cassie caught the full impact of his hard-boned profile. 'I want Cassandra. Where is she?'

The silly girl went to pieces, her hand riffling through her tousled auburn hair. 'Are you sure?' she said, a funny, breathless little catch in her voice. 'Won't I do instead?'

His mouth curved in brief acknowledgement, and Cassie drummed her fingertips restlessly on the banister. The girl was a fool. Couldn't she see he was lethal? Obviously she didn't know what she was dealing with. The man hadn't stayed a bachelor into his early thirties without knowing how to kiss and run.

Ryker's sharp gaze fastened unerringly on the stairs. 'So there you are,' he said with smooth satisfaction.

'Rats,' she muttered, shooting back into the bedroom. She heard his feet pounding the wooden boards as he took them in ultra-swift time.

Her nerves leapt as he appeared in the doorway, and she stared at him darkly through the sudden wave of dizziness that swirled in her head. He wasn't even breathing fast.

'What are you doing here?' she said directly, striving to keep cool defiance in her tone. It was her only defence against the shock of seeing him standing there, an imposing intruder in the room. She wasn't prepared for it. 'I thought you were in France. You told me you were going away.'

His slow smile did nothing to soothe her prickly emotions. 'But now I'm back,' he murmured. 'And just in time, it seems.'

She scowled. 'Did you *have* to force your way in here like that, like some hot-blooded Viking on the rampage? I'm working, Ryker; this is my territory, and your heavy-handed methods are not wanted here—*you* are not wanted here.'

The snub glanced off his hard exterior. 'So I gather. I've had warmer welcomes than this.' Mockery laced his tone, and she stiffened.

'What did you expect?' she asked grimly. 'I'm in the middle of something. What's behind this sudden appearance? How did you know where I was staying?'

He appraised her thoughtfully. 'This place belongs to a friend of mine. He was planning on making a few renovations, and, to put it mildly, he was less than pleased when he found out about all the activity that had suddenly sprung up. Seeing his property featured in the *Despatch* only intensified his desire to prosecute. Can you blame him?'

Inwardly, Cassie groaned. It couldn't have turned out worse, could it? Her new-found friends had unwittingly focused on the very circles in which Ryker moved. That was bound to mean trouble.

Coolly cynical, he went on, 'I might have guessed from the outset that you and Nick Driscoll had a hand in it. He doesn't change much, does he? The first sniff of opportunity, and he's in there, rooting.'

A tiny muscle flicked in her cheek. 'It's his job. What do you expect?'

'Nothing at all. He doesn't interest me in the slightest.' He stopped moving, his long, hard-muscled body just a hair's breadth away from her, and her eyes were instantly riveted on blue denim pulled taut across strong thighs, on the deep navy sweatshirt that closely moulded his broad chest. Hastily she dragged her gaze away, only to find it meshed with gold as he looked down at her.

'It's your part in it that concerns me,' he said. 'If it had been anyone else, I'd have had no compunction about leaving them to face the consequences. But as things stand, your father is a good friend. He's also a public figure—have you thought about how this could affect him? He isn't likely to react well to your getting yourself mixed up with the police.'

'I have to live my own life, Ryker,' she advised him softly. 'And my father's name isn't going to be drawn into this, so there's no reason for him to get himself into a state. He doesn't need to worry about my every move.'

'Is that so? Maybe he could rest easier if you didn't exhibit such a penchant for the unsavoury. Living in a squat was never going to endear him to your cause, was it?' He paused, a dry smile playing over his firm, well shaped mouth. 'I can't say that your latest crusade came as any great surprise to me when I heard about it, but it did occur to me that you were heading straight for disaster. This particular manoeuvre doesn't appear to have the glow of fortune shining over it.'

Her mouth indented with scornful amusement. 'So I suppose you're here to haul me back into line? What did you have in mind—a brash show of force leading to a tactical surrender of some sort?' She tossed her head, and the unruly cloud of dark curls quivered unsteadily. 'Do us both a favour and take off again, Ryker. I don't need you around. I can sort out my own problems.'

He shifted then, and she watched him warily, his long, vital body an inherent threat to her composure, the shimmering heat of his glance sliding over the ripe softness of her curves. 'Tactical surrender,' he repeated slowly, savouring the words on his tongue, a faint grin in his voice. 'Now there's a thought——'

'Forget it,' she snapped, sharply regretting her unguarded phrasing. 'I'm here, and I'm staying for the duration.'

He watched her consideringly, the warm, speculative gleam still lingering fathoms deep in his eyes. 'An unfortunate stand to take, I'm afraid. You ought to know by now that once I decide on a course of action I always follow it through to its logical conclusion.' He paused to let the message sink in. 'Roughly translated,' he added helpfully, 'that means I'm here now, and I'd like you to leave with me.'

Her smile was deceptively sweet. 'Isn't that too bad? I'm afraid you lost out this time. But put it down to experience, why don't you? After all, things can't always go your way, you know.'

'I wouldn't be too sure about that.' His tawny, tiger eyes mocked her. 'You never did weigh more than a sack of feathers. It wouldn't be the first time I've thrown you over my shoulder.'

Cassie's chin took on an obstinate slant, even as she backed away. Her eyes were a brittle, deep blue. 'You wouldn't dare.'

'Try me,' he challenged drily, eyeing the pert line of her smooth-fitting white jeans.

'Back off, Ryker,' she said, biting down on her uncertainty with acid tone. 'Lay hands on me and you'll live to regret it. Just remember, you're the one who taught me self-defence, and I sure as hell remember every nasty move in the book.'

'Every one?' he chuckled, moving closer. 'This I have to see.' Bending suddenly, he swooped to lift her unceremoniously over one broad shoulder.

Cassie's breath caught in sharp reaction, her senses raggedly absorbing the unexpected contact. He was all hard-muscled strength; she registered every tough sinew against the softness of her flesh, and it was only gradually that her mind began to function again. He had taken her by surprise; she had not for one minute thought he would seize her.

Belatedly, she jabbed her fists with full force into a strategic point along his back. Twisting sharply, he let her glide to the floor, his arm reaching out to steady her as she rocked back on her feet.

'Not bad,' he said, his mouth moving in that crooked, disarming way that made her pulse leap in frantic haste. 'You'll need to quicken up your reflexes, though, if you expect to win.'

She swallowed, struggling to regain her composure. As she looked at him, her teeth set in frustration. He was not supposed to find this amusing, dammit. His grin unsettled her, did alarming things to the usually even balance of her stomach. It made her nervous system shoot into overdrive, but she was darned if she'd give in to it.

She breathed in deeply. 'Look,' she said, 'I'm sure there are far more important things you could be doing than trailing around after me. You can wind down. Go home, and, while you're about it, tell my father I'm OK, I won't make any sparks, and he won't find the slightest breath of scandal attached to his name.'

His features hardened. 'I doubt he would be reassured by your word alone.' Abruptly, he walked away from her, his eyes scanning the room and the landing beyond, and Cassie watched him with smarting resentment. He was determined to interfere, no matter what she said.

He turned back to her. 'What possessed you to come here? This place is a total fire risk, according to the owner. The wiring's in a hazardous condition; there are no decent washing facilities. You don't have to live like this.'

Her look was hostile. 'That's for me to decide. I didn't ask for your interference, and I don't want it. I'm only interested in getting a good story, and to do that I need to try all the angles.'

Ryker's expression was distinctly unimpressed. 'Even to the extent of getting involved with the police?'

'I'm working,' she persisted. 'I have a job to do and I'll do whatever's necessary to get it done properly. There's no reason for you or anyone else to concern yourself with my affairs, and I'll thank you to leave me alone.' She jerked away from him, moving towards the window, the T-shirt sliding errantly down to expose the creamy smooth slope of her shoulder. Ryker's stare seared into her, burning on to her skin.

'You know me better than that, Cassie. I came to take you out of here, and I don't intend to leave empty-handed.'

'Ah, of course, there we have it,' she said, viewing him with disdain. 'I was forgetting your army roots—a mercenary, were you? I hadn't thought of offering you cash.' She began a fruitless search in the pockets of her jeans. 'Nothing there, I'm afraid. Maybe we could have a whip-round.'

His eyes hardened. 'You're pushing your luck,' he growled.

'Am I?' she seethed. 'If I was just anybody, I could do as I pleased without anyone batting an eyelid.'

He seemed to find that amusing. 'If you were just anybody,' he agreed, 'you could dance naked in the street, and damn the consequences. But you're not. You're the daughter of a very wealthy and powerful man, and getting involved in bad publicity does neither of you any good.'

'These people have every right to have their case brought out in the open,' she argued hotly. 'It isn't their fault they have nowhere to stay, and it's criminal that places like this old house stand empty for years on end while there are people in desperate need. It's time someone stood up for their rights.'

'Pity the poor students, is that it?'

'Too right,' she said with vehemence. 'They're not paid enough to live on—how are they supposed to manage on a mere pittance?'

'And are you setting yourself up as their leading light, campaigning for their cause?' His glance was filled with scepticism, and her spine stiffened.

'How does anything ever get done if no one wants to stand up and be counted?' she threw back.

'Very commendable, Cassie, but you can't take on every lame duck you come across.'

She released her breath in a short burst of exasperation. What was the point in even trying to explain anything to him? 'You don't understand.'

'I understand perfectly,' he said drily. 'You enjoy it, don't you? You thrive on trouble. You and Driscoll both. I heard he'd joined the team at the *Despatch*. What brought that on? Couldn't he keep away from you? Still drooling at your heels, is he?'

'It was a job opportunity that came his way,' she said stiffly. 'It was the paper that influenced his decision, not my presence.'

Ryker was scornful. 'That rag?'

'It's a perfectly sound paper,' she retorted.

His mouth made a dissentient twist. 'Driscoll doesn't exactly add to its integrity with his prying lens.' He sent another glance around the room. 'He's the least of my concerns, though. We have to get you away from here before the police arrive. I suggest you make a start on collecting together your belongings.'

She stood her ground. 'I am not leaving here; I thought I had made that quite clear.'

'I think you may find you want to change your mind after I've talked to the others.'

It was her turn to be scornful. 'What can you possibly say to them that will in any way change the situation?'

'Perhaps you overlook the fact that I have a few friends in the land-development business? One in particular has come up with an arrangement that will most probably suit everyone . . . an offer of accommodation for all concerned, within reach of the college, and at a rental they can all afford—provided they leave here this evening. Any confrontation with the police, and the offer will be withdrawn immediately. They'd be fools to turn it down, don't you agree?'

She drew in a long breath. She might have known that he would have everything sewn up, all the angles tied. That was the way he worked.

He moved away from her, walking out of the room, and she stared after him, trying to make sense of the seething tide of her emotions. She was bewildered by the surge of feeling he provoked in her whenever he was near, by the isolation she felt when he had gone, the blank emptiness that was left in his wake. He would never know the true intensity of her feelings for him. She could never reveal the way she felt and risk his embarrassed reaction. He had always been affectionate towards her, caring, considerate—because she was her father's daughter, the daughter of the man who had encouraged him in the early stages of his air-charter business.

Her career was what she should be concentrating all her energy on, not empty dreams of love that could never be fulfilled. Ryker was here for one reason: to take her away from the squat, and impending trouble. His presence here threatened to undermine all the work she had put in over these last few weeks.

How could she stop him? There was no way she could win once he had put his proposition to the others. Of course they wouldn't turn away a chance like that. They were being handed the golden key on a platter, weren't they? It was the answer to all their problems.

She frowned thoughtfully. Maybe it wasn't all lost. There was another slant she could try. An interview with this influential friend wouldn't go amiss some time, if she could fix it up.

Nick broke in on her preoccupation. Shorter than Ryker by three or four inches, he had the lithe frame of a man used to activity. 'What's happening?' He adjusted the strap on his camera, sliding it over his shoulder. 'Do we still have a story?'

Briefly she recounted what Ryker had said, and Nick's grey eyes narrowed. 'It's a pity we can't keep the police angle, but never mind,' he mused. 'There's still a chance I can get some good pictures, even now.' He flicked back the waving brown hair that persisted in falling down over his forehead.

'I'm not sure that's a good idea,' Cassie said. 'You know Ryker doesn't like to be involved in that kind of publicity. You could be stirring up a hornets' nest. Leave it; we can use what you already have.'

He went back downstairs, leaving Cassie to search for her holdall, and a few minutes later Ryker came back into the room. 'That's all settled, then,' he said with obvious satisfaction. 'Are you packed and ready to go?' He looked around expectantly.

'Stop gloating,' Cassie said. 'You knew you couldn't lose, you smooth-talking——'

'Language, Cassandra,' he admonished her softly. 'If you can't bring yourself to thank me for helping out, try at least to remember you're a lady.'

'*Thank* you?' she echoed tersely. 'Did you seriously expect me to thank you for what you did?' She shook her head at his folly. 'Don't hold your breath, will you? What you've done is simply to succeed in burying the problem where no one can see it for what it is. You've provided nothing more than a temporary salve to pour over the wound. What we need is publicity to get the powers that be to take notice and do something for people everywhere. It isn't enough that just a handful are fortunate enough to benefit from someone's after-dinner *bonhomie*. We need wide-scale action and results.'

'Right now, all I'm concerned about is keeping you out of the hands of the police, and out of court.' His glance shifted over the holdall. 'Is that it, then? Are you ready at last? I didn't see your car outside—I take it you still have the old Ford?'

She gave a brief nod of assent. 'I wouldn't dream of parting with it.'

He grimaced. 'Don't tell me it's at the garage again? As I recall, you always did put too much faith in it.'

Her frosty silence told him all he wanted to know, and his mouth quirked. 'I might have guessed. In that case, you can come with me. I'll give you a lift back to your flat.'

With sharp, angry movements, Cassie pushed the last of her things into the bag, and zipped it shut. Straightening, she said curtly, 'I hardly think there would be much point in doing that, since you've just effectively rendered me homeless.'

'Homeless?' he echoed, but she ignored his puzzled query, taking the stairs swiftly, her tread light and energetic. Ryker kept much too close for comfort. Reaching the hall, she watched the others troop out into the street through what was left of the door he had shattered.

'I don't follow,' he said, attempting to take the bag as they went out into the warmth of the early evening. 'Your father gave me your new address.'

Resisting, Cassie moved jerkily, and the ricochet of the loaded bag hit him in the calves.

He made a grab for her waist as she tried to walk away. 'Just stop and explain yourself,' he ordered, pulling her around to face him. His touch unnerved her, a feverish, unbidden heat racing like wildfire along her veins, and she stumbled against the hard length of him, the holdall slipping from her fingers. His lean, muscled body acted as a buffer for the softness of her curves, and the colour rose swiftly to her cheeks. Dazed, she was caught unawares by a sudden flashing light that blinded her temporarily, and she turned her head in time to see Nick disappearing down the avenue, checking his camera as he went.

He must have decided to get one last shot of the building. It was unfortunate that he had taken it just as she and Ryker emerged.

'One of these days,' Ryker said grittily, 'that man is going to answer to me. What do you mean, you're homeless?'

He was completely unaffected by their brief closeness. Cassie shifted away from the confining

hold of his strong hands, and made an effort to
bring her breathing under control. 'The builders are
working on my flat just at the moment,' she told
him. 'I've never been fond of brick dust.'

He was unperturbed. 'Then I'll take you to your
father's house,' he offered.

'You certainly will not,' she bit out. 'I am not
going to Bourton Manor. What gives you the idea
that I can take off for the North Downs at a moment's notice? It's much too far away. I've a story
to get out, or had you forgotten? Perhaps you
thought you'd done enough damage to make me
drop the whole idea—well, you're wrong. You may
have put a blight on it, but there must be something I can salvage. I'll get a room somewhere.'

'You never give up, do you?' he said tersely. 'I
suppose it was you who put Driscoll up to that
photo stunt—anything for publicity.'

'I fail to see why you should assume that,' she
retorted, hurt that he should think that way. 'And
anyway, it's hardly unexpected if Nick uses his
camera at every opportunity. It's what he's paid to
do, after all—and you are newsworthy. It's the price
you pay for shooting to the top in the world of
high-powered business. If you don't like it, you'll
simply have to resort to dark glasses and a Homburg
pulled down low over your brow.' She started to
walk away, but he was too quick for her.

'Not so fast.' His hand snaked out and tethered
her wrist. 'I said I'd give you a lift, and
I meant it.'

His car was parked alongside the pavement, a sleek sports model, built for speed. 'Get in,' he said, his mouth hard. He jerked open the passenger door and she looked at his chiselled expression and thought twice about giving him any argument for the moment. Moodily, she slid into the leather-covered seat.

'I suppose I'd better try the King's Arms first,' she muttered. 'They usually have a room available, and they're not too expensive.'

He started up the engine, and she watched his hands move on the wheel, firm and in control. He was a good driver, she had acknowledged that long ago, and after a while she leaned back, his smooth handling of the power-packed car lulling her into a brooding silence. They were headed outwards, through the busy London streets, leaving the crowded inner city behind them, and it was only as they passed by the King's Arms and kept on going that she said stiffly, 'What are you doing? I've told you where I want to go. Turn the car around.'

'A hotel doesn't strike me as a good idea. A woman alone at night in the city might be prey to all kinds of danger.'

'Aren't you taking a lot on yourself?' she remarked coldly. 'I prefer to make my own decisions. Take me back.'

'I think not, Cassandra. My place strikes me as a much better idea.'

CHAPTER TWO

CASSIE sucked in her breath. The very idea of staying with Ryker, of being in such close proximity to him for any length of time, had her nerves jumping erratically in feverish disarray, her pulse beating out a rapid tattoo. She mustn't let this happen. Over the last few years she had gone out of her way to have only the minimum contact with him, and she couldn't let him shatter her peace of mind now. Ryker at a distance she could just about cope with; Ryker by her side put altogether too much of a strain on her defences.

'I already told you,' she said with taut emphasis, 'I've no intention of going to the North Downs.'

'No, I wasn't referring to the house; I've an apartment in London now, too. I find it's convenient when I'm here on business.'

'Really? Well, I have no wish to stay with you, Ryker, and I'll thank you to stop this car and let me out. I'll take a taxi. At least cab drivers do as they're bid.'

He glanced at her obliquely. 'I fail to see quite what you're so het up about, Cassandra,' he murmured drily. 'I wasn't suggesting we set up house together, merely that I put you up for a night or two.'

He was laughing at her. Did he know what she
was feeling, how much his presence disturbed her?
Surely he could not? At any rate, she meant to keep
a tight rein on her physical reactions to him, and
she resented his calm dismissiveness.

'You're too fond of having things your own way,'
she retorted. 'You seem to think you can do just
as you please, regardless of my feelings.'

'Nonsense. Anyway, we're here now.'

They were in a secluded, tree-lined close, she saw,
where the distinctive red-brick buildings all had a
certain quiet elegance, fronted by gleaming wrought
iron and steps leading to the ground floor.

'We overlook the park,' he said. 'I like it here,
especially at this time of year.'

If he was trying to woo her into acquiescence, he
wasn't going to succeed, she thought churlishly. Her
mouth set in a firm line. Getting out of the car, she
walked purposefully towards the boot, ready to grab
her bag and go, but he had already lifted out her
holdall and was striding up the steps to the imposing mahogany door.

'Ryker,' she mouthed sharply, 'you're an inter-
fering——'

'Save it,' he said briskly. 'It's late, and we've both
had a long day.'

He disappeared into the hall with her belongings, and mounted the stairs to his second-floor
apartment. She followed with ill concealed rancour.

The lounge was long, and wide, furnished in the
cool and uncluttered manner of a man who liked
space and stylish simplicity.

'I never met a more stubborn, mulish man,' she said bitingly, going after him as he went through to the kitchen. 'First you barge in and totally destroy the article I'm working on, and now you have the utter gall to whisk me away and deposit me here without so much as a by-your-leave. It wouldn't occur to you that I prefer to be within shouting distance of my editor, would it? No, you have to come along like a raging buccaneer and snatch me away.'

'I thought you were planning on salvaging the article,' he commented, spooning coffee into a percolator, and setting the switch.

She glowered at him, and he said with needling provocation, 'I really can't see why you're making such a fuss. Am I dragging you away from Driscoll, is that the problem?' His eyes narrowed, coldly penetrating. 'It wouldn't be the first time.'

He turned away from her, picking up her holdall and taking it from the room, and she watched him go, fighting against the angry colour that stole into her cheeks. He had done it deliberately, brought up that dreadful, humiliating incident just to crush her. How could he bring up something that had happened five years ago? That day was all too deeply imprinted on her memory, wasn't it? She hadn't needed his barbed reminder.

Nothing had gone right that afternoon, she recalled. Nick had been staying at Bourton Manor for a few days. He'd been there to write up a feature on her father, and he was taking photos of their home, and the well tended estate.

'How did you get started in the newspaper business?' she'd asked urgently. 'Did you work your way up from the bottom, or did you do a course first and then apply around?' His work had fascinated her. It had been her own dream to do something like that. 'Which interests you the most—the writing, or the photography?'

Nick had laughed at her questions, shot at him rapid-fire, so keen had she been to know everything, and he'd done his best to answer. Perhaps he had been flattered by her attention.

But that particular afternoon, five years ago, she'd been thankful he was not around. The arguments between her and her father were nothing new, but she did not want her new-found friend to witness them.

James Wyatt had set ideas on what she should make of her life. Her career was mapped out—by him, on his terms—and it seemed that her wishes had no place in his decision-making.

At seventeen, she fiercely resented his attempts to mould her will to his own, and this time the bitter aftermath of their furious clash hung like a pall over the house, filling her with an overwhelming need to escape.

She was not thinking clearly when she ran from the house. Nick, returning from his trip to town, almost collided with her, but she rushed past him. All that was in her head was the beckoning tranquillity of the lake, the lush green of the grass where she could throw herself down and hide from the world behind the rambling hedgerow. Nick followed, though, curious about her sudden flight.

'What's wrong, Cassie?' he asked, questioning the slow trickle of tears she fought to hold back. 'Tell me.'

She was terribly vulnerable just then, needing the comfort of another person, and Nick was there to listen and soothe, and pour balm on her fractured soul. Perhaps that was why, after the first few wary moments, she allowed herself to be folded into his embrace.

'It's my father,' she told him haltingly. 'He's determined that I shall join the family business.' Nick smoothed back the damp tendrils of her hair, and she sniffed and said, 'It isn't what I want. He should have had a son to carry on the tradition. I can't do it. I want to write—why can't he understand that?'

'He wants you to stay in the family home,' Nick said. 'Is that so unnatural? You're going to be very wealthy one day, an heiress—isn't there a trust fund, some kind of settlement from your grandparents? Shouldn't you go along with his wishes, rather than alienate him?'

She was taken aback a little by his knowledge of their family affairs. How did he know all that? It wasn't like her father to reveal so much to someone he had only just begun to know.

'I can't do as he wants,' she muttered. 'I'll be a cipher, nothing more.'

'But a rich one,' Nick murmured. 'Isn't that worth keeping the boat steady for the next few years at least?'

Miserably, she shook her head, and he studied her thoughtfully for a moment. Then, taking her face in his hands, he kissed her gently, with slow deliberation. She was not sure she liked that kiss, but the hand stroking her hair was soothing, and she gradually succumbed to his caresses. His advances soon became increasingly passionate, and she floundered, youth and inexperience adding to her uncertainty.

Confused and unhappy, her reactions were like those of someone waking from a bad dream. Slowly her thoughts began to coalesce into a recognisable whole. She did not want this. Belatedly, she tried to call a halt, her palms pushing against his chest in futile restraint.

'Please, Nick, I——'

'It's all right, Cassie, believe me...'

The sound of bracken crackling underfoot brought her into startled awareness of their surroundings. She looked up, and saw Ryker looming over them, his features dark and forbidding, and her stomach turned a somersault.

'Am I interrupting something?' he enquired, his tone caustic, the glitter of his eyes harsh as they swept over her dishevelled state.

Mortified, Cassie tried to pull together the edges of her blouse, tremblingly conscious of his contemptuous gaze firing along the creamy slope of her breasts. Her cheeks burned. Why did he have to find her like this?

Nick stood up. 'I'd have thought,' he said with rash belligerence, 'that it was fairly obvious your company is not wanted.'

'Isn't that too bad?' Ryker gritted, deep sarcasm crusting his words. 'This happens to be my land, and I'd prefer you do your lovemaking elsewhere.'

'Your land?' Nick repeated, plainly taken aback.

'You heard what I said,' Ryker told him forcefully. 'See to it that you leave—now, unless you want me to lay on a charge of trespass.' The grim menace of his expression left no doubt that he would take the law into his own hands if necessary.

Turning his attention back to Cassie, his lancing scrutiny ripped through the already lacerated edges of her composure. She put up a hand to her hot face. As Nick began to move away, she struggled to her feet, the folds of her cotton skirt hampering her as she made to go after him.

Ryker caught her arm. 'Not you, Cassie,' he commanded. His fingers were like a band of iron around her flesh as he pulled her towards him, and she was fiercely, vibrantly aware of his strength, his powerful masculinity. 'Haven't you any more sense than to get involved with him?' he gritted harshly.

Her mind refused to work. He was devastatingly close, his touch firing her into tingling awareness. She blinked, her limbs dissolving in shocked recognition of what was happening to her. This was why she had felt nothing when Nick held her. It was Ryker, and Ryker alone, who dominated her being, scored a path through her heart.

He stared down at her, and she was stunned by the anger that burned fathoms deep in his eyes. Anger, and something else. Something she did not recognise.

'Ryker,' she began shakily, trembling as the fingers of her free hand brushed against his chest. She felt him stiffen. 'I didn't mean——'

He pushed her away. It was as though the sound of her voice had slammed down a shutter within him. 'Tidy yourself up,' he said brutally, his mouth a hard, grim line. 'Your father's on his way over here.'

'My father?' The anguished acknowledgement of her new discovery clouded her concentration. 'What—what do you mean?'

'I've already said. He's on his way over here. We have a meeting in...' he checked his watch '...five minutes.' His eyes seared her. 'Unless you want your father to see you looking as though you've just been bedded, I suggest you do something about your blouse.'

Shame coursed through her veins as she looked down at her rumpled clothing and saw herself through his eyes. Shakily, she dealt with the last of her buttons. When she had finished, she looked up and found him studying her flushed features with a dark, savage intensity that made her flinch. She had never seen him so angry, so distant.

He said tersely, 'You'd better hope he doesn't take the lakeside path. It would take more than a few minutes to wipe away that look of wanton sensuality.'

Her heart gave a painful lurch. It's you, she cried inwardly. You're the reason ...

He looked at her, cynicism etched into his hard mouth. 'What are you, Cassandra? Half child, half woman—a volatile, dangerous combination, far too dangerous to be running wild where the Driscolls of this world are concerned. I doubt very much that you can handle the consequences you reap.'

It was her feelings for him that she had never been able to handle. There was nothing childlike in her emotional response to him, nor in the way she craved his recognition of her growing love. But Ryker was never short of female attention; she had learned that very early on. Women were drawn to him like moths to the flame, and those who he chose to date all had one thing in common—they were nothing like Cassie. They were sophisticated, glamorous, wordly wise.

Even now, that knowledge had the power to cut deep. Pushing back the painful memories, Cassie sat down at the table and stared around the kitchen, the blip blip of the percolator barely encroaching on her consciousness. Ryker walked into the room and switched it off, pouring the hot liquid into two ceramic mugs.

'Daydreaming?' he enquired abrasively, and she stared at him with bitter dislike.

'I was seventeen,' she said. 'I needed your interference then as little as I need it now.'

He pushed a steaming mug across the table towards her. 'You took a risk, getting involved with him, knowing he was only in the area to do a photo feature on your father. I expect he could have made a killing on the information you sent his way. But no doubt the beguiling charms of the daughter persuaded him to be more circumspect than his usual manner.'

'Your view of things is completely warped,' she told him icily.

'Is it? He may have adhered to the rules with your father, but he's had no such scruples in the articles he's produced on me since then, has he?' He stared at her hard, his features taut. 'From the amount of detail he puts in, I think I might be forgiven for wondering just how he comes by that information.'

His words stung. What detail did he mean? His home, his background? Did he really think she would have given Nick anything that could be slanted against him? Anyway, she did not know for sure any of the intimate goings-on in his life. There was only what she read in the Press, and she shied away from those reports. She hoped they were only guesswork, nothing more.

'He didn't need me to tell him about your conquests,' she said tightly. 'It seems to be common knowledge that women are only too eager to throw themselves into your net like suicidal butterflies.' She sipped at her coffee.

Ryker smiled drily. 'Been reading your own paper, have you?'

She put down her mug with a faint snap, and got to her feet, scraping back her chair. 'Thanks for reminding me. As you said, it's late, and I have work to finish off. My editor expects an article of some sort to arrive on his desk, whether or not there's been outside interference. If you'll excuse me,' she said with exaggerated politeness, 'I'll go to my room.' She walked to a door which led off from the kitchen. 'Is it through here?'

His mouth slanted attractively. 'By all means,' he murmured. 'It does happen to be my room, but if you insist on sharing I shan't put any objections in the way.'

Amusement danced in his gleaming amber gaze, and she clenched her fingers into fists at her sides. He was making fun of her, tormenting her at every opportunity. 'Don't flatter yourself, Ryker,' she gritted.

There was only one other door, and she went through it, relieved to find herself in a small guest bedroom. Slamming the door shut, she drove the bolt home, her temperature rising like quicksilver as she heard Ryker's soft chuckle on the other side.

Sleep did nothing to improve her temper. Ryker had taken a perverse delight in annoying her, and she had been foolish enough to leave herself wide open to his devilish baiting. She found it hard to forgive herself that lapse.

Ever since he had arrived at the squat, he had played havoc with her concentration, and she could not let that state of affairs continue. As soon as she had showered, she would phone the office. Her work had been disrupted long enough.

On second thoughts, she'd do it now. There was always someone on hand at the office to take copy,

however early, and with any luck Ryker would still
be asleep. She might even be able to leave him a
note and slip away without encountering him again.
He was obviously going to take any chance he could
to provoke her, and she would simply not allow
him the pleasure any longer.

Rummaging through her bag, she lifted out her
silk robe and pulled it on over her underwear, tying
the belt firmly at her waist before she went through
to the kitchen.

Ryker, though, was standing by the window as
she walked into the room, a coffee-cup in his hand
as he looked out over the park. Her step faltered.
He was wearing casual clothes, as on the previous
day, but the cut of his beige trousers was
undeniably expensive, moulding strong thighs and
fitting smoothly over his lean torso. Her glance
flickered away distractedly.

He turned around fully then, viewing her over
the rim of his cup before he drained the last of his
coffee. His shirt collar was open, revealing the
deeply bronzed column of his throat.

'Good morning,' he murmured, replacing his cup
on the sill. His lambent gaze shifted slowly over her
slender shape, pausing to linger on the rounded
curve of hip and thigh outlined by the clinging folds
of material. She was tautly conscious of the scant
state of her dress, but she gave him a quelling stare,
resentfully remembering his teasing remark of the
previous night.

Undaunted, his wandering glance slid down to
take in the long, smooth line of her legs, the fine,

sloping arch of her bare feet. He was doing it deliberately, in order to goad her, she decided, bitterly aware of the treacherous nature of her own body as her skin warmed in response to his scorching appraisal.

'I hadn't expected to find you up yet,' she said abruptly, her mood fractious. From the appetising smell of fritters and eggs that assaulted her nostrils, she gathered he must already have breakfasted.

'I have a business to run,' he commented with laconic ease. 'Did you sleep well?'

'Well enough.'

Her tone was grouchy, and his mouth slanted in amusement. 'Not a morning person, are you, Cassie?'

Her fingers toyed with the sash of her robe. Why did he have this effect on her? Surely she had outgrown the foolish infatuation that had rendered her helpless in the past? She could see clearly now, and she would not let herself fall under his spell. Being close to Ryker was like being suspended fast within a force field; his attraction was a potent and dangerous thing. This time, though, she would not be caught by it. She was determined. It was not fair, she reasoned. When he chose to, he could charm the birds off the trees, but she would never set herself up as a source for his amusement.

'There's coffee, and more fritters in the pan,' he said, going over to the table and applying butter liberally to a crusty roll.

He had an appetite like a warrior, she thought restively, watching him eat. Yet there was not an

ounce of spare flesh on him. He burned up energy
too fast; he was all hard muscle, fit and vigorous,
his body toned like an athlete's.

'Is something wrong?' he enquired pleasantly, his
hands momentarily stilled, and she realised with a
shock that she must have been staring.

Her blue eyes skittered away. Stiff-lipped, she
asked, 'May I use your phone?'

He inclined his head in the direction of the
lounge. 'Help yourself.'

Going through to the other room, she sat cross-
legged on the couch and dialled her office, relating
her story to the typist on the receiving end. Having
dealt with that task to her satisfaction, she was just
about to ring off when Jim Harker's irascible tones
came on the line. She steeled herself for a dressing
down. Her boss was never in the best of moods
first thing.

'If you're not at the squat,' he said tightly, 'where
are you calling from?'

She told him, and there was a momentary pause.
Then, 'Ryker Haldene, did you say?' His voice took
on a note of suppressed excitement. 'Now there's
a touch of good fortune. You realise he's taking
part in the air show next week, don't you? All the
proceeds are to go to various charities, so it was a
real feather in their cap for the organisers to get
him to agree to make an appearance. Now that's a
story that will really pull our readers in. They'll be
gasping to know what makes him tick. Go for it,
girl; you're on the spot. I'll expect to hear
from you——'

'But you don't understand...' Cassie tried to get a word in. 'He doesn't—I can't——'

'You're babbling, Cassandra. Quit stalling and get on with it. You've a heaven-sent opportunity there; it's been handed to you on a plate. Another thing—I heard he might be paying a visit to one of his pursuits centres in a few weeks; he doesn't do that very often. They were something he set up before he went into the air-charter business, so it could be a new angle for us. Go along with him and see what mileage you can get out of it.'

'But I can't do that. He doesn't like the articles the *Despatch* put out—and can you blame him? If you didn't keep changing everything, giving them a different slant, it might be a different matter. It's not on, Jim; I'm not submitting any articles on him if you plan to mess them about.'

'You worry too much,' he said dismissively. 'We're here to sell papers, not nurse sensibilities. Just get on with the job, Cassandra. I need journalists who bring in the goods. Remember that.'

'Jim, it isn't——'

She was talking to the air. In his usual precipitate manner, he had already cut the call.

She glowered in angry frustration at the buzzing receiver for a moment, before slapping it back on to its base.

'Trouble?' Ryker appeared in front of her, one dark brow lifting in query.

He had startled her out of her preoccupation, and she jumped, her senses thrown into confusion by his unexpected approach.

'I—er—no.'

She frowned, and tried to pull herself together, viewing him in an abstracted fashion. Any hope she might have entertained of slipping quietly away and removing herself from the perilous mouth of the tiger's lair had just flown straight out of the window, hadn't it?

If she valued her job, she was going to have to work with him now, somehow persuade him into letting her write a piece on him, and at the same time prevent Jim Harker from tampering with it. It was stretching the bounds of possibility to hope that Ryker might agree. Any other paper, perhaps. Any other journalist... She ran a hand through her hair. Lord, what a mess.

Ryker's stare was quizzical. 'No?' he repeated. 'Are you sure? From the look on your face, anyone might think you've just been landed with an outsize problem.'

Choking slightly, she averted her head, turning her pained reaction into a cough. Problem? What problem? she derided herself inwardly. It was nothing she couldn't handle, was it, given a few months to prepare the ground?

CHAPTER THREE

'DIDN'T you say something about breakfast?' Cassie said brightly. Springing up from the sofa, she headed towards the kitchen. 'Shall I make more coffee?'

A dart of challenge flashed in the depths of his eyes. 'Deflective tactics? That was your editor you were talking to, I assume. Is everything OK?'

'Fine, fine,' she lied. 'What could possibly be wrong?'

'What indeed?' he echoed softly.

She avoided his narrowed gaze. Lifting the lid on a pan, she scooped out a couple of potato fritters and slid them on to a plate, taking them over to the table. When she was seated, she took time to glance around. 'Nice place you have here,' she murmured between mouthfuls. 'Have you had it long?'

To her relief, he accepted the change of subject without further comment. 'A few months. My visits to the capital are more frequent these days.'

'You're no stranger on the international circuit, either,' she said with a wry inflexion. 'Your air-charter business didn't just bloom, it proliferated beyond all imagining, didn't it? I guessed it would happen years ago; you were never one to let time lie idle on your hands.'

'I could say the same thing about you. You haven't exactly stayed still over the last few years, have you? University, a bright career just beginning to take off, a new home. Do you ever miss being at Bourton Manor?'

'Not at all. My place may be small, and a lot needs doing to it, but at least it's all my own, and I have my independence. There's a lot to be said for being a free agent.'

Finishing off the last of the food, she leaned back in her chair, and breathed deeply, lazily crossing one leg over the other. His gaze tracked the indolent, sensuous movement.

'That was good,' she said. 'Sheer delight, a feast of indulgence.' She linked her hands behind her head, sending the tumbled dark waves that massed around her shoulders into a flurry of disorder. 'I shall have to let you cook for me again some time.'

'Hmm.' He assessed her narrowly. 'In the meantime, maybe you had better get dressed. I have work to do.'

Her mouth made a moue of discontent, its message dissolved by the faint sparkle in her eyes. 'And I'd been hoping you might spare me some time—just a few moments—to listen to a small proposition I have to put to you.'

'I knew something was hatching in that devious brain. If it involves your newspaper, you can forget it.'

'Me? Devious? How could you think such a thing?' She sent him an affronted look.

Whatever he might have been about to reply was swallowed up in the sudden clatter made by the opening and closing of an outer door. The sound of footsteps in the hall followed.

Cassie threw him a swift glance, but he did not seem at all concerned by the intrusion.

'That will be Sophie,' he said. 'I asked her to stop by.'

The unexpected entrance of Sophie Tremayne still managed to throw Cassie a little off balance. Ryker's secretary was no stranger to her, and she was, as usual, a model of sophistication that put Cassie's own casual attire to shame. The smooth blonde chignon was immaculate, the cream linen suit cut in classic lines that made the most of her shapely figure, her well shaped feet encased in stylish leather shoes with three-inch heels.

Sophie's cold blue glance wafted over Cassie like a draught of Arctic wind. There had never, Cassie reflected ruefully, been any love lost between her and Sophie. Even though, on several occasions, she had attempted to break the ice, the barrier always remained steadfastly intact.

Turning to Ryker, Sophie said, 'I saw your car outside, so I guessed you were at home—though I hadn't realised Cassandra would be with you. I hope you didn't mind my using the key, but obviously you didn't hear my knock.'

She held out a manila file towards him. 'The notes you asked for,' she remarked. 'I think you'll find everything's in order.'

'Thanks.' Ryker took it from her, opening it up and riffling through the papers. 'That was quick work.'

She gave him a knock-out smile. 'I believe you said it was fairly urgent.'

'It is.' He weighed the package in his hand. 'Help yourself to coffee while I go and deal with this. I'm sure you and Cassie will have plenty to talk about.'

Sometimes, Cassie thought disgustedly, men could be so blind. Was he really unaware of the antipathy that existed between the two women? Sophie was older than she was by six years, and perhaps that was the reason they could find no common ground. And, of course, Sophie had been in Ryker's employ from the very beginning. Her place in his life was well established.

The door closed behind Ryker, and Sophie turned a cool gaze on Cassie. 'I suppose I should have guessed you would be here. Ryker said you were involved in some kind of scrape. It really is too much, you know. He has far more important things to do than spend time sorting you out.'

Cassie lifted a negligent shoulder. 'Am I stopping him? I didn't ask to come here.'

Sophie's mouth tightened. 'You know, you really ought to realise by now that there's no future for you with Ryker.'

Cassie raised a finely arched brow in query and Sophie smiled thinly. 'It was always perfectly obvious to me how you feel about him. But you're wasting your time.' She flicked a speck of wool from her skirt with long, manicured fingernails. 'The only reason that he bothers with you at all is because his integrity is deeply ingrained. He values the friendship he has with your father, and he'd hate to see you do anything that will cause James any adverse publicity.'

'You profess to know an awful lot about the way Ryker thinks,' Cassie remarked coolly. 'Since when did you have a through-line to his psyche?'

Sophie's tone was laced with scorn. 'Ryker and I have worked together since he moved next to Bourton Manor, had you forgotten? Don't you think that was bound to make us close?'

How could Cassie ever doubt it?

'Of course,' Sophie went on, 'we've both been far too busy following our careers to take the final step, but it's only a matter of time. At the moment, he's too much involved with other commitments, travelling the world over, but he wouldn't dream of leaving me behind.' She paused, smiling faintly. 'So you see, Cassandra, if you're hoping that your infatuation can come to something, you're hoping in vain.'

'Aren't you making a lot of assumptions?' Cassie put in sharply. 'Why on earth should you have the idea that I harbour any emotions at all where Ryker is concerned?'

Sophie laughed. 'Oh, come on, give me some credit. I'm a woman; I can see these things. But you really don't have a chance, you know. Ryker needs a woman who can smooth his path, make sure that the wheels of his life are well oiled.'

Her cold gaze skimmed over Cassie's *déshabillé*, the riotous tumble of ebony hair, the bare feet. 'Why would he look twice at you? You don't even dress the part. I'll bet you still spend all your time in jeans and T-shirts.' Her lips thinned. 'Take it from me, he might amuse himself with you for a time, but that's all it is—a temporary distraction.'

'I'm so glad you told me,' Cassie said with tight sarcasm. 'I might not have slept nights, thinking that I filled his every waking thought.'

Ryker came back into the kitchen, and she stood up, muttering tersely, 'I'm going to take a shower.'

Gathering up her clothes on the way, she headed for the bathroom, locking the door behind her.

Was there any truth in what Sophie had said? She turned the shower full on, honing it to a fierce jet. Steam filled the room. How close was his relationship with his secretary? And was it possible he might suspect how Cassie herself felt about him? Just the thought of the humiliation that would bring brought a flush of heat to her face.

It was true, she acknowledged unhappily, stepping under the sharp spray; right from the start, when he had first arrived at her father's house for a business meeting, she had been knocked for six by his powerful male presence. When he'd bought the neighbouring property, his appearances around the place had soon become the centre of her universe. The mere sound of his voice had been enough to set her pulse racing, the blood pounding her body with frantic haste.

He was ruggedly masculine, and she had been overwhelmingly attracted to him; there was no denying it. But Sophie was always there, in the background, and it was clear that a man like Ryker could have his pick of women. What chance had a naïve young girl had of gaining any prominent place in his life? He liked her, though; she knew that. From the beginning they had shared an easy friendship, and he had never objected to her wandering freely over his land. The small copse and the lake had always been her bolt-hole in times of stress, the place she retreated to when the arguments with her father became too much to bear.

She did not remember her mother, and she often wondered if things might have been easier if she had lived, if a woman's touch might have softened her father. He did not understand her. His temper, always notoriously uncertain, had plumbed new depths that summer, when she was seventeen. Unwittingly passing by the study as he'd emerged with Ryker, Cassie had caught the brunt of it.

'Where are you going?' her father grated. 'I want to talk to you. I've just received the prospectus for the business and economics course at the university and I want to go through it with you before I leave for Switzerland.' He scanned her skimpy ribbed top and her bare midriff with taut censure.

Cassie's blue eyes darkened, an ominous glitter smouldering in their depths. He thought he could intimidate her with his harsh manner, but he would not succeed.

'We've talked about this before,' she reminded him evenly, 'and you know perfectly well that I don't want to take that kind of course. I'm sorry; I've tried to take an interest in the company, but land development doesn't hold out the remotest enticement for me. Uprooting people from their homes so that an office block or a shopping complex can go in their place goes against the grain. There are other things I plan to do with my life.'

'Writing, you mean?' Disapproval edged his voice. 'Just because you've managed to put out a few short stories doesn't mean that you have any major talent for it, and I'm certainly not funding you to spend the next three or four years doodling. You can think again.'

'I've already thought it through,' Cassie said firmly, her shoulders stiff with determination. 'I'm going to study journalism, and I'll pay for it myself out of the money my grandmother left me.'

James Wyatt let out an explosive hiss. He had never enjoyed being thwarted. 'I've no time to waste on this; I have arrangements to make for my trip.' He turned to Ryker. 'Can't you talk to her? She listens to you. See if you can't get her to see sense.'

Ryker studied her thoughtfully, and her fingers twisted in agitation. She rammed her hands into the pockets of her shorts. 'My mind is made up,' she said, 'and besides, I have things to do right now.'

She left the house with the sound of her father's anger rumbling in the background, and set off along the road for the village shop. Her father had never tried to understand her point of view and these arguments always left her taut with mounting frustration. Her own temper was rapidly coming to the boil, and she had to walk it off, or burst.

After half an hour, she began to wonder if there was not a better method of dealing with her warring emotions. The oppressive warmth of the afternoon did nothing to contain her anger. The sun beat down on her without mercy, aggravating her already frayed nerves. Her father was too full of himself, his own ideals, to have time to consider other people's opinions, let alone those of his daughter.

It did not take her long to purchase the few bits of stationery that she needed, and she made the return journey at a slower pace, flagging in the sweltering heat.

Without her realising it, her steps had taken her towards the lake, close to the rickety landing-stage that had long been in need of repair. With a sigh of relief, she sat down by the water's edge, watching the golden glow of the sun spread in a molten arc over its surface. The sky was a perfect, cloudless blue, the air hot, stifling, taking her breath away.

Restively, she looked around. The water looked invitingly cool, and no one was around to disturb her. Ryker usually swam in the morning, and his work occupied him for the major part of the day. Since the episode with Nick, she had kept out of his way as much as possible, not wanting to see a return of the harsh condemnation in his eyes. But he wasn't likely to be heading in this direction, was he? Why was she hesitating? Pulling off her top, she dropped it to one side, and stepped out of her shorts, standing in her flimsy underwear looking out over the calm water. The sun blazed down on her, a flaming orb, high in the sky, searing her flesh with its incandescent flame.

The lake whispered to her, and she moved towards it slowly, stepping into its welcoming embrace. For a long, breathtaking moment, she savoured its cool, silken touch on her burning skin. After a while, she turned on her back, making waves, revelling in the lap of water on her pliant body. Idly, she gave herself up to its enveloping arms, only turning her glance towards the distant grassy bank when she felt gloriously refreshed.

Instantly, the warmth was back, an uncomfortable ripple flowing unchecked through her veins. 'Ryker?' It shocked her to the core to see him standing by the water's edge, tall and lean, his amber gaze unerringly steady.

Hastily, she pushed herself upright, thankful that now at least only her shoulders were laid bare to his scrutiny. 'What are you doing here?'

'Shouldn't I be? It is my land, after all.'

She grimaced. 'I thought you would be working this afternoon—you don't usually come down to the lake at this time.'

Her glance flickered over his white trousers, the ice-blue shirt, unbuttoned at the neck. She closed her eyes for a brief moment, shutting out his image. He was far too attractive for her peace of mind.

'If you've come to argue with me about my father,' she muttered, 'I don't want to hear it.' Her hair clung damply about her face and shoulders, small rivulets trickling down to fall in glistening droplets on her skin.

He shrugged. 'Actually, I came to repair the landing-stage.'

Her brow furrowed, and slowly she scanned the bank, her gaze coming to rest at length on a canvas tool bag alongside some obviously new planking.

'Ah.' Warm colour suffused her cheeks. Of course he wouldn't be interested in sorting out her problems. He had other things to occupy his time. She cupped water in her palms and let it flow in a cooling stream over her gold-tinted arms. 'I suppose I'm in the way,' she said, perversely resenting his indifference. 'Are you planning on throwing me off as you threatened with Nick?'

His jaw tensed, the planes of his face darkly shuttered. 'I doubt that will be necessary.' His sardonic tone sparked a fiery edge along her already smarting sensibilities.

'I'm glad,' she muttered. 'It's really much too hot to get embroiled in a tussle.'

'True. It must rate as the hottest day this summer.' His brooding glance unnerved her, slanting as it did over the naked curve of her shoulders, coming to rest with unusual preoccupation on the tiny golden birthmark that lay on one smoothly rounded slope.

Suddenly, she found she had lost all desire to remain in the water. 'I'd like to come out of here,' she said. 'Turn around, would you? While I get dressed.'

His head went back slightly, as though his mind had been elsewhere and she had startled him with her words. He laughed softly, but did as she asked.

When she was fully clothed once more, she said coolly, 'Since you obviously have work to do, I'll get out of your way. I'd hate to bother you any longer than necessary.'

'Bother me?' he murmured. 'I'll let you know when that happens.'

He was right, of course. What made her think she could possibly disturb him in any way? He was a neighbour, a business associate of her father. He probably took her father's viewpoint, too.

'You won't solve any of your problems by scowling.' His amused tones penetrated the black cloud of her thoughts, and her gaze rested on him smokily. 'You should talk it through with him, calmly. Both of you let your tempers get the better of you, and then you walk away from the issue without hammering it out properly.'

'It's pointless. He doesn't understand any viewpoint but his own, and I'm through with trying to make him listen.'

'James is not used to dealing with rebellion. Your non-conformity irritates him.'

'My father and I will never agree.'

'That's true,' Ryker confirmed. 'You're too much alike. Without some give and take on either side, you'll neither of you get very far.'

'I can't reason with him,' she insisted. 'He has it stuck in his head that I'll join the firm, and nothing will shift that idea. My feelings are of no account to him.' Her lips moved in a faint twist of disillusion. 'He dismisses my opinions as if they have no bearing on anything. That's why we're always arguing. But I can't let him have his way on this. Writing is what I feel I can do best, and if he doesn't like it, well, that's too bad.' She tossed her head back lightly, and Ryker appraised her in silence, taking in the firm set of her mouth, the grim truculence in the taut angle of her jaw.

'Maybe he needs time to adjust,' he said. 'Lately he's been away more often than he's been at home. He has to learn how to cope with a daughter who's beginning to find her voice, a voice as strong as his own. It's taken him aback.'

Her blue eyes shifted with restless frustration. 'I can't see him trying to meet me halfway, can you? He may be my father, but there's no law that says we have to get on together.' She breathed in raggedly, the curve of her breasts slowly rising with the motion. 'Anyway, there's no need for you to involve yourself any further.' She swallowed, feeling strangely at odds with herself. 'You've done his bidding, haven't you? He asked you to talk to me, to point out the error of my ways. Well, consider it done. You can get on with other things now. You can do what you came here for.' Her voice wavered. 'Don't let me disturb you any longer.'

She made to turn away and he stopped her, his hands closing on her shoulders, drawing her around to face him.

'Wait, Cassie. There's no need to upset yourself. I'm sure it can all be sorted out in the end. You need to give it a little time. Allow things to calm down.'

'You take his side,' she muttered. 'Men always stick together. You all think women can be soothed with soft words, that you'll get your own way in the end.'

She started to pull away and he wound his arms around her, holding her close. 'No, sweetheart. It isn't that way at all.'

He was smiling down at her, his eyes warm and golden, his stare roaming over her sun-flushed face. And then everything seemed to change. There was a sudden stillness. The heat must be getting to her, she reasoned abstractedly; that was why she felt so dizzy, so out of control, why there was this peculiar weakness in the pit of her stomach.

His gaze drifted down to dwell on the full curve of her soft mouth, and her heartbeat jolted to a jerky, staccato rhythm. He moved closer, his head shading out the sun, and then he was taking her startled mouth with his own. His taste was warm and male, and there was a hint of musky fragrance faintly emanating from the pores of his skin. Her fingers collided helplessly with the hard-boned contours of his shoulders, slid along the smooth, muscled perfection of his chest as he eased her against his rugged frame.

A wild, unbidden quiver of longing shuddered through her. The kiss lingered, melting the nebulous shreds of her resistance in a sweetly flowing tide, a heady wash of intoxication that would not be stemmed. She was enthralled by him, drinking in the nectar she had craved so long.

When he finally drew his mouth from hers, she looked up at him, his features swimming hazily before her, as though the brilliance of the sun had invaded her being and blinded her to everything but him. He stared at her without speaking. His thumb trailed lightly over the throbbing fullness of her lips, his glance absorbing the hectic glitter of her eyes, the warm flushed pink of her cheeks.

'You're very sweet, Cassie,' he murmured. 'Very young, and delightfully responsive. But I think you had better go.' He pushed her away from him, holding her at arm's length. 'As you said, I have work to do, and Sophie will be arriving at the house in a couple of hours. We have a dinner date.'

'D-dinner?' She stumbled over the word, needing to know, not wanting to hear.

'I promised I'd take her to the new restaurant that opened up in Wetherton last month.' He paused. 'We leave for Switzerland tomorrow. Go and make things up with your father, Cassie. Decide for yourself what you mean to do. I shan't be around long enough to help.'

He was icily remote now, cold as stone. The breath snagged in her lungs. She had not even dented his rigid self-possession. Desperately, she fought to control the sickening lurch of her stomach. How could he kiss her like that, and then send her away as though the episode had no meaning? For her, the whole world had crystallised in that tender moment of possession. But for him...

She was fooling herself, wasn't she? There was no place in his life for her. He was making that plain. He was a man on the move, his parameters were extending far beyond anything she could imagine, and he would not be taking her along with him. Why should he, when the Sophies of this world beckoned, enticing him with their smooth sophistication?

If she had any pride left at all she could not let him see how much he had hurt her by his rejection.

'I'll do that, Ryker,' she said, striving to keep her voice steady. 'But you already know what I plan to do, don't you? I'm going away, to study journalism.'

It was best, she thought achingly, if their paths crossed only fleetingly from now on. Every time she saw him, she would have to steel herself not to care.

Her glance went to the planking and the tool bag. 'I'll leave you to get on,' she said.

He nodded. 'Yes, I'd better make a start. It wouldn't do to keep Sophie waiting, would it?'

She turned and walked away from him. His knife-thrust had found its mark, and she knew that the wound would fester indefinitely, for there was no cure for a bleeding heart.

In the steamy atmosphere of the bathroom, she finished dressing in clean blue jeans and a soft cotton blouse, then pulled a comb through the damp tendrils of her hair. One thing had not changed in all these years, she decided morosely.

Sophie was still around. She even had her own key to his apartment.

A door banged somewhere, and she hoped that it meant the other woman had gone at last. Half an hour at a time was about all she could take of her company.

Deftly she applied a light touch of blusher to her cheeks, and searched through her make-up bag for lipstick. Satisfied at last with her reflection in the mirror, she dabbed a splash of her favourite perfume on her wrists and temples before going in search of Ryker. There was still the thorny subject of the air display to be dealt with, and the story her editor wanted, and she knew from past experience it was not a prospect to be relished.

She found him in a small room off the lounge that served as a study. He was sitting at a desk, frowning in concentration as he sifted through some papers.

'Are you busy?' she murmured, seating herself on the arm of his chair and looking over his shoulder at the documents that were occupying his attention. 'That looks technical. Am I in your way?'

He gave her a sideways glance. 'Even if you were, I doubt anything I said would make much difference. Once you're set on something, you can be remarkably persistent.'

She smiled and leaned forward a little, a faint cloud of perfume wafting between them as she rested one arm lightly on the back of the chair. 'Is that a bad thing?' Running her gaze over his strong profile, she resisted the temptation to slide her fingers over the tough sinews of his neck, to explore the texture of crisp dark hair at his nape.

'Not necessarily. It all depends what it is that you're after.'

'Honestly, Ryker,' she murmured, 'to hear you talk, anyone would think I always had an ulterior motive. I'm merely taking an interest in your work.'

'You're up to something. I know you too well.'

'And you're far too suspicious. It can't be good for you. It knots up the muscles, causes tension.' She moved restlessly. Perhaps sitting next to him hadn't been such a good idea. She was the one getting knotted up. He was so close, yet, for all that, he might have been light years away when it came to touching him.

'Lay it on the line, Cassie,' he said abruptly. 'I have work to do, and a meeting scheduled for half an hour's time.'

She grimaced. 'OK—but you have to give it some thought, not just deny me outright.'

His eyes narrowed, and she went on quickly, 'I'd like an interview. Your work, your life, the flying. The air show's next week, isn't it? I could do a full-page spread——'

'No.'

'But you can't dismiss it out of hand, Ryker,' she said urgently. 'It'll be a wonderful article, I promise. I'll even let you go through it before I hand it over. And think how it will enhance your image—how many people know about the pursuits centres you set up, for instance?'

'I started those centres before I went into the charter business,' he said grimly. 'I don't need the extra publicity, especially not the kind of in-depth article you're planning.'

'But you——'

'No.' Ryker's hands gripped her arms, and she registered the familiar aching hurt of rejection as he pushed her away from him. He stood up, moving over to the window, his features all hard angles, shadowed planes.

'I'm warning you, Cassie,' he gritted, 'you are not to write about me. Nor do I want you and that camera-happy sidekick anywhere near me at the air show. Is that clear?'

She got to her feet, swallowing against the painful constriction of her throat. 'Why?' she demanded huskily, endeavouring to batten down her turbulent emotions. 'Give me a reason,' she said. 'You can't still blame me for the articles that have gone out before. I told you, I had nothing to do with what Nick wrote. Besides, he's bound to be there, taking photos of the planes. You can hardly stop him from doing that. The event has to be covered, after all.'

'It's the way he chooses to go about it that concerns me.' He pulled a couple of newspapers from a drawer in his desk and slammed them down in front of her. 'He didn't exactly restrain himself there, did he?'

She looked down at the photograph splashed over one page. Ryker was pictured leaving a cottage with a woman—someone Cassie did not recognise. She read the caption and stifled a groan. 'Haldene leaves cosy love nest. Who is the mystery woman?'

'That was worth a full-page spread, wasn't it?' he bit out.

'I'm sorry,' she said. 'I had no idea. I hadn't seen it. Who is she?' She could not stop herself from asking the question.

'A friend,' he answered tersely. 'Someone I was helping out. What happens next? Headlines in the Sunday papers—"My taste in women, by Ryker Haldene. Secrets from between the sheets."'

She felt her fingers bite into the leather of the chair. 'Ryker, listen to me, will you? You've had your fair share of trouble with the Press, I concede that, and I can understand your attitude. But I'm only trying to do my job. I'd never write anything that would be hurtful to you, you know that.'

'Is that right? And has Jim Harker changed his tactics one iota since he took over at the *Despatch*? We both know he hasn't.' His expression was implacable. 'I've told you,' he said brusquely, 'keep away.'

He was demanding the impossible, she reflected bleakly. She had a job to do, and, one way or another, she had to produce something that would satisfy her boss. Knowing Jim Harker's brittle personality, it was either that, or the dole queue. She had to feed herself and pay the bills, and it was unfortunate that Ryker's strictures came a poor second in that competition.

CHAPTER FOUR

CASSIE watched the plane spiral downwards, her throat taut with anxiety as it swooped towards the ground, the plume of smoke blazoned across the heavens in its wake like a bright streamer. At the very last moment, it seemed, the nose lifted, arcing upwards, on and on into a perfect circle drawn against the backcloth of an intensely blue sky.

Her lungs were painfully constricted. Why did she let it get to her this way? Ryker was a brilliant pilot. Nothing could happen to him, could it? He had nerves of steel, and he knew what he was doing, knew the exact moment to send his craft into a mind-shattering spin.

She swallowed. Now he was banking away, getting ready to bring the plane on course to land.

'I want to get some close-ups,' Nick said at her side. 'We'll have to make our way to the enclosure.'

Cassie nodded, waiting until the gleaming, silver-winged machine coasted along the runway in the distance, and then she let out a long, shuddery breath. 'OK. I'm with you.'

It was just as well there was little more to be done this afternoon. She wouldn't be sorry to be finished here; she was strangely on edge today, had been, in fact, since she had left Ryker's flat. Or perhaps it was just the heat, sapping her of her usual verve. She would be thankful to get away from the crowds, and back to her own place.

Now, though, she had to keep her mind firmly on work. She had already interviewed the various celebrities of the day—all except one, she reflected wryly—and she checked that her notebook was safely tucked into her bag, before she started off after Nick. With luck, Ryker would have unbent enough to give one or two quotes, but she wasn't counting on it, considering his black mood when last she had seen him.

The faintest breeze fanned her hot face as she approached the enclosure with Nick, and she welcomed its cool drift. Showing their Press cards to the officials, they wandered in among the assortment of planes just as Ryker was climbing down from his own. Immediately he was surrounded by a small entourage, and the whole group began to move away towards the refreshments lounge.

He had not noticed Cassie, but of course he wouldn't, she thought with a hint of sourness as she observed Sophie winding her arm through his. The woman couldn't even wait until they were alone together before she started mauling him.

Deliberately, she turned her thoughts to the article she was working on. At least she could go and talk to the mechanic, now that Ryker was otherwise engaged. She left Nick to snap away where his fancy took him, while she went over to talk to the man who had begun a routine check of the plane.

He was more than willing to chat, she discovered, and it seemed that he knew quite a lot about Ryker's private life. She found herself wistfully hoping that he was merely embroidering reality, and at the same time she mentally cursed Jim Harker for putting her through this misery. She would stick to facts about the aircraft and his skill as a pilot. There was no way she could write anything else.

'That was a great one,' Nick said, adjusting the lens on his camera. 'Lean back against the fuselage, both of you, and I'll get another.' She hadn't noticed Nick's reappearance while she had been engrossed in conversation, but now she obliged briefly with a smile, and Nick quickly took the shot he wanted.

Hitching the camera over his shoulder once more, he came and put his arm around her waist. Unexpectedly, giving her no time for evasion, his head swooped downwards and he kissed her. When he finally released her mouth, she stared up at him in faint astonishment. Why had he done that now, in full view of anyone who cared to watch?

She wished that she could feel more for Nick, respond to him in the way that he so obviously wanted. For her, it had been a relief to see a familiar face when they had met up in London. She had just started in her new job, and they had begun to date, and she had tried so hard to make it work between them. But always, deep inside, something made her hold back, some lingering ember, perhaps, of that other fierce chemistry that burned within . . .

'How about a drink before I get this lot back to the lab?' he murmured, his hands spreading lightly over her ribcage.

'She doesn't have time for that. She and I have some unfinished business to settle.' The harsh words gave her a fierce jolt, and she turned her head, eyes widening, to look up at Ryker, who had appeared at her side out of nowhere like a prowling, malevolent tiger. Her colour must have fluctuated visibly as her temperature shot from hot to cold to hot again in the space of seconds under the needling ferocity of his stare.

With an effort, she began to assemble her scattered wits. 'Unfinished—what business? I don't recall——'

'No, you wouldn't,' he cut in savagely. 'Though if you could manage to stop making an exhibition of yourself for as long as five minutes at a time and prise yourself away from Casonova here, you might find you have less trouble with your memory.' He looked at Nick as though he might hit him, then turned on the white-faced mechanic.

'Don't you have work to be getting on with?' he gritted.

The young man made an expedient, hasty exit, and Cassie frowned after his disappearing figure. 'Was it necessary to use that tone with him?' she demanded.

'It wouldn't have been if you hadn't gone out of your way to distract him.' His attention swung blackly to Nick's hand, still draped around her waist. 'Are you having trouble ungluing yourself from Cassandra or were you waiting for me to do it for you?' His eyes burned with glittering menace, and slowly Cassie felt Nick's fingers slip away.

'You have no right,' she flung at Ryker, clenching her teeth. It wasn't as though he cared about her, was it? He just wanted to get at Nick. 'Who gave you the idea you could interfere? What business is it of yours?'

'Feeling deprived, are you?' he said, with a sneer, and her fingers itched to slap him. He had a nerve pouring condemnation on her when he had only just torn himself away from Sophie's clutches. The thought of them together made her stomach turn. 'I wouldn't advise it,' he said darkly, staring at her hands. 'I just may hit back.'

'Now look here...' Nick began, only to find himself pinned like a squirming insect under the sharp lance of Ryker's gaze.

'Still here, Driscoll?' he mouthed unpleasantly.

Nick backed off a little, and Cassie said tautly, 'You're the one who should be leaving, Ryker. Your presence is not required. You've already set a spanner in the works—isn't that enough to satisfy even you?'

'Not nearly enough,' he growled. 'You have some explaining to do.'

She ignored the dark storm raging in his eyes and glared back. 'Oh, you think so, do you? Why is that? Are you suffering some kind of ego trip?'

'Cassie,' Nick said, placing a restraining hand on her arm, 'perhaps you should——'

'Keep out of this, Nick,' she seethed, slapping his hand away, and turning with renewed belligerence towards Ryker. 'Since when do I have to account to you for my actions?'

'Since your seedy, underhand enquiries were aimed at winkling out whatever information you could get from my mechanic.'

'Seedy? Underhand?' Her tone dripped scorn. 'Look around, why don't you? This is broad daylight, or hadn't you noticed? Perhaps it's your mind that's the problem. Too many dark corners in there, with lurking monsters creeping and crawling around.'

He didn't like that. Long, hard fingers came around her wrist like a manacle, clamping the slender bones, and pulling her away from the relative protection of the plane. She had forgotten just how strong he was.

'We'll finish this conversation somewhere else,' he said, his face set like granite. 'Come on.'

Nick moved, and Ryker's teeth bared in a snarl. 'Any interference from you, Driscoll, and you'll find yourself very swiftly in no man's land.'

Nick hesitated, and Cassie could see that there would be no help forthcoming from that quarter. It served her right for slapping him away. Her breath hissed in frustration. She was on her own.

Digging her heels into the tarmac, she jerked her wrist ineffectually against the hand that held her. She was no match for him, and her temper soared as he dragged her along after him.

'I'm not going anywhere with you, you oversized bully. Who do you think you are, Haldene, coming here and throwing your weight about?' Enraged, she clenched her free hand into a fist against her side until the knuckles whitened with the strain. 'Don't think you can come here telling me what do do. If I want to wander about chatting to all and sundry I'll do it, with our without your say-so.'

Her words made no impact on him, and she was uncomfortably aware that people were beginning to turn their heads and stare after them as he propelled her across the tarmac to the car park. 'People are looking, Ryker,' she gritted fiercely. 'You're making a scene. Doesn't that bother you?'

'I'm getting used to it, around you,' he slammed back. 'You and trouble seem to be synonymous.'

Reaching his car, he opened the passenger door, and pushed her inside so that she sprawled in an untidy heap on the leather. Before she had even managed to straighten out her limbs, he had the engine up and running.

'Damn you, Ryker, you'll pay for this. This is the second time you've abducted me. It's getting to be a fetish.'

'Sure,' he said nastily. 'I can think of a few others I could get hooked on. All I need to start is a gag and a length of strong rope.'

Her teeth clamped. 'I didn't know you had such sadistic tendencies. Turns you on, does it, getting rough with helpless women?'

She felt his cynical gaze rake over her flushed features. 'You? Helpless? Don't make me laugh,' he mouthed tersely. 'You'd scare off a snake if it threatened your space.'

'Oh, that's great,' she said, stung by his harsh opinion of her. 'So now I'm some kind of Amazon, am I?'

'You're a rebel,' he said rigorously. 'You always have been. Ever since I've known you, you've lit up like a fuse in a box of fireworks whenever anyone challenged your right to do as you pleased. Don't you ever think of the consequences for other people?'

Her brows arched finely. 'I have no idea how you came by this bad opinion of me. Since when did I do anything to hurt anyone else?'

'Going behind my back and getting information out of my mechanic wasn't exactly designed to overwhelm me with joy, was it?'

They had reached their destination, it seemed. Ryker swung the car violently into the only parking space available in the vicinity of a country pub and they climbed out on to the gravelled drive.

'Is it my fault he was such a blabber-mouth?' she said. 'All I did was chat about the plane. I didn't ask him to volunteer details about your sleazy love-life.' In fact she desperately wished he hadn't. Details were the last thing she wanted to know. 'Though how you have the nerve to throw stones at me and Nick with your sheets glowing from all the heat generated I don't know. If you don't want your linen aired in public, you should try being more discreet.'

'My love-life is not sleazy. You shouldn't believe everything you're told.'

He marched her across the gravel and the smell of burgers being grilled on a barbecue made her feel faintly nauseous. With Ryker continually rocking the see-saw of her emotions, how could she ever face food again?

Her glance took in the busy forecourt. The place overlooked open fields and the drone of aircraft could be heard overhead as the air display continued. It was a hive of industry out here. People were collecting beer and snacks and heading along the footpath to the field to watch the show in comfort.

'Full, then,' she said thinly. 'Would that be a better word? Let's say your flat sees a lot of activity, with Sophie flitting in and out at all hours.' Pain stabbed at her and she went on with remorseless sarcasm, 'Not to mention all the others.'

His eyes slitted. 'You're treading on thin ice, lady. I've told you before, you shouldn't put any credence in what you read. Especially what's printed in your own paper.'

'Oh, of course,' she said, nodding in arrant disbelief. 'Well, you would say that, wouldn't you? What have you done with Sophie, by the way? I see you eventually managed to tear yourself away from her arms.'

He frowned. 'Sophie is not your concern. She merely dropped by on her way to meet some friends. She never intended to stay.'

'Hah!' Cassie exploded in sickly triumph. 'So you're the one who's feeling deprived. Now I know what this is all about. You're working out your frustration by lashing out at me. Too bad, Ryker. You'll just have to suffer.' Though she doubted his suffering would ever reach the depths she had plumbed.

'Don't be ridiculous.' He dug in his pocket for some change and ordered a couple of drinks from the outdoor sales. 'That's all beside the point, anyway. The fact is, I won't have you printing a load of rubbish about me.'

'As if I would.' His accusation made her blood boil. She felt the angry hurt fizzing inside her. 'Didn't I tell you I'd show you the copy first? What do you take me for, Ryker?'

'I think,' he said bitingly, 'that you're going out of your way to annoy me, buzzing away like a gnat that won't give up till it gets its bite of flesh. All that matters to you is getting a story at all costs. You were defeated over the squat, and you're determined not to lose out this time. Well, I'm here to tell you, you're not going to wheedle any more information out of anyone even remotely connected with me. My private life is my own; you're not going to spread it over the papers for all and sundry to pick at.'

'Thanks a lot,' she said bitterly, incensed and profoundly wounded by his casual summing-up of her character. 'As a matter of fact I did manage to produce an article on the squat, despite your interference, and it was very well received. And as to any writing about your private life, it wouldn't occur to you that your reasoning is at all faulty, would it? I've never set out to write anything bad about you. I'm sorry if Jim slants things the wrong way, but I don't go out of my way to cause you trouble, and it won't happen again, believe me.'

'I don't believe you.'

Her fingers clenched. 'It seems to me that you're determined to think the worst of me, no matter what I say or do.'

'*Especially* what you do,' he agreed savagely, tossing aside her attempt at explanation in a casual way that made her madder still. How could he have the nerve to decry her actions when he had just hijacked her?

Taking a long swallow from his beer, he thrust a drink into her hand, and for a wild moment she contemplated tipping it over him.

'Don't even think it,' he advised with taut menace, his own glass raised and ready.

Her lips flattened against her teeth. She didn't doubt that he'd do it.

He finished his drink and pushed the empty glass on to a table by the barbecue before turning towards the footpath. Did he expect her to follow? Stubbornly, she held her ground. She was astounded by the way his thinking processes were working. How could he believe her capable of such malice?

'Are you going to stay there all day?' he demanded.

'I'm considering my options,' she said. Thirstily, she drank the last of the cold cider and slammed down her glass. 'You can't seriously think I'm going to meekly trail after you so that you can continue the lecture. Just because you dragged me to this place doesn't have to mean I'm stranded.'

Broodingly, she glanced over to the car. Had he locked it? Was there the slightest chance he still kept a spare key hidden in the glove compartment? It would serve him right if his car disappeared from under his nose. Three or four minutes were all she needed.

Her dark thoughts were interrupted by the unmistakable jangle of his keys. Tormentingly, he held them out on one finger. His mouth twisted in sardonic amusement. 'You'll have to wrestle me for them.'

'You think you're so clever, don't you?' she said tightly. 'Watch your step, Ryker. You're heading for a fall.'

'Then I'll take you down with me,' he said, his voice grim.

A jet screamed overhead and they both looked up to follow its progress, shielding their eyes from the sun.

Ryker shifted abruptly. 'It's pointless standing here arguing,' he said. 'We might as well go down to the field to watch the last part of the show.'

She didn't move, and his eyes took on a steely glint. 'If you tamper with the car, you'll set off the alarm. Don't say I didn't warn you.'

He started along the footpath and after a few moody seconds of debate she went after him, picking her way over the rough ground towards the stile. Everything was going wrong, and it was all her own fault. She had made him angry by turning up this afternoon, but what else could she do? Her job was at stake. Hooking her jeans-clad leg over the wooden bar, she wondered if there was any way she could persuade him to see things from her point of view.

She manoeuvred over the stile, and when her feet touched the solid earth once more she paused for a moment, staring about her at the lush stretch of meadow. It was festooned with groups of people—couples, families with young children—all intent on making the most of the summer afternoon. There were picnic baskets scattered around, she noticed, and bottles of squash, and some people had binoculars to help them keep track of the planes droning at intervals overhead.

'I should be covering the rest of the show,' she said, going over to where Ryker had settled himself.

'Knowing you, you've already three times as much as you need.' He plucked a long blade of grass, twirling it idly in his fingers.

Dropping to sit beside him, she said, 'I really haven't any intention of writing anything that could possibly offend you.' Her mouth made a grimace. 'That's a promise, Ryker. I thought I'd concentrate the bulk of my article on the charity aspect.'

He sent her a cool glance, his jaw tightening. 'Your word had better be good.' He stretched out his long legs, and leaned back on his elbow, studying the swirling path of a biplane as it looped in the sky. 'When is the piece supposed to be featured?' he asked brusquely.

She glanced at him quickly. 'Tomorrow. I'll type it up later this afternoon and take it into the office as soon as it's ready. Most likely it will go out in the weekend edition as well. It won't take Nick long to process the photos.'

Distaste etched his features. 'He hangs around you like a pet poodle. Seems to me he's been clinging to your skirts since you were knee-high to a grasshopper.'

'I was away for three years,' she retorted. 'A lot of water's gone under the bridge in that time.' He was never going to let her forget that momentary indiscretion with Nick, was he?

'He's still around. He must have homed in on you as soon as he discovered you were in London.'

Her gaze was withering. 'We were bound to meet—we were mixing in the same circles. And now we work together, hadn't you noticed?'

'Is that what you call it? It didn't look much like work to me, the way he was wrapping himself around you.'

His tone was sneering, and she stiffened, but he hadn't finished. 'Has he moved in with you yet, or is that a delight still to come?'

'You never give up, do you?' she said tersely. 'It may be the casual sort of arrangement you'd go in for, but I want more than that.'

'Ah. You want him to do the honourable thing.' His eyes narrowed, the pupils darkening. 'Is that likely?'

'He's already proposed,' she said tautly. 'Does that satisfy your curiosity?'

Ryker's jaw clenched. 'You can't marry him. It would be the biggest mistake you ever made.'

'Why? Because you don't approve of him? The decision is mine to make.' The fact that she had turned him down need not come into it. She had known Nick for some time, but her emotions remained locked up inside her. He had tried to persuade her that love would grow if she gave it half a chance, and she had tried, but it made no difference in the end. But Ryker had no right to intrude. Who was he to judge her when it came to relationships?

'Because of your background. Some day, you're going to be a very rich young woman. When does the full bequest from your grandparents come to you? When you reach the age of twenty-five, or when you marry; isn't that the situation? And isn't there some kind of shares set-up?'

'And if there is?'

'Don't you see it makes all the difference?'

'No, I don't.' She frowned. 'Nick said he wanted to marry me. The money isn't an issue between us.'

'If you think that, then you're a fool,' he said sharply.

Cassie hesitated. Ryker had his own reasons for questioning Nick's integrity, and it would be fatal to her peace of mind if she let him believe he had planted a seed of doubt. His ego was big enough already.

'I don't want to discuss the subject,' she said.

The tension was back between them in full force, the air bristling with it, and she could not understand her own confused and troubled feelings. She glanced at Ryker's taut profile. Did he find her so unattractive that he could not understand that a man could care for her deeply? Certainly she held no appeal for him; he had made that clear years ago, and at his flat the other day—hadn't he pushed her away from him? He had even, this afternoon, she thought ruefully, compared her to a gnat.

Another plane circled the skies above them, and Ryker tilted his head back, focusing his attention on the display with the curiosity of one expert in the skill of another.

She stared at him through heavy-lidded eyes, absorbed by the way the white denim of his trousers moulded itself to his strong thighs, the way the navy T-shirt clung faithfully to his muscled chest and the flat plane of his stomach. Her glance stole to his face, and she had to curb her desperate impulse to reach out and trace the line of his jaw. Why was he so remote from her? Why did they always have to argue?

The faintly spicy fragrance of his aftershave mingled with his own indefinable clean male scent. He was near enough to her so that she could see the texture of his skin, the firmly rounded outline of his mouth, yet, for all that, there was a wall between them that could never be breached.

Her gaze jerked away like a skittish foal, small beads of perspiration breaking out on her brow. What was wrong with her? Her thoughts had gone shooting off on a crazy, outlandish track and it was all she could do to get herself under control. She was behaving like an idiot, running after something way beyond her reach. Pensively, she smoothed her fingers over the denim of her jeans. Would he ever allow her to get close to him?

Restlessly she eased her position on the grass, curling her legs beneath her. Crying for the moon was a wearing occupation; there had to be something she could do to take away the dull ache inside. It was time she took her life in hand again.

The whine of the aircraft diminished to a low throb as the plane became a mere speck in the distance, and Ryker turned to look at her. 'I feel like stretching my legs,' he said. 'Are you coming?'

He stood up, his body long and lithe, and put out a hand to pull her to her feet. To him, it was just a polite gesture, but its effect on Cassie was immediate. She could feel the ricochet of pleasure vibrating along her spine.

'How long are you staying in the area?' she asked as they set off across the field to find the footpath.

'Another day or so. I have some things to attend to and then I'm going to spend a short time at one of the pursuits centres.'

'I'd heard that.' Drat Jim Harker and his wretched story.

They had reached a wooden fence, and again he held out a hand to her as she climbed over. The touch of his fingers was like flame on her skin, the imprint burning in her mind long after he had released her. A stream flowed through the field, and they walked alongside it, Ryker's gaze fixed on the burbling, tumbling water.

She cast him a considering glance. 'I wonder,' she began slowly, 'if you would let me come along?'

He viewed her with suspicion. 'Why the sudden interest?'

'Hardly sudden,' she protested. 'It's been at the back of my mind for some time.' She grinned faintly. 'I've always thought it would be interesting to see you in action, but you weren't around to ask. Anyway,' she went on more soberly, 'Jim heard you were going and he asked me to write a piece on you and the centres, and how you came to set them up.'

'I knew it,' he drawled. 'I knew your sudden interest had some connection with your work.'

'It isn't purely because of my work,' she said.

His gaze was sceptical. 'It seems to me that the only reason for your persistence is your ruthless determination to please your editor.'

'I do have to earn a living,' she said, annoyed that he had put her on the defensive. 'But all the same, the idea does appeal to me. I think I'd quite like to immerse myself in an environment that's wild and natural and totally alien to me, something right away from the city, and the traffic, and the pollution.'

'Book yourself a holiday in the outback. That should do the trick.'

'Now you're being facetious,' she said irritably, pained by his dismissal of her. Was the thought of having her near him for any length of time so distasteful to him? 'Why are you so against me all the time? There's no reason why I shouldn't go along. It might do me a world of good—aren't these courses designed to instil self-confidence?'

'You don't need any boost to your confidence. You have more than enough already.'

She pulled a face. 'Not true,' she said. 'There's always room for improvement. What could be better for me than to join the group you'll be taking?'

'You wouldn't fit in with them.'

'Why not?' she demanded.

'They're all young men.'

'You're a chauvinist. Don't you know about equality? Women no longer spend all their time sewing samplers and singing by the piano; you do realise that, don't you? Some of us even hold down steady jobs, run a home, and, heaven forbid, drive a car.'

'Some of you,' he countered drily, 'even manage to keep the car maintained regularly so it doesn't let you down every five minutes.'

She coloured faintly. 'It isn't my fault if you men keep changing the rules. If you will insist on bringing in lead-free petrol you should see to it that all the engines work on it. Or at least keep the pumps in a separate place where people in a hurry don't get confused.'

Ryker gave a smothered cough and she sent him a sharp stare. 'Don't you dare laugh at me.'

His mouth twitched. 'I wouldn't dream of it.'

Stopping beneath the shade of a huge old sycamore, he stared down into the stream, watching the frenetic passage of the water as it cascaded in darting whorls over the weathered stones.

'Why do you keep saying no to me, Ryker?' Cassie asked huskily, coming to stand beside him, her spine angled lightly against the bark of the tree, her eyes unconsciously wide with appeal. 'It's just a little article. Just an interesting feature on what it feels like to take part on one of these courses. I give you my word, I'd be no trouble. You wouldn't even know I was there.'

'Your word, huh?' He flattened his hand against the tree and studied her thoughtfully. 'I think you could turn out to be more trouble than I ever envisaged.' He reached for her hand. 'You're no longer a tomboy, Cassie. You're a city girl, through and through. You've been pampered all your life.'

Slowly, he turned her fingers for his inspection. His thumb brushed softly, feather-light, over her palm, and a trembling started up inside her. She tried to stem the quivering reaction of her body. He didn't know what his touch was doing to her. How could he? Yet her limbs were molten; she was weak with sudden longing.

'Look at these hands,' he murmured. 'They're beautiful, manicured to perfection. How long do you think they'd stay that way?' He shook his head.

'At the first sign of discomfort, you'll be agitating to come home.'

Her eyes darkened. 'You don't know that. You might at least give me the chance to prove myself.'

He released her hand. 'You don't have to prove anything, Cassie.'

'Please, Ryker? Don't refuse me. I want to do a serious piece.'

'Even if you did, there's no guarantee Harker wouldn't turn it around.' He shook his head. 'Besides, as I said, the group is all male. Perhaps you could go along some other time, with no input for the paper.' He watched her expression. 'I'm sorry.'

'No, you're not,' she said fiercely. 'You're glad to have the chance to turn me down. You don't want me around because you think I'll cause problems. I won't, I promise. Anyway, you've taken women along before, I know you have.'

'Women,' he agreed, amicably enough. 'Not one woman, not you. You'd create too much of a diversion. I don't want you around, causing havoc.'

Her cheeks dimpled. 'Me—havoc? Now how could I do that? You know I wouldn't dream of upsetting the apple cart.'

His smile was fixed. 'Coming from the lips of Eve's handmaiden, that does nothing to reassure me. You've been practising since childhood.'

She laughed softly, but it was a wistful laugh, directed at herself. If he thought her capable of disturbing other men, why was it that she couldn't have that effect on him?

'You think so?'

He leaned towards her, a faint, answering smile on that dangerously attractive mouth, and her senses reeled, heady with a peculiar, aching excitement. Hazily, she wished that she could feel the sensuous drift of those firm lips on hers. Her breath spun out in a long, soundless sigh. The sun danced lightly over her skin; she felt the heat of it seeping into her limbs and filling her with a deep, melting languor.

Carefully she rested her head back against the tree, her soft curls spreading out in a cloudy fan about her head.

His glance narrowed on her. 'There are tiny leaves in your hair,' he said. 'You must have brushed by the hedgerow when you climbed the stile.'

The warm amber gleam of his eyes explored her features, traced the pattern of her mouth, her cheekbones, rested on the soft down of her skin. He was so close that he might almost have touched her. She found herself aching for the feel of his fingers firm about her ribcage, the brush of his hand over the waiting silk of her flesh. Fierce longing rippled through her veins. Her body arched faintly in reckless acknowledgement of her need, and his gaze wandered over the heated flush of her skin, came to dwell on the full pink curve of her mouth.

His features shaded, the planes and angles of his face dark and shuttered.

'Go back, Cassie,' he said, and there was a harsh, mocking inflexion in his voice as he moved away from her. She was bereft, stunned. 'Tell Jim Harker that there's no deal. No trip. No story.'

He started to walk along the path that led back to the car, and Cassie closed her eyes, absorbing the impact of the shock on her bewildered senses, trying desperately to focus on reality. How could she have left herself open once more to his callous indifference to her? When would she ever learn the lesson he had been trying to teach her throughout all those long, empty years? He did not want her. He would never want her.

As she sank back against the tree, the rough bark on her spine and beneath her fingers was like a scourge, underlining her folly. She should never have let her emotions get the better of her. The flame of love was fickle; it turned in on her and scorched her soul, leaving only ashes in its place. If she was to survive, she had to stifle the blaze before it raged out of control and consumed her altogether. But how was she to do that?

Work was her only salvation. Unfortunate that it must also involve Ryker, but what choice did she have? Jim was determined on this new angle, and that meant, vetoed or not, Ryker's island pursuits centre had to be her next port of call.

CHAPTER FIVE

ONCE made, there was no going back on her decision to join Ryker on the island. Cassie tried to push back the feelings of guilt that assailed her. Jim Harker had refused to listen to sweet reason, and she had thought long and hard about telling him what to do with his job, before concluding dismally that other offers of employment would be few and far between in the present climate.

It was just like Jim to have winkled out all the details of Ryker's travel plans, and Cassie already knew where he moored his sleek launch. Slipping on board in the first light of morning, without attracting attention, had been more than a little wearing on her nerves, she recalled. Even now, her heart was still pounding at the prospect of discovery.

Luckily the large mound of canvas sheeting on deck provided a reasonable refuge, though if she had to stay cooped up like this much longer she'd be too stiff to move, and that wouldn't do at all. She needed to be pretty swift on her feet if she was to keep out of Ryker's way for the next few hours. He would find out soon enough that she'd stowed away on board, but, if things went to plan, by the time all hell was let loose it would be too late for him to ship her back home.

Risking a glance from under the heavy weatherproof sheet, she was thankful to see the island come into view. She was hungry—it must be nearing breakfast-time—but she would have to wait a while before she could eat. Avoiding Ryker was top priority for the moment. Though, as he didn't own the island, he hardly had the right to forbid her presence there, and if she happened to be always in the outer edges of his vision as he worked with his group of men there was probably little he could do about it.

He was guiding the boat carefully alongside its mooring by a rough wooden quay. A few more minutes, and she would be able to free her cramped legs and get the circulation going once more.

She waited while he unloaded supplies, and as soon as he had heaved the last box from the deck and marched away with it she hauled herself stiffly on to dry land. Even at this early hour, the heat was beginning to build up, and she looked at the sky and hoped there wouldn't be a storm later on. Pulling her overloaded holdall across her shoulders, she pondered which direction to take. Ryker had headed east. It followed, therefore, that she should turn to the west.

It was a relatively small island. She could do a swift reconnaissance of his camp later, when he had settled everyone in. Though where the others actually were was something of a mystery. Perhaps they would be arriving later—an unusual divergence from the normal procedure, she would have

thought, but no doubt there was a perfectly
reasonable explanation.

An hour later, she stood on the cliff edge, looking
bleakly out over the sea crashing against the rocks
below. The island had a stark beauty, with grassy
hillocks, and rocky outcrops, and a freshwater
brook running through a winding vale. Behind her,
a small copse offered a modicum of shelter. Perhaps
she would rig up something there for the night.
Shrugging to ease the tension in her shoulders and
back, she turned her thoughts firmly to the preparations she needed to make.

'What the devil are you doing here?'

Cassie froze, rooted to the spot by the savagely
familiar tones. How had he managed to discover
her so soon? she groaned inwardly. Couldn't she
have had just another hour, at least?

'Answer me, damn you.'

Slowly, she turned around, steeling herself. 'Why,
if it isn't Ryker,' she murmured. 'What a small
world it is.'

'Don't try to be flippant with me.' The biting fury
of his tone sliced through her like a knife, and she
had to brace herself not to flinch. 'How the hell
did you get here?'

She sent him a cool stare. 'The same way as you,'
she answered. 'It seemed the logical way to travel
at the time.'

'Did it indeed?' He started towards her, menacing her with his taut, muscled frame. 'Let me tell
you,' he said through his teeth, 'your logic has a
major flaw—namely, I don't like it. I don't need

it. I won't have it messing up my plans. Am I making myself clear?'

'Perfectly.' He was still advancing on her slowly, with lethal precision, like a tiger stalking his prey. She eyed his long, powerful body with misgiving, and took a careful step backwards.

'I have no intention of "messing up your plans" as you put it. I'm here to do a little quiet research. Just pretend I'm not here, that I don't exist.'

'My life's ambition,' he grated. 'Only it's becoming all too apparent that you're out to do whatever you can to sabotage my dreams.' A muscle flicked in his jaw. 'What is it with you? Are you determined to go to any lengths to get a story?' His mouth made a sardonic curve. 'Well, your luck just ran out. This is the end of the line. You'd better grab your things and come with me.'

Defiantly, she stood her ground. 'I don't need you to tell me what to do,' she threw back tightly.

'Don't you?' He moved, swifter than light, his hand clamping her wrist. 'I have to disagree.'

'Let go of me,' she flared, struggling furiously, losing her balance as the soft earth shifted beneath her feet. 'Take your macho tactics some place else.'

He glanced over the cliff top, at the tumbling waves below, his lips making a brief, cold smile. 'Do you really want me to let you go?'

She followed his glance, a small shiver of unease rippling along her spine. She did not like the undercurrent of malice in his tone. He looked, she thought, as though he might actually enjoy dropping her over the edge.

'Take a closer look down there,' he gritted. 'Why do you think those stones are heaped up at the foot of the cliff? Like to join them, would you? Believe me, right now that would cause me very little heartache.'

Suddenly, the ground no longer felt quite so stable. Horrified, she realised that something was happening, that what she had thought was rock-solid was in fact beginning to break up beneath her feet. She felt the earth give way, felt herself begin to slip down, the toes of her shoes scrabbling against rock to find a narrow ledge. The blood drained away from her face. It was only the iron band of his fingers that held her secure, prevented her from falling.

'Ryker,' she said hoarsely, struggling frantically to keep her balance on the crumbling earth, 'I think—er—I think this is—er—some kind of land-slip... It isn't safe——'

'You said it.' His fingers gripped her like a vice. 'Not quite so self-assured now, are you, Cassandra? Do you still want me to let you go?'

'N-no. Ryker,' she said in panic, 'don't play games; this is—not funny.'

'You'd rather I helped you?'

She nodded, her eyes widening in desperation. Why was he asking such damn-fool questions?

His teeth bared. 'Say "please, Ryker,"' he drawled with silky intonation. '"Please help me, Ryker." Let me hear you say it.'

She muttered a short, heartfelt prayer as more stones dislodged beneath her feet. 'Please, Ryker,' she whispered. 'Please help me.'

At last he did as she asked. Swinging her into his arms, he lifted her up and away, walking with her to a safe distance from the edge. She clung to him, frantic with remembered terror, her breath coming in short, sharp bursts as her lungs did battle with her rattled nerves.

He set her down on her feet, but still her fingers clutched at him. Her heart was racing, pounding as fiercely as the waves that broke on the jagged rocks below. A shudder racked her body, her hands moving convulsively against his chest.

He pulled her to him, his arms fastening about her, his eyes dark and unreadable before he bent towards her and brushed her trembling mouth with his own.

Tension had locked her limbs, panicked fear still held her mind in thrall, yet gradually the sweet, slow burn of his kiss mingled with the confusion of her thoughts, until after a while the shock of what had happened to her began to ebb away.

Easing her closer to him, he deepened the kiss, pressuring her to him with the taut strength of his thighs, the binding inducement of his hand splayed out in firm possession along her spine.

Conscious thought had flown; there was only this new and bewildering sensation, this seductive, wildfire assault that scorched away the last vestiges of her fright. A tremor rippled through her, a soft sound breaking in her throat.

She felt his hands tighten on her momentarily before he dragged his mouth from hers. Heat flickered in the depths of his gaze, slowly dying away to be replaced by a darkness she could not fathom. He pushed her from him.

Dazed, she stared at him, her lips swollen and tingling from the sweet ravishment he had inflicted. Why had he done that? Why had he kissed her, then pushed her away as though he could not bear her near him? Had it been just a spur-of-the-moment thing, brought on by their sudden closeness? She was a woman, and she had clung to him, and there was no denying he was a strongly physical man; his reactions were swift and overwhelming. What had happened? Had he remembered the only woman who held any place in his life? Had he recalled that his loyalty and affection lay with Sophie?

She swallowed on the acrid taste that welled in her throat. How could he have kissed her like that, after the way he had treated her? He had taken pleasure in taunting her over that sheer drop, in tormenting her. It added insult to injury to be cast aside so readily now.

'How could you treat me like that?' she demanded, bitterness underscoring her voice.

His brow rose, and her anger grew. 'You enjoyed making me suffer,' she accused. 'I was scared out of my wits when I started to slip down that cliffside, and as far as you were concerned I might have been a sack of grain. You didn't care two pins for what I was going through.'

'Perhaps the knowledge that you had brought it on yourself had something to do with that.' His cool response brought her no satisfaction.

'I hate you for what you did,' she threw at him furiously. 'I might have been killed, and you treated it like some kind of a joke.'

'Hardly a joke,' he remarked tautly. 'I find nothing remotely funny in your presence here. I told you not to come, and you deliberately went against what I said.' His brows drew together in a dark, forbidding line. 'These places can be dangerous,' he rasped. 'As you just discovered for yourself. Lucky for you that I happened to be around. They're no playground for a tenderfoot with no training whatsoever.'

'I'm not a total idiot,' she muttered, forced to acknowledge that he had at least saved her from falling. He didn't have to relish her plight so much, though, did he? 'I wouldn't have come here without doing some reading on the subject first——'

'Reading,' he echoed, his tone sharp with derision. 'A lot of good that will do you.'

Smarting, she said, 'You talked to me about some of the survival training you did when you were in the Army...'

A gleam darted fitfully in his eyes. 'That was a long time ago. What were you? An itsy bitsy teenager with——'

'With fluff between her ears—go on, say it,' she said, resenting the easy way he thrust aside her defensive claims. 'That's what you think, isn't it?' She faced him stormily, hands on her hips, ready to do battle. Obviously the long talks they had had all those years ago meant nothing to him, though she remembered them vividly. 'You don't give me any credence,' she railed. 'Well, you'll see. I'll show you.'

Grimly he studied the slim gold watch on his wrist. 'I don't have time to take you back to the mainland now.'

'Forget it,' she said, her mouth taking on a mutinous line. 'I wouldn't go, anyway. I'm here now, and I'm staying. My being here doesn't involve any decision-making on your part.'

'Doesn't it?' His tone was caustic. 'I don't have time to play nursemaid.'

'I can take care of myself.' A faint breeze fanned her hot cheeks, disturbed the thin fabric of her soft cotton shirt. She felt its warm touch on her legs, left bare by her denim shorts.

'Sure. You just gave me a prime example of how you do that. I guess on that record all I have to do is come back in the morning and search for your body.'

His jeering tone scalded her pride. 'Don't bother,' she said. 'Just keep away from me.' Her sparking gaze took in his black jeans and the black T-shirt, the gleaming midnight hair. Why did he have to look so...powerfully male? 'If you hadn't come along threatening me like some kind of dark, avenging demon I wouldn't have strayed so close to the edge in the first place. Leave me alone, Ryker; get off my case.'

'Nothing will give me greater pleasure,' he agreed tersely. 'Return the favour, will you? I have a lot to do, and I don't need you in my hair.'

'I have no intention of getting in your way,' she muttered. 'I'm sure you have more than enough to do seeing to your protégés. No doubt they'll more than appreciate your undivided attention.'

'Which protégés did you have in mind? There's no one here but you and me.'

She stiffened. 'But—you said you were bringing a group.'

'Not to this island, and not for a few days yet. In fact, for your information, you wayward little witch, this is a new location. I'm here to complete a survey, check out the possibilities and pitfalls. As you already discovered, there's a dangerous landslip that has to be fenced off before we can let loose any raw recruits.' His smile grated on her nerves. 'So it seems,' he murmured, 'that if you were hoping to snatch any more interviews your plans are doomed to disappointment.'

She bit back her chagrin. Getting the thoughts and feelings of all the members of the group might have given her a slant that would take the pressure off Ryker. She could have come up with something to satisfy Jim Harker and at the same time keep Ryker from blowing his top. The whole thing had not sat easy with her right from the beginning, and now it seemed that it had all been for nothing.

'It looks as though Jim had his dates all mixed up,' she said dolefully.

'Doesn't it?' Ryker's obvious satisfaction needled her.

She shrugged. 'Then I shall simply have to concentrate on getting the feel of the place instead. I'll discover what it feels like to combat the elements, and try fending for myself in primitive surroundings.'

'I imagine you'll gain a good idea of that through the course of the day,' he agreed. 'Hunting out something to eat and drink will occupy a lot of your time. Unless, of course, you've stuffed that holdall with goodies.'

His disparaging glance showed he expected that was exactly what she would have done.

'I didn't have room,' she said. 'Other things seemed more important.'

His mouth twisted at that, and she felt a spark of satisfaction.

'I'm sure there's a plentiful harvest out there just awaiting my delectation,' she told him with a confidence she was far from feeling.

'True,' he agreed. 'There are plenty of berries and mushrooms on the island. Nettles, too. Try boiling them.'

'Nettles?' She stared at him. 'Don't you think I could poison myself eating those?'

His eyes glinted. 'Keep away from me if you do. I'd hate to have you throw up all over me.'

She watched as he walked away without a backward glance. That just about summed it up, didn't it? That was as much as he cared. She could drop down the cliff or writhe in agony from tasting some deadly substance, and she was crazy if she expected anything else. He was never going to toss her a declaration of undying love, was he?

This was no time to start feeling sorry for herself. Pulling her notebook and pencil from her bag, she made a few swift jottings. One way or another, she would get an article out of this.

Throughout the morning, she heard Ryker banging away at fence posts, and came across him from time to time as he strung wire in a taut line across the dangerous spots on various parts of the island.

The heat was getting more oppressive as the day wore on. She explored the whole of the west side of the island, taking notes, and collecting dry wood for a fire, so that she could boil up water for a drink. Nettle soup. Ugh. Still, she could give it a try. And Ryker was certainly right about the presence of nettles on the island. Her reddened, stinging legs were testimony to that.

She sat down on a flat rock near to the place where he had moored the boat, and looked up at the darkening sky. Rubbing a hand gingerly over the tender skin, she wondered if there was thunder in the air. Her throat was dry, her skin flushed from her exertions.

'Having second thoughts about your venture into the wilderness?'

She tensed as he came into view. 'Certainly not,' she said sharply. 'It'll take a lot more than your grouchy presence to put me off. If your recruits can put up with you, so can I.'

'Some of them actually enjoy my company.'

She shot him a dark look. 'You mean the women, I suppose. I've no doubt you put yourself out to be charming to them. After all, they do pay for the experience.'

'Careful, Cassie,' he cautioned her. 'Your sharp tongue is getting the better of you.'

She gave him a serenely innocent smile, hiding the nagging jealousy of her thoughts, then turned her gaze in the direction of the shore. Absently, she scratched at the irritation on her legs.

'What have you done?' he asked.

'Nothing.'

He bent down beside her and she swung her legs away from his hard scrutiny. 'Keep still,' he ordered, lightly slapping her thigh, 'and let me look.'

His fingers feathered over her burning calves, and she wasn't altogether sure that the heat she was experiencing came solely from the nettle sting. A faint throbbing started up in her temples; a light ripple of sensation quivered through her limbs.

'It's not as bad as it looks,' he said at last. 'I'll get something to put on it.'

He walked over to the launch, and came back a few minutes later holding a tube of ointment. Unscrewing the lid, he squeezed out a few centimetres of white cream and smoothed it over her skin. The cooling effect gave almost instant relief.

'That feels good,' she said on a sigh. 'Thanks.'

He put the lid back on the tube and dropped it into her holdall. 'If you wore something sensible, instead of flaunting yourself in those cut-off denims, you wouldn't have been stung.'

The rebuke smarted more than the inflamed skin. 'Oh, I'm sorry,' she said tartly, remembering Sophie's painful gibes. 'Is my dress sense not to your taste? I do apologise for offending you. I'll wear a yashmak and robe next time I come on one of these trips.'

'Heaven forbid there's a next time.'

She stood up, sending him a glare. 'I suppose if my name happened to be Sophie you'd have no objections. She could "flaunt herself", as you put it, in whatever she fancied.'

'I doubt very much that Sophie would want to be here, roughing it,' he said drily, 'let alone allow herself to be seen dead in frayed denims. Her taste tends to the more exotic.'

'Like Chanel perfume, and outfits by Armani and Gaultier? Is that what turns you on?'

A glinting flame sparked in the depths of his eyes. 'Janet Reger, perhaps. Why the sudden interest, Cassie?'

The softly voiced question sent a swift rush of heat to faintly colour her cheekbones. Denial followed hot on its heels.

'Interest? Me? You have to be joking. I'm merely wondering why you have such a marked antipathy to my presence here. Of course, I didn't realise my clothing would become an issue. I guess that's just one more black mark you have against me. Neither denim nor cotton lace could possibly meet your prerequisites, could they?'

His eyes raked her slowly. The nape of her neck prickled with awareness as she felt his amber gaze shift in gleaming assessment over her slender length.

'Couldn't they?'

She stared at him, wide-eyed, pushing her fingers through the silky cascade of her hair, and his lips twisted in a half-smile, his glance following the unconsciously sensuous movement of her hand.

'Why don't we put an end to this senseless arguing, and find a more pleasurable way of passing the time?' He reached for her, his hands shaping the smooth curve of her hips and drawing her towards him. 'We're quite alone; there's no one to disturb us.' His thumbs began to make slow, circling movements that burned into her flesh, even through the taut constriction of her shorts. A gleam lit his eyes, devilment lurking there, and, with a start, she came out of the hypnotic trance he had lulled her into.

'N-no,' she yelped, jumping back, away from him. He was teasing her, making fun of her, and she had almost fallen for it. 'You're just trying to sway me off course,' she muttered, 'so that you can go home telling yourself how useless I am, and how like a woman to let herself get side-tracked. Only you're wrong. It won't work. I'm going to do this properly. I have to go now; I have things to do.'

'That goes for both of us,' he said, casting a thoughtful glance around. 'There's still some fencing I have to fix in place, so I'll leave you to get on. With nightfall drawing close, you'll have a lot to see to. The temperature will probably drop quite drastically from now on—but I dare say once you have your shelter constructed you'll get by well enough.' Amusement glimmered in his eyes. 'You could always light a fire near-by, too—that might serve to keep any stray animals away.'

She repressed a shudder. He was trying to frighten her, make her show her weakness so that he could laugh in her face, but she wouldn't give him the satisfaction.

'Thanks for the advice,' she said, stiffening her shoulders. 'Don't let me keep you.' What kinds of animals did he mean? She frowned. He was making it up. There weren't any really dangerous animals in this part of the country. Were there? Of course he was making it up. She wouldn't let it bother her. Anyway, it was just as well she had stuffed some matches into her holdall. They were bound to come in useful.

She set off for the copse. The wind was getting up, but the small clearing seemed an ideal place to set up home for the night. She hoped the grey, cloud-laden sky didn't mean trouble. She pushed the thought aside. Large, leafy branches were what she needed. She'd soon have a shelter made up. Pity she hadn't been able to bring a tent along, but she'd had to travel light in the hope that Ryker wouldn't discover her.

A hack-saw would have come in handy to use on the branches, but she made do with her bare hands, breaking off what she needed, and sending her silent apologies to the maimed trees. The dry timber from the ground would serve for the fire.

He was leaning against a tree trunk as she came back into the clearing with her load. The wind buffeted her, making the task of dragging her burden more difficult. 'I thought you had pressing work to do,' she enquired coolly.

'It'll keep for a while.' He folded his arms across his broad chest. 'This promises to be far more interesting than what I had in mind.' There was glinting mockery in the way his eyes appraised her. He wanted her to make a mess of it. He was just waiting to see her fail dismally.

She ground her teeth together as she ransacked her holdall for a length of twine, scattering supplies in all directions as the fading light hampered her search. At last she found it. Knotting the branches together, she heaved them into position, her breathing laboured as she braced the overhanging boughs to form a makeshift roof. That done, she stood back and contemplated the result.

Ryker was still there, she noticed uncomfortably, his narrowed gaze shifting over her handiwork. What was he thinking? His shuttered expression told her nothing. Her fingers twisted in the belt of her shorts. She *had* remembered everything he'd told her all those years ago, hadn't she? She had listened avidly to everything he'd had to say. She had wanted to know everything there was to know about him, and now...he didn't want her anywhere near him. Her throat closed painfully on the thought.

Lord, she could do with a coffee. At least she wasn't cold now, after all that activity, but her shirt felt damp, and she realised with something of a shock that it had started to rain, and the wind was driving it her way.

'Presumably you have your shelter already made,' she said, bothered by his continuing presence. 'Why don't you go and use it?' She slammed the lid down on the treacherous hope that he might want to stay with her. 'I've no inclination to let you share mine.'

'Just as well, then, that I won't be asking. It looks as though it might be a bit cramped in there, anyway. Besides——' he glanced up at the dark, gloom-ridden sky '—I'm not altogether convinced that it would last long enough to see us through till morning.'

She threw him a sharp, questioning look. 'What's wrong with it? Why shouldn't it last? I've tied everything together.'

'So you have.'

When he made no further comment, she decided to ignore him. Holding down her flyaway curls, she dived for cover from the blustering gale and fished out her matches from her bag. He probably expected her to rub two sticks together to make a fire, but she had to draw the line somewhere. She'd already regretfully consigned the small Primus stove to the back of a cupboard at her flat. Coffee, though, she could not bring herself to do without.

With water from the canister, she could be enjoying a hot drink within minutes. If the smell of coffee tormented him and made him think what he was missing, that was just too bad; he could go and get his own. He was standing there, watching her every move, and making it perfectly clear he had no intention of helping her out. She lit the dry wood as another gust of wind hit her sanctum and the whole edifice seemed to sway. Carefully, she placed a pan of water over the flames.

Spooning sugar into her mug, she told herself Ryker could not possibly have done any better. Heavens, there was a storm blowing out there; it was bound to shift a little. Frowning, she tugged the damp shirt away from her skin, listening to the loud creaks and whines as the wind tore with mischievous fingers at her flimsy refuge. Another blast, and there was an ominous, sharp crack.

Cassie watched in choked disbelief as the pan tipped over, and the orange glow of the fire guttered and died as water doused the flames. The sound of splintering wood followed, and she cursed vehemently as the whole structure slowly collapsed on top of her.

Humiliatingly, Ryker pulled her out from the tangle of branches. His grin added to her mortification, and she slapped his hands away. 'Go away,' she said, her voice fraught. 'I don't need you. You wouldn't have done any better.'

His mouth curved wider. 'Maybe not.'

She sent him a black scowl. 'I told you before; don't you dare laugh at me.'

'As if I would.' Unholy light danced in his eyes, and her scowl deepened.

'The wood's too thin and weak,' she gritted, tugging twigs from her hair and flinging them to the ground. 'That's the problem.' He carried a saw and hammer and nails with him, didn't he? Was that what made up the thinking man's survival kit these days? Pity she hadn't had room in her bag. 'Those knots I tied were perfect; I know they were. They'd stand up to anything.'

He was still grinning, the fiend. 'Except a westerly wind. I imagine you'd have fared better over on the east side of the island.'

A dark glower shaded the twin spots of colour that burned high in her cheeks. Why hadn't she taken that into account? Of course he was right.

A low, ominous rumble of thunder sounded in the distance, and she hid a grimace. 'Don't imagine I shall let a little thing like a puff of wind throw me,' she told him. She searched the wreckage for what she could salvage, seizing on a gnarled branch. 'This is just a minor set-back,' she said, brandishing the wood like a sword in front of her. 'It isn't going to knock me off my feet.' She jumped as a streak of lightning raced across the sky. Rain hissed over the ground, plastering her clothes to her skin.

'Put the wood down,' he said, 'before it does one of us some damage.'

She viewed him abstractedly, her attention caught by another crash of thunder. The roar of blood thrummed in her ears.

Ryker bent down and retrieved her belongings from the jumble of wood on the ground.

'I have to start again,' she muttered, frowning as he straightened and purposefully removed the branch from her clenched fingers.

'No, you don't,' he said peremptorily. 'You're coming with me. We'll spend the night on my side of the island. You're getting soaked, and I don't want a case of pneumonia on my hands on top of everything else.'

'Oh, thanks; thanks a lot for that deep, heartfelt consideration,' she gritted, setting her teeth. 'But I really wouldn't like to put you to that trouble. I shall stay here and sort myself out, and if I should, by any remote chance, contract some deadly disease, I'll endeavour to expire quietly, with the minimum of fuss. Please go away, Ryker. I can manage perfectly well on my own.'

Another blinding fork of lightning seemed to split the sky in two. 'That's as may be,' Ryker said, taking her arm in a firm grip, and swinging her holdall over his shoulder. 'But I'm not prepared to take the risk. You'll spend the night with me, and if that idea doesn't appeal that's hard luck. I'm in no mood for argument. Are you coming under your own steam, or do I carry you?'

The pressure on her arm increased. 'There's no need to pull,' she said darkly. How could she refuse such a gracious invitation? He was really looking forward to her company, wasn't he? 'I know you're stronger than I am. You don't have to prove it.'

'Then get a move on.'

They walked through meadowland and across rugged outcrops of rock, heading east. At last Ryker said, 'Here we are. We can get in out of the rain and dry out a bit.'

She stood very still, and stared. 'It's a hut,' she said thickly. 'Ryker...it's a hut.' She was completely nonplussed. It was the last thing she had expected to see. 'You cheated.' Her voice rose in an outburst of disbelief. 'It's a purpose-built cabin. It was here all the time.' She sent him an accusing look. 'I thought this was supposed to be all about survival?'

'I'm not here to pit my wits against the elements,' he told her raspingly. 'I came here to do a job—to prepare the groundwork—and I shall be leaving first thing in the morning.'

He pushed open the door of the cabin and went inside. 'Once I get the fire going,' he said, as she followed him into the room, 'it will soon start to warm up in here. Take off your wet things and grab a couple of blankets from the shelf.'

Cassie's eyes widened as he went over to a woodburning stove that stood in one corner. He started a small blaze. 'Hurry up,' he said, eyeing her wet clothes with disfavour. 'You're dripping all over the floor.'

She stared around. There was a table, solid and serviceable, a camp-bed with a sleeping-bag thrown over it, and a couple of chairs. The shelves were stacked with provisions of all kinds.

His voice sounded warningly in her ears, and she jumped again. 'If I start to hear your teeth chattering, I shall take matters into my own hands. Put your things to dry near the fire.'

He started to strip off his own shirt, and she caught a stunning glimpse of his deeply tanned male torso. He was magnificent to look at, lean and tautly muscled, his skin gleaming faintly gold in a way that tugged at her senses. She felt an aching need to touch him.

Shakily, she turned away, and reached for a woollen blanket to cover herself while she undressed. He had no such qualms, it seemed. He'd have taken everything off, whether or not she had continued to stare. Hurriedly, she dealt with her garments, wrapping herself in the voluminous folds of soft wool.

'Soup, I think,' he said, and she sent him a covert glance, relieved to find that he had donned a fresh pair of jeans and a cream sweater. All her clothes had suffered in the storm raging outside. The holdall had developed a leak.

She sighed. 'Does it have to be nettle soup?' she queried tentatively. 'I think I may develop an allergy.'

He grinned. 'I can probably come up with something better than that. Hot, thick vegetable, with fresh, crusty rolls. How does that sound?'

'Wonderful.' She sent him a smoky glance. 'You're a fiend; you know that, don't you?'

He laughed. 'You were the one who wanted to fend for yourself in primitive surroundings. Who am I to stop you?'

When the soup was piping hot, and she had fixed a pot of coffee, they sat down at the scrubbed wooden table. Cassie said, 'You never did tell me what it was that made you set up these centres.'

'Didn't I?' He applied himself to his soup.

She wondered if he was reluctant to talk about it. 'It's strange, isn't it,' she said, 'that people should be interested in learning how to cope in the wild? I suppose, in a way, it's exchanging the tensions of the concrete jungle for a challenge of another kind.' Breaking off a chunk of bread, she studied him thoughtfully. 'You were doing it for real in the beginning, weren't you? When you were in the Army. I should have thought...' She paused, uncertain, then plunged on. 'After the way your father went missing, I should have thought survival techniques were the last thing you wanted to get into. Didn't it bring back awful memories? You must have been only a child when it happened.'

He did not answer for a moment, and she began to regret her hastily posed questions. Then he said quietly, 'It always haunted me, not knowing what had happened to him after his plane crashed. Although he and his friend had managed to get clear of the wreckage, there was no trace of what happened to them.'

'But surely there must have been something, some clue?'

He shook his head. 'They had registered a flight plan in the usual way, but by the time it was realised something had happened conditions had deteriorated on the mountains. Temperatures were way below freezing, and a blizzard sprang up. There was no chance of finding them.'

'Ryker, I'm so sorry.' She reached out and touched his hand briefly.

'It all happened a long time ago,' he said.

She was silent for a moment, then said quietly, 'Your mother took the news very badly, didn't she?'

'I watched her give up hope and gradually fade away. They said it was heart failure. I was angry. Why hadn't he survived? Why didn't he get back to us?'

'Is that why you joined the Army?'

He finished off his coffee. 'I had no family left, so it seemed a natural choice of career. After a while, I realised that there was something I could do during my stint in the services, something that might give more than the ghost of a chance to some unlucky soul who crash-lands in a war zone, or goes astray in unknown territory. So I specialised in training recruits in those skills for a time. It wasn't much of a compensation for my own loss, but at least it helped me keep my sanity.'

Cassie said nothing, acknowledging the deep sorrow he must have felt at losing both parents, the strength he had dragged from within himself to fight back.

'Life goes on,' he said. 'You learn that there are other challenges to meet, different mountains to conquer.'

'So when you left the Army,' she mused, 'you used the skills you had learned to set up the centres?'

'It seemed the logical thing to do at the time. And it helped to fund the charter business later. I don't have a great deal to do with the pursuits centres these days, but I enjoy overseeing them occasionally, or looking out new locations such as this.'

'Have you finished everything that you came here to do? You said you were leaving tomorrow.'

He nodded. 'Mostly. All the dangerous areas are fenced off now, so we can leave first thing in the morning. I've meetings scheduled on the mainland, so I have to get back as soon as possible.'

They would go back, she thought bleakly, and he would once more move out of her life. A shiver ran through her and she pulled the blanket more firmly around herself.

'You're still cold,' Ryker said. His gaze rested on her, and she wondered what it was that she could see in his eyes. Was it concern, affection even? Perhaps he did care for her, just a little. Perhaps— hope darted fitfully—more than just a little... Was it possible?

Ryker stood up, saying briskly, 'Come over to the stove and get warmed up.'

She stretched wearily, and walked towards the heater as he had suggested. Despite the hot soup and the growing warmth of the room, the cold seemed to have seeped into her bones. The cold of loneliness...

Unexpectedly, Ryker's arms came around her, hugging her close, his hands chafing warmth into her arms, sliding along her back. 'You should have said you were still feeling chilled,' he admonished her.

The touch of his hands, the pressuring warmth, was almost too much for her. She wished that this closeness meant more to him, that he would hold her as though that was where she belonged, with him for a lifetime. But how could that ever be, when there was Sophie...?

Her head dropped, her cheek resting against the solid warmth of his shoulder, taking what comfort she could from his nearness. Sophie was not here, and Ryker's arms were holding her safe. She would keep that thought next to her heart and cherish it.

'You're tired,' he said. 'It's been a long day, one way and another.' He moved away from her, and she felt the sudden sharp pang of loss. 'You'd better use this for tonight,' he said, unzipping the sleeping-bag. 'It's only a narrow camp-bed, but you should be fairly comfortable.'

'But what will you do?' She glanced around. 'I don't like to mess up your arrangements.'

'I'll put some blankets on the floor. It's no problem. Now, get some sleep. We need to make an early start tomorrow.'

CHAPTER SIX

RYKER said little to Cassie next morning, concentrating instead on loading supplies on to the launch, and making ready for the journey back to the mainland. Studying his broad back as she tried to help, Cassie wondered if, in the light of day, he felt a renewed surge of anger because she had gone against his wishes in going to the island. His manner seemed distant, and she was not sure whether it was purely due to his preoccupation with other matters.

'Leave that,' he ordered briskly, as she made to haul a box on deck. 'Perhaps you could see to a pot of coffee before we set off?'

Feeling that she was somehow in the way, she did as he suggested. While she waited for the water to boil, she picked up her notebook and scribbled a few hurried lines. Coming back into the cabin, Ryker sent her a steel-eyed glance that made her falter. Hastily, she pushed the book back into her holdall. She had no wish to do anything which would bring an end to the brief moments of closeness they had shared. The glowing memory of being in his arms was something she wanted to hold on to for a while longer.

Reality, though, intruded all too soon. 'Where do you want me to drop you?' he said as they drove

111

into the city some hours later. 'Are you going straight back to the flat?'

She checked her watch. 'I think I'd better call in at the office. There are one or two leads I have to follow up, and I can probably make a start this afternoon.'

The interview she pursued took longer than she had estimated, and by the time she had written up the piece it was very late. As she eased her tense limbs, it dawned on her that she had missed out on a meal, and when a few of her colleagues voted on a hot snack at the local pub it seemed like a good idea. The prospect of going back to her flat, when Ryker would not be there, was dismal, and she made an effort, instead, to join in with the banter going on around her.

When she eventually made it back to her apartment, she was too tired to do more than scrub herself clean and fling herself into bed. Last night seemed so far away now, and she closed her eyes on thoughts of Ryker, wishing he were still with her.

Morning came too soon. Slipping her silk robe over her underwear, Cassie emerged from the bathroom with a weary yawn. At least the shower had gone part way to refreshing her. She would get to grips with some writing as soon as she had eaten. Producing something on the pursuits centre would take careful thought, if Ryker was to approve. Not that there would have been any problem if Jim didn't constantly try to add his own slant.

'You're scowling,' Nick said, startling her as she walked into the kitchen. 'What brought that on?'

She looked at him, her mind disorientated for a moment or two. Puzzled, she said, 'Nick? What are you doing here?'

'You asked me to keep an eye on the place while the builders finished off, remember?' He grinned. 'It was only a few days ago; you can't have forgotten?'

'No, but——'

'They were working until late, and it took me a couple of hours to tidy up after them, so I decided I might as well stay over in your spare room—I didn't think you'd mind.'

She shook her head. 'No, of course not. I'm sorry, I don't seem to be thinking too clearly this morning. Thanks for straightening things up, though you should have left it for me. I'd have seen to it.'

'It was no trouble.' He gave her a speculative look. 'Why don't you put me out of my misery, and marry me? We go back a long way, don't we? We share the same interests—couldn't we make a go of it?'

Cassie's blue eyes clouded. 'I wish I could tell you what you want to hear, Nick. I'm sorry. I *do* like you. I've always thought of you as my friend, but I can't give you more than that.'

'It's Ryker, isn't it?' There was a bitterness in his voice. 'If he wasn't on the scene I'd be in with a chance, but ever since he came back you've been different; you've been edgy the whole time.'

'Have I? I don't know. I'm very confused about everything just now.'

'There's no future for you with him. He already has a relationship, with his secretary. Forget him, Cassie. I can make you happy.'

'Please, Nick, don't push it,' she said, her throat tight. 'I've told you before; I don't want to talk about him, and I'm not going to argue with you.' She went over to the percolator and spooned in fresh coffee.

Seeing her closed features, he bit back what he was about to say. 'OK,' he said, resignedly. 'Have it your way for now. But I shan't give up. Perhaps we can talk about this again later.' He appeared harassed. 'Right now, I have to go out on a job; there's just time for a quick shave.' He started towards the bathroom. 'Your father rang, by the way. He's been trying to reach you for some time.'

'What did he want?'

Nick shrugged. 'He didn't say, but he didn't sound in a very good mood.'

The doorbell rang as he disappeared into the bathroom, and Cassie frowned. She only hoped it wasn't her father come to take her to task. She wasn't up to dealing with him right now, not before breakfast.

It was Ryker. Seeing him standing there outside her door, large as life and twice as overpowering, made her heart leap.

'Ryker,' she murmured, staring at him, drinking in his familiar, bone-meltingly attractive features.

'Are you going to keep me standing out here all day?' he asked quizzically. 'I thought I might at least get a foot in the door.'

'Oh!' Slowly, her faculties returned. 'Of course, you want to come in.' She stood to one side, toying with the belt of her robe.

He looked at her oddly, his brows pulled together in a slight frown, and walked through to the lounge. Removing his grey leather jacket, he threw it over the settee and remarked thoughtfully, 'I take it the builders have finished now?'

She nodded, her eyes drawn to the breadth of his shoulders, his long, lean frame.

'Is something wrong, Cassie?' he murmured. 'You look a little distracted this morning.' He began to wander around her living-room, glancing over her bookshelves. He removed a paperback and flicked lightly through it.

'No.' She found her voice. 'I just hadn't been expecting you, that's all. I mean, you didn't say you'd call. I thought...' She stumbled to a halt as Nick walked into the room.

'You're about out of toothpaste,' he said. 'Shall I——? Oh...' He stopped short as he saw Ryker.

Ryker's stare was deadly, his eyes narrowing on a dangerous glitter as he looked from one to the other. Nick paled slightly under his tan.

'Now I see,' Ryker said, his voice grating in the silence that descended, 'why you were so put out by my arrival.' Throwing the book to one side, he went on, 'You didn't tell me I was interrupting something.' His face might have been chiselled from a block of ice, and Cassie braced herself against the involuntary shiver that coursed along her spine.

She said quietly, 'I think you might be jumping to conclusions, Ryker.'

'Really?' His gaze streaked over her with cold insolence, and she was tautly conscious that the flimsy robe did little to conceal her feminine curves from his roving scrutiny. 'I shouldn't have thought there was much room for ambiguity, would you?'

Nick's mouth twisted. 'Cassie doesn't need your approval or disapproval, Ryker. She's free to do whatever she wants. It's entirely her choice if she wants to share her roof with a man. I doubt very much that you consult her when you invite a woman to stay with you.'

Cassie felt sick. She did not want to think about Ryker and other women.

'If I want your opinion,' Ryker said, his jaw clenching, 'I'll let you know.'

Nick's eyes flickered slightly, and he turned to Cassie. 'Look, I have to go; I'm late already. I'll bring a few supplies back with me. You seem to be running short of one or two things.'

Cassie frowned darkly as the door closed behind him. Nick had done it deliberately—thrown down a casual remark designed to mislead, almost as though he was staking a claim. Sooner or later, they would have to have a long, serious talk.

She breathed deeply. Even though she disliked his way of tackling things, Nick did have a point. What right did Ryker have to sneer, when Sophie shared his bed? That she did so, Cassie was in no doubt. Ryker was too male to be satisfied with a platonic relationship.

'What's got into you?' Ryker demanded. A muscle flicked jerkily at the side of his mouth. 'Have you taken leave of your senses? Don't you know any better than to throw in your lot with that unscrupulous snapshot merchant?'

'Is he any worse than you?' she flung back. 'You're the last one who should be throwing stones. At least Nick treats me with tenderness and respect. He doesn't try to drop me down cliffs.'

'No,' he agreed savagely, leashed violence in his glittering stare. 'He spends all his time bedding you, doesn't he? Is that what turns you on, making out with the paparazzi?'

She gasped at the insult, the blood draining from her face, and he studied her with measured contempt. 'No wonder you're in such a scratchy mood most of the time. Too many late nights.'

'You are despicable,' she said, lacing each word with acid distaste. 'And my disposition might improve by leaps and bounds if I were to find that this was all a bad dream, that your presence here is purely a figment of my imagination. As it is, I don't have to put up with you or your nasty remarks any longer. You know where the door is—I suggest that you use it.'

'I'm not ready to go yet.'

His cold arrogance fuelled her temper. 'Aren't you? Why exactly did you come here today, Ryker? It can't only have been that you wanted to throw insults at me.'

'I came,' he said curtly, 'to look over the article you're planning.'

'I don't work with people breathing over my shoulder,' she informed him frigidly.

'Even better. Consigning the whole thing to perdition is more or less what I had in mind, anyway.'

'Then it's fortunate you don't have a say in what I choose to do. If, and when, I produce an article bearing some reference to you, I'll allow you the privilege of reading through it before I commit it to print. Until that time comes, there's little point in your idling around here. I'd appreciate it if you would go.'

He ignored her blatant hostility. 'How long has he been staying here?'

Her skin prickled with annoyance. 'That's none of your business.'

'I'm making it mine. He's no good. It's time you realised that his attitude to you is tempered by what he hopes to gain long-term. He might well be interested in you as a woman, but the fact that one day you're going to be very wealthy weighs heavily in his scheme.'

'Are you still on that tack? Why don't you give it a rest, Ryker? You've told me what you think, and I've duly filed it. My eyes are wide open, and I'm quite happy with things the way they are. I don't see any need for you to keep emphasising the point.'

'I disagree. Since I don't believe you have fully appreciated the message yet, perhaps I should drive it home a little harder. Nick isn't the one for you.

How can he be, when you return another man's kisses with such sweet enthusiasm?'

He came towards her, and, too late, she read the intent that flamed in his eyes. She swallowed. 'Ryker, you——'

'That's right, Cassie. Me. You melt so delightfully whenever you're in my arms. I think it's time we explored that intriguing fact, don't you?'

He reached for her, and she began to struggle, trying to twist away from the restricting pressure of his hands, her robe caught up by the solid weight of his thigh, her wrist clamped in his large fingers.

'Let me go, Ryker,' she said urgently, fearful of the betraying pulse of her senses, her body's treacherous response whenever he was near.

He laughed softly, a breath of sound in the back of his throat. 'I think not.'

His glance shimmered over her, taking in the tangle of silk, the smooth expanse of her naked shoulder laid bare to his gaze. 'How do you account for the way you tremble in my arms, Cassie, if he means so much to you?'

His mouth covered hers, crushing the softness of her lips with bruising intensity. She was swamped by a wave of dizziness that left her weak, her limbs without substance. A shuddery sigh racked her body, and he bound her closer to him, wrapping her firmly in the circle of his arms. The lazy flick of his tongue slowly undermined her resolve, laid waste her will-power to push him away, reminded her of all the honeyed dreams she had woven around the two of them.

As his hands caressed her, stroking along her
spine, sweet, thrilling sensation unfurled inside her,
and she yielded restlessly to the sensuous demand,
leaning into him, returning his kiss with heated,
tremulous passion. Her fingers shook, trailing
lightly over his neck, absently seeking out the strong
column of his throat.

A low moan escaped her, muffled by the slow
glide of his mouth as it drifted down to explore the
loosened edges of her robe. Fleetingly, his tongue
ran over the smooth creamy expanse of her
shoulder, pausing to nuzzle the line of her col-
larbone, and the scalloped, lacy edge of her bra.
Then, shockingly, he dipped his head to brush his
lips over the throbbing, turgid mound of her breast.
A soft, shuddery cry broke in her throat, her
fingertips gripping convulsively into the fine fabric
of his shirt. He moved, shifting his weight slightly
to angle her against the rigid support of a cupboard,
his hands stroking the rounded curve of her hips,
drawing her to him so that she could feel the hard,
raw urgency of his desire.

'How can you deny the way you feel?' he muttered roughly. 'There's no mistaking the soft, supple
invitation of your body.' The warmth of his mouth
on her throat brought heated tremors to course
through her limbs. 'You want me. I could take you
here and now,' he said huskily, 'I could lose myself
in you.'

Her untutored body quivered in response,
whispers of caution swamped by her own need, by
her recognition that this was the man she loved,

had waited for, craved for so many years that she could not bear to turn him away.

'Ryker...' She looked into his eyes, wanting his words of love, desperately longing for some sign that his feelings went as deep as her own, but her thoughts turned quickly to despair. What she read in his smouldering gaze was not love; it was pure desire, a hot, swift, demanding passion, a raging fire that would consume her and leave her shattered in its wake.

The long, shrill cry of her broken dreams sounded a jarring note in her head, echoed in some far distant place like a peal of bells. Slowly the ringing of the phone pierced her consciousness, and she heard Ryker mutter a low curse. 'You'd better answer it,' he said.

Bemused, she straightened her robe and ran a hand shakily through her hair. She swallowed, and breathed deeply several times before she could bring herself to cut off that relentless, urgent demand.

James Wyatt's voice was edged with frost. 'So I've managed to track you down at last. First you're in that wretched squat, living in a commune, your photo splashed all over the papers. If it hadn't been for Ryker arranging that new accommodation, Lord knows what would have happened. The family name would have been dragged right through the mud. I'm warning you, Cassandra, it's time this nonsense came to an end.'

He paused briefly. 'There's a job in the company open for you. There has been all along. You can start next month and we'll forget what's gone

before, but if you choose to defy mc I'll think again
about your trust fund, and you can say goodbye
to your inheritance.'

Cassie held the receiver away from her, and closed
her eyes briefly as though it would in some way
shut off the flow of words.

'And where have you been these last few days?
Chasing halfway across the country on some fool
errand, no doubt.'

'I was with Ryker,' she said. 'There was no need
for you to worry.'

'Where is he now?'

'He's here.'

'Put him on; I want to talk to him. I've an important business meeting coming up in a few weeks.
I need him to fly me up there. The fewer people
who know about it the better.'

She handed the phone to Ryker and sat down on
the couch, pulling her robe protectively around
herself.

Ryker's tone was even and unperturbed, as
though nothing had happened between them, as
though what had been momentous to her had not
even begun to ruffle the calm surface of his demeanour. He had switched off, just as quickly as
if he had snapped his fingers.

How could she even have hoped that he might
have some spark of feeling for her? The only reason
he had made love to her at all was because he
wanted to prove a point.

Ryker finished the call and looked across at her, his dark brow raised in question. 'What was all that about?'

His cool, detached manner helped to restore function to her brain once more. She sighed. 'I'm disinherited again,' she said, her mouth twisting in a rueful curve. 'He's never liked my working as a journalist. My being at the squat was the final straw.'

'Can you blame him?'

She considered him impassively. 'It's all in the past now. It won't serve anything to rake over old embers. Though I'd quite like to submit a final piece to add to the feature I wrote. Your friend, the one who supplied the accommodation, would make a likely candidate for an interview, don't you agree? It would round off the whole series of articles quite nicely.'

'Gregson?' He absorbed the cool blue challenge of her gaze. 'I dare say something could be fixed up. It would mean your coming along to the annual gathering on Saturday. He promised he'd be there.'

Her brows lifted. 'You astonish me. Isn't this an about-turn? Don't you have any objections to throw at me? I'm not used to your conceding ground so easily.'

'Somehow,' he said drily, 'I have the feeling that a refusal would make very little difference. On current showing, you'd turn up anyway.' He came over to the couch, and sat down beside her, his amber gaze shifting over her, taking in her tense form, the jutting angle of her jaw.

She registered his nearness with a darkly brooding resentment. Did he think she would be gullible enough to fall into his arms a second time that day?

She studied the hard, strong-boned lines of his face, the firm mouth that had only a short time ago wreaked such devastating havoc on her senses. Pain knotted inside her, and abruptly she thrust the hurtful thoughts away, closing her mind against the harsh imagery. Why had she deluded herself that there could ever be anything between her and Ryker? He was only here because of the article she meant to write, and now she had blown everything, made a fatal mistake. She had shown him that she could be vulnerable to his lovemaking. She had to bring things back on to an even keel.

Her lashes flickered, hiding her dark abstraction. 'As you offered so generously, I accept. I'll drive down to your place on Saturday.' She paused. 'I take it that Sophie will be there?'

Ryker hesitated, his eyes narrowing on her. 'She said she would try to make it. Why? Is that a problem?'

'Not at all,' she said, her voice faintly distant. 'But if most people are going as couples, I hope you won't have any objections if I bring someone along with me.'

'Who did you have in mind? Driscoll?' His mouth made a hard line, his eyes taking on the glitter of tempered steel. 'Why should I let——?'

'I know you don't like him,' Cassie interrupted coolly. 'You've made that quite plain on more than one occasion, but if I'm to conduct an interview I want photos too. Nick works with me. I need him to come along.'

He viewed her thoughtfully for a long moment. 'Why do I get the impression that I'm being manoeuvred?'

'Do you, Ryker?' she murmured with feigned sympathy. 'Now who's being uptight, I wonder? You really should learn to take things at face value once in a while. All this suspicion must be very wearisome. Why don't you think of it as the chance for both of you to air your feelings? I'm sure you can be civilised about it, both being grown men.' There was a hint of mischief in her tone. 'Or is that too much to ask?'

'Let me warn you, Cassie,' he said roughly, 'if there's any trouble, if he uses that camera of his to angle after a centre-page spread of my guests, he'll find himself out on the pavement.'

'I can well imagine it,' she said drily. 'Would that apply to me, too?'

His smile was brief and humourless. 'Oh, I think not, my sweet. I'm sure there are other, far more satisfying ways of dealing with you.' He paused, speculation in his prowling gaze, and she knew a vague flicker of unease. His mind was busy ticking over, and it didn't bode well for her, that was for sure. His expression held all the lethal promise of a ruthless predator.

'Ryker——' she began, but he cut her off.

'Bring him along, by all means. I have the feeling that, one way and another, Saturday could prove to be quite an interesting day.'

CHAPTER SEVEN

CASSIE pressed her finger to the doorbell, and listened as the chimes echoed faintly through the corridors of the big house, their resonance muted by the sound of music and laughter.

'He must have quite a crowd in there,' Nick said, a faint smile playing over his mouth. 'I wonder if Hal Gregson's arrived yet, and had time to mellow?'

His grey eyes silvered in the moonlight and Cassie said sharply, 'You're here to take one or two photos of him, if he gives permission. Other than that, you keep the cover firmly on the lens, is that clear? This is supposed to be a social gathering, not a news stunt.'

'Of course,' he murmured, his voice amused. 'I know that. Don't worry so much; I won't let you down.'

Her brows pulled together in a frown. 'I thought we'd mix a little, that's all—get to know a few people, make contacts, nothing more.'

'I understand that,' Nick agreed, sliding a hand around her waist. 'Relax. I reckon this could turn out to be a great idea of yours.'

Cassie wasn't so sure. She had started to have doubts about the whole thing, from the moment Ryker had been in agreement. Why had he had such a sudden change of heart, been quite happy to have

126

Nick come as her partner? He was planning something, she was certain of it, and now she couldn't think why she had been foolish enough to push it in the first place.

She could always have persuaded Hal Gregson into an interview by phoning him up in office hours. OK, so it was good to meet someone socially, and it might help to get her off to a better start, but that wasn't the real reason she was here, was it? Hadn't she, in some dark, perverse corner of her mind, wanted desperately to see Ryker again, grasped at the merest chance of a meeting? Even knowing how little he cared, some tormentor inside her had prodded her into accepting this invitation, some masochistic instinct had pushed her into this act of folly.

It was too late to be having second thoughts. The door opened, and her nervous system sent out a red alert as Ryker came into her line of vision.

'Cassie...come on in.' He nodded briefly to Nick, then stood back as they walked into the hall, his gaze travelling slowly over her. Then he smiled, a devastating, attractive smile that did something wonderful to his features and sent her lungs into a spasm of shock. All at once she was finding it difficult to breathe; her mouth was dry as dust.

He looked different, somehow. Maybe it was the suit that did it, dove-grey, the expensive tailoring sitting well on his broad shoulders, his cream silk shirt contrasting with the bronze of his throat, the grey trousers emphasising the taut, muscular strength of his legs. Or maybe it was the spark that glimmered briefly in his eyes that had disturbed her. It was the look of the hunter, she registered in growing alarm, the stealthy satisfaction of one who knew that the snare was laid, the trap was set. She moistened her lips with the tip of her tongue and tried to pull herself together. She was being fanciful. Looks could be deceptive.

Leading them through to the main lounge, Ryker furnished them both with a drink, and said thoughtfully, 'I expect you'd like me to introduce you to one or two people.' He sent a searching glance around the room, and Cassie gulped down the sparkling wine, savouring the cool liquid as it slid down her parched throat.

She watched with suspicion as Ryker took Nick to one side, saying smoothly, 'I'm sure you'd like to meet Marie Delahaie. You two have something in common, since she's extremely interested in photography, though not as a professional.'

Marie Delahaie's eyes lit warmly as she greeted Nick. She looked as though she had stepped directly from the pages of an *haute couture* magazine, Cassie thought, looking with admiration at the classic lines of her dress and jacket. The discreet gold jewellery she wore at her throat and wrist spelled out wealth and good taste.

'And you'd like to speak to Hal, wouldn't you, Cassie?' Ryker murmured, coming back to her. 'I told him that you'd be here this evening, and he's looking forward to meeting you. I think we'll find him in the study, talking to Ray.' Cassie gave her glass to a passing waiter, and Ryker guided her away from the crowded room, his hand firmly at her elbow.

'Ray's one of your board members, isn't he?' she queried, trying desperately to ignore the slow burn of his fingers on her bare skin.

'That's right. He's working out a contract for a new administrative centre with Hal, but neither of them will mind if you interrupt them. And if you don't get your business finished this evening, you can always have another word with him in the morning. He'll be staying here overnight.'

'I shan't be here. I'm going back to London later this evening.'

'Nonsense,' he said briskly. 'I know James is away for the night, and you wouldn't want to stay over in the Manor while it's empty, but I'm sure I can find room for you here. Plenty of other people are staying over, and you don't have to let your evening be spoiled by the thought of the journey back. Besides, you came in Nick's car, didn't you? Is yours in the garage again?' His mouth indented fractionally when she didn't reply. 'Anyway, I shouldn't imagine he'll be in any condition to drive in a few hours' time.'

There was probably some truth in that. Although they had agreed on returning home the same day, Nick had already been giving out hints that he wouldn't mind looking out a hotel for the night. Cassie did not want to do that, and Nick had posed her with a problem, since she wasn't sure her money would stretch to alternative travel for the distance home. She was still paying for the renovations to her flat. Even so... 'I don't think I can stay here,' she said.

Ryker came to a halt outside the door of the study, and turned her to him, his hands resting lightly on her arms. She looked at him, a question in her troubled gaze, and he said with a wry inflexion, 'Do you have to make a fight out of everything I say and do? It's no big deal staying here.' His hand went to the door. 'Go and say hello to Hal. You won't mind if I don't stay around, will you? I really should go and find Sophie.' He moved away.

What had she expected? His relationship with Sophie had lasted through all these years, hadn't it? He was bound to be dancing attendance on her this evening. She had known it, yet still she had fought against the demons of her subconscious. Having him so near...close enough to touch...knowing he belonged with someone else, was the purest agony.

She couldn't go on this way, she realised, breathing deeply. She had an interview to conduct, and she had to appear cool and professional.

Several deep breaths helped. Slowly her pulse settled to a more even rhythm, and she went inside the room, steeling herself not to reveal the chaotic confusion of her emotions to either of the two men who came to their feet as she entered.

When she emerged from the study some three-quarters of an hour later, she had a wealth of information at her fingertips, and her address book was filled with valuable contacts.

It was a good thing she had trained herself to concentrate on the task in hand, she reflected soberly, trying to ease the faint throbbing in her head with the slow, circular motion of her fingers on her temples, because the haunting spectre of Ryker and Sophie might well have been her downfall.

Helping herself to another glass of wine from a silver tray in the lounge, she looked around for Nick, and saw him ensconced in a corner with Marie. He beckoned her over.

'Marie was just telling me about her investment in Barton Development,' Nick said. 'That's the same line your father's in, isn't it, Cassie?'

'That's right.' To Marie she said, 'I doubt you'll go wrong with Bartons as part of your share portfolio.' She sipped at her drink. 'From what I gather, the price is rocketing sky-high at the moment.'

'So I understand.' Marie assessed her shrewdly. 'James Wyatt isn't doing too badly either, is he?'

'An understatement if ever I heard one,' Nick laughed, his grey eyes dancing as he looked at Cassie.

A movement at her side alerted her to Ryker's reappearance. She stiffened. He was not alone. Sophie was very much in evidence, her arm locked into his, her body draped over his side in sensual invitation. Cassie swallowed the rest of her wine, and Marie turned a considering glance in her direction.

'And do you have shares in your father's company?' she asked. 'Do you mind my asking? I expect you have one of these trust clauses that allows you so much at a coming-of-age. That's how it was with me; I had to wait until I was twenty-seven to receive the bulk of my income—an age my father considered mature enough to handle it wisely.'

She grinned at Cassie, inviting a response.

'There was something along those lines,' Cassie murmured.

'Was?'

Nick gave her an odd look, and Ryker said drily, 'There was an unfortunate family argument. Cassie's father disinherited her, so now she's quite on her own in the world with regard to finance, isn't that right, Cassie?'

She slid her wine glass on to a shelf. 'You should know,' she said shortly. 'You were there.'

Sophie's mouth thinned disparagingly. 'It was hardly an unexpected turn of events, was it? You might have known if you carried on the way you were going that James would do something about it. You can't go around living with hippies and expect him to swallow it, especially when he's given you every chance to become part of the family firm.'

Cassie's ears had begun to buzz; a tight band was slowly working its way around her head. 'Don't let it upset you, Sophie,' she murmured. 'It's my problem, but I'm sure I shan't end up sleeping rough and holding out my begging-bowl to passers-by in the street.'

Sophie looked at her with distaste. 'Time will tell,' she said.

She turned to Ryker, her mouth softening. 'Darling, I have to go. Could you possibly take me back to my flat? I hate to drag you away from your guests, but it doesn't look as though the taxi I ordered is going to arrive, and I need to pick up a few things before I go to the station. Would you mind? At least it will give us a little more time to talk.'

'It's no problem. Just give me a minute with Ray. He'll hold the fort while I'm gone.'

'I, too, must make my goodbyes,' Marie said in an apologetic tone. 'Though I don't know what's happened to my lift. She's probably gorging herself at the buffet, and won't want to leave, but I really do have to go. It's the opening week of my new bistro, and I must put in an appearance, however late. You're all very welcome to come along at any time and help me celebrate.'

'I can give you a lift,' Nick said. 'There's no need to tear your friend away if she's enjoying herself. I'm more than happy to take you.'

Marie put an affectionate hand on his shoulder. 'What a charming man you are. How kind. You must, of course, sample the food and wine at my place. I insist.' She looked encouragingly towards Cassie. 'And you too, Cassie. Would you join us?'

'I think not, if you don't mind. I said I might have another word with Hal later.'

Cassie felt a wave of nausea engulf her as she watched Ryker move away with Sophie, his hand lifting in a quick gesture of farewell. The woman was in firm possession, her lips curved in response to something Ryker was saying.

Left alone, Cassie absently took the wine that a waiter offered. She stared at the buffet laid out on long white linen-covered tables, and the sickness returned, clawing at her stomach. Sophie called to him like a siren, and he went eagerly to her side, a willing victim.

Was that what he had wanted from this evening? Was that what he had planned—to show her that Sophie had prime place in his life, that he regretted the lapse he had made when he kissed Cassie, when he had said how much he wanted her? He had been driven by male need, and now he wanted the memory pushed out of the way, forgotten as though it had never existed.

She began to walk about the room, oblivious to the people who talked and laughed, blind to the couples who swayed contentedly to the music. The stairs were ahead of her, and she took them slowly, holding her wine glass carefully, taking small sips as she went. Her head felt slightly dizzy, as though it did not quite belong to her, and she held on to the oak banister with her free hand, willing herself to go one step at a time.

This was Ryker's home, the place he came back to, the place where he ate and slept and where he had lived almost from the first time she had met him. She wanted to know it, to feel it, to absorb its atmosphere into her bones, to have this one little part of him which was all she would ever have.

Each room was stamped with his refined taste, his love of what was solid and enduring, and she examined each one, drifting through them in succession, running her fingers over polished wood, and the smooth luxury of velvet.

She found herself in a large bedroom, and decided hazily that she had come to the end of the line. The carpet beneath her feet was deep-piled and welcoming, and she slipped off her shoes, feeling the soft wool with her stockinged toes.

Sitting down on the big bed, she drained the last of her wine, the bubbles filling her nostrils, tingling the back of her throat, her head swimming with warm sensation. This was where she wanted to be. This felt right, and she lay back, her hands closing on quilted silk, her mind slowly easing into a black, dreamless void.

'Time to surface, sleepyhead, or the coffee and croissants my housekeeper has prepared will go to waste.'

She blinked, then squeezed her eyes tightly shut against the sunlight that streamed in through the undraped windows. A little hammer was working overtime inside her head; her mouth and throat felt achingly dry.

'Come on,' Ryker said firmly, 'drink up. You might try a couple of aspirin, they'll do wonders for your hangover.'

She squinted at him. 'Hangover?' she said, her voice roughened and thick. 'Who said I had a hangover?' She pressed a hand to her throbbing head, and heard Ryker's low chuckle.

Scowling, she picked up the aspirin from the bedside table and tasted the coffee. It was good. She savoured it slowly, then lay back against the pillows, closing her eyes, her limbs cushioned against the softness of the mattress, the tiredness seeping out of her body.

Some minutes later, she felt his presence by the side of the bed, and she slanted him a look. He wasn't even dressed properly. She blinked again, her blue eyes busy taking in the fact that he wore only dark trousers, and that his chest was bare and his black hair was still damp from the shower.

'Why aren't you in your room, Ryker?' she muttered. 'How can I get up and get dressed with you hovering around?'

He rubbed at his hair with a towel. 'Actually, this *is* my room. It's clear you were in such a state last night that you didn't know whose bed you climbed into. Just as well it was mine. It could have caused problems with some of the guests.' He grinned and she threw him a black look.

'I didn't climb into bed. I just . . .' Her brows met in a frown. What had she done last night? She remembered sitting on the quilt; that was clear enough in her head. The folds of her dress had caught underneath her, and she'd lain back; that had unlocked the ravels of material.

Her shoes were on the carpet where she had left them. She stared at the floor. No, she hadn't pushed them tidily under the chair; she was sure about that.

'Where is my dress?' she muttered. 'I don't recall——'

'I put it on a hanger for you,' Ryker said. 'You wouldn't have wanted it creased, would you?'

'I don't remember...' It dawned on her that, beneath the light covering of the quilt, she was wearing very little. And how had she come to be actually beneath the quilt? She stared at him, her eyes widening, and he returned her look with one of total innocence—feigned innocence, she realised with growing wrath.

'You undressed me,' she accused, a tidal wave of heat invading her from top to toe. 'How could you; how dared you?'

'You were in no state to do it yourself.' He seemed to muse a moment. 'What happened to the cotton lace, by the way? I must say, silk does have a certain quality all of its own. Not that I noticed, of course.'

His mouth began to tilt at the corners, and she aimed the pillow at him. He caught it, and placed it carefully on the end of the bed, and the gleam she saw darting in his eyes incensed her even more.

'Don't stand there tormenting me, you fiend. I didn't mean to stay here in the first place, much less in your bed. Get out of here and leave me alone. Find somebody else to annoy.'

'It's hardly my fault if you were upset by your boyfriend's defection last night, now, is it?'

'Defection?' Her voice thickened.

'Well, call it what you will. I didn't force him to leave, and it wasn't me who encouraged him to stay over at Marie's place. Money, though, does seem to have its own magnetic attraction for him. It must have come as a shock to him to find that you no longer had an inheritance.'

Her mind was working rapidly now. Was that what Ryker had been plotting all along—to get rid of Nick? He must have been instrumental in setting up the whole thing.

'You knew that would happen, didn't you?' she said, her tone becoming acrid. 'That's why you introduced them. How did you know that Marie would play into your hands?'

He shrugged, not bothering to deny it. 'She's a very good friend of mine. When I asked her to help out, she was only too happy to oblige. Like it or not, Cassie, he's no good, and when the time is right he'll find himself given very short shrift by Marie Delahaie.'

'You're quite ruthless, aren't you?' Cassie said bitingly. 'Who asked you to interfere?'

'You're better off without him. You know that, even though you're snapping at me. And he won't be back in your life in quite the same way ever again, Cassie; I hope you accept that. He'll only turn on the charm when he wants something. You may not be happy about it, but that's how it is.'

'Why should you assume that money is the only factor in our relationship?' she flung at him. 'Don't you think I have anything else to offer a man? Am I so totally devoid of attractions?'

'I didn't say that, and you're well aware that it isn't true. You don't need to fish for compliments.'

'Is that what I was doing?' she said scathingly. 'Don't run away with the idea that anything you could say would be of the slightest interest to me.'

He made a mocking salute. 'I won't, then. If you've worked off most of your aggression on me now, I think I'll go and shave.' He fingered his jaw. 'Mustn't appear downstairs looking as though I've had a heavy night, must I?'

She threw the remaining pillow at him and he side-stepped it neatly, his grin wide as he went into the adjoining small dressing-room. The hum of his electric razor started up, and she sat up in bed, jaw clenched, fizzing angrily. Oh, he was mightily pleased with himself, wasn't he? All his plans had fallen into place just the way he wanted, and he was feeling smugly satisfied.

How much of that satisfaction could be lain at Sophie's door? How long had he stayed at her flat last night? The questions pierced her like a sharp blade, the image of them twined together searing through her head like a physical pain.

Her fists clenched tightly on the bedcovers. She wasn't going to stay in this house a minute longer than she had to. Reaching for the phone on the table, she jabbed a button. Even if it cost her half her month's salary, she'd get a taxi, or rent a car to take herself home.

A strange bleeping came from the machine, and she stared at it in perplexed annoyance. A string of taped messages began to issue forth, and she prodded another button without result. How was she supposed to stop the wretched thing?

Her father's voice cut into the room. 'Top-level meeting,' he was saying. 'All hush-hush. Tyler Mason building; must be there for seven.' She searched in vain for some kind of off switch while he talked on, and then all at once Ryker was removing the receiver from her fingers, shutting off the tape.

'You didn't hear that, Cassie,' he said, his mouth hard. 'None of it, do you understand?'

'Such riveting stuff, too. How could I help it if the thing went racketing on?' she said tersely. 'I don't possess one of these gadgets. How am I supposed to know how they work?'

'Who were you trying to phone? Nick? You're wasting your time.'

'As a matter of fact,' she said stormily, 'I was aiming to get out of here. Much as it may surprise you, I have no wish to remain under your roof for another second. Even my father manages to make his presence felt here. All the more reason for making a speedy exit, don't you think? Quite apart from the fact that I have work to do. Pressing work.'

She tugged sharply at the quilt and pulled it around herself as she climbed out of bed. Lurching unsteadily, she began to cross the room, the cumbersome material hampering her movements. Ryker went after her.

'What are you doing?' he demanded, grabbing her arm as she kicked the duvet from under her feet.

Her teeth clamped. 'What do you think I'm doing? I'm trying to free myself from your over-sized quilt before it trips me up.'

His fingers closed on her arms. 'I meant what I said about the phone call. The meeting is not to be discussed; not a word is to get out. Is that clear?'

'What do you think I am?' she raged, her fury exploding in a red mist. 'Do you imagine I'm so eager to spill the beans that I'll race off to get in touch with the nearest secret agent, like some kind of Mata Hari?' She dragged in a fierce breath. 'Maybe that's not such a bad idea after all,' she gritted. 'I wonder if it pays well?'

The duvet slipped a little, providing a glimpse of one long, stockinged leg, and she stared down at it, momentarily shocked. Ryker's features became suddenly dark and unreadable, and she said shakily, 'Now there's a thing. Shall I play the vamp, Ryker, see what other secrets I can prise from you?'

The quilt began to edge away from the creamy slope of her thigh and she laughed with faint reck-lessness. 'You always did have a complex about the mysteries I might unravel, didn't you? You never trusted me when it came down to it. You were never sure what might end up in print. What on earth will you do now to counter my devious activities, I wonder? Shadow my every move?'

Her eyes glittered angrily. If he hadn't been holding her so fast, she would have swished the duvet back into place, but his hands restricted her. 'For your information,' she bit out tersely, 'I was merely heading for the shower. I had no idea I should ask your permission first.' She glared at the offending fingers. 'Or are you expecting to lay hands on me in there, too?'

He exhaled raggedly, his hold on her tightening as he pulled her towards him. 'And if I did? I wonder how long you would be fighting me, how soon it would be before you were sighing in my arms.'

She tossed her head in negation, the glossy black waves rippling over her bare shoulders. 'I don't know why I'm standing here listening to you.'

'Isn't that the point? Why are you here? Why did you choose my room, my bed?'

She shook away the thread of doubt that flickered through her mind. 'It just happened that way,' she muttered. 'It wasn't intentional. I had a little too much wine, and I was sleepy, that's all.'

'That isn't all. There were any number of rooms, yet you settled on this one.' His lips made a derisive smile. 'Not that I'm complaining, you understand. I'm quite happy to have you here, but don't think for one minute that I'm deceived by your actions. You may be confused and unhappy, but I know very well what's going on in your head. You were upset because Nick walked out with another woman, and you blamed me; you wanted to vent your spleen on me.'

His thumbs bit into the soft flesh of her arms. 'You have to think again, my sweet, and think hard about your actions. You're no longer a tender seventeen-year-old. You're a beautiful, desirable woman, and you're playing with fire. That can be a very, very dangerous thing to do.'

A hectic flush ran along her cheekbones. 'What are you saying, Ryker? What fire is this?' All the old hurt came flooding back. 'Since when were you interested in me? I don't have any part to play in your grand scenario, do I?'

He gave a harsh laugh. 'There's one part you play to perfection, my dark, provoking angel. You waft in and out of my life like sin itself, but I think now it's time to call a halt. The reckoning is due.'

'Ryker, I——'

He did not give her time to finish. He kissed away the words, taking her mouth with a hungry insistence that left her quivering with startled pleasure. Sensation flowed through her like a starburst, swift and unexpected, the flickering sweep of his tongue leaving behind a trail of flame. Warmly, his fingers curved into the soft folds of the quilt, brushing against the creamy swell of her breast. Under the drugging intimacy of that spellbinding friction, she ceased to breathe; time was suspended.

'We don't need this,' he said thickly, frowning at the cushioning silk that separated them. She barely had time to register his meaning before he was slowly, deftly tugging it from her.

For a stark, breathless moment, she stood quite still, totally defenceless as his glittering gaze raked her near-naked form. Then some scrap of her wits returned and she tried to retrieve her covering, only to have him push it away with the toe of his shoe.

There was no shield against his burning appraisal.
She stared at him, distracted, her blue eyes
widening.

When he spoke, his voice was thick with raw
passion. 'You're stunning,' he muttered,
'breathtaking...'

Pressing his palm to her shoulder, he tipped her
backwards on to the bed, and Cassie made a be-
lated, choked sound of protest that went unheeded.
His powerful body surged over her, the hard thrust
of his hips pinning her to the mattress, desire blatant
in the eyes that seared her with golden intent. His
questing mouth met hers, hotly seeking, his tongue
making deliciously melting incursions that invited
her recklessly abandoned response.

Dimly, in the midst of passion, she acknowledged the inherent threat his possession would
bring, coming, as it did, without any recognition
of her feelings. She shifted restlessly, her fingers
tangling in the soft material of his shirt. He
deepened the kiss, as though he recognised the vestiges of her resistance and would swallow it up, erase
it with the warm pressure of his mouth.

'Ryker, please...' She was gasping, panting for
breath, her lips burning from the impact of kisses
that left her weak with trembling desire. 'Not this
way...' With love, with sweet, tender possession...but not this way...

His head lowered, and he kissed her again, but
this time there was no haste, only a warm and
seeking exploration, and it seemed as though her
conscious mind had come adrift from reality; her

whole being centred on this moment in time, this pursuit of pure delight. Her mouth softened and clung, welcoming the lazy invasion of his tongue.

His hand slid possessively over her stockinged leg, caressed the smooth, bare skin of her thigh, and her body was no longer obeying the dictates of her head. His musky male scent filled her nostrils, invited her to nuzzle the warm texture of his throat, to taste the faint saltiness of his skin.

His mouth curved as he stared down at her, his fingers shifting to deal with the clasp of her bra and remove the unwanted scrap of silk. Her breasts spilled out, open to his gaze, and she twisted beneath him, intensely vulnerable under that raking stare.

'I can't believe how incredibly lovely you are,' he murmured, his hands cupping her, testing the soft weight, before his tongue came down to tease the creamy, sensitive flesh, and her body tingled in shocked excitement.

The pleasure was exquisite, a pure, aching burst of delight as his tongue slowly circled the hard nub of her breast and filled her head with a sweet, dream-like haze. His knowing mouth made a downward foray, seeking out the silken curves and hollows of her flesh, lingering with rapt attention on each newly discovered delight.

She had never known such sensation before, such a wanton ache growing within her. Her fingers explored the hard line of his shoulders with eager fascination, a soft, shuddery sigh escaping her. He was all she wanted, all she would ever need. This man, the man she had loved for a lifetime.

'You want me,' he said. 'You're trembling for me.' His voice was a low growl of husky satisfaction.

She looked at him, saw the faint glimmer of triumph that flickered in his eyes, and knew a shiver of despair. How could she not want him? Only he knew how to draw from her the soft, whimpering cries of pleasure. Hadn't he set out to do just that, to coax her into submission? And what would happen afterwards, when he was sated with her? There was no love on his part, she registered miserably. He came to her in pure need, like a man who must slake a thirst.

'I can't deny that,' she said, bleakness in her voice. 'You're very good, Ryker, really very good.' She averted her face from him, her words muffled. 'But then, you must have had a lot of practice.'

He stiffened, easing the space between them so that he could look down at her. 'You wanted me,' he said. 'It isn't something you can hide. Why this sudden change of mood? What's wrong?'

'Wrong?' She shifted away from him, snatching up her bra as she slid her legs off the bed. 'What could possibly be wrong?' Her hands fumbled with the clasp of the flimsy garment as she eased it into place.

'Cassie . . .' He came to her and she twisted away from him, moving to the wardrobe to search for her dress.

'You must be very pleased with yourself,' she said huskily. 'The methods you chose might have been different, but you managed to deal with me almost as effectively as you dealt with Nick. Well, consider it a success. I've learned my lesson. I won't make the same mistake again.'

She found her dress and stepped into it. 'You almost had me falling under your spell, losing myself in your arms.' Her fingers trembled on the zip as she dragged it up. 'Thank heaven I still have some remnant of sanity left. I have no wish to join the long line of women who have graced your bed, Ryker.'

She went to the door, and he followed her, his eyes sparking angrily. 'Don't you think we should talk this through? I'm entitled to some explanation for your sudden change in attitude.'

'I've already told you what I think,' she muttered. 'I see no reason for prolonged discussion.' She smiled thinly. 'If that raises your blood-pressure, you could always take a cold shower. I won't be using it after all. I find your price is far too high for me.'

CHAPTER EIGHT

CASSIE started down the steps to the pavement, leaving behind her the old grey stone building of the development company. She had to meet Nick for a working lunch at the pub, and she was running late. Even so, she paused for a moment, breathing in the cool, fresh air, her gaze absently wandering over the passers-by.

A man had stopped to look in a shop window, and as she took in his tall figure, the striking jet hair, her heart gave a frantic jolt.

'*Ryker*?' The word came out as a whisper. She stood very still, every nerve, every single one of her senses geared up and waiting, and then he turned, glancing around, and everything seemed to drain out of her, leaving her weak, lifeless. It was not Ryker.

She breathed in deeply. Why did this keep happening to her? That made three times this week that she had imagined she had glimpsed him striding along the street.

She began to walk towards the pub. Thinking about him was a futile occupation, she told herself. He had been furiously angry when she had left the house that day, but it could only have been rage brought on by frustration. After all, she would never mean any more to him than a woman he had wanted to bed. His future plans revolved around Sophie, didn't they? Somehow, she had to accept that, no matter how painful it might be.

'Over here, Cassie.' Nick motioned to her from the bar, and she went over to him, hiding a grimace at the dark nature of her thoughts.

'I was beginning to think you weren't coming,' he said lightly.

'I went to see Hal Gregson in his office. We talked for longer than I expected.' She gave the barman an order for a ploughman's and a glass of fruit juice with lemonade.

'I thought you spoke to him at the party a few weeks back?'

'This was a follow-on from some of the leads he gave me.'

Nick's glance was sharp. 'Has your father finally forgiven you for the squat business? I understood that was what caused the flare-up of trouble.'

Cassie shrugged. 'My father is always getting uptight about one thing or another. It's the pressure of business that causes it, I think. It soon blows over.' Spotting an empty table in a corner, she took her food over to it and sat down.

Nick was smiling when he joined her, his usual affable self once more. 'So you're on friendly terms again?' he persisted, sitting opposite her.

Cassie nodded briefly. 'Didn't you say that Marie might be joining us at some stage?' she murmured, steering the conversation away from family matters.

Hc shifted restively. 'There was no firm arrangement. I thought I might put together a feature on her bistro.'

'I see.'

'Do you?' His eyes darkened. 'You've been very cool to me just lately. I thought you might have the wrong idea—we only continued to meet because of the work angle.'

He was lying, Cassie decided, watching the quick, nervous movements of his fingers, but she said nothing.

He hesitated. 'There was nothing between us, you know. You do believe me, don't you?'

'It really doesn't matter what I think, Nick,' she answered carelessly. 'You're free to do whatever you like.'

Her cool serenity seemed to disturb him. 'But you and me, Cassie,' he said, 'we had something going between us, didn't we? I shouldn't like you to——'

'We've known each other a long time,' she cut in. 'But perhaps it's time to branch out now, go our separate ways.'

He flinched, his face paling. 'You can't mean that. And anyway, what about our work? We work well together; we're a team.'

'Look at it in a different light,' she said, quite gently. 'Wouldn't you find it refreshing to work with another partner?'

His mouth took on a sullen droop. 'It's Ryker, isn't it? He's behind all this. He's been influencing you. He wants you away from me.'

She stiffened. Coolly she said, 'I haven't seen Ryker for some time. As far as I know, he's working on setting up a new administrative centre.' Certainly he had made no move to come in search of her. But then, why would he? They hadn't parted on the best of terms. It was only her own folly that made her keep thinking of him.

Nick said, 'He's had something to do with this land-development deal your father's angling after, hasn't he?'

She looked at him thoughtfully, absently forking her salad around her plate. 'What deal is that? Ryker doesn't dabble in land.'

'Maybe it was only the charter side of things that he was concerned with, then,' Nick mused. 'But I understood that your father and a group of developers were setting something up, some crucial deal that they wanted kept strictly undercover till it's all signed and sealed.' He looked at her questioningly.

'I wouldn't know,' she said with a frown. 'Where did you hear all that?'

'Oh, just a rumour. Something someone let slip. I thought you might have a few details up your sleeve. You'd maybe want to cover the event for the paper—when it's gone through OK, of course.'

'My father doesn't confide in me,' she said dismissively.

She began to toy with the remains of her French stick, allowing her glance to travel idly around the room while her mind was busily turning things over. What was it Ryker had said? 'He'll only turn on the charm when he wants something.' Perhaps he was right, and Nick was more devious than she had imagined. He had been delving into what didn't concern him, trying to prise information out of her, and that worried her. How far would he go to get what he wanted?

Her gaze wandered around the crowded bar, troubled, unseeing, and it took a moment or two for the shock to register as she found herself staring straight at a familiar hard, lean profile. Her fingers clenched on the bread, and for the second time that day her insides started jumping about in erratic confusion.

Ryker started to work his way through the mass of people, and she felt the bread crumble between her fingers as he approached their table.

'Mind if I join you?' Without waiting for a reply, he pulled up a chair and sat down.

'You haven't...' Her voice sounded very faint, coming from a long way off, and she cleared her throat and tried again. 'This is unexpected. You haven't been in here for some time.'

'No. I've been busy.' His features were taut and unsmiling.

She said cautiously, 'Is this a planned meeting, Ryker? You didn't happen to come here merely by chance?'

'No. You're quite right. I thought you might be having lunch here. It is your usual haunt, I gather.' He stared at her plate and the heaped collection of crumbs. 'Were you planning on feeding the birds?'

'Oh.' She brushed her fingers together hastily, removing every last trace of bread. 'What a good idea,' she muttered. 'I was going to head for the park in a minute or so. The ducks can have a feast.'

'In that case, I'll walk you over there.'

'That won't be necessary.'

He ignored her sharp rejoinder. 'It will give us an opportunity to talk. You don't have to get back to the office this afternoon, do you?'

'What makes you think that?'

'I spoke to your editor.'

'You did what?' The exclamation broke from her. 'Don't you think that's going a little far?'

'Is it? I thought it was sensible in the circumstances.' He began to tip the bread into a serviette and stuffed it into the pocket of his grey jacket. He stood up. 'If you've finished, we might as well go. It seems a pity to be stuck in here when it's bright outside.'

She refused to be side-tracked. 'What circumstances?' she demanded.

'I already told you. We have to talk. The park seems as good a place as any.' He lifted a black brow. 'If you're ready.'

'Who said I was going anywhere with you?' she muttered crossly. 'Nick and I——'

'Nick was just leaving.' He sent a chilling glance in his direction. 'Weren't you, Nick?'

'I suppose you've been checking my schedule too,' Nick said, tight-lipped.

Ryker's smile did not reach his eyes. 'It may have come up in the conversation.'

Nick drained the last of his lager, and got to his feet. Cassie frowned as the two men faced each other. It had not escaped her attention that one or two people near-by were giving them interested glances, and it annoyed her intensely. It seemed to be a thing that happened around Ryker.

'I hope,' she said, sending him a flinty look, 'that you aren't going to cause a scene in here. I rather like coming to this place, and I'd hate to have to find somewhere else to eat.'

'That won't be necessary,' Ryker murmured. 'You are coming to the park, aren't you?'

'Since I've finished my drink and you seem to have commandeered the remains of my lunch,' she muttered, pushing back her chair, 'I suppose I might as well go with you.'

Nick threw her a harassed glance. 'I need to talk to you Cassie. There are things we have to settle. I'm going on a job up North for a few days, and we're supposed to be going to Europe a fortnight today to put together this new series of articles for the Sundays.'

She paused, debating the situation in her mind. There was no way she wanted to spend the next few weeks working in close contact with Nick, but her attempts to get her boss to see things from her point of view had come to nothing so far.

There must be some way to deal with the matter, surely, but this wasn't the time to start discussing it, not with Ryker standing over them like a predatory beast just waiting to pounce. He was up to something, and she wanted to know what it was. This thing with Nick would have to wait.

'We'll have a chance to meet up when you get back,' she told him. 'There are quite a few things we have to sort out in the office.'

He wasn't happy about it, that was clear, but he wasn't going to argue the point while Ryker was in the vicinity.

They left the pub, and Cassie turned with Ryker in the direction of the small local park. He said harshly, 'Haven't you any more sense than to keep up your involvement with him?'

'What does it have to do with you?' she countered, annoyed. 'I don't pass comment on your associates.'

'Don't you?' There was more than a hint of mockery in his tone. His eyes glittered. 'I thought that was exactly what you did, last time we were together.'

Her spine went rigid. 'I prefer to forget about that,' she said tersely. 'It's not something I want to dwell on. The whole situation was totally out of hand, as well you know. Besides,' she added with caustic vehemence, 'I was referring just now to your business associates, not your bedmates. Or perhaps it's the same thing with you.'

They walked in through the park gates and he said with cool curiosity, 'Perhaps you should explain. I don't think I quite understand all the animosity I've been getting from you just lately. Where did you get the idea that I had some kind of harem stashed away?'

'Don't you?' She smiled sweetly, baring her teeth.

A muscle flicked in his jaw. 'I'm a one-woman man, didn't you know?'

She studied him for a moment. 'Would that be one at a time, or one in particular?' She did not wait for his reply. Going over to the railings that bordered the pond, she looked out over the water at the family of ducks that slid with stately decorum over its smooth surface.

Ryker came alongside. 'You know, Cassie,' he said, 'you seem to be having something of an attitude problem. There are times when I'd really like to shake some sense into you.'

Her eyes frosted into chips of ice. 'Try it,' she warned, 'and I guarantee you'll be sorry.'

He laughed, a low, rumbling sound in the back of his throat, and her mouth tightened. With slow deliberation, she wound her fingers around the rail, squeezing the way she might have done if it had been his neck. 'Hand over the bread, Ryker,' she said curtly. 'The ducks look as though they could do with a good feed.'

She fed the small family until the crumbs had all disappeared. 'Why are you back in London anyway?' she asked. 'Have you finished setting up the centre, or are you here to make arrangements for my father's flight on Friday?'

'Both,' he said.

She crumpled up the serviette and tossed it into a wire bin. Clearly he hadn't made a special journey just to talk to her. The knowledge left a cold, empty place inside her.

Ryker leaned back against the railings, one arm resting along the metal bar. 'I understand you'll be seeing James again some time this week?'

'Wednesday. We're having dinner together.'

'Perhaps you could do me a favour and give him some papers. It looks as though I'll be too tied-up to make contact myself. Would you mind?'

'I suppose not.' Her glance skimmed over him. He didn't look as though he was carrying any packages. 'Where are they?'

'Back at my apartment. It won't take more than a few minutes to drive over there.'

Suspicion darkened her eyes. 'I don't think——'

'Stop looking for trouble in everything I say and do,' he said with sharp annoyance. 'We're just going to pick up some documents; it's no big deal. If you've changed your mind, I'll post them to him and risk a delay.'

'I didn't say that.' She thrust her hands into the pockets of her flower-strewn cotton skirt, disturbing the lines of the matching overblouse that she wore loose, like a jacket. He made her sound like a grouch, she thought morosely. Of course he had no ulterior motive in inviting her to go along with him. Why should he? He wasn't the least bit interested in her when Sophie was on the scene.

A band started playing from the stand somewhere over to their right, and the ducks shot away, making for the cover of the reeds. Feeling oddly desolate, she turned away and went with him to his car.

The journey, as he had said, took only a few minutes. Pushing open the door to his lounge, he dropped his jacket over a chair and walked over to a glass-fronted cabinet. 'Can I get you a drink?' he asked.

She shook her head. 'I think I'll give it a miss. Me and alcohol don't appear to mix too well just lately.'

His grin was lop-sided. 'Is that so?' he said in a low drawl. 'I can't say that I had any complaints.' His gaze swept over her, swift and all-consuming, like the lick of flame.

'I didn't come here for your entertainment, Ryker,' she muttered in aggravation, her senses heated by that flickering stare. 'Shouldn't you be hunting out those papers?'

'They're on the bureau.' His eyes continued to roam. 'You're looking good,' he murmured. 'There's something immensely appealing about you in a skirt. Ultra-feminine. I like that.'

'Do you?' She wasn't going to fall for his smooth flattery. 'You shouldn't concern yourself too closely with what I wear, you know,' she added, her voice etched with scorn. 'I really don't dress up to please you.'

'You don't have to,' he said, amusement threading his words. 'I'm quite happy to see you in nothing at all.'

She hated him for reminding her of that embarrassing episode that she wanted pushed to the back of her mind. It had meant nothing to him but the chance of a swift flirtation, a meaningless fling while the opportunity presented itself, and now he was laughing at her.

Her eyes narrowed. 'Why am I getting the treatment?' she enquired coolly. 'Are you having problems with your love-life?'

His tone was dry. 'You could say that, yes. I'm not particularly addicted to cold showers.'

'Oh, shame.' She did not bother to hide the sharp sarcasm. 'I'm sure you won't be suffering for too long. Somebody is bound to beat a path to your door.'

Going over to the bureau, she picked up a sheaf of papers. 'Are these the ones?' she asked, and, at his nod, pushed them into her bag. 'Then I'll be on my way,' she said, walking to the door and tugging it open. 'I have things to do. Goodbye, Ryker.'

'I don't think so, Cassie. Not yet.' He slammed the door back in place, leaving her staring at solid wood. Angrily, she turned to face him and he said, 'I think it's high time we straightened one or two things out. You seem to be harbouring some misconceptions about me that I'm beginning to find intensely irritating.'

His palm flattened on the wood. 'Firstly, you should get it clear in your head that there are no hordes of women queuing up at my door.'

'You're a perfect saint,' she said with rank disbelief. 'Though I don't know why you're bothering to explain yourself to me. Why should I be in the least bit interested in your sex-life?'

'You seemed to be giving it undue attention just a few short weeks ago,' he retaliated briskly. 'As it appeared to be of such great importance, I thought it best that we air the subject.'

'So there we have it.' She spread her hands in an expansive gesture. 'You've painted a wonderful picture of monkish celibacy, and now everyone's happy, aren't they? Where, precisely, does Sophie fit into all this, I wonder?'

'Sophie?' he said, his brows drawing together.

'Oh, to be cast aside so wantonly,' Cassie exclaimed with dry cynicism. 'How on earth will you explain yourself when she comes bursting into your kitchen, clamouring for your attention?'

'That's highly unlikely,' he retorted, 'since she happens to be in Paris at the moment.'

'Very nice for her, I'm sure,' she commented in a clipped tone. 'But unfortunate for you, of course, since it means you have time on your hands, if nothing else. How very sad for you.' She looked pointedly at the wood panelling. 'If you would simply remove yourself from the door and let me through, then this conversation could come to an end.'

His rakish smile sent dangerous undercurrents to lap at the edges of her confidence. 'You're in a great hurry all of a sudden,' he murmured. He reached out and cupped her chin with his fingers. 'Are you afraid of me for some reason?'

She tried to turn her mind to the question, but the slow descent of his warm mouth as he bent to take possession of her soft lips blanked everything

from her head. After the first delicious quivers of
sensation slowly unfurled, there was only the insidious melting of her bones, an awakening desire
to lean into his embrace and offer up to him the
eager response he was so pleasurably inviting. Her
mouth trembled, her lips parting beneath the tantalising stroke of his tongue, her body blending with
his in an urgent, unconscious demand.

His arms came around her, crushing her to him;
his breath was warm against her cheek, her throat,
as he paused to plant lingering kisses along her
satin-textured skin.

He smiled into her eyes, satisfaction hovering
around his mouth, but she dared not give in to the
pulse of joy that leaped within her. So many times,
things had gone wrong between them, leaving her
hopes and dreams shattered, in tiny fragments. Why
should this time be any different? Wasn't he still
taking opportunity where he found it, adding her
to his list of conquests?

'Stay a while,' he suggested softly. 'I think we
could at least talk, don't you?'

Hesitantly, she nodded, and he brushed her lips
fleetingly with his own. 'Make yourself comfortable
on the sofa,' he said. 'I'll fix us some drinks. It
won't take a moment.'

She watched him leave the room, her fingers
straying to her hot cheeks. Whenever he kissed her,
touched her, she had the same trouble. Her mind
went into a spin, and thought became a virtual impossibility. It was difficult enough to come to terms
with her confused emotions, without the added

distraction of his kisses to send her thoughts
spiralling off into the next galaxy.

She walked to the bathroom. Perhaps if she
splashed cool water over her face it would put her
in a calmer frame of mind, help her to think in a
more rational way.

Dabbing at her wet face with a towel, she reflected that she might have been misjudging him in
some ways. Hadn't he denied the long line of
women reputedly flitting through his life? And she
only had Sophie's word that the two of them were
heading towards marriage, didn't she?

Her head cleared a little, the mist of doubt beginning to recede. He wanted her. It was a start, at
least, something to wrap around the cold emptiness
of her heart.

She pulled open the door, ready to go back into
the lounge, and the faint swish of a bath-robe drew
her gaze. It was hanging from a peg and she stared
at it, her blue eyes locked in stunned disbelief on
the rose-coloured satin, the monogram em-
broidered in gold thread on the wide lapel. Her
stomach heaved in appalled recognition. Sophie's
robe. Here, in Ryker's bathroom.

Cassie felt overwhelmingly sick. What kind of
fool was she to listen to anything he had to say, to
abandon herself to his kisses as though she were
drowning and he held out the only lifeline?

Lifting the robe off the hook, she draped the offending garment over the crook of her little finger,
and held it away from her, her mouth fixed in an
expression of frozen distaste.

Ryker was placing a tray of coffee on a low table, and he looked up as she came back into the lounge.

She did not know how she managed to keep her voice steady. With icy directness she said, 'So it's to be off with the old and on with the new, is it, and to hell with small matters of unfinished business? Aren't you guilty of a little double standard here? You're perfectly ready to heap condemnation on Nick, yet here you are, treading the same slippery slope.' She tossed the robe towards him, watched it slither to the floor at his feet. 'Nice try, Ryker. But count me out.'

Leaving his apartment, she slammed the door behind her, then ran for the first bus that would take her right out of his vicinity.

Driving back from Shropshire a few days later, Cassie wearily reflected that there had been easier interviews she had been called on to conduct in the past. Still, tricky as it had been, she had a wealth of information to work on now, and the finished article should hold a lot of promise.

Deftly she eased the car into a parking slot in front of the Georgian mansion that housed her flat. It was good to be home again. Sliding out from behind the wheel of her car, she glanced along the street as she prepared to lock up. Her hand stilled, the keys clasped in her palm. Somehow she had expected that Ryker would make an appearance sooner or later, and it came as no real surprise to find him waiting for her, looming in her vision like the devil himself, dark and threatening, his face set in a harsh scowl.

Deliberately she made herself continue with the task of securing the car, steeling herself to keep the bitterness from spilling out.

'You again,' she said, pushing her keys into her pocket. 'What now? More soft persuasion, more silk-sheathed words? It won't work; haven't you learned that yet?'

'Oh, I've learned a lot these last few days,' he said with granite-edged surety. 'You make an excellent teacher, but then you know exactly what you're doing, don't you? You're not content with pushing in the knife; you have to give it a twist before you walk away laughing.'

Cassie leaned back against the gleaming bodywork of the car, shaken by his vehemence. 'Is this likely to take long?' she asked. She would not let him see that his presence disturbed her. 'I've just travelled endless miles along a congested carriageway and I'm really in no mood for your invective right now. The last forty-eight hours have been hectic to say the least.'

'You don't need to tell me that,' he grated harshly. 'I've been on the receiving end, remember? What made you do it? Explain it to me, would you? I'd really like to know.'

'What's the matter, Ryker? Can't you take a put-down? Has it never happened to you before? Think of it as a whole new experience and learn from it.' She started towards the building, shrugging him aside as he came after her. 'I don't want you, Ryker, and that's final.' It was a lie that scorched her soul.

'That goes both ways,' he assured her, icily controlled, pushing his way with arrogant aggression into her sitting-room. 'I wanted a woman, not a cold-blooded viper with no thought in her head but revenge.'

He looked at her with loathing, and she frowned, not sure of the mood he was in. Anger, yes, there was certainly that, but there was something more, an undercurrent that surged beneath the surface like a violent black tide and threatened to engulf her.

'Revenge?' she said, returning his stare with one of frigid dislike. 'I have no idea what you're talking about. And I should have thought you were the last person to be heaping condemnation on me. Shouldn't you be looking to your own behaviour, or is it quite all right in your book to be making love to another woman while your girlfriend is away?'

'How can you have the utter gall to talk about my behaviour?' he said with taut menace. 'At least I acted in a way that was human, that was born out of basic, natural instinct—but you...what you did defies all understanding——'

'Oh, come on,' she mouthed scornfully, 'what are we talking about here? You tried it on, and I walked out. That's not hard to cope with, is it? I should have thought even you could get that message without too much difficulty.'

'I got the message all right, loud and clear,' he told her savagely. 'What I can't fathom is why you had to drag your father into it too. This particular quarrel had nothing to do with him, yet, by leaking the details of his meeting, you dragged him right into the middle of it, didn't you? Not only that, but you let him believe that I was responsible for the débâcle. Why? What made you do it? Were you determined on causing friction at any cost? Was this the only way you could think of to pay me back? By losing me the respect and friendship of a man I've known for years? By inflicting on me the contempt of his colleagues?'

His mouth twisted into a cruel line. 'I've got your measure now; I know just how low you'll stoop, and there's nothing—do you hear me?—nothing you can do that will have the slightest effect on me or the way I operate. Am I getting through to you? Do *you* understand what I'm saying?'

'No.' Her face had paled; she shrank away from the brooding hostility that smouldered in the depths of his eyes. He looked at her with hatred, the leaping enmity of his gaze barely leashed. 'I don't understand any of it. Why should you assume that I had anything to do with what happened at the meeting? I know nothing about it. What makes you think it was me?'

'You were the only one who knew of the arrangements, apart from myself, but, just to make sure, I checked with one of the journalists who turned up at the event. He gave me your name.'

'It isn't true,' she said, thoroughly shaken by what he was saying. She hadn't told anyone. She had kept it all to herself. How could he think that she was capable of such an act? 'I knew how important it was. I wouldn't have done anything to jeopardise the meeting.'

'Wouldn't you?' He walked to the door and jerked it open, turning to face her. Cynicism was etched on his hard mouth; the eyes that raked her were cold and implacable. 'I'll believe that when hell freezes over.'

CHAPTER NINE

SKILFULLY manoeuvring the tray of savoury biscuits on one palm, Cassie threaded her way across the office, her mind detached, only vaguely tuned in to the buzz of conversation going on around her. It was work as usual, since the paper had to go to print no matter what minor disturbances threatened the ebb and flow of daily life, but there was more laughter today, a light release of tension brought on, no doubt, by the wine that Nick had handed around. Back from his brief excursion up North, he was in a celebratory mood. Things were going his way.

'Sorry.' Cassie lurched into him as someone squeezed past her, and the tray wobbled precariously.

'Here, let me take that.' Nick took it from her and placed it on a desk, helping himself to a cheese straw. 'Are you all packed and ready for sunny Spain?' he queried, grinning amiably.

A small line worked its way into her brow. 'I need to talk to you, Nick,' she muttered.

'Something to do with the trip?'

There was little she could do about that, she thought irritably, since her boss had proved unmoving. 'No, about my father's meeting—the one that found its way into the papers.'

Her glance strayed over the desktop, lighting on a manila file, and she ran her fingers roughly through her hair. 'Damn, I meant to take those reports down to the sales office. When I get back, I want a word with you.'

He looked at her guardedly. 'OK. I'm not going anywhere.' Cassie picked up the file and headed for the glass door, which was wedged open.

Her steps faltered as she came to the corridor. Ryker's flint-edged stare caught her unawares and she stumbled to a halt, recovering slowly.

'I hope you haven't come to cause trouble,' she said stiltedly.

'I assumed that was your forte,' he countered, his mouth straight and hard.

The accusation pained her. He had shown a complete disregard for all that she had said before, and it seemed that the intervening days had done nothing to mellow him.

'I've tried to explain,' she muttered, 'but if that's how you feel, then there's nothing more to be said, is there?'

There was derision in his tone. 'Then it's just as well—isn't it?—that I came here to see your boss and not to bandy words with you. Besides——' his gaze moved in cool assessment around the room beyond '—you obviously have other things on your mind right now. I'd hate to interrupt a party.'

His caustic tone flayed her nerves, and her knuckles clenched involuntarily, her fingers curling tightly on the folder she carried.

'It isn't a party,' she said, 'just a farewell drink.'

His wintry gaze settled on Nick. 'I take it that the trip to Europe is still on?'

'We leave the day after tomorrow.'

He said reflectively, 'It may turn out to be the best thing that can happen. I doubt even he can wreak much damage from that distance.'

'I might have expected that from you,' she remarked, her mouth tightening. 'You've always made your animosity towards him plain.'

'Have I? I thought I treated him with the respect he deserves.' His eyes were dark with censure. 'You should do the same; keep away from him, unless you want to be tarred with the same brush.'

Cassie gave a disdainful shrug, pretending a carelessness she was far from feeling. 'You should keep it in mind that you don't need to concern yourself with my life any more. I dare say you'll find it difficult to begin with; after all, old habits die hard and the temptation to interfere must still be battling beneath the surface. You'll learn, Ryker, in time.'

'And will you do the same? Haven't you come to realise yet exactly what Driscoll's about?'

'Perhaps we should forget about Nick,' she said abruptly. 'It seems to me that you have a few problems of your own to sort out. Why precisely are you here, Ryker? Isn't this something of a turnaround, your sudden friendship with my boss? I thought you hated having your name in the paper, yet here you are treading the very ground you reckon to despise.'

'It's called expediency,' he returned with bland indifference. 'Have you never heard of it?'

'You mean ethics can be dispensed with when it suits you, when you want publicity for a new enterprise.' Her eyes were smoky with scorn.

'Think of it any way you like,' he said. 'I don't have time to argue the point. I have a meeting to attend.'

She stared after him as he strode away, fighting down the emotions that raged inside her, each one warring for supremacy. There was no tenderness for her, no understanding, no chance that the love she felt for him could ever be returned. His life was mapped out before him, and there was no niche in it for her. He hadn't come here today to see her; she might never have known he'd been in the building, but for that chance meeting.

'Is that trouble brewing?' Nick asked, shooting her a questioning look as she went back into the office after delivering the file. He was half sitting, half leaning on the desk, his fingers curled around a pencil.

'Nothing I can't handle,' she said, her tone bleak.

'He didn't seem in the best of moods,' he persisted. 'Something must be wrong. Is it anything to do with this business with your father?'

'More than likely,' she said shortly. 'How did you come by all the details, Nick? Did you use my name as a sweetener? It was you who phoned in the article, wasn't it?'

'You were the one who left the package on your desk,' he said defensively.

'Are you talking about the package that was addressed to my father—the one that Ryker gave me to deliver?' She viewed him with shocked distaste.

'How could you do such a thing? You must have known it was private.'

Nick tossed the pencil to one side. 'I thought it was something to do with work. You shouldn't leave things lying around if you don't want them to be seen.'

Her jaw tightened. 'It was only there for half an hour. I didn't realise you could stoop so low. I've been blind, haven't I? Ryker was right all along.' She went over to the phone. 'I don't like being used. And I don't like your underhand methods.'

She dialled her father's number. It was the one, final thing she could do to sort out this mess, she decided as she waited for the call to be connected. Not that it would change her own situation in the least. How could it? Her fingers twisted convulsively on the receiver, and she drew herself up, breathing deeply against the constriction of her lungs. What her father did with the information was up to him. From now on, she had to put everything behind her and concentrate on the job in hand. It was the only way she could cope with the endless desolate hours that lay in store.

By six o'clock she just about ready to tidy up her desk and go home. There was nothing more she could do in the office for today, and she was feeling somehow incredibly drained.

Nick pushed a small white card into her hand. 'This just came in,' he said woodenly. 'Jim told me to give it to you. There's no one else on call.'

Wearily, Cassie took the card from him. 'What is it?'

His shoulders moved negligently. 'Some sort of leisure complex just opening, as far as I know.'

Quickly Cassie scanned the handwritten details on the card, staring at it in disbelief. 'But this place is seventy or so miles away, for heaven's sake. I'll be lucky if I get there before ten by the time I've sorted the address out on the map. And I've never heard of this man, Benedict, who's supposed to run the place. I need to know something about him. Can't it wait until tomorrow?'

Nick's manner was cold. 'Jim said he's a wealthy eccentric we've been trying to track down for ages—now that we've finally landed him he says he's going to be too busy to be interviewed over the next few days, and, if we can't fit him in today, forget it.' He lifted his jacket from the back of a chair and walked out.

Cassie pushed the card into her pocket. She wondered how much fuss Jim would make about the expenses tab if she booked into a hotel rather than drove back in the early hours. She rummaged in her bag for her car keys. And by the time she got down there, the man would most likely have changed his mind about the whole thing.

The Benedict estate was shrouded in darkness when she drove up to the imposing set of gates that marked the entrance some hours later, but, thank goodness, there was a lamp glowing in the lodge keeper's house. Turning off the ignition, she slid out of the car, and rang the bell. The night air was cool, and she shivered a little as she waited for someone to answer.

'I need to get to the main house,' she said, giving her name to the grey-haired man who at last came to the door.

'You're expected,' he acknowledged. 'But you'll have to leave your car here and go the rest of the way on foot. I'll take you up there. You won't know your way about in the dark.'

There was a deal of truth in his words, she found, some ten minutes later, as she followed the torch beam which the man threw haphazardly from side to side as they went. She was hopelessly disorientated, and it seemed as though they had travelled a weird kind of zigzag path through endless trees and shrubbery before they finally saw a glimmer of light through the woodland ahead. Talk about eccentric, she mused, chafing her arms.

'Here we are,' her guide said, pausing in front of a large stone-built house, and rapping on the brass knocker. 'You'll be all right now.'

Cassie knew a moment of uncertainty as he made to leave her. 'Are you sure?' she said quickly. 'Won't he think it a little late to be conducting an interview? What if he's changed his mind?'

'Oh, he won't do that. Though he's a law unto himself, that one.'

He started back the way they had come, and she called unhappily after his retreating figure, 'But how do I get out of here when I've finished? It looks like a maze out there.'

'That's exactly what it is.' A familiar voice sounded from behind her, deep and gritty with a hint of gravel, and she froze, her spine braced against the shock.

Turning to look up at Ryker's dark features, shaded by the moonlight, she said stiffly, 'Is this some kind of joke?'

'Not at all. It's all about survival skills,' he murmured, deliberately misunderstanding her. 'Drop someone in the middle of that, and they find their way out or starve in the attempt.'

'Why am I here?'

'You wanted an interview, didn't you? Isn't that what you've wanted all along?' His smile mocked her. 'Well, now's your chance.'

Cassie's teeth met. This must be some cruel game he was playing. 'I changed my mind. I'm not staying here.' She took a few steps away from him and peered out into the shadowed night, at the trees etched blackly against the grey skyline.

'That's up to you,' Ryker said in a lazy drawl. 'If you want to spend the night in the open, go ahead. Though you'd probably stand a much better chance of getting to the lodge if you waited until morning. No guarantees, of course.'

He made to close the door and she said with a flare of panicked anger, 'Don't you dare shut that door on me. I want to know what you're up to, Ryker. I want to know what's going on.'

'Changed your mind?' he enquired softly. He shook his head. 'The fickleness of women never ceases to amaze me, but if you're sure——' his voice dropped '—then you had better come in.'

She wasn't sure of anything. The tiger eyes gleamed at her in the darkness, undermining her resolution as she began to follow up the silky invitation to enter his lair. She had to be on her guard.

If she let him creep under her defences she would be lost forever.

'Why are you doing this?' she said once they were inside the large hall. She felt the support of the wooden door at her back.

Ryker leaned towards her, the powerful lines of his body threatening her already shaky self-possession as his hands flattened on the door. He pushed it shut, sliding the bolt home with a finality that made her blink.

'Did you imagine,' he said, his jaw taut, his mouth firm and unyielding, 'that I would stand by and let you go off to Europe with that shady character? Think again, Cassandra.'

So it was about Nick. Was he concerned about her inheritance, or did he think they would be cooking up some wild feature about him? 'Aren't you letting your dislike of him get the better of you?' she asked stonily. 'We aren't likely to be putting out any articles on you from several hundred miles' distance.' Not that she intended to work with Nick any longer. She would tell Jim Harker her mind was made up. 'How were you thinking of stopping me from going with him? By keeping me here, a virtual prisoner?'

'If that's what it takes.' He stared down at her, cool arrogance in every line of his hard-boned face.

'One day,' she said scathingly, 'you'll go just that step too far. And then you'll pay for your crimes.'

'Let's go through to the lounge, shall we?' He placed a hand in the small of her back and pushed her forwards with grim resolve.

The room was expensively furnished, she noted, with two large, comfortable sofas, and display cabinets lining one wall. She looked around, and felt him tug the jacket from her shoulders.

'I won't be staying,' she said firmly. 'Get that into your head.'

His smile was sardonic as he draped the jacket over a chair, his glance flickering over the soft cotton of her blouse and the slim fit of her linen skirt. Her stiletto-heeled shoes emphasised the shapely length of her legs, and his eyes lingered a while before he said with lazy intonation, 'I don't think you'll get far in those, do you? Is that your interview outfit? Very nice. I hate to think what I've been missing all these years.'

She evaded that scintillating scrutiny, going to stand by the couch. The jut of her mouth was mutinous. 'I meant what I said. You can't keep me here. What do you think my editor will say when I don't return? You'll find yourself in a lot of hot water, Ryker, so I should forget the whole thing if I were you.'

'I wouldn't let Jim's reaction worry you.' His tone was casually indifferent, and she sent him a suspicious glare.

'Was he in on this?' she demanded hotly.

'Let's say we had a deal going.'

'What deal?'

'I think you could guess. An interview, in return for your dropping the European bit.'

'Dropping the . . .' Her eyes widened in outrage. 'What makes you think you can interfere?' she said, incensed. It wasn't as though he cared about her, was it? she thought bitterly.

His glance moved over her, sharp and needling. 'Are you unhappy at being wrenched away from Driscoll? You'll get over it,' he said with cold unconcern. 'I told you before, he's not the one for you. You only think you love him.'

'And what would you know about that?'

He ignored her snarled question. 'Sit down. This may take some time.'

'I will not,' she said with a bite. 'You have nothing to say to me that I care to listen to. If I want to go to Europe with Nick, then I'll go, and there's nothing you can do to stop me.'

'Isn't there?' His voice was soft with hidden menace. 'I think you underestimate me, Cassie.'

'Do I? Perhaps it's you who underestimate me,' she shot back. 'I do what I want to do; haven't you realised that yet?'

He acknowledged her outburst with a dry, humourless smile. 'And right now you're spoiling for a fight, is that it? I wouldn't like to disappoint you, but I hoped we might at least be civilised in our dealings with each other. To begin with, you might allow me to thank you for going to your father and putting him right about what really happened.'

'I suppose he phoned you with the news.' Her father would have wanted to clear the air. 'I don't need thanks,' she muttered. 'I did what my conscience dictated.'

'Nevertheless, I appreciate what you did.'

'There had been a mistake and it needed to be put right,' she said with brittle control. 'You needn't imagine that it had any deep meaning.'

'I won't.' His brows met in a dark line. 'Though it had occurred to me to wonder why you went to so much trouble to sort things out.'

Pride came to her rescue. 'What is this? Are you reading into it things that aren't there? It must be the male ego at work. Is Sophie still not around to soothe your tortured libido? How distressing for you.'

Her arrant insensitivity clearly irritated him. 'What is this obsession you have with me and Sophie?' he grated. 'She works for me; you know that.'

'Oh, of course,' she retorted with cold, pained sarcasm. 'That's why she has the key to your flat so that she can come and go at all hours. How silly of me not to realise that sleeping with you is part of the job.'

A muscle jerked in his chest. 'Sophie does not sleep with me,' he said through his teeth.

Cassie's brow quirked swiftly upwards. 'Does she not? I might have known,' she said with blistering scepticism. 'You're probably far too active in bed to give her the opportunity. Poor girl. She must be exhausted.'

'I wonder,' he said, with ominous, deadly calm, 'where all this hot air is coming from? Could it be, on the one hand, that you're curious about Sophie's robe taking up space in my bathroom? Or is it that deep down you'd like to satisfy yourself about my performance in bed? From the amount of interest my activities generate in you, I'd plump for the latter. That suits me fine, sweetheart; I'm quite happy to satisfy your curiosity on that score. You had only to ask.'

'Don't kid yourself, Ryker,' she returned unevenly. 'I wouldn't touch you with a ten-foot pole.'

'That's a thought-provoking statement,' he murmured, 'but I'm sure we can work our way around it in due course. In the meantime, to clear up the other little matter that appears to be exercising your brain, Sophie does not feature as a major part of my life. In fact she has gone to Paris to attend an interview for a job—a job she will probably get, since I gave her an excellent reference, and I happen to be acquainted with the director of that particular company. She stayed at my place overnight so that she could be within reasonable distance of the airport. She *slept*——' he emphasised the word with relish ' —in a separate room from mine. As to the matter of the key, she returned it several weeks ago when I asked for it.'

'Really.' Cassie took a deep breath to still the slight shakiness of her voice. 'And what prompted you to do that? Were you having the locks changed?'

His smile was darkly brooding. 'I didn't like the idea of her being able to walk in on you and me whenever she chose. The first time she did it was one time too many, and I was determined to ensure that we would have complete privacy from now on.'

'That isn't——' she swallowed against the sudden dryness of her throat '—a problem that's likely to arise, is it?'

'Don't you think so?' His teeth bared, and once more she was reminded of the hungry predator. 'Stick around, my sweet; I think you may have a surprise coming. Just bear in mind that your being here with me has nothing whatever to do with Sophie, or her departure to Paris. The reasons are quite separate and always have been.'

'Naturally,' she said, her resentment acute. 'How could I let myself be side-tracked away from the real issue? You don't like all the publicity you've been getting lately, and that's why you made a deal with my boss. What was it to be—one final story, to be firmly vetted, and then no more?' She drew in a ragged breath. 'Well, I won't let you dictate terms to me that way,' she muttered thickly. 'I won't have my work ordered and censored to suit you; I'll——'

'You'll what? Do battle with me?' With one hand he pushed her so that she fell in a sprawling heap on to the soft cushions of the couch. 'Good. I rather think I'd like that.'

Furiously, she struggled to sit up, only to encounter once more the thrust of his hand on her shoulder, propelling her backwards. From her supine position, she stared up at him, open-mouthed, her breathing laboured.

'You can't do this,' she panted. 'You can't——'

'Why not?' he rasped. 'Give me ten good reasons——'

'But you...' she said gaspingly. 'It isn't—I...'

She stopped babbling and filled her lungs with air. 'Ryker,' she said, trying again, 'you're out of your head.'

'You may well be right.' The cushions shifted as he lowered his weight on to the sofa, and came down over her, pressuring her with his taut body into the couch. 'You're in my bloodstream, like a fever raging out of control.' His mouth claimed hers swiftly, with heated compulsion, swallowing her mumbled protest. The glide of his fingers along the smooth silk of her thigh startled her pulse into a wild, frantic beat, melted her limbs into boneless submission.

'I don't understand,' she muttered dazedly when he released her mouth long enough to make a seeking foray along the velvet column of her throat. 'I thought——'

'I'm not carved out of stone,' he said, his voice roughened. 'I'm flesh and blood, and I want you—do you know just what you do to me?' He dragged her hand to his chest, spreading her palm flat across the thin cotton of his sweatshirt. 'Feel, Cassie; go ahead, see what you've done.'

Beneath her fingers she felt the thunder of his heart, the discordant pounding that matched the frenzied race of her own.

'Now do you understand?' he growled.

'But you...' Her fingers trailed in dawning wonder over the hard bounds of his ribcage. 'This is madness...'

His muffled curse was diffused into the curve of her shoulder. 'Pure insanity,' he agreed savagely. 'I have to be crazy to keep getting tangled with you. But I can't help myself. I want you; I must have you . . .'

Cassie squeezed her eyes shut for a few hazy seconds. He was talking want and need, as though she could assuage his thirst, but there had to be more than that, more than just a fleeting fire to be tamed, surely? She pushed at his shoulders, relieved when he moved back and allowed her to ease herself into a sitting position.

She said huskily, 'Last week you hated me. You were quite happy to assume that I was in the wrong, and to consign me to the back of beyond, but now, just because you've found out otherwise, you think everything can go back to the way it was before. Well, it can't. You can't switch emotions about just as you please and expect me to go along with it.'

His eyes slanted over her, dark with impatience. 'When I arranged this set-up, I had no idea that you had talked to your father. I was furiously angry with you, that's true, but it didn't alter the way I feel about you. And hearing that you were still planning on skipping over to Europe with that dark-eyed gigolo had me madder than a crazed bull.'

'I can still do that,' she said, shifting away from him.

'No.' He ran a hand down her arm and warm, tingling sensation shimmered through her. 'I won't let that happen.' He stood up suddenly, scooping her into his arms and lifting her against his chest.

'Ryker...' She felt the hard muscles of his arms bunch, and she clung on as he marched with her through a door and into another room. Without ceremony, he dropped her on to a wide bed.

Leaving her there, he went back to the door and turned the key in the lock.

'What are you doing?' She watched, wide-eyed, as he tugged at the buttons of his shirt.

'What I should have done a long time ago,' he gritted. 'This thing with Nick is over, finished; understand? I'll make you realise that if I have to keep you here for months on end.'

'Here? In this bed, you mean?' A hectic flush gathered in her cheeks.

He pocketed the key. 'The sofa is no place for what I have in mind,' he said thickly, a look of blatant possession glittering in his eyes as he came towards her. 'I'll make you forget him.'

He slid down beside her, pinning her against the pillows with the firm pressure of his hands. 'I'll make love to you until there's no thought in your head but me, no room for anyone's kisses but mine.'

'Jealousy, Ryker?' she queried in open wonder. 'Can this be jealousy I'm hearing?' A faint surge of hope began to swell inside her.

He gripped her fiercely, crushing her into the mattress with the hard strength of his muscular thighs. 'Jealousy is pure hell,' he rasped, 'and I've been there longer than I care to remember. From the first moment I saw you with him, I wanted to break him in two.' He drew in a taut, harsh breath. 'You were mine, you had to be mine, but you were so young, and I knew that I had to wait, or lose you. I thought maybe you might have been infatuated with me for a while, but you needed time to sort your feelings out. You lived such a cloistered existence in your father's home.'

His jaw clenched. 'Then you turned to Driscoll and I felt the world come crashing down around my ears. And later, when I found that he had moved in with you, I had to restrain myself from tearing him apart. I decided it had to end. I had to do something about it once and for all.'

'You were wrong,' she said, and he stared at her, his eyes darkening.

'No—I wanted him out of your life, for good.'

'He was never part of it,' she said quietly. 'He didn't live with me; I didn't even ask him to stay that night, though he had volunteered to look after the place while the builders finished off. I only arrived home in the early hours of the morning. Apparently he cleared up after the workmen left, and decided to stay on rather than drive home late at night.'

Ryker exhaled slowly, then bent his head to kiss her hungrily, taking her soft mouth with bruising force, as though he would annihilate any scrap of resistance. 'I love you,' he said huskily. 'I've always loved you.'

Joy burst inside her, sweet and pure as honey, filling every pore of her being. 'Love?' she echoed, her eyes smokily blue. Her fingers crept beneath his sweatshirt, paused on the warm, supple skin of his chest, felt the tension in him.

'Cassie...' His voice was thick against the silky tangle of her hair. 'You have to see; you have to understand—I can't let you go...'

'I'm not going anywhere, Ryker,' she whispered. 'Tell me again—what you just said.'

He stared at her, a line furrowing into his brow. 'I love you.'

She was very still, trying to combat the dashing millrace of her heart. 'But you've never said that before. You've always been so distant, so hard on me.'

'Distant? Hard?' His frown deepened. 'You weren't exactly sweetness and light yourself. You were always so damned prickly whenever we were together, always accusing me of butting in where I wasn't wanted, telling me you hated me, insisting that there was something going on between Sophie and me.' His mouth set in a repressive line, and Cassie gave a shaky smile, her fingers tracing a delicious path of discovery beneath his shirt.

His breathing became ragged as he caught her absorbed expression. 'You,' he complained huskily, 'are a wilful, wanton, seductive witch. And I want you to know...' his fingers stroked along the soft material of her blouse, trailing a fiery path over the ripe fullness of her breasts '...that I have every intention of playing you at your own game.'

Her nipples hardened betrayingly under the subtle teasing; her lips parted on a sigh, soft and enticing, inviting the sweet possession of his kiss. 'I love you,' she whispered against the warmth of his mouth. 'There could never be anyone else for me. Nick and

I—yes, we dated, but it didn't work; it couldn't work, because you were always there in my heart. You've been the only one I ever wanted in all these years.'

Satisfaction rasped in his throat, and he deepened the kiss, his hands moving over her in a silken caress, sliding beneath the restricting folds of her skirt to draw her against his potent maleness.

'I've waited so long to hear you say that,' he muttered hoarsely.

Her body arched to meet him, helplessly rocked by the tide of desire; she was floating on a warm swell of love and longing. With eager, trembling fingers, she pushed back his shirt, and allowed her lips to seek out the smooth contours of his chest, revelling in the taste and feel of him. She felt him shudder against her pliant body, his arms tightening on her for a few seconds before he released her.

She watched him, wondering, saw the fierce ache of desire glittering in the depths of his eyes.

'Too many clothes,' he said in a husky explanation, his hands dealing unsteadily with her buttons until her blouse gave way and he could turn his attention to the clasp of her lacy bra.

'Very pretty,' he murmured, a smile in his voice, 'but we can do without it, can't we?' The garments slid to the floor one after the other, and he ravished her with his tawny gaze, his eyes flaming a path of burning intent over her creamy skin. His prowling mouth followed, seeking out the smooth crescents of her breasts, his tongue playing with absorbed fascination over the ripe centres in turn, lapping at the sensitised buds until she thought she would faint with sheer pleasure.

A small moan escaped her as he drew back from her, but he tugged gently at the zip of her skirt, easing it down over her hips, discarding it. His own clothes joined it a few moments later.

'I want to see you naked,' he said, his voice low and rough as he slid the remaining scrap of lace from her. 'You're so beautiful, Cassie, every sweet inch of you, every tiny golden freckle.'

He looked down at her, trailing kisses across the satiny expanse of her abdomen, shifting to explore the rounded curve of her hip and the smooth length of her thigh. His hands shaped her, moving in tantalising exploration over her slender body, rousing her to a pitch of breathless excitement as he discovered her secret, inner warmth and invited her helpless abandonment with the knowing delicacy of his touch.

'Ryker, please...' She wanted more; incredibly this exquisite intimacy was not enough, and she moved restlessly against him, feeling the hard strength of his arousal test the soft, moist heart of her.

Slowly he thrust into her, sheathing himself in velvet, giving her time to adjust to the strange new sensation before he began to move, the rhythm of his body creating a sensual whirlpool of need and intense, piercing desire.

The throb of heat pulsed within her, a primeval beat, spiralling towards a glorious crescendo, and then she was falling, tumbling down into the vortex, little wild cries escaping her as the waves of pleasure eddied inside her. His own explosive fulfilment came within seconds, a harsh sound strangling in his throat, a groan of ecstasy breathed against her hot cheek as together they drifted into the languorous aftermath of joy.

He held her, wrapped in his arms, their bodies swathed in the golden glow of love. 'I think,' he said softly, smiling into her eyes, 'you had better marry me very quickly. We have a lot of time to make up.'

She nuzzled against him, pressing her lips to the smooth bare skin of his shoulder. 'A long honeymoon,' she said huskily. 'Somewhere warm and peaceful, where no one can disturb us. Do you know anywhere like that, Ryker?'

He kissed the tip of her nose. 'I know just the place,' he murmured, gathering her close to him. 'But right now, this bed looks pretty much like heaven to me. What do you think?'

'Paradise,' she said on a blissful sigh. 'Sheer paradise.'

Accept 4 FREE Romances and 2 FREE gifts

FROM READER SERVICE

Here's an irresistible invitation from Mills & Boon. Please accept our offer of 4 FREE Romances, a CUDDLY TEDDY and a special MYSTERY GIFT! Then, if you choose, go on to enjoy 6 captivating Romances every month for just £1.80 each, postage and packing FREE. Plus our FREE Newsletter with author news, competitions and much more.

**Send the coupon below to:
Mills & Boon Reader Service,
FREEPOST, PO Box 236,
Croydon, Surrey CR9 9EL.**

- - - **NO STAMP REQUIRED** - - -

Yes! Please rush me 4 FREE Romances and 2 FREE gifts! Please also reserve me a Reader Service subscription. If I decide to subscribe I can look forward to receiving 6 brand new Romances for just £10.80 each month, post and packing FREE. If I decide not to subscribe I shall write to you within 10 days - I can keep the free books and gifts whatever I choose. I may cancel or suspend my subscription at any time. I am over 18 years of age.

Ms/Mrs/Miss/Mr _____ EP55R

Address _____

_____

Postcode _____ Signature _____

**mps
MAILING PREFERENCE SERVICE**

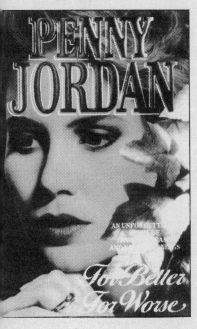

Next Month's Romances

Each month you can choose from a wide variety of romance with Mills & Boon. Below are the new titles to look out for next month, why not ask either Mills & Boon Reader Service or your Newsagent to reserve you a copy of the titles you want to buy – just tick the titles you would like and either post to Reader Service or take it to any Newsagent and ask them to order your books.

Please save me the following titles: Please tick | ✓

HEART OF THE OUTBACK	Emma Darcy	
DARK FIRE	Robyn Donald	
SEPARATE ROOMS	Diana Hamilton	
GUILTY LOVE	Charlotte Lamb	
GAMBLE ON PASSION	Jacqueline Baird	
LAIR OF THE DRAGON	Catherine George	
SCENT OF BETRAYAL	Kathryn Ross	
A LOVE UNTAMED	Karen van der Zee	
TRIUMPH OF THE DAWN	Sophie Weston	
THE DARK EDGE OF LOVE	Sara Wood	
A PERFECT ARRANGEMENT	Kay Gregory	
RELUCTANT ENCHANTRESS	Lucy Keane	
DEVIL'S QUEST	Joanna Neil	
UNWILLING SURRENDER	Cathy Williams	
ALMOST AN ANGEL	Debbie Macomber	
THE MARRIAGE BRACELET	Rebecca Winters	

If you would like to order these books in addition to your regular subscription from Mills & Boon Reader Service please send £1.90 per title to: Mills & Boon Reader Service, Freepost, P.O. Box 236, Croydon, Surrey, CR9 9EL, quote your Subscriber No:................................... (If applicable) and complete the name and address details below. Alternatively, these books are available from many local Newsagents including W.H.Smith, J.Menzies, Martins and other paperback stockists from 12 March 1994.

Name:..
Address:..
....Post Code:..........................

To Retailer: If you would like to stock M&B books please contact your regular book/magazine wholesaler for details.

You may be mailed with offers from other reputable companies as a result of this application.
If you would rather not take advantage of these opportunities please tick box   ☐

'Where do we go from here?' Richard murmured.

'To bed,' Nicola said firmly, pushing against his chest.

'That's fine by me.'

She pushed him away more vigorously. 'That's not what I meant at all!'

'It wasn't?' There was laughter in his voice.

There had been nothing tentative about his first kiss. Now, as he kissed her for the second time, she knew it would be futile to pretend she didn't want him.

Dear Reader

In February, we celebrate one of the most romantic times of the year—St Valentine's Day, when messages of true love are exchanged. At Mills & Boon we feel that our novels carry the Valentine spirit on throughout the year and we hope that readers agree. Dipping into the pages of our books will give you a taste of true romance every month...so chase away those winter blues and look forward to spring with Mills & Boon!

Till next month,

The Editor

Anne Weale was still at school when a women's magazine published some of her stories. At twenty-five she had her first novel accepted by Mills & Boon. Now, with a grown-up son and still happily married to her first love, Anne divides her life between her winter home, a Spanish village ringed by mountains and vineyards, and a summer place in Guernsey, one of the many islands around the world she has used as backgrounds for her books.

Recent titles by the same author:

THE FABERGÉ CAT

TURKISH DELIGHTS

BY

ANNE WEALE

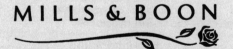

MILLS & BOON LIMITED
ETON HOUSE, 18-24 PARADISE ROAD
RICHMOND, SURREY TW9 1SR

For Angela, Katrina, Sara, Sheila and Valerie who shared the journey which inspired this story. Also for Ayhan, our guide, whose courtesy, patience and humour smoothed the way. And for M, the world's best travelling companion.

First published in Great Britain 1993
by Mills & Boon Limited

© Anne Weale 1993

Australian copyright 1993
Philippine copyright 1994
This edition 1994

ISBN 0 263 78310 3

Set in Times Roman 10 on 10½ pt.
91-9402-58286 C

Made and printed in Great Britain

CHAPTER ONE

For Nicola Temple, one of the delights of living in London was to walk down a street where, between 1851 and 1860, Charles Dickens had lived and written *Bleak House*. Or through a nearby square where, in a house destroyed by bombing in 1941, Virginia Woolf had written some of her novels.

Nicola's parents lived in the country, but close enough to London for her to commute from their home. But, once established as a junior editor, she had wanted to be independent; to enjoy the pleasures of city life rather than merely working there from nine to five.

Not that she had a nine-to-five job. Being a publisher's editor was a vocation rather than merely a means of earning her living, especially now she was a commissioning editor with her own list of authors.

One of them was coming to lunch with her today at the Café des Amis du Vin, a bistro near Covent Garden. Her expenses allowance didn't run to the elegant restaurants where the senior editorial staff entertained the best-selling authors on the Barking & Dollis list. But as this author was a suburban housewife who had written her first novel at the kitchen table while her toddler and baby were having their afternoon nap, lunch at any London restaurant was a rare treat for her.

One day in the future, Nicola hoped, they would both reach the heights of lunching at the Savoy. Her own target was a seat on the board of B & D's directors, and she felt sure that, with her encouragement, some of her authors had it in them to become famous best-sellers.

Most of the editorial staff lived on the outskirts of London and didn't arrive at the office until ten. Nicola

5

liked to be at her desk at nine in order to have a quiet hour before her telephone started to ring.

Many of the calls were internal, but sometimes her authors would ring up out of the blue and expect her to switch her mind to their problems; often their personal hang-ups as well as professional difficulties.

The reception area at Barking & Dollis was staffed by two girls: one at the switchboard dealing with almost non-stop calls and the other receiving packages brought in by motorbike messengers and directing visitors to offices on other floors. This morning an arty-looking young man with a large portfolio, probably containing roughs for a book jacket, was perched on one of the leather sofas.

Smiling at all three, Nicola said, 'Morning, Polly. Morning, Fiona.'

Aware of them eyeing her new suit—usually she came to work in a sweater and skirt—she ran up the stairs to Editorial on the second floor.

Here the whole floor was divided into glass-walled cubicles, their size depending on the status of their occupants. Later in the day the most noticeable feature of the area would be the blue screens of the computer terminals used by the secretaries and also by the editorial staff when they wanted to check the details of a contract or the current sales figures of a particular title.

At the moment the screens were blank and Nicola had the place to herself.

The first of her colleagues to arrive was Gordon, who was in charge of the crime fiction list.

'Morning, Nicola. Ready for a coffee?' The coffee machine was always his first port of call.

'Yes, please, Gordon.'

A few moments later he came back with two polystyrene beakers.

'I hear the New Broom is in town. Any day now the clean sweep will start.'

He was talking about Richard Russell, whose photograph had been in both the American and British publishing periodicals when his appointment as chief executive of Barking & Dollis was announced.

Although he had already made one or two flying visits to the firm now under his control, Nicola had been out of the office on the day he had toured the building and met the editorial staff.

There had been much speculation in the trade papers about the measures Russell would take to pull the firm out of its serious financial difficulties.

'What do *you* think he'll do?' she asked Gordon.

'Something fairly drastic, that's for sure. Neither of us has much to worry about. We pull our weight. But I——' Gordon broke off. 'That sounds like my telephone. See you...'

Watching him hurry to his office, one wall of it massed with books, including titles by several of the most popular names in crime fiction, Nicola knew he had little to fear from the man he called the New Broom. Two of Gordon's most successful authors had clauses written into their contracts ensuring that if he left Barking & Dollis they would be free to follow him. That alone was a powerful insurance. No firm, in difficult times, wanted to lose writers whose new books always reached high ratings on the best-seller lists and stayed there for many weeks.

None of the books on her own list had ever done that. But at least one of her authors had the potential to best-sell in a few years' time. So, although a great many people in publishing had lost their jobs in the past few months, Nicola wasn't too worried about her own position.

When, that afternoon, she returned to the office after lunching with her author, there was a note on her desk.

Please call Mr Russell's secretary immediately.

She picked up the internal telephone and tapped the extension number.

'This is Nicola Temple. You wanted to speak to me?'

'Mr Russell wants to see you. He's busy at the moment. I'll call you when he's free.'

Nicola checked her hair and make-up. Then she tried to get on with some work. But it was difficult to concentrate with a summons to see the chief executive looming over her.

What did he want? Merely to give her the once-over?

She was kept in suspense for only ten minutes before his secretary rang back.

'Mr Russell will see you now.'

The CE's suite was on the top floor, with the door to his secretary's office immediately opposite the lift. To the left was the boardroom, to the right a conference room.

Nicola had been on this floor only once before, for her interview with the previous CE. The same pleasant-faced, fortysomething secretary was working at a desk near the door to the inner sanctum.

Receiving a 'go ahead' nod, Nicola tapped on the door and heard a brisk voice say, 'Come in.'

A friendly smile already forming round her mouth, she turned the handle and entered.

The new chief executive was using a notebook computer of the kind she longed to own but at present couldn't afford.

For a few moments longer his fingers moved lightly over the keys. Then he stopped work and stood up. She had heard he was tall, but hadn't realised how tall. As she walked towards him, he subjected her to a scrutiny which seemed to leave no detail of her appearance unregistered. And it wasn't a friendly inspection. He didn't smile as she approached.

She had never felt her self-possession more severely tested than in the first moments of being appraised by Richard Russell's critical blue eyes.

Without shaking hands, he said, 'Sit down, Miss Temple. I wanted to see you earlier but you weren't in. Where were you?'

'Having lunch with an author.'

One of his straight black eyebrows rose into an inverted tick.

'A long lunch,' he said drily. 'You were out of the office until nearly four o'clock.'

'We had a lot to discuss. Actually we left the restaurant at three, but hadn't finished our talk so I walked to her station with her.'

'What was the purpose of this prolonged discussion? What did it achieve?' he asked.

The questions were hard to answer in the precise, quick-fire way she felt he expected.

'We talked about a lot of things...I think Margaret went home feeling encouraged and stimulated. She doesn't get much support from her husband and——'

'Long lunches are an expensive waste of time which I intend to curtail if not to ban altogether,' he cut in incisively. 'This company is in trouble, Miss Temple...or do you prefer "Ms" Temple?'

There were women on the staff who would have been infuriated by the sarcastic tone of this query and its implications. Clearly he was an arch anti-feminist and liked everyone to know it.

Well, he was the boss, and it was his privilege to impose his views on his employees if he chose. Whether, in so doing, he would get the best out of them was another matter. But that wasn't her concern. Her priority was to please him and clearly, by being absent when he sent for her, she had got off on the wrong foot.

'I answer to either,' she said pleasantly. 'Or to my first name, Nicola, if you prefer.'

'This company is in trouble,' he repeated. 'It has been for some time. Because the previous administration failed to take steps to stop the rot, there is now no option but to make stringent...extremely stringent cut-backs.'

In the harsh set of his mouth as he paused, and in the stern blue gaze fixed on her face, Nicola read signs that made her mouth and throat go dry.

'I have here——' he tapped the casing of the compact computer '—all Barking & Dollis's records since—far too late, in my view—the company started to make use of modern technology. I've spent the past two weeks studying the records of every member of staff and the profitability of every title published by B & D during the past several years. Now it's my unpleasant task to do what should have been done long ago.'

Again he paused, the merciless stare fixed on her face. She knew that at any moment he would deliver a verdict against which there would be no appeal.

'The books you have commissioned since your promotion have not performed well enough to justify their place on our list. I'm sorry to have to tell you your services are no longer required.'

Even though she had already guessed what was coming, Nicola still couldn't believe he had dismissed her.

After some moments of silence, she managed to say unsteadily, 'You mean ... I'm sacked ... just like that.'

He nodded. 'I'd prefer you to leave at once ... this afternoon. There's nothing to be gained by the staff who are leaving remaining here under notice. It's better they start job-hunting immediately.'

'I—I can't believe this,' she stammered. 'I can't believe that after three and a half years I'm being chucked out without notice. I'm not a slacker, Mr Russell. I've put in nearly as many hours in my own time as in the firm's time. And what's going to happen to my authors? Are you going to ditch them too?'

'If I had been heading this company, most of them wouldn't have been taken on,' he said curtly. 'We'll fulfil our contractual obligations but, where there is only an option to publish the next book, most of your authors will have to look elsewhere. It's tough, I know. But it's the nature of business...and publishing is a business. Not, as it once was, "an occupation for gentlemen"...or for young ladies with literary inclinations.'

'That isn't fair,' she protested. 'It may apply to a handful of the women in publishing, but it certainly doesn't to me. I'm not subsidised by rich parents...or filling in time till I marry. I see my job as a career.'

'It's no use arguing, Miss Temple. I didn't arrive at this decision without careful thought. Staff cuts are unavoidable. You would agree, wouldn't you, that as a young single woman you're in a better position to survive redundancy than a man with a wife and children to support?'

That silenced her for a moment. Then she said, 'In most cases yes, but for all you know I may be the sole supporter of an elderly parent. Many single women are.'

'I have your background notes here.'

He touched a couple of keys and swivelled the computer towards her. On the screen she saw her original CV followed by a heading 'Editorial Director's Report'. The screen wasn't large enough to show this unless Richard Russell used the scroll key. Instead he turned the screen back towards him.

Then, reading from another section of the file on her, he said, 'You spend Monday to Friday in London and most weekends at your parents' home in Kent. Your father is a branch manager for one of the major insurance companies. Your mother is secretary of a gardeners' circle and an active supporter of several local charities. You have no one dependent on you.'

'Except myself. My parents can't afford to keep me. And with all the so-called "rationalisations" there've been in publishing recently, there are more people out of work than posts to be filled. I've no hope of getting another job.'

He didn't deny it, but said calmly, 'In publishing, possibly not...at least in the immediate future. The present recession won't last forever. They never do.

Meanwhile, you have skills applicable to other occupations. Your father may be able to pull some strings for you.'

'I don't want another occupation...and I don't believe I deserve to be thrown out of this one. I can't deny that none of the books I've handled has done very brilliantly, but they haven't been disasters either. It takes time to build an author.'

'I've dipped into the books you've bought for us, Miss Temple, and they strike me as mainly reading for people such as your mother...middle-class, middle-aged housewives.'

'There are a lot of them about, Mr Russell,' she retorted. 'They——'

He cut in, 'I'm afraid I haven't time to discuss the public's reading habits. I'm too busy addressing the problem of how to save this company from going into liquidation.' He rose to his feet.

'The blame for your predicament doesn't lie with me. Your understandable ire should be aimed at the previous management who failed to foresee and prepare for the changes affecting the book industry. I'm sorry we can't continue to employ you, but I also think, from your record, that you may find yourself more comfortable in a different kind of occupation. Publishing—like the theatre and the movies—has a misleading glamour about it.'

He came round the desk and moved in the direction of the door.

'In New York, we've already had to trim our sails to the rough winds of recession. It's going to get equally tough over here. You have many excellent qualities to help you relocate and those will be emphasised in the reference which I'll sign later today and you'll receive tomorrow.' He opened the door and held out his hand. 'I wish you luck, Miss Temple.'

It was an automatic reflex to shake the hand he offered. For a moment she had the strange feeling that a powerful current of energy was actually flowing through the large firm hand enclosing her shaky one. Then the contact was broken and he was waiting for her to go.

'Goodbye.' She could feel his impatience to get on.

'Goodbye.' To her surprise, her reply sounded normal. But inside she was starting to fall apart.

His secretary said, 'You'd better sit down for a minute.' She produced a beaker of water. 'Sip this. If it's any comfort, you're not the only one,' she went on sympathetically. 'A lot of desks are being cleared this afternoon.'

It took time for the words to sink in. Nicola felt dazed, as if she had just cracked her head on something hard.

After some moments, she said, 'Who are the others?'

'Three in Editorial, two in Publicity, one in Rights and six from other departments...twelve altogether. It's the biggest shake-up I remember and I've been here for sixteen years. Maybe I'll be in the next tumbril. He may import an American secretary...or replace me with a robot. He's the first boss I've ever had who can type. He types faster than I do, would you believe? His computer taught him!'

A small gadget attached to the front of her businesslike blouse began to bleep.

'I'll have to go. He doesn't like to be kept waiting.' With a kindly pat on Nicola's shoulder, she went to answer the summons.

Terminal One was full of people with skis balanced on their luggage trolleys when Nicola arrived at Heathrow Airport soon after six a.m. on the last Saturday in January.

Joining the line at the All Destinations check-in desk, she kept a lookout for anyone else with luggage like hers: a large dark green canvas grip with 'Amazing Adventures' stencilled in fluorescent pink letters on the side of it.

When her luggage had been weighed and tagged, she slung the rucksack containing her camera and other valuables over her shoulder by one strap and went through the security barrier and Passport Control to the main departure lounge.

Her passport, issued nine years ago, was almost due for renewal. But there wasn't a lot of difference between the photograph of her at seventeen and the way she looked this morning, without make-up, her thick, fair shoulder-length hair tied back at the nape of her neck.

At seventeen she had looked mature for her age, the type of kind, sensible girl who might take up nursing or teaching or become an invaluable secretary. Not, at that age, a pretty girl, although a discriminating eye might have seen the promise of something more lasting than prettiness.

Today, casually dressed and with her clear skin bare of anything but moisturiser, she looked younger than twenty-six. The traumas of three years ago hadn't left any visible scars.

Flight BA 676 to Istanbul was called just before eight. Most of the people who assembled in the final departure area were Turkish businessmen in dark overcoats with briefcases.

But a few passengers were dressed like Nicola in walking boots, jeans, sweatshirts and padded jackets. Hers, dark blue and filled with down, was on loan from her brother.

She was idly watching the last comers having their tickets checked when suddenly her dark grey eyes widened in startled dismay.

The tall man striding into view was someone she had seen before. Only once, a long time ago, but his features were imprinted on her memory as clearly as if it were yesterday.

This was the man who, for a while, had wrecked her life—and with as little compunction as if he were stepping on an ant or swatting a house fly.

The last time she had seen him, on that unforgettable day in the chief executive's office on the top floor of the Barking & Dollis building, he had been in the clothes of a high-powered international businessman.

Today he was wearing a military-style khaki sweater with cotton reinforcements at the shoulders and elbows and a pair of the multi-pocketed Rohan trousers her brother always wore on his expeditions.

His clothing left her in little doubt that he was also a member of the Amazing Adventures group. The realisation that, of all people, Richard Russell was going to be one of her travelling companions for the next sixteen days filled her with horror.

He had no right to be here, she thought angrily. A man with his means should be jetting off to one of the ritzy winter-sun resorts where tycoons and their women foregathered at this time of year, not butting in on a holiday designed for low-budget travellers who didn't mind roughing it.

Unaware of her hostile gaze fixed on his autocratic profile, Richard Russell strolled towards the doors through which very soon everyone in the waiting area would be despatched to their aircraft.

He appeared to have timed his arrival to suit his own convenience, ignoring the instruction to be there two hours before take-off.

Not bothering to take a seat, he stood near the doorway and inspected his fellow passengers. Before his survey reached Nicola, the doors were opened and people began to go through.

The interior of the plane was divided into two sections, the more expensive seats at the front being occupied by some of the businessmen and one elegant woman. The Euro-Traveller section at the rear was where Nicola and her as yet unknown fellow trekkers would be sitting.

Richard Russell was stowing his belongings in an overhead locker when she moved hurriedly past him, her

face averted. At least she had been spared the ordeal of
sitting next to the man and had a few hours to steel
herself before being forced to shake hands with him.

As yet unheated, the aircraft felt cold. But it was
nervous tension rather than the low temperature which
made Nicola shiver as she fastened her seatbelt. Seeing
Richard Russell had brought back all the wretchedness
of the months after he had sacked her. And although
the job she had now was as well paid and reasonably
congenial, it didn't have the same prospects as the one
she had lost, nor was the work as satisfying.

She had survived. She was still independent and
solvent. But she wasn't as happy and fulfilled as she had
been before her abrupt and arbitrary dismissal.

Presently, looking out of the window, she saw that
they were flying over what looked like a fantasy world
of jagged mountains and vast frozen lakes. Actually the
lakes were the smooth surface of clouds and the fairytale
mountains were the peaks of the central European alps.

For a while the excitement of being whisked across
Europe to what had once been Constantinople, heart of
the legendary Ottoman Empire, city of Suleiman the
Magnificent, made her forget the occupant of a seat
several rows in front of her.

But thinking about some of the other rulers of
Constantinople, and their cruelty towards their in-
feriors, triggered thoughts of Richard Russell: the man
who had cut short her career in publishing, and that of
eleven of her colleagues, as ruthlessly as Sultan Mehmed
the Conqueror had ordered the drowning of seven of his
dead father's concubines.

What Richard Russell had done on the day described
in the trade Press as 'one of the blackest dates in the
history of British publishing' might not be as brutal a
crime as ordering the execution of unwanted slave girls.
But she had no doubt that, had he lived in those times,
he would have been capable of equally merciless
treatment of those in his power.

*   *   *

At Istanbul airport, Nicola was among the last to have her passport checked. By the time she passed through the barrier to the baggage reclaim area, most of the other passengers had collected their luggage and were heading in the direction of the Customs desks.

To her relief there was no sign of Richard Russell. It seemed she had been mistaken and he wasn't one of her group after all. Well, a fortnight staying in cheap *pansiyons* was certainly not the sort of holiday she would have expected him to choose from all she had heard and read about him.

His father was an American senator, his grandfather a multimillionaire whose possessions had included one of the USA's most important publishing houses.

On his mother's side he was descended from British aristocrats and, at his mother's insistence, had been educated at Eton like all his maternal forebears. On both sides of the Atlantic he sprang from the most élite strata of Anglo-American society. It was hardly likely that he would choose to fraternise with the kinds of holiday-makers who shopped around for bargain breaks and were prepared to put up with some privations in order to see the world.

Why he should have been flying Euro-Traveller instead of Business Class was a puzzle. But no doubt by now he was on his way to the famous Pera Palas Hotel or the modern luxury of the Sheraton where the kind of people he was used to mixing with would stay.

Feeling better, Nicola cast a surreptitious eye over the people who were going to be her travelling companions. Not that she really minded what they were like as long as he wasn't one of them.

When they had been through Customs and emerged into the concourse, they were met by a smiling dark-eyed girl with a cloud of curly black hair who suggested that, before leaving the airport, they might like to go to the bank at the far end of the concourse.

'You can leave your luggage here with me. I'll watch it for you.'

As they followed her directions, Nicola noticed that compared with the number of men in the building there were very few women about. Unaccustomed to being the cynosure of so many masculine eyes—particularly when she was dressed for trekking and deliberately had left off her normal make-up—she found it a little uncomfortable to be stared at so openly.

But she forgot about the stares when she saw who was standing at the cashier's window at the airport bank. Richard Russell. And on the floor by his feet was an Amazing Adventures bag.

He was one of the group after all.

When the kitbags had been stowed in the hold of the coach taking them to their overnight accommodation, and everyone was settled in their seats, the Turkish girl picked up a microphone.

'Good afternoon, ladies and gentlemen. My name is Nuray. I'm your tour guide. Your hotel is in the old part of the city near the Grand Bazaar and the famous Blue Mosque.'

As she listened, Nicola was aware of the presence of her *bête noire* two seats in front of her on the opposite side of the aisle. From where she sat, all she could see was one of Richard Russell's long legs stretched out in the aisle, part of a broad shoulder and the taut line of his cheekbone and jaw. His hair was as almost as dark as Nuray's and, judging by the colour of his skin, it wasn't long since he had spent time in the sun, possibly at Christmas. He had been lightly tanned, she recalled, the first time she'd met him.

So far he hadn't noticed her. Probably when he did he wouldn't remember her. Why should he? She had been in his presence for less than ten minutes, and she hadn't been the only person he had axed that day.

'The outskirts of large cities are never very prepos-
sessing, are they?' said the woman sitting beside her.
'I'm Hilary Goodge.'

It was hard to judge how old she was because, although
her hair was white, her skin wasn't lined except round
her friendly hazel eyes. Also she looked very fit. A quick
glance showed no ring on her wedding finger.

When Nicola had introduced herself, Miss Goodge
said, 'Is this your first visit to Turkey?'

'Yes.'

'Mine too, although not my first "amazing adventure". Last year I trekked in Nepal.'

'That must have been very exciting.'

Miss Goodge nodded. 'Very. Have you travelled with
AA before?'

'No, but my brother has. He's done their Peru trek.'

It was after four, local time, when they reached the
hotel. As they climbed down from the coach, two small
barefoot children appeared, silently begging for money
with gestures indicating hunger.

Their signals tore at Nicola's heart. At present she had
nothing in her wallet except large-denomination notes
and was obliged to ignore them, like everyone else. But
the sight of their muddy little feet, purple with cold,
distressed her very much.

'They probably make a good thing out of stationing
themselves outside a hotel frequented by first-world
tourists,' said a cynical voice from behind her. A voice
she would have recognised anywhere because of its distinctive timbre and its accent, a blend of Harvard and
Oxford.

Turning, her grey eyes blazing, she said, 'That's the
most heartless statement I've ever heard. How would
you like to have bare feet on a raw day like this?'

CHAPTER TWO

As HER angry tone caught the attention of other members of the group, Richard Russell said calmly, 'I shouldn't.'

He handed the children the money he had been about to give them when she'd flared at him.

'But actions speak louder than words,' he added drily, cocking a quizzical eyebrow at her.

He moved away to remove his kitbag from the luggage hold.

Although she hadn't expected him to recognise her, it was curiously galling to be looked at without recognition by someone who had had such a catastrophic effect on her life.

Led by the Turkish girl, they carried their kitbags into the hotel. With marble floors, chandeliers and red and gold décor, the reception area and open-plan lounge were more luxurious than Nicola had expected.

But ten minutes later, looking out of the window in the twin-bedded room on the sixth floor she was sharing with Miss Goodge, she saw that the back of the hotel overlooked flats no better than slums. Quickly she let the net curtain fall into place, at the same time remembering Richard Russell's sardonic reply to her accusation of heartlessness.

'As Nuray says the tap water in Istanbul is heavily chlorinated, I'm going out to stretch my legs and buy some bottled water,' said Miss Goodge. 'If you go out, leave our key at the desk.'

Nicola nodded. 'I'll have a shower. Hot showers may be hard to come by later on. The brochure did warn us that on parts of the trek the facilities will be primitive.'

'That won't worry me,' said Miss Goodge. 'But some of the others may not care for it. It's too soon to form firm opinions, but I shouldn't be surprised if the tall man with blue eyes is the only member of the party who will take everything in his stride. He looks a very tough cookie.'

'What makes you think that?' asked Nicola.

'He reminds me of an explorer who gave a talk to the school where I used to teach. This man has the same fine-tempered look about him. You know how the metal for swords was repeatedly heated and cooled to improve its hardness and elasticity? Life puts some people through a similar process...makes them more resilient than most of us.'

Left on her own, Nicola pondered Miss Goodge's first impression of Richard Russell. To give the devil his due, he had rescued the publishing firm from the brink of insolvency. But had it been necessary to employ such Draconian methods?

One of the salesmen sacked at the same time as Nicola had had a nervous breakdown from which he would probably never recover fully. She had met him in the street not long ago and been shocked to hear that he was still out of work and unlikely ever to recover the standard of life he had lost when Richard made him redundant.

Presently she went down to the lobby to order coffee.

'Turkish or Nescafé?' the waiter asked.

'Turkish, please.'

'Make that two, will you? You don't mind if I join you, I hope?' said a man who had been on the coach.

'Not at all,' she said politely, although there was something about him she didn't take to. His hair was combed forward, probably to disguise a receding hairline, and his sweater was a colour she disliked.

'I'm Philip Shadwell.'

'Nicola Temple.' To be friendly, she asked, 'Have you trekked before?'

He shook his head. 'I haven't had a holiday for some time. The firm I worked for—an estate agency—went bust. But I'm on my feet again now.'

Their order arrived: tall glasses of water and small glasses of black coffee with a bowl of sugar cubes.

A few minutes later they were joined by two other members of the group, a brunette in her thirties and a much younger girl with red hair. They introduced themselves as Janet Sloane and Sylvie Bond.

At the airport Nicola had noticed Janet was much better dressed than everyone else in an expensive tweed jacket over what looked like a cashmere sweater with needlecord trousers and highly polished boots. She was also wearing a lot of make-up and her nails were varnished the same deep red as her sweater.

'What's the coffee like?' Janet asked, as the waiter reappeared.

Nicola sipped it. 'Very strong.'

Janet ordered a half-bottle of white wine and Sylvie enquired about soft drinks. She had a very fair skin and, as she talked to the waiter, who was also young and looking admiringly at her, she blushed.

'I'm surprised our guide is a woman,' said Janet. 'In a Muslim country I thought we'd be led by a man.'

They were sitting not far from the lift which had just reached lobby level. As a uniformed bellboy opened the door, Richard Russell stepped out.

Although he noticed the group sitting in the lounge, he didn't stroll over to join them, With a casual wave, he made for the doors.

Nicola noticed Janet's eyes following him down the marble steps to street level. She's welcome to him, she thought.

They had dinner at a kebab house. A table for twelve had been prepared for them and Nuray sat at one end and explained the menu.

Nicola sat between Miss Goodge and Philip with Janet and Richard opposite.

'Turkish cooking is supposed to be one of the three finest cuisines in the world, but somehow I don't think this is the place to sample it at its best,' said Janet, with a critical glance round the crowded restaurant.

'This isn't supposed to be a luxury holiday,' said Miss Goodge.

For her first course Nicola chose *piaz*, a dish of hard-boiled eggs and thinly sliced tomatoes on a bed of haricot beans.

Presently, after no one had spoken for some minutes, Nicola's room-mate said in slightly raised voice, 'Shall we introduce ourselves? I'm Hilary Goodge, retired schoolmistress. My main interest now is gardening.' She looked expectantly at Janet, who was facing her. 'And you are?'

'Janet Sloane...director of a management consultancy. I don't have time for many interests outside my work, which is very demanding.'

Smiling at him, Janet passed the cue for a thumbnail CV to Richard.

He said, 'Richard Russell. I work for a UK subsidiary of an American multi-media corporation. My other interests are rock-climbing, history and architecture.'

It was a modest way of describing the chairmanship of one of the oldest and most famous publishing houses in England, thought Nicola, as he looked across the table at her.

'I'm Nicola Temple. I'm secretary to the manager of a bookshop. My interests are reading and cooking,' she volunteered.

When everyone in the group had given brief details of themselves, Miss Goodge leaned forward to address their guide.

'How is it you speak such perfect English?'

'Thank you,' said Nuray, smiling. 'I don't think my English is perfect, but the reason I speak it quite well is because one of my sisters is married to an Englishman. I've spent many holidays with them since their wedding when I was eight and my sister was twenty. We're a large family. She is the eldest and I am the youngest. I still live with my parents in another part of Istanbul.'

At the end of the meal she told them each what they owed. The food was very cheap by English standards.

'I'd have preferred to pay more for something better, wouldn't you?' Janet murmured to Richard, taking some Turkish notes from an expensive wallet.

Nicola who, like some of the others, was keeping her money in a kangaroo-bag on a belt round her waist, saw him shrug and say, 'Mine wasn't bad. It filled the gap.'

She wondered what had brought Janet on this trip. A fortnight lazing in the sun by day and dancing under the stars by night at a glitzy resort in the Caribbean seemed more her style.

In the hotel lobby Nuray said, 'I'll be here at ten o'clock tomorrow to show you the Blue Mosque and other places of interest before we board the train for tomorrow night's journey. I hope you sleep well. Goodnight.'

When she had gone, someone suggested having a drink in the lounge, a proposal which met with approval from most of the group.

Miss Goodge said to Nicola, 'I had a late night last night. But there's no reason why you shouldn't stay up as long as you like. You won't disturb me. I'm a very sound sleeper and shan't stir until my alarm clock rings in the morning.'

Thinking the older woman might like to have the bedroom and bathroom to herself for a while, Nicola said, 'I'll have a glass of wine while you're getting ready for bed and come up in about half an hour.'

In the lounge, slightly to Nicola's irritation, Philip, having sat next to her at dinner, seated himself beside her again. She had hoped to chat to other members of the group.

Never mind, there would be plenty of time to get to know everyone in the next two weeks, she thought, waiting her turn to give an order to the waiter.

The only one she didn't want to know better was Richard Russell. Some contact with him was unavoidable, but she meant to have as little to do with him as possible. Which shouldn't be too difficult as Janet obviously hoped to annex him.

Later, although the bed was comfortable and it had been a long day, she found she couldn't sleep. His presence in the group didn't make for peace of mind.

He revived so many memories she had tried to forget; not only the disruption of her career but also of her personal life. As a side-effect of losing her job, she had lost the man she had been in love with. She was over it now. Her heart was no longer irreparably broken as it had seemed to be for the first eighteen months after the split with Ian.

But the combination of losing her job and her lover had been severe blows to her self-esteem. Meeting Richard again had shown that her *amour propre* wasn't completely healed yet.

Although at first it had angered her that he hadn't the slightest recollection of ever seeing her before, now she realised it was better this way.

The situation would have been much worse if he *had* remembered her.

As he seemed a man who would normally have an excellent memory, she must hope that during the next two weeks of daily contact nothing about her would ring a bell in his mind.

It was bad enough his being part of the group. She could do without the added chagrin of having him suddenly remember that, during the purge he had instigated, she had been one of the first to be jettisoned.

*   *   *

When Nicola and Miss Goodge went in search of breakfast next morning, they expected to be the first comers. Richard Russell was ahead of them.

'Who is your room partner?' Miss Goodge asked him, when they had exchanged good mornings.

'No one. I paid the supplement for a single room to avoid finding myself with a smoker or a snorer.'

'Fortunately neither Nicola nor I fall into either of those categories,' said Miss Goodge.

He smiled. 'Actually the main reason I've arranged to have a room to myself is that I don't need a lot of sleep. Five or six hours is enough. The rest of the time I read, which would be hard lines on anyone sharing a room with me.'

Other members of the group arrived and helped themselves to the bread, white cheese, honey, butter and black and green olives set out on a side table. Coffee and tea were provided in two large urns.

After breakfast they packed their belongings, which were to be left in the hotel's luggage-room to await their return from sightseeing.

Today Janet's outfit seemed more suitable for drinking *Glühwein* or hot chocolate in the cafés of a fashionable ski resort than a day spent walking round Turkish mosques and museums.

At five minutes to ten Nuray arrived to take them to the Blue Mosque by way of the streets surrounding the legendary Grand Bazaar.

'Today being Sunday, it's closed,' she told them. 'But when you come back to Istanbul at the end of the trek you'll have plenty of time for shopping. There are one thousand shops in sixty-seven covered streets. It's easy to lose your way in the bazaar, but it's fun to explore and the shopkeepers are helpful about giving directions.'

At the Blue Mosque they took off their boots and trainers and left them on racks by the door. Nuray took a scarf from her pocket and covered her hair with it.

'This isn't essential but, if you have a scarf with you, it's respectful.'

Inside the huge multi-domed building the floor was spread with dozens, perhaps hundreds of oriental rugs given to the mosque as offerings, the most recent gifts laid over the earlier ones.

Earlier that morning, from a mosque somewhere near the hotel, Nicola had heard the voice of a muezzin calling the faithful to prayer. But at this hour the mosque was almost empty with only a few old men on their knees in the main part of the building, and three or four women praying in the area reserved for females.

Beckoning the group to gather round her, and keeping her voice low, Nuray pointed out various features of special interest, notably the twenty thousand blue Iznik tiles cladding the interior of the building, from which the mosque took its nickname.

'The feminists among you may disapprove of the sexes being segregated,' she said, looking round the group. 'But it would be wrong to assume that women's position in Turkish society is inferior. In the more backward country districts—yes, there are inequalities. But not among educated people. Here in Istanbul there are many women in important positions. Not enough of them yet. But isn't that also true of America and the countries in the European Community?'

When no one made any comment, she said, her dark eyes twinkling, 'My last group had strong feelings on this subject. But perhaps you are more sensible and re- alise it's better to travel without preconceived ideas and to form your own opinions from what you see and hear in the next two weeks.'

The rest of the morning was spent at another of the city's great landmarks, the church of St Sophia built in the sixth century.

'Ten thousand men worked for six years to make it the most magnificent building in the world,' said Nuray. 'The doors were of ivory, amber and cedar, the columns of white and green marble from Egypt and Syria. While they were making the mosaics on the walls and ceilings—four acres of them—the Byzantines invented the technique of covering a cube with gold leaf and sealing it with molten glass.'

In spite of the ravages wreaked on it during the intervening centuries, the church was still a breathtaking building. But after an hour of admiring its splendours most of the group were glad when Nuray announced it was time for lunch.

She took them to the Pudding Shop, explaining it had once been a famous meeting place for hippies in transit between Europe and India.

In the restaurant they lined up to choose from a selection of hot dishes. All the ground-floor tables being taken, the group ate in the room upstairs, split up at several tables.

Reluctantly, as she would have preferred not to be at his table, Nicola found herself with no choice but to share with Richard, Janet and the much older man called Miles.

The two men chatted knowledgeably about the construction of the church until the arrival of a bottle of wine.

Evidently Richard and Janet had agreed to share a bottle as, before he uncorked it, the waiter gave them each a wine glass.

'Two more glasses, please?' said Richard. 'Our friends might also like to try some Turkish wine.'

His reference to herself and Miles as friends was ironic in the circumstances, thought Nicola. Of course it was only a polite manner of speaking and he had no idea that to one of the people at the table he came close to being an enemy.

'Not for me, thanks,' she said, shaking her head, when the waiter returned with the additional glasses. 'I'm having apple tea.'

'The bread is first-rate,' said Miles, helping himself
to a crusty chunk from the basket. 'If the bread we've
had so far is typical, there should be no problem with
the picnics we'll be having later on. I'm looking forward
to that part of the trip. I'm not very keen on cities. You
three are all Londoners, I believe?'

'I find big cities exciting,' said Janet. She looked at
Richard. 'Don't you?'

'I have to spend a lot of my time in them and I do
enjoy certain aspects. But I was born on an island off
Cape Cod and I miss the sea when I haven't seen it for
a while.'

'How about you, Miss Temple?' Miles asked.

'Nicola,' she corrected, smiling at him. 'I was born in
the country. I'm not a true Londoner.'

As she spoke, she caught Richard looking at her more
intently than before. Could it be that Miles's use of her
surname had rung a faint bell in his memory? Was he
wondering why 'Nicola Temple' seemed vaguely familiar? Or perhaps she was only imagining a keener look
in those extraordinarily blue eyes.

'But you like it there?' Miles persisted. 'You find the
rewards offset the drawbacks, do you?'

'Like most people, I don't have much option. It's
where I earn my living.'

'If you're a secretary, your options are wide open,'
said Richard. 'Is there anyone who has a better range
of job choices than a first-class secretary? I shouldn't
think so.'

Wanting to switch the conversation away from herself,
Nicola turned to Janet. 'Does your work involve much
travel or is it mainly in London?'

'We advise anyone, anywhere, who has management
difficulties. Last year I went to Japan to study their
management systems. I love travelling, although of
course when it's business I don't "rough it" as we're
going to on this trip.'

'You sound like a dedicated career-woman,' was Richard's comment.

'I'm deeply involved in my work,' Janet agreed. 'But then I'm sure you are too.'

'What is your field, Richard?' asked Miles. 'I didn't catch everything said at the table last night.'

'I'm a publisher. And you?'

'I'm retired now. I was in the army. What sort of books do you publish?'

'A lot of non-fiction...memoirs, biography, travel. But also literary and middle-brow novels. I'm with Barking & Dollis. You probably have some of our titles on your bookshelves.'

'Indeed I have,' Miles agreed. 'You have some excellent writers. I seldom read novels myself, but my wife used to enjoy them. Unfortunately she was an invalid for the last ten years of her life, dependent on books and the radio to keep her amused. She wasn't keen on television.'

'My favourite entertainments are plays and concerts,' said Janet. 'That's why I could never live in the depths of the country, Miles. I'd miss London's cultural life. Have you seen the new play at the Haymarket, Richard?'

'Not yet.' He looked at Nicola. 'Have you?'

She shook her head. 'I don't often go to the theatre. What's good about London for me is the number of things which are free...art shows, street markets and so on. I'm gradually working my way round all the smaller museums.'

'I'm surprised we haven't run into each other. I'm a museum buff too,' he told her, smiling.

She was aware of his charm, but although it might work on Janet it had no effect on her. She knew too much about him. The virile good looks and polished manners were merely a façade. The inner man was both tough and ruthless; a worthy scion of the American forebears who had amassed a multi-media fortune and, on his mother's side, the long line of Englishmen whose ambition and cunning had brought them titles and estates.

The night train was due to leave Haydarpasa Station at half-past five. Nuray gave them the choice of crossing the Bosporus by coach via the inter-continental bridge, or by ferry.

As the day had grown steadily colder, most people chose the coach. Nicola, snug in her down-filled jacket, wasn't troubled by the falling temperature and was keen to see the city's famous skyline from the deck of the ferry. Going over the Bosporus by a bridge, inside a tour bus, seemed an unadventurous way of crossing the boundary between Europe and Asia.

When Nuray finished counting the hands of those who preferred the coach and said, 'OK, now who's for the ferry?' Nicola put up her hand, unaware that in the seats behind her only one other person had abstained from the previous vote.

The ferry dock was near Galata Bridge, the main link between the old and new parts of the city. Close by were the berths of the fishing-boats with swarthy fishermen tossing bags of fish to customers standing on the quay, and fresh fish being charcoal-grilled and sold between hunks of bread or wrapped in unleavened *pide*.

'I'll see the rest of you later,' said Nuray, when the coach had stopped. 'The driver knows where to take you.'

She climbed down to the roadway followed by Nicola and then, to Nicola's dismay, by Richard—and only Richard.

'Have I time to buy a fish sandwich?' he asked.

'Yes, if you like.'

'Shall I get three?'

Nuray shook her head. 'Not for me, thank you. But Nicola might like one.'

'No, thanks.'

Although the fish couldn't be fresher, Nicola felt it might not be wise to eat bread handled by cooks who had spent all day on the wharf. Warned by her much-travelled brother about things to avoid, she didn't want to risk picking up a bug, especially with a night on a train and the first day of trekking ahead of her.

After Richard had bought his snack, Nuray paid for the metal tokens they needed to get through the turnstile on to the landing stage.

'I'm afraid it's going to be crowded. This is a busy time of day and with Istanbul's population up to ten million our transport systems are stretched to their limits.'

At the end of a wintry afternoon, most of the passengers wanted to be under cover and the two foreigners and their guide had no difficulty in finding places by the rail on the open deck.

'At least try a small piece of fish,' said Richard, opening his sandwich and offering it to Nicola. 'Break a little bit off with your fingers. Fish straight from the heat of the grill isn't likely to carry any germs, if that worries you about street food.'

Taking off her right glove, she detached a piece of hot fish and put it in her mouth.

'It's delicious.' She licked her fingers. 'Thank you.'

Richard sank his teeth into the bread and bit off a mouthful, chewing it with obvious enjoyment. 'Mmm...the best food I've had so far,' he said presently. 'I should have bought two and kept one for later. I doubt if the train's restaurant car will have anything better to offer.'

With a blast of her siren the steamer began to move downstream.

'This waterway isn't the Bosporus. This is the Golden Horn,' said Nuray. 'If you like, when we come back to Istanbul, we can take a boat trip along the Bosporus as far as the Black Sea. Would you excuse me for a moment? I've seen someone I know. I must go and say hello.'

Although they were surrounded by people, the Turkish girl's sudden departure left Nicola sharply conscious of being alone in the company of the last man in the world with whom she wished to have a *tête-à-tête*.

'Quite a spectacular view,' he said, looking upstream at the hillsides crowded with old and new buildings, domes, minarets and towers.

She murmured agreement, inwardly amazed that she should be seeing it with him, of all people, beside her.

'That must be Seraglio Point where the sultans had their discarded concubines drowned,' said Richard, a few minutes later. 'There were often quite a number of foreign girls in the harem, I believe. Reluctant recruits who'd been captured and sold by pirates and brigands.' There was a slight glint in his eyes as he looked down at her. 'Had you been travelling without a protector in those times, you'd have stood a good chance of becoming an unwilling odalisque.'

She said, 'Most women were slaves then anyway. It probably wasn't much worse being a sultan's concubine than a European wife with a despotic husband.'

'I don't think the ones who ended up in a weighted sack at the bottom of the Bosporus would have agreed with you, poor little wretches.'

'You may feel sorry for them now, but I expect, if you'd lived in those times and been a sultan or a pasha, you'd have had a harem like everyone else with the means and opportunity,' she said crisply.

He looked amused. 'I might—yes. But it wasn't only the concubines who had a hard time. So did the sultan's younger brothers. They spent their lives in a place called the Golden Cage, and their concubines had to have their ovaries removed. If any did become pregnant, they were drowned.'

They were both leaning on the rail and suddenly he moved closer so that their arms were touching. The contact had no significance. It was forced on him by a stout man pushing between Richard and the person on the other side of him in order to spit something into the water below. Nor, because of their cold-weather clothing,

was it the intimate contact it would have been on a warm
day.

'Sorry to crowd you,' said Richard.

His apology made the fat man glance at him. He
grinned, showing appalling teeth, and said something to
Richard in Turkish, at the same time giving him a
friendly clap on the shoulder.

To Nicola's surprise, Richard answered him in what
she took to be Turkish.

It didn't seem to surprise the fat man, who responded
even more affably and then noticed Nicola. To her surprise and discomfiture he gave her the appraising look
she had seen Turkish men giving Sylvie while they were
sightseeing.

This was followed by a nudge in Richard's ribs,
another remark and a hearty guffaw, releasing a strong
gust of garlic fumes. Then with another slap on Richard's
back, he left them.

'How come you speak Turkish?' she asked, as Richard
moved back to his previous position.

'I don't... only a few useful phrases. He was obviously being friendly, so I said the Turkish equivalent
of, "Hello, glad to know you; how are you?"' He gave
her another of his amused looks. 'I understood what he
said about you because it's an old Turkish proverb. "The
beauty of a woman is measured in kilos". He mistook
the padding in your jacket for the cuddlesome curves
Turks in his age-group admire.'

'You must have a very retentive memory.' For some
things, she added mentally.

'I had the good luck to be born with what's sometimes called a photographic memory. It doesn't mean I
remember everything I see or read. But when I want to
retain something, usually I can.'

All Nicola's reasons for disliking him, which had been
in temporary abeyance, swiftly revived.

Clearly he hadn't wanted to retain the names and faces of the people he had sacked three years ago, she thought, averting her face.

Just then Nuray came back. 'I'm sorry I deserted you. Are you freezing to death?'

She looked, thought Nicola, very beautiful with her black curls blowing round her face and her olive skin given a rosy hue by the cold.

That Richard was thinking the same thing was evident in his expression as he disclaimed being cold.

'But you're not as warmly wrapped as we are. You should have stayed on the coach, Nuray. This trip is no novelty for you and we could have managed by ourselves. I have a few words of Turkish.'

'You do? That's unusual. Most tourists don't bother even to learn to say thank you.'

Nicola had bothered and had already said *tesekkür* several times, but she didn't say so.

'I expect my accent is atrocious.' Richard said something in Turkish and raised an enquiring eyebrow.

Nuray's dark eyes sparkled with laughter. 'No, your accent is good, but where did you learn to say *that*? Not from a language book, I'm sure.'

'No, from a Turk in London.'

'Ah, that explains it.'

What had he said to her? Nicola wondered. Judging by Nuray's expression, something complimentary and possibly mildly risqué. But clearly she didn't object to him flirting with her. If she had no steady boyfriend it must make her job more enjoyable when a group of trekkers included an attractive unattached man.

The ferry was approaching its berth on the far side of the straits. Very soon they would disembark in Asia.

CHAPTER THREE

BEFORE they boarded the train, Nuray held a briefing on the platform.

'There are two compartments reserved for us. The allocation of bunks is based on my experience of these journeys. It's better for the top bunks to be occupied by the most agile members of the group. As we shall be leaving the train at four-thirty in the morning, and most people sleep partly dressed, I'm sure you won't mind sharing your compartment with members of the opposite sex.'

After a pause to see if anyone disagreed, she went on, 'Here is the plan I have worked out. If you don't like my arrangements, please tell me. I don't want anyone to be unhappy.'

She held up a clipboard with two groups of names written as large as the sheet of paper would permit.

Scanning the list, Nicola saw that she had been given a middle bunk opposite Janet. Philip would be sleeping above her with Richard in the other top bunk. The bottom bunks were allocated to the married couple, Bob and Joan Tufnell.

'You'll find there's a place for your kitbags alongside the top bunks, above the train's corridor,' said Nuray. 'When the luggage has been stowed, there'll be time to buy drinks and snacks from the station kiosks before we leave at five-thirty. Please make sure you're on board at five twenty-five. We don't want anyone left behind.'

For twelve people, all with a large kitbag and most with a day-pack as well, to make their way along a narrow corridor and arrange themselves and their baggage in the confined space of two railway carriages could have resulted in a confused scrimmage and possibly some frayed tempers.

But whatever happened next door, in Nicola's compartment Richard took charge of the operation. If his self-appointed command was resented by the two other men, neither objected to being told what to do, or to the authoritative tone of a man who might give his orders in the form of suggestions but nevertheless expected to have them obeyed without argument.

Nuray appeared in the doorway. 'If you want to do some shopping, I'll keep an eye on your things. Later, when we all go to the restaurant, the conductor will lock the compartments for us.'

At one of the station kiosks, Nicola bought a bottle of water, chocolate and a ring-shaped bread roll called a *simit* scattered with sesame seeds.

She had never travelled by a night train before and found the bustle of the station, the babble of Turkish voices and the fact that she was now in Asia, *en route* to the Taurus Mountains, very exciting.

To her brother Peter this kind of adventure was commonplace. But her own foreign holidays had been limited to a school trip to Italy, a week in Spain with her ex-boyfriend and a few days in the Dordogne region of France, working on a manuscript with an author who lived there.

Remembering that book and her enthusiasm for it, she sighed as she walked back to the train.

Richard had returned to the carriage before her and was there on his own, peeling a lemon.

'Can I interest you in a gin and tonic? No ice, I'm afraid, and I'm using slices of lemon rather than twists of peel.'

Tempted by the offer, yet reluctant to be beholden to him in any way, Nicola decided that for this one night, in these special circumstances, she would try to forget they had met before and pretend he was just another trekker.

'Yes, please.'

He had just poured a generous slosh of gin into her plastic mug when Janet and Philip came back.

'Happy hour!' said Richard. 'The drinks are on me but you'll have to supply the containers.'

The train was late starting. When at last it did move, it didn't pick up much speed. Sipping a second round of drinks and eating Turkish crisps provided by Bob and Joan, they passed seemingly endless blocks of suburban apartments.

By now it had begun to snow and the daylight was fading rapidly. The temperature inside the train was starting to rise.

Nuray appeared in the corridor and slid back the door of their carriage. 'We've been discussing what time to have dinner. The restaurant isn't large. To be sure of sitting together, we should go early.'

'The sooner we eat, the sooner we can turn in,' said Bob. 'It's going to be a short night.'

Most of the tables in the restaurant car were for four people, with tables for two on the other side of the aisle. As yet there was no one there but the two check-waist-coated waiters and a man drinking tea.

Nicola sat with Miles and two people with whom neither she nor anyone else had so far had much to do. She knew their names were Stuart Ladbroke and Lorna Wood but up to now they had been engrossed in each other. Tonight they seemed more sociable and very soon Miles and Stuart discovered a mutual interest in birdlife.

This subject appeared to bore Lorna. 'I'm not crazy about ancient cities either,' she confided to Nicola. 'But Stuart had booked this holiday before we met and he didn't want to change it so I said I'd come. Last winter I went to the Seychelles. The boyfriend I had then was crazy about snorkelling. I just lay on the beach all day and in the evening we went dancing. It was great.'

But it wasn't diplomatic to mention it while her current boyfriend was monitoring their conversation with one ear, thought Nicola.

While the other girl continued to talk about the bargain-price leather coats and bags she had heard were to be found in Turkey, Nicola's thoughts turned back four years to her own experience of holidaying with a man.

That too had been a walking tour, but not with a group. She and Ian had been on their own, staying in a small Spanish *hostal* and spending their days exploring the surrounding countryside. At that time of year, late February, the almond groves had been in blossom.

Her parents had liked Ian and, although they hadn't really approved of her going on holiday with him, they had accepted that times had changed since their day and it might not be a bad thing for young people to be on the closest possible terms before committing themselves to marriage.

Oddly enough it had been her brother Peter who had disapproved of the holiday. He had never liked Ian and subsequent events had proved him right. When she had lost her job, Ian, who was also in publishing, had seemed to feel her dismissal would be prejudicial to his prospects. He hadn't actually dropped her like a hot potato, but he hadn't wanted to be seen with her at publishing functions and the time they spent together had dwindled. Eventually she had heard he was seeing someone else. When asked if it was true, he had admitted that it was. It had been the end of her first and only love-affair.

A burst of laughter from the next table brought her back to the present. Looking past Lorna, still in full spate about clothes, Nicola gathered that Richard had just told an amusing anecdote. He wasn't laughing himself, but his expression was amused and the others at his table were falling about.

Perhaps, in a way, she should be grateful to him. He had ruined her career but had saved her from a future disaster in her private life. If he hadn't sacked her, Ian might have married her, only to let her down later.

Presently, at Richard's suggestion, the women returned to the carriage to prepare for bed ahead of the men. He and Philip had lowered the six couchettes before the compartment was locked.

Janet was the first to try out the train's facilities.

'The washrooms aren't good, but the WCs are unspeakable!' she reported, with an exaggerated shudder.

'Never mind,' Joan said comfortably. 'It's only for this one night, and we knew it wouldn't be the Orient Express, didn't we? The brochure warned us to be prepared for primitive conditions at times.'

Nicola's brother had also briefed her on what he jokingly called the Turkish Loo Experience. She returned from her trip along the corridor still smiling at the thought of how various people she knew would react to it.

Joan had gone to one of the washrooms and Janet was standing in the aisle between the bunks, creaming her hands.

'You found it amusing?' she said, raising her eyebrows.

Nicola nodded. 'If you imagine the most pompous person you know crouching over a hole in the floor in a moving train, with no hand-holds, it does conjure some rather hilarious visions, don't you think?'

'No, I do not!' said Janet emphatically. 'I shall travel first class on the way back—if this ghastly train has a first class.'

'Why did you come on this holiday if you don't like roughing it?'

'If you want to meet interesting men it's no use going on a cruise or to one of the luxury resorts,' said Janet, with unexpected candour. 'Cruises are seething with widows. Luxury resorts are full of married men, elderly lechers and on-the-make toyboys. It's an unfortunate fact of life that attractive men are mainly found doing uncomfortable things like trekking, sailing and pot-holing.

I do draw the line at that, but some degree of discomfort seems inevitable.'

'Doesn't your work bring you into contact with lots of men?' Nicola asked.

'Mostly they're married. Who needs that kind of hassle? Both Richard and Philip are single. Philip's not my type, but Richard is.'

'If you're staking a claim, don't worry,' Nicola told her drily. 'Neither of them is my type.'

They were in their bunks, with the curtains drawn across the corridor windows, when a tap on the glass announced the return of the men.

Nicola was reading by the dim light from the ceiling. The couchettes had neither curtains nor individual reading lamps.

'Feel free to use my bunk as a step to get up to yours,' Janet said to Richard.

'Thanks, but that won't necessary. Bob's berth is the one we'll use.' He reached for his day-pack, took out a wet pack and disappeared again.

Philip was the first to return from his ablutions. Watching his awkward clamber into the bunk above hers made Nicola wonder why he had chosen this holiday. Although slim, he was far from agile. Maybe his reason was the reverse of Janet's: he hoped to meet the single women he didn't encounter at work or in his normal social life.

When Richard returned to the carriage, he unlaced his heavy boots, placed them neatly together by the door, stepped lightly on the edge of Bob's bunk and with a single lithe movement swung himself up to the bunk above Janet's.

There, with economical movements suggesting that it wasn't the first time he had undressed in a confined space, he shed both his shirt and trousers and folded them.

Nicola hadn't meant to watch him undress but she had been distracted from her book by the muscular movement which had taken him from the floor to the upper berth. Now, revealed by the close-fitting T-shirt he was wearing under his outer shirt, his upper arms showed powerful muscles between shoulder and elbow.

To her chagrin, he caught her looking at him. 'If you want to go on reading, I have a good flashlight you can borrow.'

'I have a torch, thanks. But I'm going to try to sleep. Goodnight.'

She closed her book, turned towards the wall and lay down.

'Is everyone ready for lights out?' he asked.

Everyone was, and after a chorus of goodnights and rustling movements there was silence in the compartment apart from the rumbling of the train's wheels and the comings and goings in the corridor.

Nicola slept fitfully, waking each time the train stopped. Sometimes she dozed but mostly she lay thinking about Janet's reason for coming on this trip and her own non-existent love-life.

She had set the alarm on her watch to go off half an hour before they were due to disembark. But what roused her from a doze was the overhead light being switched on, followed by an irritable exclamation from the bunk above her.

'Sorry, but it's time we were up,' said Richard. Already dressed, he returned his own bunk to its upright position.

This allowed the unflatteringly hard light of the fluorescent tubes to fall full on Janet. She was wearing a black silk eye-mask. Like Nicola, she had slept in silk thermals, but Nicola's top had a round neckline and she was wearing a light sports bra under it. Janet's had a low V-neck which, as she pushed up the mask and raised herself on her elbows, gave an arresting view of her unsupported breasts, their shape clearly outlined by the fine silk jersey fabric.

As he finished securing his bunk, Richard could hardly have failed to notice them, thought Nicola.

Not that his activities had been arrested by the display of Janet's opulent curves. He said, 'Show a leg, Philip. Once you're out, we can close your bunk and give Nicola some headroom.'

Muttering complaints at being disturbed, Philip landed on the floor with a heavy thud. When his bunk had been stowed and Richard had left the compartment, he said to Nicola, 'What a bloody awful time of night to be dragged out of bed. I haven't slept much, have you?'

'Enough,' she said cheerfully, slipping her feet into her boots. 'Give me a shove with my bunk, will you? Then Bob will have some headroom.'

Nuray appeared. 'When the train stops, please don't dawdle. We must get off as quickly as possible,' she warned them. 'If you look outside, you'll see there's been heavy snow in this area, so you'll need your warmest clothes. It will be cold crossing the mountains.'

With six people trying to dress and pack their belongings in a confined space, they would never have been ready if Richard hadn't organised them, especially as both Janet and Philip admitted to being useless without the cup of strong coffee they both needed to get them going.

'Coffee comes later. Right now you have to hustle or you'll be trekking solo from somewhere down the line, and that could be awkward,' Richard said, folding Janet's bedding for her.

With his help she was ready when the train began to slow down.

'Can't see any sign of a station,' said Bob, peering out of the window.

Nicola was already in the corridor with her kitbag. The conductor beckoned her to follow him. By the time they reached the door at the end of the corridor, the train was almost at a standstill.

Outside there was nothing to be seen but the thick snow lying on the ground in the area illuminated by the lights of the train. Beyond that there was only darkness.

The train stopped. The conductor climbed down and, turning, reached up for her kitbag. As she handed it to him with a grateful, *'Tesekkür,'* there was a shout from near by and someone came running up.

She was confronted by a man with a thick crop of curly black hair, snapping black eyes and a wide grin.

'Good morning...welcome. I'm Serif, your driver. Let me help you.'

As if she were a young child, he put his hands under her armpits and with no visible effort swung her off her feet and set her on the frozen grass.

'This,' said Miss Goodge, a few minutes later, 'is how I imagine Siberia. Where exactly are we, I wonder?'

As she spoke, her warm breath turned to puffs of vapour in the icy night air.

No one answered her question. Nuray and the newcomer were deep in conversation and the others were still adjusting to the sub-zero temperature.

Thankful for the loan of her brother's jacket and two pairs of socks inside her boots, Nicola watched the train starting to move and waved to the conductor as he continued his journey, leaving his two compatriots and the group of foreigners standing beside the track.

'Come along.' Serif led the way to a large four-wheel-drive truck of the type used for transport in deserts and other difficult terrain.

Leaping aboard and helping the women to hoist their baggage up the steep steps, he showed them how to open the baggage lockers under the two long rows of sideways-facing seats.

'As there aren't many of you, there's plenty of room to make yourselves comfortable. Soon we'll stop for a hot drink.'

Leaving them to decide where to sit, he sprang down the steps and went to the separate driver's cab. Moments later there was a hiss like an air brake and the double doors at the nearside rear of the truck slid into their closed position. The engine roared. The truck jolted and bounced over some yards of rough ground before turning on to a roadway. From the cab came a cheery triple blast on the horn as Serif accelerated, making it clear why the two rows of seats had sturdy metal foot-rails fitted to the floor in front of them.

The roadside café, heated by a closed stove, where they were served with glasses of sweet tea, was the Turkish equivalent of a lorry drivers' pull-in.

'Now everyone feels better—yes?' Serif asked, when the glasses were being refilled by a man who, like him, hadn't shaved since yesterday morning.

Their dark stubble made Nicola notice that the only man present with a smooth jaw was Richard. He must have shaved last thing last night.

Mrs Tufnell joined them, a cheerful-faced busty woman in her fifties, with permed brown hair turning grey.

'You're not superstitious, I hope,' she greeted them. 'With the driver, we're thirteen.'

'As far as I'm concerned, the important thing about Serif is whether he's a safe driver. He's certainly fast,' Nicola said drily.

He was standing by the stove, one hand tucked in the pocket of his black leather windcheater, the other holding a glass of tea. He caught her eye and came over.

'You know my name, but I don't know yours.'

She introduced the two older women, after which Miss Goodge asked them all to call her Hilary.

'Hilary...Joan...and Nicola,' he repeated. 'Is this your first time in Turkey?'

They told him it was and Hilary asked, 'How far are we driving today?'

'A long way. But you can sleep and later we'll stop for breakfast. I'm the only one who must stay awake,' he said, smiling. 'Don't worry. I'm not tired. I went to bed early last night.'

'You speak very good English,' said Joan.

'Of course. You don't speak Turkish, do you? So I must speak English...and German. We have many German tourists.'

When Richard joined them, Hilary said, 'With you two big chaps in the party, we should survive whatever amazing adventures the trip has in store for us. Richard, this is Serif. Serif...Richard.'

The men shook hands and smiled at each other, but it seemed to Nicola that there was a certain wariness in the looks they exchanged.

Before they could have any conversation, Serif was called away by the café's proprietor.

'He seems nice,' said Joan. 'We've struck lucky with the people in charge of us, haven't we? Bob and I've been on holidays where we hardly ever saw the couriers and they weren't all that friendly when they did condescend to appear.'

'Really? Perhaps you've been unlucky,' said Hilary. 'All the couriers and guides I've encountered have been very good at their jobs. What's your experience, Richard?'

'It's the first guided tour I've been on. I didn't choose this trip. It was booked by a friend who's interested in classical archaeology. A few days ago his father was taken seriously ill and is probably going to die. Sam couldn't leave his mother to cope on her own. He was going to cancel the holiday but I said I'd come in his place.'

'So you're here on impulse,' said Hilary.

'That's right. I needed a break, the tickets were there for the taking and here I am. Whether I'll regret it remains to be seen. We do seem to have struck an exceptionally cold spell. But maybe the weather will be better once we're over the mountains. May I get you some more tea, ladies?'

'He's very nice too,' said Joan approvingly, as he took her glass to be refilled. She gave Nicola a roguish glance. 'With him and Philip and now a good-looking driver, there's plenty of talent, as our daughter would say. It's no fun for you younger people if a group's all one sex, is it?'

'To me Serif looks as if he may be a bit of a brigand where girls are concerned,' said Hilary. 'I'd expect him to target Sylvie as being the most impressionable. She's gazing at him now.'

So was Lorna, Nicola noticed. While Stuart was talking to Philip, Lorna was eyeing Serif.

The long drive south was less of an ordeal for Nicola than for some of the others.

She had with her a sheepskin foot-muff, borrowed from her mother, and with this, and her sleeping-bag tucked round her legs, she scarcely felt the cold numbing the feet of others less well-equipped.

What none of them realised until after the tea-stop was that the truck's heater had broken down. It was warm in the driver's cab. They could see through the window at the back of it that Serif had shed his black jacket and Nuray her thick dark overcoat. But the back of the truck was like a refrigerator, and, while the two couples on board could huddle together for warmth, those on their own had only their clothes and other wrappings to protect them from the Arctic conditions.

Although the interior lights were on, they were too dim and the truck was jolting too much to make reading possible. How anyone could sleep was a mystery to

Nicola, but several people seemed to be dozing, including the two on either side of Richard.

After a while she put on her head-set and passed the time listening to music. By the time she had played both sides of the cassette the sky was starting to lighten, gradually revealing long vistas of rolling hills.

On the other side of the truck Sylvie, deep asleep, was lolling against Richard. He didn't seem to mind. Although his eyes were scanning the view through the windows in Nicola's side, she had the impression that his thoughts were elsewhere.

Full daylight brought no relief from the cold. The journey began to seem interminable. By flexing her toes and ankles inside the fleecy muff, Nicola kept the blood coursing through them. But for some of the others cold feet were becoming painful.

At last they came to a small town. To everyone's relief the truck stopped outside a café. It wasn't the sort of establishment any of them would have chosen for a coffee-stop in Europe. But this was rural Asia Minor.

'Ooh, let me get close to that stove!' Joan exclaimed, making a bee-line for the source of the café's warmth. 'My poor feet feel like lumps of ice.'

'On the other side of the mountains it will be warm,' Serif promised. 'Maybe not tomorrow, but the next day you will be swimming.'

A chorus of sceptical comments greeted this statement.

'It's true, I promise you. Look——' He unbuttoned his shirt to display a deeply tanned chest. 'This is from lying in the sun on the beach where you'll be swimming. If you don't believe me, ask Nuray.'

'The weather is usually very nice,' the Turkish girl confirmed. 'We've come a long way from Istanbul and we still have some way to go. The sun will be shining when we get to Antalya.'

'Why is the heater kaput? asked Richard. 'Can't it be repaired?'

'Serif will have it mended. I'm sorry it's cold for you. There's room for one more person in the front if anyone would like to join us.'

'I'm staying with Bob,' said Joan.

'I brought a hot-water bottle,' said Hilary. 'Would you ask them to refill it for me, Nuray?'

The Turkish girl smiled and nodded. 'Would you like to come in the front with us, Janet?' she enquired.

Richard came over to Nicola. 'What were you listening to with that rapt expression on your face?' he asked.

'It could have been one of several things. The tape is a recording made for me by my brother. It's a mixture of favourite pieces to save me bringing a lot of tapes.'

'Is your brother in the music business?'

She shook her head. 'He's an expert on travelling light.'

'If you run out of books, I have two or three you might like. Which guide book did you bring?'

'The one recommended in the Amazing Adventures travel pack.'

He said, 'I've read it. It's not as good as the one published by my people. We have an excellent travel list.'

The remark revived her antagonism. She was tempted to flash back, I had a good list too—until you scrapped it.

Common sense kept her silent. This wasn't the time or the place for a confrontation.

She restricted herself to saying, with a marked lack of interest, 'Really?' before turning to speak to someone else.

Perhaps even that was unwise. He could hardly fail to recognise the brush-off and be annoyed by it. Men like Richard Russell weren't accustomed to receiving signals that their conversation wasn't interesting.

CHAPTER FOUR

DURING breakfast, a long-distance coach drew up outside. Most of the disembarking women passengers wore headscarves arranged to cover their foreheads and fall on their shoulders. One old lady wore baggy Turkish trousers but the girl on whose arm she was leaning, perhaps her granddaughter, was dressed in jeans and a fashionable sweater.

'*Their* bus is heated,' Lorna said, pouting.

Overhearing her, Serif gave her his dazzling black-eyed smile. 'But now you've had a good breakfast and when you see our beautiful mountains you won't care about a little cold. Why not come beside me in the cab?'

'She's with me,' Stuart said curtly.

'Ah...I see.' Serif inclined his head in amused acknowledgment of the fact that Lorna was private property.

Later, as they left the restaurant, he said to Nicola, 'The man sitting next to you...is he your boyfriend?'

'I met Philip in Istanbul the day before yesterday.'

'And the girl sleeping with her head on the big guy's shoulder? Is she with him?' Clearly he had been watching the trekkers through his inside rear-view mirror.

She shook her head. 'Apart from Joan and her husband, and Stuart and Lorna, all the rest of us are singles.'

'That's good.'

'Why?'

'Because that's the reason for holidays. To make new friends...perhaps to fall in love...like Nuray's sister and her English husband. Perhaps you'll find a Turkish boyfriend. You're a lovely girl...the kind Turkish men like.'

50

Nicola laughed. 'I may have a boyfriend at home.'

'But no one important. If he existed, he wouldn't let you come here without him.'

'Everyone on board, please,' called Nuray.

There were others who hadn't yet boarded, but Nicola had the feeling the summons was directed at her. Maybe Nuray didn't like Serif flirting with the female trekkers, either because they might take him too seriously or because the Turkish girl had her own eye on him.

As the highway ascended the pass over the Taurus Mountains, it became even colder. The scenery was magnificent with snow-covered peaks and crags towering on every side, but soon the view was obscured by ice forming on the windows.

Hanging on to the overhead hand-rail, Hilary came from her place at the rear and said to Nicola, 'If you and I share your quilt, Philip can borrow my rug.'

Miles was dozing, his chin on his chest. Taking care not to disturb him, Nicola sat down in the empty seat next to his and spread her unzipped sleeping-bag across Hilary's legs and her own.

'It was foolish of Philip not to provide himself with all the necessaries,' said Hilary, the noise of the engine and the Turkish music being relayed from Serif's radio ensuring that this remark wouldn't reach his ears. 'We had clear instructions on what to bring. I suppose he didn't bother to read them. It wouldn't surprise me to find that he hasn't brought any books either. What did you bring?'

Sylvie had fallen asleep again but not, this time, with her coppery head on Richard's shoulder. Cocooned in her striped sleeping-bag, she was lying curled up across two seats.

From Sylvie, Nicola's gaze shifted to the strongly marked profile of the man she had snubbed. She regretted it now, knowing it had sprung from pique, because he had no recollection of seeing her before. And he wouldn't let it pass, she felt sure. Somehow, sooner or later, he would make that snub boomerang.

Absently studying his profile while listening to Hilary talking about Turkish literature, Nicola saw that everything she had been told about Richard Russell was there in his strongly marked profile, his intelligence indicated by the high forehead from which his dark hair sprang as thickly but without the curling disorder of Serif's hair.

Her gaze moved downwards past the bridge of his nose to the aggressive thrust of his chin. Between those two bony projections were the softer lines of his mouth, the amorous curve of the lower lip endorsing the rumours about his penchant for beautiful, stylish women.

According to the publishing grapevine, mere glamour wasn't enough. It was said that his girlfriends had to be as diverting conversationally as they were between the sheets.

A tall order, thought Nicola. I wonder if they get as good as they give?

The road was descending now. Soon the ice on the windows had turned to moisture which Richard wiped away with a cloth he found in a locker at the front of the truck.

For the next hour the way was downhill. Occasionally they passed ramshackle, isolated dwellings or small clusters of houses, but there was no sign of a café on this stretch of highway.

People were starting to grumble when suddenly the truck stopped, the rear door wheezed open and Nuray appeared.

'As it's on our way to Antalya we are going to visit the ruins of Termessos,' she told them. 'It's an easy walk which you'll like after sitting for so long.'

'I'm *starving*!' Sylvie exclaimed, emerging from her bag, her cheeks flushed from her long nap.

'You didn't eat enough breakfast,' Richard reminded her.

'I don't like cheese first thing in the morning.'

'It's what the Turks like for breakfast, so either you eat it or go hungry,' he said unsympathetically.

To Nicola's disappointment, their accommodation at Antalya wasn't a timber-built *pansiyon* in the old part of the city, but a small modern hotel off one of the main shopping streets.

Nor was she to share with Hilary as she had expected.

'For the first week of the trek we find it best for the single people to have different room-mates each time we move to a new place,' Nuray explained, before handing out their keys. 'In this way everyone makes friends more quickly—especially the shy people.'

She referred to her clipboard. 'Tonight Hilary is sharing with Sylvie, and Janet with Nicola.'

'I shouldn't think this place has been built long. Everything looks brand-new,' said Janet, flopping wearily on to one of the twin beds in their room. 'I'm bushed! Being woken in the middle of the night doesn't suit my metabolism. You can have the shower first.'

When, swathed in a large white bath-towel, her wet head wrapped in a smaller one, Nicola returned to the bedroom, Janet was asleep.

Nicola left her undisturbed while she rough-dried and combed her hair. Then, because she wanted to use her dryer and there wasn't time for Janet to have a long nap, she gave her a gentle shake.

Janet was still doing her face when Nicola went down to the lobby and walked outside to enjoy the sun on her face. Richard was there before her.

In view of her offhand response to his remark at the breakfast stop, she wondered if he would ignore her. But it seemed his punctilious manners were too deeply ingrained to allow him to be discourteous, whatever he might feel inwardly.

Rising from the low stone wall where he had been sitting, he said pleasantly, 'A hot shower is a great reviver, isn't it?'

'It was wonderful.' Impulsively, she added, 'I was rather abrupt at the café this morning. Put it down to tiredness, will you?'

For a moment or two he was silent, looking down at her with an expression she couldn't interpret. Then he said, 'No need to apologise. It was understandable.'

What did that mean? That he *did* know who she was and therefore wasn't surprised when her hostility had shown through?

'We were all a bit uptight at breakfast,' he went on. 'Being dumped off a train in the small hours and bounced up and down in that rattle-trap——' with a gesture at the nearby truck ' —is enough to jangle anyone's nerves. Here come some of the others.'

They had lunch at a *pide salonu* serving Turkish pizzas.

'If you thought pizza was an Italian idea, you were wrong,' said Nuray. 'It was a Turkish invention. We also gave the world tulips, cherries, parchment and angora wool . . . and smallpox inoculations were being given in Turkey seventy years before your Dr Jenner introduced vaccination in England. So I think we've made a good contribution to civilisation, don't you?' she asked, smiling.

The restaurant's tables being round ones, the group couldn't sit together. Nicola shared with Stuart, Lorna and Serif, who helped them to choose from the menu.

Nuray came to their table. 'Serif, will you find out what everyone wants to drink, please?'

He nodded. 'What would you like, Nicola? There's no alcohol served here.'

'Water for me, please.'

While he was away from the table and the other two were gazing at a children's programme on the large colour TV, Nicola found herself watching Richard and wondering why she had felt constrained to apologise to him.

The reason wasn't only that it seemed a tactical error to distance herself from anyone with whom she had to live at close quarters for two weeks. It was more complex.

Could it be that, in spite of what he had done to her, she was attracted to him?

When Serif returned, she asked, 'How long have you worked for the tour company?'

'Since I was a student. Our universities have only two terms: from October to January and March to June. In the vacations many students work in the tourist industry. Turkey is a young country. More than half our population is under twenty years old. We have forty universities, but every year there are seven hundred thousand applications for places. I was lucky to get a place. But of course I am very intelligent,' he added, with a grin.

'What subjects were you studying?'

'Languages ... German, French and Italian. Then the company offered me a permanent job as a driver. I know something about motors, you see. I was always interested in them and I can do running repairs if the truck breaks down.'

Nicola wondered if he had actually graduated. If he had, surely he could have got a better job than driving for a tour company? Perhaps he had failed his exams. Or even been sent down for breaking university rules.

Serif said, 'One day I shall be a famous poet.'

'A poet?' she exclaimed, startled. He seemed to have none of the attributes she associated with poets. Everything about him suggested a man of action, not an intellectual, and certainly not one who expressed his ideas in verse.

'Do you like poetry? If you're interested, I'll introduce you to some of our Turkish poets.'

Because poetry seemed an unlikely avocation for him, Nicola couldn't help wondering if this was a tactic he used to charm susceptible-looking female trekkers.

Their food arrived, for Nicola a salad and a generous circle of *pide* topped with melted cheese. The cold in the mountains and the walk to Termessos had made her very hungry and she ate it with relish. Lorna, who had chosen a meat topping, picked at hers with less enthusiasm.

When Serif tried to get a four-way conversation going, she and Stuart responded in monosyllables, apparently more interested in what was happening on the screen.

Eventually, looking at Nicola, Serif raised both eyebrows, shrugged and gave up the effort to draw a livelier response from them.

Later, when Nuray was leading a walk through town, he fell into step beside Nicola. 'The two who sat with us at lunch. Why do they come to Turkey if they only want to watch television?'

Nicola had been pondering that question herself. 'They may have had a row. They're not walking together and at lunch Stuart looked rather tight-lipped.'

'Tight-lipped? I don't know this expression.'

'It means repressing annoyance.'

'My English will improve, talking to you. You have a good vocabulary.'

His eyes were focused on her mouth. Although she felt sure it was part of his technique, she couldn't deny that it sent a faint tremor through her. He was dangerously attractive, this big black-eyed Turk. And clearly adept at seduction. It was just as well he hadn't targeted Sylvie. She wouldn't stand a chance of resisting him.

That night they dined at another small restaurant where a table for thirteen was ready for them.

Earlier Nicola had washed her cotton shirt, rolled it in a towel for half an hour and then left it suspended on a hanger in front of the hot-air unit. Apart from changing her shirt and underclothes, she was wearing the jeans and sweatshirt in which she had started the journey.

But Janet had put on clinging black stretch-velvet leggings, a loose black and silver sweater and oversize large silver hoop earrings. She had also stepped up her make-up.

Nicola sat between Miles and Stuart. Janet was sitting beside Richard, talking with great animation, the earrings catching the light with each shift of her head.

While they ate, a musician played an electronic keyboard. All the other diners were men, Nicola noticed.

The meal concluded with fresh fruit, and Serif had a glass of *raki* with his coffee. The colourless spirit clouded when he topped up the glass with water.

'We call it lion's milk. Try it.' He offered the glass to Sylvie.

She took a small sip, immediately pulling a face and saying, 'Yuck...it's horrible!'

Later, outside the restaurant, Nuray asked what they would like to do for the rest of the evening. The four older people wanted an early night. Nicola decided to join them.

Sylvie asked if the town had discos. Richard said he wanted a brisk walk and would find his own way back to the hotel. His long-legged stride had already taken him a hundred yards in the opposite direction when the five early-nighters left the others discussing the options.

'What it is to be young,' Joan said, a shade wistfully.

Bob tucked his wife's arm through his. 'Being young's not that wonderful, love. We'll have a nice drink of hot chocolate and read in bed for a bit. I reckon we'll enjoy that more than anything they'll be doing and we'll be brighter in the morning. Let's hope they come in quietly and don't disturb us.'

'I haven't the least doubt Sylvie will succeed in disturbing me,' said Hilary. 'Especially if Serif persuades her to overcome her initial aversion to *raki*.'

'Get her tight, do you mean?' said Joan. 'Oh, I don't think that's in his mind. If you ask me, Nicola is the one he fancies. He looked ever so disappointed when you said you were coming back with us, Nicola. So did Janet when Richard went off on his own.'

Nicola laughed. 'I should think Serif's only interest in any of us is guessing the size of our tips at the end of the trip. He probably has a girlfriend in Istanbul.'

'Nicola's got a head on her shoulders,' Bob said approvingly. 'It's Lorna who might take a fancy to Serif, if only to make Stuart jealous. I reckon they've got problems, those two.'

'Who hasn't?' Miles said unexpectedly. 'Problems are part and parcel of the human condition.'

They were on the wide pavement of an esplanade with room to walk five abreast. He was at the outer edge, his tall figure casting the longest shadow as they passed a street lamp.

Glancing sideways at him, it struck Nicola that he and Richard had certain similarities; that this was how Richard would look in thirty years' time.

Tall, spare, active, authoritative.

She wondered if Hilary found Miles attractive. And why, when she was better-looking than Joan, and more intelligent, she had never married.

When I'm Hilary's age, shall I still be on my own? she wondered, with an inward shiver which had nothing to do with the coldness of the night.

'Good morning.'

Alone in the breakfast-room and intent on the fashion show on the ubiquitous television, Nicola hadn't noticed Richard's entrance.

'Good morning.'

Watching him use the coffee urn, she wondered if he would sit with her or at one of the other tables.

'May I join you?'

'Please do,' she said politely.

'I'm surprised we're the only ones down. I'd have thought the muezzin would have woken the dead.'

'One would think so,' she agreed. 'But Janet was still fast asleep when I slipped out for a walk. Did you hear the others come in, or were you out late yourself?'

'I was in bed by ten-thirty. Whatever Antalya's night-life is like in high season, I don't think there's much on offer at this time of year. Not that nightclubs and discos appeal to me. Do you like them?'

She shook her head. 'I enjoy dancing at private parties, but not to mega-decibel pop in crowded clubs. Not even when I was eighteen.'

He looked sideways at her. 'How long ago was that?'

'Eight years.'

'You don't look twenty-six.'

'How old are you?'

'Thirty-four... going on forty-five,' he added wryly.

'Why do you say that?'

'The past few years have been a difficult time. A lot of publishing houses have gone to the wall. Now the power in the book industry is in the hands of the big chains of retail outlets. The firm I work for has kept afloat and solvent, but it's been tough going.'

She wondered why he spoke of the firm he worked for, rather than the firm he ran. Did he really see himself as a cog—even if a super-cog—in the UK wheel of the American mega-corporation founded by his grandfather?

Or could it be that, because he was among people who didn't operate at his level, he was deliberately playing down the power he wielded?

'But haven't you found it rewarding to keep your firm in the black when others were sliding into the red?' she asked.

'In many ways—yes. But there's a down-side. Some years ago a book came out in the States called *When Bad Things Happen to Good People*. That's the side of my work I don't like...making decisions which are going to be bad for good people in order to keep the train on the rails, as they say.'

As he spoke, he was spreading white cheese on a chunk of crusty loaf. Nicola shot a covert look at him. Did he really have no idea that sitting beside him was someone for whom one of his decisions had been catastrophic?

'Part of my problem may be that I never took the time off between school and college, or between college and my first job, that most of my contemporaries did,' he went on. 'I never back-packed around Europe or South-East Asia or wherever. Did you do that?'

'No, I went straight from school to secretarial school and then did some temping until I got my first proper job.'

'You said you worked in a bookshop. Which one?'

'Chatham's.'

She had had the job for eighteen months, having got it on the strength of her computer skills and a glowing reference from her previous employer. Chatham's was arguably the most famous bookshop in the West End of London.

'In a manner of speaking, we're in the same line of business,' said Richard.

'Don't you want to forget about business while you're on holiday?'

'Certain aspects of it, yes. But books are my pleasure as well as my work. I'm not short of other interests. But they're relaxations which have to be fitted in to a pretty tight working schedule. For instance I have a pilot's licence but most of my flying is across the Atlantic with all the other guys with briefcases and the *Financial Times* under their arms. Did you see a movie called *Out of Africa* with Redford and Streep in the main roles?'

'You mean those wonderful shots of the Rift Valley from the air?'

He nodded. 'You liked that sequence too, hmm?'

'It was brilliant...I really felt I was up there in the air with them. It was a great film...I came out of the cinema with red eyes and my bag full of damp tissues,' she admitted.

'Yes, those scenes at the funeral were moving. I had a lump in my throat.'

It surprised her that he should confess to being moved. Often men felt they must hide their deepest emotions.

Her ex-boyfriend had equated masculinity with a permanently stiff upper lip.

Yet no one could look more macho than the man beside her, his tall lithe frame set off by his serviceable walking clothes. But he wasn't ashamed to admit that the touching scene in which Meryl Streep, playing Karen Blixen, had spoken the valediction at her lover's graveside had stirred the same feelings in him as in Nicola, even if not to the extent of making him weep.

Then the moment of unexpected rapport came to an end as they were joined by Hilary.

After saying good morning, she said, 'My current room-mate has to be the most disorganised person I've ever encountered. Her side of our room looks as if a tornado has struck it. Such untidiness drives me mad. I'm sure you wouldn't like it either, Nicola. And how Janet put up with it on our first night in Istanbul is a mystery to me.'

'Perhaps it was she who suggested to Nuray that you should change partners,' said Miles, arriving in time to overhear this remark. 'Thereby spreading the burden, so to speak.'

'You may be right. But as far as I'm concerned one night with Sylvie is enough. She's a nice little thing in some ways, but obviously hopelessly spoilt by whoever brought her up. I shall have to speak to Nuray about it.'

'Today we are going to Perge,' Nuray announced, when the group had assembled outside the hotel's entrance. 'Perge was founded about a thousand years before Christ and was deliberately sited twenty kilometres inland to be safe from raids by the pirates who terrorised the coast. Now please board the truck and we'll get started.'

At Perge, Serif parked the truck outside the city's amphitheatre.

As she handed out tickets, Nuray said in her clear, carrying voice, 'The theatre could seat fourteen thousand people on forty-two levels. We'll climb to the top, where you'll be able to see what a large city this was.'

Nicola's admiration for the skills of the people who had designed and built the theatre was counterbalanced by the knowledge that their idea of entertainment had often included spectacles involving brutal slaughter.

Watching, from the arena, Richard's agile progress up the steps to the uppermost tiers, she didn't think that had he lived in those times he would have enjoyed the gladiatorial events. But perhaps he would have watched the slaves and other victims being butchered with an air of indifference if his career required it. She felt sure he would have been an achiever whatever age he had lived in.

I should have been a slave, she thought, with a wry smile.

As she climbed to the top, the steps being too high for her to leap up them as easily as he had, she found herself trying to reconcile her previous ideas about him with the impressions she was receiving on this trip.

The two didn't match, which made her feel confused and unsettled.

Although it was not yet mid-morning, the sun was sufficiently warm for everyone to start stripping down to their T-shirts.

As Nuray was allowing half an hour for them to explore the theatre and take photographs, Nicola wandered off by herself and sat down to bask in the sun.

She had emptied her mind of all thoughts and was luxuriating in a warmth not enjoyed since the previous summer when an unmistakable voice said, 'You must take care not to burn.'

'I put sun-filter on my face first thing this morning,' she said, opening her eyes to look up at Serif. 'Actually I tan quite easily. I'm not as fair-skinned as Sylvie.'

He sat down beside her. 'I've tried talking to her but she has nothing to say. She seems scared of me. Perhaps someone has warned her that Turkish men may try to seduce her.'

'Some of them might,' said Nicola.

'But not me. I don't make passes at nervous virgins.'

Nicola was inclined to doubt that Sylvie was as innocent as he thought, even if most Turkish girls of her age were.

She said, 'Surely, for you, it's not a good idea to make passes at anyone? If they complained, you could find yourself out of a job.'

'The women I make love to don't complain...they enjoy it,' Serif said, with a grin. 'I'm a very good lover.'

'Most men think they're wonderful drivers and wonderful lovers. Some of them are, some of them aren't.'

'You sound as if you've had a lot of experience.'

'Very little. I'm going by things I've read in books and magazines.' Then, hurriedly changing the subject, 'Don't you get bored, visiting these places repeatedly?'

'Sometimes...if the people we're guiding are boring. Then I stay in the truck and sleep...or write a poem.'

Nicola said, 'Turkish is a very musical language. I've listened to you and Nuray talking and the sounds aren't harsh to the ear like those of some languages.'

He slanted a teasing look at her. 'It sounds even better when it's whispered in your ear on a warm night by the sea. Perhaps one night soon I'll give you a demonstration.'

She said composedly, 'I'm sure everyone would like to hear you recite one of your poems to us, Serif. I think Nuray is signalling that it's time to move on.'

CHAPTER FIVE

FROM the theatre they walked to Perge's large stadium and then to the entrance to the city.

Leading them to a pillared square with traces of mosaic pavements, Nuray said, 'This was the *agora* or market-place, surrounded by shops. There would have been more to see at the beginning of this century. Unfortunately in the 1920s there was a building boom in a village near here and Perge offered a good supply of stone.'

'Would you mind if I snapped you, Nuray?' Richard asked, as she finished speaking.

'You'll get a better shot if I stand here.' She moved closer to a pillar, the naturalness of her pose showing she was used to being photographed.

Today she had shed her dark overcoat and was in jeans and an apricot sweatshirt with a coral scarf. The colours flattered her olive skin. Standing beside the tall stone column with the blue sky as a background, she had a dramatic beauty. Everyone took a photograph of her.

From the market they followed a long paved street lined with columns before retracing their steps to look around the Roman baths where two of the original pools had been excavated.

'For the Romans, the baths were like London's famous gentlemen's clubs,' she told them.

Before the take-over which had put Richard in charge, the London office of Barking & Dollis had been seething with gossip and speculation. Someone had found out that he was a member of the exclusive Racquets Club in New York, the equally exclusive Travellers' Club in Paris, and also had the entrée to a bastion of the British Establishment.

64

This news put some people against him before they met him. Nicola remembered one of her colleagues—a bolshie type who begrudged anyone having anything he didn't have—whingeing about Richard's privileged background. At the time she had defended him, saying that the new chief executive might give the company a badly needed injection of American drive and efficiency. Never dreaming, as she spoke, that she would be among the first to feel his axe.

As Nuray pointed out the tunnels where warm air had circulated, Nicola found herself thinking that, even if Richard had come from a humble background, he would have been born to lead, not to follow, to command rather than obey.

The very way he stood was indicative. While Stuart leaned against a wall and Philip sat slumped on a convenient ledge, Richard's stance was relaxed but upright, one hand holding the strap of the light pack slung on his shoulder, the thumb of his other hand hooked through the braided leather belt round his lean waist.

She looked away before he could catch her staring at him.

'Now you can look around by yourselves. At twelve o'clock we'll meet at the truck and go for lunch,' said Nuray.

The group dispersed. Nicola wanted to photograph an unusually fine marble capital she had noticed lying on the grass near the baths, perhaps dislodged from its column by an earthquake.

Richard had the same idea. When she had taken her picture she found him standing near by.

'I like all my shots to have someone in them. Apart from adding interest, it shows the scale of the subject,' he said. 'Would you mind posing for me, Nicola?'

With less assurance than Nuray she moved to stand by the fallen capital.

'That's fine, but there's no need to look so serious. How about a smile?' He took two snaps in quick succession before closing the lens cover. 'Thanks.'

'Not at all.' She expected him to walk away but he seemed to be waiting for her to move and, when she did, fell into step beside her.

'If we had a time machine, we could take ourselves back to 333 BC when Alexander the Great was here. This must have been a magnificent city in its day. I'd like to see that colonnaded street by moonlight.'

Reminded of Serif's remark about Turkish being at its most musical when murmured in a girl's ear on a warm night, she wondered what Richard's voice would sound like in those circumstances.

'I'm sure Nuray would lay on some moonlit ruins for you, if you asked her,' she said lightly.

'She might . . . in the line of duty. I gather that Serif's offer was of a private nature. Just the two of you.'

She gave him a startled glance. How could he possibly know that? He had been on the other side of the amphitheatre when Serif had been talking to her. She remembered noticing Richard standing on the edge of a long drop and thinking he must have a better head for heights than she had.

He said drily, 'The acoustics in the theatre are excellent. Not only is it possible to hear everything said in the arena from the highest row of seats, but—depending on the wind, I imagine—private conversations between people on one side of the theatre can be heard on the other.'

'Oh . . . I see,' she said, disconcerted. Then, recovering her self-possession, 'So presumably you heard my answer . . . that we'd *all* like to hear him recite some of his poems.'

'I'm prepared to wait till his verses have appeared in print,' Richard answered. 'For me, amateur poetry recitals have as little appeal as Morris dancing. Anyway that's not what he had in mind. He'd prefer an audience of one.'

He had been surveying the ruins, but now he looked down at her.

'If I were you I'd steer clear of a secluded rendezvous with that guy. From what I've heard, the Turks have a low boiling point.'

'That might not be clear to Sylvie, but at twenty-six one does have a rough idea on how cope with the two-legged wolves of this world,' she said mildly.

'If you say so. But the wolves of Asia Minor may be harder to handle than the European species. Because this is an old-fashioned country where nice girls definitely don't, it doesn't follow that the men don't try their luck with foreigners.'

'I expect they do. And probably—sometimes—successfully. But I think Serif's bright enough to know who might fall for his line and who won't.'

'Don't count on it.'

They had lunch in a village bar where, as usual, only men were to be seen. The long table, spread with a plastic cloth, had been decorated with sprays of wild narcissi stuck in empty Coke bottles. Both Hilary and Nicola leaned forward to inhale their delicate fragrance.

'Did you notice the wild anemones growing in the ruins this morning, Nicola?' Hilary asked.

After lunch they went back to Antalya to see, on the outskirts of town, the Düden waterfall pouring over a cliff into the sea.

Richard looked faintly bored by this spectacle. He had probably seen Niagara and other more impressive falls, thought Nicola. Or perhaps he was beginning to regret taking his friend's place on a holiday which didn't provide either the standard of comfort he was accustomed to, or the high-powered people with whom he was used to mixing.

However their next stop, the Archaeological Museum, was good enough to satisfy the most exacting traveller.

'This is one of the best collections in Turkey,' Nuray told them. 'It's only a short walk back to our hotel and your time is free until we meet for dinner at seven. I have to shop for our picnic tomorrow so I'll leave you to enjoy the museum.'

The exhibit Nicola liked best was a dancer, larger than life-size, carved from two kinds of limestone, her face and body white marble, her hair and garments pale grey.

She had been badly damaged and her feet were missing, as were parts of her swirling draperies. But what had survived had been cleverly suspended in its correct position. Poised on a pedestal and lit by concealed spotlights, the statue recaptured all the lithe grace of the girl who had posed for an unknown but brilliant sculptor centuries before.

When Nicola returned to the entrance hall, more than an hour later, she seemed to be the only one of the group left in the museum. Then, through glass doors leading to a terrace and garden at the rear, she saw Richard and Janet sitting at a table, drinking coffee.

Rather than intrude, she bought some postcards of the dancer, and left. This was evidently a time of day when the well-heeled young of Antalya met for soft drinks at the cafés along the esplanade. Most of the girls wore jeans and the sexes seemed to mix as freely as they did in Europe, she noticed.

Instead of going back to the hotel, she continued walking to the centre of the town. After wandering through a maze of narrow streets lined with shops selling gold jewellery, leather goods and cheap holiday clothes, she stopped at a stall displaying the blue beads thought to ward off misfortune. For the equivalent of fifty pence, she bought ten medium-sized beads as an inexpensive souvenir.

She wouldn't have been here at all if it hadn't been for the generosity of her godmother. Every year Aunt

Ruth—who was actually a schoolfriend of her mother's, not a relation—gave her an extravagant Christmas present. Two years ago it had been a desktop PC, last year a food processor and a course of aromatherapy treatments. This year it had been a holiday. Aunt Ruth had picked out five holidays she thought her god-daughter would enjoy, leaving the final choice to Nicola.

She had chosen the trek in Turkey mainly because it didn't conflict with the culmination of a very important spare-time project she was involved with. Also she hoped it would have a tonic effect on her vitality at the low point of the winter, and erase from her mind the last vestige of negative feeling about the past. Physically it had already done her good. Emotionally, because of Richard's presence, it had had the opposite effect.

That night the group dined at a large *restoran* near the harbour. Among the other diners, only two had their wives with them. The rest of the tables were occupied by groups of men.

The meal began with the appetisers known as *mezes* including a creamy yogurt and cucumber dip.

Serif, at one end of the table, was drinking his usual *raki*.

Richard had ordered wine. When his glass had been filled, he raised it in Serif's direction and said, '*Serefe!*'

'Is that the Turkish equivalent of cheers?' Miles asked.

'So I gather,' said Richard. 'Although literally it means "to honour"... is that correct, Serif?'

The Turk nodded. 'But this is the way you should do it.'

He picked up his *raki* with a finger and thumb on the rim of the glass, swung it casually over his left shoulder, passed it behind his head and then, bringing it forward, upside-down, over his right shoulder, replaced it on the table.

The main course tonight was a meat stew accompanied by boiled cracked wheat to soak up the juices.

'Tomorrow we're going for a long hike, so tonight you must eat well, Sylvie. You'll need a lot of energy,' Serif told her, as she poked at the chunks of meat.

'I never eat much.'

'That's why you're too thin.'

'I'm not thin...I'm slim,' she protested. 'I don't want to be fat.'

'A little more flesh on your body would be an improvement,' he told her. 'Didn't you think the statues in the museum were beautiful women?'

She pulled one of her schoolgirlish faces. 'No, I didn't! Their hips were *huge.*'

'Only compared with the hips of model girls, and what use are they, except for showing off clothes? A woman should be built for making love and having babies.' The twinkle in Serif's showed he knew it was a provocative opinion. 'You agree, don't you, Richard? And Stuart?'

'You wouldn't get away with a statement like that in the UK,' Stuart told him. 'Or in the States. The feminists would have your guts for garters. Isn't that right, Rick?'

If Richard disliked being called Rick, he gave no sign. 'Said in all seriousness, yes, probably it would cause offence. But for my taste the statue of the dancer has as much appeal now as when it was sculpted.'

There was a chorus of assent, although Sylvie's puzzled expression suggested she had passed the dancer without noticing her.

For their pudding Nuray had ordered *kadayif*, a confection which looked like fine shredded wheat, drenched in a thick honey syrup.

After dinner they all went for a stroll round the marina. With nightfall the temperature had dropped. Even when they couldn't be seen, the proximity of snow-clad mountains could be felt in the razor-sharp air. Nicola was glad of the soft cashmere muffler her mother had given her last Christmas and the knitted gloves she had bought in a London street market.

In a café they ordered drinks and practised the glass-whirling toast Serif had shown them earlier. Predictably, Richard was the quickest to master the trick of doing it without any spills.

'This is only our fourth night in Turkey. It seems far longer than that since I left home,' said Janet when, with varying degrees of success, everyone had made two or three attempts to emulate Serif's skill.

She was looking at Richard as she spoke, but it was Nuray who answered.

'It's always the same. When I meet a new group at the airport, they're not very friendly. But it doesn't take long, on a trek, for them to become friends.'

'Sometimes lovers,' Serif tacked on, his dark gaze shifting from Janet to Nicola to Sylvie before returning to Nuray's face.

What that brief survey signified Nicola wasn't sure. But she saw that it didn't please the Turkish girl.

'That's not good,' Nuray said briskly. 'Most holiday romances don't last. Abroad, people are not the same as at home. They're on their best behaviour. To love someone truly you must know them as they really are.'

Next day, after a bumpy ride along dirt tracks used by forestry workers, Serif brought the truck to a halt on a bluff overlooking a river where minerals made the water the colour of a peacock's neck feathers.

'We will walk through Köprülü canyon and Serif will drive to the shepherd's house where we'll have tea,' Nuray told them. 'All this is national park.' Her gesture embraced a long range of soaring crags, their slopes dark with evergreen forest.

After skirting the river for about half an hour, they came to some widely spaced stepping stones to the far bank.

Nicola and Hilary managed these easily, as did the men, but Lorna and Sylvie would have slipped and fallen if they hadn't been helped. Philip also lost his balance, reaching the other side with his trainers squelching water.

'That guy's on the wrong vacation. He should be in Miami or Torremolinos,' Richard said in a low-voiced aside to Hilary which Nicola overheard.

For a reason she couldn't analyse, she found herself saying, rather acidly, 'Not everyone can be Superman. Maybe he's not such a wimp as you seem to think.'

They both turned to look at her; Hilary with a faintly surprised smile, Richard with an ironical lift of the eyebrow.

'Fallen for him, Nicola?' he asked, in an amused voice.

Ignoring the quip, she said, 'Snap judgements can be wrong. I need to know people well before I decide they're worthless.'

'I don't think Richard intended to write Philip off,' Hilary said, in a placatory tone. 'But he certainly isn't equipped for this type of holiday. Nor is Sylvie.'

Richard laughed. 'That little thing isn't equipped to grapple with any eventualities. But I guess there'll always be someone around to rescue her.'

Hilary said, 'I often wish I had learned to play the helpless female when I was young instead of being trained to be sensible and capable in an era when far fewer women stood on their own feet. Today the pendulum has swung too far. Many thoroughly feminine females feel obliged to pretend they aren't. Would you agree, Nicola?'

'In what way?' said Nicola, wishing she hadn't sprung to Philip's defence. If anyone other than Richard had made that remark about him, she would have smiled agreement. It *was* hard to fathom why Philip had chosen this holiday. But Richard's disparaging comment had reminded her of his assessment of her own capabilities and prompted that foolishly pointed gibe about Superman.

'Take Lorna, for example,' said Hilary, after casting an eye behind her to make sure Lorna and Stuart were well out of earshot. 'In my day, she'd have travelled with a girlfriend, not a young man. Is that freedom really to her advantage? They're obviously having disagreements. When they get home the relationship will probably end. What will Lorna have gained by shaking off the restraints in force in her mother's and aunts' youth? Experience, yes—but at the price of disillusionment.'

She was walking alongside Nicola now, with Richard following close behind. It was he who, when Nicola remained silent, considering her reply, said, 'Isn't it better for them to find out now that they don't suit each other than on what, in an earlier era, would have been their honeymoon?'

'It's the argument usually advanced in favour of the present system,' the older woman answered. 'I'm not convinced. An incontrovertible fact is that any two people of the opposite sex are going to have problems adjusting to living together. If Stuart and Lorna *were* on their honeymoon, they would be more careful of each other's feelings. They would both take a different attitude simply because they were in an ongoing situation.'

'Any couple who chose a group trek for their honeymoon would need their heads examined,' said Richard.

Hilary laughed. 'Definitely! Although having a "structured honeymoon"—one with something to do other than making love—is a good idea. That's why, in my day, touring honeymoons were popular.'

He said, 'You're keeping very quiet, Nicola. Do you agree with Hilary?'

'I agree that Lorna would have enjoyed this trip more without Stuart as her partner.'

'That's side-stepping. We want to know where you stand on the question of unmarried people taking holidays together.'

'You haven't said where you stand,' she pointed out.

'That goes without saying...he's in favour,' Hilary answered for him. 'Most men are—except the fathers of daughters. Their views tend to be stricter. As far as young unattached men are concerned, the present moral climate is a dream come true.' She cast a teasing glance upwards at the man behind her. 'Isn't that so?'

'You could say that,' he agreed. 'But women must like it or they wouldn't go along with it. In the old days manners and mores were dictated by my sex. Not any more...at least not in the western world. You may not approve of the ways things are, Hilary, but Nicola's generation does. They still have the option to keep us at arm's length, but they don't choose to exercise it.'

'Men have never been kept at arm's length by women in love,' said Hilary. 'Not unless they were extremely closely chaperoned. Even when I was young, nice girls did...given the opportunity. But usually, if not invariably, for love. Not casually, as they do now. Not simply to be in the swing. That's what I find sad...the absence of passionate feeling in so many relationships. But of course that's the view of a spinster *d'un certain âge* and I don't expect you to share it.'

Had they been alone, Nicola would have surprised her by agreeing. But this wasn't a subject she wanted to discuss with Richard listening in.

'I don't think age or status have much to do with the validity of people's views,' he said to Hilary. 'If you were a teacher, dealing with parents as well as children, you must know a lot about human relationships.'

'I've certainly seen the pain that the failure of their parents' marriages inflicts on children,' she answered. 'Dear me, what a depressing subject for a lovely day. I'm most interested in your *métier*, Richard. Although I'm an avid reader, I know very little about publishing. What made you choose it as a career?'

'My grandfather was a publisher and my father started out as one but then changed to politics. It was expected of me.'

'Would you rather have done something else?' she asked.

'If I had, I would have done it. No, I was happy to conform to family tradition. I wouldn't be where I am now—in charge of a major imprint—if I hadn't had that background. It might have taken another ten years to get there... ten years I can be using to push through much needed reforms.'

Nicola wanted very much to hear this conversation. At the same time she knew it was risky. Any discussion of publishing increased the likelihood that her name and face would suddenly ring a bell with him.

'What reforms?' asked Hilary.

'Half the girls in publishing—and it's currently a predominantly female occupation except at the highest levels—haven't had any serious training,' he explained. 'They've picked up what they need to know, or picked up some but not all the necessary knowledge. Now steps are being taken to improve our training system.'

'If the donkey work is done by women, why aren't they reaching the top places?' Hilary asked.

'I thought they were,' said Nicola. Knowing it was probably unwise, she cited the four who had been her role models, and another who, since she had lost her own job, had broken through the so-called glass ceiling to become a chief executive.

'A few have done very well,' he conceded. 'But you're talking about a handful of exceptional women and there's still a long way to go before we see a woman heading the Publishers' Association.'

Nicola had heard it said that, in spite of being only half-British, he was in line for that distinction and might become the youngest publisher ever to be so honoured.

'I'm sorry... I've taken the wrong path,' said Nuray. 'I think it's best we go back to where I made the mistake.'

'Oh, no!' The protest came from Sylvie. 'How far is that?'

'Two or three kilometres, not more.'

Sylvie groaned. 'What's that in miles?' Her voice had the petulant whine of a fractious child.

'What makes you think this isn't the right path, Nuray?' asked Richard.

'If it were, we should be at the shepherd's house now. There's no sign of a house.'

'Have a rest-stop while Miles and I do some scouting,' he suggested. 'From the top of that rising ground, we may be able to get our bearings.'

'How come you don't know the way?' Lorna asked, when the two men had set off together.

'I've only done this walk once before. Last time, I had a bad cold and Serif led the walk through the canyon while I stayed at the shepherd's house. I'm very sorry.'

'It doesn't matter, dear,' said Joan. 'It won't be dark for a long time yet. If the worst comes to the worst, we can go back to he beginning and wait there till Serif comes to find us.'

'That's *miles* back. We'd be exhausted,' Lorna said grumpily.

'If you thought coming over the mountains with a broken heater was cold, wait till you've spent a night in the open,' said Bob.

His tone was jovial and raised a supportive laugh from his wife, Hilary and Nicola. But Sylvie looked ready to burst into tears.

'There may be bears...or wolves.' She looked nervously round her.

'Not in this part of Turkey,' Hilary said firmly. 'And the men would light a fire for us. It would be an adventure.'

Nuray looked gratefully at her. She was obviously deeply embarrassed and perhaps was worrying about the complaints some of the party might make to her employers.

'No joy. We'd better go back to the point where Nuray thinks we went wrong,' said Richard, when he came back.

'Where *she* went wrong,' Lorna muttered.

'It's easy to make a mistake when the paths through the wooded areas look so much alike.' He gave Nuray a charming smile.

The Turkish girl's anxious frown cleared.

The effect of his smile on Nicola was known only to herself, and did nothing for her peace of mind. If she could react to a smile which wasn't even directed at her, what would happen if it were? she wondered.

I will *not* be attracted to him, she told herself resolutely.

But as the group began to retrace their footsteps, some with a good grace, others with sulky expressions, she knew it was already too late.

She had been attracted to Richard Russell from the moment she had walked into his office. Which somehow had made the ensuing interview even more galling than if he had been the kind of man with thinning hair and thickening waistline more commonly found in the seats of power.

Watching his tall erect figure as he walked with Nuray at the head of the column, she thought no one would ever guess the taut and sexy backside outlined by his blue jeans spent a lot of time chair-bound. Dressed as he was, in this setting, he looked the quintessential outdoors man; every line of his body designed for strenuous action.

Stop thinking about the man, will you? she told herself impatiently. You're becoming obsessed with him.

CHAPTER SIX

IT WAS late afternoon when a herd of long-haired black goats appeared, followed by a prune-faced crone in a headscarf and Turkish trousers. A long machete-style knife was stuck through the back of the cloth wrapped round her waist.

She and Nuray greeted each other with relief on the Turkish girl's side and much toothless laughter from the goat-keeper.

'Don't fraternise with the goats,' Miles remarked, as the animals surrounded them, chewing tasty mouthfuls from the undergrowth and eyeing the strangers with calm curiosity. 'Those white things in the partings along their spines are ticks.'

Janet gave a dramatic shudder. 'What a life for the poor old thing! Living miles from anywhere with only goats for company. Thank God I wasn't born in rural Turkey.'

'She looks happy enough,' said Miles, as another cackle of laughter echoed through the woods.

'We're nearly there now,' said Nuray. 'Soon you'll be able to rest and have tea.'

'Looking at our hostess's hands, I'm not sure I want to take tea with her,' murmured Janet.

The house which came into view about ten minutes later was not the picturesque hovel they had expected. It was in the process of being rebuilt with bricks, perhaps with money sent back from Germany or Italy by immigrant sons.

On a crude wooden balcony giving access to rooms on the upper floor, Serif was asleep. As the group approached, a girl emerged from a room on the ground floor and called up to him. By the time Nuray was within speaking distance, he was on his feet, looking down at the weary walkers.

'Like a panther on a sunny branch,' Hilary remarked to Janet and Nicola.

Rather an apt analogy, thought Nicola. Showing his white teeth in a yawn, raking his fingers through his lustrous black hair and then stretching his muscular arms, Serif did bring to mind that sinuous and predatory member of the cat family.

'What kept you?' he asked. 'You're late.'

'We took a wrong turn,' Richard told him.

To which Nuray added, 'I lost the way. Never mind, we're here now. Come down and help serve the tea.'

'Aysel will do it.' Serif leaned over the balcony and spoke to the other Turkish girl.

'She looks like the cat that swallowed the canary,' said Janet. 'My guess is that, while granny was out with the goats, there've been fun and games here. The girl's very pretty. Can you see Serif wasting an opportunity like that?'

Nicola took her glass of sweet tea to a wooden platform built out over a slope which appeared to be where the family would sit in summer. It had a magnificent upward view of soaring rose-red cliffs.

'Are you tired?' Serif asked, coming to join her. Instead of looking at the view, he lounged on the rail surrounding the platform, looking at her.

'A little. But it's been a good day. This is a wonderful country.'

'Would you like to live here?'

She shook her head. 'It's too remote for me. Do you know how old the goat-lady is?'

He shrugged. 'Forty-five...fifty.'

'She looks seventy.'

'It's a hard life without electricity. All the water has to be carried to the house in buckets. Before her son went abroad, they were very poor. Now it's a little better but they still don't live the way you do.' He reached out and touched her cheek with the back of his knuckles. 'Your skin will never be like old dry leather.'

'I hope not.' She wondered how many tourists had felt that tender gesture and been told the same thing.

Serif's eyes switched from her face to a point somewhere behind her.

'We are under observation,' he murmured. 'Richard is a typical Englishman, isn't he?'

She glanced over her shoulder. Richard was standing by the corner of the house. His sunglasses made it impossible to tell if he was watching them or admiring the view.

'Actually he's an American with an English mother. Why does he strike you as being typically English?' she asked.

'The English are suspicious of foreigners, especially of foreign men who look admiringly at their women. They're also snobs. A Turkish truck driver isn't good enough to touch the cheek of an English young lady. That's what he's thinking.'

'He's far more likely to be wishing he could climb those cliffs. You're talking about Englishmen the way some of them were fifty years ago. Now we're part of the European Community and Richard himself is exceptionally cosmopolitan.'

'You're very quick to defend him. Perhaps you like him better than you like me.'

'Actually I would just as soon this were an all-women trek,' she told him, hoping to take the wind out of his sails. 'Mixed groups aren't as relaxing as a single-sex expeditions.'

Serif looked perplexed. 'Are you saying that you find women more attractive than men?'

'Not in the sense you mean. But I enjoy the company of other women, if they're intelligent and interesting. Men are happy in the company of other men. Why shouldn't we be content with our own sex?'

He disconcerted her by saying shrewdly, 'I think a man has hurt you and now you are nervous in case it happens again.'

There was an element of truth in his diagnosis. She had been bitterly hurt by Ian's reaction to her dismissal. But that was a long time ago and she wasn't aware of backing away from new relationships for fear they might turn out badly. There was always an element of risk in loving people. She knew that and accepted it.

'I'd like some more tea, if it's possible,' she said, handing him her glass.

'Of course.'

'Without sugar, please?'

He went off to fetch it and, instead of waiting for him as he probably expected her to, Nicola took the opportunity to rejoin the others.

As they were saying goodbye to the herdswoman, the old lady suddenly plunged her hand inside the collar of Janet's shirt. Pulling out a gold chain, she examined it closely before giving a nod of approval and stuffing it back in place, at the same time making a remark to Nuray.

'What did she say?' asked Janet.

'She's never seen a gold necklace as thick as yours. She thinks you must have a very rich husband.'

'If only I had,' was Janet's laughing comment.

When Nicola shook hands and said, '*Tesekkür*,' she was surprised to receive a kiss on both cheeks.

'I wish we had thought to bring a small present for her,' she said to Nuray.

'We provided the tea and sugar. There's plenty left over. She's satisfied.'

Although the next day was hot, they arrived at the beach to find it almost deserted; a mile or two of clean pale sand washed by a sparkling sea with some ruins among the wooded cliffs at the eastern end. Some upturned boats made convenient backrests.

Hilary was the first to test the temperature of the water by paddling.

'Invigorating!' she reported.

'Does that mean freezing?' Janet asked suspiciously.

'No, no...just a bit cold at first.' Hilary started to undress.

Richard had already stripped off his shirt.

'That's an expensive tan,' murmured Janet, watching him unzip his jeans.

As he took them off, revealing dark boxer-style swim shorts, powerful muscles rippled under the silky brown skin of his back and shoulders. Bob, who was changing near him, had long lost the lean elasticity which characterised Richard's physique.

They were all in the sea, Richard far out in the deep water and the rest closer to the shore, when Serif came sprinting down the beach in a brief red slip and kicked up a froth of spray before taking a running header.

He surfaced close to Nicola, his thick curls momentarily flattened before a quick flick of his head restored their springiness.

Neither Nuray nor Philip joined the swimmers, and the others had been out of the water for quarter of an hour before Richard waded ashore after his more vigorous exertions.

'An interesting contrast, those two,' said Janet, watching him talking to Serif while she and Nicola applied sun-cream. 'Quite alike in some ways and totally different in others. Which one do you prefer?'

'I don't know,' said Nicola. 'Which do you?'

'Both of them could be hard to handle. Perhaps Miles would be the best bet. Older men are more restful.'

Janet leaned back on her elbows. She had changed into another swimsuit, a red one with high-cut legs and a top which stayed up without straps.

'Sometimes I wonder if men are worth all the hassle. Hilary's managed without one and doesn't seem unhappy about it.'

Nicola's gaze returned to the two men standing with their backs to the sea and their eyes on the wooded hinterland. Now that they had no clothes on, or none that disguised their conformation, it was clear that Richard's extra two inches were in the length of his legs, which were also less hairy than Serif's.

Both had impressive shoulders but, while Serif's chest had a breastplate of coarse black hair tapering down past his navel, Richard's chest had the polished smoothness of the marble gods in the museum.

Janet was lying down, oblivious of everything but the heat of the sun on her supine body. Nicola followed her example, trying to concentrate on the soft sound of the waves brushing the beach a few yards away, and what Nuray's promised surprise for the afternoon might be.

But sunbathing was not a good way to clear the mind of erotic fancies, she found. A few moments later she sat up, reached for her shirt, and set off along the beach.

On the way back, strolling by the water's edge, she saw Richard loping towards her at a lazy run.

He slowed down as they came abreast.

'Did you enjoy your swim?'

'Very much. You obviously enjoyed yours.'

'Being desk-bound a lot of the time, I need all the exercise I can get. This trip isn't as strenuous as I'd hoped. Is it turning out as you expected?'

'More or less...except I thought there'd be more of us, including one or two Aussies and other nationalities.'

She thought he had stopped to talk to her out of politeness and would soon continue his run.

Instead he said, 'It's close to lunchtime. I'd better turn back with you. Tell me about your job at Chatham's.'

'Like Gertrude Stein's rose, a secretary is a secretary is a secretary.'

He swooped to pick up a piece of sea-polished glass. 'I often think secretaries are the only essential species in the entire business world.'

'Perhaps less essential than they used to be in these days of lap-tops and modems and personal organisers,' said Nicola.

'It's still mainly the travelling salesmen who use those aids. It's amazing how many top-level people are computer illiterates. I don't think the efficient secretary is in any danger of extinction...and I'm sure you're very efficient.'

'What makes you think so?'

'I noticed you checking the slip when you changed currency at the airport. You don't have to rummage for your passport when we check in at hotels. You're the only one who says please and thank you in Turkish. You file the illustrated tickets Nuray hands out in your guide-book.'

It was disconcerting to find she had been under close observation. But perhaps he had studied the others equally closely.

'You seem to have missed your vocation,' she said lightly. 'With your eye for clues to character, you should have been a detective.'

He laughed. 'Maybe I should. My favourite light reading is crime fiction. Do you read crime novels?'

'Sometimes. As you said you were interested in history, I'd have thought that would be your main reading.'

'It is. The crime stuff is for unwinding.'

She knew it was risky, but she couldn't resist asking, 'Do you need much unwinding? I thought Barking & Dollis were over the difficulties they had a few years ago.'

'We are. If you talk to people who've been in the book trade a long time—any business, come to that—they'll tell you that booms and busts come and go like the seasons and the weather. Been with Chatham's long?'

'Yes.' She left it at that.

'You must know our central London rep... George Morden.'

She nodded. George Morden wasn't aware she had once worked for his employers. He had joined Barking & Dollis soon after she left them, head-hunted by the man strolling beside her.

'He's the tops,' Richard said. 'It's a key job and I wanted the best man in it so I poached him from one of our rivals.'

'I gather you have a reputation for ruthlessness.'

'I have? Where have you heard that? Not from George?'

It was interesting that he called the rep by his first name. His predecessor, a publisher of the old school, had referred to the sales force by their surnames.

'No, he's loud in your praise. I've heard him telling my boss that you're the best thing that's happened to British publishing in years.'

He laughed. 'That's because I pay him more than he was getting before. Also it's part of his spiel to make people believe B & D is being run by a genius. The average book buyer doesn't know or care who a book is published by, but presumably in your job you do notice the colophon on a book you've enjoyed? What do you think of our list?'

'It's excellent,' she said truthfully. It was on the tip of her tongue to add, But presumably that's because you have some of the best commissioning editors in the business.

She repressed the comment. This conversation was already skating dangerously close to a confrontation which could only result in mutual embarrassment for the rest of the holiday.

'That's good to hear,' he said, smiling at her. 'Not that I can take much of the credit, except in the sense that authors are attracted to a publishing house where they're likely to get a fair deal and be treated in a civilised way. Most of the kudos must go to our editors.'

To steer the conversation away from editors, Nicola said, 'George Morden says your campaign against the sale-or-return system is the most important change you want to make.'

It was clearly a subject on which he had strong views. He shared them with her for several minutes before breaking off to say, 'Sorry, you didn't come on holiday to hear me riding my hobby-horse. Let's talk about cookery. What sort of things do you like to cook?'

'I'm a Sunday supplement cook. Most of the recipes I try out are clipped from the weekend papers. I learnt the basics from my mother when I was small.'

'It sounds as if you had one of those nice old-fashioned happy family childhoods that are supposed to be dying out.'

'Yes, I did. Didn't you?'

'My parents didn't get on too well. Their relationship is largely a front for my father's political career. My mother is English. When she went to live in the States, she took with her the person we call Nan who had been her nurse as a child. Nan looked after us as well...us being myself, my two brothers and my sister. She gave us the cosy home background while our parents were busy politicking and socialising. So, like you, I had a good childhood but in a different way. Do you see much of your parents now?'

'About every third weekend. They're only forty-five minutes away.'

'Is that by car or train?'

'Train. I have a driving licence and Dad lets me use his car, but there would be no point in my keeping one in London. Do you?'

He nodded. 'I spend quite a few weekends with my English grandparents. They live in Wiltshire. It would be an awkward journey by public transport. Do you know that part of England?'

When she shook her head, he went on, 'It's peaceful down there. Nothing has changed much since my grandfather was my age. It's a great place for recharging one's batteries.'

Lord Rotherhithe's gardens were said to be among the most beautiful in Britain, a fitting setting for a Tudor mansion owned by the same family for centuries. But the way Richard referred to it, it might have been a sequestered country cottage. In an age when many people lost no chance to show off, she couldn't help liking the way he played down his background.

By this time they were back with the others who were preparing to go to the *lotanka* behind the beach for lunch.

'What's on the menu today, Nuray?'

'Not a big choice today, Bob. Tomato soup, salad, spaghetti and chips. Is that all right for you?'

'Sounds fine to me,' he beamed.

'Spaghetti *and* chips!' murmured Janet, as she and Nicola pulled on their trousers. 'And bread too, no doubt. I can't take all this carbohydrate they're pushing into us.'

'Have the soup and salad and pass on the rest,' Nicola suggested.

They ate at a table outside the *lotanka* served by a smiling woman in Turkish trousers with a clean white cotton headscarf covering her hair and tied at the nape of her neck.

The beautiful setting, the toned-up feeling left by her swim and the expectation of an interesting afternoon combined to give Nicola a strong sense of well-being. There was only one fly in the ointment—Richard. And the disturbing change in her feelings towards him.

How could she be warming towards someone who had done what he had done, not only to her but to other people? It had been the act of a despot, a man to whom other people were merely pawns in the power game. There must have been a way to put the company back on its feet without all those arbitrary dismissals.

After lunch Nuray said, 'Now you can rest or swim again until four o'clock. Then we're going for a walk to see something very unusual. Those of you who have torches should bring them.'

'We're not going caving, are we?' asked Janet. 'If so, count me out. I'm claustrophobic.'

Nuray shook her head. 'But it will be dark when we come down the mountain. The track is good but a torch will be an advantage.'

Nicola decided to combine a sunbathe with writing a letter to her friend Gina Latimer. Whether the letter would reach London before Nicola did was debatable, but it would relieve her feelings to tell Gina about Richard being here.

Gina was another victim of the recession. She had worked in the PR side of publishing and now had a job in the customer relations department of a major chain store. But she found it dull compared with writing Press releases, organising author tours and liaising with the media.

Together they were involved in an enterprise they hoped would triumphantly redress their set-backs. Gina had jumped at the proposition Nicola had put to her and they had spent the past nine months giving most of their spare time to it.

Very soon their labours would bear fruit. If they pulled it off, the success of their venture would prove that both Richard Russell and the man who had laid off Gina had made a mistake as classic as that of the several publishers who had turned down the chance to buy Frederick Forsyth's massively successful book *The Day of the Jackal*.

Of course, they might *not* pull it off. But after a lot of discussion they had felt it was a risk worth taking.

If their hopes were fulfilled, Nicola knew that nothing in her life would ever give her greater satisfaction than proving Richard Russell wrong.

Dear Gina,
　　You'll never guess who's here. My No. 1 *bête noire*! He has no idea who I am. At first I thought he might

be pretending not to recognise me, but now I think it's genuine. If I didn't know what a heartless pig he can be, I might succumb to his charm, which is considerable.

I'm writing this at the beach. Later we're going on a mystery tour up a mountain, led by our Turkish guide. She seems to be boss of our outfit—though I don't think the driver likes it when she tells him what to do—but from what I've seen so far the majority of Turkish women have a long way to go to equality.

Although it's good to relax after the long hard slog of the past few months, my mind is still mainly on The Project. I can't wait for blast-off...

The track wound its way through a pine wood and then skirted a ravine, twisting and turning among outcrops of limestone and fir trees. It was an easy climb which soon had them high above sea-level.

Presently Nuray called a halt, suggesting they make themselves comfortable on flat-topped rocks.

'Some of you will have heard of the Lycian hero Bellerophon and his winged horse, Pegasus. For a long time this part of the Lycian kingdom had been terrorised by the Chimera, a fire-breathing monster with a lion's head, a goat's body and a serpent's tail.'

As she spoke, her dark eyes ranged over the group. But it seemed to Nicola that the one she looked at most often was Richard.

'The King of Lycia sent Bellerophon to kill the monster,' Nuray went on. 'Because he could fly out of its reach on Pegasus, he succeeded. According to legend, it happened higher up this mountain, and the fire from the monster's dying breath is still burning under the rocks. In a few moments you'll see the flames.'

By now it was growing dusk. They seemed a long way from the nearest human habitation as they pressed on up the track to an open space where no trees were growing. At the foot of this expanse of bare rock was a

small cluster of ruins. The air had a strange, rather unpleasant smell.

'Methane,' said Richard. 'What used to be called
marsh gas or, in coal mines, fire-damp.'

'I thought fire-damp was dangerous,' said Janet.

'It's explosive when it's mixed with air and comes into
contact with naked flame. But only in confined spaces.'

'The fires show up better in the dark,' said Serif.

He had a dry piece of brushwood in his hand. When
he held it to the flames coming from a hole in the rock
it caught alight and he was able to ignite escapes of gas
from other holes.

'Be careful where you sit down,' he told the trekkers.
'Some people find the smell makes them feel sick.'

'I don't like this place. It's creepy,' said Sylvie, looking
round as if she expected to see the fire-snarling Chimera
burst from the rocks to devour them.

'In ancient times it was thought to be a holy place,'
said Nuray. 'Now, in summer, it's a popular picnic spot.
You can see the ashes of fires where people have cooked
food.'

By the time it was fully dark, Serif had piled
brushwood near several vents and soon he had three large
fires going, their flames casting a flickering red glow over
the ruins and the faces of the trekkers.

'I think we must leave now,' said Nuray, as the blaze
began to die down. 'By the time we reach Finike and get
settled in our new rooms, it will be time for supper.'

Apart from Sylvie and Philip, everyone had a torch
to use where the trees were thick and their branches cast
dense shadows. Where there were fewer trees, moonlight
and starlight lit the way.

They set out in a crocodile but because some of the
group were more sure-footed than others the file became
more and more strung out. Soon Nuray, who was
leading, could no longer be heard talking to Miles who
was behind her.

Nicola was held up by Bob and Joan plodding cautiously down in front of her. Joan seemed particularly unsure of herself in the dark, but she didn't suggest Nicola should pass her. Perhaps she found it reassuring to have two people behind to help Bob pick her up if she missed her footing.

The last in the line was Serif, who had given the truck's keys to Nuray so that the first down wouldn't have to wait for the last-comers.

They were about halfway when Nicola heard a noise which made her check and turn. It had sounded like a thud followed by a muffled expletive.

She waited for the beam of Serif's torch to appear round the outcrop she had passed a few moments earlier. When it didn't, she wondered if he could have slipped and fallen. It didn't seem likely. He had a powerful torch and was light on his feet.

'Serif?'

When there was no reply to her call, she turned back and went round the great rock.

'*Serif*!'

He was sprawled at full length on the path.

What could have happened to knock him out? she wondered, going down on her knees beside him and shining her torch on his unconscious face.

She was drawing in her breath to give loud yell for help when his eyes opened. With a big grin, he sat up and put both arms round her.

'Did you think the Chimera had got me?'

'Oh, Serif . . . that isn't funny,' she protested. 'You're too old to play such a trick.'

'I was bored. Bob and Joan go so slowly. We can soon catch them up.'

As she tried to disengage herself, he pulled her closer and kissed her. It was only a light, playful kiss and he didn't attempt to prolong it.

'There! Wasn't that nice?' he asked softly.

It was hard to deny that being kissed by a good-looking man, especially after a prolonged dearth of kisses, *was* rather nice.

Taking her hesitation for assent, he said, 'Let's do it again.'

This time the pressure of his lips was firmer and she felt the rasp of his five o'clock shadow against her chin. But when his arms moved and he tried to hold her more closely, she resisted and struggled free.

'The others will think we've *both* been seized by the Chimera,' she said rather breathlessly. 'Come on; we must catch them up.'

He let her go and together they scrambled to their feet.

'Later…' he said. 'Later there'll be time to be together.'

Nicola let that pass. She started to hurry down the track, resolved not to fall for any more of his strategies.

'Be careful. You're going too fast,' he warned her.

She slowed slightly, wondering if Joan had noticed they were no longer close behind her. If they didn't get back to the truck at the same time as the Tufnells, it would be typical of Joan to say archly, 'What happened to you two?'

In fact she needn't have worried. Very soon she saw Joan's light ahead and the other woman didn't seem aware that the last two in the line had fallen behind for a while.

In the truck Janet was retouching her lipstick. As she settled in the seat opposite, Nicola was glad her own lips were bare. Had Serif kissed Janet, there would have been tell-tale smudges round both their mouths.

On the run to their next destination she thought about his kisses and about tactful ways to explain he was wasting his time.

Casual sex—which presumably was his objective—had never appealed to her. She believed a prerequisite of making love was feelings of genuine affection and tenderness, not just a strong physical attraction.

After the break-up with Ian, she had decided that love was a snare and a delusion. She wasn't even sure any longer that she wanted to marry and have children.

Her parents were happily married, as were most of their friends. But somehow, between her parents' generation and her own, the ability to pick the right partner and stay married for life seemed almost to have died out. Among her own circle—made up mainly of former and current colleagues—most were either living together, or separated, or second-time-around.

It was all very well for her mother to insist that true love and a life of happiness 'till death us do part' was still a viable concept. Gina, after two abortive relationships, had given up waiting for Mr Wonderful to materialise.

'Mr Dull Steady DIY-Expert is the guy I'm looking for now,' she had said once. 'Or if I do fall in love again, I'll go into it with my eyes open, knowing it won't last.'

Nicola had ageed. Yet tucked away in a corner of her heart was the tenacious longing to meet a man and live 'happily ever after'. Not just on a humdrum level of mutual convenience and tolerance, but in Shakespeare's marriage of true minds.

CHAPTER SEVEN

'TONIGHT, Sylvie, you're sharing with Nicola,' said Nuray, in the lobby of the hotel at Finike.

Nicola soon discovered for herself why Hilary had disliked sharing with the youngest member of the group. Sylvie's method of unpacking was to unload the confusion in her kitbag on to her bed and then lay claim to most of the room's inadequate storage space.

'You can have first go in the shower, if you like,' she said, dumping a jumble of cosmetics on the table between the two beds.

Nicola jumped at the offer, foreseeing that Sylvie would leave the bathroom a mess. To her dismay there was no hot water.

Feeling sticky from her swim, she forced herself to have a cold shower. Although they had been warned that hot water might not always be available, its absence came hard to anyone accustomed to an unfailing supply. But the cold shower made her feel good afterwards.

'I'm not going to torture myself,' said Sylvie, when Nicola emerged. 'I've been in the sea today. I wonder if there's a disco here? The evenings are *boring*!'

'Ask Serif. He looks like a night owl.'

'He's too old for me,' said Sylvie. 'Still, better than no one, I s'pose. I thought there'd be lots of good-looking Turkish waiters. My friend had a great time last summer.'

They ate at a restaurant on the outskirts of town, a great barn of a place which, in season, could cater for several hundred tourists. Tonight the only diners were the Amazing Adventures group and, at a smaller table, four men who looked like travelling salesmen.

94

The long table set for the group was lit by night-lights inside flowers made from thinly cut curls of orange peel. They cast a flattering golden glow on the diners' faces.

'It's a pity there's no one of Sylvie's age on this trek,' Nicola said to Nuray, as the meal began with an excellent thyme and pea soup.

The Turkish girl nodded. 'I can see she's bored, but what can I do about it? A holiday at Bodrum in summer would be better for her. She's not interested in ancient cities or beautiful scenery. She wants to dance and flirt with boys of her own age.'

Tonight the *mezes* included delicious hot courgette fritters.

When she had finished her fritters, Nuray stood up to announce, 'For our next course I've ordered a Turkish speciality called *imam bayildi*. An *imam* is the prayer leader at a mosque, and the name of this dish means "the *imam* fainted". When this dish was invented by an *imam*'s wife, it was so delicious that he fainted with pleasure. But if anyone doesn't like aubergines, there are other things you can order.'

While they were waiting for the aubergines, Nicola said, 'Serif tells me he's worked for AA since he was student. How long have you been with them, Nuray?'

'Two years. My father is very conservative. At first he didn't approve. Even in Istanbul it's still usual for Turkish girls to live with their parents until they marry.'

She was at the end of the table with Richard on her left. Turning to him, she said, 'I know that sounds old-fashioned. In London girls have more independence. I expect most of the girls in your company live away from home, don't they?'

'I would think so, yes. Does your father still disapprove?'

Tonight Nuray had on a peach-coloured shirt with the coral kerchief she had worn when he photographed her at Perge. The candlelight emphasised the length and thickness of her lashes and the lovely contour of her eyebrows. She had an irresistible smile, Nicola thought, watching her focus it on Richard.

'He's resigned to it now. Even, perhaps, a little proud of me. When I go home I have interesting things to tell him about the people I've met...this time a publisher. The next time I come to London, you must come and meet my sister. My brother-in-law is a surgeon. They live in South Kensington. Is that near you?'

'Not far away. I must show you what goes on in a publishing house.' He looked across the table. 'You too, Nicola, if you're interested. But perhaps you see too many books at Chatham's to want to see where they're generated.'

Before she could answer, Miles, who was next to her, said, 'Oh, you work at Chatham's, do you? I usually have a browse there if I have to go to London. An excellent shop. The staff are so splendidly knowledgeable.'

'My boss would be delighted to hear you say so.'

While Miles told her about his collection of gardening books, Nicola was aware of Nuray continuing to flirt with Richard.

Later, when they were leaving, Janet said in an undertone, 'Our guide was really turning the charm on Richard tonight, wasn't she? Perhaps she's hoping to emulate her sister and feels he's a likely candidate.'

'Perhaps,' agreed Nicola lightly.

Considering Janet's suggestion on the drive back, she didn't think it probable that Richard would fall for a Turkish girl, however attractive. Men with his background married within their own circle. The future Mrs Richard Russell would most likely come from his mother's aristocratic milieu or the equally exclusive 'old money' set in America.

The fact that, according to report, his girlfriends had been chosen for their intelligence and style didn't mean his bride would have those qualities. In Richard's social strata, good blood-stock applied to people as well as horses.

Earlier she had heard him talking to Hilary about riding holidays. Probably his performance on horseback was as impressive as the powerful crawl he had demonstrated in the sea this morning.

He was one of those fortunate people who, by a combination of natural gifts and intense application, excelled at everything they tried.

Except perhaps at close and lasting relationships. He was thirty-four and still unmarried. Why?

Because he had yet to meet the right girl? Because he preferred to remain free as long as possible? Because, in spite of his eligibility and surface charm, there were flaws, not apparent to those who knew him only slightly, which emerged on closer acquaintance?

Aware that she was spending more time thinking about him than about any of the others, Nicola made a conscious effort to turn her thoughts in other directions. Soon afterwards they arrived at the hotel.

On the top floor was a dining-room-cum-coffee-shop. Before supper, deprived of hot showers, the Tufnells had gone to some nearby shops and come back with various cakes, one of which they fetched from their room to share with the group.

Presently Richard said, 'I'm going for a stroll round town. Will anyone join me?'

When Janet, Philip and Sylvie had said they would, he turned an enquiring glance on the Tufnells.

'I'm going to finish my crossword and Joan's going to read,' said Bob.

Richard raised an interrogative eyebrow at Nicola.

She would have liked to join them, but said, 'If the water's hot now, I want to wash my hair.'

The others left but Nicola stayed talking to the Tufnells, who had ordered more coffee, for a few minutes.

In this hotel their rooms were on different floors instead of being all on one landing. Hers and Sylvie's was on the first floor.

On the second-floor landing Serif was reading a paper. As she came down the stairs from the coffee-shop, he folded it into a tight roll and stuck it in his back pocket.

'I thought you wouldn't be long. Let's go and find a bar. It's cold out...too cold for a walk.'

'I have to wash my hair.'

'You can do it in the morning. This is our only chance to be alone.'

Stepping in front of her, blocking her way down the stairs, he put his hands on her arms and drew her to him.

Instinctively Nicola's hands came up to hold him away from her. But he was too quick and too strong for her to fend him off. The next moment her hands were pressed uselessly against his chest and his mouth was on hers...

'Excuse me.'

The voice which made Serif stop kissing her was Richard's.

'Sorry to disturb you,' he said politely. 'Janet thinks she left her scarf upstairs.'

As they moved aside, he stepped past and went up the stairs in the easy three-at-a-time leaps of a long-legged man in a hurry.

He was already out of earshot when Nicola recovered herself sufficiently to say crossly, 'You're out of line, Serif.'

'Don't be cross. You'd liked it. So did I.' He attempted to draw her back to him but this time she was prepared and fended him away more vigorously.

'I *don't* like it,' she said vehemently. 'We are practically strangers. I'm not into casual kissing. I don't want a holiday romance. I mean that. I'm not playing hard to get.'

'Oh, come on...don't be like that. I thought you liked me?'

'I would...if you'd stop making passes.'

'A kiss isn't a pass,' he objected. 'Are you embarrassed because Richard saw us? So what? Unless you prefer him to me? Perhaps you want Richard to kiss you? Is that why you're angry?'

'Certainly not!'

The forceful retort was no sooner uttered than Richard came down the stairs with Janet's scarf in his hand.

'Sorry... not trying to cramp your style, Serif. But you have chosen a rather public place. Goodnight.'

For a moment, after he had brushed past them and turned the bend of the stairs to start down the next flight, he looked straight at Nicola.

What thoughts lay behind the enigmatic expression on his face it was impossible to tell.

Early the following morning, she went for a walk round the town.

She had slept badly, upset by the incident on the staircase. Annoyingly, Serif's kiss had stirred up feelings which, like a fire in a slow-burning stove flaring up when the draught-door was opened, had troubled her more last night than for a long time.

All the unsatisfied longings aroused by her holiday with Ian, and subsequently damped down, had revived. But what had kept her awake was not the possibility that in Serif's arms she might at last find the fulfilment which had eluded her in Spain.

It could be that he was a more accomplished lover than Ian. But as she was not in love with him she would never find that out.

In fact, after Richard had passed them for a second time, she had spoken to Serif in a tone which might have been so offensive to a Turkish man's pride that he wouldn't speak to her again.

Well, if he's in a huff now that's just too bad, she thought.

Serif's opinion was unimportant. It was what Richard thought that she minded.

Why?

Why should she care what he, of all people, thought? On the basis of her CV and her seniors' reports, he hadn't rated her at all highly. In fact her personal impact on him had been so slight that three years later neither her name nor her face meant a thing to him. So what did it matter that he'd caught her being kissed by Serif? Or that he must also have overheard her strenuous denial on being asked if she wanted *him* to kiss her?

The answer, which she had spent much of the night avoiding but now admitted to herself, was that she was suffering from a physical attraction so strong it amounted to infatuation.

One which was likely to prove even more abortive and painful than her previous involvement with a man.

Later that day they walked in rugged country which in past times might have sheltered brigands. Compared with English landscapes, this terrain was awesome in its wildness.

After about an hour's steady tramping, while they paused to admire a fine view, Nuray announced that in another thirty minutes they would come to a place to have tea.

'And I have some biskwits in my pack to share with you,' she added.

'What sort of biskwits?' asked Richard.

'Why are you laughing at me?' she asked, recognising, as Nicola did, the slight crinkling round his eyes and the hint of a smile at one corner of his mouth.

'The u is silent, Nuray. The English pronounce the word as if it were spelt b-i-s-k-i-t-s. In America we call them crackers.'

'Thank you for correcting me. I know I make many mistakes.'

'On the contrary, your English is very nearly perfect. I was only teasing you. In future whenever I have a "biskwit" with my tea, I'll remember you.' He put an arm round her shoulders and gave her a hug.

Had she needed confirmation of her condition, the sharp thrust of pain Nicola felt as she watched them would have told her what was the matter with her.

To the others the hug would have seemed a fraternal gesture. She suspected a deeper significance. Richard might not be falling for Nuray in any serious sense, but obviously he found her attractive. It would have been strange if he didn't. With her luxuriant black hair, flashing dark eyes and tawny skin, she *was* the most attractive woman present.

Perhaps Richard had every attention of tasting Nuray's pretty lips before the trek was over. The fact that she still lived at home, and possibly had less experience than girls of her age in western countries, might be a challenge to him.

The bar of the mountain hamlet where they stopped for tea had a beaten earth floor and open rafters. Several locals were already there, countrymen muffled against the cold in old overcoats and an assortment of other warm clothing. One had a shawl round his shoulders. Their hands were like roots, gnarled and ingrained with soil, the nails black and broken. But their faces were cheerful, their talk punctuated with chuckles and guffaws.

All the Turks were smoking. Soon Nicola found that the fug was making her eyes smart. Like Miles and Hilary, she went outside. As they were deep in conversation, she didn't join them but moved away and stood contemplating the view and sipping apple tea.

A week tomorrow some of the group would be returning to London. She had been able to book a two-day extension because, on the Monday when she should have returned to work, her boss would be in Scotland at his mother's ninetieth birthday party. As he was away that day, he had said she could take advantage of the option to extend her holiday.

'It's too smoky in there for me too.'

As Richard joined her, Nicola gave a slight jump.

'Did you ever smoke?'

She shook her head. 'My father offered a huge bribe if I stayed clear until I was nineteen. By then I had the sense to see what an expensive shackle the habit is. Have you smoked?'

'Yes... But I decided to stay with alcohol. Beer in those days. Mainly wine now. Although anyone with their ear to my wall last night would have heard the tell-tale glug-glug of the gin bottle. It was hellishly cold, didn't you think?'

She nodded. 'I wore my down jacket to read in bed. I couldn't get the hot-air thing to work properly.'

'They're all suffering from various degrees of burn-out. This is a much poorer country than I'd realised. Like Spain in the Sixties, they need the prosperity mass tourism can bring. It will be a pity if they let all their coasts be colonised by third-rate architects designing for barbarian developers.'

'I suppose it's inevitable. Countries never seem to learn from each other's mistakes.'

Discussing the impact of tourism, Nicola relaxed. At first she had thought he intended to talk about the scene on the stairs last night; perhaps to punish her for that emphatic 'Certainly not!'.

She felt a surge of regret that they couldn't have met like this, but with the difference that she was still in publishing but had never worked for Barking & Dollis. They would have had so much in common, so many things to talk about.

'There seems to be something about you the Turks find irresistible.'

Both the statement and the sudden change in Richard's tone and expression made her realise she had relaxed too soon. 'It could make your life complicated if you were here on your own.'

Refusing to be drawn, she said, 'You're really working on your Turkish. The old men in there were delighted to find a foreigner speaking some of their language.'

'I'm trying, but you know what they say about languages.'

'No?'

'The best place to pick them up fast is in bed. I'm sure Serif would be pleased to give you some private tuition.'

'Perhaps, but I'm not interested.'

'In improving your Turkish...or in Serif?'

'I have as much Turkish as I need, and brief encounters aren't my style.'

Janet came out of the bar and strolled over to join them. 'I'm getting a sore throat in there. I hear we're having fresh trout for dinner...at that place where we left the truck. I feel sorry for Lorna, being stuck there for four hours,' she added.

Lorna had opted out of the afternoon walk.

'She has Serif with her,' said Richard. 'He's good company, isn't he, Nicola?'

She could tell that he didn't believe her claim to be indifferent to the Turk. If only he knew who really had the power to turn her on. But that, thank God, was something he would never suspect if she could help it.

'It looks as if we're on the move,' he said. 'Shall I take your glass back for you?'

As the empty tea-glass changed hands, their fingers were in fleeting contact. Her reaction to his touch was a mixture of pleasure and despair. How could this have happened to her so quickly?

On the return walk she came to the conclusion that any holiday of this kind must act as a forcing house for all human relationships. Mainly it was friendship which flourished more quickly than in normal conditions. Possibly, sometimes, animosities sprouted. But who would have thought that, not quite a week after seeing him at Heathrow, her feelings about Richard Russell would have changed so dramatically? From intense dislike to unwilling attraction in six days. It didn't seem possible, but it was so.

'This time last week we were packing to come away,' said Janet. 'This time next week we'll be on the train back to Istanbul.'

Nicola knew that the next seven days would be a bittersweet time which her head would want to pass as quickly as possible, while her foolish infatuated senses would treasure every hour, dreading the end of the journey.

By half-past ten the next day they were hurtling along the coast on a road blasted out of undulating red cliffs rising from the sea. The water lapping the many small empty beaches tucked in the curves of the cliffs looked invitingly clear.

Serif was in high spirits. The rock and roll tape he was playing was being relayed to the trekkers. Through the rear window of the cab they could see him beating time on the steering-wheel.

Every few minutes he took a bend perilously close to the edge of the tarred surface and a twenty-foot drop into the sea.

Nicola was sitting on the offside of the vehicle, leaning forward to peer at a cluster of holiday villas under construction on the clifftop, when the truck swung sideways to avoid an oncoming lorry. The movement sent loose objects flying, made Joan give a cry of alarm and pitched Nicola across the aisle.

She was fielded by Richard, sitting opposite. He grabbed her by both upper arms and for a few seconds his fingers felt like steel clamps.

'I'm sorry,' she said, as he rose from his seat and lifted her back into hers.

'No problem.' He let her go and bent to retrieve a book which had fallen from the seat beside hers.

Before resuming his place he moved to the front of the truck, holding the overhead rail, and switched off the relay outlet, silencing Serif's choice of music.

'You mean thing! I like that tape,' Sylvie objected.

'You may, but the grown-ups don't.'

He smiled as he said it. Nicola, watching, saw Sylvie pull a face, in much the same way that Nicola, in her teens, had sometimes reacted to being told off by her brother.

'Would you like to borrow my head-set, Sylvie?' she offered.

'What sort of music is it? I don't go for classical stuff.'

'It's a mixture. Give it a trial for ten minutes. You might like some of it.'

'OK.'

About mid-morning they stopped on the outskirts of Kale where, in an open space, a large number of people were assembling.

After Serif had leaned from his window to speak to some bystanders, Nuray came back to tell the group what was happening.

'There's a market here today and also, soon, *deve güresi* . . . camel fighting.'

'I certainly don't wish to see *that*,' Hilary said firmly. 'The market—yes. But animals being made to fight is not my idea of entertainment.'

Most people murmured agreement. Nuray said, 'OK, we'll look round the market and then drive through the town to see the rock tombs in the cliffs.'

Many of the market stalls were festooned with lengths of fabric for the traditional baggy trousers called *samlar* worn by the women. There were also stands selling track suits, trainers and the cheap plastic toys to be found in markets worldwide.

'Serif seems to take the view that women don't mind a little forceful persuasion.'

Nicola looked up to find Richard beside her. No one else from the group was near by. She replaced the string of beads she had been looking at. 'He would lose his job if he barged into our bedrooms. Anyway, why should he need to? I'm sure he has girlfriends galore. There's probably one of them waiting for him at Kas.'

'It was you he was kissing at Finike the night before last.'

'He was just trying it on. Men do. Haven't you . . . in the past?'

'I'm thirty-four, Nicola, not sixty-four. My wild oats aren't that far behind me.'

'I know that,' she said unguardedly. 'They're still being sown, so one hears.'

'They are? It's news to me. Where did you pick that up?'

'I don't remember.'

'I think you do,' he said shrewdly. As she moved on to the next stall, his hand fell on her shoulder, lightly but making it clear she was not going to get away until she had provided a more satisfactory answer to his question.

'I probably read something about you in one of the trade papers. My boss leaves them lying around and I sometimes look through them in my lunch break.'

'I read them too and I don't recall any references to my personal life.'

'Perhaps it wasn't a direct reference to you. It may have been in that column where the writer makes oblique digs at the well-known people in publishing. Perhaps it was someone else at Barking & Dollis he called a Casanova.'

'It must have been,' he said drily, removing his hand from her shoulder. 'It certainly wasn't me.'

A small Turkish child standing on a box behind the next stall gave them a big smile. 'Hello.'

'Hello.' Richard leaned his tall frame over the wares on display to ruffle the child's curly head.

Other children, playing in the space between the two lines of stalls, ran up to demonstrate that they too knew foreign greetings.

'Hello. *Bonjour, monsieur. Guten tag.*'

'Do you like children, Nicola?' he asked.

'I haven't had much to do with them. My brother isn't married yet. Both my parents were only children, so we don't have any cousins.'

'I have seven small nephews and nieces and a lot of my friends have children, except those whose wives have careers and are putting it off.' His tone was neutral, giving no clue to where he stood on that issue. 'I already have four godchildren. So that's eleven birthdays to be remembered. Fortunately my computer warns me ahead of time.'

'Perhaps you'll be able to stock up with presents at the Grand Bazaar next Saturday.'

'Maybe, although Nuray says a better place to shop is a newly built mall in the suburbs. Tell me, was it because you were under a misapprehension about my attitude to women that you were noticeably stand-offish at the beginning of the trip?'

She had thought they were back on safe ground and was disconcerted.

'I was? Perhaps you imagined it.'

'I don't think I did. If I'm wrong, why didn't you tell me you knew who I was? It would have been the natural thing to do—if you hadn't already decided to dislike me.'

He was right, of course. Had he been at the helm or on the staff of any other publishing company, she *would* have made friendly overtures. She would probably have mentioned her connection with Barking & Dollis.

In the publishing trade as a whole, there had been a great deal of sympathy for the victims of the purges. Some—mainly people more senior than herself—had been taken on by rival companies, one or two actually being promoted to better positions than the jobs they had lost.

She decided the only way to deal with this interrogation was to turn it around and throw a question at him.

'Did it bother you?'

CHAPTER EIGHT

'NATURALLY. Any normal person is bothered by a hostile reaction...especially from someone they don't know.' After a pause, Richard added, 'And particularly from someone they'd like to know better.'

His tone made Nicola's heart flip. Was she reading more into the statement than he intended? Probably he was only referring to the connection between publishing and bookselling.

In her most casual tone, she said, 'Now we *all* know each other better. Considering the diversity of our ages, backgrounds and everything, we've homogenised well, haven't we? That's probably one of the best things about this type of holiday—the opportunity to get to know people one would never normally meet.'

'And, in some cases, wouldn't want to,' was Richard's sardonic comment.

On the way back to the truck, the trekkers couldn't avoid seeing two of the camels fighting.

But it wasn't the gory battle Nicola and Hilary had envisaged. In fact the bout in progress as they passed was rather less violent than two women elbowing each other in a scrimmage for sale bargains. Held by their owners, the camels lurched sideways at each other. Both were frothing at the mouth.

'But because their bits are uncomfortable, I should think, rather than because their blood is up,' said Hilary.

Standing or squatting in a wide circle around the beasts engaged in desultory combat were two or three hundred Turks, the female spectators segregated on a bank of gravel forming a convenient grandstand.

When Stuart paused to photograph one of the hobbled animals, its owner came rushing up to demand a fee.

Stuart was annoyed. 'To hell with that,' he said crossly.

Richard laughed. 'Come on, Stuart. Give the guy a thousand *lira*. You'd pay that for a postcard.'

'That's different. This is a rip-off.'

'OK, it's a rip-off. But you have to give him marks for trying. I expect he has a lot of mouths to feed.'

'Not at my expense.' Stuart stalked off.

Richard shrugged and exchanged looks with Hilary. Watching them walking ahead of her, Nicola envied their easy companionship.

On the other side of town, with the group gathered round her, Nuray said, 'These Lycian rock tombs you can see in the cliffs behind me are among the most beautiful and interesting antiquities in Turkey. In summer this place would be swarming with visitors. Today we are the only people here. Before you explore the Greco-Roman theatre and climb up to the tombs, let's refresh ourselves with orange juice.'

As the orange-juice seller had only a hand-press and it was going to take some time to make juice for everyone, Nicola thought she would explore first and have a drink later.

Presently, trying to find her way towards the tombs without going back to the main entrance to the theatre, she came to a place where the stone ledge on which she was standing was about four feet above the grassy path below.

It was too far to jump. Before she could sit on the edge and lower herself down, Serif appeared.

'Do you want to come down? I'll help you.' He held out his arms to her.

It was difficult to refuse without seeming rude. Reluctantly she put her hands on his shoulders and let him swing her off the ledge. Then, instead of letting her go, he kept his hands on her waist.

'Are you still angry because I kissed you?'

There were people near by. She could hear several voices.

'No, but please let me go.'

Instead his hold on her tightened. As she turned her face sideways, trying to elude his mouth, he slid one arm further round her, using the other hand to turn her face towards him. He wasn't rough, but he was strong, and determined their lips were going to meet. Short of methods the situation didn't justify, there was nothing she could do to stop him.

Knowing from the sound of the voices that they weren't going to be alone for much longer, Nicola gave in and let him kiss her.

'Ooh, I say! What's going on here?'

Mrs Tufnell's voice behind him—half excited, half shocked—made Serif raise his head.

'Oh, it's you two,' Joan said, as he and Nicola moved apart. 'I didn't recognise you for a minute.'

With her were Philip and Bob.

'It's a bit early in the day for that sort of thing, isn't it, lad?' her husband remarked, in a jocular tone. 'Still, you're only young once.' He gave Nicola a wink. 'And it's not a proper holiday without a dash of romance, is it?'

Later, on the way to the next night stop, they spent half an hour playing energetic beach football.

Richard scored his goals with an amused shrug, not the jubilant clasping of hands over heads which were Serif's and Stuart's reactions when they kicked the ball into the improvised goals ineffectively defended by Philip at one end of the pitch and by Bob at the other.

'You lot look like lobsters. Joan and I are freezing,' said Janet, when the others returned to the truck. 'It's high time the heater was mended. Serif should have fixed it this morning instead of chasing Nicola around the ruins.'

Richard heard the remark and raised an eyebrow.

'Chasing you, Nicola?'

'Janet's exaggerating.'

At this point, as she had earlier, Hilary smoothed over what, from Nicola's point of view, was Janet's gaffe.

'Perhaps the heater can be attended to while we're at Kas. Why don't you and Miles have a word with Serif this evening, Richard? It certainly ought to be mended before we go back over the mountains.'

'We'll do that,' said Richard. 'Serif does seem to be letting his duties as driver-mechanic take second place to his social activities,' he added, with an enigmatic glance at Nicola.

She had thought Serif attractive when they had met and, in his audacious black-eyed way, he was. But the way she felt now about Richard made her impervious to the Turk's charisma. He had become a complication and a nuisance. Even the way he played football seemed to her too flamboyant compared with the more relaxed style of the tall American.

Before they arrived at the next place on the itinerary, Serif stopped the truck for Nuray to join the group.

'In Turkish, K-a-s is pronounced like your word cash,' she told them. 'Kas is the site of the ancient city of Antiphellos and we know that in Roman times it was famous for its sponges. A few years ago it was a fishing port. Now it caters to many tourists, but not at this time of year.'

The Oteli Ekici, their base for the next two nights, was a newly built hotel. With its rows of small balconies, it resembled the thousands of hotels constructed to house package-tourists in resorts all round the Mediterranean. Its only distinguishing feature was a lobby floor spread with colourful rugs.

Here, to their mutual pleasure, Nicola and Hilary were assigned to the same room.

'Janet is neat and considerate, but I don't find her as compatible,' said Hilary, as they unpacked their belongings.

Although the radiators weren't on, the water in the bathroom was hot and they both had a shower and washed out their smalls, pegging them out on a rack provided for that purpose on the minuscule balcony.

Their room overlooked a colony of similar hotels, all the others closed up for the winter. However, on leaving the hotel they discovered that, in the opposite direction, lay an attractive harbour and beside it a triangular space with some trees and a statue of Kemal Atutürk, the founder of modern Turkey.

While they were exploring, they met Richard, who was looking for a bottle of Turkish brandy, and found a small bottles of cheap *kanyak* in a shop near the vegetable market. From there the three of them wandered around, discovering a cobbled street of attractive old timber houses with a beautiful Lycian tomb at the top of it.

'How about a pre-dinner drink in my room?' said Richard, when they returned to the hotel.

Later, when they were tidying themselves for supper, Hilary said, 'He's rather an enigma, isn't he? Far more at ease than Philip, far more outgoing than Miles, and yet I sense a reserve . . . a part of himself he holds back. What do you think about him, Nicola?'

'I don't know. He's out of my league. I'm not used to hobnobbing with chief executives.'

'Most people haven't reached those heights at Richard's age. He must be exceptionally clever.'

There had been a time, immediately after her dismissal, when Nicola had felt that nepotism had a good deal to do with Richard's early eminence. Since then she had changed that view. There could be no doubt that his incisive leadership had saved Barking & Dollis from disaster.

His innovative ideas and the reforms he had instituted were the talk of the trade. This year the firm was expected to win the coveted Publisher of the Year award. Considering how recently it had been in the doldrums, to receive that accolade would be a remarkable achievement.

'I've heard people in the book trade speak highly of him,' she said, in a neutral tone.

She knew Hilary was very perceptive and didn't want her to guess how she felt about Richard. She valued Hilary's opinion of her and felt sure the older woman would think it foolish to succumb to an attraction so quickly. And she would be right.

They had dinner at a small restaurant on the waterfront. The meal started with *sigara boregi*, hot, crisp 'cigarettes' of fine pastry filled with cheese. These were followed by spinach in a savoury gravy and then by grilled meat with mushrooms.

When everyone had finished the main course, Nuray said, 'I suggest we leave here now and go to a place near the post office where they serve cakes and hot chocolate.'

It was on the way to the cake bar that Sylvie tripped and fell over. She picked herself up, unhurt except for her hand which was badly grazed.

'I'll come back to the hotel and dress it for you,' said Nicola. As it was Sylvie's right hand, she wouldn't be able to deal with the injury herself. 'Explain to the others what's happened, will you, Hilary?'

The group had left the restaurant together but some had walked faster than others and the three of them had stopped to look in the window of a shop selling china.

At the hotel it emerged that Sylvie had come away without even a sticking plaster in her baggage. Fortunately Nicola had a basic first-aid kit, so they went to her room.

By the time they got there, the clean tissues she had given Sylvie to stop blood dripping on her clothes were soaked.

Sylvie had tripped on a chunk of breeze block half hidden in a mound of grit by a building site. When she saw how much grit was embedded in the heel of her hand, she paled, her eyes brimming with tears.

'Don't watch if it makes you feel queasy,' Nicola advised.

Cleaning the wound was going to be painful. She wished the group included someone more expert than herself.

Sylvie was crying, and Nicola was trying to be both gentle and quick, when there was a knock at the door.

Wondering if the desk clerk who had given them their keys, and seen the bloody tissues wrapping Sylvie's hand, could have sent for a doctor, Nicola left the younger girl perched on the lid of the lavatory while she opened the door.

'I thought you might need help,' said Richard. He was carrying a plastic box and a mini immersion heater.

'I'm trying to get all the grit out of Sylvie's hand. It's a bit tricky.'

The bathroom wasn't large. With Richard there it seemed even smaller. But his presence put a brake on Sylvie's tears and cries of pain.

'You need a cup of tea. Nicola will make it while I finish doing your hand,' he said, taking charge.

Nicola was only too willing to relinquish control. As she carried out his instruction to make tea, she realised that as soon as she saw him standing outside she had felt a wave of relief. It wasn't that she was unequal to coping with a minor emergency if she had to, but she knew Richard would be better at subjecting Sylvie to pain now to prevent infection later.

Presently she emerged, her hand neatly bandaged.

'Richard's cleaning the basin.'

'Sit down and drink this.' Nicola put a mug of tea into her good hand. 'If I were you, I'd go to bed. It's cold out and you've had a shock.'

Richard emerged from the bathroom.

'Are you up to date with your shots, Sylvie?'

She looked blank until Nicola asked, 'When did you last have a tetanus booster?'

'Oh... not long ago.' Sylvie put aside the mug. 'I'm all right now. Let's go back to the others.'

Richard shook his head. 'You're going to bed. Doctor's orders.'

'I'm not going to stay behind while everybody else has fun.'

'I doubt if you're missing anything wonderful and we're staying too, aren't we, Nicola? We're going down to the bar, and you're going to swallow this pill and get a good night's rest. It's a big day tomorrow... the boat trip.'

Nicola felt sure that if she had prescribed an early night Sylvie would have rebelled. When Richard laid down the law, she grumbled but obeyed.

On their way downstairs, he said, 'It was good of you to come back with her. When Hilary told us what had happened, I thought I'd follow in case Sylvie was giving you trouble. She's not the type to bite the bullet.'

'I was very glad to see you,' Nicola admitted.

'Good... we're making headway.' The remark, and the tone in which he said it, made her pulses quicken.

The hotel did not have a bar as such. Drinks were served at the sofas in the reception-cum-television lounge. The desk clerk was watching a programme but responded to Richard's request for coffee with cheerful alacrity.

'While he's out of the way, let's turn the volume down,' said Richard.

He succeeded in reducing the noise level but, even though they chose a sofa with a pillar between it and the TV, the sound of a Turkish game show was still intrusive.

When the clerk returned with their tray, Richard said, 'Let's take it up to the first-floor landing. I noticed a sofa there and we shan't have to compete with the noise from the box.'

The sofa he meant was at the junction of two long corridors, facing the door of the lift.

'Not where I should choose to have coffee, but it seems to be our only option,' said Richard. There being no table, he put the tray down on the middle of the sofa's three squabs.

'And we can intercept Sylvie if she tries to sneak out in the hope of seeing that Tasmanian boy who was chatting her up in the restaurant,' said Nicola. 'Although I don't think she will. She's quite in awe of you.'

'You can't blame her for wanting more action than the trip offers anyone of her age. But before we leave Kas, so Nuray tells me, we're going to eat at the town's smartest dine-and-dance place.' He poured out the coffee. 'I suspect it's the only one open at this time of year. In summer the harbour will be full of private and charter yachts. Instead of sitting up here, we'd be at a table on the waterfront, watching the world go by.'

He handed her a cup. As he picked up the other, he said, '*Mutluluga* . . . to happiness.'

'*Mutluluga*,' she echoed, knowing she would rather be here, in the dimly lit and unheated corridor of an almost empty hotel with this man, than in the most glamorous place in the world with another man.

The only thing better would be to be in Richard's room, in his bed, in his arms.

Was that his objective? she wondered. Was he, like Sylvie, impatient to see more action than the holiday had offered so far? Had he decided that, of the three available women, she would be the least trouble, not only to get into bed but also to drop when the trek ended?

Being the first down to breakfast, Nicola chose a chair facing the sea and sat thinking about last night.

Was she glad or sorry Richard hadn't made a pass at her? It was one of those questions to which there was no cut-and-dried answer.

Her feelings about the way the evening had ended were a mixture of relief, disappointment, pique, puzzlement and unsatisfied longing. She wanted Richard more than she had ever wanted Ian. And, last night, desire might have proved stronger than discretion had Richard tried to coax her to spend the night with him.

But perhaps he had remembered what she had temporarily forgotten: that what he did at night was his own affair, but *her* absence from her room would be noticed and might even cause some alarm if Hilary failed to grasp the reason for it.

Whatever his reason for *not* making a pass—the most obvious one being that he wasn't sufficiently attracted to her—he had seemed to find her company enjoyable. They had talked until Hilary had stepped out of the lift, having left the others still talking at the cake bar.

After a short conversation, Hilary had taken the room-key and five minutes later Nicola had said goodnight to Richard and followed her.

There was snow on the tops of the foothills through which they drove to reach the village of Üçagiz where a boat would be waiting to take them to Kekova Island.

Üçagiz had only recently been connected to the coastal road system. Before that, access had been by boat and rough track, which had kept the village from being spoilt. Now its long seclusion was ending and, because of its picturesque situation, it was in danger of being ruined. Nuray said they might be among the last people to see it untarnished by tourism.

In an open square in the centre of Üçagiz—which Nuray said was pronounced Uchaz—several girls and two older women were awaiting the arrival of the bus with shallow baskets filled with cotton scarves similar to the ones on their own heads.

It was a short walk to the jetty where a fisherman, whom Nuray called Uncle Arif—uncle being a courtesy title—kept his boat. The small foredeck was spread with a rug and the seats along the sides with Turkish runners.

Soon everyone was aboard, the engine was throbbing and they were moving away from the wharf and beginning to see Üçagiz in its entirety, a huddle of small, red-roofed houses against a backcloth of arid hills and blue sky, the dominant feature being a white minaret topped by an emerald-green spire.

'We're going to a place where you can bathe,' said Nuray, as the boat neared a rocky cove.

Nicola leaned over the side and dabbled her hand in the water. It felt cold but was clear as stained glass, the pebbles on the bed as distinct as if they were inches rather than feet below the surface.

With the boat moored to a convenient rock, the passengers scrambled ashore. There were plenty of places where those who wanted to swim could undress.

The sun felt gloriously warm on Nicola's bare back as she stood on one leg to buckle a plastic sandal on the other foot.

Richard and Miles were already in the sea when she plunged in, stifling a shriek as the cold water embraced her. But it wasn't long before her body adjusted. After some energetic swimming all the bathers came out feeling invigorated and chiding the others for missing a great experience.

'Nicola . . . are you decent?'

Miles's voice brought her out from behind the rock where she had been changing to find him offering her a biscuit.

'Oh, lovely . . . digestives . . . my favourites. Thanks, Miles.'

'Richard's dispensing brandy, if you fancy a tot.'

'Why not? Although I'm not cold now . . . gloriously warm.'

They made their way to where Richard was pouring out *kanyak*.

He had replaced his wet shorts with a towel wrapped round his lean hips. In the bright morning light, his skin had a burnished sheen which made her long to run her fingers over the powerful contours of his shoulders and chest.

She found it difficult to keep her eyes off him. It seemed almost unfair that, with all his other advantages, he should also be good to look at. But she mustn't allow herself to watch him. If she did, it would soon be noticed, and she couldn't bear anyone to guess that she found him wildly attractive.

Back in the boat, they were taken to see an island which had been the site of a long-submerged city. Its quay and other ruined buildings were still visible in the clear water. But according to Miles and Hilary the most memorable feature of the place was the vivid green euphorbia bushes growing above the drowned city to a much greater size than either of the group's two keen gardeners had ever seen before.

Simena, where they were to lunch, was built on the side of a hill crowned by the crumbling walls of a large castle.

As she stepped ashore, Nicola noticed a beautifully carved stone capital standing upside-down on the quay, topped by a plant in a can which had once held paint for the boats pulled up on the nearby hard.

They ate out of doors on a terrace which in summer would be shaded by cane blinds spread across the rafters overhead.

Cane-shaded light bulbs wired to the rafters indicated that, later in the year, meals were also served here after dark. It was easy to imagine the sea gleaming in the moonlight, the black silhouettes of the islands, and the coloured riding lights of visiting yachts moored down in the harbour.

Nicola found herself thinking what a lovely place it would be for a seagoing honeymoon. Angry with herself for indulging in wishful thinking, she passed the empty chair next to Richard and sat next to Miles.

CHAPTER NINE

THE following afternoon they were taken to see a display of handmade carpets. The shop's owner, said Nuray, would also explain how the rugs were made and what the patterns signified.

The seating consisted of two narrow stone benches built along right-angled walls which, hung with rugs, served as backrests. Nicola found herself squeezed between Richard and Bob.

The display began with the service of apple tea, after which the young bearded dealer, speaking excellent English, began to unfold the neat stacks of flat-weave kilims and hand-knotted pile rugs, some new, some antique.

He had the enthusiasm of a man with a deep knowledge and love of the wares he sold. Very soon the floor of the shop was piled knee-high with a profusion of rich colours and fanciful patterns.

'Are you going to buy one?' Nicola murmured, while a second tray of tea was being served.

Bob thought she was speaking to him. 'That depends what he's asking. Joan'll know if they're reasonable. A very keen shopper is my wife.'

Nicola glanced enquiringly at Richard. To take up a minimum of space, he was sitting with his shoulders pulled forward as much as possible and his hands clipped between his long thighs.

'I think so. What about you?'

She shook her head. 'I'd like to but can't afford it...even if they are bargains. All my resources are already earmarked.'

She wondered what he would say if he knew about The Project. He would probably tell her she and Gina were mad.

The rug in which Richard was interested was the one Nicola would have chosen had money been no object. It was an intricate design of many strange birds and animals worked in sophisticated colours on a ground of off-white silk. Intended to cover a wall rather than a floor, not surprisingly it was more expensive than the rugs already priced.

Had she not been committed to The Project, she would have enjoyed buying a rug as a present for her parents. But she and Gina had agreed to cut out all self-indulgence in order to minimise the amount they were borrowing from their banks. Nicola wouldn't have been here but for Aunt Ruth's generosity. But now, ten days away from wintry London, breathing an unpolluted mixture of mountain and sea air, eating well, walking a lot, swimming, she was feeling very much peppier than when she had set out.

Outside the shop, Hilary said, 'Nuray, are those firm prices he gave us? Or are we meant to bargain?'

'They're good prices; better, I believe, than you'll find in Istanbul. And he's a reputable dealer who supplies several of the best specialist rug shops in London. If you want the rug mailed to you, you can rely on its arrival.'

Standing behind her, Serif said, 'Turkish rugs are a very good souvenir of your holiday. Better than Turkish delight…"a moment on the lips, a lifetime on the hips".'

'Where did you learn that expression?' Joan asked.

'From an American lady.'

'I'm going for a walk round the block, Nicola, and then I shall look at "my" rug again,' said Hilary. 'I'll see you later.'

As the group dispersed, Serif fell into step with Nicola who was heading uphill. 'You didn't see anything you liked?

'Several I liked very much. But I haven't the money to buy one.'

'You don't need money. You can pay with your credit card.'

'A card isn't a magic wand, Serif. I'd have to find the cash later.'

That seemed to puzzle him. 'If you were poor, you wouldn't be here,' he said. 'This holiday isn't expensive, but for what it costs you in England many people in Turkey could live for a long time.'

'I'm not poor. But I don't need a rug and the money I earn is being put by for something else.'

'A car?' he asked.

'No, not a car. I don't need one.'

'I'd like a Mercedes sports model . . . a beautiful car,' he said, half closing his eyes. Then, looking sideways at her, 'Would you like me better if I had a Mercedes?'

'Possibly a lot less. An expensive car might make you insufferably pleased with yourself. You don't suffer from an inferiority complex as things are,' she added, laughing.

'My word, I wouldn't have recognised you,' said Hilary, when she came up to change for the evening and found Nicola ready to go down. 'You look quite different with your hair up and all that make-up.'

'Too much make-up, do you think?' Nicola had borrowed some from Sylvie.

Hilary studied her for a moment. 'No, probably not. Certainly no more than most young things wear at parties, and Janet puts on all the time. I'm just not used to seeing it on you.'

Nicola gave herself a final inspection in the dressing-table mirror. She had put up her hair with a pair of tortoiseshell clips and was wearing a pair of flamboyant silver and gilt earrings Peter had brought back from a visit to Java. Her silk T-shirt was grey, the same colour as her eyes. Tonight she had on her best jeans and, instead of the braided leather belt usually slotted through the loops on the waistband, she had pulled through a long Indian scarf in grey and two shades of blue.

There was no one in the reception lounge when she went downstairs. She sat on one of the sofas, feeling increasingly jittery as the moment when Richard might finally recognise her approached.

Although her hairstyle tonight was not the same as the cut she had had the day he'd sacked her, it was closer to that style than the casual ponytail she had worn since the trek started. And the make-up and earrings must make her look more like the Nicola Temple he had met three years ago.

Usually he was one of the first to appear whenever the group assembled. Would he be early tonight?

To relax the tight knot of tension inside her, she made herself take some deep breaths. Anyone would think she was waiting for an important interview on which her future depended.

When Richard came down the stairs, she saw him before he saw her, half hidden by one of the large columns between the foot of the staircase and the corner where she was sitting.

He was dressed in a low-key style with grey trousers and a grey sweater, with a striped shirt showing at the V-neck and his anorak over his arm.

As she rose and stepped into view, he stopped short on his way to desk.

'Nicola!' he exclaimed, in an odd tone. As he took in her upswept hair, made-up face and silk top, his eyebrows rose. 'You're a knockout!'

'Thank you.'

'This is your London persona, I take it?'

She nodded. 'Hilary claimed not to recognise me. Does a little more make-up really make so much difference?'

He gave her a long, intent look. She waited, holding her breath, for the penny to drop. If it did, how would he handle the situation?

But what he finally said was, 'No, not really. You remind me of a line in one of my favourite books. I doubt if you would have read it. It's an American biography of a man called Maxwell Perkins. He was an editor for Scribner's, one of the great US publishing houses. It was Perkins who discovered and nurtured Ernest Hemingway and F. Scott Fitzgerald and other famous writers of the inter-war period.'

Nicola had read the book many times. Maxwell Perkins was one of her heroes, as much for his qualities as a man as for his place at the head of her former profession. But she didn't tell Richard she knew the book almost by heart.

'What's the line I remind you of?'

'It's a quotation from Virgil. *Dea incessu patuit*. But I won't tell you what it means. Read the book when you get back to London. I'm sure Chatham's will have it.'

The lift door opened and Lorna and Stuart stepped out, followed by Philip. Otherwise Nicola's face might have shown she already knew what the words meant and was thrown completely off balance by them.

Lorna was wearing a clinging black body and black tights with a short tiger-striped lamé wrap-around skirt.

'All ready for our rave-up?' she asked brightly. Then, giving Stuart a nudge, 'What about a drink while we're waiting for the others to come down?'

It wasn't until later, when they were walking to the restaurant, that Nicola had a chance to think about what Richard had said to her earlier.

The Latin phrase he had quoted came from a part of the biography which dealt with Maxwell Perkins' first meeting with the woman most people thought to have been the love of his life.

In a note to her, he had written, 'I always greatly liked the phrase "*dea incessu patuit*". But I never really knew its meaning till I saw you coming toward me through our hall the other night.'

Translated, the words meant 'she revealed herself to be a goddess'.

Could Richard really have meant that he thought *she* looked like a goddess? Nicola wondered disbelievingly. Yet what other construction was there to put on his statement?

A log fire was adding its cheerful blaze to the glow of a line of candles on the long table prepared for them at a restaurant overlooking the harbour. Turkish music was playing. An appetising aroma was wafting from the kitchen. All the staff seemed pleased to see them, hurrying to help with coats, pull out chairs and take orders for drinks. It was the most welcoming place they had been to so far.

Or was her impression coloured by the astounding compliment she had received? Nicola asked herself as she sat down. A compliment she wasn't supposed to have understood.

Whether by chance or contrivance Richard took the chair next to hers. They were both on the outer side of the table, the people opposite having their backs to a wall.

When everyone was seated, Nuray tapped a glass with a spoon. As the chatter of voices muted, she said, 'Tonight, as a special treat, we're going to have *kalamar* for our main course. But the food isn't ready yet, so why don't we all dance?'

Whereupon she and Serif moved into the space between the tables and began dancing together in a style which combined western disco with spasms of vigorous belly-dance shoulder-shaking and hip-grinding.

The party went on till late, a few locals coming in to eat, or to drink at the bar, and the staff joining in the dancing after the kitchen had closed.

The first to leave were the Tufnells, followed a little later by Miles, Hilary and Janet. Nicola didn't notice Stuart and Lorna leaving, or Philip. Suddenly it was midnight and the only people left from the group were Serif and Nuray, herself and Richard, and Sylvie who was being partnered by a young member of the staff.

'I think I'll call it a night.' Nicola got down from her stool at the bar where, at Serif's insistence, she had been trying some *raki*.

'I'll come with you,' said Richard, draining his glass.

After the noise and the warmth of the restaurant, it seemed very cold and quiet in the street outside. In spite of her padded jacket, she shivered and stepped out briskly.

'It was a good evening, didn't you think?' she said.

'Yes . . . a lot of fun.'

'I'd love to have a video of Hilary dancing with Serif.'

'She's a good sport,' Richard agreed.

He sounded slightly abstracted, making her wonder if really the evening had bored him. It had not, by sophisticated standards, been anything remarkable. And, even if he was not a regular nightclubber, he must in his time have been to all the best places in New York, London and many other cities with famous nightspots.

They walked up the hill in silence. There were not many lights on now. In summer the people of Kas stayed up late in the service of the new tourist industry. But at this time of year they reverted to traditional habits. Probably in the whole town not more than a dozen people were still awake.

At the corner where the road went in four directions, a tree made a patch of black shadow. As they reached it, Richard took her lightly but firmly by the shoulders and swung her against him.

'This is what I've been waiting for.'

He kissed her.

* * *

'Where do we go from here?' he murmured, a little while later, his lips against her cheek.

Nicola, who was feeling as if she had drunk several glasses of *raki* in rapid succession, made an effort to sound clear-headed.

'To bed,' she said firmly, pushing against his chest.

He loosened his hold on her slightly but kept her in the circle of his arms. 'That's fine by me. As long as you don't mind Hilary knowing about us?'

She pushed him away more vigorously. 'That's not what I meant at all!'

'It wasn't?' There was laughter in his voice. 'Well, maybe you're right. We'll be back in Istanbul soon, and meanwhile I can at least kiss you.'

He kissed her again, this time with even more assurance.

There had been nothing tentative about his first kiss. He had known she would respond, and she had. Now, as he kissed her for the second time, she knew it would be futile to pretend she didn't want him. All she could do was hope he would never discover the real reason for her rapid response.

She would rather be taken for an easy conquest than have him guess the truth: that she was helplessly infatuated.

The desk clerk was watching a chorus line of scantily clad girls on TV when they entered the hotel. He gave Richard his key and went back to his seat as they turned towards the stairs.

As they reached the landing, Nicola wondered if he would try to coax her to end the evening in his room. Probably Hilary was asleep by now. There was really nothing to stop her staying out as long as she pleased . . . until five o'clock in the morning, if she felt like it.

Halfway along the corridor, where the bedrooms were unoccupied and no one would be disturbed by the murmur of voices, he said in a low tone, 'If we must say goodnight, we'd better do it here.'

After he had kissed her in the street, the shadow of the tree had masked the expression on his face. But even here, close to a wall light, she found it impossible to guess the thoughts in his mind as he looked down at her.

Was this, on his side, merely a physical attraction? Or something more?

Richard took her face between his palms and moved them lightly over her cheeks for a moment. Then his fingers slid to the back of her head and she felt him unfastening her hair.

He must have done it before, with other women. When he had taken off the clips he felt for the pins, putting them into the pocket of her jacket before spreading her hair over her shoulders.

'You don't look much older than Sylvie with your hair down. Maybe it's just as well you do have a chaperon.'

'Maybe it is.' She slipped both arms round his neck, drew his head down and gave him a warm kiss.

But when he would have prolonged it, she broke away and said firmly, 'Goodnight, Richard. See you tomorrow.'

He had already eaten his breakfast when Nicola and Hilary arrived in the dining-room next morning. By the time they had made their selections from the buffet, he was leaving the room.

'Good morning. I'm going to the bank to cash some traveller's cheques,' he told them.

The remark was addressed to them both and there was nothing in the smiling glance he gave Nicola to distinguish it from the way he looked at Hilary. When he had gone and she was starting her breakfast, she could almost believe she had dreamed last night's kisses.

Conversation at the table was mainly about how much money would be needed for the remainder of the trip. Nicola's preoccupation wasn't whether she was going to

need more Turkish *lira*, but what Richard had had in
mind when, last night, he had said, 'We'll be back in
Istanbul soon...'

Was he going to suggest they spend the final nights
of the trip together, away from the others? Was she going
to fall in with that plan? Was it his intention to see more
of her after they returned to London? Or was it strictly
a holiday affair which would end when they parted
company in the baggage hall at Heathrow?

Somehow, between now and Thursday evening, when
they would be catching the train back to the city, she
had to make up her mind exactly where she stood and
what she intended to do.

Lunch was a picnic eaten among the ruins of the hilltop
city of Xanthus, looking down at a river from a height
of several hundred feet.

They ended the day at Fethiye, a yachting centre and
the last place they were to stay before heading back towards Istanbul.

On their last night on the coast, Nicola went to bed
in a quandary. Had Richard's kisses at Kas, the night
before last, been merely an impulse he had since regretted and didn't intend to repeat?

Neither last night nor today had he made any noticeable effort to spend time alone with her.

That night the temperature dropped. They woke up
to a cold, wintry morning. The breakfast waiter was
wearing a woolly ski cap with a scarf wrapped round
the lower part of his face when Nicola and Hilary went
up to the top-floor restaurant for breakfast. His response to their smiling, '*Günaydin*,' was an unintelli-
gible mumble.

Spreading her hands above the warmth of the paraffin
heater, Hilary said, 'You know *not* moving on every few
days is going to seem rather dull. This trip has brought
out the gypsy in me. Good morning, Richard.'

'Good morning.' He came to stand by the stove but kept his hands in his pockets.

'I was just saying to Nicola that I'm getting used to being in perpetual motion, but perhaps you've had enough and will be glad to stay put.'

'I shan't be staying put for long. I have to fly to New York early next week. My normal life is fairly mobile.'

'My everyday life is extremely settled and orderly,' said Hilary. 'Which is why I choose adventurous holidays. Will you be glad to get back, Nicola?'

'You're talking as if it were over,' said Nicola. 'There's still Pamukkale to see...and another night on the train...and Topkapi and the Grand Bazaar.'

'Who knows?' said Richard. 'Our second look at Istanbul could be the high spot of the trip.'

As he spoke, he looked at her mouth. It was almost as if he had leaned across the stove and kissed her.

The most direct route to Pamukkale had been blocked by heavy snowfalls, Serif reported. The alternative route would take longer.

For Nicola it was a morning of intense visual pleasure. There had not been many really white winters in her lifetime. When snow had fallen thickly, it had never stayed immaculate for long. In London it quickly turned to unpleasant grey slush. Even in the country town where she had grown up, roads were salted and swept, pavements and pathways shovelled, the illusion of a changed world lost.

But here, once they had left the main highway to follow the detour, they entered a Christmas-card world where it wouldn't have seemed surprising to see a Dickensian stage-coach coming in the opposite direction.

After driving from eight until eleven at a much slower speed than usual, they came to a small town where Nuray announced a coffee stop.

'Who would have expected to find a cake shop in these backwoods?' said Hilary, looking with surprise at the range of confectionery in the glass display counter as Serif shook hands with the proprietor.

'Here the best drink is *salep*,' he told her, putting one arm round her shoulders and the other round Nicola's. 'Shall I order it for you?'

'What is *salep*?' asked Hilary.

'We drink it in winter to keep out the cold... and to cure colds. It's made from the root of a wild orchid mixed with hot milk and sprinkled with cinnamon... delicious.'

Both women agreed to try it, but when, a few minutes later, Nicola took a sip from her cup, she found it unbearably sweet.

The café had tables for four and she and Hilary were sitting with Stuart and Lorna. Richard was at the table alongside theirs and, although she had kept her reaction to the drink to herself he leaned over and murmured, 'Not nice?'

'Too sweet for my taste.'

'Have my coffee.'

Without waiting for her assent, he exchanged her cup for his.

'But you may not like it either,' she protested.

Leaning across for the second time, his hand on the back of her chair, he said in her ear, 'Anything your lips had touched would taste like nectar to me.'

It was obviously meant as a joke, but although she smiled and said lightly, 'That sounds like one of Serif's lines,' she was aware of another, deeper response.

If he could make her quiver when he was being facetious, how would she react to serious love-talk? But perhaps there wouldn't be any. Perhaps he was one of those men who, when making love, carefully avoided saying anything which might be construed as a commitment.

* * *

The journey continued across a great plain ringed by mountains. Most of the way they had the road to themselves. The few cars they saw had chains on their wheels.

Presently they came to a vast and desolate-looking lake. By now the back of the truck was thickly coated with snow thrown up by the rear wheels. Soon, in spite of the heater, the side-windows began to ice over. Deprived of a view, the more restive members of the party began to grumble.

For Nicola, music was an effective antidote to boredom. She and Richard had swopped cassettes and she spent the rest of the morning listening to his tape of Beethoven's Fifth and trying to make up her mind what to do about him when they reached Istanbul.

It was late afternoon when they came to Pamukkale, an immense petrified waterfall thousands of years old.

As the truck chugged up the hill alongside the great white cascade which had already been visible from several miles away, Nuray explained what it was.

'At the top of the hill are the ruins of ancient Hierapolis. Among them is a spring. The water is full of calcium bicarbonate. As it flows over the edge of the plateau, carbon dioxide is given off and the calcium carbonate turns to hard chalk... travertine. In summer this is one of Turkey's biggest tourist attractions. To save it being damaged, shoes are forbidden on the terraces. If you want to explore them, you must do it with bare feet.'

'Is the travertine slippery?' Janet asked.

Nuray shook her head. 'It may look like ice but you won't slip, and the water is warm.'

After paddling in the shallow pools on the cascade, they swam in the warm water of what had once been a sacred pool and was now a public swimming-bath surrounded by attractive semi-tropical gardens. Scattered on the floor of the pool were columns and blocks of stone, the remains of a large portico.

'Nicola...what have you done to yourself?' Hilary exclaimed, as they came out of the water together.

Nicola looked at blood trickling down her right leg. 'Oh, dear...how did that happen?'

'You must have grazed yourself on one of the submerged pillars.'

'It's nothing much. I didn't even feel it.'

In the changing-room she mopped up the blood with a tissue and stuck a plaster over the small laceration. Then she dried and dressed, but left off her jeans in case blood oozed through the plaster and stained them.

Leaving the baths with her towel wrapped like a sarong round her hips and thighs, she encountered Richard.

'What did you think of it?' he asked. 'I found it rather unpleasant...like swimming in soup. But I've never much cared for jacuzzis. Although maybe, if the Pera Palas has private spa tubs, I'd enjoy relaxing in one with you. How do you feel about that?'

CHAPTER TEN

THERE was an electric pause. Nicola felt mentally pole-
axed by the unexpected proposition.

Richard was looking down at her, and for once she
could read his mind. He was visualising her lying in a
bubbling spa tub in the luxurious bathroom of his hotel
in Istanbul.

She hadn't expected to have to commit herself yet.
The two sides of her nature—the rational and the
reckless—were still locked in subconscious conflict. She
was no nearer a decision than she had been several days
ago.

'Hilary says you've hurt yourself, Nicola,' said Miles,
from behind her.

She turned. 'It's nothing serious. Perhaps water at
ninety-five degrees desensitises one's nerve-ends. I didn't
feel a thing.'

'All the same, it would be a good idea to put some
antiseptic on it,' said Richard.

When they got back to the truck, he insisted on removing the plaster to have a look at the place. Then he
covered it with a better plaster from his own first-aid
pack.

For a few minutes they had the truck to themselves,
the others still being in the baths or on their way to the
café.

'You haven't answered my question,' he reminded her.
'This trip has been fairly spartan. Shall we reward ourselves with a spot of *grande luxe* at the Pera?'

He made it sound like a decision to splurge on a bottle
of champagne rather than ordering tea. Surely he must
know that, for her, it was far more momentous? Perhaps

135

not. Perhaps he was used to girls who didn't make a big
deal out of this kind of proposition.

To her astonishment, she heard herself saying, 'Why
not?' and then, 'But isn't the Pera Palas likely to be
fully booked?'

'Not in February. Anyway, I already have a booking.
I'll call them tonight from the station and tell them
there'll be two of us.'

Serif put his head inside the truck. 'We must leave the
station soon. Have you seen Nuray? I'd better find her.'

'After wearing trousers for nearly a fortnight,' said
Nicola, 'I'm beginning to forget what it feels like to wear
tights and a skirt.'

She stepped into her jeans and pulled them up under
the towel before discarding it. 'Will jeans be all right at
the Pera Palas? I didn't bring any smart clothes.'

'Nor did I. If we don't pass muster for the dining-
room, we'll get room service to feed us.'

The train was already standing at the platform in the
station at Denizli.

'This time we have three compartments reserved for
us. With only four people in each, you'll be more
comfortable,' said Nuray. 'I've put Hilary, Janet, Nicola
and Sylvie together. In the men's compartment are Miles,
Richard, Philip and Stuart. I am sorry to separate you,
Stuart and Lorna, but it's only for one night. Lorna and
I will be sharing with Bob and Joan. You won't mind
being the only man with three women, will you, Bob?'

'Nothing I'd like better, love.' He cleared his throat.
'And now the moment has come to say thank you, on
behalf of us all, to our driver. We've had a few hairy
moments but here we are, safe and sound at the end of
a very enjoyable trip, and we'd like to show our appreciation of the way you've looked after us, lad. Don't
spend it all on lion's milk.'

Clapping Serif on the shoulder, he handed him an envelope containing the group's contributions to Serif's tip.

'It's very kind of you. Thank you. I've enjoyed the trip too,' said Serif, putting the envelope inside his leather jacket.

Later, after several people had taken group photographs, and everyone had supplied themselves with snacks and bottles of water from a kiosk on the platform, he shook hands with the men and kissed the women on both cheeks.

Soon after the train had pulled out of the station, it stopped at a smaller station where a boy was grilling chunks of meat over a charcoal brazier. As Nicola and Janet watched, a passenger from the train appeared with a large *pide* loaf which the boy filled with ten or twelve meat-laden skewers.

'I wonder what's on the menu in the dining-car?' said Janet.

'You were going to travel first class on the way back,' Nicola reminded her.

'Miles dissuaded me.' A few minutes later, when both Hilary and Sylvie had left the compartment, Janet said, 'Do you remember what else I said to you?'

'Remind me.'

'I said if one wanted to meet interesting men it was no use going on a cruise or to one of the luxury resorts because men like doing uncomfortable things like rafting and trekking. I was right, wasn't I? Philip's a dead loss, but Miles and Richard are both worth a bit of suffering, wouldn't you say?'

'They're interesting men,' Nicola agreed.

'Come off it,' said Janet. 'Richard's a real prize. I would have bagged him for myself, but I'm not his type. At first I thought Nuray was, but now it's obviously you he fancies. I don't suppose you need warning that he probably isn't serious. But it'll be great while it lasts.

Even if Richard had been a possibility, I'd still have gone for Miles. There's a lot to be said for an older man, especially if he's in good shape, which Miles is.'

'But what about Hilary?' said Nicola.

'What about her?'

'She likes him too.'

'I'm sure she does. He's an attractive man... too attractive to settle for her. I'm not saying she isn't a nice woman, but sexually she's long past her sell-by date.'

Nicola's affection for Hilary made her resent this casual dismissal of her friend's claims to Miles's interest. But Hilary's return put an end to the conversation. It left Nicola disturbed and worried.

In her opinion, Hilary was a far more suitable partner for Miles than Janet. Miles would have to be out of his mind not to realise that.

As perhaps I am out of mine, she thought anxiously.

Later, stretched in her bunk, listening to the rattle of the wheels carrying them back to Istanbul, she flicked on her torch to check the time by her watch.

This time tomorrow she would be in bed with Richard. He would probably be asleep after making love to her.

Would she also be asleep? Or lying awake regretting her decision to join the list of his girlfriends?

She woke to find herself alone in the compartment with the other three couchettes returned to their daytime position.

She looked at her watch. Nine o'clock. The others must be having breakfast. Why hadn't they woken her? And why was the train still trundling through open country? Surely they should be back in Istanbul by now?

As she sat up and stretched, the door opened and Hilary held back the curtain screening the compartment from the view of passers-by.

'I thought you might like a glass of tea,' she said. 'You were so deeply asleep we decided not to disturb you. The train has been delayed by the snow. We'll be arriving late... much to the annoyance of those who are panting to go to the Grand Bazaar.'

'How kind you are...thank you.' Nicola took the glass and saucer. 'I couldn't get to sleep last night, hence my total torpor this morning. Did you sleep well?'

'I don't think anyone did.' Hilary sat down on the opposite seat. 'At least the delay means our rooms should be ready for us. I'll have a hot shower before I go to the bazaar. What about you?'

It was on the tip of Nicola's tongue to tell her she wouldn't be going back to the hotel with the rest of them. But something made her keep silent. Perhaps the feeling that Hilary would disapprove and hence a desire to postpone the loss of her good opinion until the last possible moment.

No one could accuse the older woman of being narrow-minded. Her tolerance had been demonstrated many times during the trek. At the same time it had been clear that she didn't like some modern manners and morals and wasn't afraid to say so.

As she was under the impression that Richard and Nicola had met for the first time a fortnight ago to-morrow, Hilary was bound to think it impetuous, if not lax, for Nicola to be spending the weekend with him.

When Hilary had gone, she dressed and dealt with the couchette. Luckily the conductor was in the corridor and she made signs asking him to lock the compartment while she went to the washroom.

When she returned, he had disappeared. She was wondering whether to wait or go in search of him when Richard appeared at the end of the corridor.

In the moments it took him to reach her, she made a decision.

'Locked out?' Richard asked. 'I'll go and find the conductor for you.'

'No...wait. I want to speak to you...privately. There may not be another chance.'

He raised an eyebrow. 'Changed your mind?'

'Not completely.'

'What does that mean?'

'I...I've decided I'd rather the rest of the group didn't know about...our arrangement. So I'll spend tonight with them and join you tomorrow.'

He received this announcement in silence. After a pause, he said, 'As you wish. In that case, shall I invite Miles and Hilary to join us for dinner?'

'That's a good idea.'

Her first reaction was relief that he wasn't annoyed. But when he had gone to find the conductor, it struck her that for him to accept the change of plan so easily showed that becoming her lover was far less important to him than to her.

The conductor came back and unlocked the door. When Nicola was in the compartment, Richard stood in the doorway and said, 'I don't want you to do anything you're not happy with, Nicola. If you'd rather not come to the Pera, you have only to say so.'

Perversely, now that he was offering her an escape, she felt as if something wonderful were about to be snatched away.

'Are you having second thoughts?' she prevaricated.

Richard glanced along the corridor in the direction of the dining-car. Then he stepped into the compartment and took her in his arms.

'Does that answer your question?' he asked, a few moments later, releasing her.

Her lips tingling from the unexpected and passionate kiss, she could only nod.

'But you haven't answered mine,' he reminded her. 'That you don't want the others to know about us suggests you aren't entirely comfortable with our arrangement.'

'I just don't feel it's their business. I prefer being discreet about these things.'

'Do you do "these things" often?' he asked.

Before she could reply, Janet appeared in the corridor behind him.

'What a bore this delay is. I was planning to dump my kit at the hotel and take a taxi to Ataköy Galleria, the new shopping mall. It sounds more my style than a bazaar full of tourist tat. Would you like to come with me, Nicola?'

'I'm not sure. I'll see what Hilary is planning. Excuse me, I'm going for breakfast.'

Richard had already stood aside for Janet to enter the compartment. Nicola avoided his eyes as she passed him. She needed time to compose herself after that vigorous demonstration of his attitude to their time together. She hoped he wouldn't follow her to the dining-car.

To her relief he didn't, and the rest of the group were filling in the AA questionnaires and didn't notice her sitting down at an unoccupied table for two.

Her breakfast had been served and she was drinking another glass of tea and looking at the snowy landscape when Nuray brought her a questionnaire.

'May I join you for a few minutes?'

'Of course, Nuray. You must be looking forward to being back with your family and having a few days' rest, aren't you? When do you start your next trek?'

'I have a new group arriving on Monday, on the same aircraft that you and Richard will be going home on. But they'll be doing a different trek. I shan't be repeating this one until next month.'

After signalling to the waiter to bring her another glass of tea, she said, 'Normally on Sunday I take the people who have booked the weekend in Istanbul on a boat trip along the Bosporus to the Black Sea. But Richard says that, as there are only the two of you, he thinks you can manage without me. Are you happy with that arrangement?'

Nicola nodded. 'You ought to have one full day off between treks. The company work you hard, don't they?'

Nuray smiled. 'Most people think my job is all holiday.'

'There's a lot of responsibility involved. When are you likely to be visiting your sister again?'

'It depends how busy the company is. Sometimes there aren't enough bookings and a trek is cancelled. May I have your telephone number? I'd like to visit the bookshop where you work and say hello to you.'

'We could have lunch together.'

'What was it like in the women's part of the *hamam*?' asked Richard, when he and Miles met Hilary and Nicola for drinks in the lobby before going out for dinner that evening.

The two women looked at each other and laughed.

'Interesting!' said Hilary. 'The building was fascinating architecturally, but we were rather less keen on the ministrations of the masseuses—especially the rubdown with an abrasive glove. If I went again, I'd buy a new *kese* beforehand. The ones used on Nicola and me looked as if they had abraded a lot of bodies. How was it for you two?'

'We had the place to ourselves. Miles had the chief masseur and I had his assistant,' said Richard. 'Apparently it's not done for men to strip off completely. We were issued with a loin cloth called a *pestamal* and a pair of wooden clogs which weren't too easy to walk in.'

Nicola said, 'We were given a towel later on, but nothing like your *pestamal*. Turkish women kept their briefs on.'

'We could have done with our own shampoo,' added Hilary. 'The brand they use in the *hamam* stings when it gets in your eyes. I thought it was like being shampooed by a friendly gorilla, didn't you, Nicola?'

'It was certainly *nothing* like the aromatherapy treatments my godmother gave me the Christmas before last. But I wouldn't have missed it. What did you think of it, Miles?'

He had been looking in the direction of the lifts. Now, instead of answering her question, he suddenly rose to his feet. 'I've asked Janet to join us,' he said. 'Here she comes now.'

During the afternoon, Janet had had her hair done.

'How do you like my new outfit? I bet there was nothing like this in the Grand Bazaar,' she said, showing off a quilted gilet and matching skirt of velvet-soft caramel suede, worn with a paler silk shirt. She had also bought a bronze bag and shoes.

Although she looked very smart, Nicola found it hard to believe that quiet, kind and seemingly wise Miles could be more taken with her than with Hilary. Which just went to show that physical attraction could warp anyone's judgement, she thought uneasily.

'I'm looking forward to seeing the Topkapi Palace tomorrow morning,' said Hilary, while they were undressing.

There was nothing in her cheerful manner to betray that she might be hurt by the fact that all evening Miles had allowed Janet to monopolise him.

'How fast this fortnight has flown,' she went on. 'I can't believe that this time tomorrow I shall be back in my own bed.'

And I shall be in Richard's, thought Nicola, with mingled anticipation and apprehension.

The pear-shaped Kasikci diamond was said to have been found in the rubble of the Blachernae Palace by an impoverished spoonmaker who sold it for a few *lira*.

Now flashing and glittering in the light of a concealed spotlight, it lay on a bed of black velvet which rocked gently back, forth and sideways to show off the brilliance contained in the huge stone.

Displayed on its own in a large alcove, protected by a pane of thick glass and probably by a sophisticated alarm system, the eighty-six-carat diamond and the rest

of the treasure amassed by the Ottoman sultans made
the jewellery in Bond Street shop windows seem like mere
trinkets.

In other circumstances, Nicola could have spent all
day feasting her eyes on the inspired designs and superb
workmanship of what had to be the world's most magnificent collection of jewels.

But these were not the only things Nuray wanted them
to see before, at noon, the rest of the group left for the
airport. And although Nicola had been looking forward
to this visit to Topkapi Palace, now she was here she
found it hard to concentrate on the wonders of the
sultans' domain when, in a few hours' time, she and
Richard would be alone at the Pera Palas.

It was a very cold day. The museum attendants were
wearing dark blue overcoats and standing close to radiators, although these did little to raise the temperature
in the vast kitchens where meals for the five thousand
inhabitants of the palace had once been prepared and
which now housed wonderful displays of Chinese celadon
and Japanese porcelain.

On the way to the most famous part of Topkapi, Nuray
stopped to address them. 'The word harem means "forbidden". Today you'll be shown only a few of the four
hundred rooms. For centuries the harem here was a
mystery guarded by Sudanese eunuchs. It wasn't until
about thirty years ago that the compound was opened
to the public. At one time there were nearly seven
hundred female slaves in the harem, but many of them
used to die from diseases carried by vermin or from our
cold winters.'

They entered the harem by the Court of the Black
Eunuchs leading to the legendary Golden Road to the
Selamlik, the private quarters of the sultans.

As they moved through the empty rooms, once
crowded with hundreds of women, Nicola wondered
what it had been like to be brought here against one's

will and, perhaps, selected for the bed of a man one had
never seen and might find repulsive.

At least it was by her own choice that tonight she
would share Richard's bed. Even so, she couldn't pretend
to feel totally sanguine about it.

When the coach taking the rest of the group to the airport
had disappeared round the corner, Richard said, 'I'll or-
ganise a taxi.'

On the way to his hotel, she tried to look calmer and
more relaxed than she felt. Why *was* she flustered? This
was something other people did all the time without
making a big deal of it. So why did it feel a major commitment to her?

She hadn't been nervous the first time she went away
with Ian. Perhaps because she had thought he was her
future husband. She didn't think that about Richard.

In fact she had no idea what his long-term intentions
were, if indeed he had any. For all she knew this could
be a two-night stand, after which he would say goodbye
and erase her from his memory as effectively as he had
before.

It was then, as the taxi sped over Galata Bridge to the
modern side of the city where the luxury hotels and the
embassies were located, that in a sudden flash of understanding she knew she was here because—no matter what
he felt—she was in love with Richard.

And before she had come to terms with this realisation she was hit by a second stroke of enlightenment.
She had been in love with him from the moment of
setting eyes on him three years ago.

People said it couldn't happen; that you couldn't fall
in love with a stranger. But it had happened to her. She
could see it clearly now. She had walked into his office
and recognised instantly that he was the man she had
been waiting for, the man she could love for the rest
of her life.

And her instinct had been right. The past two weeks
had confirmed that he did have the qualities she admired, that he *could* be the love of her life. Apart from
one small crucial detail. That he might never feel the
same way about her.

'You're very quiet, Nicola.' He reached out and took
one of her hands, giving it a slight squeeze.

'I—I was thinking about the others...wondering if
their flight would take off on time.'

'I liked Miles and Hilary. The rest...' He shrugged.

The taxi drew up outside the imposing green façade
of the Pera Palas, and the other members of the group
were driven from Nicola's mind by the likelihood that
the next thing on Richard's agenda might be to make
love to her.

The lift must have been installed when the hotel was
built in 1892. Flanked by potted palms in brass urns on
ornate torchères in the form of elephants' heads, it had
an elaborate wrought-iron gate. Inside it was panelled
with dark wood and equipped with a small sofa.

'Later I'll show you the room Kemal Atutürk used
when he stayed here. They've made it into a museum,'
said Richard, as they were borne upwards. 'This place
has an interesting guest list. As well as kings, queens,
maharajahs and several prime ministers, they've looked
after Mata Hari and Sarah Bernhardt, Josephine Baker
and Garbo, and of course Agatha Christie.'

The porter carrying Nicola's kitbag had Richard's key.
He unlocked a door on the second floor. But the room
into which he led them wasn't a bedroom but a spacious
and comfortable, if rather old-fashioned, sitting-room.
As the porter disappeared into an adjoining room, Nicola
went to one of the windows. It had a fascinating view
of the Golden Horn.

When she turned round Richard was tipping the porter.
As the door closed behind him, Richard took off his
windcheater and tossed it on to a chair. He beckoned

her to him. 'Do you realise it's more than twenty-four hours since I kissed you?'

She went to him, trembling inside. Was this it? Was this the beginning of having all her dreams realised ... or shattered?

He took her face in his hands. 'Have you wanted this as much as I have ... to be alone together?'

'Yes.' Her heart was pounding so hard that she felt sure he must hear it.

As he bent his head she closed her eyes.

She was in his arms on the sofa when there was a tap at the door.

'I ordered some coffee.'

Gently, Richard disengaged himself and went to admit a waiter carrying a tray.

To Nicola's relief, the man didn't look at her as he placed it on a low table. Not that she was dishevelled, but she felt it must be obvious that his knock had interrupted a passionate embrace.

When the waiter would have poured out the coffee for them, Richard said something which stopped him. With an obsequious bow and a magician's dexterity in palming the tip, he whisked himself out of the room as swiftly and silently as his colleague.

'You've learnt far more Turkish than I have,' she said, watching Richard fill the cups.

'You forget ... I don't need much sleep. It was a distraction at night when I was trying not to think about you. But I shan't be improving my Turkish vocabulary tonight,' he added, handing a cup and saucer to her.

'Thank you.'

He picked up the other cup. Instead of returning to the sofa, he removed himself to an armchair a few yards away.

'If we're going back to the bazaar, I had better keep my distance. There's a Turkish proverb which says that the longer a pleasure is postponed, the more intense it becomes. It may be true.'

She was tempted to say, Let's forget the bazaar. Let's go to bed. It was what part of her wanted; the secret side of her nature which had always been controlled and repressed by her more decorous side.

But her decorous side was still dominant, making her answer lightly, 'I'd better get my things unpacked. I'll take my coffee through to the bedroom.'

He rose to open the door for her, but he didn't follow her in.

The bedroom was as spacious as the sitting-room, dominated by a large double bed, the floor spread with fine Turkish carpets. Her kitbag had been placed on a luggage rack. She unlocked the padlock.

As she began distributing her belongings, she wondered what her father and mother would think if they could see her now; what Gina would think.

There wasn't much doubt about her parents' reactions. They might not be shocked, but they would be concerned. They wouldn't want her to be hurt.

Gina would be aghast. She knew from the photographs of Richard in the book trade Press that he was attractive. But she would find it incredible that, having professed to loathe him for the past three years, Nicola could undergo a dramatic volte-face and, after only two weeks, end up in bed with him.

I ought to tell him who I am, she thought, as she took her washbag to the bathroom. I should have told him before.

Compared with yesterday's group visit to the Grand Bazaar, exploring the labyrinth of covered streets and narrow alleys with Richard was a much richer experience.

He had a good-humoured way of dealing with the salesmen who, whenever anyone paused to look at their wares, immediately started a spiel in the appropriate language.

Even today, when the most luxurious shops were located elsewhere, it was easy to visualise the time when heavily veiled women had come here to choose silks and pearls from the Orient and be shown the latest innovations from the West.

At the heart of the maze was Ic Bedestan, the old bazaar, a survival from the fifteenth century with small cave-like shops filled with rugs, camel bells, brass platters, antique tiles and old silver.

In the street of the quilt-makers, Richard chose two beautiful hand-stitched quilts to be shipped to his sister in Boston.

Afterwards they found their way to the smaller Spice Bazaar where the familiar scents of vanilla and cloves mingled with more exotic seasonings. Nicola noticed a jar labelled 'Aphrodisiac des Sultanes' and wondered what was in it, and if Richard had noticed it. She was grateful to him for not rushing her to bed at the first opportunity, as Ian had. She had enough misgivings about this weekend already without being made to feel like a latter-day odalisque.

They had a late lunch at a restaurant up some stairs near the entrance to the spice market. It had been recommended to Richard by a friend who lived in New York and there were several Americans eating there.

'If we'd had more time,' he said, as they finished their meal, 'We could have taken a ferry to the Princes' Islands. They're only an hour or two offshore. One of my mother's forebears spent a couple of years in Turkey with Sir Henry Bulwer, who was British Ambassador here in the 1850s. He bought the island called Yassiada and built a castle there. Travelling and living abroad must have been a lot more interesting then than now.'

'Apart from my great-grandfather who served in France in World War One, I don't think any of my forebears ever set foot out of England,' said Nicola. 'Even my parents aren't keen on going abroad. They've never been further afield than the Highlands of Scotland and the west coast of Ireland.'

'Sensible people...they know what they like and stick to it. Half the people who travel today don't really want to see the world. They're just keeping up with their neighbours, or going one better,' he said. 'You can bet your life Bob and Joan will be glad to get home this afternoon. So will Lorna and Sylvie. They'll all be delighted to get back to the telly, and sliced bread, and cornflakes for breakfast.'

'At least Sylvie now knows that olives can be black as well as green,' said Nicola.

They both smiled at the memory of Sylvie helping herself to olives at breakfast one morning, under the impression that they were cherries, and reacting with her usual disgust to the unexpected taste.

Signalling to the waiter, Richard said, 'Shall we go back to the hotel now?'

CHAPTER ELEVEN

LESS than half an hour later they were back in his suite.

'Siesta time,' he said, closing the outer door. While collecting the key from the porter's desk, he had asked for a bottle of Veuve Clicquot to be sent up.

'I'd like a shower,' said Nicola.

'Why not have a tub... more relaxing? I'll bring you a glass of champagne. Drinking chilled wine in a hot bath is my sister's favourite way of unwinding.'

'It·sounds good.'

In the bedroom she unlaced her walking boots. Her fingers were trembling slightly and her heart was beginning to beat in slow, heavy thumps.

In the bathroom she turned on the taps and started to undress. Unlike some of the hotels they had stayed at during the trek, the Pera Palas didn't expect its guests to restrict their ablutions to certain hours. Steaming water gushed from the hot tap.

Noticing the various freebies included a small bottle of bubble bath, Nicola unscrewed the top and tipped the contents into the cascade. Normally she didn't like foam baths, preferring fragrant oils which left her skin feeling silky. But at this stage of the relationship she needed the screen of bubbles to help her through the initial awkwardness of being naked.

Perhaps Richard would think her absurdly shy, even prudish. Prudish she wasn't, but shy—yes. Given her limited experience, how could she not be?

Instead of using the shower cap provided—did anyone look good in a shower cap?—she clipped her hair high on the crown of her head, and stepped into the still filling bath.

She had turned off the taps and the bubbles were frothing round her shoulders, concealing the rest of her body, when there was a tap at the door.

'Come in.'

Richard came in, a glass of champagne in each hand, and shouldered the door shut behind him. 'I've hung the Do Not Disturb notice on our door and told the switchboard we aren't taking calls,' he said, as he handed one of the glasses to her.

'Nobody knows I'm here. Are you expecting any calls?'

'No, and it's not likely anyone will call, but some people do know I'm here. Before I came away, I didn't foresee that on——' he checked the date by his watch '—February the eighth I'd want to be incommunicado.' He sat down on the edge of the bath, by her feet. Lifting his glass, he said, 'To Amazing Adventures, and to my friend Sam, without whom I wouldn't have met you.'

It was her cue to say, 'Well, actually we've met before, but you don't remember it.' But this wasn't the moment. She would tell him later...afterwards.

'To Amazing Adventures.' She took a swig of champagne, hoping it would slow her pulse-rate.

Richard ran a hand over his jaw. 'Would you mind if I shave while you're in there?'

'Go ahead.'

He took his glass to the basin at the far end of the bathroom. As he took off his shirt, his tanned back rippled with muscle. She felt her insides contract. What was she worrying about? Whatever the outcome of this weekend, she was here with this gorgeous man. Very soon she would be in his arms again. Forget the past. Don't think about the future. Enjoy the here and now.

'Like some music?' Richard asked.

She hadn't noticed before that the bathroom had a radio.

'Yes, please.'

When he switched it on, two Turkish male voices were
having what sounded like an argument. He found a
station playing western orchestral music.

'How's that?'

'Fine...lovely.' After a pause she added, 'Your sister's prescription works.'

It wasn't, strictly speaking, true, but she could see that
it would work...for ordinary tensions. Surprised to see
him lathering his chin the way her father did, she said,
'I thought you'd use an electric razor.'

'I was expecting to stay at *pansiyons* which might not
run to shaver plugs.' He looked at her through the mirror.
'I have a fairly stiff beard. I don't want to rough up your
skin.'

She sipped her champagne and watched the swift,
practised movements and steady hands with which he
removed the creamy soap from the taut brown planes
of his cheeks and chin.

'You'd be a good subject for a sculptor. You have the
kind of head which translates well into bronze.'

He laughed, showing a flash of white teeth. Then his
expression changed. In the act of rinsing his razor, he
paused to give her a long look.

'And you should have sat for Renoir. You aren't as
plump as most of his lovely ladies, but you look every
inch as luscious.'

If his eyes had been teasing, she would have echoed
his laugh. But they weren't. He sounded sincere.
Luscious—me? she thought, startled. It wasn't a word
she would ever have applied to herself.

Richard bent over the basin to sluice his face, neck
and ears with handfuls of running water. When he
straightened, his eyelashes were sticking together in spiky
clusters, as if he had been swimming. She had a fleeting
impression of the way he must have looked at eighteen.

Then he reached a long arm for one of the old-
fashioned huckaback hand towels, with 'Pera Palas'
woven into their borders. When his face was dry it

became the one she was used to; that of a confident, worldly man who knew far more about women than she knew about men.

Whistling softly to the music, Richard spread toothpaste on his brush. He sounded happy.

Damn right he's happy! What other mood d'you expect when you've fallen into his lap like a ripe plum...?

The voice in her head was her brother's.

Richard brushed his teeth, the movements of his hand and arm reactivating the exciting play of muscles on his back. He left the basin neat, folded the towel and drained his glass of champagne.

'More champagne for you?'

'Please.'

He left the room for a moment to fetch the bottle and ice-bucket. After refilling both their glasses, he put his on the floor next to the bath and then dabbled his hand in the bath water.

'More hot water?'

She nodded, sensing that he was playing with her, deliberately postponing the moment all this was leading up to.

'Mind your feet,' he said, before turning on the tap.

She drew up her legs, her knees appearing like islands in the sea of foam. But his warning hadn't been necessary. The bath was a large one. She could have lain flat on the bottom with room to spare.

When he judged the temperature was right, he turned off the tap. Straightening, he unbuckled his belt.

'I'll come in with you ... if you don't mind?'

Although he amended the statement into a question, it was obvious he didn't expect a negative answer. Disconcerted—this wasn't what she had expected—she said nothing. She had dim memories of playing in the bath with Peter when they were both small, but had never shared a bath with an adult man.

Richard unzipped his jeans. 'Move forward, will you?'

As she sat up and edged forward, she was aware of a pair of long suntanned legs, of spilling some of her champagne, of the displacement of water as he slid down behind her, making the layer of foam quake and seem for a moment in danger of overflowing.

'Right... now you can lie back again,' he said, as the upsurge stabilised.

With one hand he retrieved his glass, with the other, spread over her midriff, he pressed her backwards until she was lying against his chest.

'How's that? Comfortable?'

'You're laughing at me.'

'No, no... I wouldn't do that.' She felt the vibration of his chuckle against her shoulder-blades. 'Well, yes... maybe a little. Why are you being so serious? We're here to enjoy... be happy together.'

He pressed a soft kiss on her temple, then gently nibbled the lobe of her ear. 'For me, this is the best part of the trip. Would you agree?'

She nodded, catching her breath as, under the water, his hand slid away from her waist and began to explore the rest of her body, starting with her breasts.

For a big man, he had an incredibly gentle touch. Nicola closed her eyes and let her head tilt back on to his muscular shoulder, her inhibitions evaporating as the slow movements of his fingers sent flashes of exquisite pleasure streaking along her nerves.

'I want to look at you,' he murmured presently, close to her ear.

Moments later she realised he must have opened the outlet with his foot. Beneath the foam, the water was draining away, leaving her covered with bubbles. As the bathwater ebbed, the foam began to evaporate. He accelerated the process by trickling some of his champagne over her breasts.

'Richard! It's cold!' she protested, not really minding.

He put the glass back on the floor, and hers with it. 'Turn around. I want to kiss you properly.'

She wriggled round to face him. They kissed. Suddenly it seemed the most natural thing in the world to be in his arms, in a bath, in a famous foreign hotel where princes and presidents had stayed. The only unnatural factor was not to be able to say, between kisses, I love you.

When Nicola opened her eyes on Sunday morning, she knew it was much later than her usual getting-up time.

Hardly surprising, she thought, smiling to herself.

Judging by the feel of Richard's body, curled round behind her, he was still deeply asleep.

That too had been predictable. After last night he might not wake up until noon!

She lay still, savouring the unaccustomed cosiness of sharing a bed, and remembering that first amazing hour after he had lifted her out of the bath, enveloped her in a large bath-sheet, carried her to bed and made love to her in a way she would never forget.

If only he had been her first lover, she thought wistfully. If only she had waited for him.

If only he could become her final and forever lover.

Quickly she pushed this thought to the back of her mind. The best way to live today was as if it were her last. One glorious butterfly-short span, worth more than a lifetime of mundane beetle-days.

'Nicola?' Richard's voice, soft but not drowsy, broke into her thoughts.

Without moving, she said equally quietly, 'I'm not asleep. I thought you were.'

As she spoke, he rolled on to his back, leaving her free to straighten her legs and stretch.

Last night, on his instructions, a waiter had used his pass key to open the outer door and wheel in a damask-clothed trolley while they were still in the bedroom. They had eaten in the sitting-room, wrapped in dry bath-towels. After a delicious light supper, and another bottle of champagne, they had come back to bed and made love...and made love...and made love. Until finally, exhausted by bliss, she had gone to sleep in his arms.

'What time is it?' she asked.

He reached out to take his watch from the night table.

'Almost nine-thirty. Time to make a move if we're going on that river trip.' He rolled back towards her, raising himself on one elbow to look down into her eyes. 'How did you sleep, lovely one?'

'Need you ask?'

Although, last night, he had swept aside her inhibitions, this morning she still felt a little residual shyness. Indeed now she had more to be shy about than before.

Last night she had startled herself. She had always known that, deep down, there was a wanton streak in her. But she hadn't expected it to surface quite so rapidly, so wildly.

He smiled. 'You were delicious...figuratively... literally...every way there is.' He bent to drop a kiss between her eyebrows. 'Let's brush our teeth and try out the shower. But first I'll order breakfast. What would you like?'

While he was calling room service, she couldn't resist running her hands over his smooth brown skin. Her touch wasn't intended to arouse him but it had that effect.

As soon as he had put the receiver back on its rest he began to return her caresses, his touch deliberately sensuous.

Suddenly last night's passion was flaring into new life. But this morning, unlike the first time, he didn't need to be gentle. Her desire was as urgent as his. Their bodies fused in a single swift fluid movement. Their hearts beat as one. They moved to the same eager rhythm, driving each other to the same breathless frenzy...sharing the same ecstatic free-fall.

*   *   *

By the time they were ready to go out, the river mist seen from their room while they were breakfasting had cleared. The sun was shining.

On the advice of the helpful receptionist, instead of taking the two-hour boat-trip to the upper end of the Bosporus, where eventually it merged with the Black Sea, they took a taxi for the outward journey.

Although Richard talked to the driver most of the way, he also held Nicola's hand. From time to time he gave her looks which were hard to meet without revealing the full extent of her feelings.

The thought of a second night with him made her heart lurch in her chest.

Then she remembered that this time tomorrow they would be airborne for London, and on Tuesday he was flying to the States. For all she knew, the delights he had shown her last night might, for him, be a commonplace experience. What had seemed to her exceptional and wonderful might, in his life, be the norm.

They had lunch at a seafood restaurant on the waterfront at Rumeli Kavagi on the European side of the strait. A Genoese fortress was visible on the Asian side, a fiddler was playing background music and pleasure boats, ferries, several cargo ships and even a winter cruise liner added interest to the scene. The other customers were mainly cheerful family parties of Istanbullus.

At this time of year the last boat back to the city left soon after three o'clock, but luckily it wasn't crowded. They found somewhere to sit with a good view of both shores.

'Two weeks ago today, we were on that other ferry,' said Nicola. 'I thought then it was Nuray you fancied.'

'And I thought you couldn't stand me,' Richard said drily. 'Talk about hostile vibes . . .'

It was a perfect opportunity to explain the reason for her initial hostility. She was about to do so when a man selling sweetmeats came up to them and Richard bought a box of *lokum*, the proper name for Turkish Delight.

The youth who was selling it wanted to practise his English and it was quite a long time before he moved on. By then Nicola had changed her mind, deciding to postpone her confession, if it could be called that, until she had some indication that this was a lasting relationship which had to be put on a straightforward footing.

If it was not going to last, what was the point of raking over the ashes?

The journey back was delightful. She felt sorry the rest of the group had missed it.

In places the Bosporus was wide, a mile and a half from bank to bank, both sides having castles and forts strategically placed on the heights above small clustered fishing villages and the painted or weather-bleached waterside summer-houses called *yalis*.

She wished Richard would put his arm around her. She was beginning to realise that, although she had loving parents and many friends, for a long time she had been starving for the special affection between a man and a woman. She wanted to take his hand and hold it to her cheek, to rest her head on his shoulder, to feel his arm round her waist.

But Richard, although he talked to her, was intent on the passing scene. She felt sure that, had he been in love with her, he would have been looking at her as often as at the view.

As soon as they got back to the hotel, he was as attentive and romantic as she could have wished, sweeping her back to bed and making masterful love to her.

But when he had gone for a shower, leaving her lying in a daze of satisfied languor, her doubts began to creep back. Surely, by now, if this was more than an affair, he would have given some hint of deeper feelings?

Later they dined at a small intimate restaurant famed for its Turkish cuisine but without a rigid dress code.

'My guest would like *bülbül göbegi*,' said Richard, when the head waiter asked if they wished for a sweet.

'I don't even know what it is,' she said, a few moments later.

'It's a nightingale's nest,' he said, smiling. 'Not a real one...it's made from *kadayif*, which I know you like, with pistachio nuts for the eggs. Wasn't I right? If you'd seen "nightingale's nest" on the menu in English, isn't it what you'd have chosen?'

She had to admit that it was. While she ate the nightingale's nest, Richard drank strong but unsweetened Turkish coffee.

Somehow she couldn't help feeling that the choice he had made for her and what he had chosen for himself might reflect the difference in their characters, and have a bearing in the nature of their relationship.

On the flight to England, Nicola assumed they would share a taxi to central London, one of them dropping the other off. It didn't work out that way.

Where the Customs hall debouched into the airport's main concourse someone from Barking & Dollis—a man she had never seen before—was waiting for Richard.

Apparently a crisis had blown up during the morning. Mr Kenton's mission was to brief Richard about it. He had come in a chauffeur-driven car and, when they reached it, said to her, 'You won't mind sitting in front, will you, Miss—er——? This matter is rather confidential.'

'Not that confidential, Kenton,' Richard told him impatiently. 'Miss Temple is the soul of discretion.' He smiled at her. 'Aren't you?'

Nicola said, 'I don't mind sitting in front if Mr Kenton wants to talk to you privately.'

The chauffeur was holding the rear door. Before Richard could argue, she opened the front one and got in. If they weren't going to be by themselves, it didn't really make much difference where she sat.

On the fast road through open country between the airport and the edge of the city, she retouched her lipstick, using the mirror attached to the back of the passenger's sun-visor.

As she'd hoped, it gave her a glimpse of Richard. He had started the trek with a tan and now, after two weeks of outdoor life, his face was strikingly bronzed compared with the office pallor of the man who had come to meet him.

But she also saw a subtle change from the way Richard had looked on the opposite side of the breakfast-table this morning, and in the seat next to hers on the flight. His relaxed expression had gone, replaced by a sterner mien. Now he looked more like the man who had sacked her three years ago.

Perhaps, as he listened grave-faced to whatever Mr Kenton was telling him, he was mentally passing sentence on someone else.

They were almost back in the metropolis when the glass panel opened and Mr Kenton instructed the driver to take the young lady wherever she wanted to go before returning to the office.

When the car stopped outside the house where Nicola lived, the driver got out to unlock the boot where her kitbag was stowed. As she got out, so did Richard.

'I'm sorry about this, Nicola.'

'It doesn't matter. I hope the trouble is nothing too serious.'

He shook his head, saying in a low tone the man in the car wouldn't hear, 'An in-house storm in a teacup, probably. But I'll have to sort it out before going Stateside tomorrow. I'll call you as soon as I can. Got your house key?'

She nodded, hating to have to say goodbye to him, especially in front of other people.

The driver was placing her kitbag on the doorstep. 'There you go, miss.'

'Thank you...and goodbye.' She bent to speak through the open rear door. 'Goodbye, Mr Kenton.' Straightening, she held out her hand. 'Goodbye,

Richard.' Her voice was husky as she added, 'And thanks
for a marvellous weekend.'

He took her hand in his larger one. She had the feeling
he wanted to sweep her into his arms and kiss her the
way he had kissed her before leaving their room at the
Pera Palas that morning.

But instead he lifted her hand to his lips.

'Thank you for sharing it with me. Take care of
yourself.'

He stepped back inside the car. The driver closed the
door and returned to his own seat. Richard looked at
her through the window, his expression inscrutable, until
the vehicle glided off. Then after a final wave he turned
away to resume his conversation with Kenton.

She had been in the flat for ten minutes when the telephone rang.

'Hello?'

'Oh, good...you're back.' The voice was Gina's. 'How
was the trip?'

'Fine. How are things with you?'

'Terrific! It's nearly knocking-off time. Shall I come
round and bring you up to date?'

'Yes, do.'

'I'll be there in half an hour.'

By the time the doorbell rang, Nicola had been to the
nearest shop to buy bread, milk, fruit and a bunch of
early daffodils for the vase on the coffee-table. She had
also flicked round with a duster, run the cold tap to clear
the water in the pipe before filling the kettle and unpacked a jar of apple tea granules.

'You look wonderful,' said Gina, after hugging her.
'So how did things go between you and the Beast of B
& D? Were you able to avoid him?'

'I'll tell you all that later. First tell me what's been
happening while I've been away.'

'The main thing is that The Project is now public
knowledge...the first two trade ads have appeared.' Gina
delved in her tote bag and produced a copy of *The*

Bookshop and the tabloid-size *Bookworld News*. 'Here they are.' She opened both periodicals and laid them side by side on the coffee-table. 'Don't they look good?'

Nicola had already seen and approved the layouts designed for them by an ex-boyfriend of Gina's who worked for an advertising agency. But this was how they had been seen by booksellers up and down the country.

Her eyes skimmed the familiar text of the advertisement, every word of it carefully thought out, all the stale clichés of publishing avoided.

'Margaret's over the moon with excitement,' said Gina. 'Especially about the editorial feature, which she knows is worth ten advertisements. Look...how does that grab you?'

'They've used the photo!' Nicola exclaimed.

Another of Gina's contacts, an up-and-coming photographer, had taken the picture of Gina and Nicola sitting on either side of Margaret, all three of them beaming at the camera as radiantly as if Margaret's novel were already at No. 1 on the best-seller lists.

The article below the photograph not only filled the page but continued overleaf.

'You can read it properly later,' said Gina. 'Most of it's a rehash of my Press release with some editorial comments worked in. They also rang Margaret for quotes and, predictably, she sang your praises and said she would never have finished such a long, ambitious book without your encouragement...especially after B & D had rejected the outline she submitted to them.'

'I must call her,' said Nicola. 'Just to let her know I'm back.'

She picked up the telephone, dialled the number and had a short conversation with her excited author who, fired by their confidence in her, was now at work on another long novel.

'How about some coffee?' said Gina, when Nicola replaced the receiver. 'Now I look at you closely, you look a bit bushed. Did you have to crawl out of bed at an ungodly hour this morning?'

'Not specially. I've had some late nights. Instead of coffee, try apple tea.' Nicola had left Gina's parcel on the worktop near the kettle. 'Here's a small present for you. Nothing lavish, I'm afraid.'

Gina, who liked to make the most of her handspan waist, was delighted with the silver-buckled belt. 'I hope you bought something for yourself and didn't spend all your pennies on me.'

'I've got some Turkish beads, but they're still in my luggage.'

They took their mugs to the sitting area. Gina slipped off her loafers and made herself comfortable at one end of the sofa. 'So now tell about your trip... from the beginning. You said in your letter that Richard Russell hadn't recognised you. But that was only a few days into the trek. Did he cotton on later... or did you tell him who you were?'

'Neither... he still doesn't know.'

'Are you serious?' Gina exclaimed. 'How come?'

'There never was a good moment to bring it up and have it out.'

'He's going to know before long... as soon as he sees the trade papers. Did you have much to do with him? What sort of terms were you on by the end of the trip?'

Nicola had already debated whether to tell her friend how her time in Turkey had ended. But although she and Gina were close they had had too much else to talk about to spend much time discussing their love-lives in detail.

She said, 'Quite friendly terms actually. I... I changed my mind about him. That may sound strange after all the bad things I've said about him in the past, but when you're with someone every day from breakfast to bedtime you get to know them pretty well. He's a much nicer person than I imagined.'

'He's still the guy who sacked you,' said Gina. 'I don't understand how you could spend two weeks with him and not bring that up... not ask him to justify himself. You say by the end you were on "quite friendly terms". How friendly? Are you going to see him again? Did you exchange telephone numbers?'

'Everyone did. Whether Richard will call I don't know. He's off to America tomorrow. He'll be away for ten days. His brothers and sisters are there, apart from B & D's parent company.'

'Well, even if his *amour propre* is only half as sensitive as the average male ego, he's not going to like being made to look foolish,' said Gina, with a gesture at the trade periodicals.

'What do you mean? How does Richard come into it?'

'The fact that he sacked you is mentioned. It does add spice to the story from a journalistic point of view.'

'I'd better read what they've written.'

Nicola reached for *The Bookshop* and started reading the rest of the article which had appeared the previous Friday.

Margaret Wanstead's second novel *The Gothick Window*, to be published by Trio in simultaneous hardback and paperback in May, is a bold experiment by three women who, not long ago, were victims of the 'rationalisation' which left many publishing people redundant and some 'mid-list' authors without a publisher.

Margaret Wanstead and her editor, Nicola Temple, were both with Barking & Dollis until the advent of B & D's new CE, Richard Russell.

But although B & D weren't impressed by the outline of Wanstead's second book and waived their option on it, Temple was convinced the novel was a winner.

She and former PR-girl Gina Latimer, another victim of the recession, decided to pool their resources and publish the book themselves, calling their imprint Trio.

The story went on to describe the smallness of their initial investment, the big input of time and energy on top of their regular jobs, their problems with distribution and their innovative ideas about marketing.

It was first-class free publicity; but, as Gina had indicated, it wasn't going to please Richard.

Although it didn't go as far as to credit Nicola with statements she had never uttered, it was certain to leave everyone who read it with the feeling that he had blundered, and that a major part of her motivation was a determination to prove him wrong.

CHAPTER TWELVE

NICOLA spent the following weekend with her parents. Soon after her arrival her mother said, 'You know that unpleasant man who sacked you from Barking & Dollis...?'

Nicola tensed. 'What about him?'

'There was an article on him in a bundle of magazines I was given for the white elephant stall at next month's coffee morning.'

Nicola tried to sound casual. 'Have you still got them?'

'No, I've passed them on to Mrs Finsbury who's running the stall.'

'Oh.' Nicola hoped her disappointment wasn't visible.

'But I cut the article out for you. It's in my desk. I'll fetch it.'

In her methodical way Mrs Temple had made a note of which magazine it came from and the date of the issue. The feature, part of a series on London's eligible bachelors, had appeared eighteen months ago.

'I know one can't believe all one reads, but it makes him sound a dreadful womaniser,' said Mrs Temple. 'I don't like that type of man. There's no such thing as a reformed rake, in my opinion. They can never resist another conquest, which makes life hell for their poor wives.'

It wasn't until after lunch, when she and her father had dealt with the washing-up, that Nicola was able to retreat to her room and study the article in detail.

With several small pictures of him escorting different but equally gorgeous girls, there was a large picture of him looking heartbreakingly attractive in a dinner-jacket.

Reading the text made it clear why the feature had increased her mother's dislike for him. But Nicola couldn't relate this image of Richard to the way he had been in Turkey.

She felt sure that Gina, who kept a close eye on all the glossies, would have known about the feature but decided to keep it to herself.

One result of the piece in *The Bookshop* was that a number of would-be writers having difficulty finding a publisher made contact with Nicola by writing care of the trade paper.

She also heard from several published authors who weren't happy where they were and thought she sounded more *simpatica* than their present editors.

But the one person she wanted to hear from remained silent. Although she knew he might be extremely busy, she had hoped he would find time to telephone her from America. But ten days passed and no call came.

She had been back at work for two weeks and was wondering if she ought to make contact with him when, on Friday evening, someone rang the downstairs doorbell.

As she wasn't expecting anyone, she felt sure it had to be him and hurried to use the entryphone.

'Who is it?'

'Richard Russell.'

Nicola's heart contracted. 'Come up. It's the top floor.' She pressed the button to unlock the street door.

Knowing it wouldn't take him long to reach her front door, she dashed to the bedroom to run a comb through her hair.

Richard's loud double rap on the door had something peremptory about it. When she opened the door and saw him standing on the landing, his forbidding expression confirmed her fear that he had been furious to find himself mentioned in the article in *The Bookshop*.

'Good evening.' His tone was formal. 'I hope it's a convenient moment to talk to you.'

'Of course...come in.' She stood aside so that he could enter. 'How was your trip to the States?'

Ignoring the question, he walked to the centre of the room, casting a cursory glance around her living quarters. Then, turning to face her, he said curtly, 'Why didn't you tell me who you were?'

It was a moment she had foreseen and mentally rehearsed many times.

She said quietly, 'At first I thought you must know who I was. When I realised you didn't, it seemed more tactful to say nothing.'

'Tactful!' he exclaimed explosively. 'You lied to me...made a fool of me.'

She shook her head. 'That isn't true. I—I acted as I thought best...to spare us both embarrassment. What, really, was the point of dredging up our first meeting if you had no memory of it?'

'I suppose that depends on how highly one rates the truth. Clearly it isn't a matter of priority with you,' he said cuttingly.

His tone flicked her like a whiplash.

'I think my regard for the truth is as high as most people's. It was an awkward situation. Surely if anyone has a right to feel aggrieved it's me, not you.'

'How do you make that out?' he asked tersely.

'It is rather galling to discover that someone who's had a major impact on your life has absolutely no recollection of ever seeing you before.'

'So you took your revenge by making me look a fool in front of the entire industry.'

'That's neither fair nor true,' she protested. 'I was as surprised as you to find your name mentioned in the pieces about Trio in the trade Press. There was nothing about you in Gina's original Press release, apart from a reference to the fact that Margaret's first novel was published by Barking & Dollis who decided not to take up an option on her second book. It was the journalists who wrote those articles who dragged your name in.'

'Which doesn't exonerate you,' he told her coldly. 'Your deception might be forgivable if we'd remained no more than holiday acquaintances. But we didn't. Which makes your behaviour devious to say the least. I repeat...you lied to me. That it was a lie by default doesn't make it any more acceptable.'

The bite in his tone made Nicola's temper start to simmer. 'I did *not* lie,' she retorted. 'I simply didn't remind you of circumstances most men of feeling would have remembered for themselves. To accuse me of lying is as wild an exaggeration as...as my saying you seduced me.'

'As to that, I'd be interested to know just why you agreed to spend the final two days at the Pera with me. In the light of what I've learned since, I don't think it was for the reason I thought at the time.'

'And what reason was that?' she asked.

He was silent for several seconds, his blue eyes slightly narrowed and locked with hers so that she found it impossible to look away.

'For love,' he said harshly. 'Love or lust are the usual reasons why people go to bed together. In Istanbul I assumed that, with you, it would have to be love.'

If, by the smallest hint, he had indicated any tender feelings towards her, she would have admitted instantly that his assumption had been correct.

But his judgemental frown was so like the man who had sacked her and so unlike her companion at the Pera Palas that she found herself saying in a flippant tone, 'You've missed out another reason...curiosity.'

He looked momentarily baffled. 'Curiosity?'

'After reading a piece about you in one of the glossies, I couldn't resist finding out if you really were the great lover you were cracked up to be.'

Her riposte made a subtle change to the look on his lean face: the difference between hot anger and icy rage. She knew she had gone too far and had only herself to blame for whatever he did next.

'I see. And did I pass muster?' he asked, in a tone which made her quail inwardly.

When she didn't answer he crossed the space between them in a couple of strides and took her roughly by the shoulders. 'Come on ... how did you rate me?'

'Richard ... please ... I wasn't serious.'

He misunderstood what she meant.

'Clearly! In which case it's just as well you were playing games with a well-known stud. A nicer guy could have been seriously hurt, thinking you might be serious about him.'

Bending his head, he kissed her hard on the mouth; a kiss of deliberate and brutal sensuality from which she instinctively recoiled as if it were a stranger trying to force a response from her.

At that moment he *was* a stranger, not the demanding but never ungentle lover he had been in Istanbul.

For a horrible moment she thought that, in this new guise, he might try to take her again and, in so doing, ruin every memory of that brief two-day idyll.

But, to her relief, he didn't. As suddenly as he had grabbed her, he let her go.

'It's all right. Don't panic,' he said sardonically. 'I've got the message. You only let your hair down on holiday ... not on home ground.'

He stormed past her and was gone, banging the door behind him.

The following week she had a day off from the shop. She was reading a manuscript which had been forwarded to her when the doorbell rang. Could it possibly be Richard?

Full of hope, she dashed to the entryphone speaker. 'Hello ... who is it?'

'Parcel post for Miss N. Temple,' said an unknown male voice.

Her spirits sinking back to the rock-bottom level which had been the norm since their row, she said, 'I'll be right down.

'Are you sure it's for me?' she asked, when the parcel turned out to be not another typescript but something large and heavy.

'If you're Miss N. Temple it is,' said the driver. 'Sign here, please.'

It wasn't until Nicola had dumped the parcel on the floor in her living-room that she saw that the stamps were Turkish. The only people she knew in Turkey were Serif and Nuray. Why should either of them send her a present?

Opening the parcel took several minutes. What it contained was a rug folded with its underside outwards. When she spread it out on the floor she recognised it as the expensive rug she would have bought had she been able to afford it.

In the centre of the rug was an envelope containing a note. 'For Nicola, from Richard—a memento of Kas.'

'Nicola! What's wrong?' Gina demanded, arriving for supper that evening and seeing at a glance that her friend had been crying.

Later, when Nicola had confided the whole story to her, Gina said, 'You know what you should do? Go to see him. The rug is a perfect excuse. In the circumstances you can't keep it. So return it to him...in person.'

'What good will that do?'

'He's had time to cool down...think things over. He may regret what he said, but not feel like making the first move. Men find it harder to say they're sorry than we do. Their upper lips are stiffer and so are their necks. If you appear on his doorstep looking fragile and wan, probably he won't just climb down...he'll jump down in one easy movement.'

'I doubt that,' said Nicola.

'It's worth a try, isn't it? As it's going to cost the equivalent of the taxi fare to his place to post the rug back to him, what have you got to lose?'

The following evening, with the rug rolled into a cylinder and fastened with plastic sticky tape, Nicola stood in the street waiting for a taxi.

It was a fine dry evening and under her coat she was wearing what, in Gina's opinion, was the most feminine outfit in her wardrobe: a honey-coloured dress with a nipped-in waist and full skirt.

'Go to town on your eyes, but go easy on the lipstick,' Gina had advised, the night before. 'You don't want to look as if your whole world has crashed, but you don't want to look cheerful either. And when he invites you in—only an arrant boor would grab the rug and slam the door—first off let *him* do the talking. I would guess he's been feeling a heel ever since he stamped out. Give him a chance to say so. Don't rush in and abase yourself first. What you did—or rather what you didn't do—wasn't so terrible.'

A taxi drew up alongside her and the driver jumped out and came round to the pavement. 'Let me give you a hand with that, love. Where do you want to go?'

Less than ten minutes later she was outside Richard's door, preparing to press the bell.

If he wasn't at home, Gina had advised repeating the visit until she did catch him in.

'If you're serious about the man, so what if it costs you money to get back together with him?' she had said.

However, it seemed that he was in because, as she waited for the door to open, she could hear music playing.

But it wasn't Richard who opened the door. It was a girl in the checked cotton trousers and starched white tunic of a chef.

Nicola knew instantly who she was. Her name was Jane Stonebridge. She was the daughter of a North

Country landowner and, after taking a cordon bleu course in Paris, she had started cooking for private parties.

She had been cited as Richard's latest *amour* in the article in the glossy.

'Hello,' she said, smiling. 'Richard's still in the shower. I'm Jane...the cook. Goodness, what an exciting-looking present——' her eyes on the rug. 'Come in. The party doesn't start until half-past eight, actually. But it doesn't matter that you're a little ahead of time. He's already opened the wine and he won't be more than ten minutes. He came home early tonight.'

It was not quite a quarter to eight. Nicola had checked the time in the taxi. But, although there might be a gap of half an hour between Richard's finishing dressing and the arrival of the first guests, this was not the time to confront him. Especially not in the presence of a former girlfriend, who might now be current again.

'Is it heavy? Shall I take one end?' the other girl asked.

'No, it isn't very heavy... and I'm only delivering it, not coming to the party.'

'Oh, I see.' Jane took charge of the parcel. 'Is there a card inside?'

'No, but he'll know who it's from. Actually it's not a present... just something I'm returning. Goodbye.'

Nicola turned and hurried away.

It wasn't until she got home that she wondered why she had been so stupid. By leaving the rug there, she had lost the only reason ever to see him again.

With her wits about her, she could have pretended to be looking for someone called Henry Jones and brought the rug away with her. If Richard had heard the doorbell and asked Jane who had called, she would have said, Someone with the wrong address.

At ten o'clock the telephone rang.

'Oh…you're home,' said Gina, when Nicola answered it. 'I hoped you'd still be out. What happened? How did it go?'

When Nicola told her, she said, 'That wasn't very bright, Nicola.'

'I know, but I was confused when the girl called Jane came to the door. They may be back together again. For all I know they may never have been apart.'

'The chances are she was there in her professional capacity. The magazine may have exaggerated his interest in her,' Gina said bracingly. 'Write a note to him now and post it first thing tomorrow. Say you were overwhelmed by his marvellous present, that you would have loved to keep it, but, knowing the way he feels about you, you felt that you couldn't. Explain about hoping to see him but not wanting to intrude on the party. Hey, I've got a better idea. Tomorrow, send him some flowers or a plant as a late birthday present. Then he'll have to make contact with you.'

'I can't do that,' said Nicola. 'It's too much like trying to ensnare him. If he wants me, he'll get in touch. He's not the shy, diffident type. Richard's a man who knows what he wants and goes for it. If he wanted me, he'd have been round here days ago.'

'I'm not so sure,' said Gina. 'Men are a very strange species. Some are tigers and some are pussycats, and sometimes falling in love turns a pussycat into a tiger and vice versa.'

'I'll think about it,' said Nicola.

'That's a large part of your trouble,' Gina told her. 'You think too much. If you could only bring yourself to do what comes naturally instead of endlessly analysing your feelings and speculating about his, you'd be a lot better off. Do you know what I'd do in your place?'

'What?'

'I'd ring him up—now!—and tell him how miserable I felt. Cry a little. Why not? What have you got to lose?

At worst he can only cut you off. At best he might rush round to comfort you.'

'Is it likely...in the middle of a party? I have a better idea. I'm going to do some work. It's work, not love, which really makes the world go round...and we aren't going to make our fortunes out of one book, however well it sells. So the sooner I get back to the slush pile the better.'

Her eyes went to the stack of unsolicited manuscripts waiting to be read.

'Goodnight, Gina. Thanks for your sympathetic ear. Don't worry; I'm not going to pine and die.'

CHAPTER THIRTEEN

THE days that followed gave Nicola an uncomfortable insight into the reasons why people in deep depressions lost the energy even to get out of bed and get dressed.

There were several mornings when she felt like pulling the bedclothes over her head and staying where she was instead of facing another day at the shop. She still had her family and her friends, but the only person she really needed was Richard. Without him, the world was a wilderness and the future as terrifying to contemplate as being imprisoned for life.

Her unhappiness over Ian had been nothing like this. Even the trauma of being sacked had not been as bad, for then she had been sustained by anger and a sense of injustice.

What she was going through now was both deserved and self-inflicted. She had brought it on herself by her own lack of moral courage. No wonder Richard despised her.

The launch party for *The Gothick Window* was held at the Royal Over-Seas League.

The room booked for the party overlooked the garden at the back of the building and, beyond, the taller trees and open spaces of Green Park.

Nicola was the first to arrive. She hadn't seen Gina for a week although they had talked by telephone while Gina was shepherding Margaret round the provinces on a promotion tour.

It had had to be done on a shoestring because they didn't have the funds to do it in style like the major publishing houses. Instead of travelling first class on trains to the nearer cities and by air to the distant centres, they had done the trip by car.

It must have been quite exhausting, especially for Margaret, who wasn't used to rushing from place to place. But already it had produced some excellent newspaper and local radio interviews as well as valuable publicity on regional television chat shows.

The time on the invitation cards was six to eight-thirty p.m. After which Nicola and Gina would take Margaret and her husband out to supper.

Standing at one of the tall windows while, behind her, the League's staff put the finishing touches to the buffet table, Nicola looked out at the golden-green light of a perfect spring evening and wondered what Richard was doing.

Perhaps he was still at his desk, or striding homewards to change for a dinner party or a date. It might be that he wasn't in London at the moment. Wherever he was, he wouldn't be thinking of her.

Oh, God, how can I bear it . . . this terrible aching longing for him? she thought forlornly.

'Hi, there! How's it going?' said Gina, from behind her. 'Oh, don't you look nice . . . and so relaxed! I feel totally frazzled. Does it show?'

'Not a bit,' Nicola assured her. 'If you're frazzled, how about Margaret? Where is she?'

'In the Ladies' . . . changing. On our first day out she was nervous, but after that she enjoyed it. I was amazed at how well she handled the interviews. By the end of the week you'd have thought she'd been doing it for years.'

When she judged that all the guests who were important from a publicity point of view had arrived, Gina mounted a step-stool which made her visible to everyone in the crowded room and rang a small bell to claim their attention.

'Ladies and gentlemen, Margaret and Nicola and I would like to thank you for coming to what, for many of you, is just another publishing party, but for us is a

very special occasion. Already we have grounds for believing that Margaret's book is going to be a big success.'

With justifiable pride, she announced the number of
copies 'subscribed' by bookshops up and down the
country.

She concluded her speech by saying, 'To borrow a
phrase often used in authors' dedications, there is one
person without whom none of this would have happened. His contribution to our new imprint, Trio, illus-
trates the truth of the proverb that it's an ill wind that
blows no one any good.

'As most of you know, at the end of Eighties, the
wind of change blew through the publishing world. For
some of us it seemed an ill wind...a *very* ill wind.
Actually, for Margaret, Nicola and me, that spell of adversity was good for us. It galvanised us into proving
ourselves. It challenged us to tackle something we would
never have attempted in the normal course of events.
The first to feel the spur was Nicola and, for a while,
the man who applied it wasn't her favourite person. But
she feels differently now.'

Gina paused to look round her audience.

'Have you guessed who I'm talking about? Please join
me in giving a warm welcome to one of the most dynamic influences in publishing and, in a way, the prime
mover of Trio...Mr Richard Russell of Barking & Dollis.'

As Gina started to clap and other people followed suit,
Nicola felt a wave of panic at the realisation that she
was going to have to face Richard in front of all these
people. Her second reaction was anger that Gina, and
Margaret as well, had conspired to arrange his presence
without consulting her. In those moments it seemed a
unforgivable betrayal.

Then the people near her drew back to allow the unexpected guest to make his way to Gina's side. And the
sight of him, taller and browner than any of the other
men there, swept aside every thought but the joy of seeing
him again.

She watched him shake hands with Gina before she stepped down from the stool. Richard did not take her place on it. He didn't need to. His height made him easily seen.

As the clapping died down, he said, 'Good evening, ladies and gentlemen. You're probably as surprised to see me here as I was to be invited. As Gina has indicated, to two of the principals of Trio I should be *persona non grata*. However, there are few publishers who haven't made similar errors of judgement. I'm very glad that in this instance my unwise decision to dispense with Nicola Temple's services has led to this happy occasion.'

He turned to smile at Margaret. 'Gina gave me an advance copy of Mrs Wanstead's novel, which I've read with great interest and enjoyment. It's a matter for regret that it isn't on Barking & Dollis's list. I haven't any doubt it will be extremely successful. Not only because it's being published with exceptional verve, but because anyone who reads it will want their friends to read it. As everyone in publishing knows, enthusiastic readers, especially if some of them are booksellers, can sell a book far faster than any amount of expensive hype.'

His blue eyes ranged over his audience. 'In my opinion too many second-rate books have been hyped as surefire best-sellers in recent years. But *The Gothick Window* is not, as we so often hear, written "in the tradition" of any established author. Margaret Wanstead has her own style and her own special view of the world.'

After a pause, he continued, 'One good book doesn't make a list, but a resounding success is a fine way to start. I'm sincere in wishing this new imprint well. It seems highly probable that—having already turned adversity to their advantage—Gina and Nicola are destined to do great things. There are not many people who, in similar circumstances, would have had the magnanimity to include me in these celebrations. My congratulations and best wishes to both of you and to your first publication.'

There was another burst of applause, curtailed when Margaret mounted the stool and signalled that she had something to say.

'Thank you for the nice things you've said about my book, Mr Russell. I'd just like to add that if it weren't for my editor, Nicola Temple, I might never have finished it. There were many, many times when I felt I had bitten off more than I could chew. Nicola was an unfailing source of encouragement when I was tired, depressed or having problems with my plot. I owe a tremendous debt to these two remarkable girls. Thank you both for everything.'

Blowing a kiss to Gina with one hand, and another to Nicola with the other, she stepped down.

'Would you like to say something, Nicola?' Gina asked, under cover of the clapping.

Nicola shook her head. 'You might have warned me——' she began, in an undertone.

Gina didn't let her finish. She jumped back on the stool. 'Right; that's the formal part over. Now I'm sure most of you would like to meet our author, and, if anyone here hasn't already received a complimentary copy of *The Gothick Window*, please help yourself from the stack on the table over there.'

As she began to introduce people to Margaret, Richard turned to Nicola.

'That was a very nice compliment Mrs Wanstead paid you.'

Even a close observer would have seen nothing in his manner to hint at the rift between them.

'Yes, wasn't it,' she agreed. 'Let me get you a drink.'

But it was Richard who caught the eye of a waiter circulating with a tray of wine and put a glass into her hand before taking one for himself.

'To Trio!' he said, raising his glass.

'Thank you.' She lifted hers in acknowledgement.

How had Gina induced him to come? What was his reason for coming? What was he really thinking behind the urbane front he was putting on? Why couldn't she be equally civilised instead of standing here tongue-tied, unable to think of a single polite nothing to utter?

'Did you know I was coming?'

She searched for an evasive reply but failed to find one. 'Er...no...actually I didn't. But I'm very glad you're here.'

'Are you?' he said, his eyes sceptical. 'You look like someone who has read that, when unexpectedly confronted by a large and dangerous wild animal, the only thing to do is to stand one's ground.'

'Richard...how nice to see you again,' said Hilary, appearing beside them.

Discreetly made up, in a black dress with pearls round her neck and in her ears, and a beautiful antique paste brooch pinned to her shoulder, she looked more like an elegant Londoner than a green-fingered countrywoman.

'Hilary! Good to see *you*.' Richard bent to kiss her.

The three of them had been chatting for a few minutes when Miles came into view and, with him, Janet.

'Where's Richard?' asked Gina.

'I think he's gone.' Nicola surveyed the room. The party was thinning out now. 'I don't see him anywhere.'

'Gone? You mean you let him go?' her friend expostulated.

'We weren't together when he left.'

'You damn well should have been!' Gina said crossly. She lowered her voice. 'I didn't go to all that trouble to get him here for you to louse things up again.'

'What trouble? What are you talking about?'

'I delivered his invitation in person. I didn't make an appointment. I just showed up at B & D and sent in my card with "in partnership with Nicola Temple" scribbled on it. Although he had someone with him, I got the red carpet treatment. By the way, his secretary said how pleased she had been to read the piece about us in *The*

Bookshop because she remembered how shattered you'd looked the day he sacked you.'

At this point Gina broke off to say to some people on their way out, 'Thank you so much for coming.'

'When I was shown in to see him,' she continued, 'he couldn't have been nicer.'

'He usually is, I gather, with attractive women.'

'There are times, Nicola, when I could shake you,' Gina said, through clenched teeth. 'The man is in love with you. That's why he came tonight. Don't you realise what strength of character it took for him to come here and admit to a major error of judgement in front of all those people? It takes a real man to do that, and the reason he did it is because he's crazy about you.' .

'Did he tell you that?'

'Don't be a dope. Of course not. Men like Richard don't expose their deepest feelings to anyone but the woman they love—and you're not giving him any encouragement to tell you. Far from looking overjoyed to see him tonight, you looked as if a giant anaconda had just slithered in.'

As this tallied with Richard's description of her reaction, Nicola had to accept that she had looked markedly unwelcoming.

'It wouldn't surprise me if his reaction to this caper is to go home and get smashed out of his mind,' said Gina. 'Except that he isn't the type to drown his sorrows in Scotch. If you've any sense you'll go round there and tell him you thought it was wonderful of him to come tonight.'

'How can I do that? We're taking Margaret and Keith out to dinner.'

'I can cope with them on my own. Margaret will understand if I tell her you've got a headache. She's beginning to feel bushed herself. So am I. We shan't be making a night of it.'

Nicola hesitated. She still wasn't sure that Gina was right about Richard's motive for coming to the party. If she were, why had he left early?

Her friend read her mind. 'Look, I know you very well, and now I've met him and talked to him at some length. You're obviously made for each other. If you had the guts to launch Trio—it was *your* idea, re-member?—what's stopping you saying that you love him? I mean, are women equal or aren't they? Do we still have to sit around twiddling our thumbs, waiting for men to stick their necks out? He's done that once—asking you to stay at the Pera Palas with him. This time why not stick *your* neck out?'

Nicola's mind was made up not by Gina's homily but by the realisation that if she didn't take a chance the future would remain a void of lonely nights and quietly desperate days. Her only joy would be work, and even that satisfaction would be diminished by the emptiness in her heart.

'I'll go. I'll try it,' she said, suddenly decisive.

Gina let her shoulders sag as if she had just ac-complished an uphill task.

'And if he's not there,' she said, straightening, 'camp on his doorstep till he shows up.'

He was not at home when she arrived at his house. There were no lights showing and no response to the bell.

Nicola found the nearest pub. He wasn't there.

It struck her that the most likely place for him to go if he didn't want to be alone was to his club, particularly as it was a short walk from the Over-Seas League. She wouldn't be allowed to enter that masculine stronghold, but presumably they would give him a message. She took a taxi back to St James's Street.

The porter at the club shook his head in response to her query.

'Mr Russell isn't here at present, miss.'

'If he should come in later, could you tell him I was looking for him? I need to see him rather urgently.'

'If you'd care to write a message, miss, I'll see that Mr Russell gets it if he should come in this evening.'

From the club, Nicola returned to Richard's house in the hope that he might be there now. She hung about for half an hour and then scribbled another note.

Dear Richard,

I was so taken aback by your unexpected presence at the party that I don't think I made it clear what a wonderful surprise it was. Why did you leave early? I was going to ask you to join us for a post-party supper. I would like very much to iron out our misunderstandings and get back on our Istanbul footing. It's now nine forty-five p.m. and as you haven't come home yet, and are not at your club or the pub round the corner—I checked both—I'm going back to my place. Please call me.

Nicola.

She remembered Gina urging her to stick her neck out. After a moment's hesitation she added a postscript. 'I love you.'

Quickly she pushed the note through his letter-box before she could change her mind.

Then, for the fifth time that evening, she waved to a cruising taxi.

A familiar figure was pacing the pavement not far from her front door when the taxi turned into her street. There was no other traffic about and Richard heard the cab stopping and checked his stride to look back. When he saw Nicola climbing out he came hurrying towards her.

'I've been looking everywhere for you. How long have you been here?' she asked.

'Since I left the party. I have to talk to you.' He bent to speak to the driver. 'How much?'

'Four pounds, sir.'

'I have it here,' said Nicola, before Richard could pull out his wallet.

She handed the driver the fare and a tip. 'Thank you. Goodnight.'

Her smile at him was radiant. For Richard to be here had to mean Gina was right.

'I'm sorry you had to wait. Actually I was supposed to have supper with Gina and Margaret after the party, but I asked to be excused,' she said, handing him her latch-key. 'If only I'd come straight home you wouldn't have had this long wait.'

'It doesn't matter. You're here now.'

He unlocked the door and stood back for her to enter the hall. She turned on the light, time-switched to allow her to reach her own front door before it went out.

They went up the stairs without speaking and Richard, who still had her key-ring, unlocked the door at the top.

To hide her nervousness, she said, 'You must be longing to sit down. Let me fix you a drink.'

'What are you going to have?'

'A brandy and ginger, I think. I try not to mix grape and grain.'

'A brandy and ginger sounds great. This is a nice place you have here.' He moved towards the coffee-table and put her keys on it.

'It must seem poky compared with your house, but it's conveniently central and I like living at tree-top level.' She opened the fridge and took out a large bottle of chilled dry ginger and a tray of ice cubes.

'You've made it very comfortable...very personal. When I was here before I was in too much of a temper to take it in. I behaved very crassly that time...and have regretted it ever since.'

'You were entitled to be angry and I didn't handle it well.' She handed him his drink. 'Let's relax. It's been an exhausting day.'

They sat down at either end of her sofa. But Richard didn't lean back and stretch his long legs. He sat on the edge of the seat, his elbows on his knees and the glass held between them.

'I wondered if I'd ever come here again,' he said, glancing round at the bookshelves and pictures. 'After what happened last time, and then when you sent the rug back, it seemed unlikely.'

'I didn't send the rug back. I brought it in person. Didn't Jane Stonebridge tell you that?'

'She said a glamorous blonde in a hurry had dropped it off. It sounded as if you were on your way to a date. The fact that you returned it seemed quite significant. I knew you had liked it at Kas.'

'I loved it. I wanted to keep it. But how could I when you were furious with me?'

Richard put his untouched drink on the low table in front of him. Then he moved closer and took the glass from her hand. Holding both her hands in his, he said, 'I was angry because I had fallen in love with you. I wanted to tell you while we were in Istanbul. But I guess when you're thirty-four and you've never met the right girl and a lot of your friends have already been divorced from the wrong girl it makes caution seem a good idea. By the time we'd been apart a week, I was missing you badly. But a long-distance call is not the best way to tell a girl you love her, so I waited. And then of course when I got back the whole office was buzzing with the news about Trio.'

'Oh, Richard, if *only* I had told you before we left Istanbul. But you see, I thought if you loved me you would say so... and *then* I would tell you. When you didn't say what I wanted to hear, I was forced to conclude that on your side it was just a holiday affair.'

'I know. I must have been crazy. But I was only going to be away ten days and we'd known each other for two weeks—or so I thought. The irony of the situation is that when we arrived in Istanbul and something about you seemed familiar I thought it was because you were the girl I'd been waiting for all my life.'

'Yet the real first time you saw me I made no impression at all,' she said ruefully.

'Well, that's not surprising. I was preoccupied with the unpleasant task of sacking people. You were an unknown girl to whom I had to break some bad news. And you weren't the last on my hit-list,' he added. 'I had others to see after you.'

'How you must have hated it. You're such a kind person really. But I suppose you can't be kind if you're running a business.'

'Not if it's been mismanaged as badly as B & D before I took over. When things have been let go and are totally out of control, the remedies have to be drastic. But I didn't come here to talk about publishing. We have—or I hope we have—the rest of our lives to do that.' For the first time he smiled at her. 'What I want to discuss at the moment is a permanent merger of our private lives.'

4 FREE

Romances and 2 FREE gifts just for you!

You can enjoy all the heartwarming emotion of true love for FREE! Discover the heartbreak and happiness, the emotion and the tenderness of the modern relationships in Mills & Boon Romances.

We'll send you 4 Romances as a special offer from Mills & Boon Reader Service, along with the opportunity to have 6 captivating new Romances delivered to your door each month.

Claim your FREE books and gifts overleaf...

An irresistible offer from Mills & Boon

Become a regular reader of Romances with Mills & Boon Reader Service and we'll welcome you with 4 books, a CUDDLY TEDDY and a special MYSTERY GIFT all absolutely FREE.

And then look forward to receiving 6 brand new Romances each month, delivered to your door hot off the presses, postage and packing FREE! Plus our free Newsletter featuring author news, competitions, special offers and much more.

This invitation comes with no strings attached. You may cancel or suspend your subscription at any time, and still keep your free books and gifts.

It's so easy. Send no money now. Simply fill in the coupon below and post it to -
Reader Service, FREEPOST, PO Box 236, Croydon, Surrey CR9 9EL.

— NO STAMP REQUIRED —

Free Books Coupon

Yes! Please rush me 4 FREE Romances and 2 FREE gifts! Please also reserve me a Reader Service subscription. If I decide to subscribe I can look forward to receiving 6 brand new Romances for just £10.80 each month, postage and packing FREE. If I decide not to subscribe I shall write to you within 10 days - I can keep the free books and gifts whatever I choose. I ma cancel or suspend my subscription at any time. I am over 18 years of age.

Ms/Mrs/Miss/Mr _____ EP56

Address _____

_____

Postcode _____ Signature _____

mps
MAILING
PREFERENCE
SERVICE

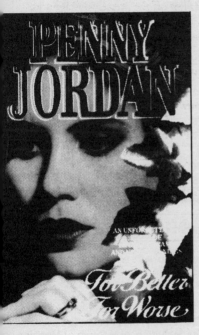

Next Month's Romances

Each month you can choose from a wide variety of romance with Mills & Boon. Below are the new titles to look out for next month, why not ask either Mills & Boon Reader Service or your Newsagent to reserve you a copy of the titles you want to buy – just tick the titles you would like and either post to Reader Service or take it to any Newsagent and ask them to order your books.

Please save me the following titles: **Please tick**

Title	Author	✓
HEART OF THE OUTBACK	Emma Darcy	
DARK FIRE	Robyn Donald	
SEPARATE ROOMS	Diana Hamilton	✓
GUILTY LOVE	Charlotte Lamb	
GAMBLE ON PASSION	Jacqueline Baird	
LAIR OF THE DRAGON	Catherine George	
SCENT OF BETRAYAL	Kathryn Ross	
A LOVE UNTAMED	Karen van der Zee	
TRIUMPH OF THE DAWN	Sophie Weston	
THE DARK EDGE OF LOVE	Sara Wood	
A PERFECT ARRANGEMENT	Kay Gregory	
RELUCTANT ENCHANTRESS	Lucy Keane	
DEVIL'S QUEST	Joanna Neil	
UNWILLING SURRENDER	Cathy Williams	
ALMOST AN ANGEL	Debbie Macomber	
THE MARRIAGE BRACELET	Rebecca Winters	

If you would like to order these books in addition to your regular subscription from Mills & Boon Reader Service please send £1.90 per title to: Mills & Boon Reader Service, Freepost, P.O. Box 236, Croydon, Surrey, CR9 9EL, quote your Subscriber No:..................................... (If applicable) and complete the name and address details below. Alternatively, these books are available from many local Newsagents including W.H.Smith, J.Menzies, Martins and other paperback stockists from 12 March 1994.

Name:...

Address:..

....Post Code:..........................

To Retailer: If you would like to stock M&B books please contact your regular book/magazine wholesaler for details.

You may be mailed with offers from other reputable companies as a result of this application. If you would rather not take advantage of these opportunities please tick box ☐